THE
THOUSANDFOLD
THOUGHT

Also by R. Scott Bakker

THE PRINCE OF NOTHING SERIES

The Darkness That Comes Before

The Warrior Prophet

The
Thousandfold
Thought

The Prince of Nothing
Book Three

R. Scott Bakker

The Overlook Press
Woodstock & New York

First published in the United States in 2006 by
The Overlook Press, Peter Mayer Publishers, Inc.
Woodstock & New York

WOODSTOCK:
One Overlook Drive
Woodstock, NY 12498
www.overlookpress.com
[for individual orders, bulk and special sales, contact our Woodstock office]

NEW YORK:
141 Wooster Street
New York, NY 10012

Cataloging-in-Publication Data is available from the Library of Congress

Manufactured in the United States of America
ISBN 1-58567-705-1
2 4 6 8 10 9 7 5 3 1

To Tina and Keith
with love

In pursuing yonder what they have lost, they encounter only the nothing they have. In order not to lose touch with the everyday dreariness in which, as irremediable realists, they are at home, they adapt the meaning they revel in to the meaninglessness they flee. The worthless magic is nothing other than the worthless existence it lights up.

—THEODOR ADORNO, *MINIMA MORALIA*

All progressions from a higher to a lower order are marked by ruins and mystery and a residue of nameless rage. So. Here are the dead fathers.

—CORMAC McCARTHY, *BLOOD MERIDIAN*

Contents

APPENDICES

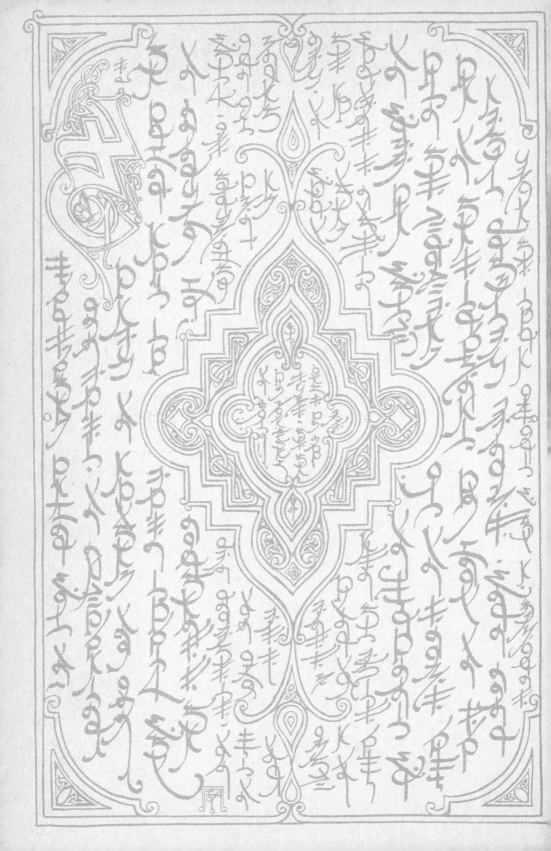

What has come before ...

The First Apocalypse destroyed the great Norsirai nations of the North. Only the South, the Ketyai nations of the Three Seas, survived the onslaught of the No-God, Mog-Pharau, and his Consult of generals and magi. The years passed, and the Men of the Three Seas forgot, as Men inevitably do, the horrors endured by their fathers.

Empires rose and empires fell: Kyraneas, Shir, Cenei. The Latter Prophet, Inri Sejenus, reinterpreted the Tusk, the holiest of artifacts, and within a few centuries, the faith of Inrithism, organized and administered by the Thousand Temples and its spiritual leader, the Shriah, came to dominate the entire Three Seas. The great sorcerous Schools, such as the Scarlet Spires, the Imperial Saik, and the Mysunsai, arose in response to the Inrithi persecution of the Few, those possessing the ability to see and work sorcery. Using Chorae, ancient artifacts that render their bearers immune to sorcery, the Inrithi warred against the Schools, attempting, unsuccessfully, to purify the Three Seas. Then Fane, the Prophet of the Solitary God, united the Kianene, the desert peoples of the southwestern deserts, and declared war against the Tusk and the Thousand Temples. After centuries and several jihads, the Fanim and their eyeless sorcerer-priests, the Cishaurim, conquered nearly all the western Three Seas, including the holy city of Shimeh, the birthplace of Inri Sejenus. Only the moribund remnants of the Nansur Empire continued to resist them.

Now war and strife rule the South. The two great faiths of Inrithism and Fanimry continually skirmish, though trade and pilgrimage are tolerated when commercially convenient. The great families and nations vie for military and mercantile dominance. The minor and major Schools squabble and plot, particularly against the upstart Cishaurim, whose sorcery, the Psûkhe, the Schoolmen cannot distinguish from the God's own world. And the Thousand Temples pursue earthly ambitions under the leadership of corrupt and ineffectual Shriahs.

The First Apocalypse has become little more than legend. The Consult, which had survived the death of the Mog-Pharau, has dwindled into myth, something old wives tell small children. After two thousand years, only the Schoolmen of the Mandate, who relive the Apocalypse each night through the eyes of their ancient founder, Seswatha, recall the horror and the prophecies of the No-God's return. Though the mighty and the learned consider them fools, their possession of the Gnosis, the sorcery of the Ancient North, commands respect and mortal envy. Driven by nightmares, they wander the labyrinths of power, scouring the Three Seas for signs of their ancient and implacable foe—for the Consult.

And as always, they find nothing.

Book One: *The Darkness That Comes Before*

The **Holy War** is the name of the great host called by Maithanet, the Shriah of the Thousand Temples, to liberate Shimeh from the heathen Fanim of Kian. Word of Maithanet's call spreads across the Three Seas, and faithful from all the great Inrithi nations—Galeoth, Thunyerus, Ce Tydonn, Conriya, High Ainon, and their tributaries—travel to the city of Momemn, the capital of the Nansur Empire, to become Men of the Tusk.

Almost from the outset, the gathering host is mired in politics and controversy. First, Maithanet somehow convinces the Scarlet Spires, the most powerful of the sorcerous Schools, to join his Holy War. Despite the outrage this provokes—sorcery is anathema to the Inrithi—the Men of the Tusk realize they need the Scarlet Spires to counter the heathen Cishaurim, the sorcerer-priests of the Fanim. The Holy War would be doomed without one of the Major Schools. The question is one of why the Scarlet Schoolmen would agree to such a perilous arrangement. Unknown to most, Eleäzaras, the Grandmaster of the Scarlet Spires, has waged a long and secret war against the Cishaurim, who for no apparent reason assassinated his predecessor, Sasheoka, some ten years previously.

Second, Ikurei Xerius III, the Emperor of Nansur, hatches an intricate plot to usurp the Holy War for his own ends. Much of what is now heathen Kian once belonged to the Nansur, and Xerius has made recovering the Empire's lost provinces his heart's most fervent desire. Since the Holy War gathers in the Nansur Empire, it can only march if provisioned by the Emperor, something he refuses to do until every leader of the Holy War signs his Indenture, a written oath to cede all lands conquered to him.

Of course, the first caste-nobles to arrive repudiate the Indenture, and a stalemate ensues. As the Holy War's numbers swell into the hundreds of thousands, however, the titular leaders of the host begin to grow restless. Since they war in the God's name, they think themselves invincible, and as a result see little reason to share the glory with those yet to arrive. A Conriyan noble named Nersei Calmemunis comes to an accommodation with the Emperor, and convinces his fellows to sign the Imperial Indenture. Once provisioned, most of those gathered march, even though their lords and a greater part of the Holy War have yet to arrive. Because the host consists primarily of lordless rabble, it comes to be called the Vulgar Holy War.

Despite Maithanet's attempts to bring the makeshift host to heel, it continues marching southward, and passes into heathen lands, where—precisely as the Emperor has planned—the Fanim destroy it utterly.

Xerius knows that in military terms, the loss of the Vulgar Holy War is insignificant, since the rabble that largely constituted it would have proven more a liability than an advantage in battle. In political terms, however, the Vulgar Holy War's destruction is invaluable, since it has shown Maithanet and the Men of the Tusk the true mettle of their adversary. The Fanim, as the Nansur well know, are not to be trifled with, even with the God's favour. Only an outstanding general, Xerius claims, can assure the Holy War's victory—a man like his nephew, Ikurei Conphas, who, after his recent victory over the dread Scylvendi at the Battle of Kiyuth, has been hailed as the greatest tactician of his age. The leaders of the Holy War need only sign the Imperial Indenture, and Conphas's preternatural skill and insight will be theirs.

Maithanet, it seems, now finds himself in a dilemma. As Shriah, he can compel the Emperor to provision the Holy War, but he cannot compel him to send Ikurei Conphas, his only living heir. The first truly great Inrithi potentates of the Holy War—Prince Nersei Proyas of Conriya, Prince Coithus Saubon of Galeoth, Earl Hoga Gothyelk of Ce Tydonn, King-Regent Chepheramunni of High Ainon—arrive in the midst of this controversy, and the Holy War amasses new strength, though it remains a hostage in effect, bound by the scarcity of food to the walls of Momemn and the Emperor's granaries. To a man, the caste-nobles repudiate Xerius's Indenture and demand that he provision them. The Men of the Tusk begin raiding the surrounding countryside. In retaliation, the Emperor calls in elements of the Imperial Army. Pitched battles are fought.

In an effort to forestall disaster, Maithanet calls a Council of Great and Lesser Names, and all the leaders of the Holy War gather in the Emperor's palace, the Andiamine Heights, to make their arguments. Here Nersei Proyas shocks the assembly by offering a many-scarred Scylvendi Chieftain, a veteran of past wars against the Fanim, as a surrogate for the famed Ikurei Conphas. The Scylvendi, Cnaiür urs Skiötha, shares hard words with both the Emperor and his nephew, and the leaders of the Holy War are impressed. The Shriah's Envoy, however, remains undecided: the Scylvendi are as apostate as the Fanim, after all. Only the wise words of the Prince Anasûrimbor Kellhus of Atrithau settle the matter. The Envoy reads the decree demanding that the Emperor, under pain of Shrial Censure, provision the Men of the Tusk.

The Holy War will march.

Drusas Achamian is a sorcerer sent by the School of Mandate to investigate Maithanet and his Holy War. Though he no longer believes in his School's ancient mission, he travels to Sumna, where the Thousand Temples is based, in the hope of learning more about the mysterious Shriah, whom the Mandate fears could be an agent of the Consult. In the course of his probe, he resumes an old love affair with a harlot named Esmenet, and despite his misgivings he recruits a former student of his, a Shrial Priest named Inrau, to report on Maithanet's activities. During this time, his nightmares of the Apocalypse intensify, particularly those involving the so-called "Celmomian Prophecy," which foretells the return of a descendant of Anasûrimbor Celmomas before the Second Apocalypse.

Then Inrau dies under mysterious circumstances. Overcome by guilt, and heartbroken by Esmenet's refusal to cease taking custom, Achamian flees Sumna and travels to Momemn, where the Holy War gathers under the Emperor's covetous and uneasy eyes. A powerful rival of the Mandate, a School called the Scarlet Spires, has joined the Holy War to prosecute its long contest with the sorcerer-priests of the Cishaurim, who reside in Shimeh. Nautzera, Achamian's Mandate handler, has ordered him to observe them and the Holy War. When he reaches the encampment, Achamian joins the fire of Xinemus, an old friend of his from Conriya.

Pursuing his investigation of Inrau's death, Achamian convinces Xinemus to take him to see another old student of his, Prince Nersei Proyas of Conriya, who's become a confidant of the enigmatic Shriah. When Proyas scoffs at his suspicions and repudiates him as a blasphemer, Achamian implores him to write Maithanet regarding the circumstances of Inrau's death. Embittered, Achamian leaves his old student's pavilion certain his meagre request will go unfulfilled.

Then a man hailing from the distant north arrives—a man calling himself *Anasûrimbor* Kellhus. Battered by his recurrent dreams of the Apocalypse, Achamian finds himself fearing the worst: the Second Apocalypse. Is Kellhus's arrival a mere coincidence, or is he the Harbinger foretold in the Celmomian Prophecy? Achamian questions the man, only to find himself utterly disarmed by his humour, honesty, and intellect. They talk history and philosophy long into the night, and before retiring, Kellhus asks Achamian to be his teacher. Inexplicably awed and affected by the stranger, Achamian agrees ...

But he finds himself in a dilemma. The reappearance of an Anasûrimbor is something the School of Mandate simply has to know— few discoveries could be more significant. But he fears what his brother Schoolmen will do: a lifetime of dreaming horrors, he knows, has made them cruel and pitiless. And he blames them, moreover, for the death of Inrau.

Before he can resolve this dilemma, Achamian is summoned by the Emperor's nephew, Ikurei Conphas, to the Imperial Palace in Momemn, where the Emperor wants him to assess a highly placed adviser of his—an old man called Skeaös—for the Mark of sorcery. The Emperor himself, Ikurei Xerius III, brings Achamian to Skeaös, demanding to know whether the old man bears the blasphemous taint of sorcery. Achamian sees nothing amiss.

Skeaös, however, sees something in Achamian. He begins writhing against his chains, speaking a tongue from Achamian's ancient dreams.

Impossibly, the old man breaks free, killing several before being burned by the Emperor's sorcerers. Dumbfounded, Achamian confronts the howling Skeaös, only to watch horrified as his face peels apart and opens into scorched *limbs* ...

The abomination before him, he realizes, *is a Consult spy,* one who can mimic and replace others without bearing sorcery's telltale Mark. A skin-spy. Achamian flees the palace without warning the Emperor and his court, knowing they would think his conviction nonsense. For them, Skeaös can only be an artifact of the heathen Cishaurim, whose art also bears no Mark. Senseless to his surroundings, Achamian wanders back to Xinemus's camp, so absorbed by his horror that he fails to see or hear Esmenet, who has come to rejoin him at long last.

The mysteries surrounding Maithanet. The coming of Anasûrimbor Kellhus. The discovery of the first Consult spy in generations ... How could he doubt it any longer? The Second Apocalypse is about to begin.

Alone in his humble tent, he weeps, overcome by loneliness, dread, and remorse.

Esmenet is a Sumni prostitute who mourns both her life and her dead daughter. When Achamian arrives on his mission to learn more about Maithanet, she readily takes him in. During this time, she continues to take and service her customers, knowing full well the pain this causes Achamian. But she really has no choice: sooner or later, she realizes, Achamian will be called away. And yet she falls ever deeper in love with the hapless sorcerer, in part because of the respect he accords her, and in part because of the worldly nature of his work. Though her sex has condemned her to sit half naked in her window, the world beyond has always been her passion. The intrigues of the Great Factions, the machinations of the Consult: these are the things that quicken her soul.

Then disaster strikes: Achamian's informant, Inrau, is murdered, and the bereaved Schoolman is forced to travel to Momemn. Esmenet begs him to take her with him, but he refuses, and she finds herself once again marooned in her old life. Not long after, a threatening stranger comes to her room, demanding to know everything about Achamian. Twisting her desire against her, the man ravishes her, and Esmenet finds herself answering all his questions. Come morning he vanishes as suddenly as he appears, leaving only pools of black seed to mark his passing.

Horrified, Esmenet flees Sumna, determined to find Achamian and tell him what happened. In her bones, she knows the stranger is somehow connected to the Consult. On her way to Momemn, she pauses in a village, hoping to find someone to repair her broken sandal. When the villagers recognize the whore's tattoo on her hand, they begin stoning her—the punishment the Tusk demands of prostitutes. Only the sudden appearance of a Shrial Knight named Sarcellus saves her, and she has the satisfaction of watching her tormentors humbled. Sarcellus takes her the rest of the way to Momemn, and Esmenet finds herself growing more and more infatuated with his wealth and aristocratic manner. He seems so free of the melancholy and indecision that plague Achamian.

Once they reach the Holy War, Esmenet stays with Sarcellus, even though she knows that Achamian is only miles away. As the Shrial Knight continually reminds her, Schoolmen such as Achamian are forbidden to take wives. If she were to run to him, he says, it would be only a matter of time before he abandoned her again.

Weeks pass, and she finds herself esteeming Sarcellus less and pining for Achamian more and more. Finally, on the night before the Holy War is to march, she sets off in search of the portly sorcerer, determined to tell him everything that has happened. After a harrowing search, she finally locates Xinemus's camp, only to find herself too ashamed to make her presence known. She hides in the darkness instead, waiting for Achamian to appear, and wondering at the strange collection of men and women about the fire. When dawn arrives without any sign of Achamian, Esmenet wanders across the abandoned site, only to see him trudging toward her. She holds out her arms to him, weeping with joy and sorrow ...

And he simply walks past her as though she were a stranger.

Heartbroken, she flees, determined to make her own way in the Holy War.

Cnaiür urs Skiötha is a Chieftain of the Utemot, a tribe of Scylvendi, who are feared across the Three Seas for their skill and ferocity in war. Because of the events surrounding the death of his father, Skiötha, some thirty years previously, Cnaiür is despised by his own people, though none dare challenge him because of his savage strength and his cunning in war. Word arrives that the Emperor's nephew, Ikurei Conphas, has invaded the Holy Steppe, and Cnaiür rides with the Utemot to join the Scylvendi horde on the distant Imperial frontier. Knowing Conphas's reputation, Cnaiür senses a trap, but his warnings go unheeded by Xunnurit, the chieftain elected King-of-Tribes for the coming battle. Cnaiür can only watch as the disaster unfolds.

Escaping the horde's destruction, Cnaiür returns to the pastures of the Utemot more anguished than ever. He flees the whispers and the looks of his fellow tribesmen and rides to the graves of his ancestors, where he finds a grievously wounded man sitting upon his dead father's barrow, surrounded by circles of dead Sranc. Warily approaching, Cnaiür nightmarishly realizes he *recognizes* the man—or almost recognizes him. He resembles Anasûrimbor Moënghus in almost every respect, save that he is too young ...

Moënghus had been captured thirty years before, when Cnaiür was little more than a stripling, and given to Cnaiür's father as a slave. He claimed to be Dûnyain, a people possessed of an extraordinary wisdom, and Cnaiür spent many hours with him, speaking of things forbidden to Scylvendi warriors. What happened afterward—the seduction, the murder of Skiötha, and Moënghus's subsequent escape—has tormented Cnaiür ever since. Though he once loved the man, he now hates him with a deranged intensity. If only he could kill Moënghus, he believes, his heart could be made whole.

Now, impossibly, this double has come to him, travelling the same path as the original.

Realizing the stranger could make possible his vengeance, Cnaiür takes him captive. The man, who calls himself Anasûrimbor Kellhus, claims to be Moënghus's son. The Dûnyain, he says, have sent him to assassinate his father in a faraway city called Shimeh. As much as Cnaiür wants to believe this story, however, he's wary and troubled. After years of obsessively pondering Moënghus, he's come to realize the Dûnyain are gifted with preternatural skills and intelligence. Their sole purpose, he now knows, is domination, though where others used force and fear, they used deceit and love.

The story Kellhus has told him, Cnaiür realizes, is precisely the story a Dûnyain seeking escape and safe passage across Scylvendi lands would tell. Nevertheless, he makes a bargain with the man, agreeing to accompany him on his quest. The two of them strike out across the Steppe, locked in a shadowy war of word and passion. Time and again, Cnaiür finds himself drawn into Kellhus's insidious nets, only to recall himself at the last moment. Only his hatred of Moënghus and knowledge of the Dûnyain preserve him.

Near the Imperial frontier, they encounter a party of hostile Scylvendi raiders. Kellhus's unearthly skill in battle both astounds and terrifies Cnaiür. In the battle's aftermath, they find a captive concubine, a woman named Serwë, cowering among the raiders' chattel. Struck by her beauty, Cnaiür takes her as his prize, and through her he learns of Maithanet's Holy War for Shimeh, the city where Moënghus supposedly dwells ... Can this be a coincidence?

Coincidence or not, the Holy War forces Cnaiür to reconsider his original plan to travel around the Empire, where his Scylvendi heritage will mean almost certain death. With the Fanim rulers of Shimeh girding for war, the only possible way they can reach the holy city is to become Men of the Tusk. They have no choice, he realizes, but to join the Holy War, which, according to Serwë, gathers about the city of Momemn in the heart of the Empire—the one place he cannot go. Now that they have safely crossed the Steppe, Cnaiür is convinced Kellhus will kill him: the Dûnyain brook no liabilities.

Descending the mountains into the Empire, Cnaiür confronts Kellhus, who claims he has use of him still. While Serwë watches in horror, the two men battle on the mountainous heights, and though Cnaiür is able to surprise Kellhus, the man easily overpowers him, holding him by the throat over a precipice. To prove his intent to keep their bargain, he spares Cnaiür's life. After so many years among worldborn men, Kellhus claims, Moënghus will be far too powerful for him to face alone. They will need an army, he says, and unlike Cnaiür he knows nothing of war.

Despite his misgivings, Cnaiür believes him, and they resume their journey. As the days pass, Cnaiür watches Serwë become more and more infatuated with Kellhus. Though troubled by this, he refuses to admit as much, reminding himself that warriors care nothing for women, particularly those taken as the spoils of battle. What does it matter that she belongs to Kellhus during the day? She is Cnaiür's at night.

After a desperate journey and pursuit through the heart of the Empire, they at last find their way to Momemn and the Holy War, where they are taken before one of the Holy War's leaders, a Conriyan Prince named Nersei Proyas. In keeping with their plan, Cnaiür claims to be the last of the Utemot, travelling with Anasûrimbor Kellhus, a Prince of the northern city of Atrithau, who has dreamed of the Holy War from afar. Proyas, however, is far more interested in Cnaiür's knowledge of the Fanim and their way of battle. Obviously impressed by what he has to say, the Conriyan Prince takes Cnaiür and his companions under his protection.

Soon afterward, Proyas takes Cnaiür and Kellhus to a meeting of the Holy War's leaders and the Emperor, where the fate of the Holy War is to be decided. Ikurei Xerius III has refused to provision the Men of the Tusk unless they swear to return all the lands they wrest from the Fanim to the Empire. The Shriah, Maithanet, can force the Emperor to provision them, but he fears the Holy War lacks the leadership to overcome the Fanim. The Emperor offers his brilliant nephew, Ikurei Conphas, flush from his spectacular victory over the Scylvendi at Kiyuth, but only—once again—if the leaders of the Holy War pledge to surrender their future conquests. In a daring gambit, Proyas offers *Cnaiür* in Conphas's stead. A vicious war of words ensues, and Cnaiür manages to best the precocious Imperial Nephew. The Shriah's representative orders the Emperor to provision the Men of the Tusk. The Holy War will march.

In a mere matter of days, Cnaiür has gone from a fugitive to a leader of the greatest host ever assembled in the Three Seas. What does it mean for a Scylvendi to treat with outland princes, with peoples he is sworn to destroy? What must he surrender to see his vengeance through?

That night, he watches Serwë surrender to Kellhus body and soul, and he wonders at the horror he has delivered to the Holy War. What will Anasûrimbor Kellhus—a Dûnyain—make of these Men of the Tusk? No matter, he tells himself, the Holy War marches to distant Shimeh—to Moënghus and the promise of blood.

Anasûrimbor Kellhus is a monk sent by his order, the Dûnyain, to search for his father, Anasûrimbor Moënghus.

Since discovering the secret redoubt of the Kûniüric High Kings during the Apocalypse some two thousand years previously, the

Dûnyain have concealed themselves, breeding for reflex and intellect, and continually training in the ways of limb, thought, and face—all for the sake of reason, the sacred Logos. In the effort to transform themselves into the perfect expression of the Logos, the Dûnyain have bent their entire existence to mastering the irrationalities that determine human thought: history, custom, and passion. In this way, they believe, they will eventually grasp what they call the Absolute, and so become true self-moving souls.

But their glorious isolation is at an end. After thirty years of exile, one of their number, Anasûrimbor Moënghus, has reappeared in their dreams, demanding they send to him his son. Knowing only that his father dwells in a distant city called Shimeh, Kellhus undertakes an arduous journey through lands long abandoned by men. While wintering with a trapper named Leweth, he discovers he can read the man's thoughts through the nuances of his expression. Worldborn men, he realizes, are little more than children in comparison to the Dûnyain. Experimenting, he finds that he can exact anything from Leweth—any love, any sacrifice—with mere words. So what of his father, who has spent thirty years among such men? What is the extent of Anasûrimbor Moënghus's power?

When a band of inhuman Sranc discovers Leweth's steading, the two men are forced to flee. Leweth is wounded, and Kellhus leaves him for the Sranc, feeling no remorse. The Sranc overtake him, and after driving them away, he battles their leader, a deranged Nonman, who nearly undoes him with sorcery. Kellhus flees, racked by questions without answers: Sorcery, he'd been taught, was nothing more than superstition. Could the Dûnyain have been wrong? What other facts had they overlooked or suppressed?

Eventually he finds refuge in the ancient city of Atrithau, where, using his Dûnyain abilities, he assembles an expedition to cross the Sranc-infested plains of Suskara. After a harrowing trek he crosses the frontier, only to be captured by a mad Scylvendi Chieftain named Cnaiür urs Skiötha—a man who both knows and hates his father, Moënghus.

Though his knowledge of the Dûnyain renders Cnaiür immune to direct manipulation, Kellhus quickly realizes he can turn the man's thirst for vengeance to his advantage. Claiming to be an assassin sent to murder Moënghus, he asks the Scylvendi to join him on his quest. Overpowered by his hatred, Cnaiür reluctantly agrees, and the two men set out across the Jiünati Steppe. Time and again, Kellhus tries to secure the trust he needs to possess the man, but the barbarian continually rebuffs him. His hatred and his penetration are too great.

Then, near the Imperial frontier, they find a concubine named Serwë, who informs them of a Holy War gathering about Momemn—a Holy War for *Shimeh*. The fact that his father has summoned him to Shimeh at the same time, Kellhus realizes, can be no coincidence. But what could Moënghus be planning?

They cross the mountains into the Empire, and Kellhus watches Cnaiür struggle with the growing conviction that he's outlived his usefulness. Thinking that murdering Kellhus is as close as he'll ever come to murdering Moënghus, Cnaiür attacks him, only to be defeated. To prove that he still needs him, Kellhus spares his life. He must, Kellhus knows, dominate the Holy War, but he as yet knows nothing of warfare. The variables are too many. Though Cnaiür's knowledge of Moënghus and the Dûnyain renders him a liability, his skill in war makes him invaluable. To secure this knowledge, Kellhus starts seducing Serwë, using her and her beauty as detours to the barbarian's tormented heart.

Once in the Empire, they stumble across a patrol of Imperial cavalrymen; their journey to Momemn quickly becomes a desperate race. When they finally reach the encamped Holy War, they find themselves before Nersei Proyas, the Crown Prince of Conriya. To secure a position of honour among the Men of the Tusk, Kellhus lies, and claims to be a Prince of Atrithau. To lay the groundwork for his future domination, he claims to have suffered dreams of the Holy War—implying, without saying as much, that they were *godsent*. Since Proyas is more concerned with Cnaiür and how he can use the barbarian's knowledge of battle to thwart the Emperor, these claims are accepted without any real scrutiny. Only the Mandate Schoolman accompanying Proyas, Drusas Achamian, seems troubled by him—especially by his name.

The following evening, Kellhus dines with the sorcerer, disarming him with humour, flattering him with questions. He learns of the Apocalypse and the Consult and many other sundry things, and though he knows Achamian harbours some terror regarding the name Anasûrimbor, he asks the melancholy man to become his teacher. The Dûnyain, Kellhus has come to realize, have been mistaken about many things, the existence of sorcery among them. There is so much he must know before he confronts his father ...

A final gathering is called to settle the issue between the Lords of the Holy War, who want to march, and the Emperor, who refuses to provision them. With Cnaiür at his side, Kellhus charts the souls of all those present, calculating the ways he might bring them under his thrall. Among the Emperor's advisers, however, he observes an expression he cannot read. The man, he realizes, possesses a *false face*. While Ikurei Conphas and the Inrithi caste-nobles bicker, Kellhus studies the man, and determines that his name is Skeaös by reading the lips of his interlocutors. Could this Skeaös be an agent of his father?

Before he can draw any conclusions, however, his scrutiny is noticed by the Emperor himself, who has the adviser seized. Though the entire Holy War celebrates the Emperor's defeat, Kellhus is more perplexed than ever. Never has he undertaken a study so deep.

That night he consummates his relationship with Serwë, continuing the patient work of undoing Cnaiür—as all Men of the Tusk must be undone. Somewhere, a shadowy faction lurks behind faces of false skin. Far to the south in Shimeh, Anasûrimbor Moënghus awaits the coming storm.

Book Two: The Warrior-Prophet

Free of the Emperor's machinations, the Lords of the Holy War fall to squabbling among each other, and the **Holy War** fractures into its various nationalities as it marches toward the heathen frontier. Contingent by contingent, it gathers beneath Asgilioch on the heathen frontier.

But Prince Saubon, the leader of the Galeoth contingent, is too impatient, and on the prophetic advice of Prince Kellhus, he marches with the Tydonni, the Thunyeri, and the Shrial Knights. The Imperial Army under Ikurei Conphas and the Conriyans under Prince Proyas remain at Asgilioch, awaiting the Ainoni and the all-important Scarlet Spires.

Skauras, the leader of the Kianene host, surprises Saubon and his impetuous peers on the Plains of Mengedda. A desperate battle follows, where, just as Prince Kellhus predicted, the Shrial Knights suffer grievously saving the Holy War from a cadre of Cishaurim. As the day wanes, the rest of the Holy War appears in the hills, and the Fanim host is completely routed.

The Governorate of Gedea falls, though the Emperor manages to take her capital, Hinnereth, through trickery. The Men of the Tusk continue south. Broken by their defeat on the Plains of Mengedda, the Kianene fall back to the south bank of the River Sempis, yielding northern Shigek to the Inrithi invaders. Prince Kellhus begins giving regular sermons beneath the famed Ziggurats of Shigek. Many in the Holy War begin referring to him as the "Warrior-Prophet."

With Cnaiür as their general, the Men of the Tusk cross the Sempis Delta, and a second great battle is fought beneath the Kianene fortress of Anwurat. Despite the dissolution of Cnaiür's command and the martial cunning of Skauras, the Men of the Tusk prevail once again. The sons of Kian are hacked to ruin.

Anxious to press the advantage, the Great Names then lead the Holy War south across the coastal deserts of Khemema, depending on the Imperial Fleet to keep them supplied with fresh water. The Padirajah, however, surprises the fleet at the Bay of Trantis, and the Men of the Tusk find themselves stranded in the burning wastes without water. Thousands upon thousands die. Only Prince Kellhus's discovery of water beneath the dunes saves the Inrithi from total annihilation.

The remnants of the Holy War drift from the desert and descend upon the great mercantile city of Caraskand. After a number of abortive assaults, the Men of the Tusk prepare for a long siege. The winter rains come, and with them, disease. At the height of the plague, hundreds of Inrithi perish every night. Only a Fenim traitor allows the Holy War to breach Caraskand's mighty fortifications. The Men of the Tusk show no quarter.

But even as the city falls, Kascamandri, the Padirajah himself, approaches with another great host. Suddenly the besiegers find themselves besieged in a sacked city. Diseases of malnutrition, then outright starvation soon begin afflicting them. Meanwhile, the tensions between traditional Inrithi and those acclaiming Prince Kellhus as a prophet—the Orthodox and the Zaudunyani—grow to the point of riot and violence.

Incited by the accusations of Sarcellus and Ikurei Conphas, the Lords of the Holy War turn against Prince Kellhus. He is denounced, declared a False Prophet, and, in accordance with *The Chronicle of the Tusk*, seized and bound to the corpse of his wife, Serwë, who is executed by Sarcellus. He is then lashed to an iron ring—a circumfix—and hung from a tree. Thousands gather in solemn vigil.

After Cnaiür reveals Sarcellus as a skin-spy, the Men of the Tusk repent, and the Warrior-Prophet is cut down from the Circumfix. Moved by a profound fervour, they assemble outside the gates of Caraskand. The Grandees of Kian charge their grim ranks and are utterly undone. The Padirajah himself falls before the Warrior-Prophet, though his son, Fanayal, survives to flee east with the remnants of the heathen army.

The road to Holy Shimeh is now open.

But far to the north, in the shadow of dread Golgotterath, the Consult rides openly once again, torturing those Men they find with a single, implacable question: "Who are the Dûnyain?"

Drusas Achamian faces a dilemma, the greatest he's ever encountered. Using the Cants of Calling, he contacts the Mandate and informs them of his dread discovery beneath the Andiamine Heights, but he says nothing of Anasûrimbor Kellhus, even though the man's name could very well mean the Celmomian Prophecy—that an Anasûrimbor would return at the end of the world—has been fulfilled.

The omission torments him, but the more time he spends teaching Kellhus on the march, the more he finds himself in awe of the man. With strokes of a stick across the ground, Kellhus rewrites classical logic, devises new and more subtle geometries. He regularly anticipates the insights of Eärwa's greatest thinkers, even extends them in astonishing ways. And he never forgets anything.

Achamian, especially after the debacle with Inrau in Sumna, is under no illusions regarding his School. He knows what they would do with Prince Anasûrimbor Kellhus. So he convinces himself that he needs time to determine whether Kellhus is in fact the Harbinger of the Apocalypse. He decides to betray the Mandate, to risk the very future of humanity, for the sake of a single, remarkable man.

While the Holy War awaits the arrival of the last stragglers about Asgilioch, he turns to drink and whores to silence his misgivings, only to find Esmenet among the camp-followers. Their reunion is both ardent and awkward. Afterward, Achamian takes her to his tent as his wife. After a lifetime of fruitless wandering, he finds himself terrified by the prospect of happiness. How can anyone be happy in the shadow of the Apocalypse?

As the Holy War marches ever deeper into Fanim territory, he continues teaching Kellhus. During this time, Achamian and Esmenet make a game of interpreting Kellhus, becoming more and more convinced of his divinity. In the course of these ruminations, Achamian confesses his fear that Kellhus may be one of the Few—those who can work sorcery. When Kellhus claims as much shortly after, Achamian insists on proof, using a small, demon-haunted Wathi Doll he obtained in High Ainon. Xinemus is outraged by the blasphemous demonstration, and Achamian finds himself estranged from his old friend.

When the Holy War reaches Shigek, Kellhus finally asks Achamian to teach him the Gnosis—something that would complete his betrayal of the Mandate. Needing solitude, Achamian travels alone to the Sareotic Library, where the sorcerers of the Scarlet Spires ambush and abduct him.

The torment drags on for weeks. Iyokus, the lead interrogator, even captures and blinds Xinemus in an attempt to wring more information from Achamian. The Scarlet Spires, it seems, have learned of the events beneath the Andiamine Heights. They know about Skeaös and the skin-spies, and with the very future of his School at stake, Eleäzaras is desperate to extract as much intelligence as possible.

Despite his sorcerous constraints, Achamian is able to call out to his Wathi Doll, which has been buried in the ruins of the Sareotic Library. After a long wait the Doll arrives and breaks the Uroborian Circle that imprisons him. Achamian at last shows the Gnosis to the Scarlet Spires. Though Iyokus escapes his vengeance, he and Xinemus are at last free.

After recuperating, the two friends set out to rejoin the Holy War, their relationship now marred by the resentment Xinemus bears for losing his eyes. They find the Men of the Tusk trapped and starving in Caraskand and learn of the Circumfixion of Kellhus and Serwë. Achamian immediately sets out to find Esmenet, relieved beyond words to discover that she survived the desert.

He finds her with the Zaudunyani. She tells him that she is pregnant with Kellhus's child.

Achamian goes to the ring-bound Kellhus thinking only of murder. Instead he learns that Consult skin-spies riddle the Holy War. Kellhus, it seems, can see them. He tells Achamian that the Second Apocalypse has in fact begun.

Despite his sorrow and hatred, Achamian goes to Proyas arguing that Kellhus must be saved. Proyas agrees to summon the other Great Names, and Achamian presents his case, arguing that the world is doomed without Anasûrimbor Kellhus, only to be made a laughingstock by Ikurei Conphas.

He fails to convince the Lords of the Holy War.

Thinking Achamian has repudiated her, **Esmenet** loses herself in the Holy War and eventually joins a troop of camp prostitutes. But at Asgilioch, she finds Achamian kneeling in the crowds, drunk and beaten. Never has she seen him so desperate. They reconcile, even though she cannot confess the truth of her affair with Sarcellus.

He tells her about Skeaös and the events beneath the Andiamine Heights, about his failure to tell the Mandate about Kellhus. She consoles him even as she struggles to grasp the dread import of his words. He insists the Second Apocalypse is coming, and though it seems something too horrific, too abstract, to be real, she finds herself believing him. She joins him in his humble tent, and becomes his wife in spirit if not in ritual.

Achamian introduces her to Kellhus, Serwë, Xinemus, and everyone else about their motley yet extraordinary camp fire. At first she regards Kellhus with suspicion, but she soon finds the wonder of the man as irresistible as everyone else.

As the Holy War marches across Gedea, she watches as Kellhus grows in prestige and reputation, becoming more and more convinced that he must be the prophet he claims not to be. During the same time her love of Achamian deepens, though she has difficulty trusting it.

Then, in Shigek, Kellhus asks Achamian to teach him the Gnosis. Since this would represent a final, ultimate betrayal of the Mandate, Achamian leaves for the Sareotic Library to meditate alone. He and Esmenet exchange hard words. The following night Kellhus awakens her with grim tidings: the Sareotic Library burns, and Achamian is missing.

She mourns him the way she once mourned her dead daughter. While the Men of the Tusk assail the South Bank, she remains alone in Achamian's tent, refusing, despite Xinemus's entreaties, to rejoin the Holy War. How would Achamian find her if she moved? After the Battle of Anwurat, Kellhus comes to her with Serwë, and with reason and compassion convinces her to join them on the continued march.

She finds their company awkward at first, but Kellhus is able to make sense of her melancholy, to give shape to the morass of accumulated sorrow that burdens her heart. He begins teaching her how to read—as a way to distract her, she suspects. As the weeks pass and the Holy War begins its disastrous march across the desert, she starts to resign herself to the fact that Achamian is dead.

She also finds herself more and more attracted to Kellhus.

Despite her shame, despite her resolutions, the chance intimacies accumulate. His words seem to carve her at the joints, cutting ever closer to truths she cannot bear. She admits her affair with Sarcellus, all her small betrayals of Achamian. Then, at last, overcome by shame and grief, she confesses the truth about her daughter: Mimara didn't die all those years ago. Esmenet sold the girl to slavers to forestall starvation.

She and Kellhus make love the following morning.

The long suffering in the desert seems to sanctify their relationship. Everything appears transformed. She even casts away her Whore's Shell, the contraceptive charm used by most prostitutes, something she never even considered with Achamian. Esmenet becomes the Warrior-Prophet's second wife. For the first time in her life she feels shriven—pure.

Caraskand is besieged and overcome. Serwë gives birth to the infant Moënghus. And Kellhus yields Esmenet more and more power within the growing ranks of Zaudunyani, raising her above even his closest disciples, the Nascenti. She becomes pregnant.

Then suddenly everything seems to collapse. The Padirajah traps the Holy War in Caraskand. Misery and riot own the streets. The Great Names execute Serwë and condemn Kellhus to the Circumfix. All seems lost ...

Until Achamian returns.

Cnaiür urs Skiötha's torment deepens. Though the Men of the Tusk mean nothing to him, he sees his own undoing in their slow capitulation to Kellhus. He alone knows the truth of the Dûnyain, which means he knows that Kellhus will eventually betray him in the prosecution of his obscure ends. Just as he knows the man will betray the Holy War.

As the Holy War marches deeper into Fanim territory, he tries to teach Prince Proyas the rudiments of war as practised by the Kianene. Assigned by Proyas to command a cohort of Conriyan outriders, he returns to the camp he shares with Kellhus, Achamian, and the others of the less and less. He knows that Kellhus now possesses Serwë body and soul, and when he returns, he finds himself punishing her for Kellhus's outrage. Secretly he loves her, or so he tells himself.

In the arid highlands of Gedea, he decides he can tolerate no more. He refuses to share Kellhus's fire, and demands that Serwë, whom he claims as his prize, come with him. Kellhus denies him. Since concern for women is unmanly, Cnaiür relinquishes her, though she continues to tyrannize his thoughts. His madness burns brighter. Some nights he roams the countryside, raping and murdering indiscriminately.

After the Holy War seizes the north bank of the River Sempis, the Lords of the Holy War assign Cnaiür the task of planning the assault on southern Shigek. Impressed by his insight and cunning, they acclaim him their general for the impending battle. Kellhus comes to him, offering Serwë in exchange for the secrets of battle. Cnaiür knows that his knowledge of war is the last advantage he possesses over the Dûnyain, the only thing Kellhus still needs from him, but Serwë has somehow become more important than anything. She is his prize, his proof ...

Cnaiür agrees. Riven by recriminations, he teaches Kellhus the principles of war.

Despite all his efforts, Skauras outwits him on the battlefield; only determination and good fortune save the Holy War from defeat. Something breaks within Cnaiür. At the height of the crisis he leaves Kellhus and the others, abandons his command to collect his prize. But when he finds Serwë, *another Kellhus* is beating her, demanding information. He surprises the second Kellhus, stabbing him in the shoulder. The man flees, but not before Cnaiür glimpses his face crack open ...

Cnaiür seizes Serwë, begins dragging her to his camp. She rages at him, tells him that he beats her because she lies with Kellhus the way he had lain with Kellhus's father. She tries to cut her own throat.

Bewildered and undone, Cnaiür wanders aimlessly through the camp. Later that night, as the Men of the Tusk celebrate their victory, Kellhus finds him at the edge of the Meneanor, howling at the breakers. Thinking he is Moënghus, Cnaiür begs him to end his misery. The Dûnyain refuses.

Throughout the disastrous desert march and the siege of Caraskand, madness rules Cnaiür's heart. Not until the city falls does he recover some semblance of his former self. Fomenting against Kellhus, the Great Names come to him, hoping to confirm rumours that Kellhus is not a true prince of Atrithau. The estrangement between Cnaiür and Kellhus is no secret. Thinking the Holy War doomed, Cnaiür decides to take what compensation he can. He names Kellhus a "prince of nothing."

Only when Serwë is murdered by Sarcellus does he realize the consequences of his betrayal. "Lie made flesh," Kellhus calls out to him before he is seized. "The hunt need not end." Cnaiür flees, and in a moment of resurgent madness cuts a swazond across his own throat.

He obsesses over the Dûnyain's final words. When the Mandate Schoolman confronts the Lords of the Holy War with the severed head of a Consult skin-spy, he finally grasps their meaning. He follows Sarcellus, who hastens from the assembly to the temple-complex where his brother Shrial Knights guard Kellhus upon the Circumfix. Knowing he intends to kill the Dûnyain, Cnaiür intercepts him, and they duel before the starving masses gathered about the dying Warrior-Prophet. But the skin-spy is too fast, too skilled. Cnaiür is saved only when Gotian, the Grandmaster of the Shrial Knights, distracts Sarcellus by demanding to know how he learned to fight so. Exhausted, bloodied, Cnaiür beheads the counterfeit Shrial Knight.

Raising its severed head to the sky, he shows the Holy War the true face of the Warrior-Prophet's adversary. The hunt for Moënghus need not end.

Anasûrimbor Kellhus requires three things to prepare for his father in Shimeh: knowledge of battle and of sorcery, and possession of the Holy War.

From the outset, he uses his claim to caste-nobility to insinuate himself into the councils of Proyas and the other Great Names. He proceeds cautiously, patiently laying the groundwork of his domination. From his readings of Inrithi scripture, he learns what the Men of the Tusk expect from a prophetic figure, so he sets out to emulate—as far as he can—all of those characteristics. He becomes a pilot of souls, crafting others' impressions of him with subtle inflections of word, tone, and expression. Soon, almost all those who know him find themselves in *awe*. Throughout the Holy War men whisper that a prophet walks among them.

At the same time, he plies Achamian with particular care. While mining him for his knowledge of the Three Seas, Kellhus subtly conditions him, instilling the passions and beliefs that will eventually force him to do the impossible: teach Kellhus the Gnosis, the deadly sorcery of the Ancient North.

In the course of his study, however, he discovers dozens of skin-spies mimicking men in various positions of power. He realizes, moreover, that they now *know* he can see them. One of them, a high-ranking Shrial Knight called Sarcellus, approaches him, probing for details. Kellhus uses the opportunity to make himself even more enigmatic, into a puzzle the Consult will be loath to destroy before solving. As long as he remains a benign mystery to the Consult, Kellhus realizes, they will not move against him.

He needs time to consolidate his position. Until the Holy War is his, he cannot risk an open confrontation.

He says nothing to Achamian for much the same reason. He knows the Mandate Schoolman believes him to be the Harbinger of the Second Apocalypse, and that the only thing preventing Achamian from telling this to his Mandate handlers is the recent death of his former student, Inrau, as a result of their machinations. Knowing that Kellhus could actually *see* Consult agents in their midst would prove too much. And as Achamian himself admits, the Mandate would likely seize Kellhus rather than treat with him as an equal.

Once the Holy War secures Shigek, Kellhus begins asserting himself more and more, giving what are called the Sermons of the Ziggurat. Though many now refer to him openly as the Warrior-Prophet, he continues to insist he is simply a man like any other. Knowing that Achamian has succumbed—that he believes him to be the world's only hope—Kellhus finally asks the Schoolman to teach him the Gnosis. But when Achamian leaves for the Sareotic Library to meditate on this request, he is abducted by the Scarlet Spires.

Assuming Achamian lost, Kellhus turns to Esmenet, not out of any errant sense of lust, but because her extraordinary native intelligence makes her useful both as a subordinate and as a potential mate. The differences between the Dûnyain and the worldborn makes his bloodline invaluable. He knows that whatever sons he produces, especially by a woman of Esmenet's intellect, will prove powerful tools.

So he begins seducing her by teaching her to read, by showing the hidden truths of her own heart, and by drawing her ever deeper into his circle of power and influence. Far from proving an obstacle, her bereavement actually facilitates his plan by rendering her more emotionally vulnerable and prone to suggestion. By the time the Holy War enters the desert, she has willingly joined him and Serwë in their bed.

Despite its calamities, the journey across the desert provides ample opportunity for him to exercise his otherworldly abilities. He rallies the Men of the Tusk with demonstrations of indomitable will and courage. He even saves them, using his preternatural senses to find well-springs beneath the sand. By the time the remnants of the Holy War fall upon Caraskand, thousands upon thousands openly hail him as the Warrior-Prophet. At long last he yields to the title.

He names his followers the Zaudunyani, the "Tribe of Truth."

But now he faces an added danger. As the numbers of Zaudunyani swell, so too do the misapprehensions of the Great Names. For many, following the dictates of a living—as opposed to a long-dead—prophet proves too much. Ikurei Conphas becomes the de facto leader of the Orthodox, those Men of the Tusk who repudiate Kellhus and his revisionary Inrithism. Even Proyas finds himself increasingly troubled.

The Consult, as well, have been watching Kellhus with growing trepidation. In the confusion of Caraskand's fall, Sarcellus leads several of his brother skin-spies in an assassination attempt that very nearly costs Kellhus his life. Knowing that it might prove useful, Kellhus saves one of their severed heads.

Shortly after this attempt, Kellhus is finally contacted by one of his father's agents: a Cishaurim fleeing the Scarlet Spires. He tells Kellhus that he follows the Shortest Path, and that soon he will comprehend something called the Thousandfold Thought. Kellhus has innumerable questions, but it is too late: the Scarlet Spires approach. To avoid compromising his position, Kellhus beheads the man.

When the Padirajah arrives and seals the Holy War up within Caraskand, the situation becomes even more dire. According to Conphas and the Orthodox, the God punishes the Men of the Tusk for following a False Prophet. To defuse their threat, Kellhus plots the assassination of both Conphas and Sarcellus. Neither attempt succeeds, and General Martemus, Conphas's closest adviser, is killed.

The dilemma now facing Kellhus is almost insuperable. The Holy War starves. The Zaudunyani and the Orthodox stand upon the brink of open war. And the Padirajah continues to assail Caraskand's walls. For the first time, Kellhus is confronted by circumstances he cannot master.

He sees only one possible way to unify the Holy War under his leadership: he must let the Men of the Tusk condemn him and Serwë, and trust that Cnaiür, driven to avenge Serwë, will save him. Only a dramatic reversal and vindication can possibly win over the Orthodox in time.

He must make a leap of faith.

Serwë is executed, and Kellhus is bound to her naked corpse. Then he is lashed to a circumfix and hung from a great tree to die of exposure. Visions of the No-God plague him, as does Serwë pressed dead against him. Never has he suffered so ...

For the first time, Anasûrimbor Kellhus weeps.

Achamian comes to him wild with rage because of Esmenet. Kellhus tells him about the skin-spies, about his visions of the impending Apocalypse.

Then, miraculously, he is cut down, and he knows that at last the Holy War is his, and that they will have the ardour and conviction they need to overcome the Padirajah.

Standing before the exultant masses, he grasps the Thousandfold Thought.

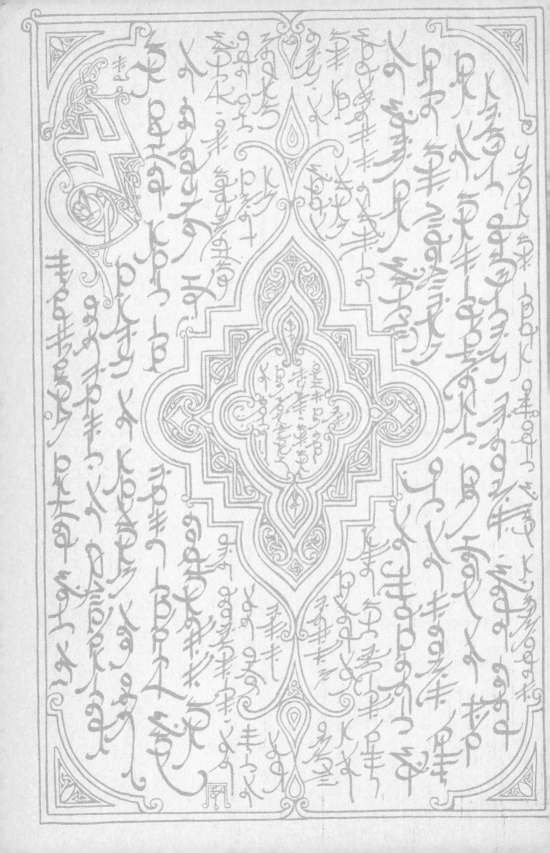

The
Final
March

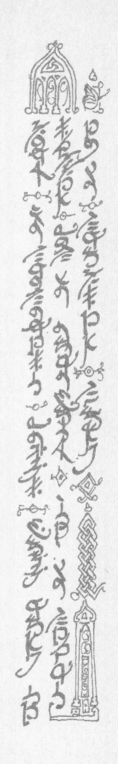

CHAPTER ONE

CARASKAND

*My heart shrivels even as my intellect bristles. Reasons—I find
myself desperate for reasons. Sometimes I think every word written
is written for shame.*
—DRUSAS ACHAMIAN, *THE COMPENDIUM OF THE FIRST HOLY WAR*

Early Spring, 4112 Year-of-the-Tusk, Enathpaneah

There had been a time, for Achamian, when the future had been a habit,
something belonging to the hard rhythm of his days toiling in his father's
shadow. His fingers had stung in the morning, his back had burned in the
afternoon. The fish had flashed silver in the sunlight. Tomorrow became
today, and today became yesterday, as though time were little more than
gravel rolled in a barrel, forever brightening what was the same. He
expected only what he'd already endured, prepared only for what had
already happened. His past had enslaved his future. Only the size of his
hands had seemed to change.

But now …

Breathless, Achamian walked across the rooftop garden of Proyas's
compound. The night sky was clear. The constellations glittered against
the black: Uroris rising in the east, the Flail descending to the west. The
encircling heights of the Bowl reared across the distance, a riot of blue
structures pricked by distant points of torchlight. Hoots and cries floated

up from the streets below, sounding at once melancholy and besotted with joy.

Against all reason, the Men of the Tusk had triumphed over the heathen. Caraskand was a great Inrithi city once again.

Achamian pressed through a hedge of junipers, fouled his smock in the sharp branches. The garden was largely dead, the ground rutted and over-turned during the height of the hunger. He stepped across a dusty gutter, then stomped about, making a carpet of grasses gone to hay. He knelt, still searching for his breath.

The fish were gone. His palms no longer bled when he clenched his fists in the morning. And the future had been … unleashed.

"I am," he murmured through clenched teeth, "a Mandate Schoolman."

The Mandate. How long since he had last spoken to them? Since it was he who travelled, the onus was on him to maintain contact. His failure to do so for so long would strike them as an unfathomable dereliction. They would think him mad. They would demand of him impossible things. And then, tomorrow …

It always came back to tomorrow.

He closed his eyes and intoned the first words. When he opened them, he saw the pale circle of light they cast about his knees, the shadows of grass combed through grass. A beetle scrambled through the chiaroscuro, mad to escape his sorcerous aspect. He continued speaking, his soul bending to the sounds, giving inner breath to the Abstractions, to thoughts that were not his own, to meanings that limned the world to its foundation. Without warning, the ground seemed to pitch, then suddenly here was no longer *here*, but everywhere. The beetle, the grasses, even Caraskand fell away.

He tasted the dank air of Atyersus, the great fortress of the School of Mandate, through the lips of another … *Nautzera*.

The fetor of brine and rot tugged vomit to the back of his throat. Surf crashed. Black waters heaved beneath a darkling sky. Terns hung like miracles in the distance.

No … not here.

He knew this place well enough for terror to loosen his bowels. He gagged at the smell, covered his mouth and nose, turned to the fortifications ... He stood upon the top tier of a timber scaffold. A shroud of sagging corpses loomed over him, to the limits of his periphery.

Dagliash.

From the base of the walls to the battlements, wherever the fortress's ramparts faced the sea, countless thousands had been nailed across every surface: here a flaxen-maned warrior struck down in his prime, there an infant pinned through the mouth like a laurel. Fishing nets had been cast and fixed about them—to keep their rotting ligature intact, Achamian supposed. The netting sagged near the wall's base, bellied by an accumulation of skulls and other human detritus. Innumerable terns and crows, even several gannets, darted and wheeled about the macabre jigsaw; it seemed he remembered them most of all.

Achamian had dreamed of this place many times. The Wall of the Dead, where Seswatha, captured after the fall of Trysë, had been tacked to ponder the glory of the Consult.

Nautzera hung immediately before him, suspended by nails through his thighs and forearms, naked save for the Agonic Collar about his throat. He seemed scarcely conscious.

Achamian clutched shaking hands, squeezed them bloodless. Dagliash had been a great sentinel once, staring across the wastes of Agongorea toward Golgotterath, her turrets manned by the hard-hearted men of Aörsi. Now she was but a way station of the world's ruin. Aörsi was dead, her people extinct, and the great cities of Kûniüri were little more than gutted shells. The Nonmen had fled to their mountain fastnesses, and the remaining High Norsirai nations—Eämnor and Akksersia—battled for their very lives.

Three years had passed since the advent of the No-God. Achamian could feel him, a *looming* across the western horizon. A sense of doom.

A gust buffeted him with cold spray.

Nautzera ... it's me! Ach—

A harrowing cry cut him short. He actually crouched, though he knew no harm could befall him, peered in the direction of the sound. He gripped the bloodstained timber.

On a different brace of scaffolding farther down the fortifications, a Bashrag stooped over a thrashing shadow. Long black hair streamed from the fist-sized moles that pocked its massive frame. A vestigial face grimaced from each of its great and brutal cheeks. Without warning, it stood—each leg three legs welded together, each arm three arms—and hoisted a pale figure over the heights: a man hanging from a nail as long as a spear. For a moment the wretch kicked air like a child drawn from the tub, then the Bashrag thrust him against the husk of corpses. Wielding an immense hammer, the monstrosity began battering the nail, searching for unseen mortises. More cries pealed across the heights. The Bashrag clacked its teeth in ecstasy.

Immobilized, Achamian watched the Bashrag raise a second nail to the man's pelvis. The wails became raving shrieks. Then a shadow fell across the sorcerer. "Anguish," a deep voice said, as close as a whisper in his ear.

Intake of breath, sharp and sudden. The incongruent taste of warm Caraskandi air …

For an instant his Cant faltered at this memory of the world's true order, and Achamian glimpsed the Heights of the Bull framed by a field of stars. Then there he was—*Mekeritrig*—standing over him, staring at Nautzera where he hung flushed and alive among gaping mouths and groping limbs.

"Anguish and degradation," the Nonman continued, his voice resonant with inhuman tones. "Who would think, Seswatha, that *salvation* could be found in these words?"

Mekeritrig stood in the curiously affected manner of Nonmen Ishroi, his hands clasped and pressed into the small of his back. He wore a gown of sheer black damask beneath a corselet of nimil that had been worked into circles of interlocking cranes. Tails of nimil chain followed the gown's pleats to the ground.

"Salvation …" Nautzera gasped in Seswatha's voice. He raised his swollen gaze to the Nonman Prince. "Has it progressed so far, Cet'ingira? Do you recall so little?"

A flicker of terror marred the Nonman's perfect features. His pupils became thin as quill strokes. After millennia of practising sorcery, the Quya bore a Mark that was far, far deeper than that borne by any Schoolmen—like indigo compared with water. Despite their preternatural beauty, despite the porcelain whiteness of their skin, they seemed blasted, blackened, and withered, a husk of cinders at once animate and extinct. Some, it was said, were so deeply Marked that they couldn't stand within a length of a Chorae without beginning to salt.

"Recall?" Mekeritrig replied with a gesture at once plaintive and majestic. "But I have raised such a *wall* ..." As though to emphasize his declaration, the sun flared across the wall's length, warming the dead with crimson.

"An obscenity!" Nautzera spat.

The nets flapped about the nailed corpses. To his right, near to where the wall curved out of sight, Achamian glimpsed a carrion arm waving back and forth, as though warning away unseen ships.

"As are all monuments, all memorials," Mekeritrig replied, lowering his chin toward his right shoulder—the Nonman gesture of assent. "What are they but prostheses that pronounce our impotence, our debility? I may live forever, but alas, what I have lived is mortal. Your suffering, Seswatha, *is* my salvation."

"No, Cet'ingira ..." Hearing the strain in Seswatha's voice filled Achamian with an eye-watering ache. His body had not forgotten this Dream. "It need not be like this! I've read the ancient chronicles. I studied the engravings along the High White Halls before Celmomas ordered your image struck. You were great once. You were among those who raised us, who made the Norsirai first among the Tribes of Men! You were not this, my Prince! You were never this!"

Again the eerie sideways nod. A single tear scored his cheek. "Which is why, Seswatha. Which is why ..."

A cut scarred where a caress faded away. In this simple fact lay the tragic and catastrophic truth of the Nonmen. Mekeritrig had lived a hundred lifetimes—more! What would it be like, Achamian wondered, to have every redeeming memory—be it a lover's touch or a child's warm squeal—blotted out by the accumulation of anguish, terror, and hate? To understand the soul of a Nonman, the philosopher Gotagga had once written, one need only bare the back of an old and arrogant slave. Scars. Scars upon scars. This was what made them mad. All of them.

"I am an Erratic," Mekeritrig was saying. "I do that which I hate, I raise my heart to the lash, so that I might remember! Do you understand what this means? You are *my children!*"

"There must be some other way," Nautzera gasped.

The Nonman lowered his bald head, like a son overcome by remorse in the presence of his father. "I am an Erratic ..." Tears sheened his cheeks when he looked up. "There is no other way."

Nautzera strained against the nails impaling his arms, cried out in pain, "Kill me, then! Kill me and be done with it!"

"But you *know*, Seswatha."

"What? What do I know?"

"The location of the Heron Spear."

Nautzera stared, eyes rounded in horror, teeth clenched in agony. "If I did, you would be the one bound, and I would be your tormentor."

Mekeritrig backhanded him with a ferocity that made Achamian jump. Droplets of blood sailed down the wall's mangled length.

"I will strip you to your footings," the Nonman grated. "Though I love, I will upend your soul's foundation! I will release you from the delusions of this word 'Man,' and draw forth the beast—the soulless beast!—that is the howling Truth of all things ... You *will* tell me!"

The old man coughed, drooled blood.

"And I, Seswatha ... *I will remember!*"

Achamian glimpsed fused Nonman teeth. Mekeritrig's eyes flared like spears of sunlight. Orange-burning circles appeared about each of his fingertips, boiling, seething with fractal edges. Achamian recognized the Cant immediately: a Quya variant of the Thawa Ligatures. With volcanic palms, Mekeritrig clenched Seswatha's brow, serrated both body and soul.

Nautzera howled in voices not his own.

"Shhhh," Mekeritrig whispered, clutching the old sorcerer's cheek. He squeezed away tears with his thumb. "Hush, child ..."

Nautzera could only gag and convulse.

"Please," the Nonman said. "Please do not cry ..."

And Achamian howled, *Nautzera!* He couldn't watch this, not again, not after the Scarlet Spires. *You dream, Nautzera! You dream!*

Great Dagliash stood mute. Terns and crows swept and battled through the air about them. The dead stared vacant across the thundering sea.

Nautzera turned from Mekeritrig's palm to Achamian, heaving, heaving chill air. "But you're dead," he gasped.

No, Achamian said. *I survived.*

Gone was the scaffolding and the wall, the stench of rot and the shrill chorus of scavenger birds. Gone was Mekeritrig. Achamian stood nowhere, struck breathless by the impossibility of the transition.

How is it you live? Nautzera cried in his thoughts. *We were told the Spires had taken you!*

I ...

Achamian? Akka? Is everything okay?

Why did he feel so small? He had reasons for his deception— reasons!

I—I ...

Where are you? We'll send someone for you. All will be made right. Vengeance will be exacted!

Concern? Compassion for him?

N-no, Nautzera. No, you don't understand—

My brother has been wronged! What more must I know?

An instant of mad weightlessness.

I lied to you.

Then long, dark silence, at once perfect and raucous with inaudible things.

Lied? Are you saying the Spires didn't seize you?

No—I mean, yes, they did seize me! And I did escape ...

Images of the madness at Iothiah flashed through the blackness. Iyokus and his dispassionate torments. The blinding of Xinemus. The Wathi Doll, and the godlike exercise of the Gnosis.

Remembered men screamed.

Yes! You did well, Achamian—well enough to be written! Immortalized in our annals! But what's this about lies?

There's a—his body in Caraskand swallowed—*there's a fact ... a fact I've hidden from you and the others.*

A fact?

An Anasûrimbor has returned ...

A long pause, strangely studied.

What are you saying?

The Harbinger has come, Nautzera. The world is about to end.

The world is about to end.

Said enough times, any phrase—even this one—was sure to be leached of its meaning, which was why, Achamian knew, Seswatha had cursed his followers with the imprint of his battered soul. But now, confessing to Nautzera, it seemed he'd never uttered these words before.

Perhaps he'd simply never *meant* them. Certainly not like this.

Nautzera had been too shocked to be outraged by his admission of betrayal. A troubling vacancy had dogged the tone of his Other Voice—even a premonition of senility. Only afterward would Achamian realize that the old man had simply been terrified, that, like Achamian himself a mere few months earlier, he feared himself unequal to the events unfolding before him.

The world was about to end.

Achamian began by describing his first meeting with Kellhus, that day outside Momemn's walls when Proyas had summoned him to appraise the Scylvendi. He described the man's intellect—even explained the man's improvements on Ajencis's logic as proof of his preternatural intelligence. He narrated Kellhus's inexorable rise to ascendancy in the Holy War, both from what he himself had witnessed and from what he'd subsequently learned through Proyas. Nautzera had heard, apparently through informants near to the Imperial Court, that a man claiming to be a prophet had grown to prominence among the Men of the Tusk, but the name Anasûrimbor had become Nasurius by the time it reached Atyersus. They had dismissed it as simply one more fanatic contrivance.

Then Achamian described everything that had happened in Caraskand: the coming of the Padirajah, the siege and starvation, the growing tension between the Orthodox and the Zaudunyani, Kellhus's condemnation as a False Prophet—and ultimately, the revelation beneath dark-boughed Umiaki, where Kellhus had confessed to Achamian even as Achamian confessed now.

He told Nautzera about everything except Esmenet.

After he was freed, even the most embittered of the Orthodox fell to their knees before him—and how could they not? The Scylvendi's duel with Cutias Sarcellus—the First Knight-Commander a skin-spy! Think, Nautzera! The Scylvendi's victory proved that demons—demons!—had sought the Warrior-

Prophet's death. It was exactly as Ajencis says: Men ever make corruption proof of purity.

He paused, a peevish part of him convinced Nautzera had never read Ajencis.

Yes yes, the old sorcerer said with soundless impatience.

He came upon them like a fever after that. Suddenly the Holy War found itself unified as never before. All of the Great Names — with the exception of Conphas, that is — knelt before him, kissed his knee. Gotian openly wept, offered his bared breast to the Anasûrimbor's sword. And then they marched. Such a sight, Nautzera! As great and terrible as anything in our Dreams. Starved. Sick. They shambled from the gates — dead men moved to war …

Images of the already broken flickered through the black. Gaunt swordsmen draped in strapless hauberks. Knights upon the ribbed backs of horses. The crude standard of the Circumfix snapping in the air.

What happened?

The impossible. They won the field. They couldn't be stopped! I still can't rub the wonder from my eyes …

And the Padirajah? Nautzera asked. *Kascamandri. What of him?*

Dead by the Warrior-Prophet's own hand. Even now, the Holy War makes ready to march on Shimeh and the Cishaurim. There's none left who might bar their passage, Nautzera. They've all but succeeded!

But why? the old sorcerer asked. *If this Anasûrimbor Kellhus knows of the Consult, if he too believes the Second Apocalypse is nigh, why would he continue this foolish war? Perhaps he said what he said to deceive you. Have you considered that?*

He can see them. Even now, the purges continue. No … I believe him.

After Sarcellus's death, over a dozen men of rank and privilege had simply vanished, leaving their clients astonished and delivering even the most fanatical of the Orthodox to the Warrior-Prophet. In the wake of the Padirajah's overthrow, both Caraskand and the Holy War had been ransacked, but as far as Achamian knew, only two of the abominations had been found and … exorcized.

This … this is extraordinary, Akka! What you say … soon all the Three Seas will believe!

Either that or burn.

There was grim satisfaction in thinking of the dismay and incredulity that would soon greet Mandate embassies. For centuries they'd been a laughingstock. For centuries they'd endured all manner of scorn, even those insults that jnan reserved for the most wretched. But now ... Vindication was a potent narcotic. It would swim in the veins of Mandate Schoolmen for some time.

Yes! Nautzera exclaimed. *Which is why we mustn't forget what's important. The Consult is never so easily rooted out. They'll try to murder this Anasûrimbor—there can be no doubt.*

No doubt, Achamian replied, though for some reason the thought of further assassination attempts hadn't occurred to him.

Which means that first and foremost, Nautzera continued, *you must do everything in your power to protect him. No harm must come to him!*

The Warrior-Prophet has no need of my protection.

Nautzera paused. *Why do you call him that?*

Because no other name seemed his equal. Not even Anasûrimbor. But something, a profound indecision perhaps, held him mute.

Achamian? Do you actually think the man's a prophet?

I don't know what I think ... Too much has happened.

This is no time for sentimental foolishness!

Enough, Nautzera. You haven't seen the man.

No ... but I will.

What do you mean? His brother Schoolmen coming here? The thought troubled Achamian somehow. The thought that others from the Mandate might witness his ...

... humiliation.

But Nautzera ignored the question. *So what does our cousin School, the Scarlet Spires, make of all this?* There was a note of sarcastic hilarity in his tone, but it seemed forced, almost painfully so.

At Council, Eleäzaras looks like a man whose children have just been sold into slavery. He can't even bring himself to look at me, let alone ask about the Consult. He's heard of the ruin I wrought in Iothiah. I think he fears me.

He will come to you, Achamian. Sooner or later.

Let him come.

Every night the ledgers were opened, the debtors called to account. There would be amends.

There's no room for vengeance here. You must treat with him as an equal, comport yourself as though you were never abducted, never plied ... I understand your hunger for retribution—but the stakes! The stakes of this game outweigh all other considerations. Do you understand this?

What did understanding have to do with hatred?

I understand well enough, Nautzera.

And the Anasûrimbor—what do Eleäzaras and the others make of him?

They want him to be a fraud, I know that much. What they think of him, I don't know.

You must make it clear to them that the Anasûrimbor is ours, Achamian. You must let them know that what happened at Iothiah is but a trifle compared with what will happen if they try to seize him.

The Warrior-Prophet cannot be seized. He's ... beyond that. Achamian paused, struggled with his composure. *But he can be purchased.*

Purchased? What do you mean?

He wants the Gnosis, Nautzera. He's one of the Few. And if I deny him, I fear he might turn to the Scarlet Spires.

One of the Few? How long have you known this?

For some time ...

And even then you said nothing! Achamian ... Akka ... I must know I can trust you with this matter!

As I trusted you on the matter of Inrau?

A long pause, fraught with guilt and accusation. In the blackness, it seemed to Achamian that he could see the boy looking to his teacher in fear and apprehension.

Unfortunate, to be sure, Nautzera said. *But events have borne me out, wouldn't you agree?*

I will warn you just this once, Achamian grated. *Do you understand?*

How could he do this? How long must he wage two wars, one for the world, the other against himself?

But I must know I can trust you!

What would you have me say? You haven't met the man! Until then, you can never know.

Know what? Know what?

That he's the world's only hope. Mark me, Nautzera, he's more than a mere sign, and he'll be more than a mere sorcerer—far more!

Harness your passions! You must see him as a tool—a Mandate tool!—nothing more, nothing less. We must possess him!

And if the Gnosis is his price for "possession," what then?

The Gnosis is our hammer. Ours! Only by submitting—

And the Spires? If Eleäzaras offers him the Anagogis?

Hesitation, both outraged and exasperated.

This is madness! A prophet who would pit School against School for sorcery's sake? A Wizard-Prophet? A Shaman?

This word forced a silence, one filled by the ethereal boiling that framed all such exchanges, as though the weight of the world inveighed against their impossibility. Nautzera was right: the circumstances were quite mad. But would he forgive Achamian the madness of the task before him? With polite words and diplomatic smiles Achamian had to court those who had *tortured* him. What was more, he was expected to woo and win a *prophet*, the man who had stolen from him his only love ... Achamian beat at the fury that welled up through his heart. In Caraskand, twin tears broke from his sightless eyes.

Very well, then! Nautzera cried, his tone disconcertingly desperate. *The others will have my hide for this ... Give him the Lesser Cants—the denotaries and the like. Deceive him with dross into thinking you've traded our deepest secrets.*

You still don't understand, do you, Nautzera? The Warrior-Prophet cannot be deceived!

All men can be deceived, Achamian. All men.

Did I say he was a "man"? You haven't yet seen him! There's no other like him, Nautzera. I tire of repeating this!

Nevertheless, you must yoke him. Our war depends upon it. Everything depends upon it!

You must believe me, Nautzera. This man is beyond our abilities to possess. He ...

An image of Esmenet flashed through his thoughts, unbidden, beguiling.

He possesses.

———⟨⟩———

The hills teemed with the herds of their enemy, and the Men of the Tusk rejoiced, for their hunger was like no other. The cows they butchered for the feast, the bulls they burned in offerings to flint-hearted Gilgaöl and the other Hundred Gods. They gorged themselves to the point of sickness, then gorged again. They drank until unconsciousness overcame them. Many could be found kneeling before the banners of the Circumfix, which the Judges had raised wherever men congregated. They cried out to the image; they cried out in disbelief. When bands of revellers passed one another in the darkness, they shouted, "We! *We* are the God's fury!" in the argot of the camp. And they clasped arms, knowing they held their brothers, for together they had held their faces to the furnace. There were no more Orthodox, no more Zaudunyani.

They were Inrithi once again.

The Conriyans, using inks looted from Kianene scriptoriums, tattooed circles crossed with an X on their inner forearms. The Thunyeri, and the Tydonni after them, took knives drawn from the fire to their shoulders, where they cut representations of three Tusks—one for each great battle—scarring themselves in the manner of the Scylvendi. The Galeoth, the Ainoni—all adorned their bodies with some mark of their transformation. Only the Nansur refrained.

A band of Agmundrmen discovered the Padirajah's standard in the hills, which they immediately brought to Saubon, who rewarded them with three hundred Kianene *akals*. In an impromptu ceremony at the Fama Palace, Prince Kellhus had the silk cut from the ash pole and laid before his chair. He planted his sandals upon the image, which may have been a lion or a tiger, and declared, "All their symbols, all the sacred marks of our foemen, you shall deliver to my feet!"

For two days the Fanim captives toiled across the battlefield, piling their dead kinsmen into great heaps outside Caraskand's walls. Innumerable carrion birds—kites and jackdaws, storks and great desert vultures—harassed them, at times darkening the sky like locusts. Despite the bounty, they squabbled like gulls over fish.

The Men of the Tusk continued their revels, though many fell ill and a hundred or so actually died—from eating too much after starving for so long, the physician-priests said. Then, on the fourth day following the Battle of Tertae Fields, they made a great train of the captives, stripping them naked to make manifest their humiliation. Once assembled, the Fanim were encumbered with all the spoils of camp and field: caskets of gold and silver, Zeümi silks, arms of Nenciphon steel, unguents and oils from Cingulat. Then they were driven with whips and flails through the Gate of Horns, across the city to the Kalaul, where the greater part of the Holy War greeted them with jeers and exaltation.

By the score they were brought to the black tree, Umiaki, where the Warrior-Prophet sat upon a simple stool, awaiting their petitions. Those who fell to their knees and cursed Fane were led as dogs to the waiting slavers. Those who did not were cut down where they stood.

When all was finished and the sun leaned crimson against the dark hills, the Warrior-Prophet walked from his seat and knelt in the blood of his enemies. He bid his people come to him, and upon the forehead of each he sketched the mark of the Tusk in Fanim blood.

Even the most manly wept for wonder.

Esmenet is his …

Like all horrifying thoughts, this one possessed a will all its own. It snaked in and out of his awareness, sometimes constricting, sometimes lying still and cold. Though it seemed old and familiar, it possessed the urgency of things remembered too late. It was at once a screeching call to arms and a grievous admission of futility. He had not simply lost her, he had lost her to *him*.

It was as though his soul only had fingers for certain things, certain dimensions. And the fact of her betrayal was simply too great.

Old fool!

His arrival at the Fama Palace had thoroughly flummoxed the Zaudunyani functionaries. They treated him with deference—he was their master's erstwhile teacher—but there was also trepidation in their manner, an *anxious* trepidation. Had they acted suspicious, Achamian would have attributed their reaction to his sorcerous calling; they were religious men, after all. But they didn't seem unnerved by him so much as they seemed troubled by their own thoughts. They knew him, Achamian decided, the way men knew those they derided in private. And now that he stood before them, a man who would figure large in the inevitable scriptures to follow, they found themselves dismayed by their own impiety.

Of course, they knew he was a cuckold. By now the stories of everyone who had broken bread or sawed joint at Xinemus's fire would be known in some distorted form or another. There were no intimacies left. And his story in particular—the sorcerer who loved the whore who would become the Prophet-Consort—had doubtless come quick to a thousand lips, multiplying his shame.

While waiting for the hidden machinery of messengers and secretaries to relay his request, Achamian wandered into an adjoining courtyard, struck by the other immensities that framed his present circumstance. Even if there were no Consult, no threat of the Second Apocalypse, he realized, nothing would be the same. Kellhus would change the world, not in the way of an Ajencis or a Triamis, but in the way of an Inri Sejenus.

This, Achamian realized, was Year One. A new age of Men.

He stepped from the cool shade of the portico into crisp morning sunlight. For a moment he stood blinking against the gleam of white and rose marble, then his eyes fell to the earthen beds in the courtyard's heart, which, he was surprised to note, had been recently turned and replanted with white lilies and spear-like agave—wildflowers looted from beyond the walls. He saw three men—penitents like himself, he imagined—conferring in low tones on the courtyard's far side, and he was struck that things had become so sedate—so *normal*—so quickly. The week previous, Caraskand had been a place of blight and squalor; now he could almost believe he awaited an audience in Momemn or Aöknyssus.

Even the banners—white bolts of silk draped along the colonnades—spoke of an eerie continuity, a sense that nothing had changed, that the Warrior-Prophet had always been. Achamian stared at the stylized likeness of Kellhus embroidered in black across the fabric, his outstretched arms and legs dividing the circle into four equal segments. The Circumfix.

A cool breeze filtered through the courtyard, and a fold rolled across the image like a serpent beneath sheets. Someone, Achamian realized, must have started stitching these before the battle had even begun.

Whoever they were, they had forgotten Serwë. He blinked away images of her bound to Kellhus and the ring. It had been so very dark beneath Umiaki, but it seemed he could see her face arched back in rigour and ecstasy …

"He is as you said," Kellhus had confessed that night. *"Tsuramah. Mog-Pharau ..."*

"Master Achamian."

Startled, Achamian turned to see an officer decked in green and gold regalia stepping into the sunlight. Like all Men of the Tusk, he was gaunt, though not nearly as cadaverous as many of those found outside the Fama Palace. The man fell to his knees at Achamian's feet, spoke to the ground in a thick Galeoth accent. "I am Dun Heörsa, Shield-Captain of the Hundred Pillars." There was little courtesy in his blue eyes when he looked up, and a surfeit of intent. "He has instructed me to deliver you."

Achamian swallowed, nodded.

He ...

The sorcerer followed the officer into the gloom of scented corridors.

He. The Warrior-Prophet.

His skin tingled. Of all the world, of all the innumerable men scattered about all the innumerable lands, he, Anasûrimbor Kellhus, communed with the God—the *God!* And how could it be otherwise, when he knew what no other man could know, when he spoke what no other man could speak?

Who could blame Achamian for his incredulity? It was like holding a flute to the wind and hearing song. It seemed beyond belief ...

A miracle. A prophet in their midst.

Breathe when you speak to him. You must remember to breathe.

The Shield-Captain said nothing as they continued their march. He stared forward, possessed of the same eerie discipline that seemed to characterize everyone in the palace. Ornate rugs had been set at various points along the floor; the man's boots fell silent as they crossed each.

Despite his nerves, Achamian appreciated the absence of speech. Never, it seemed to him, had he suffered such a throng of conflicting passions. Hatred, for an impossible rival, for a fraud who had robbed him of his manhood—of his wife. Love, for an old friend, for a student who was at once his teacher, for a voice that had quickened his soul with countless insights. Fear, for the future, for the rapacious madness that was about to descend upon them all. Jubilation, for an enemy momentarily undone.

Bitterness. Hope.

And awe ... Awe before all.

The eyes of men were but pinholes—no one knew this better than Mandate Schoolmen. All their books, even their scriptures, were nothing more than pinholes. And yet, because they couldn't see what was unseen, they assumed they saw everything, they confused pinpricks with the sky.

But Kellhus was something different. A doorway. A mighty gate.

He's come to save us. This is what I must remember. I must hold on to this!

The Shield-Captain escorted him past a rank of stone-faced guardsmen, their green surcoats also embroidered with the golden mark of the Hundred Pillars: a row of vertical bars over the long, winding slash of the Tusk. They passed through fretted mahogany doors and Achamian found himself on the portico of a much larger courtyard. The air was thick with the smell of blossoms.

In the sunlight beyond the colonnade, an orchard soaked bright and motionless. The trees—some kind of exotic apple, Achamian decided—twined black beneath constellations of blooming flowers, each petal like a white swatch dipped in blood. At different points through the orchard, great sentinels of stone—dolmens—towered over the surrounding queues, dark and unwrought, more ancient than Kyraneas, or even Shigek. The remnants of some long-overthrown circle.

Achamian turned to Captain Heörsa with questioning eyes, only to glimpse movement through braces of leaf and flower. He turned—and there she was, strolling beneath the boughs with Kellhus.

Esmenet.

She was speaking, though Achamian could only hear the memory of her voice. Her eyes were lowered, thoughtfully studying the petalled ground as it passed beneath her small feet. She smiled in a manner at once rueful and heartbreaking, as though she answered teasing proposals with loving admissions.

It was the first time, Achamian realized, that he'd seen the two of them together. She seemed otherworldly, self-assured, slender beneath the sheer turquoise lines of her Kianene gown—something fitted, Achamian had no doubt, for one of the dead Padirajah's concubines. Graceful. Dark of eye and face, her hair flashing like obsidian between the golden ribs of her headdress—a Nilnameshi Empress on the arm of a Kûniüric High King. And wearing a Chorae—a *Trinket!*—pressed against her throat. A Tear of God, more black than black.

She was Esmenet and yet she wasn't Esmenet. The woman of loose life had fallen away, and what remained was more, so much more, than she'd been at his side. Resplendent.

Redeemed.

I dimmed her, he realized. *I was smoke and he ... is a mirror.*

At the sight of his Prophet, Captain Heörsa had fallen to his knees, his face pressed to the ground. Achamian found himself doing the same, though more because his legs refused to bear him.

"So what will it be the next time I die?" he had asked her that night she had broken him. *"The Andiamine Heights?"*

What a fool he'd been!

He blinked womanishly, swallowed against the absurd pang that nettled the back of his throat. For a moment the world seemed nothing more than a criminal ledger, with all he'd surrendered—and he'd surrendered so much!—balanced against *one* thing. Why couldn't he have this *one* thing?

Because he would ruin it, the way he ruined everything.

"I carry his child."

For a heartbeat her eyes met his own. She raised a hesitant hand only to lower it, as though recalling new loyalties. She turned to kiss Kellhus's cheek, then fled, her eyes seemingly closed, her lips drawn into a heart-frosting line.

It was the first time he had seen the two of them together.

"So what will it be the next time I die?"

Kellhus stood before one of the apple trees, watching him with gentle expectation. He wore a white silk cassock patterned with a grey arboreal brocade. As always, the pommel of his curious sword jutted over his left shoulder. Like Esmenet, he bore a Trinket, though he had the courtesy to keep it concealed against his chest.

"You need never kneel in my presence," he said, waving for Achamian to join him. "You are my friend, Akka. You will always be my friend."

His ears roaring, Achamian stood, glanced at the shadows where Esmenet had disappeared.

How has it come to this?

Kellhus had been little more than a beggar the first time Achamian had seen him, a puzzling accessory to the Scylvendi, whom Proyas had hoped to use in his contest with the Emperor. But even then there had been something, it now seemed, a glimpse of this moment in embryo. They had wondered why a Scylvendi—and of Utemot blood, no less—would seek employ in an Inrithi Holy War.

"*I am the reason,*" Kellhus had said.

The revelation of his name, Anasûrimbor, had been but the beginning.

Achamian crossed the interval only to feel strangely bullied by Kellhus's height. Had he always been this tall? Smiling, Kellhus effortlessly guided him between a gap in the trees. One of the dolmens blackened the sun. The air hummed with the industry of bees. "How fares Xinemus?" he said.

Achamian pursed his lips, swallowed. For some reason he found this question disarming to the point of tears.

"I—I worry for him."

"You must bring him, and soon. I miss eating and arguing beneath the stars. I miss a fire nipping at my feet."

And as easy as that, Achamian found himself tripping into the old rhythm. "Your legs always were too long."

Kellhus laughed. He seemed to shine about the pit of the Chorae. "Much like your opinions."

Achamian grinned, but a glimpse of the welts about Kellhus's wrists struck the nascent humour from him. For the first time he noticed the bruising about Kellhus's face. The cuts.

They tortured him ... murdered Serwë.

"Yes," Kellhus said, ruefully holding out his hands. He looked almost embarrassed. "Would that everything healed so quickly."

Somehow these words found Achamian's fury.

"You could see the Consult all along—all along!—and yet you said nothing to me ... Why?"

Why Esmenet?

Kellhus raised his brows, sighed. "The time wasn't right. But you already know this."

"Do I?"

Kellhus smiled while pursing his lips, as though at once pained and bemused. "Now, you and your School must parlay, where before you would have simply seized me. I concealed the skin-spies from you for the same reason you concealed me from your Mandate masters."

But you already know this, his eyes repeated.

Achamian could think of no reply.

"You've told them," Kellhus continued, turning to resume their stroll between the blooming queues.

"I've told them."

"And do they accept your interpretation?"

"What interpretation?"

"That I'm more than the sign of the Second Apocalypse."

More. A tremor passed through him, body and soul.

"They think it unlikely."

"I should imagine you find it difficult to describe me ... to make them understand."

Achamian stared for a helpless moment, then looked to his feet.

"So," Kellhus continued, "what are your interim instructions?"

"To pretend to give you the Gnosis. I told them you would go to the Spires otherwise. And to ensure that nothing"—Achamian paused, licked his lips—"that nothing happens to you."

Kellhus both grinned and scowled—so like Xinemus before his blinding.

"So you're to be my bodyguard?"

"They have good reason to worry—as do you. Think of the catastrophe you've wrought. For centuries the Consult has hidden in the fat of the Three Seas, while we were little more than a laughingstock. They could act with impunity. But now that fat has been cooked away. They'll do anything to recover what they've lost. *Anything.*"

"There have been other assassins."

"But that was before ... The stakes are far higher now. Perhaps these skin-spies act on their own. Perhaps they're ... directed."

Kellhus studied him for a moment. "You fear one of the Consult might be directly involved ... that an Old Name shadows the Holy War."

He nodded. "Yes."

Kellhus did not immediately reply, at least not with words. Instead, everything about him—his stance, his expression, even the fixity of his gaze—grew sharp with monumental intent. "The Gnosis," he finally said. "Will you give it to me, Akka?"

He knows. He knows the power he would wield. Somewhere, beneath some footing of his soul, the ground seemed to fall away.

"If you demand it ... though I ..." He looked to Kellhus, somehow understanding that the man already knew what he was about to say. Every path, it seemed, every implication, had already been travelled by those shining blue eyes. *Nothing surprises him.*

"Yes," Kellhus said with a peculiar moroseness. "Once I accept the Gnosis, I yield the protection afforded by the Chorae."

"Exactly."

In the beginning Kellhus would possess only the vulnerabilities of a sorcerer, none of the strengths. The Gnosis, far more than the Anagogis, was an analytic and systematic sorcery. Even the most primitive Cants required extensive precursors, components that damned nonetheless for being inert.

"Which is why you must protect me," Kellhus concluded. "Henceforth you will be my Vizier. You will reside here, in the Fama Palace, at my disposal." Words spoken with the authority of a Shrial Edict, but infused with such force of certainty, such inevitability, that it seemed they *described* more than they demanded, that Achamian's compliance was some ancient and conspicuous fact.

Kellhus did not wait for his reply—none was needed.

"*Can* you protect me, Akka?"

Achamian blinked, still trying to digest what had just happened. "*You will reside here ...*"

With her.

"F-from an Old Name?" he sputtered. "I'm not sure."

Where had this treacherous joy come from? *You will show her! Win her!*

"No," Kellhus said evenly. "From yourself."

Achamian stared, glimpsed Nautzera screaming beneath Mekeritrig's incandescent touch. "If I cannot," he said with a voice that seemed a gasp, "Seswatha can."

Kellhus nodded. Motioning for Achamian to follow, he abruptly turned, pressing through interlocking branches, crossing rows. Achamian hastened after him, waving at the bees and fluttering petals. Three rows over, Kellhus paused before an opening between two trees.

Achamian could only gape in horror.

The apple tree before Kellhus had been stripped of its blossoming weave, leaving only a black knotted trunk with three boughs bent about like a dancer's waving arms. A skin-spy had been pulled naked across them, bound tight in rust-brown chains. Its pose—one arm trussed back and the other forward—reminded Achamian of a javelin thrower. Its head hung from drawn shoulders. The long, feminine digits of its face lay slack against its chest. Sunlight showered down upon it, casting inscrutable shadows.

"The tree was dead," Kellhus said, as though in explanation.

"What ..." Achamian began in a thin voice, but halted when the creature stirred, raised the shambles of its visage. The digits slowly clawed the air, like a suffocating crab. Lidless eyes glared in perpetual terror.

"What have you learned?" Achamian finally managed.

The abomination masticated behind lipless teeth. "*Ahh,*" it said in a long, gasping breath. "*Chigraaaa ...*"

"That they are directed," Kellhus said softly.

"*Woe comes, Chigraaa. You have found us too late.*"

"By whom?" Achamian exclaimed, staring, clutching his hands before him. "Do you know by whom?"

The Warrior-Prophet shook his head. "They're conditioned—powerfully so. Months of interrogation would be required. Perhaps more."

Achamian nodded. Given time, he realized, Kellhus *could* empty this creature, own it as he seemed to own everything else. He was more than thorough, more than meticulous. Even the swiftness of this discovery— wrested, no less, from a creature that had been forged to deceive— demonstrated his ... inevitability.

He makes no mistakes.

For a giddy instant a kind of gloating fury descended upon Achamian. All those years—centuries!—the Consult had played them for fools. But now—*now!* Did they know? Could they sense the peril this man represented? Or would they underestimate him like everyone else had?

Like Esmenet.

Achamian swallowed. "Either way, Kellhus, you must surround yourself with Chorae bowmen. And you need to avoid large structures, anyplace where—"

"It troubles you," Kellhus interrupted, "to see these things."

A breeze had descended upon the grove, and countless petals spun through the air as though along unseen strings. Achamian watched one settle upon the skin-spy's pubis.

Why bind the abomination here, amid such beauty and repose—like a cancer on a young girl's skin? Why? It seemed the act of someone who knew nothing of beauty ... nothing.

He matched Kellhus's gaze. "It troubles me."

"And your hatred?"

For an instant it had seemed that everything—who he was and who he would become—wanted to love this godlike man. And how could he not, given the sanctuary of his mere presence? And yet intimations of Esmenet clung to him. Glimpses of her passion ...

"It remains," he said.

As though provoked by this response, the creature began jerking, straining against its fetters. Slick muscle balled beneath sunburned skin. Chains rattled. Black boughs creaked. Achamian stepped back, remembering the horror of Skeaös beneath the Andiamine Heights. The night Conphas had saved him.

Kellhus ignored the thing, continued speaking. "All men surrender, Akka, even as they seek to dominate. It's their nature to submit. The question is never *whether* they will surrender, but rather *to whom* ..."

"Your heart, Chigraa ... I shall make it my apple ..."

"I—I don't understand." Achamian glanced from the abomination to Kellhus's sky-blue eyes.

"Some, like so many Men of the Tusk, submit—*truly* submit—only to the God. It preserves their pride, kneeling before what is never heard, never seen. They can abase themselves without fear of degradation."

"I shall eat ..."

Achamian held an uncertain hand against the sun to better see the Warrior-Prophet's face.

"One," Kellhus was saying, "can only be tested, never degraded, by the God."

"You said 'some,'" Achamian managed. "What of the others?" In his periphery he saw the thing's face knuckle as though into interlocking fists.

"They're like you, Akka. They surrender not to the God but to those like themselves. A man. A woman. There's no pride to be preserved when one submits to another. Transgress, and there's no formula. And the fear of degradation is always present, even if not quite believed. Lovers injure each other, humiliate and debase, but they never *test*, Akka—not if they truly love."

The thing was thrashing now, like something brandished in an invisible fist. Suddenly the bees seemed to buzz on the wrong side of his skull.

"Why are you telling me this?"

"Because part of you clings to the hope that she tests you ..." For a mad moment it seemed Inrau watched him, or Proyas as a boy, his eyes wide and imploring. "She does not."

Achamian blinked in astonishmen. "What are you saying, then? That she degrades me? That *you* degrade me?"

A series of mewling grunts, as though beasts coupled. Iron rattled and screeched.

"I'm saying that she loves you still. As for me, I merely took what was given."

"Then give it back!" Achamian barked with savagery. He shook. His breath cramped in his throat.

"You're forgetting, Akka. Love *is like sleep*. One can never seize, never force love."

The words were his own, spoken that first night about the fire with Kellhus and Serwë beneath Momemn. In a rush, Achamian recalled the sprained wonder of that night, the sense of having discovered something at once horrific and ineluctable. And those eyes, like lucid jewels set in the mud of the world, watching from across the flames—the same eyes that watched him this very moment ... though a different fire now burned between them.

The abomination howled.

"There was a time," Kellhus continued, "when you were lost." His voice seethed with what seemed an inaudible thunder. "There was a time when you thought to yourself, 'There's no meaning, only love. There's no world ...'"

And Achamian heard himself whisper, "Only her."

Esmenet. The Whore of Sumna.

Even now, murder stared from his sockets. He couldn't blink without seeing them together, without glimpsing her eyes wide with bliss, her mouth open, his chest arching back, shining with her sweat ... He need only speak, Achamian knew, and it would be all over. He need only sing, and the whole world would burn.

"Not I, not even Esmenet, can undo what you suffer, Akka. Your degradation is your own."

Those *grasping* eyes! Something within Achamian shrank from them, beseeched him to throw up his arms. *He must not see!*

"What are you saying?" Achamian cried.

Kellhus had become a shadow beneath a tear-splintered sun. At long last he turned to the obscenity writhing across the tree, its face clutching at sun and sky.

"This, Akka ..." There was a blankness to his words, as though he offered them up as parchment, to be rewritten as Achamian wished. "This is your test."

"*We shall cut you from your meat!*" the obscenity howled. "*From your meat!*"

"You, Drusas Achamian, are a Mandate Schoolman."

After Kellhus left him, Achamian stumbled to one of the massive dolmens, leaned against it, and vomited into the grasses about its base. Then he fled through the blooming trees, past the guards on the portico. He found some kind of pillared vestibule, a vacant niche. Without thinking, he crawled into the shadowy gap between wall and column. He hugged his knees, his shoulders, but he could find no sense of shelter.

Nothing was concealed. Nothing was hidden. *They believed me dead! How could they know?*

But he's a prophet ... Isn't he?

How could he not know? How—

Achamian laughed, stared with idiot eyes at the dim geometries painted across the ceiling. He ran a palm over his forehead, fingers through his hair. The skin-spy continued to thrash and bark in his periphery.

"Year One," he whispered.

HAPTER TWO

CARASKAND

I tell you, guilt dwells nowhere but in the eyes of the accuser. This men know even as they deny it, which is why they so often make murder their absolution. The truth of crime lies not with the victim but with the witness.

—HATATIAN, *EXHORTATIONS*

Early Spring, 4112 Year-of-the-Tusk, Caraskand

Servants and functionaries screamed and scattered as Cnaiür barged past them with his hostage. Alarums had been raised throughout the palace—he could hear them shouting—but none of the fools knew what to do. He had saved their precious Prophet. Did that not make him divine as well? He would have laughed had not his sneer been a thing of iron. If only they knew!

He halted at a juncture in the marmoreal halls, jerked the girl about by the throat. "Which way?" he snarled.

She sobbed and gasped, looked with wide, panicked eyes down the hallway to their right. He had seized a Kianene slave, knowing she would care more for her skin than her soul. The poison had struck too deep with the Zaudunyani.

Dûnyain poison.

"Door!" she cried, gagging. "There—there!"

Her neck felt good in his hand, like that of a cat or a feeble dog. It reminded him of the days of pilgrimage in his other life, when he had strangled those he raped. Even still, he had no need of her, so he released his grip, watched her stumble backward then topple, skirts askew, across the black floor.

Shouts rang out from the galleries behind them.

He sprinted to the door she'd indicated, kicked it open.

The crib stood in the nursery's centre, carved of wood like black rock, standing as high as his waist, and draped with gauze sheets that hung from a single hook set in the frescoed ceiling. The walls were ochre, the lamplight dim. The room smelled of sandalwood—there was no hint of soil.

All the world seemed to hush as he circled the ornate cradle. He left no track across the cityscapes woven into the carpet beneath his feet. The lamplights fluttered, but nothing more. With the crib between himself and the entrance, he approached, parted the gauze with his right hand.

Moënghus.

White-skinned. Still young enough to clutch his toes. Eyes at once vacant and lucid, in the way only an infant's could be. The penetrating white-blue of the Steppe.

My son.

Cnaiür reached out two fingers, saw the scars banding the length of his forearm. The babe waved his hands, and as though by accident caught Cnaiür's fingertip, his grip firm like that of a father or friend in miniature. Without warning, his face flushed, became wizened with anguished wrinkles. He sputtered, began wailing.

Why, Cnaiür wondered, would the Dûnyain keep this child? What did he see when he looked upon it? What *use* was there in a child?

There was no interval between the world and an infant soul. No deception. No language. An infant's wail simply *was* its hunger. And it occurred to Cnaiür that if he abandoned this child, it would become an Inrithi, but if he took it, stole away, and rode hard for the Steppe, it would become a Scylvendi. And his hair prickled across his scalp, for there was magic in that—even doom.

This wail would not always be one with the child's hunger. The interval would lengthen, and the tracks between its soul and its expression would multiply, become more and more unfathomable. This singular need would be unbraided into a thousand strands of lust and hope, bound into a thousand knots of fear and shame. And it would wince beneath the upraised hand of the father, sigh at the soft touch of the mother. It would become what circumstance demanded. Inrithi or Scylvendi ...

It did not matter.

And suddenly, improbably, Cnaiür understood what it was the Dûnyain saw: a *world* of infant men, their wails beaten into words, into tongues, into nations. Kellhus could see the measure of the interval, he could follow the thousand tracks. And *that* was his magic, his sorcery: he could close the interval, answer the wail ... Make souls one with their expression.

As his father had before him. Moënghus.

Stupefied, Cnaiür gazed at the kicking figure, felt the tug of its tiny hand about his finger. And he realized that though the child had sprung from his loins, it was more *his* father than otherwise. It was his origin, and he, Cnaiür urs Skiötha, was nothing but one of its possibilities, a wail transformed into a chorus of tortured screams.

He remembered a villa deep in the Nansurium, burning with a brightness that had turned the surrounding night into black. Wheeling to the laughing calls of his cousins, he had caught a babe on sword point ...

He yanked his finger free. In fits and starts, Moënghus fell silent.

"You are not of the land," Cnaiür grated, drawing high a scarred fist.

"Scylvendi!" a voice cried out. He turned, saw the sorcerer's whore standing on the threshold of an adjoining chamber. For a heartbeat they simply stared at each other, equally dumbfounded.

"You *will not!*" she suddenly cried, her voice shrill with fury. She advanced into the nursery, and Cnaiür found himself stepping back from the crib. He did not breathe, but then it seemed he no longer needed to.

"He's all that remains of *Serwë*," she said, her voice more wary, more conciliatory. "All that's left ... Proof that she *was*. Would you take that from her as well?"

Her proof.

Cnaiür stared at Esmenet in horror, then glanced at the child, pink and writhing in blue silk sheets.

"But its *name!*" he heard someone cry. Surely the voice was too womanish, too weak, to be his.

Something's wrong with me ... Something's wrong ...

Her brows furrowed and she seemed about to speak, but at that instant the first of the guardsmen, garbed in the green-and-gold surcoat of the Hundred Pillars, burst through the shambles of the door Cnaiür had kicked in.

"Sheathe your weapons!" she cried as they tumbled into the chamber. They turned to her, stunned. *"Sheathe!"* she repeated. Their swords were lowered and stowed, though their hands remained ready upon the pommels. One of the guardsmen, an officer, began to protest, but Esmenet silenced him with a furious look. "The Scylvendi came only to kneel," she said, turning her painted face to Cnaiür, "to honour the first-born son of the Warrior-Prophet."

And Cnaiür found that he was on his knees before the crib, his eyes blank, dry, and so very wide.

It seemed he had never stood.

Xinemus sat at Achamian's battered desk, squarely facing a wall whose fresco had largely sloughed away; aside from a speared leopard, random eyes and limbs were all that remained. "What are you doing?" he asked.

Achamian wilfully ignored the warning in his tone. He spoke to his humble belongings, which he had spread across his bed. "I already told you, Zin ... I'm gathering my things, going to the Fama Palace." Esmenet had always teased him about the way he packed, for taking inventories of what he could count on his fingers. *"Better hike your tunic,"* she would always say. *"The little things are the easiest to forget."*

A bitch in heat ... What else could she be?

"But Proyas has forgiven you."

This time he noticed the Marshal's tone, but it caught his ire more than his concern. All the man did was drink anymore. "I haven't forgiven Proyas."

"And me?" Xinemus finally said. "What of *me?*"

Achamian's scalp prickled. There was always something about the way drunks said *me.* He turned to the man, trying to remind himself that this was his friend ... his only friend.

"What of you?" he asked. "Proyas still has need of your counsel, your wisdom. *You* have a place here. I don't."

"That isn't what I meant, Akka."

"But why would I ..." Achamian trailed, suddenly realizing what his friend had in fact meant. He was accusing Achamian of abandoning him. Even still, after everything that had happened, the man dared blame. Achamian turned back to his pathetic estate.

As though his life weren't madness enough.

"Why don't you come with me?" he ventured, only to be shocked by the insincerity of his tone. "We can ... we can *talk* ... talk with Kellhus."

"What need would Kellhus have of me?"

"*You* need, Zin. You need to talk with him. You need—"

Somehow, Xinemus had vacated the desk without making a sound. Now he loomed over Achamian, wild-haired, ghastly for more than the absence of his eyes.

"*You talk to him!*" the Marshal roared, seizing and shaking him. Achamian clawed at his arms, but they were as wood. "I begged you! Remember? I begged, *and you watched while they gouged out my fucking eyes!* My fucking eyes, Akka! My fucking eyes are *gone!*"

Achamian found himself on the hard floor, scrambling backward, his face covered in warm spittle.

The great-limbed man sagged to his knees. "*I can't seeeee!*" he at once whispered and wailed. "*I-haven't-the-courage-I-haven't-the-courage ...*" He shook silently for several more moments, then became very still. When he next spoke, his voice was thick, but eerily disconnected from what had racked him only moments before. It was the voice of the old Xinemus, and it terrified Achamian.

"You need to talk to him for me, Akka. To Kellhus ..."

Achamian lacked the will either to move or to hope. He felt bound to the floor by his own entrails.

"What do you want me to say?"

———— ❧ ————

The first flutter of the eyes against the morning light. The first tasted breath. The drowsy ache of cheek against pillow. These, and these alone, connected Esmenet to the woman—the whore—she had once been.

Sometimes she would forget. Sometimes she would awaken to the old sensations: the anxiousness floating through her limbs, the reek of her bedding, the ache of her sex—once she had even heard the tink-tink-tinking of the copper-smithies from the adjoining street. Then she would bolt erect, and muslin sheets would whisk from her skin. She would blink, peer across the dim chamber at the heroic narratives warring across her walls, and she would focus on her body-slaves—three adolescent Kianene girls—prostrate on the floor, their foreheads pressed down in morning Submission.

Today was no different. Squinting in disorientation, Esmenet arose to the fussing of their hands. They chattered in their curiously soothing tongue, venturing to explain what they said in broken Sheyic only when their tone prompted Esmenet to fix one of them—usually Fanashila—with a curious look. They brushed out her hair with combs of bone, rubbed life back into her legs and arms with quick little palms, then waited patiently as she urinated behind her privacy screen. Afterward, they attended to her bath in the adjacent chamber, scrubbing her with soaps, oiling and scraping her skin.

As always, Esmenet endured their ministrations with quiet wonder. She was generous with her praise, delighted them with her own expressions of delight. They heard the gossip, Esmenet knew, in the slaves' mess. They understood that captivity possessed its own hierarchy of rank and privilege. As slaves to a queen, they had become queens—of a sort—to their fellow slaves. Perhaps they were as astounded as she was.

She emerged from the baths light-headed, slack-limbed, and suffused with that sense of murky well-being only hot water could instill. They dressed first her then her hair, and Esmenet laughed at their banter. Yel and Burulan teased Fanashila—who possessed that outspoken earnestness that condemned so many to be the butt of endless jokes—with light-hearted mercilessness. About some boy, Esmenet imagined.

When they were finished, Fanashila left for the nursery, while Yel and Burulan, still tittering, ushered Esmenet to her night table, and to an array of cosmetics that, she realized with some dismay, would have made her weep back in Sumna. Even as she marvelled at the brushes, paints, and powders, she worried over this new-found jealousy for things. *I deserve this*, she thought, only to curse herself for blinking tears.

Yel and Burulan fell silent.

It's just more ... more that will be taken away.

It was with awe that Esmenet greeted her own image in the mirror, an awe she saw reflected in the admiring eyes of her body-slaves. She was beautiful—as beautiful as Serwë, only dark. Staring at the exotic stranger before her, she could almost believe she was worth what so many had made of her. She could almost believe that all this was real.

Her love of Kellhus clutched at her like the recollection of an onerous trespass. Yel stroked her cheek; she was always the most matronly of the three, the quickest to sense her afflictions. "Beautiful," she cooed, staring at her with unwavering eyes. "Like goddess ..."

Esmenet squeezed her hand, then reached down to her own still-flat belly. *It is real.*

Shortly before they finished, Fanashila returned with Moënghus and Opsara, his surly wet nurse. Then a small train of kitchen slaves entered with her breakfast, which she took in the sunlit portico while asking Opsara questions about Serwë's son. Unlike her body-slaves, Opsara continually *counted* everything she rendered to her new masters: every step taken, every question answered, every surface scrubbed. Sometimes she fairly seethed with impertinence, but somehow she always managed to fall just short of outright insubordination. Esmenet would have replaced her long ago had she not been so obviously and so fiercely devoted to Moënghus, whom she treated as a fellow captive, an innocent to be shielded from their captors. Sometimes, as he suckled, she would sing songs of unearthly beauty.

Opsara made no secret of her contempt for Yel, Burulan, and Fanashila, who for their part seemed to regard her with general terror, though Fanashila dared sniff at her remarks now and again.

After eating, Esmenet took Moënghus and retreated back to her canopied bed. For a time she simply sat, holding him on her knees, staring into his dumbstruck eyes. She smiled as tiny hands clutched tiny toes.

"I love you, Moënghus," she cooed. "Yes I do-I-do-I-do-I-*dooo*."

Yet again, it all seemed a dream.

"You'll never be hungry again, my sweet. I promise ... I-do-I-do-I-*dooo*!"

Moënghus squealed with joy beneath her tickling fingers. She laughed aloud, smirked at Opsara's stern glare, then winked at the beaming faces of her body-slaves. "Soon you'll have a little brother. Did you know that? Or perhaps a sister … And I'll call her *Serwë*, just like your mother. *I-will-I-will-I-will!*"

Finally she stood and, returning the babe to Opsara, announced her imminent departure. They fell to their knees, performed their mid-morning Submission—the girls as though it were a beloved game, Opsara as though dragged down by gravel in her limbs.

As Esmenet watched them, her thoughts turned to Achamian for the first time since the garden.

∽∾∽

By coincidence she met Werjau, scrolls and tablets bundled in his arms, in the corridors leading to her official chambers. He organized his materials while she mounted the low dais. Her scribal secretaries had already taken their places at her feet, kneeling before the knee-high writing lecterns the Kianene favoured. Holding the Reports in the crook of his left arm, Werjau stood between them some paces distant, in the heart of the tree that decorated the room's crimson carpet. Golden branches curled and forked about his black slippers.

"Two men, Tydonni, were apprehended last night painting Orthodox slogans on the walls of the Indurum Barracks." Werjau looked to her expectantly. The secretaries scribbled for a furious moment, then their quills fell still.

"What's their station?" she asked.

"Caste-menial."

As always, such incidents filled her with a reluctant terror—not at what might happen, but at what she might conclude. Why did this residue of defiance persist?

"So they could not read."

"Apparently they simply painted figures written for them on scraps of parchment. It seems they were paid, though they know not by whom."

The Nansur, no doubt. More petty vengeance wreaked by Ikurei Conphas.

"Well enough," she replied. "Have them flayed and posted."

The ease with which these words fell from her lips was nothing short of nightmarish. One breath and these men, these piteous fools, would die in torment. A breath that could have been used for anything: a moan of pleasure, a gasp of surprise, a word of mercy ...

This, she understood, was power: the translation of word into fact. She need only speak and the world would be rewritten. Before, her voice could conjure only custom, ragged breaths, and quickened seed. Before, her cries could only forestall affliction and wheedle what small mercies might come. But now her voice had *become* that mercy, that affliction.

Such thoughts made her head swim.

She watched the secretaries record her judgement. She had quickly learned to conceal her astonishment. She found herself yet again holding her left hand, her tattooed hand, to her belly, clutching as though it had become her totem of what was real. The world about her might be a lie, but the child within ... A woman knew no greater certainty, even as she feared.

For a moment Esmenet marvelled at the warmth beneath her palm, convinced she felt the flush of divinity. The luxury, the power—these were but trifles compared with the other, inner transformations. Her womb, which had been a hospice to innumerable men, was now a temple. Her intellect, which had been benighted by ignorance and misunderstanding, was becoming a beacon. Her heart, which had been a gutter, was now an altar to him ... to the Warrior-Prophet.

To Kellhus.

"Earl Gothyelk," Werjau continued, "was thrice heard cursing our Lord."

She waved in a gesture of dismissal. "Next."

"With all due respect, Consort, I think the matter warrants further scrutiny."

"Tell me," Esmenet said testily, "whom *doesn't* Gothyelk curse? As soon as he *stops* cursing our Lord and Master, then I shall worry." Kellhus had warned her about Werjau. The man resented her, he said, both because she was a woman and because of his native pride. But since both she and Werjau knew and accepted his debility, their relationship seemed more that of combative yet repentant siblings than antagonists, as they most surely would have been otherwise. It was strange to work with others knowing that no secrets were safe, that nothing petty could be concealed. It made their interactions with outsiders seem tawdry—even tragic—by comparison. Amongst themselves, they never feared what others thought, because Kellhus made sure they always knew.

She graced the man with an apologetic smile. "Please continue."

Werjau nodded, his expression bemused. "There was another murder among the Ainoni. One Aspa Memkumri, a client of Lord Uranyanka."

"The Scarlet Spires?"

"Our source insists this is the case."

"Our source … you mean Neberenes." When Werjau nodded in assent, she said, "Bring him to me tomorrow … discreetly. We need to know precisely what they're doing. In the meantime, I will speak to our Lord and Master."

The flaxen-haired Nascenti marked something on his wax tablet, then continued. "Earl Hulwarga was observed performing a banned rite."

"Irrelevant," she said. "Our Lord does not begrudge the faithful their superstitions. A strong faith does not fear for its principles, Werjau. Especially when the believers are Thunyeri."

Another switch of his stylus, mirrored by those of the secretaries.

The man moved to the next item, this time without looking up. "The Warrior-Prophet's new Vizier," he said tonelessly, "was heard screaming in his chambers."

Esmenet's breath caught. "What," she asked carefully, "was he screaming?"

"No one knows."

Thoughts of Achamian always came as small calamities.

"I will deal with this personally … Understood?"

"Understood, Consort."

"Is there anything else?"

"Just the Lists."

Kellhus had called on all Men of the Tusk to attend to their vassals and peers—even their betters—so they might report any inconsistencies of appearance or character, anything that might suggest recent substitution by a skin-spy. The names so volunteered were marked on the Lists. Every morning, dozens if not hundreds of Inrithi were numbered, then marched beneath the all-seeing eyes of the Warrior-Prophet.

Of all the thousands so far listed, one had killed the men sent to retrieve him, two had disappeared before arrest, one the Hundred Pillars had seized for interrogation, and another, a Baron client to Count-Palatine Chinjosa, they had affected to overlook, hoping to uncover the greater ring. It was a blunt and inelegant instrument, to be sure, but short of Kellhus risking exposure, it was all they had. Of the thirty-eight skin-spies Kellhus had been able to identify before revealing his hand, fewer than a dozen had been taken or killed.

The most they could do, it seemed, was to wait for them to surface behind other faces.

"Have the Shrial Knights gather them as always."

Following the Summary of Reports, Esmenet walked the circuit of the western terrace, both to bask in the sunlight and to greet—albeit at a distance—the dozens of adulants gathered on the rooftops below. She found their attention both distressing and exhilarating. Even as she despaired over her worthiness, she tried to think of ways she might reward their unwarranted patience. Yesterday, she had several guardsmen distribute bread and pepper-soup. Today, thanking Momas for the sea breeze, she cast them two crimson veils, which twisted like eels in water as they floated over their palms. She laughed as they scrambled.

Afterward she oversaw the afternoon Penance with three of the Nascenti. Originally, the rite had been intended to shrive those of the Orthodox who had fomented against the Warrior-Prophet, but against expectations many Men of the Tusk began *returning*, some once or twice, some day in and day out. Even Zaudunyani—including those initiated in the first secret Whelmings—started to attend, claiming to have suffered doubts or malice or some such during the misery of the siege. As a result, the numbers who gathered had increased to the point where the Nascenti had to start administering Penance outside the Fama Palace.

At the direction of the Judges, the attendees stripped to the waist and assembled in long, uneven rows, where they knelt upright, their backs slick and burnished in the setting sun. While the Nascenti recited the prayers, the Judges methodically worked their way among the penitents, lashing each man three times with a branch shorn from Umiaki. With each stroke they cried out, in succession:

"For wounding that which heals!"

"For seizing what would be given!"

"For condemning that which saves!"

Esmenet still wrung her hands as she watched the dark branches rise and fall. The bleeding unnerved her, though most received no more than welts. Their backs, with protruding spine and ribs, seemed so frail. But it was the *way* they watched her, as though she were a milestone that marked some otherwise immeasurable distance, that troubled her the most. When the Judges struck, some even arched back, their faces riven with expressions whores knew well but no woman truly understood.

Averting her gaze, she spied Proyas kneeling in the rearmost line. For some reason he seemed so much more naked than the others. Possessed of an old animus, she glared at him, but he seemed incapable of meeting her eyes. After the Judge had passed, he buried his face in his hands, shook with sobs. To her dismay, Esmenet found herself wondering whom he repented, Kellhus or Achamian.

She did not attend that evening's ceremonial Whelming, opting to take a private dinner in her apartments instead. Kellhus, she was told, remained preoccupied with the Holy War's imminent march on Xerash, so she dined and joked with her body-slaves instead, siding with Fanashila in what—she gathered—was a dispute regarding coloured sashes. Let Yel be teased for a change, she thought.

Fanashila could scarce contain herself, so overwhelmed was she with gratitude.

Afterward Esmenet ducked into the nursery to check on Moënghus, then crossed the hall to what she had come to think of as her private library ...

Where Achamian had been recently installed.

The Fama Palace was a place of architectural flourish and extravagance, sheathed in the finest marbles and displaying the elegant sensibilities of the Kianene at every turn, from the bronze fretting that shuttered the windows to the lines of inset mother-of-pearl that traced every pointed arch. At its outskirts the complex consisted of a radial network of courtyards, compounds, and galleries that stacked higher as the structure climbed the various faces of the summit. She and Kellhus occupied the suite of apartments on the height's pinnacle—the highest point in Caraskand, she liked to tell herself—overlooking the Apple Garden with its ancient teeth of stone. This, Kellhus had said, exposed them to unconventional means of attack. Sorcery, it seemed, paid no heed to walls or elevation. And this was why Achamian had to reside so painfully close.

Close enough, she realized, to hear her cries on the wind.

Akka ...

She stood before the panelled door, realizing in a rush the lengths to which she had gone to avoid all thought of him. He'd not been real that first night he had come to her. Not at all. He'd been real enough when she glimpsed him in the Apple Garden, but he'd seemed *perilous* as well, as though his mere image might strip away all that had happened since the Holy War's march from Shigek.

How could seeing someone old peel the years from one's eyes?

What am I doing?

Fearing she would lose her nerve, she rapped on the wood with her left hand, staring at the bruised serpents tattooed across its back as she did so. For the briefest of instants, before the door swung open, she was sure that it wasn't Achamian but *Sumna* that would greet her on the far side. She could almost feel the brick of her window's sill pressing cold against the back of her naked thighs. And she remembered, with a visceral intensity, what it was like *being* her wares.

Then Achamian's face floated into view, more grizzled perhaps, but as stout and heartwarming as she remembered. There was far more grey in his pleated beard: the fingers of white had joined into a palm of sorts. His eyes, though ... they belonged to someone she didn't know.

Neither of them spoke a word. The awkwardness was like ice in her throat. *He lives ... he really lives.*

Esmenet fought the need to touch him, to ... reassure herself. She could smell the River Sempis, the bitter of black willows on the hot Shigeki wind. She could see him leading his sad mule, receding into the distance that had, she thought, swallowed him forever. *What brought you back to me?*

Then his eyes fell to her belly, lingered for a heartbeat. She glanced away, looking airily to the shelved walls beyond him. "I've come for *The Third Analytic of Men.*"

Without a word, Achamian strode to a brace of shelves along the southern wall. He withdrew a large chapped folio, which he hefted in his hands. He tried to grin, but his eyes would have none of it. "You can come in," he said.

She took four tentative steps past the threshold. The room smelled of him, a faint musk she had always associated with sorcery. A bed had been erected where her favourite settee had been—where she had first read *The Tractate*.

"Translated into Sheyic, even," he said, pursing his bottom lip in appreciation. "For Kellhus?"

"No ... for me."

She had meant to say this with pride, but it had sounded spiteful instead. "He taught me how to read," she explained, more carefully. "Through the misery of the desert, no less."

Achamian had blanched. "Read?"

"Yes ... Imagine, a *woman*."

He scowled in what could only be confusion.

"The old world is dead, Akka. The old *rules* are dead ... Surely you know this."

He blinked as though struck, and she realized it had been her tone and not her assertion that had prompted his scowl. Achamian had never begrudged her her sex.

He looked to the embossed lettering across the cover. There was a curious, endearing reverence to the way he drew his fingers over it. "Ajencis is an old friend of mine," he said, holding out the book. His smile was genuine this time, but afraid. "Be gentle with him."

Taking care to avoid his touch, she lifted the thing from his hands, swallowed at the thickness in her throat.

A moment of locked gazes. She thought to murmur something—a word of thanks, maybe, or a stupid joke, like those they'd used to cement so many loose moments between them—but she found herself walking toward the door instead, hugging the leather tome to her breast. There were just too many old ... comforts between them, too many habits that would see her in his arms.

And he knew this, damn him. He *used* them.

He called out her name, and she paused at the threshold. When she turned, her eyes were forced down by the stricken expression on his face. "I ..." he began. "I was your *life* ... I know I was, Esmi."

She bit her lip, resisted the instinct to deceive.

"Yes," she said, staring at her blue-painted toes. For some perverse reason she decided she would have Yel change their colour tomorrow.

What does he matter? His heart was broken long before—

"Yes," she repeated, "you were my life." When she raised her face, it was with weariness, not the ferocity she had expected. "And *he* is my world."

———— ∞ ————

She stared across the broad planes of his chest, followed the grooves of his stomach into the downy gold of his pubis, where she could see the base of him shining in the erotic gloom of partially drawn sheets. For some reason he always seemed so vast when she laid her cheek on his shoulder. Like a new world, both beguiling and terrifying.

"I saw him tonight."

"I know … You were angered."

"Not by him."

"Yes … by him."

"But why? Save loving me, what has he done?"

"We betrayed him, Esmi. *You* betrayed him."

"But you said—"

"There are sins, Esmi, that not even the God can absolve. Only the injured."

"What are you saying?"

"That this is why he angers you."

It was always the same with him, always the same remembrance of things beyond human memory. It was as though she—like every other man, woman, and child—awakened every moment to find herself stranded, and only he could tell her what had come before.

"He will not forgive," she whispered.

There was indecision in his look, frightening for its rarity. "He will not forgive."

———— ∞ ————

The Grandmaster of the Scarlet Spires turned, too numb to possess any force of person and too drunk not to. "You live," he said.

Iyokus stood dumbstruck at the threshold. Eleäzaras watched the red-irised eyes survey the smashed pottery and congealing wine. He snorted, neither in humour nor disgust, then turned to look back out over the balustrade, at the Fama Palace, dun and inscrutable upon its hill.

"When Achamian returned," he drawled, "I had assumed you were dead." He leaned forward, glanced back at the wraith once again. "Even more," he said, raising a finger, "I had *hoped* you dead." He returned his gaze to the walls and buildings encrusting the opposite heights.

"What happens, Eli?"

He tried his best not to laugh. "Can't you see? The Padirajah is dead. The Holy War prepares to march on Shimeh. *We* prepare to march on Shimeh ... Our foot lies upon the neck of our enemy."

"I've spoken to Sarothenes," Iyokus said, unimpressed, "and to Inrûmmi ..."

A mawkish sigh. "Then you know."

"I confess, I find it difficult to believe."

"Believe it. The Consult *exists*. All this time, laughing at the Mandati, and it was *we* who were the mumming fools."

A long, accusatory silence. Iyokus had always told him he should heed their claims more seriously. It seemed plain enough ... now. Everything they knew about the Psûkhe suggested it was a blunt instrument, far too cumbersome to fashion something like these ... demons.

Chepheramunni! Sarcellus!

In his soul's eye he saw the Scylvendi, bloodied and magnificent, hoisting the faceless head for all to see. How the mobs had roared.

"And Prince Kellhus?" Iyokus asked.

"Is a prophet," Eleäzaras said softly. He had watched him—*he had seen*—after they had cut the man down from the Circumfix ... Eleäzaras had watched him reach into his chest and pull out his fucking heart!

Some kind of trick ... it had to be!

"Eli," Iyokus said, "surely this—"

"I spoke to him myself," the Grandmaster interrupted, "and at quite some length ... He's a true prophet of the God, Iyokus ... And you and I ... well, we're quite damned." He looked at his Master of Spies, his face screwed into an expression of pained hilarity. "Another little joke we seem to have found ourselves on the wrong side of ..."

"Please," the man exclaimed. "How could you—"

"Oh, I know. He sees things ... things only the God could see." He swung at one of the earthenware decanters, caught it, shook it in the air to listen for the telltale slosh of wine. Empty. "He showed me," he said, casting it against the wall, where it shattered. He smiled at Iyokus, letting the weight of his bottom lip draw his mouth open. "He showed me *who I am.* You know all those little thoughts, all those half-glimpsed things that scurry like vermin through your soul? He catches them, Iyokus. He catches them and holds them squealing in the air. Then he names them, and tells you what they mean." He turned away once more. "He sees the *secrets.*"

"What secrets? What are you saying, Eli?"

"Oh, you've no need to worry. He cares nothing whether you fuck little boys or press broomsticks up your ass. It's the secrets *you keep from yourself,* Iyokus. Those are his interest. He sees ..." A pang gripped his throat so violently he had to look at Iyokus and laugh. He felt tears spill hot across his cheeks. His voice cracked. "He sees what breaks your heart."

You have doomed your School.

"You're drunk," the chanv addict said, his tone both unnerved and disgusted.

Eleäzaras raised his hand in a foppish wave. "Go speak to him yourself. He'll discern more than pickled meat through your skin. You'll see—"

He heard the man snort, then kick away a metal bowl as he withdrew.

The Grandmaster of the Scarlet Spires reclined in his settee, resumed his study of the Fama Palace through the afternoon haze. The network of walls, terraces, and Fanic colonnades. The faint smoke rising from what had to be the kitchens. The clots of distant penitents filing beneath the square gates.

Somewhere ... He's in there somewhere.

"Oh, yes, and Iyokus?" he abruptly called.

"What?"

"I would beware the Mandate Schoolman if I were you." He absently pawed the table beside him, looking for more wine—or something. "I think he plans to kill you."

CHAPTER THREE

CARASKAND

If soot stains your tunic, dye it black. This is vengeance.

—EKYANNUS I, 44 EPISTLES

Here we find further argument for Gotagga's supposition that the world is round. How else could all men stand higher than their brothers?

—AJENCIS, DISCOURSE ON WAR

Early Spring, 4112 Year-of-the-Tusk, Caraskand

The dry season. On the Steppe, it betrayed its coming with a variety of signs: the first sight of the Lance among the stars on the northern horizon; the quickness with which the milk soured; the first trailers of the *caïnnu*, the midsummer wind.

At the beginning of the rainy season, Scylvendi herdsmen ranged the Steppe in search of the sandy ground where the grasses grew quicker. When the rains waxed, they drove their herds to harder ground, where the grasses grew slower but remained green longer. Then, when the hot winds chased the clouds to oblivion, they simply followed the forage, always searching for the wild herbs and short grasses that made for the best meat and milk.

This pursuit always caught someone, particularly those who were too greedy to cull wilful animals from their herd. Headstrong cattle could lead an entire herd too far afield, into vast tracts of over-grazed or blighted pasture. Every season, it seemed, some fool returned without horse or cattle.

Cnaiür now knew himself to be that fool.

I have given him the Holy War.

In the council chamber of the dead Sapatishah, Cnaiür sat high on the tiers that surrounded the council table, watching the Dûnyain intently. He did his best to ignore the Inrithi crowding the seats about him, but he found himself continually accosted—congratulated. One fool, some Tydonni thane, even had the temerity to kiss his knee—his knee! Once again they called out "Scylvendi!" as though in salute.

Flanked by hanging gold-on-black representations of the Circumfix, the Warrior-Prophet sat upon a raised dais, so that he looked down upon the Great Names sitting about the council table. His beard had been oiled and braided. His flaxen hair tumbled across his shoulders. Beneath a stiff knee-length vestment, he wore a white silk gown embroidered by the forking of silvery leaves and grey branches. Braziers had been set about him, and in their light he seemed aqueous, surreal—every bit the other-worldly prophet he claimed to be. His luminous eyes roamed the room, stirring gasps and whispers wherever they passed. Twice his look found Cnaiür, who cursed himself for looking away.

Wretched! Wretched!

The sorcerer, the woman-hearted buffoon whom everyone had thought dead, stood before the dais to the Dûnyain's left, wearing an ankle-length vest of crimson over a white linen frock. He, at least, wasn't festooned like a slaver's concubine—as were the others. But he had a look in his eyes that Cnaiür recognized, as though he too couldn't quite believe the lot fortune had cast him. Cnaiür had overheard Uranyanka on the tier below saying that the man, Drusas Achamian, was now the Warrior-Prophet's Vizier, his teacher and protector.

Whatever he was, he looked obscenely fat compared with the rakish Inrithi caste-nobles. Perhaps, Cnaiür thought, the Dûnyain planned to use his bulk as a shield should the Consult or Cishaurim attack.

The Great Names sat about the table as before, though now stripped of the hauteur belonging to their station. Where once they had been bick-ering kings, the Lords of the Holy War, they were now little more than counsellors, and they knew it. They were silent for the most part, pensive. Occasionally one of them would lean to mutter something in his neigh-bour's ear, but nothing more.

In the course of a single day, the world these men had known had been struck to its foundation, utterly overturned. There was wonder in that—Cnaiür knew this only too well—but there was an absurd uncertainty also. For the first time in their lives they stood upon trackless ground, and with few exceptions they looked to the Dûnyain to show them the way. Much as Cnaiür had once looked to Moënghus.

As the last of the Lesser Names hunted seats across the tiers, the rumble of hushed voices trailed into expectant silence. The air beneath the corbelled dome seemed to whine with a collective discomfort. For these men, Cnaiür realized, the Warrior-Prophet's presence collapsed too many intangible things. How could they speak without praying? Disagree without blaspheming? Even the presumption to advise would seem an act of outrageous conceit.

In the safety of unanswered prayers, they had thought themselves pious. Now they were like boasting gossips, astounded to find their story's principal in their midst. And he might say *anything*, throw their most cherished conceits upon the pyre of his condemnation. What would they do, the devout and self-righteous alike? What would they do now that their hallowed scripture *could talk back?*

Cnaiür almost barked with laughter. He lowered his head and spat between his knees. He cared not if others marked his sneer. There was no honour here, only advantage—absolute and irremediable.

There was no honour—but there was *truth*. Was there not?

The insufferable ritual and pageantry, which seemed obligatory to all things Inrithi, began with Gotian reciting the Temple Prayer. He stood as rigid as an adolescent in vestments that appeared newly made: white cloth with intricate panels, each embroidered with two golden tusks crossing a golden circle—yet another version of the Circumfix. His voice shook as he spoke, and he halted once, overcome with passion.

Cnaiür found himself looking about the chamber, his breath tight in his chest, quietly astounded that men wept rather than jeered. And then, for the first time, the depths of the dread purpose that moved these men became *palpable*.

He had seen it. He had witnessed it on the fields beyond Caraskand's wall—the lunatic determination, enough to shame even his Utemot. He had watched men vomit boiled grass as they stumbled forward. He had seen others who could scarce walk throw themselves upon the weapons of the heathen—just to disarm them! He had seen men smile—cry out in joy!—as the mastodons descended upon them. He could remember thinking that these men, these *Inrithi*, were the true People of War.

Cnaiür had seen it, but he had not understood—not fully. What the Dûnyain had wrought here would never be undone. Even if the Holy War should perish, the *word* of these events would survive. Ink would make this madness immortal. Kellhus had given these men more than gestures or promises, more even than insight or direction. He had given them *dominion*. Over their doubts. Over their most hated foes. He had made them strong.

But how could *lies* do such a thing?

The world these men dwelt within was a fever-dream, a delusion. And yet it seemed as real to them, Cnaiür knew, as his world seemed to him. The only difference—and Cnaiür was curiously troubled by the thought—was that he could, in meticulous detail, track the origins of their world within his, and only then because he knew the Dûnyain. Of all those congregated in this room, he alone knew the ground, the treacherous footing, beneath their feet.

Suddenly everything Cnaiür witnessed was parsed in two, as though his eyes had become enemies, one against the other. Gotian had completed the Temple Prayer, and several of the Dûnyain's high priests, his Nascenti, had begun a Whelming for those among the Lesser Names who'd been too ill to partake in the ceremony previously. A flaming basin of oil had been set before the Warrior-Prophet, who sat idol still. The first of the initiates, a Thunyeri by the look of his braids, knelt beside the tripod, then exchanged inaudible orisons with the administering priest. Though his face had been battered by pestilence and war, his eyes were those of a ten-year-old, pinned wide in hope and apprehension. In a single motion the priest dipped his hand into the burning oil then drew it across the Thunyeri's features. For a heartbeat the man gazed from a face aflame, until a second priest doused him with a wet towel. The room thundered with exultant cries, and the thane, his expression bent by profound passion, staggered into the jubilant arms of his comrades.

For the Inrithi, the man had crossed an intangible threshold. They had watched a profound transformation, a base soul raised to the assembly of the elect. Where before he'd been polluted, now he was cleansed. And they had witnessed this *with their own eyes*. Who could question it?

But for Cnaiür, the only threshold crossed was that between foolishness and outright idiocy. He had watched an instrument, not a sacred rite—a mechanism, like the elaborate mills he had seen in Nansur, a way for the Dûnyain to grind these men into something he could digest. And this too was something he had seen with his own eyes.

Unlike the Inrithi, he did not stand within the circle of the Dûnyain's deceit. Where they saw things from within, he saw them from without. He saw *more*. It was strange the way beliefs could have an inside and an outside, that what looked like hope or truth or love from within could be a scythe or a hammer, things wielded for other ends, when seen from without.

Tools.

Cnaiür breathed deeply. This thought had tormented him once. It had been one too many.

He leaned forward, elbows on knees, absently watching the farce unfold.

The Inrithi, Proyas had told him once, believed it was the lot of men to live within the designs, inscrutable or otherwise, of those greater than themselves. And in this sense, Cnaiür realized, Kellhus truly *was* their prophet. They were, as the memorialists claimed, willing slaves, always striving to beat down the furies that drove them to sovereign ends. That the designs—the tracks—they claimed to follow were authored in the Outside simply served their vanity, allowed them to abase themselves in a manner that fanned their overweening pride. There was no greater tyranny, the memorialists said, than that exercised by slaves over slaves.

But now the slaver stood among them. What did it matter, Kellhus had asked as they crossed the Steppe, that he mastered those already enslaved?

There was no honour, only advantage. To believe in honour was to stand *inside* things, to keep company with slaves and fools.

The Whelming had come to a close, and Saubon, the titular King of Caraskand, was standing—called to account by the Warrior-Prophet.

"I will not march," the Galeoth Prince said in a dead voice. "Caraskand is mine. I will not relinquish it—even if I be damned as a result."

"But the Warrior-Prophet has *demanded* that you march," silver-haired Gotian cried. Something about the way the man said "Warrior-Prophet" made Cnaiür's hackles rise—something febrile and unmanly. The Grandmaster of the Shrial Knights, who had been the Dûnyain's most implacable foe before the exposure of Sarcellus, had since become his most fervent devotee. Such fickleness of spirit only deepened Cnaiür's contempt for these people.

"I will not march," Saubon repeated, as though speaking from a night-mare. The Galeoth Prince, Cnaiür noted, actually had the temerity to wear his iron crown to this particular Council. Even though tall, ruddy with sun and warlike health, the man looked an adolescent playing king beneath the Warrior-Prophet. "By my hand I have seized this city, and by my hand I shall keep it!"

"Sweet Sejenus!" Gothyelk cried. "By *your* hand? And a thousand others, maybe!"

"I opened the gates!" Saubon retorted fiercely. "I delivered the city to the Holy War!"

"You delivered precious little that you haven't kept," Lord Chinjosa quipped. He looked pointedly at the iron crown as he spoke, smirking as though recalling a joke traded in secret.

"Headaches," Gothyelk added, clenching a grey-haired fist. "He's delivered many a headache ..."

"I simply demand what's mine by *right!*" Saubon snarled. "Proyas—you agreed to support me, Proyas!"

The Conriyan Prince glanced uneasily at the Dûnyain, then stared evenly at the would-be Caraskandi King. During the siege, he had refused to eat more than his men, so he was gaunt, and he looked older now that he was growing his beard out square like his father's kinsmen. "No. I'll not renege on my pledge, Saubon." Indecision slackened his handsome face. "But things ... have changed."

The debate was a sham, the preserving of certain motions to advance a sense of continuity. Proyas had fairly shouted this, though he would never admit to it. Only one decision mattered.

All eyes had climbed to the Warrior-Prophet. Fierce before his peers, Saubon now seemed petulant—a king unmanned beneath the vaults of his own palace.

"Those who carry the war to Holy Shimeh," the Warrior-Prophet said, his voice falling upon them like a knife-prick, "must do so freely ..."

"No," Saubon said hoarsely. "Please, no."

At first this answer escaped Cnaiür, then he realized the Dûnyain had forced Saubon to choose his own damnation. He returned their choices to them only when he needed them to be accountable. Such maddening subtlety!

The Warrior-Prophet shook his leonine head. "There is nothing to be done."

"Strip him of his throne," Ikurei Conphas said abruptly. "Have him dragged into the streets." He shrugged in the manner of long-suffering men. "Have his teeth beaten from his head."

Astonished silence greeted his words. As the first among the Orthodox conspirators—and as Sarcellus's confidant, no less—Conphas had become an outcast among the Great Names. In the Council preceding the battle, he'd contributed little, and when he did talk, it was with the awkwardness of one forced to speak an unfamiliar tongue. It seemed that his patience had at last been exhausted.

The Exalt-General looked to his astounded peers, snorted. He wore his blue mantle in the Nansur fashion, thrown up and across the stamped gold of his breastplate. Among all those assembled, he alone seemed unmarked, unscarred, as though mere days had passed since that fateful Council on the Andiamine Heights.

He turned to the Warrior-Prophet. "Such things lie within the scope of your power, do they not?"

"Insolence!" Gothyelk hissed. "You don't know what you're saying!"

"I assure you, old fool, I always know what I'm saying."

"And what," the Warrior-Prophet said, "what might that be?"

Conphas managed a defiant smile. "That this—all of this—is a sham. That you"—he glanced again at the surrounding faces—"are a fraud."

Whispers of hushed outrage rifled through the chamber. The Dûnyain merely smiled.

"But this is *not* what you say."

It seemed that Conphas sensed, for perhaps the first time, the impossible dimensions of the Dûnyain's authority over the men surrounding him. The Warrior-Prophet was more than their centre, as a general might be; he was their centre and their *ground*. These men had to trim not only their words and actions to conform to his authority, but their passions and hopes as well—the very movements of their souls now answered to the Warrior-Prophet.

"But," Conphas said blankly, "how could another—"

"Another?" the Warrior-Prophet asked. "Don't confuse me with any 'other,' Ikurei Conphas. I am here, with you." He leaned forward in a way that made Cnaiür catch his breath. "I am here, *in you*."

"In me," the Exalt-General repeated.

He had tried to sound contemptuous, Cnaiür knew, but he sounded frightened instead.

"I realize," the Dûnyain continued, "that you speak these words out of impatience, that you've chafed at the changes my presence has wrought in the Holy War. I know that the strength I've delivered to the Men of the Tusk threatens your designs. I know that you're unsure as to how to proceed, that you don't know whether to offer the same pretence of submission that you offer your uncle or to discredit me with open words. So now you deny me out of desperation, not to prove to others that I'm a fraud but to prove to yourself that *you are in fact my better*. For an obscene arrogance dwells within you, Ikurei Conphas, the belief that you are the measure of all other men. It is this lie that you seek to preserve at all costs."

"Not true!" Conphas cried, bolting from his chair.

"No? Then tell me, Exalt-General, how many times have you thought yourself a *god*?"

Conphas licked tight lips. "Never."

The Warrior-Prophet nodded sceptically. "It is peculiar, isn't it, the place you find yourself standing? To preserve your pride before me, you must endure the shame of lying. You must *conceal* who you are, in order to *prove* who you are. You must degrade yourself to remain proud. At this moment you see this more clearly than at any other time in your life, and yet still you refuse to relinquish, to yield to your tormented pride. You trade the anguish that breeds anguish for the anguish that breeds release. You would rather take pride in what you are not than take pride in *what you are*."

"Silence!" Conphas screeched. "*No one* speaks to me this way! *No one!*"

"Shame is a stranger to you, Ikurei Conphas. An unbearable stranger."

Wild-eyed, Conphas stared at the congregated faces. The sound of weeping filled the room, the weeping of other men who'd recognized themselves in the Warrior-Prophet's words. Cnaiür watched and listened, his skin awash with dread, his heart pounding in his throat. Ordinarily, he would have taken deep satisfaction in the Exalt-General's humiliation—but this was of a different order. Shame *itself* now reared above them, a beast that devoured all certainties, that wrapped cold coils about the fiercest souls.

How does he do this?

"*Release*," the Warrior-Prophet said, as though a word could be the world's only unbarred door. "All I offer you, Ikurei Conphas, is *release*."

The Exalt-General stumbled back a step, and for a mad moment it almost seemed that his knees would buckle—that the Emperor's nephew might *kneel*. But then a curious, almost blood-chilling laugh escaped his throat; a hidden madness flashed through the cracks of his mien.

"*Listen* to him!" Gotian hissed plaintively. "Don't you *see*, man? He's the *Prophet!*"

Conphas looked at the Grandmaster without comprehension. His beauty seemed all the more astonishing for the blankness of his expression.

"You are among friends here," Proyas said. "Brothers."

Gotian and Proyas. Other men and other words. These apparently broke the spell of the Dûnyain's voice for Conphas as much as for Cnaiür.

"Brother?" he snarled. "I'm no brother to slaves! You think he *knows* you? That he speaks the hearts of men? He does not! Trust me, my 'brothers,' we Ikurei know a thing or two about words and men. He plays you, and you know it not. He tacks 'truth' after 'truth' to your heart to better yoke the blood beating underneath! Gulls! Slaves! To think I once congratulated myself on your company!" He turned his back to the Great Names, began shouldering his way toward the crowded entrance.

"Halt!" the Dûnyain thundered.

Everyone, including Cnaiür, flinched. Conphas stumbled as though struck. Arms and hands clasped him, turned him, thrust him into the centre of the Warrior-Prophet's attention.

"Kill him!" someone to Cnaiür's right cried.

"Apostate!" pealed from the benches below.

Then the tiers fairly erupted in hoarse outrage. Fists pounded the shivering air. Conphas looked about him, more stunned than terrified, like a boy struck by a beloved uncle.

"Pride," the Warrior-Prophet said, silencing the chamber like a carpenter sweeping sawdust from his workbench. "Pride is a sickness ... For most it's a fever, a contagion goaded by the glories of others. But for some, like you, Ikurei Conphas, it is a defect carried from the womb. For your whole life you've wondered what it was that moved the men about you. Why would a father sell himself into slavery, when he need only strangle his children? Why would a young man take the Orders of the Tusk, exchange the luxuries of his station for a cubicle, authority for servitude to the Holy Shriah? Why do so many *give*, when it is so easy to take?

"But you ask these questions because you know nothing of strength. For what is *strength* but the resolve to deny base inclinations—the determination to *sacrifice* in the name of one's brothers? You, Ikurei Conphas, know only *weakness*, and because it takes strength to acknowledge weakness, you call your weakness strength. You betray your brother. You fresco your heart with flatteries. You, who are less than any man, say to yourself, 'I am a god.'"

The Exalt-General's reply was little more than a whisper, but it resounded across every crook and span of the chamber. "No ..."

Shame. Wutrim. Cnaiür had thought that his hatred of the Dûnyain was without measure, that it could be eclipsed by nothing, but the *shame* that filled this room, the bowel-loosening humiliation, knocked his rancour from him. For an instant he saw the *Warrior-Prophet*, not the Dûnyain, and he stood in awe of him. For an instant he found himself *inside* the man's lies.

"Your Columns," Kellhus continued, "will disarm. You will then decamp for Joktha, where you will await passage back to the Nansurium. You are no longer a Man of the Tusk, Ikurei Conphas. In truth, you never were."

The Exalt-General blinked in astonishment, as though *these words* had offended his person and not those preceding. The man, Cnaiür realized, did suffer some defect of the soul, just as the Dûnyain had said.

"Why?" the Exalt-General asked, recovering the force of his old voice. "Why should I accede to these demands?"

Kellhus stood, approached the man. "Because I *know*," he said, stepping from the dais. For some reason, leaving the illumination of the braziers did nothing to diminish his miraculous bearing. He wore all light to his advantage. "I know the Emperor has struck treaties with the heathen ... I know that you plan to betray the Holy War before Shimeh is regained."

Conphas shrank before his aspect, retreated until caught in the arms of the faithful. Cnaiür recognized several among them—Gaidekki, Tuthorsa, Semper—their eyes bright with something more than hatred. For some reason, they looked a thousand years old, ancient with certitude.

"Because," Kellhus continued, looming over him, "if you fail to comply, I *will* have you flayed and hung from the gates." The tenor of his voice was such that the word "flay" and the skinless images it conjured seemed to linger.

Conphas stared up in abject horror. His lower lip quivered, and his face broke into a soundless sob, only to stiffen, then break again. Cnaiür found himself clutching his breast. Why did his heart race so?

"Release him," the Warrior-Prophet murmured, and the Exalt-General fled through the entranceway, shielding his face, waving his hands as though pelted with stones.

Again Cnaiür stood outside the Dûnyain's machinations.

The accusations of treachery, he knew, were likely a contrivance, nothing more. What would the Emperor gain from abetting his ancestral enemies? Everything that had transpired, Cnaiür realized, had been premeditated. *Everything.* Every word, every look, every insight, had some *function* ... But for what end? To make an example of Ikurei Conphas? To remove him? Why not simply cut his throat?

No. Of all the Great Names, only Ikurei Conphas, the far-famed Lion of Kiyuth, possessed the force of character to retain the loyalty of his men. Kellhus would brook no competitors, but neither would he risk what remained of the Holy War in internecine conflict. That alone had preserved the Exalt-General's life.

Kellhus had withdrawn, and the Men of the Tusk stood and stretched on the tiers, calling, laughing, wondering. And once more Cnaiür found himself watching them with two sets of eyes. The Inrithi, he knew, would see themselves forged and reforged, their temper improved for the want of impurities. But he knew otherwise ...

The dry season had not ended. Perhaps it never would.

The Dûnyain simply culled the wilful from his herd.

⊗∾∾⊗

Struggling to remain stationary in the crush of bodies, Proyas scanned the milling crowds once again, searching for the Scylvendi. Only moments earlier the Warrior-Prophet had withdrawn to thunderous acclaim. Now the Lords of the Holy War rumbled amongst themselves, exchanging exclamations of hilarity and outrage. There was much to discuss: the Ikurei plot uncovered, the Nansur Columns cast out of the Holy War, the Exalt-General humiliated—*debased* ...

"I wager the Imperial Loincloth warrants changing!" Gaidekki cried out from a nearby knot of Conriyan caste-nobles. Laughter boomed through the packed antechamber. It was both merciless and full-hearted—though not, Proyas noted, without strains of apprehension. The triumphal looks, the shrill declarations, the avid gestures and protestations, all spoke to the youth of their conversion. But there was something else as well, something Proyas could feel haunting the corners of his own aching face ...

Fear.

Perhaps this was to be expected. As Ajencis was so fond of observing, habit ruled the souls of men. So long as the past governed the present, those habits could be depended on. But the past had been overturned, and now the Men of the Tusk found themselves stranded with judgements and assumptions they could no longer trust. They had learned that the metaphor cut both ways: to be reborn, Proyas had come to realize, one must murder who one was.

It seemed such a small price—ludicrously small—given what they had gained.

With the Scylvendi nowhere in sight, Proyas sorted the faces into those who had condemned Kellhus and those who had not. Many, like Ingiaban, stood quiet between outbursts, their eyes wide with contrition, their lips pinched in chagrin. But others, like Athjeäri, spoke with the easy bravado of the vindicated. Watching them, Proyas felt envy claw through him, forcing his eyes downward and away. Never, it seemed, had the need to *undo* so overwhelmed him. Not even with Achamian …

What had he been thinking? How could he, a man who had meticulously hammered his heart into the very shape of piety, have come so close to murdering the *God's own voice?*

The thought still dizzied him, struck him nauseous with shame.

Conviction, no matter how narcotic its depth, simply did not make true. This was a hard lesson, made all the harder by its astounding conspicuousness. Despite the exhortations of kings and generals, despite the endless lays, belief unto death was cheap. After all, the Fanim threw themselves against the spears of their enemies as readily as the Inrithi. *Someone* had to be deluded. So what ensured that that someone was *someone else?* Given the manifest frailty of men, given the long succession of delusions that was their history, what could be more preposterous than claiming oneself the least deluded, let alone privy to the absolute?

And to make such obvious conceit the grounds of condemnation … of murder …

In all his life, Proyas had never wept so hard as he had at the Warrior-Prophet's feet. For he, who had decried avarice in all its forms, had proven the most avaricious of all. He had coveted nothing so much as the truth, and since truth had so roundly eluded him, he had turned to his beliefs. How could he not when he'd spent a lifetime abasing himself before them, when they afforded him such luxury of judgement?

When they were so much *who he was.*

The promise of rebirth was at once the threat of murder, and Proyas, like so many others, had opted to kill rather than die.

"Hush," the Warrior-Prophet had said. Mere hours had passed since Kellhus had been cut down from Umiaki. Blood still soaked the bandages about his wrists, forming black rings. "You need not weep, Proyas."

"But I tried to *kill* you!"

A beatific smile, jarring given the obvious pain it contradicted. "All our acts turn upon what we assume to be true, Proyas, what we assume *to know*. The connection is so strong, so thoughtless, that when those things we need to be true are threatened, we try to *make* them true with our acts.

We condemn the innocent to make them guilty. We raise the wicked to make them holy. Like the mother who continues nursing her dead babe, we act out our refusal."

Kellhus had paused in the breathless way he so often did, as if communing with voices that others could almost hear. He raised his hand in a curious gesture—as though to ward away hard words. Proyas could still remember the blood smeared like ink into the whorls of his palm, dark against the gold that haloed his outstretched fingers.

"When we believe without ground or cause, Proyas, conviction is all we possess, and acts of conviction become our only demonstration. Our *beliefs* become our God, and we make sacrifices to appease them."

And as simply as that, he had been absolved, as though to be known was to be forgiven ...

Without warning, the Scylvendi floated into view, towering above those crowded about the entrance to the audience chamber. Rather than a shirt, he sported a vest of coins netted in leather string—to let his wounds breathe, Proyas imagined. He wore the same iron-plated girdle as he had from the first, cinched over a kilt of black damask. His scarred arms were things of statuary, and Proyas noticed several flinch from them, as though the slaughter they signified might be contagious. Without exception, the Men of the Tusk shrank from his path, as dogs might before a lion or tiger.

There was something about the Scylvendi, Proyas knew, that sent panic muttering through the bones of even the most granite-hearted. It was more than his barbarous heritage, more than the feral power that seemed to emanate from every cord of his frame—more even than the air of brooding intelligence that lent such profundity to his look. There was a sense of void about Cnaiür urs Skiötha, an absence of constraint that suggested any brutality could be possible.

The most violent of men. That was what Kellhus had called him. And he had told Proyas to take care ...

"Madness has claimed him."

For not the first time, Proyas considered the puckered wound about the barbarian's throat.

Heeding his gaze, Cnaiür soon hulked before him, his glacial eyes all the more striking for the black of his crazed mane. He nodded curtly when Proyas bid him follow. As Proyas turned, Xinemus caught his elbow, and the Conriyan Prince found himself leading both men through the red-glazed galleries of the Sapatishah's Palace. No one said a word.

Pausing in the long shadows of the processional courtyard, he turned to the Scylvendi, resisted the urge to step outside the circuit of his reach.

"So ... what did you think?"

"That Conphas will laugh himself to sleep," Cnaiür snapped contemptuously. "But you did not summon me to sound my thoughts."

"No."

"Proyas?" Xinemus asked, as though only now realizing the impropriety of his presence. "I should leave you two ..."

He came because there was nowhere else to go.

Cnaiür snorted.

The Scylvendi, Proyas imagined, had little use for the maimed. "No, Zin," he said. "I trust you as no other."

The barbarian scowled in sudden recognition. For an instant Proyas glimpsed something untoward in his eyes, an incestuous fury, as though the man berated himself for overlooking a mortal danger.

"*He* sent you," Cnaiür said.

"He did."

"Because of Conphas."

"Yes ... You're to remain with Conphas in Joktha, while the Holy War continues to Shimeh."

For a long time the Scylvendi said nothing, though his look and pose spoke of howling rage. The barbarian even trembled. At last, with unnerving calm, he said, "I am to be his nursemaid."

Proyas breathed deep, frowned at the solicitations of several passersby. "No," he replied, lowering his voice, "and yes ..."

"What do you mean?"

"You are to kill him."

———— ⬥ ————

The smell of blossoms in the dark.

"Await him here," the attendant said, then without another word withdrew the way they had both come. A hinge pealed as the doors ground shut.

Iyokus peered across the grove, but the black beneath the trees confounded his eyes. Moonlight showered down in pale mockery of the sun, etching the flowering crowns. The blossoms were blue and black.

He was not alone. From the absences pitting his perception, Iyokus knew that some two dozen Chorae bowmen had been positioned throughout the porticoes surrounding the grove. Even now they watched him, strings drawn.

It was an understandable precaution, especially given recent events.

Iyokus could scarce credit what he had seen and heard this day. He had entertained many apprehensions over the course of his journey from Shigek. The harrowing tales of what the Holy War—and by extension, the Scarlet Spires—had endured had plagued him with premonitions of catastrophe. As the pilot had guided his ship into Joktha's harbour five days before, he had braced himself for any number of disastrous revelations ...

But surely not this. The Holy War yoked to the whims of a living prophet. The Consult made fact—the *Consult*!

And yet Iyokus had always been a meticulous man, long before the chanv had wrapped its cool and luxurious coils about his heart. Things, he understood, possessed their own intrinsic order. It would take days for him to learn the extraordinary particulars of their new circumstance, and even longer for him to grasp the implications. He would not, as had Eleäzaras apparently, despair before understanding. He would not break beneath their weight.

Such a waste. Eli had been a great man, an inspired Grandmaster— once ... The other Rank-Principals would have to be consulted, and perhaps someone new elected ... someone *rational*. But first he had to sound this so-called Warrior-Prophet. This man with a two-thousand-year-old name: Anasûrimbor.

For the first time, Iyokus noticed the great stone dolmens rearing into moonlight from the obscurity of trees, and for a moment he pondered the long-dead people who had raised them. Such remnants, he thought, were the metric of ages, the pilings of the present. They spoke of a time when no Caraskand had encompassed these hills, a time when his own ancestors had ranged the endless plains beyond the Great Kayarsus. To lay eyes upon such monuments, he knew, to truly see them, was to understand the terrifying dimensions of what had been forgotten.

Iyokus had always lamented the fact that for the Scarlet Spires the past was little more than a resource, something to be looted of knowledge and authority. For his brothers, ruins were quarries, nothing more. In their eagerness to claim superiority over the Mandate, they had even gone so far as to make a *virtue* out of forgetfulness. "The past cannot be bribed," they would say, "and the future cannot be buried."

This, he suspected, was about to change. The No-God. The Second Apocalypse ... What if these things were *real*?

Iyokus reeled at the thought. Images blighted his soul's eye: corpses bobbing down the River Sayut, Carythusal burning like some lurid scene from *The Sagas*, dragons descending on their hallowed Spires ...

First things first, he reminded himself. *Alacrity in thought. Patience in knowledge ...*

A breeze descended on the grove. It wheezed through the trees, combing thousands of petals into the air. For a moment they described the twists and eddies of various gusts, the way flotsam might reveal currents in water. Iyokus knew they should be beautiful. Then he sensed the Mark ... another sorcerer approaching through the dark lanes between the apple trees.

Who? Iyokus resisted the urge to illuminate the courtyard, recalling the Chorae trained upon him. Peering, he discerned a shadowy silhouette striding between black boughs, glimpsed the brow and left cheek of a bearded face in white moonlight.

Yes. Another rumour transformed into mad fact: that the Mandate Schoolman now served as Prince Kellhus's Vizier. That he taught him the Gnosis. There was no end to the absurdities, it seemed.

"Achamian," he called out. How it must pain the man, he thought, having to treat with those who'd so wronged him. Iyokus had told Eleäzaras that nothing good would come of abducting the man. So many miscalculations! It was a miracle their School yet possessed the strength it did.

More shadow than man, Achamian paused some fifteen paces away, gazed at Iyokus through hunched tree limbs. His voice was hard. "If an eye offends thee, Iyokus ..."

A bolt of terror struck the chanv addict. What was this? Eleäzaras's drunken warning rang loud in his ears. "*Beware the Mandate Schoolman ...*"

"Where is Prince Kellhus?"

The silhouette remained motionless. "Indisposed."

"But I was told ..." Iyokus trailed. His breath had grown cold and hard about his heart. Eleäzaras knew, he realized. *He gave me to them ... That was why he dra*—

"You were deceived," the Mandate Schoolman said.

"What do y—"

"Do you remember what you felt that night in Iothiah? You must have heard me coming for you. You must have heard the others screaming, calling for your help."

There had been nightmares.

"What is this?" the Master of Spies demanded. "What happens here?"

"He's given you to me, Iyokus. The Warrior-Prophet. I asked for vengeance. I *begged*."

Somehow Achamian had muttered something between these words, and his eyes and mouth flared incandescent.

"And he said *yes*."

Iyokus stiffened. "You begged?"

The fire-coal eyes lowered in an unseen nod. Branches and blossoms were etched blood-red against the greater black. "Yes."

"Then," Iyokus said, "I shall not."

There were rules for overmatched sorcerers, rules that Iyokus did not follow. There was no retreat from this place, not while his death lay pinched on bowstrings about him. He had been trapped.

The same as Achamian in the Sareotic Library.

A turret of translucent stone leapt into existence about him: his reflexive Wards. Then the air reverberated with his arcane mutter-song, a guttural counterpoint to the more keening cadences of Achamian.

To either side of the Mandate Schoolman, two thunderheads unfolded from nothingness, each black-hearted, each tilted to the axis of the man's position—the Houlari Twin-Tempests. A flare of lightning. Gossamer threads of incandescence danced in spasms about Achamian's spherical Wards. Shadows swung like maces about the feet of the surrounding colonnades. Momentary light gleamed across the Chorae poised within the portico. Carved white as salt behind his abstract defences, Achamian continued chanting.

Iyokus sang faster, yoked his desperation to the tortured meanings that tumbled from soul into voice. Passion became semantics, and semantics *became real*. Lightning forked and flashed, its fury redoubled, until Achamian looked a ghost suspended in a half-buried sun. Limbs snapped. Blossoms exploded skyward, wheeled like burning moths against the firmament. The surrounding trees erupted in flame, became shining pillars of fire. The dolmens loomed orange from the black.

Achamian stepped forward, past the blasted trees.

Horrified, Iyokus realized that Achamian toyed with him. The chanv addict abandoned the Houlari, seized on the great maul of his School: the Dragonhead.

A scaled neck reared into existence above him. The unseen maw dipped, vomited a cataract of golden fire. Crying out his song, Iyokus watched the deluge part about the man's Wards. Ropes of fire glided down and away, as though burning oil had been cast across a sphere of glass. But there were *cracks*, fractures that bled sheets of faint vertical light.

Again the Dragonhead struck, illuminating the entirety of the grove, blowing petals skyward in locust-clouds. And still the Mandate Schoolman *advanced*, stepping through coiling wreaths of flame, singing that mad, incomprehensible song. The fractures had multiplied, deepened ...

Iyokus screamed the words, but there was a flash of something brighter than lightning. The pure dispensation of force, unmuted by image or interpretation.

Geometries scythed through the air. Parabolas of blinding white, swinging from perfect lines, all converging upon his Ward. Ghost-stone shivered and cracked, fell away like shale beneath a hammer ...

An explosion of brilliance, then—

Heedless of the dark, the Chieftain of the Utemot rode from the Gate of Horns and into the surrounding Enathpanean hills. He hobbled his horse, a Eumarnan black apportioned to him following the destruction of Padirajah's host, then struck a fire atop a high promontory overlooking the city. The hollow in his belly had crept into his chest, where it congealed, clawing—like the crow his mad grandmother always said lived within her breast. He lay awhile, his broad back against a still-warm boulder, his arms out and swaying, his fingertips teased by trembling grasses. He savoured the warmth and breathed. Gradually the crow ceased thrashing.

And he thought, *So many stars.*

He was no longer of the People. He was more. There was no thought he could not think. No act he could not undertake. No lips he could not kiss ... Nothing was forbidden.

Staring into the infinite fields of black, he drifted asleep. He dreamed that he was bound to Serwë upon the Circumfix, pressed hard against her—within her ... And it seemed no coupling could be more profound. "You're mad," she whispered, her breath moist with urgency.

"I am yours," he gasped in an outland tongue. "You are the only track remaining."

A corpse's gaping grin. *"But I'm dead."*

These words struck like stone, and he awoke, curled half naked across gravel and grasses. He scrambled, bleary and numb, to his feet. He drunkenly brushed grit and chaff from his skin. What dreams were these? What kind of man—

Then he saw her.

Standing above his fire, wearing a simple linen shift, her skin orange and lithe and flawless, like an Inrithi goddess conjured from the flames. Her eyes shone with miniature conflagrations. Sheets of hair twined about her chin and cheeks, as blonde as slaves ...

Serwë.

Cnaiür shook his head and mane, clawed his cheeks. He opened his mouth, but breath would not come. The wind seemed glacial.

Serwë.

She smiled, then leapt into the blackness that framed her.

Snarling, he sprinted after her, fully expecting to find nothing. Pausing where she had stood, he kicked through the grasses as though searching for a lost coin or weapon. The sight of her footprint knocked him to his knees.

"Serwë?" he cried, peering across the dark. He stumbled to his feet. *"Serwë!"*

Then he saw her again, leaping from rock to rock down the shadowy slope, silver in moonlight. Suddenly all the world seemed *steep*, a concatenation of cliff faces. He glimpsed her silhouette slip between the fists of two great boulders. Caraskand sprawled across the distances below her, a labyrinth of turquoise and black. He lurched forward, began racing down the darkling slopes, leaping into the void. He crashed into a stand of dwarf yuccas, tripped through a grotesquerie of limbs. A brace of thrushes exploded into the black sky, screeching. He rolled to his feet, then ran, seemingly without breath or heartbeat, his feet magically finding their sandalled way across the murky ground.

"*Serwë!*"

He paused between the boulders, scanned the moonlit terrain. There! Her willowy figure, racing like a hare across the footings of the hill.

Spring grasses whisking across bare shins. Great loping strides, like a wolf across a killing field. Then he was skidding across gravel, flying over sudden plummets. Leaning low, he threw himself at her distant figure, his many-scarred arms scything to and fro at his side, chest heaving, spittle trailing across his chin and cheeks. The night roared. But he could not close the interval. She sprinted across fallow earth, disappeared over the lip of a terraced meadow.

"*You're mine!*" he howled.

Before him, Caraskand grew until it riddled the whole horizon with snaking streets and innumerable rooftops. The forward bastions of the Triamic Walls loomed larger, swallowing the city's nearer quarters. Soon only the heights and their monumental structures were visible.

He glimpsed her shape again, just before she vanished into the blackness harboured by a grove of olive trees. He dashed after her, through the rush of stationary limbs. When he broke the grove's far side, he found himself on the battlefield, near the remains of a burned-out byre. She was little more than a thread of white, climbing the roll of dead fields, heading toward the great heaps where the Fanim dead had been thrown.

For a moment part of him despaired. His head swam, his limbs burned with the strain of his exertions. His wind had abandoned him, yet his legs still pounded across the rutted earth. The moon cast his shadow before him, and with reckless limbs he raced it, leaping dead horses, bruising mats of spring clover. He lost sight of her among the dead, but somehow he knew she would wait.

It seemed he no longer breathed, but he could smell the dead as he willed himself up the last fallow slope. The stench soon became overpowering, a sourness so raw, so earthen deep, it clawed convulsions from his stomach. It possessed a flavour that could be tasted only on the bottom of the tongue.

So holy.

He stumbled to his knees and retched, then found himself staggering across a landscape of corpses. In some places they merely matted the ground, a macramé of stripped limbs, but elsewhere they'd been heaped dozens, even hundreds, deep—into mounds that seeped something like bone-oil from their base. Moonlight fell plain across naked skin, gleamed across exposed teeth, probed the hollows of innumerable gaping mouths.

He found her standing alone in a clearing rutted by the wains that had been used to gather the dead. Her back was turned to him. He approached warily, wondering at her nightmarish beauty. Beyond her, above a black screen of trees, a signal fire glittered atop one of Caraskand's towers.

"Serwë," he gasped.

She whirled and her face flew apart, as though snakes had been braided about her skull. He charged into her, bore her down, and for an instant he was inside her impossible expression, saw gums reaching, pink and moist, to wild lidless eyes. They rolled among the dead, until he threw himself free with an inarticulate roar. He staggered backward ...

There was no time for horror.

She twirled in the air and something exploded across his jaw. He sailed headfirst into the corpses. He clutched a cold hand in the scramble to regain his feet. He tripped on a bloated torso, reached back, braced himself against the mud of dead faces.

The skin-spy regarded him, reassembled its features into those of another. As Cnaiür watched, the blonde hair fell from its pate in a feathery cascade, drawn away by the breeze, and for some reason this seemed the most horrific of all.

He stood, slicked by sweat, gasping for breath. He was unarmed, and though part of him had shouted this from the beginning, it seemed he realized it only now. *I'm dead.*

But the thing turned to the sky instead of attacking, drawn by the sound of beating wings.

Cnaiür followed its gaze, saw a raven descending in the dark. To the right of the skin-spy, one corpse lay askew a heap of others, its elbows bent out backward, its face turned toward Cnaiür, eyes drooling from sunken sockets, lips drawn back from black-leather gums. The bird landed on its grey cheek. It regarded him with a white *human* face, no larger than an apple.

Cnaiür cursed, stumbled backward. What new outrage was this?

"Old," the tiny face said in a reedy voice. "Old is the covenant between our peoples."

Cnaiür stared in horror. "I belong to no people," he said blankly.

A vertiginous silence. It peered at him with an avian canniness, as though forced to revisit certain long-standing assumptions.

"Perhaps," it said. "But *something* binds you to him. You would not have saved him otherwise. You would not have killed my child."

Cnaiür spat. "Nothing binds me!"

It craned its tiny face to the side, bird-curious.

"But the past binds us all, Scylvendi, as the bow binds the flight of an arrow. All of us have been nocked, raised, and released. All that remains is to see where we land … to see whether we strike true."

He couldn't breathe. It seemed agony simply to look, as though everything chattered with a million masticating teeth. Everything *real*. Why could nothing be simple? Why could nothing be pure? Why must the world continually heap indignities upon him, and obscenities about … How much must he endure?

"I know whom you hunt."

"Lies!" Cnaiür raved. "Lies upon lies!"

"He came to you, didn't he? The father of the Warrior-Prophet." Diminutive amusement flickered across the creature's face. "The *Dûnyain*."

The Chieftain of the Utemot gazed at the thing, his thoughts battered senseless by a chorus of conflicting passions: confusion, outrage, hope … Then at last he recalled the only track remaining—the only *true* track— though his heart had known it all along. The one certainty.

Hate.

He grew very calm. "The hunt is over," he said. "Tomorrow the Holy War marches for Xerash and Amoteu. I am to remain behind."

"You have been moved, nothing more. In benjuka, every move bespeaks a new rule." The small face regarded him, its bald scalp shining beneath the white moon. "We are that new rule, Scylvendi."

Eyes tiny and impossibly old. An intimation of power, rumbling through vein, heart, and bone.

"Not even the dead escape the Plate."

When Achamian found Xinemus in his rooms, the Marshal was as drunk as he had ever seen him.

Xinemus coughed—a sound like gravel crashing across the planked box of a wain. "Did you do it?"

"Yes ..."

"Good—good! Were you injured? Did he hurt you in any way?"

"No."

"Do you have them?"

Achamian paused, unsettled that Xinemus hadn't said "Good" in response to his second answer as well. *Does he want me to suffer?*

"Do you have them?" Xinemus exclaimed.

"Y-yes."

"Good ... good!" Xinemus said. He bolted from his chair, but with the same rigid aimlessness with which he seemed to do everything now that he had no eyes. "Give them to me!"

He had shouted this as though Achamian were a Knight of Attrempus.

"I ..." Achamian swallowed. "I don't understand ..."

"Leave them ... Leave me!"

"Zin ... You must help me understand!"

"*Leave!*"

Achamian started, such was the intensity of his cry.

"All right," he muttered, moving for the door. His stomach heaved and hitched as though the floor pitched asea. "All right ..." He yanked the door wide, but for some perverse reason simply stood still for a heartbeat then slammed it shut as though leaving in fury. He stood breathless, watching his friend turn and stride toward the westward wall, his left hand pawing the air before him, his right clutching tight the bloodstained cloth.

"*Finally,*" Xinemus muttered under his breath, either sobbing or laughing. "*Finalleeee ...*"

He stamped palm and fingers across the wall, moving to his left. He left a trail of blood-prints across the cerulean panels, then the Nilnameshi pastoral. When he reached the mirror, he stopped, his finger fluttering across the ivory frame as he positioned himself squarely before it. He became very still—so much so that Achamian feared he would hear the breath that rasped so loudly in his own ears. For a time it seemed Xinemus gazed into the phlegmatic pits where his eyes had once laughed and fumed. There was an air of longing to his blind scrutiny.

With horror Achamian watched him fumble with the cloth, then bring one hand to each of his sockets. When he drew away his hands, Iyokus's weeping eyes stared askew from phalanges of angry skin.

Walls and ceiling lurched.

"Open!" the Marshal of Attrempus wailed. He jerked his dead and bloody gaze about the room, pausing for a heart-stopping moment on Achamian. "*Ooopen!*"

Then he began thrashing through his apartments.

Achamian slipped through the door and fled.

In the dark, Eleäzaras clutched his friend, rocked him back and forth, knowing that he held a far greater dark in his arms.

"Sh-shhhh ..."

"E-Eli," his Master of Spies gasped. The man shook and blubbered, yet somehow seemed wane even in his anguish. "Eli!"

"Shhhh, Iyokus. Do you remember what it is to see?"

A shudder passed through the addict's form. The translucent head rolled in a drunken nod. Blood spilled from the linen dressings, traced dark lines across his transparent cheek.

"The words," Eleäzaras hissed. "Do you remember *the words?*"

In sorcery, everything depended on the purity of meaning. Who knew what blinding might do?

"Y-yessss."

"Then you are whole."

CHAPTER FOUR

ENATHPANEAH

Like a stern father, war shames men into hating their childhood games.

—PROTATHIS, *ONE HUNDRED HEAVENS*

I returned from that campaign a far different man, or so my mother continuously complained. "Now only the dead," she would tell me, "can hope to match your gaze."

—TRIAMIS I, *JOURNALS AND DIALOGUES*

Early Spring, 4112 Year-of-the-Tusk, Momemn

Perhaps, Ikurei Xerius III mused, tonight would be a night of desserts.

From the vantage of the Imperial Apartments on the Andiamine Heights, the Meneanor seemed a vast shining plate beneath the moon. Xerius could scarce remember ever seeing the Great Sea so preternaturally calm. He considered summoning Arithmeas, his augur, but decided against it—more out of hubris than generosity. The man was a fawning charlatan. They all were. As his mother would say, every man was a spy in the end, an agent of contrary interests. Every face was made of fingers …

Like Skeaös.

69

Despite the vertigo, he leaned against the balustrade, staring, clutching tight a mantle of fine-brushed Galeoth wool against the chill. As always, his eyes were drawn southward, to the dark sockets of the coast. Shimeh lay out there—and Conphas. It seemed perverse, somehow, that men might plot and strive so far beyond his capacity to see or know. Perverse and terrifying.

He heard the approach of sandalled feet behind him.

"God-of-Men," his new Exalt-Captain, Skala, said in a hushed voice. "The Empress wishes to speak with you."

Xerius exhaled, surprised to find he'd been holding his breath. He turned, looked up into the towering Cepaloran's face, which seemed ugly or handsome by turns of shadow or light. His blond hair tumbled about his shoulders, crimped into tails with silver bands—a sign of some fierce tribe or other. Skala wasn't the most pleasing ornament, but he'd proven an able replacement ever since Gaenkelti's death.

Ever since that mad night with the Mandate sorcerer.

"Show her in."

He drained his bowl of Anpleian red. Seized by a sudden recklessness, he cast it at the southern horizon, as though daring the distances to be anything other than what they appeared. Why shouldn't he be suspicious? The philosophers said this world was smoke, after all. *He* was the fire.

He watched the golden bowl pirouette out, then sink into the obscurity of the lower palace. The faint ring and clatter brought a smile to his lips. He felt such contempt for things.

"Skala?" he called to the withdrawing man.

"Yes, God-of-Men?"

"Some slave will steal it ... that bowl."

"Indeed, God-of-Men."

Xerius belched, though with decorum. "Whoever it is, have him flogged."

Expressionless, Skala nodded, then turned to the golden interior of the Imperial Apartments. Xerius followed, struggling not to reel. He directed the flanking Eothic Guardsmen to close the folding doors and draw the drapes behind him. There was nothing to see out there, save calm seas and endless stars. Nothing.

He lingered over the flames of the nearest tripod, warming his fingers. Already his mother was ascending the steps from the lower suites, and he found himself clenching his thumbs, trying to purge the slop from his thoughts. Only wit, Xerius had learned long ago, could preserve him from Ikurei Istriya.

Peering over stair and past tapestried wall, he glimpsed her giant eunuch, Pisathulas, looming over his Guardsmen in the antechamber. Not for the first time he found himself wondering whether she ever fucked the oiled whale. He *should* be wondering at her motives, he knew, but she had seemed so … predictable of late, and besides, the mood had come upon him. Had she but pestered him moments later, he was sure he would have been … indisposed.

She did look beautiful, for an old hag. A headdress of wings worked in mother-of-pearl adorned her dyed hair, with a veil of tiny silver chains hanging just past her painted brows. Bound tight against her figure with golden ribbon, her gown was both simple and traditional, though the printed blue silk, he imagined, had cost him a war galley. He knew he needed to blink the wine from his eyes, but she seemed more supple than wiry …

How long had it been?

"God-of-Men," she said, cresting the last step. She lowered her head in perfect jnanic form.

For a moment Xerius stood speechless, quite disarmed by this uncharacteristic display of respect. "Mother," he said carefully. When a vicious dog nuzzled one's hand, it meant it was hungry—very hungry.

"The Saik have been here to see you."

"Thassius, yes … He must have passed you on his way out."

"Not Cememketri?"

Xerius snorted. "What is it, Mother?"

"You've heard something," she said stridently. "Conphas has sent a message."

"Bah!" He smacked his lips, turning from her. Bitch. Always yelping over her bowl.

"I *raised* him, Xerius! He was my ward—far more than he was ever yours! I deserve to know what happens. I deserve."

Xerius paused, keeping her figure in his periphery. It was strange, he thought, the way the same words could infuriate him at one moment yet strike a tender chord at another. But that was what it all came down to in the end, wasn't it? His whims. He looked her full in the face, struck by how luminous, how *young* her eyes seemed in the lantern light. He liked this whim …

"They know," he said. "This imposter, this … *Warrior-Prophet* or whatever they're calling him, accused Conphas—accused *me*!—of plotting to betray the Holy War. Can you imagine?"

For some reason, she seemed unsurprised. It occurred to Xerius that *she* could be the one who had betrayed their plans. Why not? Hers was an unnatural commingling of the masculine and the feminine intellect, driven by both an excessive need for approval and an equally excessive obsession with security. As a result, she saw rashness and cowardice everywhere she looked. In her son most of all.

"What has happened?" she asked, her tone lilting in concern.

Oh yes, one mustn't forget her precious nephew's skin.

"Conphas has been turned out. He and what remains of his Columns are to be interned at Joktha to await transport back to the Nansurium."

"Good," she said, nodding. "So your madness ends."

Xerius laughed. "My madness, Mother?" He graced her with a smile all the more cutting for its genuineness. "Or Conphas's?"

The Empress sneered. "And what's that supposed to mean, hmm, my dear son?"

The ravages of age. He had watched it happen to his father's contemporaries, watched their skulls scraped as hollow as clam shells, until their decrepit bodies seemed positively virile compared with their addled souls. Xerius found himself suppressing a shudder. These games of word and wit, they were *her* legacy. When had she fallen so many steps behind?

And yet …

"It means, Mother, that Conphas *has the field*." He shrugged amiably. "I haven't recalled him."

"What are you saying, Xerius? They *know* now … know what you intend! It would be madness!"

He stared at her, wondering how she managed it after so many years.

"Indeed. I'm sure the Great Names think much the same."

How could a crone look so … so *virginal*?

She closed her long-lashed eyes, smirking in her coquettish way. For once, it didn't seem a vain travesty. "I see," she said, sighing in the manner of a world-weary lover.

Even still, after all this time, he could remember her hand that first night, like ice stroking his baffled fire. That first night ...

Sweet Sejenus, but he was hard—so pulsing hard!

He set down his bowl and turned to her. Suddenly he found himself pressing her back toward his canopied bed. She didn't melt into compliance beneath his clasp, like a slave might, but neither did she resist. She smelled young ... Tonight *would* be a night of desserts!

"Please, Mother," he heard himself murmuring. "It's been so long. I've been so lonely ... Only you, Mother. *Only you understand.*"

He laid her across the great Black Sun embroidered into his coverings. His hands trembled as he fussed with her gowns. His groin throbbed so sweetly he feared he might soil his robes.

"You do love me," he gasped. "You do love ..."

Her painted eyes had become drowsy, delirious. Her flat chest heaved beneath the fabric. Somehow he could see through the skein of wrinkles that made a mask of her face, down to the serpentine truth of her beauty. Somehow he could see the woman who had driven his father mad with jealousy, who had shown her son the ecstasy of secrets bundled between sheets.

"My *sweet son*," she gasped. "My *sweet* ..."

His fingers and palm found warm skin. His heart became a thunderclap. He ran his hand along her calves, which she shaved in the fashion of the Ainoni, then across her still-smooth thighs. Could it be? He clutched at her groin, squeezed the haft of her erection—

There was no air for shouting. He toppled back across the floor and worked his mouth soundlessly, and she stood and smoothed her gowns and he scrambled backward, somehow managing to scream for his guards.

The first to arrive were too dumbfounded to do much more than die. A face imploded. A throat torn and gushing. It all seemed so ridiculous. Pisathulas, her giant eunuch, tried to restrain her, bawling out in some incomprehensible tongue. She broke his neck as easily as twisting a melon on the vine.

Then she had a sword.

She seemed a spider, her two limbs becoming eight with flashing grace. She danced and twirled. Men crumpled and cried out. Boots skidded across blood. Blue-tattooed limbs slapped against the floor, bruising dead bone.

Xerius turned, scrambling toward the door. There was no fear—that required comprehension—only an all-encompassing urgency, a primal need to remove himself from such sights, such circumstances.

He fought his way past two Guardsmen. His limbs floated. He ran shrieking down the gilded corridor. Slippers! Slippers! How could anyone *run* in fucking slippers?

Steaming censers whipped past him, but he could smell only the rank of his own bowel. How his mother would cackle! Her boy shitting his Imperial Regalia ...

Run! Run!

Somewhere he could hear Skala bawling commands. He vaulted downstairs only to tumble, thrashing like a dog sewn into a sack. Moaning, blubbering, he found his feet, lurched back into a run. What happened? Where were his Guardsmen? Tapestries and gilded panels swam about him. There was shit on his knuckles! Then something bore him face-first into the marmoreal tiles. A shadow upon his back, a dozen hyenas laughing through its throat.

Iron hands about his face. Nails scoring his cheek. A meaty pop in his neck. An impossible glimpse of her—*Mother*—blood-spattered and dishevelled. There was no—

Early Spring, 4112 Year-of-the-Tusk, Sumna

Sol looked up, blinking and scowling. How early was it?

"Come-come!" Hertata cried from the mouth of the alley. "Maithanet comes! They say Maithanet comes to the stone quays!"

There was something in Hertata's eyes when he said this, a hope or a longing that had grown too great. Though Sol was only eleven, he saw this, even without words to comprehend it. "But the slavers ..."

The slavers were always a worry, especially at the stone quays where they held their markets. For slavers, finding a young orphan was like finding a coin dropped in the street.

"They wouldn't dare-dare! Not with Maithanet coming! They would be damned-damned!"

Hertata always said things twice, even though the others so harshly teased him for it. They called him Hertata-tata or, more cruel still, Echo.

Hertata was strange.

"It's *Maithanet*, Sol!" There were tears in his eyes. "They say he's leave-leaving, that he's sailing across the sea-sea!"

"But the winds—"

"Started this morn! They've come, and now he's sailing across the sea, across the sea-sea!"

Why should he care for Maithanet? Men with gold rings gave no copper, unless they wanted to stick them. Why should he care for Maithanet, who would just try to stick him if he could? Fucking priests, anyway.

But the tears in Hertata's eyes ... Sol could see he was afraid to go alone.

Groaning, Sol stood and kicked about his rag bedding. He tried his best to sneer at Hertata's beaming face. He'd seen Hertata's ilk before. Always whimpering "Mommy" in the middle of the night. Always crying. Always getting sticked for food because he was too afraid to steal. They never survived. None of them. Just like his little brother ...

But not Sol! His feet were rabbit-quick.

Not far from their alley lay a large fullery, and they stopped to piss in the giant bowls arrayed before it. The façade was always crowded, especially in the morning. They did their best to avoid looking at the beggars with "fuller's feet"—the rot that resulted from years of mashing laundry—though they could hear their curses and catcalls. Even cripples despised those poorer than themselves. Finishing, the boys cut across the sulphurous reek of the fullers' yard, laughing at the rows of men stomping up and down in cement basins arranged in batteries. The air fairly thundered with the slap of wet fabric across the drying-stones. They darted past the drovers who crowded the far entranceway with their donkeys and laundry-carts.

"Will there be food?" Sol asked Hertata.

"Petals," the younger boy assured him. "They always throw petals when the Shriah walks-walks."

"I said *food*," Sol snapped, even though he knew he would eat petals
if he could.

The boy's brown eyes remained fixed on his feet. He had no idea. "It's
him, Sol ... *Maithanet* ..."

Sol shook his head in disgust. Fucking Hertata-tata. Fucking Echo.

They passed through the more affluent, porticoed streets immediately
adjacent to the Hagerna. Vendors opened their shops, joking with their
slaves as they drew heavy wooden shutters from grooves in the burnt-brick
thresholds. Periodically the two boys glimpsed the great monuments of the
Holy Precincts between the posh tenements fencing the sky. Every glimpse
of the Junriüma's turrets set them to pointing and whistling with wonder.

Even orphans could hope.

They dared not enter the Hagerna itself for fear of the Shrial Knights,
so they followed the surrounding streets toward the harbour. For a time
they walked along the wall itself, gawking at its immensity. Vines sheeted
most of it in leafy green, and they took turns guessing what the other
thought the patches of bare and ancient stone most resembled: rabbits,
owls, or dogs. In the Porampas Market they overheard two women say
that Maithanet's ship was berthed in the Xatantian Basin—the hexago-
nal harbour some old emperor had excavated from the shores of Sumna's
natural harbour long, long ago.

They made their way to the warehouse district, amazed that even as far
out as the Milleries Street the way was crowded with people walking in
the same direction. They paused to savour the smell of fresh bread and to
chortle at the mules they could see in the shadowy interiors all about
them, plodding round and round their millstones. The air had taken on a
carnival atmosphere, rumbling with laughter and animated discussion,
punctuated by the squeal of children and the bawling of infants. Despite
himself, Sol scowled less and less at Hertata's ridiculous comments. He
even laughed at the boy's jokes.

Though he would never admit it, Sol was happy he had listened to
Hertata. Being surrounded by glad-hearted people all walking the same
direction made him feel as though he *belonged* to something, as if
through some inarticulate miracle he had found his way back inside
from the filth and cold and contempt.

How long had it been since his father's murder?

A band of musicians joined their impromptu migration, and Sol and Hertata danced their way past the storehouses with their ramped entrances and slitted windows. They paused in the shadow of the Great Warehouse, which Hertata had never seen, and Sol explained how his dear friend, the Emperor Ikurei Xerius III, used it to hoard grain for him against times of famine. Hertata howled with laughter.

With the crowds thickening about them, they decided to run so they might beat the crush. As quick as he was, Sol took the lead, and Hertata chased him, laughing. They darted about families, dodged along the narrow ways that drifted and twined through crowds of people. Sol allowed Hertata to almost catch him twice, and the boy squealed in a way that made Sol both cringe and laugh. Finally, he let Hertata tackle him.

They wrestled for a moment, cursed each other with mock insults. After easily pinning him, Sol pulled Hertata to his feet. They were close to the harbour now. Gulls screeched through the sky above them. The air smelled of water and swollen wood. They wandered about, suddenly anxious. Walking vendors—old harbour men, mostly—were selling halved oranges to mask the stink, and the boys were lucky enough to find a few discarded rinds, which they gobbled, savouring the bitter.

"I told you," Hertata said, chewing, "there was food-food."

Sol closed his eyes and smiled. Yes, Hertata had spoken true.

Without warning, the sonorous peal of the Summoning Horns rang across the city, at once so familiar and strangely threatening, as though a besieging army signalled its assault.

"Come-come!" Hertata cried. He grabbed Sol by the hand, began pulling him deeper into the milling crowds. Sol frowned—only babies and stickers held hands—but he let the boy lead him through the labyrinth of waists and elbows nonetheless. He found himself studying Hertata, who continually looked back, smiling with manic encouragement. From where had his sudden courage come? Everyone knew Hertata was a cringer, yet here he was, barging toward an almost certain beating. Why would he risk such a thing? For Maithanet? As far as Sol was concerned, nothing was worth getting a beating—or even worse, getting clapped by slavers. He would sooner be sticked.

And yet there was something in the air, something that made Sol feel uncertain in a way he had never felt uncertain before. Something that made him feel small, not in the way of orphans or beggars or children, but in a *good* way. In the way of souls.

He could remember his mother praying the night his father had died. Crying and praying. Was that what drove Hertata? Could he remember his mother praying?

They pressed through limbs and curses, and despite several swats suddenly found themselves staring about the armoured flanks of a Shrial Knight. Sol had never been so close to a Knight of the Tusk before, and he fairly trembled with dread. The white of the man's surcoat was so clean, the gold embroidery so brilliant. He wore a hauberk of silvered mail, beneath which he seemed impossibly solid, rooted like a tree. Like most boys he knew, Sol feared warlike men as much as he envied them. But Hertata seemed entirely unimpressed; he poked his head past the Knight as though staring around a stone column.

Plucking up his courage, Sol followed Hertata's lead and leaned forward to look up and down the street. Hundreds of Shrial Knights held the gathering masses in check. Others on horseback rode slowly along their lines, scanning the crowds as though expecting unwanted relatives. He was about to ask Hertata if he could see any sign of the Shriah when, without a word, the Knight gently pressed the two of them back into the midst of the other onlookers.

Hertata chattered endlessly about all the things his mother had told him about Maithanet. How he had cleansed the Thousand Temples, how he had smashed the heathen with his Holy War, how he slept on a mat beneath the Tusk-Tusk. How the *God himself* blessed his every word-word, his every glance-glance, and his every foot-fall-fall. "He need only see me, Sol! He need only look-look!"

"And then what?"

But Hertata would not say.

Suddenly they were hooting and cheering. They had both turned to the sound of a distant roar striated with faint cries of *"Maithanet!"* Then, for no reason Sol could fathom, they were roaring themselves. Hertata actually bounced up and down—that is, until the crowds pressed them forward into the Shrial Knight, who had locked arms with his holy brothers to either side. The cacophony seemed to go on and on, and for a time Sol feared his heart might burst for excitement.

The Shriah! The Shriah was coming! Never had he stood so close to the Outside.

The shouts waxed on and on, slowly leached of their fervour by fatigue. Then, just as Sol decided all their commotion was stupid—who cheered the invisible?—he glimpsed sunlight flashing across jewelled rings ...

The Shrial Procession.

His heart hammered in his chest. The sun seemed to spin in the sky above. Though breathless, he cried out, and it seemed his lungs, his mouth, his voice were innumerable.

Three lavishly garbed priests crossed the narrow slot of their view. Then *he* stepped into sight. Younger. Taller. Paler. A full beard. Wearing only a simple vestment, so white it pained the eyes to look. A thousand pleading hands reached out toward him, to greet, to implore, to touch. Hertata was fairly shrieking, trying to gain his majestic attention. He merely walked, but it seemed he moved *so fast*, as though the ground itself pulled him forward. For some reason, Sol raised his hands and reached out, not to touch the luminous image before him but to jab his fingers at his friend—to point at the one soul that needed to be seen more than any other.

Perhaps it was that Sol alone, of all those lining the avenue, gestured to another. Perhaps it was that Maithanet somehow knew. Whatever the reason, the bright eyes flickered toward him. *Saw.*

It was the first total moment in his entire life. Perhaps the only.

As Sol watched, Maithanet's eyes were drawn by his pointing fingers to Hertata, wailing and jumping beside him. The Shriah of the Thousand Temples smiled.

For a breathless moment he held the boy's gaze, then the Knight's form swallowed his hallowed image.

"Yessss!" Hertata howled, fairly weeping with disbelief. "Yes-yes!"

Sol clutched his hand and laughed. Still cheering, they both turned to a shadow.

From nowhere, it seemed, a man loomed above and against them. His beard was full and square, which meant he was a foreigner. He stank of people. More ominous still, he stank of ships. He held a halved orange in his right hand and the back of Hertata's filthy tunic bunched in his left.

"Where're your parents?" he boomed with predatory good nature.

They had to ask that now. Whenever a real child disappeared, they always searched the slavers first. Slavers were hanged for stealing real children, just like the stickers were hanged for sticking them.

"O-o-over there-there," Hertata whimpered, holding out a tentative finger.

Sol could smell his piss.

"You say?" the man laughed, but Sol was already running, past the Knights and into the crowds on the far side of the procession.

He was Sol. He was fleet.

Afterward, huddling between stacked amphorae, he wept, always throwing a cautious eye to be sure no one could see. He spat and spat, but the taste of orange peel would not go away. Finally he prayed. In his soul's eye he glimpsed the flash of sunlight across jewelled rings.

Yes. Hertata had spoken true.

Maithanet was sailing across the sea.

Early Spring, 4112 Year-of-the-Tusk, Enathpaneah

They were few—only some forty thousand of them remained—but in their breasts beat the hearts of many.

Beneath the slapping banners of Household, Tusk, and Circumfix, the Holy War departed from mighty Caraskand and left behind a city scarcely inhabited. There had been much furore in the Councils at Saubon's decision to remain behind. The other Great Names petitioned the Warrior-Prophet to at least demand that Saubon allow his subordinates to march if they so desired. Many did so of their own accord anyway, including the tempestuous Athjeäri. In the end, only some two thousand Galeoth would remain behind with their King and his empty city. They said that Saubon wept as the Warrior-Prophet rode from the Gate of Horns.

A far different Holy War climbed the ways into the Enathpanean countryside. The newcomers, decked in the traditional tabards and surcoats of their homelands, provided the most stark measure of this transformation. Word of the Holy War's straits in Caraskand had inspired several thousand Inrithi to dare winter seas and make for Joktha. They began arriving at the gates shortly after the breaking of the siege, posturing, boasting, just as those watching upon the walls had once postured and boasted beneath the gates of Momemn and Asgilioch. They fell silent, however, upon entering the city, appalled by the battered faces and perpetual stares that greeted them. The ancient customs were observed— hands were shaken, countrymen embraced—but it was all a pretence.

The original Men of the Tusk—the survivors—were now sons of a different nation. They had spilled whatever blood they once shared with these men. The old loyalties and traditions had become tales of a faraway country, like Zeüm, a place too distant to be confirmed. The hooks of the old ways, the old concerns, had been set in fat that no longer existed. Everything they had known had been tested and found wanting. Their vanity, their envy, their hubris, all the careless bigotries of their prior lives, had been murdered with their fellows. Their hopes had been burned to ashes. Their scruples had been boiled to bone and tendon—or so it seemed.

Out of calamity they had salvaged only the barest necessities; all else had been jettisoned. Their spare manner, their guarded speech, their disinterested contempt for excess, all spoke to a dangerous thrift. And nowhere was this more evident than in their eyes: they stared with the blank wariness of men who never slept—not peering, not watching, but *observing*, and with a directness that transcended "bold" or "rude."

They stared as though nothing stared back, as though all were objects.

Among the newcomers, even the costumed caste-nobles seemed unable or unwilling to match their gaze. Many tried to maintain appearances—the wry glances, the nods of acknowledgment—but their looks always returned to their boots or sandals. To stand in the sight of such men, they somehow understood, was to be *measured*, not by something as flawed and as arbitrary as a man, but by the length and breadth of what they had suffered.

Their very look had become judgement, so much had they witnessed.

Thoroughly unnerved by their so-called brothers, only a few hundred newcomers dared question the Holy War's other profound transformation: the Warrior-Prophet. Those of power and influence, such as Dogora Teör, the Tydonni Earl of Sumagalt, were eased into the Tribe of Truth by the Warrior-Prophet himself. Others found themselves befriended by Judges from their various homelands, who spirited them to sermons and Whelmings. Those who continued dissenting were separated from their fellows and assigned to companies of faithful. And the worst agitators, it was said, were brought before the Consort, never to be seen again.

The Inrithi found Enathpaneah abandoned by the enemy. Gothyelk, who marched along the coastline with his Tydonni, encountered the burned ruins of nearly a hundred villas. Though most of the native Enathi, a people of ancient Shigeki stock, remained shut in their villages, not one of their Kianene lords could be found. No heathen patrols loitered in the distances. No dwelling of scale survived intact. When Athjeäri and his Gaenri came to the ends of Enathpaneah, the old forts that guarded the tracks into Xerash were still smoking, but the enemy was nowhere to be seen.

The heathen's back had been broken—just as the Warrior-Prophet had said. Save a triumphal march, it seemed nothing stood between them and Holy Shimeh.

The first elements of the Holy War descended into Xerash and camped across the Plains of Heshor, where they held a great celebration. Xerash figured large in the narratives of *The Tractate*—so much so that many argued they had already entered the Sacred Lands. Men gathered to listen to readings from the Book of Traders, the account of the Latter Prophet's years of exile among the depraved Xerashi. It seemed a thing of awe to at last stand so close to those places named.

But names change over the centuries, and many spent long hours debating points of scripture and geography. Was not the town of Bengut actually the city of Abet-goka, where Amoti merchants concealed the Latter Prophet from the wrath of the Xerashi King? Were not the massive ruins reported near Pidast the remains of the great fortress of Ebaliol, where Inri Sejenus was imprisoned for prophesying the "thousand temples"? Throughout the following days, impromptu pilgrimages set out from the main columns to visit various sites. And even though the pilgrims were invariably disappointed by the stubborn silence of the ruins they found, the eyes of most would burn with fervour when they returned. For they walked the ways of Xerash.

At Ebaliol, the Warrior-Prophet climbed the broken foundations and addressed thousands. "I stand," he cried, "where my brother stood!"

Twenty-two men died in the delirious crush. It would prove an omen of what was to follow.

For millennia the so-called Middle-Lands had been coveted by the Kings of Shigek to the north and the Kings of Old Nilnamesh to the south. After inflicting a crushing defeat on the Shigeki, Anzumarapata II, the Nilnameshi King of Invishi, settled the Plains of Heshor with untold thousands of his people, hoping to secure his empire through forced resettlement. These dark-skinned people brought with them their indolent Gods and their promiscuous customs. They raised Gerotha, the greatest city of Xerash, in the heart of the plains, and bent their backs to the fields as they had done in humid Nilnamesh.

By the Latter Prophet's time, Xerash was an old and powerful kingdom, demanding and receiving tribute from both Amoteu and Enathpaneah. The Amoti in particular thought the Xerashi an obscene race, a blight upon the land. For the authors of *The Tractate*, it was a land of innumerable brothels, fratricidal kings, and rampant homosexuality. And though the blood and custom of the Nilnameshi had been thinned into extinction long ago, for the Men of the Tusk "xeratic" still meant "sodomite," and they punished the Fanim of Xerash for the trespasses of others long dead. The Xerash that the Inrithi wandered through was a place of old and labyrinthine evils. And her people found themselves called to account not once, but twice.

Reports of massacre became common. There was the great fortress of Kijenicho along the coast, where Earl Iyengar had his Nangaels throw the garrison from the walls onto the breakers below. And the walled town of Naïth high in the Betmulla foothills, which Earl Ganbrota and his Ingraulish burned to the ground. There were the refugees along the Herotic Way—the very road to Shimeh!—who were ridden down for sport by Lord Soter and his Kishyati Knights.

The Warrior-Prophet reacted quickly, dispatching edicts forbidding all acts of murder and rapine, and censuring those responsible for the most wanton atrocities. He even sent Gotian to have Lord Uranyanka, the Ainoni Palatine of Moserothu, flogged. Apparently the man had ordered his archers to massacre an enclave of lepers near the town of Sabotha.

But it was too late. Athjeäri soon returned, bearing word that Gerotha had scorched her fields and plantations. The Kianene had fled, but all Xerash was closed against them.

Despite the dread implications, despite all the astonishing differences, the journey to Xerash reminded Achamian of nothing so much as his days as Proyas's tutor in Aöknyssus. Or so he told himself at first.

On one occasion, after Esmenet's palfrey was lamed while descending a precarious switchback trail in the Enathpanean hills, Achamian watched as some dozen knights offered to *give* her their chargers—something tantamount to giving her their honour, since their mounts were their means of waging war. Achamian had witnessed much the same while accompanying Proyas and his mother to her dowager estates in Anplei. On another occasion, they encountered a party of Tydonni footmen—some of Lord Iyengar's Nangaels, it turned out—bearing a fresh boar hoisted above them on the points of some seven or eight spears, an ancient rite of vassalage that Achamian had once witnessed in the court of Proyas's father, Eukernas II.

But there was something more general, a myriad of smaller recognitions, that seemed to remind him of those more youthful days—despite the daily battery of riding so near Esmenet. For one, others in the Sacral Retinue treated him with deference and respect, their manner so grave it sometimes verged on the comic. He was, after all, the *teacher* of the Warrior-Prophet—an occupation that had quickly morphed into the preposterous honorific—Holy Tutor. For another, he no longer *walked*. Even more than slaves, horses were the yardstick of nobility, and Achamian, lowly Drusas Achamian, now found himself with his own: a sleek black—allegedly from Kascamandri's own stock—whom he called Noon in memory of poor old Daybreak.

In fact, he found himself awash in small riches: Damask tunics, muslin gowns, felt robes—a wardrobe that included access to a pool of body-slaves for his frequent ceremonial fittings. A silvered corselet, restitched with leather pleats to accommodate his girth. An ivory jewel box containing rings and earrings that he felt too foolish to wear, as well as two black-pearl broaches that he secretly gave away. Ambergis from

Zeüm. Myrrh from the Great Salt. Even a genuine bed—a bed on the trail!—for those few hours of sleep he could steal.

Achamian had disdained such comforts during his tenure at the Conriyan court. After all, he was a Gnostic Schoolman, not some "anagogic whore." But now, after the innumerable deprivations he'd endured ... The life of a spy was hard. To finally *have* things, even things he couldn't bring himself to enjoy, eased his heart for some reason, as though they were balm for unseen wounds. Sometimes, when he ran his hands over soft fabric or yet again searched through the rings for one he might wear, a clutching sadness would come upon him, and he would remember how his father had cursed those who carved toys for their sons.

And there were the politics, of course, though they were largely confined to the jnanic posturing of the caste-nobles who continually drifted in and out of the Sacral Retinue. All manoeuvring, no matter what its stripe, would instantly collapse into uniform servility whenever Kellhus appeared, and just as quickly leap back into effect when he departed. Occasionally, when something particularly sour seemed to be brewing, Kellhus would call the principals to account, and everyone would watch with rigid wonder as he explained things—*people*—he could not possibly know. It was as though the writ of their hearts had been inked across their faces.

This no doubt explained the near-total absence of politicking among those who formed the core of the Sacral Retinue: the Nascenti, with their Zaudunyani functionaries, and the Liaisons, the caste-noble representatives of the different Great Names. In Aöknyssus, the closer one came to Proyas's father, the quicker the knives had flashed—as one might expect. Politics, after all, was the pursuit of advantage within communities of men. One need not be Ajencis to see this. The more powerful the community, the greater the advantage; the greater the advantage, the more vicious the pursuit. It was axiomatic, something Achamian had witnessed time and again in courts across the Three Seas. And yet it in no way applied to the Sacral Retinue. All knives were sheathed in the Warrior-Prophet's hallowed presence.

Among the Nascenti, Achamian found a camaraderie and a candour unlike anything he'd known before. Despite the inevitable lapses, they largely approached one another as men should: with humour, openness, understanding. For Achamian, the fact that they were as much *warriors* as apostles or apparati made it all the more remarkable ... and troubling.

Usually, as they rode in clots or files, they would joke and argue—or make wagers, endless wagers. Sometimes, they simply sang the gorgeous hymns Kellhus had taught them, their eyes bright, devoid of oily thought or inclination, their voices clear and booming. And Achamian, though embarrassed at first, soon found himself joining them, wonderstruck by the words, the phrasing, and suffused with a joy that would seem impossible afterward—too simple, too profound. Then he would glimpse Esmenet rocking in her saddle amid her servants, or he would see another corpse mute in the surrounding grasses, and he would recall the purpose of their journey.

They rode to war—to kill. To conquer Holy Shimeh.

In these moments, the differences between his present circumstance and his time as Proyas's tutor would loom stark before him, and the fleecy sense of reminiscence that seemed to permeate everything would grow hard with cold and dread. What was it he remembered?

Several days into the march, as the Holy War wound through one of the endless ravines that scored the Enathpanean countryside, a group of long-haired tribesmen—Surdu, Achamian would later learn—were brought to Kellhus under the sign of the Tusk. For centuries, they said, they had preserved their Inrithi heritage, and now they wished to pay obeisance to those who had come to deliver them. They would be the eyes of the Holy War, if they could, showing the Men of the Tusk secret ways through the low ranges of the Betmulla. Achamian missed most of what followed for the crowds, but he was able to see the Surdu chieftain curl over his knees on the earth while offering up an iron sword that had been bent into a V.

Inexplicably, Kellhus ordered the tribesmen seized. They were subsequently tortured, whereupon it was discovered that Kascamandri's son, Fanayal, had sent them. Apparently, he had seized his father's title, and was even now assembling what dregs he could at Shimeh. The Surdu were indeed Inrithi, but Fanayal had abducted their wives and children to compel them to lead the Holy War astray. The new Padirajah, it seemed, was desperate for time.

Kellhus had them flayed alive—publicly.

The image of the chieftain kneeling with the bent sword nagged Achamian for the remainder of the day. Once again he was certain he'd witnessed something remarkably similar—but not in Conriya. It couldn't be ... The sword he remembered had been *bronze*.

Then in a rush he understood. What he thought he recalled, what had suffused fairly everything with a ghostly air of familiarity, had nothing to do with his years as Proyas's tutor in the Conriyan court. In fact, it had nothing to do with *him* at all. It was ancient *Kûniüri* he remembered. The time Seswatha spent campaigning with that other Anasûrimbor ... High King Celmomas.

It always jarred Achamian, realizing that so much of what he was he in fact wasn't. Now he found himself terrified by the contrary realization: that more and more he was *becoming* what he wasn't—what he must never be. That he was becoming Seswatha.

For so long the sheer scale of the Dreams had offered him an immunity of sorts. The things he dreamed simply didn't happen—at least not to the likes of him. With the Holy War, his life had taken a turn to the legendary, and the distance between his world and Seswatha's closed, at least in terms of what he witnessed. But even then, what he *lived* remained banal and impoverished. "Seswatha never shat," the old Mandate joke went. The dimensions of what Achamian lived could always fall into the dimensions of what he dreamed like a stone into a potter's urn.

But now, riding as Holy Tutor at the Warrior-Prophet's left hand?

In a way, he was as much as Seswatha, if not more. In a way, *he no longer shat either.* And knowing this was enough to make him shit.

Strangely enough, the Dreams themselves had become more bearable. Tywanrae and Dagliash continued to predominate, though as always he couldn't fathom why they should follow this or any other rhythm of events. They were like swallows, swooping and circling in aimless patterns, sketching something almost, yet never quite, a language.

He still woke mouthing cries, but their force had been blunted somehow. At first he attributed this to Esmenet, thinking each man had a certain allotment of torment, and that like wine in the bottom of a bowl, it could be tipped this way and that, but never increased. The problem was that painful days had never made for restful nights in the past. So he decided it had to be Kellhus, and as with all realizations involving the Warrior-Prophet, it seemed painfully obvious after the fact. Through Kellhus, the scale of the present not only matched the scale of his Dreams, it counterbalanced them with hope.

Hope ... Such a strange word.

Did the Consult know what they had created? How far could Golgotterath see?

Augury, Memgowa had written, said more about men's fear than about their future. But how could Achamian resist? He slept with the First Apocalypse—she was an old and taxing lover. How could he not daydream about the Second, about the terrible power slumbering in Anasûrimbor Kellhus, and the overthrow of his School's ancient Enemy? There would be glory this time. Victory would not come at the cost of all that mattered.

Min-Uroikas broken. Shauriatis, Mekeritrig, Aurang and Aurax—all of them destroyed! The No-God unresurrected. The Consult a memory stamped into the muck.

Despite their opiate glamour, there was something terrifying about these thoughts. The Gods were perverse. Natter as they might, the priests knew nothing of their malicious whims. Perhaps they *would* see the world burn just to punish the hubris of one man. Nothing, Achamian had long ago decided, was quite so dangerous as boredom in the absence of scruples.

And Kellhus, with his cryptic responses, only aggravated these apprehensions. Whenever Achamian asked him why he continued to march on Shimeh when the Fanim were no more than a distraction, he always said, "If I'm to succeed my brother, I must reclaim his house."

"But the war isn't here!" Achamian once exclaimed in exasperation.

Kellhus merely smiled—for it had become a kind of game at this point—and said, "But it must be, since the war is everywhere."

Never had mystery seemed so taxing.

"Tell me," Kellhus said one night following their Gnostic lessons, "why is it the future that plagues you?"

"What do you mean?"

"Your questions always turn on what *will* happen, and very rarely on what I have already wrought."

Achamian shrugged, too weary to care much for anything beyond sleep. "Because I dream the future every night, I suppose … That, and I have the ear of a living prophet."

Kellhus laughed. "So it's like hash and peaches," he said, repeating the off-colour Nansur expression for irresistible combinations. "Even still, out of all the men who dare ask me questions, you're entirely unique."

"How so?"

"Most men ask after their souls."

Achamian could not speak. It seemed his heart could scarce beat, let alone his lungs breathe.

"With me," Kellhus continued, "the Tusk *is rewritten*, Akka." A long, ransacking look. "Do you understand? Or do you simply prefer to think yourself damned?"

Though he could muster no retort, Achamian knew.

He preferred.

During this period he cast the Cants of Calling no fewer than three times, though he was only able to report to Nautzera once. Apparently the old fool was having difficulty sleeping. The man was imperious and obsequious by turns, as though at once denying and recognizing the sudden shift in the balance of power between them. As a member of the Quorum, Nautzera formally possessed absolute authority over Achamian—he could even command his execution, if he thought the mission warranted such drastic measures. But in fact, the situation was quite the reverse. The Consult had been rediscovered, an Anasûrimbor had returned, and the Second Apocalypse was nigh. These were the very things that gave their School meaning, the very *mandate* from which they derived their name, and for the moment only one of their number—a discontent, no less—secured their connection to them. During one peevish and heady moment of their discussion, Achamian realized that in a sense he had become their de facto Grandmaster.

Another unsettling parallel.

As Achamian expected, the Mandate was in an uproar. Their agents around the Three Seas had been notified. The Quorum had organized an expedition that was set to leave for the Sacred Lands as soon as the *ochala* winds began—a thought that filled Achamian with more than a little trepidation. But otherwise, they really had no idea as to how they should proceed. Two thousand years of preparation, it seemed, had left them utterly unprepared.

And it showed in Nautzera's relentless questions, which ranged from the asinine to the disconcertingly shrewd. How was it the Anasûrimbor could see the skin-spies? Did he truly hail from Atrithau? Why did he continue marching against Shimeh? What had convinced Achamian of the man's divinity? How fared his old grudges? Whom did he serve?

To this last he answered, "Seswatha."

My brother.

He understood Nautzera's undertones well enough: the Quorum feared for his sanity, though given his new-found pre-eminence they had no doubt gilded their concerns in absolving explanations. *Think of what the red whores did to him! Think of what he's suffered!* Achamian knew how it worked. Even now they concocted rationales to relieve him of the burden they themselves coveted. Men forever argued their desires, forever made what the Near Antique logicians called the Inference to the Purse, which, they claimed, had secured more conclusions for more men than mere truth ever could. As the Cironji were fond of saying, if it jingled, then it was true.

Despite his obvious suspicion, Nautzera also voiced many ostensibly heartening sentiments. *We would have you know you're not alone in this, Akka. Your School stands with you.* Only to follow them with sentiments such as: *You've accomplished so much! Take pride, brother. Take pride!*

Which was to say without saying, *You've done enough.*

Then came the admonitions, which swiftly became recriminations. *Beware the Spires* turned into *You were told to set aside your vengeance!* In the space of breaths, *Take care in what you teach him* became *Many think you betray our School!*

When Achamian could tolerate no more, he finally said: *The Warrior-Prophet has asked me to relay a message to the Quorum, Nautzera ... Would you hear it?*

Achamian took the following silence for ethereal sputtering. They were powerless, and once again Nautzera had been reminded. *Speak,* the old sorcerer finally replied.

He says: "You are players in this war, nothing more. The balance remains precarious. Recall what it is you dream. Recall the ancient errors. Do not act out of conceit or ignorance."

Another pause. Then, *That's it?*

That is—

What? Does he imply that he possesses this war? Who is he compared with what we know, what we dream?

All men were misers, Achamian reflected. They differed only in the objects of their obsession.

He, Nautzera, is the Warrior-Prophet.

CHAPTER FIVE

JOKTHA

To indulge it is to breed it. To punish it is to feed it. Madness knows no bridle but the knife.

—SCYLVENDI PROVERB

When others speak, I hear naught but the squawking of parrots. But when I speak, it always seems to be the first time. Each man is the rule of the other, no matter how mad or vain.

—HATATIAN, *EXHORTATIONS*

Early Spring, 4112 Year-of-the-Tusk, Joktha

Strange, this feeling. Curiously childlike, though when he racked his soul, Ikurei Conphas could find no resembling childhood memory. It was as though he'd been bruised beneath the skin, on his heart, or even his soul. A strange sense of fragility dogged his every look, his every word. He no longer trusted his face ... It was as though certain muscles had been removed.

"*For some it is a defect carried from the womb ...*"

What did that mean?

The disarming of his men occurred beyond Caraskand's walls, across a fallow millet field. There were no incidents, though Conphas very nearly

92

snapped his teeth presiding over it. Columnaries who could sleep in formation suddenly found the most basic commands unintelligible. Several watches passed before all the various units were numbered and disarmed. When it was completed, his Columns, shorn of armour and insignia, looked little more than an assembly of half-starved beggars. Innumerable onlookers jeered from the walls.

Riding along their forward lines, Nersei Proyas called on those who had given themselves to the Warrior-Prophet to abandon their ranks. "The nations of our birth," he cried, "no longer command us. The customs of our fathers no longer command us. Our blood has ceased answering to what has come before ... *Destiny*, not history, is our master!"

There was a moment of accusatory indecision, then the first defectors began pressing their way through their Orthodox brothers. The traitors gathered behind Proyas, some defiant, others mute, and for a moment it seemed the formations would dissolve in a mass exodus. Conphas watched stone-faced, his innards churning. Then, as though a soundless horn had pealed, the defections stopped. Conphas could scarce believe his eyes: the ranks remained intact. Fewer than one in five had left their places. Fewer than one in five!

Obviously vexed, Proyas spurred his horse down a lane between the formations, shouting, "You are Men of the Tusk!"

"We are veterans of Kiyuth!" someone bawled in a drill-master's voice.

"We answer to the Lion!" another cried.

"The Lion!"

For a heartbeat Conphas could scarce believe his ears. Then, as one, the hard-hearted survivors of the Selial and Nasueret Columns roared their approval. The shouting continued, growing in desperation and fury. Someone threw a stone, which clipped Proyas's helm. The Prince retreated, swearing in fury.

Conphas raised his forearm in Imperial salute, and his men raised theirs in thundering reply. Tears clouded his eyes. The bruise of his indignities began to fade, especially when he heard Proyas declare the terms extended by the Warrior-Prophet.

Conphas could scarcely conceal his glee. Apparently the Scarlet Spires had managed to relay a message to their mission in Momemn via Carythusal, and thence to Xerius. This meant that a forced march back across Khemema—which, perils aside, would have seriously compromised his timetable—was no longer necessary. Instead, he and the remnants of his Columns would be interned at Joktha, where they would await a fleet of transports that had been dispatched by his uncle.

No matter who threw the number-sticks, it seemed, he owned the results.

The following march along the River Oras to Joktha was uneventful. He spent much of the ride lost in thought, reviewing explanation after explanation. His staff followed at a discreet distance, watching with strange eyes, never daring to speak unless directly addressed. Periodically, he asked them questions.

"Tell me, what man doesn't aspire to godhead?"

The consensus was, not surprisingly, absolute. All men, they said, sought to emulate the Gods, though only the most bold, the most *honest*, dared voice their ambitions. Of course, the fools simply mouthed what they thought he wanted to hear. Ordinarily this would have incensed Conphas—no command could tolerate sycophants—but his uncertainty made him curiously indulgent. After all, according to the so-called Warrior-Prophet, his was a marred soul, a deformation born of the womb. The famed Ikurei Conphas was not quite human.

The strange thing was that he understood full well what the man had meant. His entire life, Conphas had known he was different. He never stammered in embarrassment. He never blushed in the presence of his betters. He never minced his words with his worries. All around him, men jerked this way and that, pulled by hooks that he knew only by reputation: love, guilt, duty ... Though he understood how to *use* these words well enough, they meant nothing to him.

And the strangest thing of all was that he didn't care.

Listening to his officers oblige his vanity, Conphas came to a powerful realization: his beliefs mattered nothing, so long as they delivered what he wanted. Why make logic the rule? Why make fact the ground? The only consistency that mattered, the only correspondence, was that between belief and *desire*. If it pleased him to think himself divine, then so he would think. And Conphas understood that just as he possessed the remarkable ability to *do* anything, no matter how merciful or bloodthirsty, he also possessed the ability to *believe* anything. The Warrior-Prophet could hang the ground vertical, make all things fall toward the horizon, and Conphas need only point sideways to restore the order of up and down.

Perhaps the sorcerer's tales of the Consult and the Second Apocalypse were true. Perhaps the Prince of Atrithau was some kind of saviour. Perhaps his soul *was* deformed. It simply did not matter if he did not care. So he told himself that his life was his witness, that ages had passed without producing a soul such as his, that the Whore of Fate lusted for him and him alone.

"The fiend couldn't attack you outright," General Sompas ventured, "not without risking more bloodshed, more losses." The caste-noble raised a hand against the sun to look directly at his Exalt-General. "So he heaped infamy on your name, kicked dirt across your fire, so that he alone might illumine the councils of the great."

Even though he knew the man simply flattered him, Conphas decided that he *agreed*. He told himself that the Prince of Atrithau was the most accomplished liar he'd ever encountered—a veritable Ajokli! He told himself that the Council had been a *trap*, the product of thorough rehearsal and painstaking premeditation.

So he told himself, and so he *believed*. For Conphas, there was no difference between decision and revelation, manufacture and discovery. Gods made themselves the rule. And he was one of them.

By the time he sighted Joktha's staunch towers on the fourth day, the bruise had utterly vanished. The old iron smirk reassumed command of his expression. *I, Conphas* thought to himself, *have willed this*.

Peering through the scattered hemlock trees, he idly surveyed his prison. Unlike most cities encountered by the Men of the Tusk, Joktha's curtain walls largely ignored the advantages of terrain. The location had been chosen for its natural harbour—which was merely the largest on a coastline pocked with several such harbours. The landward fortifications formed a long, wandering line, grey as bands of iron in the sun, inter-sected by the small city's single gate: the great barbican of the Tooth—so named because of the white tile adorning its exterior.

From his vantage on the banks of the Oras, Conphas could see little of the city save for the hazy heights of what was called the Donjon Palace, the stronghold of the city's masters. The surrounding countryside, though green and overgrown, betrayed the turmoil of the past season. Not a field had been planted. The orchards had been hacked to stumps. The encircling hills loomed dark, lined with ancient terracing and dotted with derelict villas. An abandoned Ceneian fort occupied a low promontory to the south, its stone so battered that it looked more a work of nature than of man. Only glimpses of sky through an intact window revealed its origins.

The world seemed as blasted as it should.

Suddenly they were riding through a loose stand of peppertrees, and Conphas found himself wondering at the wash of their sweet scent in the wind. Old Skauras had kept peppertrees, an entire grove of them, back when Conphas had been his hostage. It had been a notorious rendezvous, particularly for the seduction of slaves. He would need to hold on to such memories, Conphas realized, to preserve his resolve through the weeks to come. A captive had to always recall those he had mastered, lest he become one of them.

Another of Grandmother's lessons.

The road they followed veered away from the wooded banks of the Oras, and Conphas led his great and miserable train across denuded and fallow ground, directly toward the Tooth. What looked like two or three hundred Conriyan knights awaited them, arrayed to either side of the dark gate. His jailers. He was heartened, even amused, by their lacklustre appearance and numbers.

The sight of the Scylvendi leaning on his pommel, however, struck his amusement dead.

The man wore his hauberk bare, save for the thick Scylvendi girdle about his waist. His black hair tangled about the folds of his mail hood, a complement to the Kianene scalps that fluttered from his horse's bridle.

Why him?

The Prince of Atrithau was a fiend—a cunning, cunning fiend! Even still.

Even still.

"Exalt-General ..."

Scowling, Conphas turned to his General. "What is it, Sompas?"

"How ..." the man sputtered. His eyes flashed with scarcely restrained fury. "How does he expect ..."

"The conditions are clear. I retain my freedom, so long as I remain within Joktha's walls. I retain my staff, and all the slaves that service it. I'm heir to the *Mantle*, Sompas. To antagonize me is to antagonize the Empire. So long as they think me neutered, they'll play their game by the rules."

"But …"

Conphas scowled. Martemus had never hesitated with his questions, but then neither had he feared Conphas. Not really. Perhaps Sompas was the smarter man.

"You think we've been humiliated?"

"This is an outrage, Exalt-General! An outrage!"

It was the Scylvendi, Conphas realized. The disarming had been salt enough, but to submit to a *Scylvendi*? He mused for a moment, surprised that he'd thought only of the implications and nothing of this slight. Had the past months sheared away so many of the old intuitions? "You're mistaken, General. The Warrior-Prophet does us a favour."

"*Favour?* How …" Sompas trailed as though horrified by his own vehemence. The man was forever forgetting and remembering his place. Conphas found it quite amusing, actually.

"Of course. He's returned to me my most precious possession."

The fool could only stare.

"My men. He's returned to me my men. He's even culled them for me."

"But we are *disarmed*."

Conphas looked back at the great train of beggars that was his army. They looked shadowy in the dust, at once dark and pale, like a legion of wraiths too insubstantial to threaten, let alone harm.

Perfect.

He glanced one last time at his General. "Hold on to your worries, Sompas …" He turned back to the Scylvendi, raising his hand in the mockery of a salute. "Your dismay," he muttered askance, "lends the stamp of authenticity to these proceedings."

I'm forgetting something.

The terrace was broad. The marmoreal paving stones were cracked here and there, as might be expected in a nation that suffered frost, but not in Enathpaneah. Even in the dark they were clearly visible, like rivers inked across maps. Cracks. No doubt the original residents had their slaves cast carpets over the offending stones, at least while entertaining guests. No Fanim Prince would tolerate such a defect. No Inrithi Lord.

Only an Utemot Chieftain.

Cnaiür nodded, rubbed his eyes, stamped his foot in an effort to stay awake. Blinking, he stared over the balustrade and out across the city and port. Rooftop piled onto rooftop, climbing the near and distant slopes, and forming a broad basin about the piers and quays that ringed the inner harbour. A dishevelled landscape of structure, struck by streets like river canyons, all leading to the sea.

Joktha ... He need only blink to see it burn.

Above, innumerable stars dusted the firmament, curving into a perfect bowl so vast, so hollow, that it seemed a single twitch might send him floating skyward, falling. It reminded him of awakening at Kiyuth. He could almost smell his kinsmen sprawling dead in ever-widening gyres.

I'm forgetting ...

He drowsed. His copper wine bowl slipped from his fingers and rolled across the cracked stone. Events from the previous evening slurred through his soul. Conphas baiting him at the gates. Conphas arguing the terms of his internment. Conphas restrained by his Generals. His cuirass glaring white in the sunlight. His long-lashed eyes.

I'm ...

The Scylvendi stirred in sudden remembrance, rolled his head about his massive shoulders.

I'm Cnaiür ... Breaker-of-horses-and-men.

He laughed, drowsed some more, dreamed ...

He walked toward Shimeh, though it was identical to the Utemot camp of his youth, a congregation of several thousand yaksh. Herds ranged the surrounding plains, but no cattle dared approach him. He passed the first of the yaksh, their hides tight against their poles, like skin about the ribs of dogs. The Utemot crowded the lanes between, limbs hanging from rotted sockets, viscera draped across their thighs. He saw all of them: his father's brother, Bannut, his brother-in-law, Balait, even Yursalka and his crippled wife. They watched him with the parchment eyes of the dead. He came across the first of his butchered chattel—a brown foal with his threefold mark. Then three cows, their throats cut, followed by a four-year-old bull, its head cudgelled. Soon he found himself climbing across mounds of horse and cattle carcasses, all of them bearing his mark.

For some reason, he felt no surprise.

Then at last he came to the White Yaksh—the very heart of Shimeh. A spear had been driven into the ground next to the entrance. His father's head adorned the haft, pale skin drawn like water-sodden linen. Cnaiür tore his gaze away, drew aside the doeskin flap. Somehow he already knew that Moënghus had made a harem of his wives, so he was neither shocked nor outraged. But the blood unnerved him, as did the fishlike way Serwë opened and closed her mouth ... Anissi was screaming.

Moënghus looked up from his passion and grinned a broad and welcoming grin. *The Ikurei still lives*, he said. *Why don't you kill him?*

"The time ... the time ..."

Are you drunk?

"Nepenthe ... All that the bird gave to me ..."

Ah ... so you yearn to forget after all.

"No ... not forget. Sleep."

So why not kill him?

"Because *he* wants me to."

The Dûnyain? You think this is a trap?

"His every word is a feint. His every look a spear!"

Then what's his intent?

"To keep me from his father. To deny me my hate. To betray—"

But all you need do is kill the Ikurei. Kill him, and you are free to follow the Holy War.

"No! There is something! Something I'm ..."

You're a fool.

Somehow Cnaiür raised his face to the muck of wakefulness, peered through ocean-swimming eyes, and saw *it* perched on the balustrade before him, its scalp polished in starlight, its feathers shot with black silk, the world floating like smoke beyond it.

"Bird!" he cried. "Devil!"

The tiny face leered. The eyes became heavy-lidded, like a demon dreaming.

"Kiyuth," it said, "where the Ikurei humiliated you and your People. Avenge the Battle of Kiyuth!"

I'm forgetting something.

How could absent things remain? How could they *be*?

Each swazond a dead man grinning. Each night a dead woman's embrace ...

Days passed, and Cnaiür tried hard to fathom the depths that pitched about him. Conphas and his Nansur were his immediate concern—or should have been. Proyas had given him the barons Tirnemus and Sanumnis with their 370-odd client knights, as well as the 58 survivors of his old band from Shigek. Like all Men of the Tusk, they were battle-hardened, but they made no effort to conceal their dismay at having been left behind. "Blame the Nansur," Cnaiür told them. "Blame Conphas." They were thoroughly outnumbered by their Nansur charges, and Cnaiür needed as much aggression as they could muster.

When Baron Sanumnis expressed misgivings, Cnaiür reminded him that these men had conspired to betray *the Holy War,* and that no one knew when the Emperor's transports would arrive. "They can overwhelm us at will," he said. "So we must strip their will from them."

Of course, he said nothing of his true motives. These men had chosen Ikurei Conphas over the *Dûnyain* ... One must always chain the dog before murdering the master.

A squalid camp of sorts was struck along Joktha's walls, far enough from the Oras to keep a good number of the Columnaries occupied with drawing and delivering water. Knowing well the organizational strengths of the Imperial Army, Cnaiür segregated the older soldiers—the Threesies as they were called—from the younger. The officers he interned in a different camp altogether. Because of the mutual enmity between the largely caste-noble cavalrymen and the caste-menial infantrymen, Cnaiür had the Kidruhil dissolved and scattered through the Columns. As a further measure, he had his Conriyans continually circulate rumours: that Conphas had been overheard blubbering in his chambers, that the officers had rioted when they learned their rations were no different from the enlisted men's—the kinds of rumours that gnawed at every army's heart. Even when universally dismissed, they served to distract idle souls and to drown those truths that did surface.

Cnaiür restricted Conphas and the forty-two men of his immediate coterie to the city—as per the Conditions of Internment. He forbade all contact with his Columnaries, for obvious reasons. Since imprisoning him outright could provoke a revolt, he allowed the Imperial Nephew what liberty Joktha provided. Even as he obsessively pondered the man's murder.

He understood why Kellhus wanted Conphas dead: the Dûnyain suffered no rivals. Likewise, he understood why Kellhus had chosen *him* as his assassin. Of *course* the savage had killed the Lion. Was he not *Scylvendi?* Was he not a survivor of *Kiyuth?*

What tormented him was what these understandings implied. If murdering Moënghus was Kellhus's sole mission, then preserving the Holy War should be his sole concern. Why assassinate Conphas when he need only remove him from the game—as he had? And why use Cnaiür to conceal his involvement, when the consequences—open war with the Empire—would have no bearing on the imminent conquest of Shimeh?

And Cnaiür realized ... There was no way around it: the Dûnyain was looking beyond the Holy War—*past Shimeh.* And to see past Shimeh was to see past *Moënghus.*

Men draped assumptions, endless assumptions, about their acts; they could scarce do otherwise, given their errant hunger for meaning. Since the beginning, Cnaiür had conceived their journey as a *hunt*, as a collusion of enemies in pursuit of a greater foe. Their quest had always seemed an arrow fired into darkness. No matter how deep his misgivings, he had always come back to this understanding. But now ... Now it seemed like nothing other than a *collar*; that Moënghus and Kellhus, father and son, were but different ends of a mighty torc that he, Cnaiür urs Skiötha, had bent about the very neck of the world. A slaver's collar.

Something ... something ...

He found himself scrutinizing Tirnemus and Sanumnis whenever the opportunity afforded. Baron Tirnemus, he quickly decided, was an outright fool, a man more bent on recovering the belly he had lost at Caraskand than anything else. Sanumnis, on the other hand, was both clever and taciturn, and seemed to wield an obvious, yet inexplicable, authority over his stouter countryman. He was a watcher.

Had they been given secret orders? Orders that made one the senior? That would explain why Tirnemus deferred and Sanumnis watched. What, after all, would be the penalty for murdering the Nansur Emperor's only heir? For contravening the Warrior-Prophet's solemn vow?

I've been sent to murder myself. The thought made Cnaiür cackle. Small wonder Proyas had been so unnerved relaying the Dûnyain's murderous instructions.

The fact that he had been assigned a Schoolman only provided further confirmation of his suspicions. Saurnemmi he was called, a young Scarlet initiate with a fey and chronic cough. He had arrived the day after Conphas, accompanied by a sorcerer-of-rank, Inrûmmi, who departed immediately and inexplicably after inspecting his student's quarters. Saurnemmi, the older sorcerer had told Cnaiür, was to be his link to the Holy War. "The boy," as the pompous fool referred to him, was to sleep until noon every day so they might converse through sorcerous dreams. Saurnemmi, in other words, was to be the Dûnyain's eyes in Joktha.

Depths! Everywhere he turned—mad, unfathomable depths!

Provoked by Saurnemmi's presence, Cnaiür ordered Tirnemus to gather Conphas and his staff in the Petition Hall of the Donjon Palace, the citadel where Cnaiür had made his headquarters. He bid the young sorcerer study their captives from the balcony. Then, once the Exalt-General and his men had assembled, Cnaiür strode into their very midst, staring hard into various faces and taking pleasure in the way they blanched. The Nansur were such predictable scum, courageous in excess when armed in mobs, but cowering fawns when outside formation.

He found himself circling Conphas, who stood ramrod straight in full military dress. "You see your brothers on my arms," he declared to the others. "Your wives ..." He spat at the feet of those nearest. "How it must gall—"

"How many of your brothers," Conphas cried out, "do I bear on *my*—?"

Cnaiür struck him. The Exalt-General sailed backward, tripped to the ground. Cnaiür whirled to the sound of slapping sandals, caught an arcing wrist. He seized his assailant's cuirass, smashed the man's face against his forehead. The dagger the fool had concealed clattered across the shining tiles.

These dogs had to be broken! Broken!

The sound of swords whisking from sheaths. Tirnemus's Conriyans suddenly appeared about him, blades outstretched. The Nansur backed away, ashen-faced. Several called out to their Exalt-General, who had rolled onto all fours, spitting blood.

"Make no mistake," Cnaiür roared over their cries, "you will heed me!" He brought a boot down on the head of the man jerking at his feet. The ingrate went still, as though wrinkles had been smoothed from his limbs. Hot blood slipped along the cracks between tiles.

A moment of wilting silence.

"Do not," Cnaiür said, raising his great banded arms, "make me the ledger of your folly!"

He could almost see them shrink. Suddenly they seemed children—frightened children—beneath the soaring pillars. His heart hammering in exultation, Cnaiür spat again, then raised his face to Saurnemmi, who watched from the gallery above, his adolescent frame bundled in silken crimson. His beard, Cnaiür noted, was little more than a mummer's gag. "Which one?" he called.

Saurnemmi coughed the inane way he always did, then nodded toward the back of the crowd, at the men milling about General Sompas. "That one," he said. "The one with"—another ceremonial cough, too soft to cut real phlegm—"with the silver bindings about his cuirass."

Grinning, Cnaiür reached beneath his girdle, extracted his father's Chorae.

Without warning, the slender man to Sompas's right bolted across the polished floors. He was felled after five strides, a shaft jutting from the back of his neck. He cried out, began screaming words that made smoke of sound. His eyes flared bright. But Cnaiür was already upon him …

Incandescence, searing every surface chalk-white. Men raised arms, cried out.

The Nansur blinked and gaped. Cnaiür turned to them, away from the broken salt-statuary at his feet. He spat and grinned, then strode towering into their midst. He made for Conphas. The Exalt-General sputtered, shrank from his approach, but Cnaiür merely brushed past him, continued wordlessly up the monumental stair. One did not trade words with whipped dogs. It was mummery, Cnaiür knew, but then *everything* was mummery in the end. Another lesson learned at the Dûnyain's heel.

Afterward, he found himself screaming in his apartments. He understood why, of course: if not for the Scarlet Schoolman's arrival, he would never have thought that Conphas too had a sorcerer. But the why of this understanding escaped him ... It always escaped him.

Was something wrong with him?

Enemies! All about him, enemies! They even dwelt within ...

Even Proyas ... Could he bring himself to break his neck as well?

He sent me to murder myself!

At night, Cnaiür drank—heavily—and the spears that lay hidden beneath every surface were blunted. The terrors, rather, oozed from the cracks in the floor. Despite the censers, the air smelled of yaksh: earth, smoke, and mouldering hides. He could hear Moënghus whisper through the dim interiors ...

More lies. More confusions.

And the bird—the fucking bird! It seemed a knot, a yanking of all things foul into a single form. His chest tightened simply thinking of it. But of course it couldn't be real. No more than Serwë ...

He told her as much, every night she came to his bed.

Something ... something is wrong with me.

He knew this because he could see himself as the Dûnyain saw him. He understood that Moënghus had knocked him from the tracks of his People, that he had spent thirty years kicking through the grasses searching for the spoor of his own passing. For a way back.

Thirty accursed years! These too he understood. The Scylvendi were a *forward* people—as were all people save the Dûnyain. They listened to their storytellers. They listened to their hearts. Like dogs, they barked at strangers. They judged honour and shame the way they judged near and far. In their inborn conceit, they made themselves the absolute measure. They could not see that honour, like nearness, simply depended on where one stood.

That it was a lie.

Moënghus had lured him onto different ground. How could his kinsmen not think him an obscenity when his voice came to them from darknesses unseen? How could he rediscover their tracks when all grounds had been trampled? He could never be of the People, not after Moënghus.

He could never think or curse himself back to their savage innocence. He had been a fool to try ... Ignorance was ever the iron of certainty, for it was as blind to itself as sleep. It was the absence of questions that made answers absolute—not knowledge! To ask, this was what Moënghus had taught him. Simply to ask ...

"Why follow this track and not another?"

"Because the Voice demands it."

"Why follow this Voice and not another?"

That *everything* could be overthrown so easily. That all custom and conviction could lay so close to the brink. That outrage and accusation could be the only true foundations ... All of it—everything *that was man*—perched on swords and screams.

Why? cried his every step. *Why?* cried his every word. *Why?* cried his every breath.

For some reason ... There must be some reason.

But why? Why?

The world itself had become his rebuke! He was no longer of the Land, but he could not beat the Steppe from the cant of his limbs. He was no longer of the People, but he could not wash his father from his blood. He cared nothing for the ways of the Scylvendi—nothing!—yet still they howled within him, railed and railed. He was not of the People! Yet still his degradations choked him. Still his longings clawed at his heart. Wutrim! Shame!

Absent things! How could absent things remain?

Each time he shaved, his thumb unerringly found the swazond puckered about his throat. He would track its ginger course. *Something ... I'm forgetting something ...*

There were two pasts; Cnaiür understood that now. There was the past that men remembered, and there was the past that *determined*, and rarely if ever were they the same. All men stood in thrall of the latter.

And knowing this made them insane.

Timing. Few things did Ikurei Conphas ponder more.

The Lords of the Holy War might begrudge them these lands, but the Nansur still held the keys. Joktha was an old Imperial possession with old

Imperial ways. Familiar with the perils of governing conquered peoples, long-dead Nansur planners had excavated hundreds of tunnels in hundreds of different cities. Walls, after all, could be retaken; corpses could only be burned.

Nevertheless, escaping the city had proven far more stressful than Conphas had expected. Though he was loath to admit it, the incident with the Scylvendi in the Donjon Palace had rattled him—almost as much as losing Darastius, his Saik Caller, had inconvenienced him. The savage had *struck* him, batted him to the floor as easily as a woman or child. And against all expectation, Conphas had been paralyzed—utterly incapacitated—with fear. Lean, wild with unnameable hungers, Cnaiür urs Skiötha had seemed the very reaver worshipped by his people. He even *stank* of the Steppe, as though somehow, bound within that astounding frame, lay earth ... Scylvendi earth.

Conphas had thought himself dead. Of course, he realized this was precisely the reaction the barbarian wanted. Frightened men, as the Galeoth said, thought with their skins. But for some reason, *knowing* this had made precious little difference. A thought-numbing dread had dogged every turn of their escape. Waiting for nightfall. Passing through the streets to the necropolis. Excavating the entrance to the tunnels. Only when he and Sompas crossed the River Oras did breath come to him easily—and even then ...

Now, accompanied by a small band of Kidruhil, they waited at the designated rendezvous, an overgrown cairn located near the heart of what had been Imbeyan's hunting preserve, several miles to the south and east of Joktha. The site had been Conphas's choice—as it should be, since *he* inevitably would occupy the heights of the drama to follow.

A series of titanic gusts broke and fumbled across the earth. The ragged evergreens answered, bending back like girls with their faces to the wind. Winter detritus flew, caught up in the sweeping of invisible skirts. Distant treetops shook, as though concealing some monstrous feud beneath their bowers. Everything, it seemed, had conspired to create the sensation of depth. So often the world seemed flat to Conphas, like something painted across his eyes. Not so today, he mused. Today would be *deep*.

Sompas's chestnut snorted, shook its head and mane to shoo a wasp. The General cursed in the petulant way of those who keep score with animals. Suddenly Conphas found himself mourning the loss of Martemus. Sompas was useful—even now, his pickets combed the countryside, searching for the Scylvendi's spies—but his value lay more in his availability than his quality. He was an able tool, not a *foil* as Martemus had been. And all great men required foils.

Especially on occasions such as this.

If only he could forget the accursed Scylvendi! What was it about the man? Even now, in some small corner of his soul, a beacon fire burned at the ready in case of his return. It was as though the barbarian had somehow stained him with the force of his presence, and now it clung, like an odour that must be scrubbed rather than rinsed away. Never had any man possessed such an effect on him.

Perhaps this, Conphas mused, was what *sin* felt like for the faithful. The intimation of something greater watching. The sense of disapproval, at once immense and ineffable, as near as fog and yet as distant as the world's rim. It was as though anger itself possessed eyes.

Perhaps faith was a kind of stain as well ... a kind of odour.

He laughed aloud, not caring what Sompas or the others thought. His old self had returned, and he *liked* his old self ... very much.

"Exalt-General?" Sompas said.

Biaxi fool. Always so desperate to be on the *inside* of things.

"They come," Conphas said, nodding to the distance.

A band of riders, perhaps twenty-strong, had cleared the bowers of a cypress stand and were filing down the opposing slope, picking their way between the hummocks that jutted from the pasture like the moles on a dog's chin. Affecting boredom, Conphas stole a glance at his small retinue, saw the first brows furrow in confusion and concern. He almost cackled aloud. What was he up to, their godlike Exalt-General?

This day had been planned long in advance. The Prince of Atrithau had wasted no time securing his authority over the Holy War. Whatever spleen the Orthodox yet possessed had been gutted by his victory over the Padirajah. Conphas still blinked in wonder thinking of that day. That such ... *certainty* could take root in such desperation. Even his own men had fought with the fury of the possessed.

Conphas had played his role and, given the narrow margins involved, had no doubt been instrumental to the Holy War's success.

But any fool could see his days as a Man of the Tusk were numbered. So he had taken … measures. Arranging this assignation through Cironji intermediaries was one of them. So too was secreting a company of Kidruhil in the wilds of Enathpaneah. Of course, he had told no one of his intentions, least of all Sompas. The long view could not be trusted to those without vision. They must first blunder across the frontier.

"Who?" Sompas asked of no one in particular. The others likewise peered, and though they sat stiff and still in their saddles, Conphas knew they clawed their insides in anticipation, like children hankering for honeycakes. The fact that the approaching riders were dressed as Fanim meant nothing. With the exception of the Nansur, all Men of the Tusk dressed like Fanim. Conphas could not help but wonder what Martemus would think. Life had seemed more careful when reflected in his shrewd eyes. Less reckless.

"Exalt-General!" Sompas abruptly cried. He made for his sword—

"Hold!" Conphas barked. "Draw no weapons!"

"But they're *Kianene*!" the General exclaimed.

Fucking Biaxi. Small wonder they never managed to seize the Mantle.

Conphas spurred forward, wheeling his mount about to face them. "Who but the *wicked*," he cried, "would cast out the righteous?"

To a man they stared at him, stupefied. They were all Orthodox, which meant they despised the Prince of Atrithau as much as he. But their resolve was born of mundane earth, not heaven. Conphas knew he could never ask too much of them—the bag of possible acts had no bottom when it came to men—but he could always ask too *soon*. These men would murder their mothers for him …

It was simply a matter of timing.

Conphas smiled as one who had shared their many straits. He shook his head as if to say, *So here we find ourselves again.*

"I've marched you to the frontiers of Galeoth. I've led you into the heart of the dreaded Scylvendi Steppe. I've taken you to the very threshold of Kian's destruction! *Kian*. How many battles have we fought together? Lassentas. Doerna. Kiyuth. Mengedda. Anwurat. Tertae … How many *victories*?"

He shrugged, as though at a loss how to make the obvious self-evident.

"And now look at us ... *Look at us*! Imprisoned. The lands of our fathers stolen. The Holy War in the grip of a False Prophet. Inri Sejenus forgotten! You know as well as I the demands of War. The time has come for you to decide whether you're the equal of those demands."

Another gust wheeled across the slope, whisking through grasses, buffeting branches, forcing him to squint against the grit. "Your *hearts*, my brothers. Ask them."

It all came to their hearts, in the end. Even though Conphas had no clue what "heart," used in this sense, actually meant, he did know that it could be trusted, like any other well-trained dog. He smiled inwardly, realizing the issue had been decided long before he had spoken. They were already committed. The genius of most men lay in finding reasons *after* their actions. The heart was ever self-serving, especially when the beliefs served involved sacrifice. This was why the great general always sought consent in the instant of commission. Momentum did the rest.

Timing.

"You are the Lion," Sompas said.

Then, as though baring their necks to the executioner, the others lowered their faces and held them there, chins to the red-lacquered breastplates they wore over their chain hauberks. They let a long moment pass. A jnanic sign of deep and reverent respect.

Even worship.

Grinning, Conphas wheeled his mount to the sound of approaching horsemen. There was a wild, unbridled air about the way they reined to a halt before him, as though the merest of whims had stayed their charge. Despite the many colours of their khalats and the glint of their corselets, they seemed shadowy and threatening. It was more than the leather of their dark desert skin, or the oiled lustre of their long-braided goatees. There was a haggard ferocity to their look. Their eyes gleamed with the manic resolve of put-upon peoples.

A speechless moment passed, filled with the grunts and snorts of warhorses. Conphas almost laughed at the thought of his uncle confronting their ancestral foe in such a way. A mole bargaining with falcons ...

As opposed to a lion.

"Fanayal ab Kascamandri," he said in a clear and resonant voice. "Padirajah."

The young man he addressed bowed his head far too low; Fanayal outranked all save Xerius or Maithanet now.

"Ikurei Conphas," the Padirajah of Kian said, his voice rich with lilting Kianene cadences. There was kohl about his dark eyes. "Emperor."

———— ❧ ————

When the rain stopped, he left her slumbering in their bed. Serwë, her face as perfect as it was false.

Cnaiür wandered from his apartments onto the terrace, breathed deep the cavernous after-storm air. Joktha and her narrow ways extended into the distance, subdued beneath the clearing sky. It resembled a vast amphitheatre, its tiers smashed and rutted. He stared for a time at Conphas's compound on the far and opposite slopes, pondered it as though it were an uncharted shore.

A burst of flapping startled him. Shadows flitted across the surrounding pools of water. Fleeing, sand-doves swept above, winging across the crescent moon then jerking downward as though bound by strings to the terrace. Trilling in alarm, they vanished below.

A voice rasped from his periphery, "You perplex me, Scylvendi."

Demons, Cnaiür now knew, had many guises. They were everywhere, mauling the world with their anarchic appetites, outraging with their impersonations. Birds. Lovers. Slaves …

And most of all, *him.*

"Kill the Ikurei," the voice keened, "and the dogs will be loosed. Why do you stay your hand?"

He turned to the abomination. To the bird.

Certain peoples, Cnaiür knew, revered and reviled certain birds. The Nansur had their holy peacocks, the Cepalorans their prairie grouses. All Inrithi butchered kites and falcons in their rites of war. For the Scylvendi, however, birds were nothing more than signs of weather, wolves, and seasons. That, and a food of last resort.

So what was this thing? He had struck bargains with it. Exchanged promises.

"You speak to me of killing," Cnaiür said evenly, "when the Dûnyain's death should be your only concern."

The little face scowled. "The Ikurei plots the Holy War's destruction."

Cnaiür spat, turned to the plate of the Meneanor, to the great finger of moonlight that divided its black back. "And the Dûnyain?"

"We need him to find the other ... Moënghus. He's the greater threat."

"Fool!" Cnaiür exclaimed.

"I eclipse you, mortal!" it replied with bird-vehemence. "I am a son of a more violent race. You cannot conceive the compass of my life!"

Cnaiür turned his profile to it, glanced at it sidelong. "Why? The blood that pulses through my veins is no less ancient. Nor are the movements of my soul. You are not so old as the Truth."

He could fairly hear the creature's sneer.

"You still do not understand them," Cnaiür continued. "Before all, the Dûnyain are *intellect*. I do not know their ends, but I do know this: they make instruments of *all things*, and they do so with a way beyond the ken of me or even you, Demon."

"You think I underestimate them."

Cnaiür turned his back to the sea. "It is inevitable," he said, shrugging. "We are little more than children to them, imbeciles drawn from the womb. Think on it, Bird. Moënghus has dwelt among the Kianene for thirty years. I know not your power, but I do know this: he lies far beyond it."

Moënghus ... Simply speaking the name cramped his heart.

"As you say, Scylvendi, you know not my power."

Cnaiür cursed and laughed. "Would you like to know what a Dûnyain would hear in your words?"

"And what might that be?"

"Posturing. Vanity. Weaknesses that betray your measure and offer innumerable lines of assault. A Dûnyain would grant you your declarations. He would encourage you in your confidence. In all things, he would dispense flattering appearances. He would care nothing whether you thought him your lesser, your slave, so long as you remained ignorant."

For a moment the abomination simply stared, as though implications could only file singly through its apple-sized skull. Its face screwed into a miniature simulacrum of contempt. "Ignorant? Ignorant of what?"

Cnaiür spat. "Your true circumstances."

"And what are my true circumstances, Scylvendi?"

"That you are being played. That you flounder in nets of your own making. The circumstances you struggle to master, Bird, have long ago mastered you. Of course you think otherwise. Like men, power stands high among your native desires. But you are a tool, as much as any Man of the Tusk."

It crooked its head to the side. "How, then, am I to become my own instrument?"

Cnaiür snorted. "For centuries you have manipulated events from the dark, or so you claim. Now you assume that you must do the same, that nothing has changed. I assure you, *everything* has changed. You think yourself hidden, but you are not. Chances are he already knows you have approached me. Chances are he already knows your ends and your resources."

Even the ancient things, Cnaiür realized, would suffer the Holy War's fate. The Dûnyain would strip them the way the People stripped the carcasses of bison. Flesh for sustenance. Fat for soap and fuel. Bone for implements. Hide for shelter and shields. No matter how deep they ran, the ages themselves would be consumed. The Dûnyain was something new. Perpetually new.

Like lust or hunger.

"You must abandon your old ways, Bird. You must strike across trackless ground. You must surrender brute circumstance to *him*, because in this you cannot hope to match him. Instead, you must watch. Wait. You must become a student of opportunity."

"Opportunity ... for what?"

Cnaiür held out a scarred fist. "To kill him! To kill Anasûrimbor Kellhus while you still can!"

"He is naught but a trifle," the bird crowed. "So long as he leads the Holy War to Shimeh, he works our will."

"Fool!" Cnaiür cackled.

The bird held forth its wings in wrath. *"Do you not know who I am?"*

The pools about Cnaiür's feet flared bright with images: of Sranc loping through fire-gilded streets, of Dragons climbing tormented skies, of human heads smoking about bronze rings, and of a high-winged monstrosity ... Blazing eyes and translucent flesh.

"Behold!"

But Cnaiür held his Trinket fast in his fist. He was not cowed. "Sorcery?" he laughed. "You merely toss shanks to the wolves of my argument. Even as we speak, *he learns sorcery!*"

The light vanished and only the bird remained, its human head white in the moonlight.

"The Mandate Schoolman," Cnaiür said in explanation. "He teaches him—"

"It will take him years, you fool ..."

Cnaiür spat, managed to shake his head ruefully despite the mad disproportion between the thing before him and the aura of its might. Pity for the powerful—did that not make one great?

"You forget, Bird. He learned my people's tongue in four days."

Kneeling naked in his apartments, he neither moved nor started at the sound of approaching footsteps. He was Ikurei Conphas I. And though he had no choice but to continue this obscene pantomime with the Scylvendi—surprise was ever the grist of victory—his subordinates were a different matter altogether. At long last the days of censoring his words and rationing his actions were over. His uncle's spies were now *his* spies, and he knew quite well the length and beam of his own sedition.

"The Saik Grandmaster has arrived," Sompas said from the darkness behind him.

"Just Cememketri?" Conphas replied. "No one else?"

"Your instructions were explicit, God-of-Men."

The Emperor smiled. "Wait with him. I come shortly."

Never had he been so desperate for information. The anxiousness was so acute that he had no choice but to master it. The hunger that whined the loudest should always be the last fed. One must have discipline about the Imperial Table.

He barked into the gloom after the General had departed. A naked Kianene girl crept forward, her eyes wide in terror. Conphas patted the rug before him, watched impassively as she assumed the position—knees spread, shoulders down, peach raised—before him. Hiking his kilt, he knelt between her orange legs. He need only strike her once before she learned to hold the mirror steady. But as he began to minister to her, another far better idea came upon him. He bid her hold the mirror before *his* face, so that her own reflection stared down upon her.

"Watch yourself," he cooed. "Watch, and the pleasure will come ... I swear it."

For some reason the cold press of silver against his cheek fanned his ardour. They climaxed together, despite her shame. It made her seem more than the animal he knew her to be.

He would make, he decided, a far different Emperor from his uncle.

Seven days had passed since his meeting with Fanayal, and still the point had not taken. Conphas was not one to fret over omens—he had watched his fool uncle twist from that wire for far too long—but he could not help but mourn the *circumstance* of his investiture. To rise to the Mantle of the Nansurium while prisoner of a Scylvendi—a *Scylvendi!* And to learn of it from a Kianene—from the *Padirajah*, no less! Though the humiliation meant nothing to him, it was an irony too sharp not to smack of the Gods. What if his candle had burned to the stub? What if they did begrudge their brothers?

The timing was all wrong.

Momemn was almost certainly in an uproar. According to Fanayal's sources, Ngarau, his uncle's Grand Seneschal, had taken matters in hand, hoping to secure Conphas's favour upon his return. Fanayal had insisted that his succession was secure—that no one either on or off the Andiamine Heights would dare foment against the great Lion of Kiyuth. And though Conphas's vanity assured him this was true, he could not overlook the fact that this was precisely what the newly anointed Padirajah *needed* him to believe. Though the Holy War lay far from Nenciphon and the White-Sun Palace, Kian stood upon the brink of an abyss. And if Conphas rushed to Momemn to secure his claim, Fanayal would be doomed.

What Son of the Salt would not say anything to save his nation?

Two things had convinced him to remain in Joktha and continue this farce with the Scylvendi: the prospect of crossing Khemema once again, and the fact that, according to Fanayal, it had been his *grandmother* who had killed Xerius. As mad as the notion seemed, and as much as Fanayal's protestations had provoked his suspicion, he somehow knew that this simply had to be what had happened. Years before, she had killed her husband to install her beloved son. And now she had killed her son to install her beloved grandson ...

And, perhaps more importantly, *to bring him home.*

From the beginning, Istriya had balked at the notion of betraying the Holy War. Conphas had forgiven her this, knowing that the old have eyes keen for encroaching shadows. What dusk does not bring thoughts of dawn? It was the intensity of her aversion that worried him. Claws such as hers did not grow brittle with age, as his uncle had apparently discovered.

The murder was entirely consistent with her character, of course. Canine avarice was ever the hook from which all her motives hung. She had assassinated Xerius, not for the sake of the Holy War, but for the sake of her precious *soul*. Conphas found himself snorting in derision whenever the thought struck him. One might sooner wash shit from shit than cleanse a soul so wicked!

But in the absence of facts to fix them, these thoughts and worries could do naught but cycle round and round, quickened by the mad stakes and the perverse unreality of it all. *I'm Emperor,* he would think. *Emperor!* But as things stood, he was a prisoner of his ignorance—far more so than of the Scylvendi. And with his Saik Caller, Darastius, dead, there was nothing to be done about it. Save wait.

He found the old man prostrate on the floor beneath the impromptu dais and chair Sompas had arranged for him. The Scylvendi had installed him and his officers in a burnt-brick manse near the centre of Joktha—an old Nansur exchange house, as luck would have it—and though technically he was free to wander where he might, a watch had been set on all the building's entrances. Fortunately for them, the Conriyans were a civilized people, sharing a civilized appreciation for bribes.

Conphas took his place on the dais, stared across what had once been a moneychanger's floor. In the gloom, bland mosaics wandered across the walls, conjuring a peculiar sense of home. An acrid edge of smoke plagued his every breath; thanks to the Scylvendi, they had been reduced to burning furnishings. Sompas stood discreetly in the same outer gloom as the slaves. Between four glowering braziers, the man lay face-first on a gold and purple prayer mat—pillaged from some tabernacle, Conphas supposed. Despite the thousand questions that raced through his soul, he gazed at him in silence for a long moment, noted the shine of his pate through strings of white hair.

Finally he said, "I take it you've heard as well."

Of course, the man said nothing. Clever as he was, Cememketri was a savant when it came to the finer points of Court etiquette. According to ancient custom, the Emperor was not to be addressed without explicit consent. Few Emperors bothered with the Antique Protocol, as it was called, but now, with Xerius dead, ancient precedent was all that remained. The crossbow had been fired, now everything had to be reset.

"You have my leave to rise," Conphas said. "I hereby rescind the Antique Protocol. You may look me in the eye whenever you wish, Grandmaster."

Two milk-white slaves, Galeoth or Cepaloran, ducked in from the dark to raise the man by his elbows. Conphas was vaguely shocked: the past months had been hard on the old fool. Hopefully he had the strength Conphas required.

"Emperor," the white-haired sorcerer murmured while the slaves brushed the wrinkles from his black silk gown. "God-of-Men."

There it was ... His new name.

"So tell me, Grandmaster, what does the Imperial Saik make of these events?"

Cememketri studied him in the narrow way that, Conphas knew, had always unnerved his uncle. *But not me.*

"We've waited long," the frail Schoolman said, "for one who might truly wield us ... for an *Emperor*."

Conphas grinned. Cememketri was an able man, and able men chafed under the rule of ingrates. The man could boast no ancestor scroll—but then sorcerers rarely could. He was Shiropti, a descendant of those Shigeki who had fled following the Imperial Army's disastrous defeat at Huparna centuries before. The fact that he had risen to the rank of Grandmaster despite these defects—Shiropti were widely seen as thieves and usurers—spoke to his ability.

But could he be trusted?

Of all the Schools, only the Imperial Saik answered to mundane powers, only they remained an organ of their state. Since Xerius believed all men as vain and treacherous as himself, he simply assumed they secretly resented their servitude, when in reality it had been his distrust they despised. The Imperial Saik, Conphas knew, revered their traditions. They took deep pride in the fact that they alone honoured the old Compactorium, the ancient indenture that had bound all the Schools to Cenei and her Aspect-Emperors in Near Antiquity. The Saik alone had kept this venerable faith. They thought the others, especially the Scarlet Spires, little more than usurpers, reckless arrogates whose greed threatened the very existence of the Few.

All men recited self-aggrandizing stories, words of ascendancy and exception, to balm the inevitable indignities of fact. An emperor need only repeat those stories to command the hearts of men. But this axiom had always escaped Xerius. He was too bent on hearing his own story repeated to learn, let alone speak, the flatteries that moved other men.

"I assure you, Cememketri, the Imperial Saik will be wielded, and with all the respect and consideration accorded by the Compactorium. You alone have prevailed over what is base and wanton. You alone have kept faith with the glory of your past."

Something akin to triumph brightened the man's mien. "You honour us, God-of-Men."

"Is all ready?"

"Very nearly so, God-of-Men."

Conphas nodded and exhaled. He reminded himself to be methodical, disciplined. "Has Sompas told you of Darastius?"

"Darastius and I shared the same Compass in Momemn, so I learned that he'd fallen silent while in transit. For a time I feared the worst, God-of-Men. It brings me immeasurable relief to find you—and your designs—intact."

Caller and Compass, the two poles of every sorcerous communication. The Compass was the anchor, the Schoolman who slept in the place known by the Caller, who entered his dreams bearing messages. This, Conphas knew, was but one of many reasons his uncle had harboured such suspicion of the Saik: so many of the Empire's communications passed through them. He who controlled the messenger controlled the message as well. Which reminded him ...

"You know of the Scarlet Schoolman assigned to the Scylvendi? Saurnemmi, his name is. No word of what happens here can reach the Holy War." He let his gaze communicate the stakes.

Cememketri's eyes had grown porcine with age, but they were sharp still. "If you deliver him alive, God-of-Men, we can ensure that the Scarlet fools will think all is well in Joktha. We need only incapacitate him before his assigned contact time—our Compulsions will do the rest. He will tell his handlers whatever you wish. And Darastius will be amply avenged, I assure you."

Conphas nodded, realizing for the first time that it was *Imperial* favour he dispensed now. He hesitated, only for a heartbeat, but it was enough.

"You wish to know what happened," Cememketri said. "How your uncle fell ..." He stooped for a moment, then drew upright in what seemed a breath of resolution. "I know only what my Compass has told me. Even so, there's much we must discuss, God-of-Men."

"I imagine there is," Conphas said, waving with indulgent impatience. "But the near before the far, Grandmaster, the near before the far. We have a Scylvendi to break ..." He stared at the Schoolman with bland humour. "And a Holy War to annihilate."

CHAPTER SIX

XERASH

Of course we make crutches of one another. Why else would we crawl when we lose our lovers?

—ONTILLAS, ON THE FOLLY OF MEN

History. Logic. Arithmetic. These all should be taught by slaves.

—ANONYMOUS, THE NOBLE HOUSE

Early Spring, 4112 Year-of-the-Tusk, Xerash

Kellhus's tactics and the Enathpanean terrain were such that Achamian had few opportunities to appreciate the Holy War's diminished size. Despite the spoils of their victory on the Tertae Plains, Kellhus commanded that they forage as they go, forcing the Holy War to disperse across the rugged countryside. From what Achamian could glean from those conversations he cared to overhear, the Fanim in no way resisted their advance. Aside from hiding their daughters and what grain and livestock remained to them, all the villages and towns of eastern Enathpaneah capitulated.

The Men of the Tusk, with their plundered apparel and sun-bitten faces, looked far more Fanim than Inrithi. Aside from their shields and banners, only their weapons and armour distinguished them. Gone were the long war-skirts of the Conriyans, the woollen surcoats of the Galeoth, and the waist-bound mantles of the Ainoni. Almost without exception, they wore the many-coloured khalats of their enemy. They rode his sleek horses. They drank his wine from his vessels. They slept in his tents and bedded his daughters.

They had been transformed, and in ways that struck far deeper than mere accoutrements. The men Achamian recalled, the Inrithi who'd marched through the Southron Gates, were but the ancestors of the men he saw now. Just as he could no longer recognize the sorcerer who'd wandered into the Sareotic Library, they could no longer recognize the warriors who'd marched singing into the Carathay Desert. Those other men had become strangers. They might as well have brandished weapons of bronze.

The God had culled the Men of the Tusk. Over battlefield and desert, through famine and pestilence, He had sifted them like sand through His fingers. Only the strongest or the most fortunate survived. The Ainoni had a saying: breaking *enemies*, not bread, made brothers. But *being broken*, Achamian realized, was more potent still. Something new had arisen from the forge of their collective suffering, something hard and something sharp. Something Kellhus had simply lifted from the anvil.

They're his, Achamian would often think, watching their grim ranks file across ridge and hillside. *All of them*. So much so that if Kellhus were to die ...

With rare exceptions, Achamian spent every moment either directly attached to Kellhus in the Sacral Retinue or in his vicinity within the canvas warrens of the Umbilica, as the Inrithi had started calling their Prophet's stolen pavilion. Until they learned something specific to the contrary, they could only assume that the Consult would eventually hazard some kind of assassination attempt. Kellhus's ascendancy threatened far more than it had already exacted.

With the Holy War afield, the opportunities to interrogate the two captive skin-spies became sporadic at best. The abominations travelled under Spires guard with the baggage, each in a covered wain, trussed upright in a network of hanging iron shackles. Achamian now participated in all the interrogations, plying the creatures with those few Gnostic Cants of Compulsion he knew—to no avail. The various torments Kellhus devised were likewise ineffective, though for hours afterward Achamian could scarce blink without glimpsing these sessions. The things convulsing in the fecal darkness, screaming and squealing, their voices fractured into bestial choruses. Then, through throats of gravel and mud, laughing. "*Chigraaaaa ... Woe comes, Chigraaaaa ...*"

Achamian couldn't decide what unnerved him more: their many-fingered faces clenching and unclenching, or the hallowed calm with which Kellhus regarded them. Never, not even in his Dreams of the First Apocalypse, had he witnessed such extremes of good and evil. Never had he felt more certain.

Achamian also attended Kellhus's every audience with the Scarlet Spires—for the predictable reasons. They struck him as strange, bumbling affairs. Eleäzaras, it was obvious, had taken to drink, which had the effect of rendering his manner stiff and awkward—a startling contrast to the loquacious contempt that had so characterized him at Momemn. Gone were the despotic self-assurance, the measuring looks, the demonstrations of jnanic expertise. Now he seemed little more than a juvenile come to realize the fatal enormity of his boasts. At long last the Holy War marched on Shimeh, the stronghold of the Cishaurim. There would be no more begging out of battle. Soon the Scarlet Spires would close with their mortal foe, and their Grandmaster, Hanamanu Eleäzaras, was terrified ... of making mistakes, of burning in Cishaurim fire, of destroying his storied School.

Against all reason, Achamian actually pitied the man, the way those of hale constitution might pity those of weak in times of sickness. There was no accounting for it. The temper of every man in the Holy War had been tested. Some survived stronger. Some survived broken. Some survived bent. And all of them knew who was who, and which was which.

At no time did the chanv addict, Iyokus, attend any of these meetings, nor was he mentioned—small mercies for which Achamian was thankful. As much as he hated the man, as much as he had wanted to kill him that night in the Apple Garden, he could do no more than exact a fraction of what he was owed. When the Hundred Pillars had taken the knife to his red-irised eyes, Iyokus had suddenly seemed a hapless stranger ... an *innocent*. The past became smoke, and retribution an act of abominable conceit. Who was he to pass final judgement? Of all the acts committed by men, only murder was absolute.

Had it not been for Xinemus, Achamian doubted he would have done anything at all.

The practical concerns of the march monopolized Kellhus's days. A continuous train of Inrithi caste-nobles conferred with him, bearing intelligence of the lands ahead, disputes that required resolution, and, more and more once the Holy War crossed the frontier into Xerash, counsel on matters of war.

Achamian typically found himself floating in and out of the various parties that formed about Kellhus. Sometimes, out of curiosity, he would pay heed to the issues discussed. Since he often remained while others arrived and departed, he was able to witness, time and again, the prodigious depths of Kellhus's intellect. He would listen to him recite, word for word, messages and admonitions that had been delivered days previously. There was not a man whose name he failed to recollect, not a detail that he missed, even when it came to mundane matters of supply. Achamian lost count of the times he turned to others—particularly Kellhus's Seneschal-Secretary, Gayamakri—in disbelief. They would grin and shake their heads, their brows pinned high in joy and awe. Their astonishment became their confirmation. "What have we done," the man once said to him, "to deserve such wonder?"

Aside from discussions involving Great Names, Achamian soon lost interest in these small dramas. His thoughts would wander much as they had before, when he'd marched with the livestock and baggage. The arriving caste-nobles would still acknowledge him, but he would quickly fade into the fluid backdrop that constituted the Sacral Retinue.

In spite of his lack of interest, the absurd gravity of his charge was not lost upon Achamian. Sometimes, during moments of boredom, an odd sense of detachment would overcome him as he watched Kellhus. The surreal glamour would fall away and the Warrior-Prophet would seem as frail as the warlike men about him—and far more lonely. Achamian would go rigid with terror, understanding that Kellhus, no matter how godlike he seemed, was in fact *mortal*. He was a man. Was this not the lesson of the Circumfixion? And if something were to happen, nothing would matter, not even his love for Esmenet.

A strange zeal would creep through his limbs then, one utterly unlike the nightmare-born fervour of Mandate Schoolmen. A fanaticism of *person*.

To be devoted to a cause alone was to possess momentum without direction or destination. For so long, *wandering* had been his twilight mission, beaten forward by his dreams, leading his mule down road and track, and never, not once, *arriving*. But with Kellhus all this had changed. This was what he could not explain to Nautzera: that Kellhus was the *incarnation* of the abstractions that gave their School purpose. In this one man lay the future of all mankind. He was their only bulwark against the End of Ends.

The No-God.

Several times now, Achamian thought he had glimpsed golden haloes about Kellhus's hands. He found himself envying those, such as Proyas, who claimed to see them all the time. And he realized that he would gladly die for Anasûrimbor Kellhus. He would begrudge no sacrifice, despite his unrequited hate.

To his dismay, however, Achamian found it increasingly difficult to sustain these feelings across the seasons of the day. His thoughts began wandering, so much so that he sometimes doubted his ability to protect Kellhus should the Consult attack. He would shake his head, eye the distances with a hawkish scowl. He would try to scrutinize every petitioner who approached Kellhus.

As always, Esmenet remained his greatest distraction.

Some days she rode, and though uncertain at first, she'd swiftly learned both beast and saddle. Even attached to Kellhus's immediate entourage at the fore of the Sacral Retinue, Achamian saw her regularly. Sometimes he would wax melancholy, silent while Kellhus and his caste-noble commanders droned in the background. Sometimes he would simply wonder—at the mere sight of her, at her acts of mannish boldness, at the way she wielded unquestioned authority over those in her train. Everything about her would seem brisk and decisive. She would seem a stranger.

Usually, however, Esmenet travelled in what others began to call the Black Palanquin, a luxurious litter borne on the backs of some sixteen Kianene slaves. A scribe would ride with her, and throughout the day Achamian saw men on horseback come to confer with her on inscrutable matters. He saw her physically only when Kellhus rode alongside the Palanquin, bearing questions or instructions. Through intervening limbs and torsos, he would glimpse her painted lips beneath the curve of bundled sheers, or her forearm across a raised knee, her fingers hanging from a relaxed wrist. The urge to crane his neck, or even to call out her name, often struck him with the force of pain. He almost never saw her eyes.

Most of their encounters occurred after the march, in the moat of activity that encircled the Umbilica. As these meetings were public, she typically afforded him little more than a courteous nod. Achamian had thought her cruel at first, suspecting that she, like so many, nursed grudges to better cultivate hate. What better way to eradicate the remains of their love? But after a time he realized she behaved this way for *his* sake as much as for hers. Everyone knew they'd been lovers before Kellhus had taken her. Though no one dared mention it, he saw it in their looks from time to time—especially with Proyas. A sudden consciousness of another's shame. A sudden pity.

Any warmth she showed him would simply remind others of his humiliation. His disgrace as a cuckold.

Five days out of Caraskand, after the slaves had hoisted and furnished the great pavilion, Achamian withdrew to his chambers so he might change into his evening attire, and *there she was*, standing in the canvas gloom, waiting for him, dressed in a panelled robe of gold and black, her hair bound in a Girgashi headdress. "Achamian," she said, not "Akka."

He struggled with his composure, beat down the desire to sweep her into his arms.

To his dismay, she spoke only on matters regarding the security of Kellhus's person. He half expected her to cite the articles of his service, as though she were an empress and he a foreign counsel on indenture. Achamian found himself playing along, answering her questions concisely, astonished at the absurdity of their new circumstance, impressed by the rigour and insight of her interrogation.

And *proud* … so very proud of her.

You've always been my better.

Where others were simply walls to him, Esmenet was an ancient city, a maze of little streets and squares, where once he had made his home. He knew her hospices and her barracks, her towers and her cisterns. No matter where he wandered, he always knew that this direction led here and that direction there. He was never lost, though outside her gates all the world might confound him.

He knew the habit of lovers, their inclination to make scripture out of self-deception. There was little difference, he had often thought, between the devotional verse of Protathis and the graffiti that marred the bath-house walls. Love was never so simple as the marks with which it was written. Why else would the terror of loss come upon lovers so often? Why else would so many insist on calling love pure or simple?

What he and Esmenet had shared had been inexplicable, as was what she shared with Kellhus now. Achamian would often overlook the innumerable horrors she had endured. The death of her daughter, Mimara. The hungry seasons. The anger in all the faces grimacing over her. The bruises. The danger. With the exception of Mimara, she would speak of these things with dismissive humour—something that Achamian, for his part, had encouraged. How could he bear her burdens when he could scarce bear his own? The honesty would come later, in the way she squeezed his fingers, or in the momentary terror that flickered through her gaze.

He knew this, and yet he said nothing. He shrank from the work of understanding. He put his trust in the inexplicable. *I failed her*, he realized.

Small wonder she'd failed him in turn. Small wonder she had ... succumbed to Kellhus.

Kellhus ... These were the most selfish—and therefore the most painful—thoughts.

Esmenet had loved joking about cocks. She marvelled at the way men fussed over them, cursing, congratulating, beseeching, coaxing, commanding, even threatening them. Once she told Achamian about a deranged priest who had actually held a knife to his member, hissing, "You must listen!" After that, she said, she understood that men, far more than women, were other to themselves. He had asked her about the temple prostitutes of Gierra, who believed that despite the hundreds of men who used them, they coupled with only *one*, Hotos, the Priapic God. She laughed, saying, "No deity could be so inconsistent."

Achamian had been horrified.

Women were windows through which men could peer into other men. They were the unguarded gate, the point of contact for deeper, more defenceless selves. And there had been times, Achamian could now admit, when he feared the raucous crowd that scrutinized him through her almost guileless eyes. All that had consoled him was the fact that he was the *last* to bed her, would always be the last.

And now she was with *Kellhus.*

Why was this thought so unbearable? Why did it cramp his heart so?

Some nights he would lie awake and remind himself, over and over, of just *who* it was that Esmenet had chosen. Kellhus was the *Warrior-Prophet.* Before long he would demand sacrifices of all men. He would demand lives, not just lovers. And if he took, then he gave as well—such gifts! Achamian had lost Esmenet, but he had *gained his soul.* Had he not?

Had he not?

Other nights Achamian would toss to and fro, silently howl with jealousy, knowing that she gasped and bucked upon *him*, that he used her in ways Achamian never could. Her climax would ring higher. Her limbs would tingle longer. And afterward she would make jokes about sorcerers and their stubby little cocks. What was she thinking, rolling with a fat old fool like Drusas Achamian?

But most of the time he simply lay still in the darkness, smelling the extinguished candles and censers, longing for her as he'd never longed for anyone or anything. If only he could hold her, he would tell himself, recounting recent glimpses of her the way the greed-stricken might count coins. If only he could hold her one last time, she would see, would she not? She had to see!

Please, Esmi ...

One night, lying exhausted after the Holy War's first march into the Xerashi plains, Achamian was struck numb by thoughts of her unborn child. He ceased breathing, understanding that this, more than anything else, was the measure of the difference between her love for him and her love for Kellhus. She had never surrendered her whore's shell for Achamian. She had never even mentioned the possibility of children.

But then, he realized with a tear-blinking smile, neither had he.

With this recognition, something either broke or mended within him; he could not tell which. The following morning he sat at one of the slave fires, watching two nameless girls tear up stalks of mint for tea. For a time he stared in a blinking stupor, still awakening. Then he looked past them, where he saw Esmenet standing in the near distance with two Nascenti in the shadow of dark horses. She caught his eyes, and this time, rather than nod without expression or simply look away, she smiled a shy and dazzling smile. And somehow he just knew ...

Her gates had been closed. She was a direction his heart could no longer go.

Memories of that other fire ...

They came to Achamian as an affliction now. Esmenet leaning against him in laughter. Serwë clapping her hands in delight, her face beaming innocence. Xinemus with his eyes. Kellhus saying, "I was scared!"

"You were *scared*? Of a horse?"

"The thing was drunk. And it was looking at me! You know ... the way Zin looks at his mare."

"What?"

"Like something to be ridden ..."

How they had loved teasing Kellhus! What joy they'd found in his feigned frailties! And that was the least of what they had lost.

That other fire. So different from this one, with its silk and awkward misery. Now they reclined with ghosts.

Achamian had come to Proyas's pavilion out of boredom more than anything else. He could tell from the Kianene body-slave's reaction that all was not right with his presence, but he'd been drinking, and he felt belligerent. The idea of annoying another struck him as justice.

The gold-chased streamers were drawn aside. He saw Proyas, dressed in a robe more appropriate to convalescence than to entertaining, sitting before a small iron-grilled fire-pot. Xinemus sat to his left, and a woman sat across from him.

Esmenet.

"Akka," Proyas said with a nervous and telling glance at the Consort. His face was drawn. After a moment's hesitation he said, "Come in. Please join us."

"I apologize. I'd hoped to find you alo—"

"He said 'come in'!" Xinemus barked with that antagonistic good nature only inveterate drunks could master. He had his profile turned to the air, as though he aimed his left ear.

"Yes," Esmi said.

Her voice sounded forced, but her eyes looked sincere. It was only as Achamian drew up a reluctant pillow that he realized she'd spoken more out of pity for Xinemus than out of any real desire for his company. He was such a fool.

She, on the other hand, looked a breathtaking beauty. It almost galled him to glance at her, not only because all men secretly rank the relative beauties of women they've lost, but because she had been but a lovely weed when she was with him, and now she seemed an astonishing flower. Pearls on silver strings. Hair like shining jet, fixed high on her head with two silver pins. A gown with a shimmering print. Dark and troubled eyes.

The body-slave busied himself collecting spent bowls and plates. Both Proyas and Esmenet paid the man extravagant attention. Everyone seemed stricken, with the exception of Xinemus, who gnawed meat from sawed ribs—pork stewed in some kind of sweet bean sauce. It smelled delicious.

"How are the lessons?" Proyas asked, as though just recalling his manners.

"Lessons?" Achamian repeated.

"Yes, with …" He shrugged, as if unsure of their old ways of referring. "With Kellhus."

Simply speaking the name had become something like twisting a tourniquet.

Achamian brushed at his knees, even though he could see nothing that blemished them. "Good." He did his best to sound lighthearted. "If I somehow live to write a book about these days, I'll call it *On the Varieties of Awe.*"

"You stole my title!" Xinemus exclaimed, reaching out to fumble for some more wine. Proyas quickly intervened, pouring a deep bowl for him, smiling despite the brittle exasperation in his eyes.

"Why?" Esmenet asked. Achamian winced at the sharpness of her tone. Blind as he was, Xinemus saw slight everywhere. He had become worse than the Scylvendi. "What's your title, Zin?"

Xinemus slurped some wine, then in his classic deadpan muttered, *"On the Varieties of Ass."*

They howled with laughter.

Achamian looked from face to beaming face, pressing away tears with his thumb. Memories flooded him. For a moment it seemed that Esmi need only reach out and clasp his hand, press the pad of her thumb against the nail of his own, and everything would be undone. Everything that had happened since Shigek.

All of them are here ... all the people I love.

"My sense of smell!" Xinemus protested. "I'm telling you, my sense of smell reaches farther than my eyes ever did! Into the deepest of cracks ... You, Proyas, you think you ate mutton last night ..." He looked to empty spaces, grimacing. "But it was really goat."

Esmenet rolled back on her cushions, chortling, kicking her small feet. Xinemus swung his head toward the sound of her laughter. He wagged a knowing finger, which he then brought to his nose. "There's beauty—so much beauty—in what we see," he said with mock eloquence. "But there's *truth* in what we smell."

Their laughter became brittle then, suddenly keen to a dangerous shift in his manner. In a moment it trailed away altogether.

"Truth!" Xinemus cried with savagery. "The world stinks of it!" He made as though to stand up, but rolled back onto his rump instead. "I can smell all of you," he said, as if in answer to their shocked silence. "I can smell that Akka's afraid. I can smell that Proyas grieves. I can smell that Esmi wants to fuck—"

"Enough!" Achamian cried. "What's this madness? Zin ... who's this fool you've become?"

The Marshal laughed, possessed of a sudden, improbable lucidity. "I'm the same man you knew, Akka." He shrugged in a drunk's exaggerated manner, holding his palms out. "Just minus my eyes."

Achamian fairly gaped. How had it come to this? *Zin ...*

"My world," Xinemus drawled on, smirking in a lurid approximation of good humour, "has been shorn in half. Before, I lived with men. Now, I dwell with asses."

No one laughed.

Achamian found himself standing, thanking Proyas for his hospitality. The Conriyan Prince sat as one broken, silent as the grave. Despite his fluster, Achamian understood that the Prince had made Xinemus his punishment. By overturning all the old reasons, Kellhus had rewritten the regrets of many, many men.

Xinemus coughed, and Achamian saw Esmenet start at the sound.

More than foul humours ailed the Marshal. He seemed worse every time Achamian saw him.

"Yes," Xinemus said, "by all means, *flee*, Akka." His sneer seemed hale despite his pallor.

"I'll return with you," Esmenet said to Achamian, who could only nod and swallow.

What's happened to us?

"Be sure to ask her," Xinemus growled as they hurried to the threshold, "why she's fucking Kellhus."

"Zin!" Proyas cried, more in terror than anger.

His thoughts buzzing, his face burning, Achamian turned to his former study, but in his periphery he could see that Esmenet had turned to *him*, blinking tears. *Esmi ...*

"What?" Xinemus laughed with mock good humour. "Is the blind man the only one who can see? Do the ancient tropes so rule us?"

"Whatever it is you suffer," Proyas said evenly, "I *will* endure its course—I've sworn this to you, Zin. But I'll tolerate no blasphemy. Do you understand?"

"Ah, yes, Proyas the Judge." The Marshal leaned back into his drink and cushions. When he continued, it was with a strange, dislocated voice—one that had discarded hope. "So he bade Horomon," he quoted, "to offer his cheeks into his hands, saying to the others, 'This man, who has put out the eyes of his enemy, the God has struck blind.' Then he spit once into each socket and said, 'This man, who has sinned, I have made clean.' And Horomon cried out in wonder, for he had been sightless, and now he could see."

He quoted *The Tractate*, Achamian realized, the famed passage where Inri Sejenus restored the sight of a notorious Xerashi criminal. For many Inrithi, "seeing with Horomon's eyes" was synonymous with "revelation."

Xinemus turned from Proyas to Achamian, as though from a lesser to a greater enemy. "He cannot heal, Akka. The Warrior-*Prophet* ... He cannot heal."

Achamian had hoped the air outside Proyas's pavilion would be free of the cramped smells and madnesses of the air within. It was not. The sky was clear, though not as sharp as the arid nights of Shigek. A haze of smoke, bitter with the scent of wet wood, washed across the deserted clearing, as did a scattered chorus of nearby voices—Conriyans drinking about their fires. He looked to Esmenet, grinning as though in relief. But she was staring at the shadows. In a tent somewhere nearby, someone was muttering with the concentrated rage of a drunk.

He cannot heal, Akka.

Neither of them uttered a word as they walked side by side through the dark lanes. The various tents and pavilions loomed out of the darkness. The fires glared. His left hand tingled with memories of holding her right. He cursed himself for the longing that filled him. How could he walk in the midst of so much dread wonder and yet feel only the tug of her? The world clamoured, encircled him with a thousand dire claims, and yet he could listen only to her silence. *I walk*, he reminded himself, *in the shadow of the Apocalypse.*

"Zin," Esmenet abruptly said. She spoke hesitantly, as though after a long and inconclusive reverie. "What's happened to him?"

Achamian's heart leapt, so violently he found himself dumbstruck. He had resolved himself to silence. To walk with her alone in the dark was torment enough—but to speak?

He looked to his sandalled feet.

"You think the question stupid?" Esmenet snapped. "You think—"

"No, Esmi."

There had been too much honesty in the way he spoke her name—too much pain.

"You ... you've no idea what Kellhus has shown me," she said. "I too was Horomon, and now—the world that I see, Akka! The world that *I see!* The woman you knew, the woman you loved ... you must know, that woman was—"

He couldn't bear these words, so he interrupted. "Zin lost more than his eyes in Iothiah."

Four silent steps in the dark.

"What do you mean?"

"The Cants of Compulsion, they ... they ..." His voice trailed.

"If I'm to be Master of Spies, I need to know these things, Akka."

Esmenet was right—she did need to know these things. But she pressed the issue, Achamian knew, for far different reasons. The estranged always resorted to talk of third parties. It was the most convenient course between insincere pleasantries and dangerous truths.

"The Cants of Compulsion," Achamian continued, "are misnamed. They're not, as many seem to think, 'torments of the soul,' as though our soul were some kind of miniature thing, something vulnerable to sorcerous instruments the way the body is to physical. The Compulsions are different. Our *soul* is different ..."

She studied his profile, but looked away when he dared glance at her.

"Souls compelled," he continued, "are souls *possessed*."

"What are you saying?"

Achamian cleared his throat. She had spoken as one accustomed to cutting through the verbal dross of underlings. "They used him against me, Esmi. The Scarlet Spires ..." He blinked, saw the Hundred Pillars Guardsman gouge out Iyokus's eyes. "They used him against me."

They had passed near a crowded bonfire. He could see her face in the intermittent firelight. Her look narrowed, but in the careful way of those sceptical of someone they pity.

She thinks me weak.

He stopped, glared at her impossibly grand aspect. "You think I fish for sympathy."

"Then what's your point?"

He beat down the anger that welled through him. "The great paradox of the Compulsions is that their victims *in no way feel compelled*. Zin sincerely *meant* everything he said to me, *he chose to say them*, even though others spoke the words."

Whenever Achamian had explained this in the past, the questions and challenges had been immediate. How could such a thing be possible? How could men take compulsion for choice?

Esmenet asked only, "What did he say?"

He shook his head, graced her with a false smile. "The Scarlet Spires ... Trust me, they know which words wield the sharpest edges."

Like Kellhus.

There was compassion in her eyes now ... He looked away.

"Akka ... what did he say?"

Figures passed to and fro before the bonfire, and shadows swept the ground between them. When he matched her gaze, it seemed he was falling. "He said ..." A pause. He cleared his throat. "He said that pity was the only love I could hope for."

He saw her swallow, blink. "Oh, Akka ..."

Of all the world, only she truly understood. Of all the world.

Longing crashed about the pilings of his resolution—to crush her in his arms, to press her back tenderly then kiss the faint saddle of freckles across her nose.

He resumed walking instead, found peevish relief in the way she obediently followed.

"H-he said things," Achamian continued, coughing against a voice-cracking ache. "He said things without hope of forgiveness. Now he can't bring himself to stop."

Esmenet seemed baffled. "But that was months back."

Blinking, Achamian looked to the sky, saw the Round of Horns glittering in an arc over the northern hills. It was an ancient Kûniüric constellation, unknown to the astrologers of the Three Seas. "Think of the soul as a network of innumerable rivers. With the Cants of Compulsion, the old banks are swamped, dikes are washed away, new channels are cut ... Sometimes when the floodwaters recede, things resume their old course. Sometimes they don't."

Four silent steps in the dark. When she replied, there was genuine horror in her voice. "Are you saying ..." Her brow slackened in incredulous astonishment. "Are you saying the Zin we knew is dead?"

The thought had never occurred to Achamian, as obvious as it was. "I'm not sure. I'm not sure what I'm saying."

He turned to her, reached out to clasp her forbidden hand. She didn't resist. He tried to say something, but his jaw could only jerk back and down, as though something different, something deeper than his lungs, demanded breath. He pulled her against him, amazed that she remained so light.

Then the old habits seized them, locked them together like hands. She bent to him, as she had a thousand times. He fell into her lips, her smell. He wrapped himself around her trembling frame ...

They kissed.

Then she was fighting him, striking him about the face and shoulders.

He released her, overcome by rage and ardour and horror. "N-no!" she sputtered, beating the air as though fending off the mere idea of him.

"I dream of murdering him!" Achamian cried. "Murdering Kellhus! I dream that all the world burns, and I rejoice, Esmi, *I rejoice*. All the world burns, and I exult for love of you!"

Her eyes were wide and uncomprehending.

Every part of him beseeched her. "Do you love me? Esmi, I need to know!"

"Akka ..."

"Do you love me?"

"He *knows me*! He knows me like no other!"

And suddenly he understood. It seemed so clear! All this time mourning, thinking he had nothing to offer, nothing to lay at the foot of her altar. "That's it! Don't you see? That's the *difference*!"

"This is madness!" she cried. "Enough, Akka. Enough! This cannot be."

"Please, listen. You must listen! He knows *everyone*, Esmi. *Everyone*!"

She was the *only one*. How could she not see? Like a kicked scroll, the logic of it rolled through him: love required ignorance. Like any candle, it needed darkness to burn bright, to illuminate. "He knows everyone!" His lips were still wet with the taste of her.

Bitter, like tears across cosmetics.

"Yes," Esmenet said, retreating step after step. "And *he loves me*!"

Achamian looked down to gather his wits, his breath. He knew she would be gone when he looked up, but somehow he had forgotten the others—the Inrithi—who had walked and caroused about them. More than a dozen of them stood like sentinels in the firelight, staring at him, their faces blank. Achamian thought of how easily he could destroy them, blast the flesh from their bones, and he matched their astonished scrutiny with this knowledge in his eyes. To a man they looked away.

That night, he beat the matted earth in fury. He cursed himself for a fool until dawn. The arguments were assembled and were defeated. The reasons railed and railed. But love had no logic.

No more than sleep.

When next he saw her, he could find no trace of this encounter, save perhaps for a certain blankness in her expression. It was mad, the moment they had shared—as she had said—and for days afterward Achamian half expected the Hundred Pillars to bring charges against him. For the first time he realized the dimensions of his plight, that he had lost her not simply to another man but to a nation. There would be no outbursts of jealous rage, no confrontations, only cloaked officials in the night, discharging their writ without passion.

Just as when he'd been a spy.

He wasn't surprised when no one came, just as he wasn't surprised when Kellhus said nothing, even though he most certainly knew. The Warrior-Prophet needed him too much—that was the bitter explanation. The other was that he *understood*, that he too mourned the contested ground between them.

How could one love one's oppressor? Achamian didn't know, but he loved nonetheless. He loved them both.

Every evening, following a typically lavish meal with the Nascenti, Achamian would wend his way through the hanging corridors of the Umbilica to a leather chamber in the lesser wing—what the Nascenti had come to call, for no reason Achamian could fathom, the Scribal Room. At the entrance, a lantern-bearing guard would always lower his face and murmur either "Vizier" or "Holy Tutor" in greeting. Once within, Achamian would spend time rearranging the rugs and cushions so that he and Kellhus could sit comfortably face to face instead of peering about the pole in the room's centre. Twice he'd upbraided the slaves, but they never learned. Then he would wait, staring across the woven pastorals set, as was the fashion for the Kianene, in a geometric maze of panels. He wrestled with the inevitable demons.

Protecting Kellhus had been the charge of his School. As real as it was, the prospect of a Consult attack seemed to concern Kellhus little. Achamian often worried that Kellhus merely tolerated him out of courtesy, as a way to build trust with a formidable ally. Teaching Kellhus the Gnosis, however, was an altogether different matter. This was the Warrior-Prophet's own charge. Even before their first lesson together, Achamian had known these exchanges would be things of wonder and terror.

From the very first, even as far back as Momemn, there had been something remarkable about Kellhus's company. Even then he'd been someone whom others sought to please, as if they grasped without knowing what it meant to stand tall in his eyes. The disarming charisma. The endearing candour. The breathtaking intellect. Men opened themselves to him because he lacked all those deficiencies that led brother to injure brother. His humility was invariable, utterly disconnected from the presence of other men. Where others crowed or fawned depending upon whose company they kept, Kellhus remained absolute. He never boasted. He never flattered. He simply described.

Such men were addicting, especially for those who feared what others saw.

Long ago, Achamian and Esmenet had made a game of sorts out of their attempts to understand Kellhus—particularly after they had acknowledged his divinity. Together they had watched him *grow*. They had watched him struggle with truths that everyone else had secretly accepted. They had watched him set aside his immaculate humility, his desire to be less than he was, and take up his calamitous destiny.

He was the Warrior-Prophet, the Voice and Vessel, sent to save Men from the Second Apocalypse. And yet somehow he remained Kellhus, the lackland Prince of Atrithau. He commanded obedience, certainly, but he never *presumed*, no more than he had about Xinemus's fire. And how could he, when presumption measured the gap between what was demanded and what was justified? Kellhus had never exacted anything beyond his due. It just so happened all the world fell within the circle of his authority.

Sometimes Achamian found himself joking with him in the old way, as though the revelations of Caraskand had never happened. As though Esmenet had never happened. Then something—a glimpse of a circumfix embroidered on a sleeve, a whiff of feminine perfume—would strike him, and Kellhus would be transformed before his eyes. An unbearable intensity would shine from his aspect, as though he were a kind of lodestone made flesh, drawing things unseen yet palpable into his orbit. Silences seethed. Words thundered. It was as though every passing moment resonated with the unvoiced intonations of a thousand thousand priests. Sometimes Achamian gripped his knees against the sensation of vertigo. Sometimes he blinked against the glimpse of haloes about his hands.

To sit in his presence was overwhelming enough. But to teach him the Gnosis?

To limit Kellhus's vulnerability to Chorae, they had agreed they should start with everything—linguistic and metaphysical—short of actual Cants. As with the exoterics, instruction in the esoterics required prior skills, arcane analogues to reading and writing. In Atyersus, teachers always started with what were called denotaries, small precursor Cants meant to gradually develop the intellectual flexibility of their students to the prodigious point where they could both comprehend and express arcane semantics. Denotaries, however, bruised students with the stain of sorcery as surely as any Cant, which meant that in some respects Achamian had to start backward.

He began by teaching him Gilcûnya, the arcane tongue of the Nonmen Quya and the language of all the Gnostic Cants. This took less than two weeks.

To say that Achamian was astonished or even appalled would be to name a confluence of passions that could not be named. He himself had required three years to master the grammar, let alone the vocabulary, of that exotic and alien tongue.

By the time the Holy War marched from the Enathpanean hills into Xerash, Achamian started discussing the philosophical underpinnings of Gnostic semantics—what were called the Aeturi Sohonca, or the Sohonc Theses. There was no bypassing the metaphysics of the Gnosis, though they were as incomplete and inconclusive as any philosophy. Without some understanding of them, the Cants were little more than soul-numbing recitations. Whether Gnostic or Anagogic, sorcery depended on *meanings*, and meanings depended on systematic comprehension.

"Think," Achamian explained, "of how the same words can mean different things to different people, or even different things to the same people in different circumstances."

He racked his memory for an example, but all he could recall was the one his own teacher, Simas, had used so many years ago. "When a man says 'love,' for instance, the word means entirely different things depending not only on who listens—be it his son, his whore, his wife, the God—but on who he is as well. The 'love' spoken by a heartbroken priest shares little with the 'love' spoken by an illiterate adolescent. The former is tempered by loss, learning, and a lifetime of experience, while the latter knows only lust and ardour."

He could not help but wonder in passing what "love" had come to mean for him? As always, he dispelled such thoughts—thoughts of *her*—by throwing himself into his discourse.

"Preserving and expressing the pure modalities of meaning," he continued, "*this* is the heart of all sorcery, Kellhus. With each word, you must strike the perfect semantic pitch, the note that will drown out the chorus of reality."

Kellhus held him with his unwavering gaze, as poised and motionless as a Nilnameshi idol. "Which is why," he said, "you use an ancient Nonman tongue as your lingua arcana."

Achamian nodded, no longer surprised by his student's preternatural insight. "Vulgar languages, especially when native, stand too close to the press of life. Their meanings are too easily warped by our insights and experiences. The sheer otherness of Gilcûnya serves to insulate the semantics of sorcery from the inconstancies of our lives. The Anagogic Schools"—he tried to smooth the contempt from his tone—"use High Kunna, a debased form of Gilcûnya, for the same reason."

"To speak as the Gods do," Kellhus said. "Far from the concerns of Men."

Following a fleet survey of the Theses, Achamian moved on to the Persemiota, the meaning-fixing meditative techniques that Mandate Schoolmen, thanks to the Seswathan homunculus within them, largely ignored. Then he delved into the technical depths of the Semansis Dualis, the very doorstep of what had been, until the coming of the man who sat before him, a final precursor to damnation.

He explained the all-important relation between the two halves of every Cant: the inutterals, which always remained unspoken, and the utterals, which always were spoken. Since any single meaning could be skewed by the vagaries of circumstance, Cants required a *second*, simultaneous meaning, which, though as vulnerable to distortion as the first, braced it nonetheless, even as it too was braced. As Outhrata, the great Kûniüric metaphysician, had put it, language required two wings to fly.

"So the inutterals serve to fix the utterals," Kellhus said, "the way the words of one man might secure the words of another."

"Precisely," Achamian replied. "One must think and say two different things at once. This is the greatest challenge—even more so than the mnemonics. The thing that requires the most practice to master."

Kellhus nodded, utterly unconcerned. "And this is why the Anagogic Schools have never been able to steal the Gnosis. Why simply reciting what they hear is useless."

"There's the metaphysics to consider as well. But, yes, in all sorcery the inutterals are key."

Kellhus nodded. "Has anyone experimented with further inutteral strings?"

Achamian swallowed. "What do you mean?"

By some coincidence two of the hanging lanterns guttered at the same time, drawing Achamian's eyes upward. They instantly resumed their soundless illumination.

"Has anyone devised Cants consisting of *two* inutteral strings?"

The "Third Phrase" was a thing of myth in Gnostic sorcery, a story handed down to Men during the Nonman Tutelage: the legend of Su'juroit, the great Cûnuroi Witch-King. But for some reason, Achamian found himself loath to relate the tale. "No," he lied. "It's impossible."

From this point, a strange breathlessness characterized their lessons, an unsettling sense that the banality of what Achamian said belied unthinkable repercussions. Years ago he had participated in a Mandate-sanctioned assassination of a suspected Ainoni spy in Conriya. All Achamian had done was hand a folded oak leaf containing belladonna to a scullery slave. The action had been so simple, so innocuous ...

Three men and one woman had died.

As always with Kellhus, Achamian needed only to gloss the various topics, and then only once. Within the course of single evenings Kellhus mastered arguments, explanations, and details that had taken Achamian years to internalize. His questions always struck to the heart. His observations never failed to chill with their rigour and penetration. Then at last, as the first elements of the Holy War invested Gerotha, they came to the precipice.

Kellhus beamed with gratitude and good humour. He stroked his flaxen beard in an uncharacteristic gesture of excitement, and for an instant resembled no one so much as Inrau. His eyes reflected three points of light, one for each of the lanterns suspended above Achamian.

"So the time has finally come."

Achamian nodded, knowing his apprehension was plain to see. "We should start with some basic Ward," he said awkwardly. "Something you can use to defend yourself."

"No," Kellhus replied. "Begin with a Cant of Calling."

Achamian frowned, but he knew better than to counsel or contradict. Breathing deeply, he opened his mouth to recite the first utteral string of the Ishra Discursia, the most ancient and most simple of the Gnostic Cants of Calling. But for some reason no sound escaped his lips. It seemed he should be speaking, but something … inflexible had seized his throat. He shook his head and laughed, glancing away in embarrassment, then tried once again.

Still nothing.

"I …" Achamian looked to Kellhus, more than baffled. "I cannot speak."

Kellhus watched him carefully, peering first at his face, then apparently at an empty point in the air between them. "Seswatha," he said after a moment. "How else could the Mandate have safeguarded the Gnosis for so many years? Even with the nightmares …"

An unaccountable relief washed through Achamian. "It—it must be …"

He looked to Kellhus helplessly. Despite all his turmoil, he truly *wanted* to yield the Gnosis. Somehow it had become oppressive in the manner of shameful acts, and for whatever reason, all secrets clamoured for light in Kellhus's presence. He shook his head, lowered his face into his hands, saw Xinemus screaming, his face clenched about the knifepoint in his eye.

"I must speak with him," Kellhus said.

Achamian gaped at the man, incredulous. "With Seswatha? I don't understand."

Kellhus reached to his belt and drew one of his daggers: the Eumarnan one, with a black pearl handle and a long thin blade, like those Achamian's father had used for deboning fish. For a panicked instant Achamian thought that Kellhus meant to debone *him*, to cut Seswatha from his skin, perhaps the way physician-priests sometimes cut living infants from dying mothers. Instead he merely twirled the pommel across the table of his palm, holding it balanced so that the Seleukaran steel flashed in the light of their fire-pot.

"Watch the play of light," he said. "Watch only the light."

With a shrug, Achamian gazed at the weapon, found himself captivated by the multiple ghosts that formed about the spinning blade's axis. He had the sense of watching silver through dancing water, then ...

What followed defeated description. There was a peculiar impression of *elongation*, as though his eyes had been drawn across open space into airy corners. He could remember his head falling back, and the sense that, even though he still owned his bones, his muscles belonged to someone else, so that it seemed he was *restrained* by the force of another in a manner more profound than chains or even inhumation. He could remember speaking, but could recollect nothing of what he said. It was as though his memory of the exchange had been affixed to the edges of his periphery, where it remained no matter how quickly he snapped his head. Always just on the threshold of the perceptible ...

Unknown permissions.

He began to ask Kellhus what had happened, but the man silenced him with a closed-eye grin, the one he typically used to effortlessly dismiss what seemed to be crucial questions. Kellhus told him to try repeating the first phrase. With something akin to awe, Achamian found the first words tumbling from his lips—the first utteral string ...

"Iratisrineis lo ocoimenein loroi hapara ..."

Followed by the corresponding inutteral string.

"Li lijineriera cui ashiritein hejaroit ..."

For a moment Achamian felt disoriented, such was the ease of reciting these strings apart. How thin his voice felt! He gathered his wits in the ensuing silence, watching Kellhus with something between hope and horror. The air itself seemed numb.

It had taken Achamian seven months to master the simultaneous inner and outer expressions of the utteral and the inutteral strings, and even then he'd started with the remedial semantic constructions of the denotaries. But somehow, with Kellhus ...

Silence, so absolute it seemed he could hear the lanterns wheeze their white light.

Then, with a faint otherworldly smile upon his lips, Kellhus nodded, looked directly into his eyes, and repeated, *"Iratisrineis lo ocoimenein loroi hapara,"* but in a way that rumbled like trailing thunder.

For the first time Achamian saw Kellhus's eyes *glow*. Like coals beneath the bellows.

Terror clawed the breath from his lungs, the blood from his limbs. If a fool such as him could bring down ramparts of stone with such words, what could this man do?

What were his limits?

He remembered his argument with Esmenet in Shigek long ago, before the Library of the Sareots. What did it mean for a *prophet* to sing in the God's own voice? Would that make him a shaman, as in the days described in the Tusk? Or would it make him a *god*?

"Yes," Kellhus murmured, and he uttered the words again, words that spoke from the marrow of existence, that resonated at the pitch of souls. His eyes flashed, like gold afire. Ground and air hummed.

And at last Achamian realized ...

I have not the concepts to comprehend him.

CHAPTER SEVEN

JOKTHA

Every woman knows there are only two kinds of men: those who feel and those who pretend. Always remember, my dear, though only the former can be loved, only the latter can be trusted. It is passion that blackens eyes, not calculation.

—ANONYMOUS LETTER

It is far better to outwit Truth than to apprehend it.

—AINONI PROVERB

Early Spring, 4112 Year-of-the-Tusk, Joktha

They ate in the privy dining chambers of the dead Grandee who had once ruled the Donjon Palace. The room possessed all the features Cnaiür had come to associate with Kianene, as opposed to merely Fanim, decor. The threshold had been carved in the imitation of elaborately thatched mats. The single window opposite the entrance was shuttered with iron fretwork, which no doubt had once carried the same blooming vines he saw on similar windows throughout the city. And the walls were frescoed with geometric designs rather than images, stylized or otherwise.

143

The centre of the room dropped three steps, so that the table—which stood no higher than Cnaiür's knee—appeared to have been hewn from the floor. It was carved of mahogany and so polished that, given the proper angle, it possessed a mirror sheen. With a battery of candles as their only source of illumination, it seemed they sat in a sunken nest of pillows, surrounded by a shadowy gallery.

All of them were at pains not to rub knees—the perennial problem of dining at Kianene tables. Cnaiür occupied the head. Conphas sat to his immediate right, followed by General Sompas of the Kidruhil, then General Areamanteras of the Nasueret Column, General Baxatas of the Selial Column, and lastly General Imyanax of the Cepaloran Auxiliaries. To Cnaiür's immediate left sat Baron Sanumnis, followed by Baron Tirnemus, then Troyatti, the Captain of the Hemscilvara. The slaves hovered in the surrounding gloom, refilling wine bowls or removing spent plates. Two Conriyan knights in full battledress watched from the entrance, their silver war-masks drawn down.

"Sompas says lights were sighted on your private terrace," Conphas remarked. His tone was offhand in the probing way of devious family members. "What was it?" he asked, glancing at the man. "Some four or five days ago?"

"The night of the rain," the General said, barely looked up from his plate. He obviously harboured reservations, regarding either his Exalt-General's feckless manner or the whole notion of dining with their Scylvendi captor. Probably both, Cnaiür mused—and much more besides.

Conphas stared in open expectancy of some kind of reply. Cnaiür matched his gaze, sheared the meat from a drumstick with exposed teeth, then returned his attention to his plate. He had suffered an unaccountable hankering for fowl of late.

He slurped back more unwatered wine, glimpsing the Exalt-General as he did so. There were still signs of bruising about his left eye. Like his Generals, he wore ceremonial military dress: a tunic of black silk chased in silver embroidery under a cuirass stamped with stylized falcons about a colourless Imperial Sun. That the man had managed to have his wardrobe dragged across the desert, Cnaiür mused, spoke volumes.

Every time he closed his eyes, he saw blood arcing across the walls.

Cnaiür had ostensibly summoned Conphas and his Generals here to discuss the arrival of the transports and the subsequent embarkation of his Columns. Twice now, he had quizzed the man on the matter, only to realize afterward that the answers the fiend provided only made apparent sense. But in truth, he cared nothing for the transports.

"*Unnatural* lights," Conphas continued, still staring at Cnaiür in expectation of an answer. Of course, Cnaiür's earlier refusal to reply—as obvious as it was—had accomplished nothing. Men such as Ikurei Conphas, the Utemot Chieftain understood, did not embarrass.

Fear, however, was a far different matter.

He took another deep drink, watched Conphas's canny eyes following his wine bowl. There was cleverness to his look—an appraisal of potential weakness—but there was worry also. The matter with the sorcerer had spooked him, as Cnaiür had known it would.

Was this, he wondered, how the Dûnyain felt?

"I wish," Cnaiür said, "to speak of Kiyuth."

Conphas pretended to occupy himself with his meal. He ate in the effete twin-fork manner of the Nansur caste-nobility, drawing each piece of food as though searching for pins. Given the circumstances, perhaps he did search for pins. His eyes were hooded when he looked up, but the taint of elation was unmistakable. In fact, there had been something ... *exultant* about his manner since his arrival.

He plans something. He thinks me already doomed.

The Exalt-General shrugged. "What about Kiyuth?"

"I'm curious ... What would you have done if Xunnurit had not attacked you?"

Conphas smiled in the manner of men who saw entire conversations from beginning to end. "Xunnurit had no choice," he said. "That was the genius of my plan."

"I don't understand," Tirnemus said, spilling duck from the corners of his mouth as he did so.

"The Exalt-General had taken every factor into account," Sompas explained with a soldier's first-hand confidence. "The seasons and the demands of their herds. Their sense of honour and the acts that would incite them. And most importantly, their arrogance ..." Sompas cast a quick glance at Cnaiür as he said this, one that somehow managed to seem both vicious and worried.

Of all the Generals present, Biaxi Sompas puzzled Cnaiür the most. The Biaxi were the Ikurei's traditional rivals in the Congregate, yet the man could scarce speak without licking Conphas's balls.

"The Scylvendi think buggery taboo," General Imyanax exclaimed in his thick accent, "the greatest of obscenities ..." He had lifted his eyes ceiling-ward while saying "greatest"; now he fixed Cnaiür with a gloating look. "So the Exalt-General had all our captives raped in open view."

Sompas blanched, while Baxatas scowled at the pugnacious Norsirai fool. Areamanteras laughed into his wine bowl but otherwise didn't dare look down the table. Both Sanumnis and Tirnemus cast discreet glances at their commander.

"Yes," Conphas said blithely as he worked his forks. Tap-tap. Scrape-scrape. "So I did."

For a long moment no one dared utter a word. Devoid of expression, Cnaiür watched the Exalt-General chew.

"War ..." Conphas continued, as though it were only natural that men should hang on his enlightened discourse. He paused to swallow. "War is no different than benjuka. The rules depend on the moves made, no more, no less."

Before he could continue, Cnaiür said, "War is intellect."

Conphas paused, carefully set aside his silver forks.

Cnaiür pushed his own plate aside. "You wonder where I heard that."

The man pursed his lips and shook his head. He dabbed his chin with his nap. "No ... You were there that day ... when I explained my tactics to Martemus. You were there, weren't you? Among the dead."

"I was."

Conphas nodded as though an old and arcane suspicion had been confirmed. "I'm curious ... It was just Martemus and I that day ..." He looked at Cnaiür significantly. "We had no escort."

"You wonder why I did not kill you?"

The Exalt-General smirked. "I was going to say 'try.'"

A slave's youthful hand reached from the darkness, drew Cnaiür's plate away. Gold and bones.

"The grasses," he said. "They knotted about my limbs. They bound me to the earth."

A door had opened somewhere. He could see it clearly in all their eyes—even in those of his so-called subordinates. A door had opened, and terror had stepped into their midst.

I see you.

Only Conphas seemed oblivious. It was as though he lacked the required organs.

"But of course," he said, grinning. "The field was *mine*."

No one laughed.

Cnaiür leaned back, stared down into the palms of his great hands. "Leave us," he commanded. "Everyone."

At first no one moved—no one even breathed. Then Conphas cleared his throat. With an intrepid scowl he said, "Do it ... do as he says."

Sompas began to protest.

"Now!" the Exalt-General barked.

When they were gone, Cnaiür's eyes clicked onto the man's chiselled face. His own brow, even his nose, were ghosts on the fringes of his periphery ... a reminder of what watched.

Cnaiür urs Skiötha ...

Conphas nodded as though he entirely understood. "I would have lost Kiyuth," he said, "had you been King-of-Tribes."

... most violent of all Men.

"That," Cnaiür said, "and more."

The man chuckled into his wine bowl. Arching his eyebrows, he said, "The Empire as well, I suppose."

Cnaiür studied him, suffused with a faint kind of wonder. The voice was the same, yet it seemed impossible that the boy before him could be the Imperial Exalt-General who had surveyed Kiyuth that morning so long ago. That man had been all-conquering. He had towered over the pastures, and the innumerable dead had all mouthed his name. The Great Ikurei Conphas.

And now here he was, the "Lion of Kiyuth." His neck as slender as any Cnaiür had broken.

The Exalt-General pushed back his plate, turned to him in a manner at once jocular and conspiratorial. "What is it that resides in the hearts of hated foes, hmm? Save the Anasûrimbor, there's no man I despise more than you ..." He leaned back with a friendly shrug. "And yet I find this ... unlikely repose in your presence."

"Repose," Cnaiür snorted. "That is because the world is your trophy room. Your soul makes flattery of all things—even me. You make mirrors of all that you see."

The Exalt-General blinked, then cackled in laughter. "Let's not mince words, Scylvendi."

Cnaiür hammered his knife into the heavy table. Bowls, platters, and Conphas all jumped. *"This,"* he grated. "This! This is what the world is in truth!"

Conphas swallowed, somehow managed to maintain his façade of good humour. "And what might that be?"

The barbarian grinned. "Even now, it moves you."

Ikurei Conphas licked his lips. Fine features tightened about clenched teeth. Why did anger always look so bland on beautiful faces? "I can assure you," Conphas said evenly, "I fear no—"

Cnaiür struck, cuffed him so hard he toppled backward.

"You act as though you live this life a second time!" Cnaiür leapt into a crouch upon the table, sent plates and bowls spinning. Eyes as round as silver talents, Conphas scrambled backward through the cushions. "As though you were assured of its outcome!"

Conphas had turned, was fighting his way clear of the depression. "Somp-Somp—!" Cnaiür vaulted across the table, hammered the back of his head. The Exalt-General went down. Cnaiür unfastened his belt, snapped it free. He yanked it about the sobbing man's neck, hoisted him to his knees. He wrenched him back to the table, threw him onto his chest. He smashed his face against its own reflection—once, twice ...

He looked up, saw the slaves cringing in the shadows, their arms upraised. One of them wept.

"I am a demon!" he cried. "A *demon!*"

Then he turned back to Conphas shuddering on the table beneath him.

Some things required literal explanation.

Sunrise. Light speared through the eastward columns, glazing them orange and rose. A faint breeze carried the scent of cedar and sand. It seemed he could hear all Joktha stir to the touch of morning.

Cnaiür swatted a wine bowl from the sheets. It clanged across tiles before being silenced by the carpets. He sat at the edge of the bed, pinching the bridge of his nose, then strode to the bronze washbasin set into the west wall. He stared at the geometric frescoes—ovals interlocking—while rinsing away the blood and soil smeared across his thighs. Then he walked naked onto his terrace, into the sunlight. Like a bead of oil dropped in water, Joktha spread outward as he approached the balustrade, stark and silent in the early morning light. Sand-doves squabbled on the eaves. To the east, black against the silver-gold sea, a fleet of ships lay anchored beyond the mouth of the harbour. *Nansur* ships.

So, it would be today.

He dressed without his body-slaves, though he dispatched one with a summons for Troyatti. The Captain intercepted him on his way to the barracks' mess.

"Send men out to those transports," Cnaiür said. "We lower the harbour chain only when each and every one has been searched. Then I want you personally to gather Conphas and his Generals, bring them to the harbour—the Grand Quay. Take as many men as can be spared."

The taciturn Conriyan had listened dutifully, scratching the swazond across his right forearm as he did so. He crushed his beard to his chest with a nod.

"And Troyatti—no matter what happens, make sure you secure the Ikurei."

"Something worries you," the Captain said.

For a heartbeat Cnaiür found himself wondering whether they were friends, Troyatti and himself. Ever since riding with him in Shigek, Troyatti and the others had called themselves the Hemscilvara, the Scylvendi's Men. He had taught them the ways of the People—they had seemed important then—and with the strange capacity of the young to worship, they had followed, and had continued to follow even after Proyas had reassigned them.

"This fleet ... it has arrived too soon—I think. There is a chance it was dispatched *before* Conphas's expulsion."

Troyatti frowned. "Instead of retrieving Conphas, you think it brings him reinforcements?"

"Think of Kiyuth ... The Emperor only sent a fraction of the Imperial Army with Conphas. Why? To guard against my kinsmen, when they have been ruined? No. He saved his strength for a reason."

The Captain nodded, his eyes bright with sudden understanding.

"Secure Conphas, Troyatti. Spill as much blood as you have to."

After sending word to Sanumnis and Tirnemus, Cnaiür rode with several of the Hemscilvara to the so-called Grand Quay, which was essentially a stone and gravel berm built out into the water, set about with wooden docks like hoardings upon curtain walls. Discarded oyster shells cracked beneath his sandals as he strode out to its terminus. His men fanned out, press-ganging the Enathi squatters, fishermen mostly, who continually availed themselves of unused berths. Cnaiür's presence ensured the absence of incident. Drying nets were dragged away. Shanties were kicked down.

The air smelled of dank and rotting fish. Raising a hand against the sun, he watched a handful of boats row out toward the mouth of the harbour, drawing closer to the foremost Nansur carrack. They looked like overturned beetles, legs pitching water in time. Red-throated gulls drifted through the sky above, their screeches near and jarring. What had Tirnemus called them? Yes, gopas ...

He watched as more and more boats gained the fleet.

Sanumnis arrived shortly after in full battledress, accompanied by a Thunyeri chieftain named Skaiwarra, who had disembarked three days earlier with some 300-odd kinsmen—Men of the Tusk all. A combination of Eumarnan wine and diarrhea, Sanumnis explained, had delayed their departure. The chieftain was a stout, blond-braided man possessing the same pocked fierceness that characterized so many of his countrymen. He spoke no Sheyic whatsoever, but between his and Sanumnis's smattering of Tydonni, Cnaiür was able to bargain with him. It seemed Skaiwarra was a pirate of recent conversion, and as such had an abiding hatred of the Nansur and their pious fleets. He agreed to tarry yet one more day.

A messenger from Troyatti appeared during their exchange. Imyanax, Baxatas, and Areamanteras were even now being escorted to the harbour, the man said, but Conphas and Sompas were nowhere to be found. Apparently Conphas had been severely beaten the night before, and Sompas had taken him elsewhere in the city, searching for a physician.

Cnaiür matched Sanumnis's dark gaze. "Seal the gates," he said. "Man the walls ... If anything happens, the city is yours—as is the Warrior-Prophet's charge."

The Baron flinched from the intensity of his look, then nodded in resignation. Cnaiür turned back to the sunlight as he and Skaiwarra withdrew. The first of the boats was returning, rowing between the towers of the harbour's mouth, over the chain where it dipped in the water. The sun had climbed high enough for him to discern the crimson of the transport's sails, bundled against black-painted masts.

Tirnemus and his entourage arrived moments before Troyatti's men escorted the Nansur officers onto the berm. The man smelled of wine and fried pork. Cnaiür told him to muster his men along the docks. "If all is well," he said, "you will need to organize the embarkation."

"Is all well?" the Baron asked with open apprehension. They could all smell it now.

Cnaiür turned his back on the man, waved for his Hemscilvara to bring the captives to the end of the quay. Their arms were bound behind their backs, which meant they had resisted.

He glared at the Nansur Generals as they were prodded forward. "You had better pray these transports are empty ..."

"Dog!" old Baxatas spat. "What do you know of prayer?"

"More than your Exalt-General."

A moment of silence.

"We know what you did," Areamanteras said, not without some caution.

Scowling, Cnaiür approached the General, pausing only when he towered over him. "What did I do?" he asked, his voice strange. "There was blood when I awoke ... blood and shit."

Areamanteras fairly quailed in his shadow. He opened his mouth to answer, then tried to purse away trembling lips.

"Fucking swine!" Baxatas cried to Cnaiür's immediate right. "Scylvendi pig!" Despite his fury, there was fear in his eyes as well.

The gopas dipped and screamed in the air above.

"Where is he?" Cnaiür asked. "Where is the Ikurei?"

None of the three said a word, and only Baxatas dared meet his gaze. At one point he seemed about to spit at him, but apparently thought better of it.

Cnaiür turned back to the nearest boat's approach. He looked down to the black water beyond the dock's edge, watched it slap about the pilings. He saw a branch reaching up from the murk, its forking tip waving just above the surface, like fingers ringed by foam.

The boatmen were shouting across the water. The transports were empty.

By mid-afternoon all the carracks and their escort of war galleys had been piloted into the harbour. Cnaiür kept the gates sealed, not willing to expose himself in any way until he had Conphas in his clutches. He had set Tirnemus and his men to join Troyatti in ransacking the city.

The Admiral of the Nansur fleet, a man called Tarempas, explained that the seasonal winds that so determined travel across the Three Seas had been unexpectedly favourable. He was far more worried about his return trip—or so he claimed. He was one of those restless, small-statured men who, given the way their eyes darted, seemed far more interested in their surroundings than their interlocutors. It was as though he continually sized everything up.

Some time afterward, the Columnaries in the main camp began rioting. They had caught word of the fleet's early arrival. When noon came without any official word, they organized a protest. Several times in the course of his travels across the city, Cnaiür had actually heard their commotion: raucous shouts followed by booming cheers. As much was to be expected from homesick men, he supposed, especially after nearly three weeks of internment.

Then word of their Exalt-General's disappearance leaked out.

With Sanumnis and Skaiwarra in tow, Cnaiür climbed the curtain walls overlooking the camp. Gaining the heights was like stepping from a calm grotto into the heart of battle, such was the clamour. A slum of hovels and tents extended from the wall's footings, filling a great swath of earth denuded by the milling of countless feet. The bare earth funnelled southward, drawn into a track running across abandoned fields to the Oras River, which wound blue and black behind hazy screens of trees. A vast mob had gathered along the westward regions of the camp, thousands of men in soiled red tunics, shaking fists at a thin line of Conriyan knights arrayed some hundred paces distant on the far side of a razed orchard. With the exception of their helms and masks, they looked for all the world like Kianene horsemen.

Sanumnis whistled in grim appreciation. "Should we cut them down?" he ventured.

"Your men would be swallowed whole. You would simply be arming them."

"Leave them, then?"

Cnaiür shrugged. "I see no siege towers ... Just keep them hemmed in, away from their officers. Give a mob a head and it becomes an army. If they start forming ranks—if they remember their discipline—summon me immediately."

The Baron nodded in what seemed grudging admiration.

Word arrived from Troyatti not long afterward. The Captain was in the city's crammed necropolis in the largely abandoned Kianene Quarter, where his men had apparently found some kind of tunnel. The certainty of it had coalesced long before Cnaiür found the man standing, shirtless, hands on hips, at the mouth of the half-ruined sepulchre.

Conphas was gone.

"It runs several hundred yards beyond the walls," the Conriyan said in grim explanation. "They had to excavate some to breach the surface ... Some." He grimaced as though to say, *At least he got his hands dirty.*

Cnaiür studied the man for a moment, pondered the absurdity of Inrithi scarring themselves in the manner of Scylvendi. It made him seem more a man somehow. He glanced across the necropolis, at the leaning obelisks, sagging ash-houses, and leering images—all Nansur or Ceneian. He felt none of the dread that had prevented the Fanim from reclaiming this ground. Shouts echoed from the nearby streets: the Hemscilvara calling to one another.

"Call off the search," Cnaiür said. He nodded to the entrance of the sepulchre. "Collapse it. Close the tunnel."

He turned to search the harbour, but the burnt-brick façade of a tenement obscured it. Conphas had orchestrated all this ... After so long with the Dûnyain, he knew the smell of premeditation.

This would not be another Kiyuth.

Something ... something ...

Without a further word to Troyatti, he galloped the short distance to the Donjon Palace. He strode through the ornate halls, shouting for the Scarlet Schoolman, Saurnemmi. He found the Initiate just as he stumbled from his chambers, eyes swollen from slumber.

"What Cants do you know?" he barked.

The insipid fool blinked in astonishment. "I-I—"

"Can you burn wood from a distance? Ships?"

"Yes—"

A lone Conriyan horn pealed from some hidden distance—the signal Sanumnis was to use to summon him. There was some kind of emergency along the walls.

"Get to the harbour!" Cnaiür snarled, already running. As he rounded the marble banister, he caught a final glimpse of Saurnemmi, standing awkward and dumbstruck, clutching the front of his silk nightshirt.

He rode hard to the Tooth, where the horn seemed to issue. It rang out three more times, metallic and mournful. He shouldered his way through the knights milling in the open mall about the Tooth's inner gates. Shouting men waved to him from the barbican's summit.

"Quickly," Baron Sanumnis exclaimed as he crested the final stairs. "Come."

Leaning between the floriated battlements, Cnaiür saw that the Columnaries had abandoned their camp and were making their way north. He saw clots of them scattered across the distance, jumping irrigation ditches, filing through groves ...

"There," Sanumnis said, clutching his beard with one hand and pointing to the first broad bend in the River Oras with the other.

Peering between black-boughed sand willows, Cnaiür saw a band of armoured horsemen riding in loose formation. They bore a crimson banner with a Black Sun halved by a horse head ... Kidruhil.

"And there," Sanumnis said, this time pointing to the hills, past a series of green-mottled slopes. Though they marched in valley gloom, Cnaiür could see them clearly: ranks of infantrymen.

"You've doomed us," Sanumnis said in his periphery. His tone was strange. There was no accusation in his voice. Something worse.

Cnaiür turned to the man, saw immediately that Sanumnis understood their straits all too well. He knew that the Imperial transports had set ashore in one of the natural harbours to the north of the city, and there disembarked who knew how many thousands—an entire army, no doubt. And he knew, moreover, that Conphas could not afford to let even one of them escape alive.

"You were supposed to kill him," Sanumnis said. "You were supposed to kill Conphas."

Weeper! Faggot weeper!

Cnaiür frowned. "I am not an assassin," he said.

Unaccountably, the Baron's eyes softened. Something almost … kindred passed between them.

"No," the man said, "I suppose you're not."

Weeper!

As though prompted by some kind of premonition, Cnaiür turned and stared down the Pull, the broad thoroughfare that opened onto the Tooth, all the way to the harbour. Over the welter of rooftops he could see the farthest of the black clapboard transports. The nearer ones were only masts.

A flash of light, glimpsed through a slot between walls. Cnaiür blinked. The thunderclap followed moments after. All those lining the parapet turned in astonishment.

More lights, glimpsed over obscuring buildings. Sanumnis cursed in Conriyan.

Schoolmen. Conphas had hidden Schoolmen on his transports. Imperial Saik. Cnaiür's thoughts raced. He turned back to the formations advancing through the valley. Glanced at the setting sun. More cracks rumbled across the sky. "Chorae bowmen," he said to the Baron. "You have, what, four Chorae bowmen?"

"The Diremti brothers and two besides. But they would be dead men … The Imperial Saik! Sweet Sejenus!"

Cnaiür grasped both his shoulders. "This treachery," he said. "The Ikurei must kill all who might testify against him. You know this."

Sanumnis nodded, expressionless.

Cnaiür released his grip. "Tell your Trinketmen to situate themselves in the buildings surrounding the harbour—to hide. Tell them they need kill only *one*—one of them—to pen the Saik in the harbour. With no infantry to prise their way, they'll be loath to advance. Sorcerers are fond of their skins."

The man's eyes brightened in understanding. Cnaiür knew that Conphas had likely commanded the Schoolmen in the harbour to remain on their ships, that their primary purpose was to render escape impossible. The Exalt-General was not so foolish as to risk his most powerful and delicate tools. No, Conphas *meant* to come through the Tooth. But there was no harm in letting Sanumnis and his men think they had forced this on him.

A brilliant flash deflected their attention to the harbour. No doubt Tirnemus and his men—those who yet survived—were fleeing into the city.

"It will be dark," Cnaiür shouted over the resulting thunder. "It will be dark before the Nansur can organize an assault on the Tooth. Aside from spotters, we must abandon the walls. We must withdraw into the city."

Sanumnis frowned.

"The Saik can do nothing so long as we stand in the midst of their countrymen," Cnaiür explained. "That is cause to hope ..."

"Hope?"

"We must *bleed him*! We are not the only Men of the Tusk."

The Baron suddenly bared clenched teeth—and Cnaiür saw it, the spark he had needed to strike. He glanced down the length of the parapet at the dozens of anxious faces that stared back at him. Others, mostly Thunyeri, watched from the Tooth's cobbled mall below. He looked to the harbour, saw curtains of smoke rolling orange and black in the setting sun.

He strode to the wall's inner brink, held out his arms in grand address. "Listen to me. I will not lie to you. The Nansur can afford no quarter, because they can afford no Truth! We all die this night!"

He let these words ring into silence.

"I know nothing of your Afterlife. I know nothing of your Gods or their greed for glory. But I do know this: In days to come, widows shall curse me as they weep! Fields shall go to seed! Sons and daughters shall be sold into slavery! Fathers shall die desolate, knowing their line is extinct! This night, I shall carve my mark into the Nansurium, and *thousands shall cry out for want of my mercy*!"

And the spark became flame.

"Scylvendi!" they roared. "*Scylvendi!*"

The mall behind the Tooth had been a market of some kind before the coming of the Holy War. An expanse of some twenty lengths extended from the base of the barbican to the mouth of the Pull. An ancient tene-ment of Ceneian construction fronted the Pull's north side, its base riddled with derelict shops and stalls. Cnaiür had concealed himself oppo-site, in one of the smaller buildings that ran along the south. If he peered, he could make out the glint of arms belonging to the shadowy myriad crowded within the tenement. A small window in the western wall afforded him a view across the gravel and dust of the mall, but since the moon rose to the west, the inner wall and barbican were little more than monoliths of impenetrable black.

Behind him, Troyatti whispered to the Hemscilvara, detailing the weaknesses in Nansur armour and tactics that Cnaiür had described to him, Sanumnis, Tirnemus, and Skaiwarra earlier. Outside, the shouts of Nansur officers echoed through the clear night air: Conphas making final preparations.

As Cnaiür had expected, the Saik had refused to leave their transports, which meant they owned the harbour and nothing else. While keeping a close eye on the arriving Columns—so far the Faratas, the Horial, and the famed Mossas had assembled—Cnaiür had dispersed teams of men throughout the buildings surrounding the Tooth, armed with what sledges and pickaxes they could muster. In a few short hours they had managed to knock out hundreds of walls, transforming, in effect, a broad tract of the western city into a labyrinth. Then, fumbling their way through the dark, they had taken up positions—and waited.

This was not, Cnaiür realized, what the Dûnyain would do.

Either Kellhus would find a way—some elaborate or insidious track—that led to the domination of these circumstances, or he would flee. Was that not what had happened at Caraskand? Had he not walked a path of miracles to prevail? Not only had he united the warring factions *within* the Holy War, he had given them the means to war without.

No such path existed here—at least none that Cnaiür could fathom.

So why not flee? Why cast his lot with doomed men? For honour? There was no such thing. For friendship? He was the enemy of all. Certainly there were truces, the coming together of coincidental interests, but nothing else, nothing *meaningful*.

Kellhus had taught him that.

He cackled aloud when the revelation struck, and for a moment the world itself wobbled. A sense of *power* suffused him, so intense it seemed something *other* might snap from his frame, that throwing out his arms he could shear Joktha's walls from their foundations, cast them to the horizon. *No reason* bound him. Nothing. No scruple, no instinct, no habit, no calculation, no *hate* ... He stood beyond origin or outcome. He stood *nowhere*.

"The men wonder," Troyatti said cautiously, "what amuses you, Lord."

Cnaiür grinned. "That I once cared for my life."

Even as he said this, he heard something, a surreal muttering like the susurrus of insects through the riddled world around them. Words coiled through the sounds, the way flames glowered through smoke, and it bent the soul somehow simply hearing them, as though meaning had become contortion ...

Brilliance. A concatenation of fires boiled over the parapets. Suddenly the barbican seemed a shield held against a blinding light. One of the spotters toppled, thrashing flames all the way to the ground.

They were coming.

Within the barbican, lines of brilliance sketched the seams about the iron-banded doors. A thread of gold flared down their centre, and in a blink both were blown outward against the portcullis. Iron screeched. Stone cracked. Another burst. Like sound from a horn, light blasted from the underpass. The portcullis sailed into the old Ceneian tenement. A wave of smoke rolled outward and upward, across buildings and down the Pull.

Cnaiür blinked spots from his eyes. Everything had gone dark. His warriors coughed, beat the air with their hands. They fell still when they heard the growing roar ... Shouting men. Thousands of them.

Cnaiür motioned for everyone to shrink back into the blackness.

It seemed to drone on for an extraordinary length of time, but the roar lost none of its ardour, and ever so gradually it became louder—and louder ... Columnaries, spears out, square-shields tight, materialized from the black maw of the barbican. They ran screaming, rank after rank of them, setting up shield-walls to either flank, hacking at the doors to the barbican and rushing forward down the Pull. Cnaiür knew how they had been trained: strike hard and deep, cut upon your enemy's flank, sever him from his kinsmen. "The wise spear," their officers bawled, "finds the back!"

The heartbeats that followed were absurd. Like gleaming shadows, Nansur after Nansur flashed past the opening of their abandoned stall. Hundreds rushed down the Pull, their helms glossed in moonlight, their pale calves dancing in the gloom. Then a horn—the first—sounded in the blackness. Across the way, Cnaiür saw wild-haired Thunyeri dropping from the tenement's second-storey windows, hooting their unnerving war cry.

The ring of steel. The clap of shields. Then all became roaring clamour.

Almost as one, the Nansur stopped and turned. Some even jumped to better glimpse the axes pitching to their left. A few canny souls turned apprehensively to black windows and entrances about them.

Then the second horn sounded, and Cnaiür leapt, screaming the war cry of his fathers. They crashed into the backs of the stunned infantry-men. He caught the first man in the jaw as he turned, the second in the armpit as he struggled to free his spear. Within seconds, hundreds had died. Then suddenly the Conriyans on the south found themselves facing the Thunyeri on the north.

A ragged cheer was raised, which Cnaiür silenced with his raving voice. "Off the streets! *Off* the streets!"

The unholy muttering had started anew.

The battle that followed was unlike any Cnaiür had experienced. The pitch of night struck in the hues of sorcerous light. Catching unawares and being so caught. Hunted and hunting through a labyrinthine slum, then warring in open streets, hilt to hilt, spitting blood from one's teeth. In the dark, his life hung from a thread, and time and again only his strength and fury saved him. But in the light, whether by moon or, more likely, the burning of nearby structures, the Nansur flinched from him and attacked only with the haft of their spears.

Conphas wanted him.

Cnaiür had not the arms for the swazond he earned that night.

The last he saw of Skaiwarra, the chieftain-thane and a band of his wild-haired axemen had butchered a company of infantrymen and turned to face down a Kidruhil charge. Sanumnis actually died in his arms, coughing blood and spittle in the gloom. Troyatti, and many of the other Hemscilvara, fell in a rain of sorcerous naphtha that left Cnaiür himself untouched. He would never learn what happened to Tirnemus or Saurnemmi.

In the end, he and a handful of strangers—some three Conriyans, like eerie automatons with their war-masks drawn, and six Thunyeri, one with the shrunken heads of Sranc swinging from his flaxen braids—found themselves driven from the flaming wreck of a millery back onto a broad stair beneath the ruins of a Fanim tabernacle. They hacked and hammered at the rush of Columnaries until only Cnaiür and the nameless Thunyeri stood, chests heaving, shoulder to shoulder. The dead formed a skirt of tangled limbs across the steps below them; the dying rocked and kicked like drunks. All the world seemed slicked in blood. Officers bawled through the dark ranks arrayed below them. Framed by the burning millery, the Nansur charged them again. The Norsirai laughed and roared, hewing and crushing with great swings of his battleaxe. A spear caught him in the neck and he stumbled into the threshing of swords.

Cnaiür howled in exultation. They came at him with the butts and hafts of their spears, their faces screwed in terror and determination. Cnaiür leapt into their midst, scarred arms hacking. "Demon!" he roared. *"Demon!"*

Hands clutched for his arms and he shattered wrists, punctured faces. Forms tackled his torso and he snapped necks, crushed spines. He tossed lifeblood skyward, nailed beating hearts still. All the world had become rotted leather, and he the only iron. The only *iron.*

He was of the People.

Without warning, the Nansur relented, crowded back into the shields of those behind, away from the advance of his dripping aspect. They stared in horror and astonishment. All the world seemed afire.

"For a thousand years!" he grated. "Fucking your wives! Strangling your children! Striking down your fathers!" He brandished his broken sword. Blood spilled in loops from his elbow. "For a thousand years I have stalked you!"

He threw aside the blade, kicked a spear into his hand, then cast it at the soldier before him. It punched through his shield, through his banded cuirass, and erupted from the small of his back.

Cnaiür laughed. The roaring flames took up his voice, made it sorcerous with dread.

Cries and shouts. Some even dropped their weapons.

"Take him!" a voice was shrieking. "You are *Nansur! Nansur!*"

A familiar voice.

It exerted a collective force, a consciousness of shared blood.

Cnaiür lowered his chin, smiled ...

They came as one this time, an encompassing wave of blows and clutching hands. He hammered and wrenched, but they bore him down. Everything became eye-watering numbness. They seemed howling apes, dancing and punishing, dancing and punishing.

Afterward, they cleared a path for their all-conquering Exalt-General. Smoke towered into the firmament beyond the battered beauty of his face, shrouding stars. His eyes were the same, though they appeared unnerved—very unnerved. "No different," his broken lips spat. "No different than Xunnurit after all."

And as the darkness came swirling down, Cnaiür at last understood. The Dûnyain had not sent him to be Conphas's assassin ...

He had sent him to be his victim.

CHAPTER EIGHT

XERASH

That hope is little more than the premonition of regret. This is the first lesson of history.

—CASIDAS, THE ANNALS OF CENEI

To merely recall the Apocalypse is to have survived it. This is what makes The Sagas, *for all their cramped beauty, so monstrous. Despite their protestations, the poets who authored them do not tremble, even less do they grieve. They celebrate.*

—DRUSAS ACHAMIAN, THE COMPENDIUM OF THE FIRST HOLY WAR

Early Spring, 4112 Year-of-the-Tusk, Xerash

At the bidding of the Warrior-Prophet, the disparate elements of the Holy War began to converge on Gerotha. Using the Herotic Way, Lord Soter and his Kishyati were the first to spy the city's black curtain walls. The imperious Ainoni Palatine rode directly to the gate that the Men of the Tusk would come to call the Twin Fists and demanded to parley with the Sapatishah-Governor. The Xerashi told him that it was only fear of atrocity that moved them to bar their gates. Lord Soter laughed at that, and without further word withdrew to the cultivated plains surrounding the city. He struck the first camp of the siege in the middle of a trampled sugar cane field.

The Warrior-Prophet, along with Proyas and Gotian, arrived early the following day. By evening the Gerothans had sent an embassy, as much simply to *see* the False Prophet who had struck down the Padirajah as to barter with him. They had no heart for hard bargains. Apparently, the Sapatishah of Xerash, Utgarangi, and all the surviving Kianene had evacuated the city days previously. Hours later the embassy returned to the Twin Fists, convinced they had no choice but to surrender, and to do so without condition.

After a long forced march, Gothyelk and the bulk of the Tydonni arrived during the night.

The following morning found the men of the Gerothan embassy strung from the battlements of the great gate, their entrails sagging to the foundations. According to defectors who managed to escape the city, there had been a coup that night, led by priests and officers loyal to their old Kianene overlords.

The Men of the Tusk began preparing their assault.

When the Warrior-Prophet rode to the Twin Fists to demand an explanation, he was greeted by an old veteran calling himself Captain Hebarata. With a vitriol only the old can summon, the man cursed the Warrior-Prophet as false and threatened the Solitary God's retribution as though it were merely another coin in his purse. Then, at the end of his tirade, someone fired a crossbow bolt …

The Warrior-Prophet snatched it from the air just short of his neck. To the wonder of all, he raised the missile aloft. "Hear this, Hebarata," he cried. "From this day I count!" A cryptic statement that troubled even the Inrithi.

During this time, Coithus Athjeäri ranged ever eastward with his hardened Gaenri Knights. They blundered into their first Kianene patrol south of a town called Nebethra. After a sharp melee, the Kianene broke and fled toward Chargiddo. Interrogating the survivors, the Galeoth Earl learned that Fanayal himself was in Shimeh, though none knew whether he planned to remain there. The Kianene claimed to have been sent out to gather intelligence on sites the Inrithi thought holy. According to one of the captives, the Padirajah hoped that securing and despoiling these places "would provoke the False Prophet to acts of stupidity."

This deeply alarmed the pious young Earl. That night he held a council with his captains, where it was decided that if any man should be provoked to rashness, it should be Coithus Athjeäri. Using copies of antique Nansur maps, they staked out a route from holy place to holy place. After kneeling for the Temple Prayer, they joined their mailed kinsmen about the bonfires. Their Eumarnan and Mongilean chargers were led out of the darkness, and they mounted with a myriad of shouts. Then, wordlessly, they rode into the moonlit hills.

So began what came to be called Athjeäri's Pilgrimage.

He rode first to survey Chargiddo, on the footings of the Betmulla. Since entering Xerash, the Men of the Tusk had heard much of this ancient fortress, and the Warrior-Prophet had bid Athjeäri send him a report. After dispatching messengers with sketches and estimates, he struck through the foothills, twice surprising and scattering Kianene under the banner of Cinganjehoi. They found the hilltop village and shrine of Muselah—where the Latter Prophet had returned to Horomon his sight—a smoking ruin.

Upon that ground they swore a mighty oath.

In the meantime, all but the last elements of the Holy War joined their brothers outside the walls of Gerotha. The fact that the Xerashi made no sorties attested to their weakness, and in the Council of Great and Lesser Names both Hulwarga and Gothyelk pressed for an immediate assault. But the Warrior-Prophet chided them, saying that the nearness of their destination and not their confidence motivated their anxiousness to attack. "Where hopes burn bright," he said, "patience is quickly consumed."

They need only wait, he explained, and the city would fall of its own accord.

⸺⸺⸺◆⸺⸺⸺

Music. This was the first thing Esmenet heard the day she began reading *The Sagas*.

She hovered in that moment of consciousness that immediately follows awakening, a kind of twilight of thought, bereft of self or place, yet painfully alert. And there was *music*. She smiled in groggy recognition. The finger-drumming, the punctuated bow strokes, bold and dramatic: it was Kianene music, she realized, being played somewhere within the many-chambered Umbilica.

"Yes! Yes!" a muffled voice called as the performance continued. She listened carefully, hoping to discern *his* voice somewhere beneath the music and above the ambient rumble of the stirring encampment. He always spoke between sounds, it seemed. The song faltered, only to be drowned by the sound of laughter and sporadic clapping.

It was the morning of their fourth day encamped about Gerotha and her stubborn walls. After vomiting, she struggled with her breakfast while her body-slaves fussed over her attire. With Yel and Burulan rolling their eyes, Fanashila explained the earlier music in her broken, but improving, Sheyic. Apparently three Xerashi captives, enslaved as porters, had petitioned Gayamakri for an opportunity to demonstrate their musical skills. What was more, the girl continued, one of them was more handsome than even the Conriyan Prince, or "Poyus," as she called him. Yel had laughed aloud at that.

After a moment's pause Fanashila blurted, "Slave may marry slave, no, Mistress?"

Esmenet smiled, but because of a pang in her throat she could do no more than nod.

Afterward, she weathered Opsara's glare as she visited Moënghus. As always, she marvelled at the way he seemed to grow from morning to morning, even as she avoided looking too long into his turquoise eyes. Their colour was not changing. She thought of Serwë, cursed herself for not missing the girl. Then she thought of the spark that burned within her own womb.

After learning the latest details of the siege from Captain Heörsa, she joined Werjau for the Summary of Reports. Everything seemed deceptively routine, from the kinds of incidents reported to the continuing challenges of maintaining a network of contacts and informants in an army on the march. They had all learned to stand on marbles by now, but every day it seemed someone disappeared and someone else re-emerged. Aside from the Xerashi musicians, the only matter of concern regarded Lord Uranyanka and his Moserothi clients. Though he'd publicly repented the massacres at Sabotha, he continued to rail against the Warrior-Prophet in private. Uranyanka was an evil, black-hearted fool.

More than once Esmenet had counselled his arrest, but Kellhus had deemed the Ainoni Palatine too important, one of those who had to be mollified rather than admonished.

Her duties as Intricati busied her long into the afternoon. She had grown accustomed to them enough to become bored, especially when it came to administrative matters. Sometimes her old eyes would overcome her and she would find herself gauging the men about her with the carnal boredom of a whore sizing up custom. A sudden awareness of clothing and distance would descend upon her, and she would feel *inviolate* in a way that made her skin tingle. All the acts they could not commit, all the places they could not touch ... These banned possibilities would seem to hang above her like the smoke hazing the canvas ceilings.

I am forbidden, she would think.

Why this should make her feel so pure, she could not fathom.

Late in the afternoon she baffled Proyas by laughingly calling him Lord Poyus during an extended briefing on the latest intelligence coming in from the field. Her bouts of impish humour were lost on him, she realized, not only because he was Conriyan, and so suffered an over-elaborate sense of gallantry, but because he continued to grieve their earlier animosity. Their parting was awkward. Then, following an update from Werjau regarding the Xerashi musicians, she somehow escaped the Nascenti and their endless requests, and discovered that she had nothing to do. This was how she found her way to *The Sagas.*

She still thought of reading as "practice," though she'd found it quite effortless for some time now. In fact, she not only hungered for opportunities to read, she often found herself simply staring at her humble collection of scrolls and codices, suffused with the same miserly feelings she harboured toward her cosmetics chest. But where the paints merely balmed the fears of her former self, the writings were something altogether different—something transformative rather than recuperative. It was as though the inked characters had become rungs on a ladder, or an endlessly uncoiling rope, something that allowed her to climb ever higher, to see ever more.

"You've learned the lesson," Kellhus had said on one of those rare mornings when he shared her breakfast.

"What lesson might that be?"

"That the lessons never end." He laughed, gingerly sipped his steaming tea. "That ignorance is infinite."

"How," she asked, at once earnest and delighted, "can anyone presume to be certain?"

Kellhus smiled in the devilish way she so adored.

"They think they know me," he said.

Esmenet had thrown a pillow at him for that, and it had seemed a thing of wonder. Throwing a pillow at a prophet.

She knelt before the ivory-panelled chest that contained her library, raised and pressed back the lid. As always, she savoured the smell of oiled bindings. There were few books within; the Fanim of Caraskand had possessed little interest in idolatrous works, let alone Sheyic translations of them. Because none of her slaves could read, she'd been forced to pack the works herself, sifting through the shelves and scroll racks in what had been Achamian's room. She'd been reluctant to stow *The Sagas* then, and now, spying the scrolls beneath Protathis, she felt that same reluctance. Scowling, she gathered them and carried them to her bed, wondering that the Apocalypse could feel so light. She propped herself against her favourite barrel-pillow. Then, running her fingers along the soon-to-be-unrolled parchment, she glimpsed the tattoo across the back of her left hand.

It seemed a kind of charm or totem now—her version of an ancestor scroll. That woman, that Sumni harlot who had hung her legs bare from her window, was a stranger to her now. Blood joined them, perhaps, but little else. Her poverty, her smell, her degradation, her simplicity—everything seemed to argue against her.

The trappings, let alone the facts, of her power would be enough to make the old Esmenet weep for wonder. Within the concentric scheme of Nascenti and Judges that Kellhus had grafted onto the old Shrial and Cultic hierarchies, she, Consort and Intricati, occupied the second most powerful ring. Gayamakri answered to her. Gotian answered to her. Werjau ... Even potentates in their own right, men such as Proyas and Eleäzaras, had to bow chin to chest. She had rewritten *jnan*! And this, Kellhus had promised her, was but the beginning.

Then there was the strength of her faith. The old Esmenet, the cynical harlot, would find this the most difficult to comprehend. Her world had been dark and capricious, a place where significance was apportioned only to those caught within some dread whimsy of the Gods. The old her wouldn't fathom the indwelling awe that now accompanied her every heartbeat. If anything, her whorish hackles would rise, and in private moments she would counsel doubt and suspicion. She had lain with too many priests.

The old Esmenet would never accept an understanding indistinguishable from trust.

And the pregnancy, the thought that she carried not merely a son but a *destiny* within her womb ... How she would laugh!

But what would strike the old Esmenet the most, she had no doubt, would be the *knowledge*. In that one respect, she'd been extraordinary. Very few pondered their ignorance as she had. Their conceit compelled them to prize only what they knew beforehand. And since significance *followed from* the already known, they always thought they possessed everything relevant to any question of truth. Obliviousness made obvious.

She had always understood that her world, for all its grand immensity, was a sham. This was why she had made her custom into apertures, windows onto the world's various corners. This was why she had used Achamian as a doorway to the past. And now Kellhus ...

He had rewritten the world down to its very foundations. A world where all were slaves of repetition, of the twin darknesses of custom and appetite. A world where beliefs served the powerful instead of the true. The old Esmenet would be astounded, even outraged. But she would come to believe—eventually.

The world indeed held miracles, though only for those who dared abandon old hopes.

Breathing deeply, Esmenet untied the leather string about the first scroll.

Like *The Third Analytic*, *The Sagas* were one of those works familiar even to illiterate caste-menials such as herself. She found it strange recalling her impressions of such things before Achamian or Kellhus. The "Ancient North," she knew, had always seemed weighty and profound, a phrase with a palpable, skin-prickling air. It lay like cold lead among the other names she knew, a marker of loss, hubris, and the implacable judgement of ages. She knew of the No-God, the Apocalypse, the Ordeal, but they were little more than curiosities. The Ancient North was a *place*, something she could point to. And for whatever reason, everyone had agreed that it was one of *those* words, enunciations that, like "Scylvendi" or "Tusk," bore the whiff of overarching doom. *The Sagas* had been little more than a rumour attached to that word. Books, to be certain, were frightful things, but in the way of snakes to city dwellers. Something safely ignored.

Those times Achamian mentioned *The Sagas*, he did so only to dismiss or disparage. For a Mandate Schoolman, he said, they were like pearls strung across a corpse. He spoke of the Apocalypse and the No-God the way others described running arguments with their relatives, with a thoughtless, first-hand immediacy, and in terms and tones that would often set her hair on end. With Achamian, the "Ancient North," which for all its dread had remained blank and obdurate, became something intricate and encompassing, a frame for what seemed an inexhaustible litany of extinguished hopes. By comparison, *The Sagas* had come to seem something foolish, perhaps even criminal. Those rare times she heard others mention them, she would smile inwardly and scoff. What could they know of these things? Even those who could read ...

But as much as she had learned about the Apocalypse, the fact remained that she knew nothing of *The Sagas* themselves. The moment she gingerly unrolled the first section of scroll, that ignorance struck her with the curious force of undone deceptions. Despite the title, she was surprised to discover that *The Sagas* consisted of a number of different works written by a number of different authors, though only two, Heyorthau and Nau-Ganor, were named. There were nine "sagas" in total, starting with "The Kelmariad." Some, she would later discover, were verse epics while others were prose chronicles. She chided herself for her surprise. Once again she'd found complexity where she had expected simplicity. Was that not always the way?

She had no idea where Kellhus had obtained the scroll, but it was very old, and as much painted as inked—the prize of some dead scholar's library. The parchment was uterine, soft and unmottled. Both the style of the script and the diction and tone of the translator's dedicatory seemed bent to the sensibilities of some other kind of reader. For the first time she found herself appreciating the fact that this history was itself *historical*. For some reason she had never considered that writings could be part of what they were about. They always seemed to hang ... *outside* the world they depicted.

It was strange. Here she lay curled on her marriage bed, her head propped on silk-threaded pillows, the scroll at a lazy angle before her. But when she read the opening invocation,

> *Rage—Goddess! Sing of your flight,*
> *From our fathers and our sons.*
> *Away, Goddess! Secret your divinity!*
> *From the conceit that makes kings of fools,*
> *From the scrutiny that makes corpses of souls.*
> *Mouths open, arms thrown wide, we beseech thee:*
> *Sing us the end of your song.*

everything about her—the wrought canopy, the dim grottoes behind the screens, the hanging panels—disappeared. Reading, she realized, *resituated*. It made gauze of what was immediate, and allowed what was ancient and faraway to rise into view. It unpinned here from the senses, and made it everywhere. It released now from the cage of the present, and lent it the aspect of eternity.

Infected by a kind of floating wonder, she fell into the first of *The Sagas*.

She found the going both difficult and curiously erotic, as though, aside from the masturbatory solitude of reading, her struggle to accommodate the writer's ancient assumptions was something too intimate not to be carnal. The realization that "The Kelmariad" was actually the history of *Anasûrimbor* Celmomas stole her breath—and sparked her first premonition of dread. This was not only the story of Achamian's dreams, it was also the story of Kellhus's blood. These times and places, she realized, were neither so ancient nor so faraway as she might have wished.

She gathered that the Dynasty of Anasûrimbor was old and venerable even in those days of Far Antiquity. In fact, the verses were replete with references to times and places—the Cond Yoke, the God-Kings of Ûmerau, the Rape of Omindalea—of which she knew nothing. For some reason, she had always thought of the First Apocalypse as the beginning of history rather than the end of one. Once again, what had been blank and monolithic became encompassing, a mansion with many rooms.

The birth of Celmomas II had been as ill-starred as any birth could be: he was the twin of a stillborn brother, named Huörmomas. The line,

His rosy wail could not stir his brother's blue slumber,

made her restless with thoughts of Serwë and Moënghus. And the way the poet used this macabre image to explain the High King's flint-hearted brilliance made her inexplicably anxious. Huörmomas, the poet insisted, ever stalked his brother's side, chilling his heart even as he quickened his intellect:

Grim kinsman, frosting the breath of his every counsel.
Dark reflection! Even the Knight-Chieftains bundle their cloaks
When they catch your glint in their Lord's eye.

After this, the strange intensity that had nagged everything, from the mere thought of reading *The Sagas* to the weight of the scrolls in her palm, took on the character of a compulsion. It was as if something—a second voice—whispered beneath what she read. Once she even bolted from the bed and pressed her ear to the embroidered canvas walls. She enjoyed stories as much as anyone. She knew what it was to hang in suspense, to feel the tug of some almost-grasped conclusion. But this was different. Whatever it was she thought she heard, it spoke not to some climactic twist, nor even to some penetrating illumination—it spoke to *her*. The way a person might.

The next four days would be haggard. Jealousy, murder, rage, and doom before all … The First Apocalypse engulfed her.

She quickly realized that, despite all her discussions with Achamian, her understanding of the Old Wars was merely episodic. "The Kelmariad" struck them into the shape of the Kûniüric High King's life, beginning with the dire warnings of his arcane counsellor, Seswatha, and culminating with his death on the Eleneöt Fields. In many ways it began as a common tale: Seswatha was the Doomsayer, the only one who could correctly read the gathering signs. Celmomas, meanwhile, was the Arrogant King, the one who could see only what was self-serving.

Apparently, long before, a fugitive Gnostic School called the Mangaecca had somehow pierced the ancient glamour the Nonmen Quya had used to conceal Min-Uroikas, the legendary stronghold of the Inchoroi. While Celmomas was still a young man, emissaries of Nil'giccas, the Nonman King of Ishterebinth, approached Seswatha, the High King's childhood friend and Vizier. The Nonmen worried that the Inchoroi, whom they had driven to the four corners of the world in the days of Cu'jara Cinmoi, had found their way back to Min-Uroikas and with the Mangaecca had renewed their harrowing studies. They told him of the rumours they had extracted from their long-dead captives. They told him of the No-God.

So Seswatha began his Long Argument, his attempt to convince the Ancient Norsirai Kings of the impending Apocalypse.

Though none of the sagas took Seswatha as its subject, he surfaced and resurfaced throughout, like something continually kicked up in the rolling flotsam of events. In "The Kelmariad" he was a principal, the stalwart of a mighty and inconstant king. The same was true of "The Kayûtiad," the verse epic of Celmomas's youngest and most glorious son, Nau-Cayûti, where Seswatha was both teacher and surrogate father. In "The Book of Generals," the prose inventory of events following Nau-Cayûti's death, his was the most powerful and most resented voice in council after council. In "The Trisiad," the verse account of Trysë's destruction, he was a shining beacon on the parapets, clawing dragons from the sky with sorcerous light. In "The Eämnoriad" he was the scheming foreigner who, for all his grand declarations, fled on the eve of the No-God's approach. In "The Annal Akksersa" he was hope incarnate, the Raised Shield of High King Cundraul III. In "The Annal Sakarpa" he was a lunatic refugee, cast out after cursing King Hûruth V for not fleeing to Mehtsonc with the Chorae Hoard. And in "The Anaxiad," the grand and tragic saga of Kyraneas's fall, he was nothing less than the world's saviour, the Bearer of the Heron Spear.

Hated or adored, Seswatha was the pin in the navigator's bowl, the true hero of *The Sagas*, though not one cycle or chronicle acknowledged him as such. And each time Esmenet encountered some variant of his name, she would clutch her breast and think, *Achamian*.

It was no small thing to read of war, let alone apocalypse. No matter how pressing her daily routine, images from *The Sagas* dogged her soul's eye: Sranc armoured in mandibles freshly cut from their victims. The burning Library of Sauglish and the thousands who'd sought refuge within her hallowed halls. The Wall of the Dead, the cloak of corpses draped about the seaward ramparts of Dagliash. Foul Golgotterath, her golden horns curving mountainous into dark skies. And the No-God, Tsurumah, a great winding tower of black wind ...

War and more war, enough to engulf every city, every hearth, to sweep up all innocents—even the unborn—into its merciless jaws.

The thought that Achamian continually *lived* these things oppressed her with an evasive, even cringing, sense of guilt. Each night, he saw the horizon move with hordes of Sranc; he shrank beneath the pitch of dragons swooping from black-bellied clouds. Each night, he witnessed Trysë, the Holy Mother of Cities, washed in the blood of her bewildered children. Each night, he literally relived the No-God's dread awakening, he *actually heard* the mothers wail over their stillborn sons.

Absurdly, this made her think of his dead mule, Daybreak. She had never understood, not truly, how much weight that name must have possessed for him. Such poignant hope. And this, she realized with no little horror, meant that she'd never understood *Achamian himself*—not truly. To be used night after night. To be debased by hungers vast, ancient, and rutting. How could a *whore* fail to see the outrage that had been heaped upon his soul?

You are my morning, Esmi ... my dawn light.

What could it mean? For a man who lived and relived the ruin of all, what could it mean to awake to her touch, to *her face*? Where had he found the courage? The trust?

I was his morning.

Esmenet felt it then, overpowering her, and in the strange fashion of moving souls, she struggled to ward it away. But it was too late. For what seemed the first time, she *understood*: his pointless urgency, his desperation to be believed, his haggard love, his short-winded compassion— shadows of the Apocalypse, all. To witness the dissolution of nations, to be stripped night after night of everything cherished, everything fair. The miracle was that he still loved, that he still recognized mercy, pity ... How could she not think him strong?

She understood, and it terrified her, for it was a thing too near to love.

That night, she dreamed that she floated over the deeps, stranded in the heart of some nameless sea. Terror pulled at her, like rocks bound about her ankles. But when she peered down, she could only see shadows in the blackening water beyond her feet. They bewitched her with their almost-clarity. Ponderous and vast, coiling about enormities. Though at first she refused to countenance it, her eyes gradually adjusted, and the monstrous forms became more and more distinct. Never had she felt so small, so exposed. The entire sea, beyond all the drowned horizons, lay placid and sun-green above black-boiling deeps. Flexing movement. Great milky eyes. Palisades of translucent teeth. And there, pale and naked, floating like a tuft through the midst of it ... *Achamian*.

His arm waved dead in the current.

Suddenly she was gasping and shaking in Kellhus's perfumed embrace. He shushed her, stroked hair from her eyes, explained that it was all a nightmare.

The desperation with which she held him shocked her. "I don't want to share you," she whispered, kissing the soft curls about his neck.

"Nor I you," he said.

She had never told him about Achamian, about their kiss that horrid night with Proyas and Xinemus. But it was not a secret between them— merely something unspoken. She had spent hours pondering his silence, and hours more cursing her own. Why, when Kellhus had so consistently coaxed her every weakness from her, would he pass over this one in silence? But she dared not ask. Especially not while labouring through *The Sagas*.

She could see it all so clearly now. The derelict cities. The smoking temples. The strings of dead that marked the slave roads to Golgotterath. She followed the Nonmen Erratics as they rode across the countryside hunting survivors. She saw the Sranc digging up the stillborn and burning them on raised pyres. She watched it all from afar, more than two thousand years too late.

Never had she read anything so dark, so despairing, or so glorious. It seemed poison had been poured into wonder's own decanter. *This*, she thought time and again, *is his night* ...

And though she tried to beat the words from her heart, they rose nonetheless, as cold as accusatory truth, as relentless as earned affliction. *I was his morning.*

One evening, shortly before completing the last of the cantos, she happened upon Achamian sitting oblivious on a tilted table of stone, soaking his feet in the green of the Nazimel River. A gladness of heart struck her, so sudden and so simple that she actually gasped. Her dismay was equally abrupt, and far more complicated. She would have called out something like, "Killing the river now, are we?" for the man was nothing if not ripe. She would have plopped her bum alongside him, traded lame jokes as they swished the water together. She would have quietly crept up behind him and shouted "Look out!" in his ear. But now, just watching him seemed ... menacing.

It was his fault for dying! If only he had stayed, if only Xinemus had said nothing of the Library, if only her hand hadn't lingered in Kellhus's lap ... She felt his heart hush for terror.

Esmi, he had said the night of his return from the dead, *"it's me ... Me."*

Beyond him a band of Thunyeri stripped nude, hopping as they struggled with their leggings. One of them ran howling, vaulted from a boulder into the burnished water. On the far shore, where the water trilled across gravel shallows, several women—slaves laundering clothes—held their sides in laughter. Out where the shade of the catalpa trees reached across the water, the Thunyeri broke the surface with a triumphant roar. Either ignoring the ruckus or insensible to it, Achamian leaned forward to scoop water into his palms. He splashed it across his face, grimaced and blinked. Sunlight winked from the black curls of his beard.

As though stunned, he stared into the waters, opening and shutting his eyes.

She had the abrupt sensation of awakening, as if the past months had been naught but one of those devious nightmares that somehow cloaked acts of horror in thoughtless normality. She had never succumbed to Kellhus. She had never repudiated Achamian. And she could call out, "Akka!"

But it was no dream.

Kellhus ran his warm palm from her shoulder to her breast, and she gasped as he pinched her nipple. Then his hand swept down across her belly to the bone-smooth curve of her hip, along her outer thigh, then around ... inside. She raised and spread her legs ... and Akka wept, clawed his beard in horror and disbelief. "Esmi!" he cried—he shrieked. "Esmi, please! It's me! It's me!

"I'm alive."

Tears had blurred him into the sepia glare. She stood upon stony earth and yet she plummeted, for she understood that her betrayal was without bottom, that her infidelity was without compare. The buzzing thoughts, the flush through face and thighs, that afternoon when Kellhus had accidentally brushed her breast. The hammering heart, the stinging breath, that night when Kellhus had hardened against the touch of her hand. The secret looks, the wanton reveries. The wonder of awakening beside him. The slick warmth between her legs when all was desert dry. The rapture of taking him, inside her knees, her womb—her heart. The strength of him, bearing into her. The moans.

The horror in Achamian's eyes.

Who was that base and treacherous woman? For Esmenet *knew* she could never do such a thing. She simply wasn't capable. Not to *Akka*. Not him!

Then she recalled her daughter, somewhere out *there* across the seas. Sold into slavery.

Reaching back to hook a sandal, Achamian pulled a foot from the water. He hunched against his knee, began lacing the leather strings. There was resignation in his manner, and tragedy too, as though his acts were both aimless and irresistible. Breathless, her hands pressed to her belly, Esmenet stole away.

She abandoned him by the river, a sole survivor of the Apocalypse, a man grieving his single trust, his one beauty.

Mourning the whore, Esmenet.

That night she returned to *The Sagas*, slack of limb and heart. She wept when she finished the final canto ...

The pyres gutted, the towers fallen and black,
The foeman glutted, our glory slung 'cross his back,
The world's keel broken, our blood thinner than our tears.
The story spoken, as though the dead possessed ears.

She wept and she whispered, *"Akka."* For she was his world, and all lay in ruin.

Akka. Akka, please ...

According to Nonman legend, the falling of the Incû-Holoinas, the Ark-of-the-Skies, had cracked the world's mantle, striking wedges into the endless dark. Seswatha now knew this legend to be true.

With Nau-Cayûti at his side, Achamian crouched in the darkness, peering across the yawning fall before them. For days they had groped through the black, too terrified to dare any light. At times it seemed they climbed through blackened lungs, so choked and multitudinous were the tunnels. Their elbows bled from crawling on their bellies.

During the years of the Great Investiture, the Sranc had burrowed out from Golgotterath far beneath the armies camped across the surrounding plains. When the siege was broken, the Consult had forgotten the mines, thinking themselves invincible. And why would they not? The Ordeal, the holy war called by Anasûrimbor Celmomas against Golgotterath, had dissolved in acrimony and cannibal pride. And the unholy advent was near. So very near ...

Who would dare what Seswatha and the High King's youngest son now dared?

Please wake up.

"What is it?" Nau-Cayûti murmured. "A postern of some kind?"

Lying prone, they stared over the lip of an upturned ledge, across what could only be a mighty chasm. Entire mountains seemed to hang about them, cliff from towering cliff, plummet from plummet, dropping down into blackness, reaching up to pinch a great curved plane of gold. It loomed above them, impossibly immense, wrought with never-ending strings of text and panels, each as broad as a war galley's sail, engraved with alien figures warring in relief. The lights from below cast a gleaming filigree across its expanse.

They looked upon the dread Ark itself, Seswatha knew, rammed deep into the sockets of the earth. They had reached the deepest pits of Golgotterath.

Below their vantage, across some hundred lengths of cavernous space, there was a door set perpendicular to the fall. Stonework had been raised beneath it, a platform with two immense braziers whose fires had blackened the Ark's surface where it bowed above them. A network of landings and stairs twined into the black obscurity below. Partially screened by curtains of fire, several Sranc reclined and rutted on the gate's threshold. Yammering squeals rang through the emptiness.

Akka ...

"What should we do?" Seswatha whispered. The exercise of sorcery couldn't be risked, not here, where the slightest bruise would be sure to draw the Mangaecca. His mere presence was fatal.

With characteristic decisiveness, Nau-Cayûti had already started stripping his bronze armour. Achamian watched the profile of his face, struck by the contrast between his pitch-blackened skin and the blond of his thickening beard. There was determination in his eyes, but it was born of desperation, not the zest and confidence that had made him such a miraculous leader of men.

Achamian turned away, unable to bear the falsehoods he had told him. "This is madness," he murmured.

"But she's *here*!" the warrior hissed. "You said yourself!"

Wearing only his hide kilt, Nau-Cayûti stood and ran his hands across the immediate stone faces. Then, clutching thin lips of rock, he hauled himself over the abyss. His heart in his throat, Seswatha watched him edge out across the gaping spaces, his back and calves shining with exertion and sweat.

Something—a shadow—above him.

Akka, you're dreaming ...

A spark of light, frail and glaring.

"Please ..."

At first she seemed an apparition before him, a glowing mist suspended in void, but as he blinked, he saw her lines drawn off into darkness, the lantern illuminating her oval face.

"Esmi," he croaked.

She knelt beside his bed, leaning over him. His thoughts reeled. What was the time? Why hadn't his Wards awakened him? The horror of Golgotterath still tingled through his sweaty limbs. She had been crying, he could see that. He raised his hands, sheepish with slumber, but she pulled away from his instinctive embrace.

He remembered Kellhus.

"Esmi?" Then, softer, "What is it?"

"I ... I just need you to know ..."

Suddenly his throat ached. He glimpsed her breasts, like smoke beneath the sheer fabric of her shift. "What?"

Her face crumpled, then recomposed. "That you are *strong*."

She fled, and once again all was dark and absolute.

It flew at night, wary of the ground below. It beat its way higher, and higher, until the air became needles, and tears fractured the million-starred void. Then it coasted, wings wide and scooping.

Urgency did not come easily to such an ancient intellect.

It pondered in the manner of its race, though its thought balked at the limits of its Synthese frame. Millennia had passed since last it had warred across such a benjuka plate. The Mandate vindicated. Their children discovered, dragged into the light. The Holy War reborn as an instrument of unknown machinations ...

That vermin could be so cunning! Mad the Scylvendi might be, but the testimony of events could not be denied. These Dûnyain ...

The rushing air had grown warm, and the ground rose as though upon a swell. Trees and bracken sunned their backs beneath the cold moon. Slopes pitched and dropped. Streams roped along dark and stony courses. The Synthese wound over and through the shadowy landscape, unto the ends of Enathpaneah.

Golgotterath would not be pleased with this new disposition of pieces. But the rules *had* changed ...

There were those who preferred clarity.

CHAPTER NINE

JOKTHA

*In the skins of elk I pass over grasses. Rain falls, and I cleanse my
face in the sky. I hear the Horse Prayers spoken, but my lips are far
away. I slip down weed and still twig—into their palms I pool. Then
I am called out and am among them. In sorrow, I rejoice.*

Pale endless life. This, I call my own.

—ANONYMOUS, *THE NONMAN CANTICLES*

Early Spring, 4112 Year-of-the-Tusk, Joktha

Somehow, he awoke more ancient.

Once, while raiding the South Bank in Shigek, Cnaiür and his men
had rested their horses in the ruins of an ancient palace. Since kindling a
fire was out of the question, they had unrolled their mats in the darkness
beneath a ponderous section of wall. When Cnaiür awoke, the morning
sun had bathed the limestone planes above him, and he found himself
staring at figures in relief, their faces worn to serenity by the seasons, their
poses at once stiff and indolent in the manner of age-old representations.
And there, impossibly, at the head of a long file of captives, was a scarred-
arm figure kissing the heel of an outland king.

A Scylvendi from another age.

"Do you know," a voice was saying, "that I actually felt pity as the last
of your people perished at Kiyuth?" It was a voice that liked its own

180

sound—very much. "No … pity isn't the right word. Regret. *Regret.* All the old myths collapsed at that moment. The world became weaker. I studied your people, deeply. Learned your secrets, your vulnerabilities. You see, even as a child I knew I would humble you one day. And there you were! Tiny figures in the distance, loping and howling like panicked monkeys. The People of War! And I thought, 'There's nothing strong in this world. Nothing I cannot conquer.'"

Cnaiür gasped, tried to blink away the tears of pain that clotted his eyes. He lay on the ground, his arms bound so tight he could scarce feel them. A shadow leaned over him, wiped his face with a cool, wet cloth. Who?

"But you," the shadow continued. It shook its head as though at an endearing yet infuriating child. "You …"

His eyes clearing, Cnaiür absorbed his surroundings. He lay in some kind of field tent. Canvas panels bellied into an apex above him. A heap of blood-caked refuse lay in the far corner—his hauberk and accoutrements. A table with four camp chairs framed the man ministering to him, who had to be an officer of some kind given the splendour of his armour and weapons. The blue mantle meant he was a general, but the bruising about his face …

The man wrung rose-coloured water into a copper basin set near Cnaiür's head. "The irony," he was saying, "is that you mean nothing in this matter. It's this Anasûrimbor, this *False Prophet*, who is the sole object of the Empire's concern. Whatever significance you possess, you derive from him." A snort. "I knew this, and still I let you provoke me." The face momentarily darkened. "That was a mistake. I can see that now. What are the abuses of flesh compared with glory?"

Cnaiür glared at the stranger. Glory? There was no glory.

"So many dead," the man said with rueful humour. "Was it you who devised that strategy? Knocking holes through walls. Forcing us to chase you and your rats into your burrows. Quite remarkable. I almost wish it had been you at Kiyuth. Then I would *know*, wouldn't I?" He shrugged. "That's how the Gods prove themselves, isn't it? The overthrow of demons?"

Cnaiür stiffened. Something involuntary thrashed through him.

The man smiled. "I know you aren't human. I know that we're kin."

Cnaiür tried to speak, but croaked instead. He ran his tongue across scabbed lips. Copper and salt. With a concerned frown the man raised a decanter, poured blessed water into his mouth.

"Are you," Cnaiür rasped, "a god?"

The man stood, looked at him strangely. Points of lantern light rolled like liquid across the figures worked into his cuirass. His voice possessed a shrill edge. "I know you love me ... Men often beat those they love. Words fail them, and they throw their fists into the breach ... I've seen it happen many times."

Cnaiür rolled his head back, closed his eyes for pain. How had he come to be here? Why was he bound?

"I know also," the man continued, "that you hate *him*."

Him. There could be no mistaking the word's intensity. The Dûnyain. He spoke of the Dûnyain—and as though he were his enemy, no less. "You do not want," Cnaiür said, "to raise arms against him ..."

"And why would that be?"

Cnaiür turned to him, blinking. "He knows the hearts of men. He seizes their beginnings and so wields their ends."

"So even you," the nameless General spat, "even you have succumbed to the general madness. *Religion* ..." He turned to the table, poured himself something Cnaiür couldn't see from the ground. "You know, Scylvendi, I thought I'd found a *peer* in you." His laugh was vicious. "I even toyed with the idea of making you my Exalt-General."

Cnaiür scowled. Who was this man?

"Absurd, I know. Utterly impossible. The Army would mutiny. The mob would storm the Andiamine Heights! But I cannot help but think that, with someone such as you, I could eclipse even Triamis."

Dawning horror.

"Did you know that? Did you know you stood in the *Emperor's* presence?" He raised his wine bowl in salute, took a deep drink. "Ikurei Conphas I," he gasped after swallowing. "With me the Empire is *reborn*, Scylvendi. I am Kyraneas. I am Cenei. Soon all the Three Seas will kiss my knee!"

Blood and grimaces. Roaring shouts. Fire. It all came back to him, the horror and rapture of Joktha. And then there he was ... *Conphas*. A god with a beaten face.

Cnaiür laughed, deep and full-throated.

For a moment the man stood dumbstruck, as though suddenly forced to reckon the dimensions of an unguessed incapacity. "You play me," he said with what seemed genuine bafflement. "Mock me."

And Cnaiür understood that he'd been *sincere*, that Conphas had meant every word he said. Of course he was baffled. He had recognized his brother; how could his brother not recognize him in turn?

The Chieftain of the Utemot laughed harder. "Brother? Your heart is shrill and your soul is plain. Your claims are preposterous, uttered without any real understanding, like recitations of a mother's daft pride." Cnaiür spat pink. "Peer? Brother? You have not the iron to be my brother. You are a thing of sand. Soon you will be kicked to the wind."

Without a word Conphas strode forward, brought a sandalled heel down on his head. The world flashed dark.

Cnaiür cackled even as the blood spilled hot across his teeth. With what seemed impossible clarity, he heard the Exalt-General retreat, the creak of leather about his stamped cuirass, the rasp of his scabbard across his leather skirts. The man swept aside the flap then strode into the greater camp, already shouting names. And Cnaiür could feel himself slipping between immensities—the earth that pressed so cruelly against his battered frame and the commotion of men and their fatal purposes.

At last, something deep laughed within him. *At last it ends.*

General Sompas entered moments after, his face grim, his knife drawn. Without hesitation he knelt at Cnaiür's side and began sawing through his leather bonds.

"The others await," he said in hushed tones. "Your Chorae is on the table."

Cnaiür could only reply in a cracked whisper. "Where are you taking me?"

"To Serwë."

The General had no problem leading the Scylvendi captive to the dark edge of the Nansur camp. They passed through a gallery of sentries and boisterous, celebratory camps. No one questioned the fact that the General wore a Captain's uniform. They were the army of a brilliant and eccentric leader. Not once had his strange ways failed to deliver victory and vengeance. And Biaxi Sompas was *his* man.

"Is it always this easy?" Cnaiür asked the creature.

"Always," it said.

In the blackness beneath a stand of carob trees, Serwë and another of her brothers awaited them, along with eight horses laden with supplies. Dawn had not yet broken when they heard the first of the horns, faint in the distance behind them.

A word dogged Emperor Ikurei Conphas, a word he had always regarded from the outside.

Terror.

He sat weary, leaning against the pommel of his saddle, watching the torches bob through the dark trees before him. Sompas waited quietly to his right, as did several others. Shouts echoed through the encampment behind them. The darkness teemed with searching lights.

"Scylvendi!" Conphas found himself crying out to the black. "*Scylvendi!*" He need not look to his officers to see their questioning expressions.

What was it about this man—this fiend? How had he affected him so? For all the hatred the Nansur bore toward the Scylvendi race, they were perversely enamoured of them as well. There was a mystique to them, and a virility that transcended the myriad rules that so constricted the inter-course of civilized men. Where the Nansur wheedled and negotiated, the Scylvendi simply took—seized. It was as though they had embraced violence whole, while the Nansur had shattered it into a thousand pieces to set as splinters across the multiform mosaic of their society.

It made them seem … more manly.

And this one Scylvendi, this Utemot Chieftain. Conphas had witnessed it, as much as any of the Columnaries who'd quailed before him in Joktha. In the firelight the barbarian's eyes had been coals set in his skull. And the blood had painted him the colour of his true skin. The swatting arms, the roaring voice, the chest-pounding declarations. They had all seen the God. They had all seen dread Gilgaöl rearing about him, a great horned shadow …

And now, after wrestling him to the ground like some lunatic bull, after the wonder of capturing him—capturing War!—*he had simply vanished.*

Cememketri insisted no sorcery was involved, and for the first time Conphas appreciated his uncle's manic suspicion of the Saik. Could they have done it? Or could it be, as Cememketri had nervously suggested, the Faceless Ones? Several of his soldiers maintained they had seen *Sompas* leading the Scylvendi through the camp—a rank impossibility, given that Conphas himself had gone to the man immediately after leaving the Scylvendi.

Faceless Ones ... Skin-spies the Mandate Schoolman had called them. Since learning from Cememketri that Xerius had been murdered by one of these things posing as his grandmother, Conphas had found himself rehearsing the Mandate fool's arguments from that day in Caraskand when they had debated the Prince of Atrithau's fate. They were not Cishaurim, Conphas had conceded that much. It was even more clear now that Xerius was dead. Why would the Cishaurim murder the only man who might save them?

They weren't Cishaurim, but did that make them *Consult*, as the Mandati had insisted? Were these truly the opening hours of the *Second Apocalypse*?

Terror. How could he not be terrified?

All this time Conphas had assumed that he and his uncle had stood at the root of all that happened. No matter how the others plotted, they but thrashed in the nets of his hidden designs—or so he thought. Such errant conceit! All along, *others* had known, others had watched, and he hadn't the slightest inkling of their intentions!

What was happening? Who ruled these events?

Not Emperor Ikurei Conphas I.

His aquiline face outlined by torchlight, Sompas looked at him expectantly, but he kept his counsel like the others. They could sense his humour, understood that it was more than merely "foul." Conphas scanned the moon-blanched countryside, felt the despairing twinge all men felt when confronted by the dimensions of the world that had swallowed those they desired. Were he one, were he alone, it would be hopeless.

But he was not one. He was *many*. The ability to cede voice and limb to the will of another—herein lay the true genius of men. The ability to *kneel*. With such power, Conphas realized, he was no longer confined to the here and now. With such power, he could reach across the world's very curve! He was Emperor.

How could he not cackle? Such a wondrous life he lived!

He need only make things *simple*. And he would start with this Scylvendi … He had no choice.

That he was *Scylvendi* could be no coincidence. Here Conphas stood on the cusp of restoring the Empire to all her past glory, only to discover that everything turned on killing a son of his ancestral enemy, the people who had overthrown the pretensions of his race time and again. He had said it himself, hadn't He? He was Kyraneas. He was Cenei …

No wonder the savage had laughed!

The Gods were behind this—Conphas was certain of it. They begrudged their brother. Like children of a different father, they *resented*. There was a message to this—how could there *not* be? He had been served some kind of warning. He was Emperor now. A move had been made. The rules had been changed …

Why? Why hadn't he killed the fiend? What vice or vanity had stayed his hand? Was it the iron hand clamped about his neck? The burn of the man's seed upon his back?

"Sompas!" he fairly cried.

"Yes, God-of-Men?"

"How does 'Exalt-General' suit you as a title?"

The ingrate swallowed. "Very well, God-of-Men."

How he missed Martemus and the cool cynicism of his gaze. "Take the Kidruhil—all of them. Hunt down this demon for me, Sompas. Bring me his head and *that* shall be your title … Exalt-General, Spear-of-the-Empire." His eyes narrowed in menace as he smiled. "Fail me and I shall burn you, your sons, your wives—every Biaxi breathing. I shall burn you all *alive*."

———— ⤬ ————

Relying on Serwë's preternatural vision, they led their horses through the pitch of night, knowing their only advantage lay in whatever distance they could travel before sunrise. They picked their way across high scrub and grass slopes, then down into a wooded vale where the bitter of cedars braced the air. Despite his injuries, Cnaiür shambled after them, drawing on something as inexhaustible as lust or fear. About him, the world reeled more and more, and simple things became nightmarish with intent. Dark trees clutched at him, drew nails across his cheeks and shoulders. Unseen rocks kicked at his sandalled toes. The ringed moon laid him bare.

Thought slurred into thought. He spat blood continually. The path before him, shadowy and granular, rolled beneath his staggering legs. A greater dark unfolded through the night, and he passed out of memory, wondering, how could souls flicker?

Then Serwë was staring down at him. He felt her thighs beneath his neck, firm and warm through her linen tunic. She leaned forward and her breast brushed his temple. She retrieved a waterskin, used it to wet a rag. She had been tending to the cuts on his face.

She smiled and a ragged breath stole through him. There was such sanctuary in the lap of woman, a stillness that made the world, with all its threshing fury, seem small instead of encompassing, errant instead of essential. He winced as she dabbed a cut above his left eye. He savoured the sense of cool water warming against his skin.

The black plate of night was beginning to grey. Looking up, he saw the faint nimbus of hair about her jaw. He reached up to brush it, but hesitated when he glimpsed the scabs across his knuckles. He became alarmed. Though the pain of his wounds lay like a weight upon him, he jerked himself upright, coughed, and spat a mouthful of bloody sputum. They sat upon a grassy round on the summit of some hill. The east warmed to the unseen sun. Ridgelines wandered across the intervening miles, dark with vegetation, pale with nude stone faces.

"I'm forgetting something," he said.

She nodded and smiled the blithe and jubilant way she always did when she knew some answer.

"The one you hunt," she said. "The murderer."

He felt his face darken. "But *I* am the murderer! The most violent of all men! They slouch forward in chains. They ape their fathers, just as their fathers aped their fathers before them, all the way back to the beginning. Covenants of earth. Covenants of blood. I stood and found my chains were smoke. I turned and saw the void ... I am unfettered!"

She studied him for a moment, her perfect face poised between thought and moonlight. "Yes ... like the one you hunt."

What were these shallow creatures?

"You call yourself my lover? You think yourself my proof? My prize?"

She blinked in dread and sorrow. "Yes ..."

"But you are a knife! You are a spear and hammer. You are nepenthe—opium! You would make a haft of my heart, and brandish me. Brandish me!"

"And me," a masculine voice said. "What of me?"

One of her brothers had sat to his right—only it wasn't one of her brothers. It was *him* ... the serpent whose coils ever tightened about his heart: Moënghus, the murderer, wearing the armour and insignia of a Nansur infantry captain.

Or was he Kellhus?

"You ..."

The Dûnyain nodded, and the air became yaksh dank—yaksh sour. "What am I?"

"I ..."

What kind of madness? What kind of devilry?

"Tell me," Moënghus said.

How long had he hidden in Shimeh? How long had he prepared? It did not matter. It did not matter! Cnaiür would crack open the sun with his hate! He would carve out its heart and bury all the world in endless black!

"Tell me ... what do you see?"

"The one," Cnaiür grated, "that I hunt."

"Yes," Serwë said from behind him. "The *murderer*."

"He murdered my father with words! Consumed my heart with revelation!"

"Yes ..."

"He set me free."

Cnaiür turned back to Serwë, filled with a longing so great it seemed his chest must implode. Crevasses opened across her forehead, cheek, and chin; knuckled limbs reared from the perfect planes of her outer face. With a gentle tug, they pulled their tips apart. Her lips vanished. She leaned forward with a slow, encompassing ardour. Limbs, long and gracile, drew back, stretched outward, then clasped the back of his skull. As though within a fist, she held him tight to her hot mouth. Her true mouth.

He drew his legs beneath him, then effortlessly hoisted her into his banded arms. So light ... The dawn sun flashed across their intertwined forms.

"Come," Moënghus said. "The track awaits us. We must run down our prey."

In the distance they heard horns. Nansur horns.

Knowing Conphas would spare nothing to capture them, they rode as far as they could press their horses, heeding the cycles of exhaustion rather than those of sun, moon, and stars. According to the creatures, Conphas had sent a Column south of Joktha immediately after debarking. His plan relied on the Holy War's ignorance, and since Saubon was certain to discover his treachery, Conphas needed to bar all the ways between Caraskand and Xerash. This meant that the Nansur lay both behind and *before* their small party. The best they could do was strike due south, slipping across Enathpaneah, then work their way eastward through the Betmulla, where the terrain would make interdiction unlikely and pursuit difficult.

Occasionally, Cnaiür spoke to them, learned something of their lean ways. They called themselves the Last Children of the Inchoroi, though they were loath to speak of their "Old Fathers." They claimed to be Keepers of the Inverse Fire, though the merest question regarding either their "keeping" or their "fire" pitched them into confusion. They never complained, save to say they hungered for unspeakable congress, or to insist they were falling—always falling. They declared he could trust them, because their Old Father had made them his slaves. They were, they said, dogs that would sooner starve than snap meat from a stranger's hand.

They carried, Cnaiür could see, the spark of the void within them. Like the Sranc.

As a child, Cnaiür had been fascinated by trees. Given their rarity on the Steppe, he only saw them in the winter months, when the Utemot moved their camp into the Swarut, the highlands that bounded the sea the Inrithi called Jorua. Sometimes he would stare at the bare trees for so long, they would lose their radial dimensions and seem something *flat*, like blood smeared into the wrinkles about an old woman's eyes.

Men were like this, Cnaiür realized, binding their manifold roots then branching in a thousand different directions, twining into the greater canopy of other men. But these things—these *skin-spies*—were something altogether different, though they could mimic men well enough. They did not bleed into their surroundings as men did. They struck through circumstances, rather than reaching out to claim them. They were *spears* concealed in the thickets of human activity. Thorns ...

Tusks.

And this lent them a curious beauty, a dread elegance. They were simple in the way of knives, these skin-spies. He envied them that, even as he loved and pitied.

"Two centuries ago I was Scylvendi," it said once. "I know your ways."

"Who else have you been?"

"I have been many."

"And now?"

"I am Serwë ... your lover."

The determination of Conphas's pursuit became evident the third night of their southward flight. Along the Enathpanean frontier, they crossed hills arranged like longitudinal dunes, with sharp, wandering ridgelines and steep slip faces. Everything was green, but in the way of tenacious rather than lush things. Carp grasses choked the clearings, thronging along the cracks of even the sheerest of escarpments. Thickets of catclaw thatched the slopes, and stands of carob dominated many of the valleys, though it was too early in the year for them to offer any forage. At dusk, while filing along the crest of one of these hills, Cnaiür saw several dozen fires winking orange on a flat top some miles to the north.

The nearness of the fires didn't surprise him; if anything, he was comforted by the distance. The Nansur, he knew, had intentionally chosen the highest ground possible, hoping to spook them into pressing their horses too hard. It was the *numbers* that troubled him. If they had tracked them this far, they knew their party hadn't fled to Caraskand to shelter with Saubon, which meant they knew Cnaiür meant to cleave east at some point. Whoever commanded the pursuit had likely already dispatched bands to the southeast in hopes of cutting them off. It would be like shooting arrows in the dark, certainly, but his quiver looked deep.

Over the course of the following day, they encountered an Enathi goatherd. The old fool surprised them, and before Cnaiür could utter a word, Serwë had killed him. The soil was too rocky to effectively bury the man, so they were forced to tie the body to one of the spare horses—which of course further tired the beast. Even then, the vultures, which forever soared the margins of the world and the Outside, found and followed them. With vultures circling, they might as well have carried a banner as high as the clouds. That night they paused in one of the valleys, and though the sky was clear and moonbright, they burned the body.

They continued across the rugged Enathpanean countryside for a week, avoiding all signs of men save for one meagre village, which they plundered for sport and supplies. For two consecutive nights the skies were overcast and the darkness impenetrable. Cnaiür cooked his blade in a small fire, then scarred his shoulders and chest with the lives he had taken at Joktha. He avoided looking at Serwë and the other two creatures, who sat opposite, as silent and watchful as leopards. When he finished, he raved at them, only to weep in remorse afterward. There had been no judgement in their eyes, he realized. No humanity.

On no fewer than three different nights, they saw the fires of what had to be their Nansur pursuers, and though it seemed to Cnaiür they were more distant each time, he was not heartened. It was a strange thing, fleeing the pursuit of unseen men. Things unseen could not be pinned with the foibles and debilities that made men *mere* men. They lay unfixed and restless in the soul. As such, they had the habit of expanding into principle, into something that transcended the mundane world and lorded over it.

Each time Cnaiür saw the fires of the Nansur, they seemed markers of something greater. And even though *he* was the one who rode with abominations, it seemed all obscenity lay on the horizon behind him. The North became despotic, the West tyrannical.

They wandered red-eyed, exchanging moon-pale landscapes for sun-bright, and Cnaiür fell to reckoning the oddities of his soul. He supposed he was insane, though the more he pondered the word, the more uncertain its meaning became. On several occasions he had presided over the ritual throat-cutting of Utemot pronounced insane by the tribal elders. According to the memorialists, men went *feral* in the manner of dogs and horses, and in like manner had to be put down. The Inrithi, he knew, thought insanity the work of demons.

One night during the infancy of the Holy War—and for reasons Cnaiür could no longer recall—the sorcerer had taken a crude parchment map of the Three Seas and pressed it flat over a copper laver filled with water. He had poked holes of varying sizes throughout the parchment, and when he held his oil lantern high to complement the firelight, little beads of water glinted across the tanned landscape. Each man, he explained, was a kind of *hole* in existence, a point where the Outside penetrated the world. He tapped one of the beads with his finger. It broke, staining the surrounding parchment. When the trials of the world broke men, he explained, the Outside leaked into the world.

This, he had said, was madness.

At the time, Cnaiür had been less than impressed. He had despised the sorcerer, thinking him one of those mewling souls who forever groaned beneath burdens of their own manufacture. He had dismissed all things *him* out of hand. But now, the force of his demonstration seemed indisputable. Something *other* inhabited him.

It was peculiar. Sometimes it seemed that each of his eyes answered to a different master, that his every look involved war and loss. Sometimes it seemed he possessed *two* faces, an honest outer expression, which he sunned beneath the open sky, and a more devious inner countenance. If he concentrated, he could almost feel its muscles—deep, twitching webs of them—beneath the musculature that stretched his skin. But it was elusive, like the presentiment of hate in a brother's glance. And it was profound, sealed like marrow within living bone. There was no distance! No way to frame it within his comprehension. And how could there be? When it *thought*, he *was* …

The bead had been broken—there could be no doubt of that. According to the sorcerer, madness all came down to the question of *origins*. If the divine possessed him, he would be some kind of visionary or prophet. If the demonic …

The sorcerer's demonstration seemed indisputable. It accorded with his nagging intuitions. It explained, among other things, the strange affinities between madness and insight—why the soothsayers of one age could be the bedlamites of another. The problem, of course, was the Dûnyain.

He contradicted all of it.

Cnaiür had watched him ply the roots of man after man and thus command their branching actions. Nursing their hatred. Cultivating their shame and their conceit. Nurturing their love. Herding their reasons, breeding their beliefs! And all with nothing more than mundane word and expression—nothing more than worldly things.

The Dûnyain, Cnaiür realized, acted as though *there were no holes* in the sorcerer's parchment map, no beads to signify souls, no water to mark the Outside. He assumed a world where the branching actions of one man could become the roots of another. And with this elementary assumption he had conquered the acts of thousands.

He had conquered the Holy War.

This insight sent Cnaiür reeling, for it suddenly seemed that he rode through *two different worlds*, one open, where the roots of men anchored them to something beyond, and another closed, where those selfsame roots were entirely *contained*. What would it mean to be mad in such a closed world? But such a world could not be! Ingrown and insensate. Cold and soulless.

There had to be more.

Besides, he couldn't be mad, he decided, because *he possessed no origins*. He had kicked free of all earth. He didn't even possess a past. Not really. What he remembered, he always remembered *now*. He—Cnaiür urs Skiötha—was the ground of what came before. He was his own foundation!

Laughing, he thought of the Dûnyain and how, upon their fatal reunion, this would overthrow him.

He tried—once—to share these ruminations with Serwë and the others, but they could offer him only the simulacrum of understanding. How could they fathom his depths when they themselves possessed none? They were not bottomless *holes* in the world, as he was. They were animate, yet they did not live, not truly. They, he realized with no little horror, *had no souls*. They dwelt utterly within the world.

And for no reason, his love of them—his love of *her*—became all the more fierce.

Several more days passed before they sighted the first true peaks of the Betmulla, though Cnaiür suspected they had crossed out of Enathpaneah sometime earlier. They made toward them, intending to traverse the great sloping aprons piled across their northern faces. They crossed a rugged tableland, then followed the winding course of a braided stream, riding beneath the bowers of water birches. As the mountains loomed ever greater and darker above them, Cnaiür could not help but recall the Hethantas and his harsh use of Serwë. He had been a fool then, a free man trying to make himself a slave of his people, but he knew not the words that would make her understand.

"Our child," he called lamely, "was conceived in mountains like these."

When she said nothing, he cursed himself and the sensitivities of women.

Later that afternoon, one of their horses was lamed descending a slope of earth and shale. They left it behind rather than put it down, for fear of vultures giving their path away. Leading their mounts, they continued long into the darkness, exploiting the preternatural sight of the skin-spies. Barring disaster, there was no way the fires behind them, no matter how dread their abstraction, could hope to overtake them.

Come morning, the ramps of the Betmulla towered into the southwestern sky. They came across a dead lake, its depths swollen with crimson algal blooms. Not far away, on a promontory rising from a pure stand of canyon oak, they found the ruined footings of some shrine. Faceless forms jutted from the rolling carpets of fallen leaves. An artesian spring trickled from the altar, and they refilled their skins. Some kind of deer grazed the slopes about the lake, and with great mirth Cnaiür watched Serwë and her brothers run a juvenile down on foot alone. Afterward, he stumbled across some cousin of orpine while making mud in the brush. The tubers, though far from ready, tasted delicious with the venison.

Their fire, as small as it was, proved a mistake. The wind was blowing directly from the west, across the lake. The skin-spies smelled them first, but far too late.

"They come," Serwë said suddenly, looking to her brothers. Within a heartbeat, it seemed, the two of them vanished into the canopy's recesses.

Then Cnaiür heard the distinctive snort and chop of horses labouring up a humus slope, the clink and clatter of gear filtering through the gloomy interior of the wood.

Knowing Serwë would follow, he sprinted up to the flat foundation of the shrine. The first of the Kidruhil cleared the oaks just as he turned upon the lip. They began hooting when they caught sight of him. Dozens materialized behind them, their uncaparisoned mounts throwing spittle from their bits as they worked their heads up and down. The Kidruhil in the forward ranks drew their longswords—

A shriek pealed through the trees.

Cnaiür saw cavalrymen yank on their reins, wheel their mounts about in confusion. He saw one fall, a crimson smear where his face should be … They were looking up now, shouting in alarm. Then Cnaiür glimpsed them, the brothers, sweeping down and out of the layered canopy, scooping up lives every time. The rearmost Kidruhil were panicking now.

To a man those galloping toward him were looking over their shoulders, veering to their right as they slowed. Cnaiür could hear an officer shouting, "Out of the trees! Out of the trees!" But his men needed no encouragement, they were already pounding across the smoking campsite. Riderless horses scattered in all directions.

Then Cnaiür noticed the bows … recurved, like the Scylvendi, drawn from lacquered leather cases set low and back on their saddles—also just like the Scylvendi. Renewing their shouts, the Kidruhil fanned back up the slope, guiding their mounts with spur and knee. The first three drew and released, raising and lowering their bows in the draw—again, just like the People. Serwë swept her arms in front of him, batting the first shaft from his path, ignoring the second, which whistled past him, and catching the third in the meat of her forearm.

Stunned, Cnaiür stepped back, fell to one knee. There was no cover. "Serwë!" he cried.

The Kidruhil had split into two streams, one to each side of the shrine. Instinctively, Cnaiür scrambled to the back left corner of the ancient platform, crouched low, using the angles to shield himself from one band while exposing himself to the other. Almost immediately the riders to his left galloped into view, yelling "Hup-hup-hup!" to their horses, raising their bows …

Somehow, Serwë was in front of him. For an instant she stood, a poised beauty, arms out, flaxen hair gleaming in the mountain sun—

She danced for him.

Shielding, leaping, striking. She kept her back turned to him, as though in observance of some ritual modesty. Her sleeves snapped like leather. Shafts clattered across the platform. Others buzzed about his shoulders and head. She dipped, rolled her arms about. A shaft appeared in the palm of her hand. She kicked, swung her heel down from her raised knee. A shaft jutted from her calf. The fletching of two more materialized in her back. She cartwheeled, kicked an arrow away even as three others thudded into her chest and abdomen. She cycled her hands outward, batted away four in succession, threw her head back, thrust out her arms, caught one in the back of her right hand. Another in her left forearm.

She jerked her head to the left. An arrowhead popped from the back of her neck. She whimpered, as a little girl might.

But she never ceased moving. Blood flew out in beads and lines, flashed in arcs beneath the sun.

Meanwhile the chorus of shouts and cries grew louder and louder. A horn pealed out, then was cut short. But Cnaiür could see nothing save her dance. Limbs lithe and pale beneath threads of crimson, pierced and weeping. The linen of her shift taut and bloody about her swaying breasts. *Serwë …*

His prize.

The cries faltered. Hooves rumbled down the slopes …

She stopped. As though preparing for prayer, she slumped to one knee. She craned her head forward, silently gagging. She raised a pierced arm, snapped the birch shaft in her mouth. Her motions were deliberate—stiff. She reached back, fumbled for the arrowhead jutting from the base of her skull, pulled the shaft clear on a stream of blood.

Then she turned to look at him. Her smiling eyes shimmered with tears. She tried to wipe at the blood pulsing from her lips, only to scratch her neck with the arrow piercing her hand. She looked at him, unpuzzled, then slouched forward across the platform. Cnaiür heard the pop of buried wood.

"Serwë!" he cried.

When he shook her, her perfect face fell apart.

Numb, desolate, he stood, stared in horror at the carnage across the slopes. The brothers stood amid the dead Nansur, watching him without expression. Both had several arrows buried in their limbs, but they seemed ... unconcerned.

Over a dozen riderless horses wandered the near distance, but he could see no sign of the Kidruhil.

"We must bury her," he called.

Serwë helped him.

CHAPTER TEN

XERASH

Souls can no more see the origins of their thought than they can see the backs of their heads or the insides of their entrails. And since souls cannot differentiate what they cannot see, there is a peculiar sense in which the soul cannot self-differentiate. So it is always, in a peculiar sense, the same time when they think, the same place where they think, and the same individual who does the thinking. Like tipping a spiral on its side until only a circle can be seen, the passage of moments always remains now, the carnival of spaces always sojourns here, and the succession of people always becomes me. The truth is, if the soul could apprehend itself the way it apprehended the world—if it could apprehend its origins—it would see that there is no now, there is no here, and there is no me. In other words, it would realize that just as there is no circle, there is no soul.

—MEMGOWA, *CELESTIAL APHORISMS*

You are fallen from Him like sparks from the flame. A dark wind blows, and you are soon to flicker out.

—SONGS 6:33, *THE CHRONICLE OF THE TUSK*

Early Spring, 4112 Year-of-the-Tusk, Xerash

The long mule-trains of the Scarlet Spires finally arrived several days into the siege of Gerotha. As though on cue, a new embassy issued from the city—this one walking in the manner of abject petitioners. The gates were not closed behind them. As the Warrior-Prophet had promised, the ancient capital of Xerash had capitulated of her own accord.

As a gift, the embassy brought the twelve heads of those who had orchestrated the earlier closing of the gates, including that of Captain Hebarata, who had mortally offended the Warrior-Prophet. But the Lords of the Holy War were not appeased, and the Warrior-Prophet spoke harshly to the Gerothans, saying that some example had to be set, some sacrifice made, both to atone for and to warn against what had happened. As though justice were to be found in the clarity of proportion, he announced his Toll of Days, saying that since four days had passed since Gerotha had shut its gates against him, so four out of ten Gerothans had to forfeit their lives.

"By dawn's light tomorrow," he decreed, "twenty thousand heads must be hung from the battlements of your city walls. If you do not do this, verily you shall all perish."

That night, while the Holy War celebrated, all Gerotha screamed. Dawn's light found her walls slicked in blood, their entire circuit ornamented with severed heads, thousands of them, either bundled in fishing nets or strung through the jaw along hanging ropes of hemp. When the heads were counted, it was found that the Gerothans had exceeded their measure by 3,056.

In all of Xerash, no city, town, or fortress would bar her gates against the Holy War again.

Athjeäri, meanwhile, became the first Lord of the Holy War to enter the Sacred Lands. Some time passed before he and his Gaenri realized they had actually entered Holy Amoteu. There was little to distinguish the Xerashi—or the Sons of Shikol, as they called them—from the Amoti in appearance or tongue. They crossed the tablelands of Jarta, whose people had once waged generational war against the ancient Amoti, then descended into a war of their own.

With no more than five hundred thanes and knights, Athjeäri battled his way ever deeper into Holy Amoteu. His sunburned Galeoth found the Amoti to be treacherous and supportive by turns. Though most called themselves Fanim, they had no love of the Kianene, and after months of dreadful rumours many thought the idolaters and their False Prophet invincible. The Padirajah himself had fallen. The great Kascamandri was dead, and here came none other than the mercurial kinsmen of Saudoun, the ruthless Blond Beast of Enathpaneah.

There were encounters at Gim, the famed Anothrite Shrine, Mer-Porasas ... Athjeäri himself was wounded in the knee at Girameh, where the Latter Prophet's mother had been born. Soon their blood-smeared standard, a Circumfix over the Red Horse of Gaenri, became a general sign of panic and terror. And though Fanayal sent more and more of his Grandees to hunt him, the Earl of Gaenri either vanished or, even worse, prevailed.

Hurall'arkeet, the desert men began to call him—the "Wind Has Teeth."

Finally, on the Day of Palms, the iron-clad knights rode into Besral, the ancestral home of the Latter Prophet's now-extinct line. Though the Inrithi mission had fled long ago, many Amoti gathered to cheer the haggard wayfarers.

For such hearts, they told one another, had to be holy.

They walked before him, talking as though oblivious to Achamian's presence mere paces behind.

Esmenet and Kellhus.

What was already being called the Toll of Days had been exacted, and the city was strangely mute, either for the want of voices or out of collective shock. Along the visible length of the alley, onlookers shrank or fell to their knees. The Xerashi in particular were careful to keep their black-ringed eyes to the ground as the Sacral Retinue filed past. The Warrior-Prophet toured Gerotha as much to be seen, Achamian imagined, as to inspect his prize.

In *The Tractate*, Gerotha was sometimes called The City of a Hundred Villages, and after two thousand years the epithet still suited.

The alleys were as narrow and as numerous as those of the Worm in Carythusal. But unlike the Worm, where the ways followed the illogic of countless disconnected decisions over countless years, these continually converged onto what the Xerashi called "smalls"—miniature bazaars where the sun actually baked the cobbles—as if Gerotha were indeed a collection of intertwined villages, grown into one another like spots of mould on bread.

Esmenet had been telling Kellhus of her morning audience with the Scarlet Spires. According to Saurnemmi, routine remained the rule in Joktha, either because or in spite of the Scylvendi's harsh ways. Otherwise, Eleäzaras claimed to have spoken to Palatine Uranyanka personally, warning him of the arcane consequences of any sedition, perceived or otherwise. "The Grandmaster," she said, "wanted me to assure you that the Palatine of Moserathu will cause you no more troubles."

Achamian could only watch and listen with dismay and admiration. It was a marvel to see her thus. There was her appearance, of course, her hair pinned in a jewelled brace, her gown—a Kianene chiton—sewn for the courts and pleasure gardens of the White Sun Palace in Nenciphon. But there was her bearing as well. Upright. Guileless. Penetrating and ironic. She was a match, and an easy one at that, for her new-found station.

It made breathing difficult. *I have to stop this!*

Before, it had been just the two of them. Before, he could simply reach out, place a relaxed hand upon her waist, and she would turn into his arms. Now everything had been put to rout. Somehow, Kellhus had become the centre, the waystation that all must cross to find one another—to find themselves. Somehow everything had been dragged into the brilliant light of his judgement. And now Achamian found himself trailing after *them*, like some heartbroken beggar …

Why would she call him strong?

"Eleäzaras insulted you," Kellhus said, turning to her, so that Achamian could see his bearded profile. He wore a magnificent sleeved gabardine over his tunic—an ornamental version of those worn by the Girgashi—with vertical bands of gold that flashed whenever he walked through sunlight. It looked altered about the shoulders, as one might expect given the dead Padirajah's reputed bulk.

"He fairly called me a whore," Esmenet said.

"You should expect such. You're unfamiliar coin to them."

Her smile was bland and cynical. "So where's the moneychanger?"

Kellhus laughed. Achamian watched the gratification break across the faces of those about him. Some of them laughed as well, creating a melancholy echo. Everywhere Kellhus went, a part of him passed through others. Like a stone tossed into calm waters.

"Men are simple," he replied. "They think primarily in terms of *things*, not relations. This is why they think it's the gold or silver that makes coins valuable, not the *obedience* they command. Tell them the Nilnameshi use pottery for their coins and they scoff."

"Or," Esmenet said, "that the Warrior-Prophet uses a woman."

A sliver of sunshine flickered across her, and for an instant everything about her, from the pleats along her chiton to her red-painted lips, gleamed silk. The two of them seemed something otherworldly in that moment—too beautiful, too *pure*, for the dingy brick and unkempt hearts that surrounded them.

"Exactly," Kellhus said. "They ask, 'Where's the gold?'" He grinned at her sidelong. "Or in your case ..."

"'Where's the *thumb*?'" Esmenet said ruefully.

Thumb. Sumni slang for "phallus." Why did it pain him so, listening to her speak in the old way?

Kellhus grinned. "They can't see that gold is only relevant insofar as it plays a role within our expectations—insofar as *we make it relevant* ..." He paused, his eyes sparkling with mirth. "The same," he continued, "might be said of thumbs."

Esmenet grimaced. "Even one named Eleäzaras?"

The Sacral Retinue had crowded to a stop. They had come to one of the many smalls that knotted the labyrinthine alleyways of Gerotha. Blank faces seemed to watch from every window. A few Men of the Tusk gazed adoring from their knees. The ever-present guardsmen of the Hundred Pillars stood pensive, staring down adjoining alleys as though they could see around corners. Someone had painted lotus vine along the weathered cornices of several buildings. A babe cried.

Shaking his leonine head, the Warrior-Prophet laughed to the heavens. And though Achamian could feel the laughter's contagion, its preternatural *demand* to celebrate things great and small, grief struck all breath from him. Anasürimbor Esmenet glanced about, her look shy with joy. Her eyes clicked away the instant she met his desolate gaze.

She took her husband's hand.

———— ✤ ————

Charaöth. The ancient stronghold of the Xerashi Kings.

The Lords of the Holy War gathered in its ruined halls, staring about in wonder and impatience as they awaited their Warrior-Prophet. Achamian overheard Palatine Gaidekki claiming that King Shikol's raving could be heard on the night wind. He saw a man—some client of Gothyelk's—gathering chips of marble into a cloth.

As the only feature visible above Gerotha's black curtain walls, Achamian had found himself pondering Charaöth from the first day of the Holy War's siege. He knew it had been abandoned with the ascendancy of the Thousand Temples in the days of the Ceneian Empire, but he had always assumed that the Fanim would have demolished it. Afterward he would learn from Gayamakri that the Kianene actually revered it as one of their holiest shrines. And why not, when so many Inrithi thought it the very heart of malevolence?

The original walls had been pulled down, so that from within Gerotha's bone-coloured expanse could be clearly seen. The voluptuous imprint of Nilnamesh was unmistakable, in the bellied columns and pilasters, in the curving stairs that ended nowhere, and in the four-winged Ciphrang that flanked every threshold. Even roofless and ruined, the architecture seemed over-heavy, though in a manner strangely at odds with the post-and-lintel monstrosities of ancient Kyraneas or Shigek. The surviving shoulder-arches proved that the antique Xerashi builders had understood the rudiments of stress and load. But the heaviness was different, as though everything had been constructed to bear weights unseen.

Could it simply be that *Shikol* had once ruled from this place? Like most Inrithi children, Achamian had been weaned on tales of the lecherous old king. "Behave," his mother always warned, "or he will find you, do unspeakable things!"

Achamian waited, doing his best to ignore Esmenet, who sat on a gilded chair not four paces to his left. He stood on the broad arc of what had been the dais of the primary audience hall. A series of steps and a ring of pilasters, their false lintels still intact, separated it from the great floor. According to *The Tractate,* the Xerashi Kings had ruled from their beds, and Shikol in particular was famed for making sport with children as his court peered through the sheers ringing his dais. Knowing the way histories tended to paint their antagonists, Achamian had always dismissed the tale as propaganda. But there, dead centre in the dais, was an ancient stone footing for what looked like a bed.

Probably an altar of some kind.

Across the great floor below, the Great and Lesser Names milled beneath the fat columns, decked in the regalia of the lands they had conquered. White banners bearing the Tusk and Circumfix in black and gold had been roped between the free-standing columns about them. The rumble of their talk thinned. Wondering whether they had glimpsed Kellhus, Achamian glanced over his shoulder, following the stair that rose from the dais's rear to the ruined gallery above and behind him. He saw nothing of Kellhus, though he spied something, a point of fluttering black, hanging over the distant network of streets and alleyways that rose up into the haze. He blinked, frowning … Was that the *Mark* he sensed?

A sorcerous bird?

"We have *arrived,*" a resonant voice called.

Startled, Achamian glanced back to the stair, saw Kellhus descend to the first landing, his beard plaited in the fashion of ancient Shir, his white vestments chased with shimmering gold. It was strange—even terrifying—to sense the Mark on him as well. It dirtied him somehow, even as it augured an unthinkable future.

Achamian turned back to the sky, but the bird was nowhere to be seen.

"At long last," Kellhus continued, casually descending the final turn of the stair, "we tread the very ground of scripture."

Achamian's thoughts raced. What should he do? Was the Consult planning an attack, or was it simply the Scarlet Spires, up to some damnable scarlet mischief? He resolved to remain wary, to ignore the tidal pull of Kellhus's oratory.

The Warrior-Prophet crossed the dais to Esmenet, placed what seemed a luminous hand on her shoulder. "From this very place," he said, "old Shikol looked to his debauched court and asked, 'Who is this menial who speaks as King?'" He gestured to ruined Charaöth—an expansive wave. "From this very place—*here*—Shikol raised the Gilded Thighbone ...

"He judged my brother."

As always, Kellhus spoke as though his words had no significance outside the Truth that shone through them—as though they were consumed by their meaning. *Attend only to these simple things*, his tone said, *and you shall be astonished.*

Achamian struggled to remain alert.

"At long last, we holy travellers, we Men of the Tusk, tread the very ground of scripture." Kellhus's expression darkened, and he looked about, to the lintel hanging above, to the columns queued across the floors before him. What had been hushed expectation escalated into something more profound, as though all present had become as breathless as the stone about them. "*This*, this is the very house of my brother's oppressor. This is the house of he who would murder Inri Sejenus, asking 'Who is this menial who speaks as King?'"

"Think! Think of how far we have come. Think of all the lands, both sumptuous and severe. Think of all the steaming cities. Think of all that we have *conquered*! And now we have arrived at the very *gates* ..." He reached out to the eastern haze with his right hand, and again Achamian saw it, the disc of ethereal gold, the halo ...

Someone cried out in rapture.

"One last horizon!" Kellhus cried, his voice at once rumbling from the skies and whispering into every ear. "One last horizon and we shall see the Sacred Land. One final march, and at last, *at long last*, we shall raise sword and song to Holy Shimeh! Even now *we rewrite the scripture of this place!*"

The Great and Lesser Names, who had watched rapt, erupted in shouts of ardour and worship. And Achamian could not but wonder what they must sound like to the Gerothans skulking the alleys below. The mad conquerors ...

"Never!" Kellhus thundered. "Never has the world seen such a band as we ... We Men of the Tusk." Suddenly he swept his sword, Certainty, from its sheath. It glared milk-white in the sun. Achamian watched its reflected light bounce across the Lords of the Holy War. Men squinted and blinked.

"We are the God's own *knife*, cast in the crucible of plague, thirst, and starvation, tempered by the hammers of war, doused in the blood of countless enemies!

"We ..." He trailed without warning, smiled as though caught in the commission of some harmless vice. "It is the wont of Men to boast," he said ruefully. "Who among us hasn't whispered lies in a maiden's ear?" Laughter rumbled through the headless pillars. "Anything that might make them ponder the swing of our kilts ..." More laughter, this time booming. Gone was the high oratory; the Warrior-Prophet had become the Prince of Atrithau, their wry and even-handed peer. He shrugged, grinned like a man among those about to drink.

"Even still, what is, is ... War watches through our eyes. Doom itself echoes in our call.

"What is, *is*. The glory of our undertaking will outshine that belonging to *any* of our forefathers. It will be a beacon through the Ages. It will astonish and gratify, and yea, it will even outrage. It will be recited by a thousand thousand lips. It will be committed to memory. And the children of our children's children will take up their ancestor lists and invoke our names with reverence and awe, for they shall know their blood is blessed—blessed!—by our greatness.

"We, we Men of the Tusk, are *more*. We are giants! *Giants!*"

Roaring exultation. Captured by the momentum of his words, Achamian found himself crying out as well. Wry to resounding ... from where had this bursting passion come? He saw tears course down Esmenet's cheek.

"So who?" Kellhus bellowed through the trailing thunder. "Who is this menial who speaks as King?"

Sudden silence. The buckled stone, with its lattice of weeds and grasses, seemed to hum. The Warrior-Prophet held out both shining hands—a welcome, an appeal, a breathtaking benediction. And he whispered ...

"*I am.*"

Without exception, men submitted to the hierarchy of the moving and the immovable. They stood *upon* the earth, they travelled over the land.

But with Kellhus, even this fundamental orthodoxy was upended: with his every step he seemed to *carry* the world with him.

So when he descended the dais and gestured to Incheiri Gotian to lead the Lords of the Holy War in prayer, it seemed the world itself was bent. As the intonations boomed between the walls, Achamian blinked the sweat from his eyes, breathed deep the humid air. He thought of Esmenet lying with such a man, and he found himself fearing for her, as if she were a petal falling into a great fire … *He's a prophet!*

So what did that make of Achamian's hate?

From paths cut through the scree, slaves produced a long table and several chairs, which they set in the centremost aisle between the columns for Kellhus and the Great Names. With the Tusk and Circumfix hanging above, they sat as if for a ritual dinner, though they drank only watered wine. Achamian stood rigid throughout the ensuing discussions. It seemed surreal, but it was the conquest of *Amoteu* they plotted—the approaches to Shimeh! What Kellhus had said earlier was true …they *had* arrived. Almost.

The proceedings were remarkably civil; gone were the days of bickering fuelled by wounded or overweening pride. Even if Saubon and Conphas had been present, Achamian couldn't imagine any of the Great Names resorting to their old antics. Kellhus dwarfed them in a manner so absolute that, much as children, they had lost all care for the cubits between them. They were his unto death … Kings and disciples.

Disagreements arose, to be certain, but the dissenters were neither scorned nor judged for merely expressing contrary opinions. As Kellhus himself said, where Truth was tyrant, the clear-eyed need fear no oppression. Proyas, especially, asked hard questions, and old Gothyelk somehow managed to restrict his outbursts to exasperated groans. Only Chinjosa seemed to play with his number-stick beneath his hand. Reasons were demanded and given, alternatives were explored and criticized, and as though by magic, the *best way* seemed to unfold of its own volition.

Prince Hulwarga was given the honour of the van, since it was deemed that his Thunyeri would be the most able to weather any possible Fanim surprise. Count-Palatine Chinjosa and his Ainoni, along with Proyas and his Conriyans, were to constitute the Holy War's main body. They would march directly on Shimeh, gathering food and siege materials as they went. Gotian and the Shrial Knights were to ride with them, as the personal guard of the Warrior-Prophet and his Sacral Retinue. Earl Gothyelk and his Tydonni, meanwhile, were given the task of isolating and overcoming Chargiddo, the Kyranean Age fortress that commanded the southwestern reaches of the Amoti and Xerashi frontier.

No one, not even Kellhus, seemed to know what the heathen had planned. All reports, especially those provided by the Scarlet Spires through Chinjosa, suggested that the Psûkari, the Cishaurim, would not abandon Shimeh. This meant that Fanayal would either contest their advance into Amoteu or fall back on the Holy City. Either way, he would give battle. The survival of the Cishaurim hung in the balance, which meant the survival of *Kian* hung in the balance. There could be no doubt that even now Fanayal mustered all possible means to overthrow them. Though Proyas counselled caution, the Warrior-Prophet was adamant: the Holy War must strike with all haste.

"We diminish," he said, "while they grow."

Several times Achamian dared glance at Esmenet in her nearby seat. A string of discreet functionaries came and went, kneeling at her side, either asking questions or bearing tidings. By and large, however, she remained attentive to the discussions on the floor before her. Achamian found himself studying the white-robed Nascenti, who stood in a group immediately behind their Warrior-Prophet—Werjau and Gayamakri foremost among them. And the strangeness of it dawned on him, the way the Holy War, which had been little more than a migratory invasion led by a raucous council of chieftains, had somehow reorganized itself into an imperial court. This was no Council of Great and Lesser Names; Kellhus merely consulted his generals, nothing more. *All of them* had been ... redeployed. And true to benjuka, the rules governing their conduct had been completely rewritten. Even the ones that held Achamian motionless, here, as vizier to a prophet ...

It was too absurd.

The sun hung low over the humid countryside by the time Kellhus dissolved the Council. His head buzzing from the heat, Achamian waited out the obligatory prayers and rounds of self-congratulation. The combination of sun and inaction made him want to scream. Perversely, he found himself hoping that the bird from earlier did omen some kind of Consult attack. Anything but this … stage.

Then, as if everyone had suddenly found themselves in agreement, the Council was over. The stone hollows between the ruins rumbled with shouts of greeting and casual conversation. Rubbing his neck, Achamian walked to the dais steps and unceremoniously dropped to his rump. He could feel Esmenet's gaze prickle the small of his back, but Inrithi caste-nobles were already climbing the dais to pay her homage, and he was too weary to do much more than pad the sweat from his face with his saffron sleeves.

A hand brushed his shoulder, as though someone had thought to clasp him but then reconsidered. Achamian turned to see Proyas. With his deep brown skin and silk khalat, he could have been a Kianene prince.

"Akka," he said with a perfunctory nod.

"Proyas."

An awkward moment passed between them.

"I thought I should tell you," he said, obviously discomfited. "You should see Zin."

"Did he send you?"

The Prince shook his head. He looked strange, far more mature, with his beard grown and plaited. "He asks about you," he said lamely. "You should go see—"

"I cannot," Achamian replied, far more sharply than he had wished. "I'm all that stands between Kellhus and the Consult. I can't leave his side."

Proyas's eyes narrowed in anger, but Achamian could not help but think that something had broken within the man. With Xinemus, he had abandoned seeking penance on his terms. He was someone who would no longer discriminate between afflictions. He would bear everything if he could.

"You've left his side before," Proyas said evenly.

"Only at his request, and against my objections."

Why this sudden need to punish? Now that Proyas required something of him, he was compelled to show him a reflection of his own callous disregard—to visit his own sins upon him. Even still, even after all Kellhus had taught him, Achamian carried the old ledgers in his heart, continued to tick off settled scores. *Why do I always do this?*

Proyas blinked, pursed his lips as though about sour teeth. "You should go see Xinemus," he said, this time making no attempt to disguise his bitterness. He left without saying farewell.

Too numb to think, Achamian watched the assembled caste-nobles. Gaidekki and Ingiaban fenced jokes—no surprise there. Iryssas stammered to keep up; sometimes he alone seemed unchanged from Momemn. Gotian upbraided some young Shrial Knight. Soter and several other Ainoni seemed to be laughing at the sight of Uranyanka kissing the Warrior-Prophet's knee. Hulwarga stood mute in the shadow of his dead brother's groom, Yalgrota. Everybody talking and belonging, forming little interlocking circles, like the links of some greater armour ...

The thought struck Achamian without warning.

I'm alone.

He knew nothing of his family, save that his mother was dead. He despised his School almost as much as his School despised him. He had lost his every student, in one way or another, to the blasted Gods. Esmenet had betrayed him ...

He coughed and swallowed, cursed himself for a fool. He called out to a passing slave—a surly-looking adolescent—told him to fetch some unwatered wine. *See,* he thought to himself as the boy ran off, *you have one friend.* His forearms against his knees, he stared down at his sandals, frowned at his untrimmed toenails. He thought of Xinemus. *I should see him ...*

He did not turn when the shadow joined him sitting on the steps. The air suddenly smelled of myrrh. Somewhere, in a treacherous and juvenile part of his soul, he leapt with joy, even though he knew it wasn't Esmenet. The shadow was too dark.

"Is it time?" Achamian asked.

"Soon," Kellhus said.

Achamian had come to fear their nightly sessions with the Gnosis. To intuitively grasp logic or arithmetic might be a thing of wonder, but to do the same with ancient War-Cants was something altogether different. How could he not dread, when the man so effortlessly outran his ability to compare or categorize?

"What troubles you, Akka?"

What do you think? something within him spat. Instead he turned to Kellhus and asked, "Why Shimeh?"

The clear blue eyes studied him in silence.

"You say you've come to save us," Achamian pressed. "You admit as much. So then *why*, when our doom resides in Golgotterath, do we continue on to Shimeh?"

"You're tired," Kellhus said. "Perhaps we should resume our studies tomorr—"

"I'm fine," Achamian snapped, only to be dismayed by his presumption. "Sleep and Mandate Schoolmen," he added lamely, "are old enemies."

Kellhus nodded, smiled sadly. "Your grief ... It still overcomes you."

For some treacherous reason Achamian said, "Yes."

The numbers of Inrithi had dwindled. Several personages had gathered at a discreet distance, obviously awaiting Kellhus, but he dismissed them with a gesture. Soon Achamian and Kellhus were quite alone, sitting side by side on the dais's lip, watching the shadows swell and congregate in the crotches of the surrounding ruin. A dry wind dropped from the skies, and for a time Achamian closed his eyes, savouring its cool kiss across his skin, listening to it whisper through the sumacs that thronged beyond the floor. An occasional bee buzzed in and out of hearing.

It reminded Achamian of hiding from his father in the gullies far from the beaches. The hush concealed between the throng of living things. The sense of slowing light. The limitless sky. It seemed a moment outside consequence, where the profound repose of what was put flight to all thoughts of past or future. He could even smell the stone as it cooled in the lengthening shadows.

It seemed impossible that Shikol had dwelt in this place.

"Did you know," Kellhus said, "that there was a time when I listened to the world and heard only noise?"

"No ... I didn't."

Kellhus raised his face to the sky, closed his eyes. Sunlight curled into the silky depths of his hair. "I know different now ... There's more than noise, Akka. There is *voice*."

Shivers unrolled like wet strings across Achamian's skin.

His eyes fixed on the horizon, Kellhus pressed his palms across his thighs, drawing folds into arcs. Against the silk, Achamian thought he glimpsed the golden discs about his fingers.

"Tell me, Akka," Kellhus said. "When you look into a mirror, what do you see?" He spoke as a bored child might.

Achamian shrugged. "Myself."

A teacher's indulgent look. "Are you so certain? Do you see yourself *looking* through your eyes, or do you simply see your eyes? Strip away your assumptions, Akka, and ask yourself, what do you really see?"

"My eyes," he admitted. "I simply see my eyes."

"Then you don't see yourself."

Achamian could only stare at his profile, dumbfounded.

Kellhus's grin shouted intellectual mischief. "So where are you, if you can't be seen?"

"Here," Achamian replied after a moment of hesitation. "I'm here."

"And just where is this 'here'?"

"It's …" He frowned for a moment. "It's *here* … inside what you see."

"Here? But how could you be here," Kellhus laughed, "when *I'm* here, and you're over *there*?"

"But …" Achamian scratched his beard in exasperation. "You play games with words!" he exclaimed.

Kellhus nodded, his expression at once cryptic and bemused. "Imagine," he said, "that you could take the Great Ocean, in all its immensity, and fold it into the form and proportion of a man. There are depths, Akka, that go *in* rather than down—in without limit. What you call the Outside lies *within us*, and it's everywhere. This is why, no matter where we stand, it's always *here*. No matter where we dare tread, *we always stand in the same place*."

Metaphysics, Achamian realized. He spoke of metaphysics.

"Here," Achamian repeated. "You're saying here is a place outside place?"

"Indeed. Your body is your surface, nothing more, the point where your soul breaches this world. Even now, as we look upon each other from across this span, from two different places, we also stand in the same place, the same nowhere. I watch myself through your eyes, and you watch yourself through mine—though you know it not."

Somehow, at some point, insight had become a species of horror. He fairly stammered. "W-we're the same person?" *Kellhus* was speaking this madness ... Kellhus!

"Person? It would be more precise to say we're the same *here* ... But in a manner, yes. Just as there's but one Here, there's but one Soul, Akka, breaching the world in many different places. And almost always failing to apprehend itself as itself."

Nilnameshi foolishness! It had to be ...

"This is just metaphysics," he said, the very instant Kellhus whispered, *"This is just metaphysics ..."*

Achamian gaped at the man, utterly dumbstruck. His heart hammered, as though struggling to recover its rhythm through violence of action. For a moment he tried telling himself that Kellhus alone had spoken, but the taste of the words was too fresh on his tongue. The silence whined with a strange horror, a sense of dislocation unlike any he had ever experienced, a sense of things once sacred and intact now broken ... Just *who* had spoken?

The world reeled through refracted sunlight.

He is me ... How else could he know what he knows?

As though nothing untoward had happened, Kellhus said, "Tell me, how can some words work miracles, while others can't?"

Achamian swallowed, tried to recover himself in his knowledge. "The Nonmen once believed it was the language that made sorcery possible. But when Men began reproducing their Cants in bastard tongues, it became clear this wasn't so ..." He breathed deeply, realizing that with this one question Kellhus had made plain not only Achamian's ignorance but the ignorance of every sorcerer living. *I really do understand nothing.*

"It's the *meanings*," he continued. "The meanings are different somehow. No one knows why."

Kellhus nodded and looked down to the hem of his robe. When he glanced up, Achamian found his brilliant eyes impossible to match. "The word 'love,'" he said, "does it mean what it has always meant, or is the meaning different for you?"

Reward the intellect and punish the heart. It was always the same with Kellhus.

"What are you saying?"

"That the meaning is different because what it recollects is different."
Esmenet.

"So you're suggesting that sorcerous words *recollect* something other words do not?" Achamian asked this with more heat than he'd intended. Derision had stolen across his expression. "But what could *words* remember? Words aren't ..." He trailed, his voice silenced by sudden understanding. *One soul ...*

"Not words, Akka. *You.* What could *you* remember that might make miracles of mere words?"

"I-I don't understand ..."

"But you do."

Achamian blinked at the preposterous tears in his eyes. He thought of the Scarlet Spires and their compound in Iothiah, of the world flying apart beneath his outstretched fingers. And he remembered the *meanings* that had thundered from his chest and soul, his world-racking song, compelling fire from empty air, light from black shadow, and the obliteration of all that offended. The words! The words that were his calling—his curse! The words that exacted the *impossible* ...

Penance from the world.

How could a mere man say such things?

"We kneel before idols," Kellhus was saying, "we hold open our arms to the sky. We beseech the distances, clutch at the horizon ... We look outward, Akka, always outward, for what *lies within* ..." He splayed a hand against his chest. "For what lies *here*, in this Clearing that we share."

The sun had crossed the crimson threshold. The air seemed to purple, and the ruins were burnished in failing reds. The earlier breeze had faded to a sun-warm draft.

"The God," Achamian said, but the voice was not his own. "You're saying that this ... this one soul that looks out from behind all our eyes is the God." Even though he spoke these words, even though he knew quite well what they meant, they escaped him somehow, fell from him without force of thought or comprehension. Achamian clutched his shoulders, felt a shudder pass through his portly frame.

"We are all God," Kellhus said, now both solemn and enthused—like a father heartening a beaten son. "The God is always here, watching through your very own eyes, and from the eyes of those about you.

But we forget who we are, and we begin to think of here as another *there*: detached, isolate, abject before the immensities of the world. We forget ... But we don't all forget equally." Kellhus fixed him with an implacable look. "Those who forget the least, we call the Few."

There had been a moment, walking the fiery hallways of Iothiah, when Achamian's wrath had been checked, when he'd faltered, realizing he no longer recognized himself. He had cried out in Seswatha's voice, and had uttered words that had transcended the circle of even that ancient individuality—Cants that had made milk of what was hard, what was *real* ...

Who had he been? Who?

"To speak sorcery, Akka, is to speak words that recollect the Truth."

"Truth," Achamian numbly repeated. He understood what Kellhus said, he *knew*, and yet something within him refused to *grasp*. "What truth?"

"That this place behind our face, though separated by nations and ages, is the same place, the same *here*. That each of us witnesses the world through innumerable eyes. That *we* are the God we would worship."

And it seemed to Achamian that he *could* remember, that across sea, mountain, and plain he saw the God blink a thousand times before a thousand hearths. A daughter gazing upon her slumbering father. An ancient wife clutching her husband's arm in spotted hands. A man spitting blood, beating an earthen floor in anguish. Here, now, in this one place ... How else could one explain the Cants of Calling or Compulsion? How else could one explain Seswatha's Dreams?

"For so long," Kellhus was saying, "you thought yourself a pariah, an outcast. And though your tongue was ever ready to accost those who would condemn you, you lived in shame. You would watch them, and you would curse yourself for hoping. Always stronger in the estimation of others—so they seemed. Always so certain. And always unable to see— the fools!—how extraordinary you truly were. They spat when they looked upon you. They laughed, and though you made their derision evidence of their stupidity, in the secret moments you grieved, you wept, and you asked, 'Why must I be cursed? Why must I be damned?'"

And Achamian thought, *He is! He is* me!

Kellhus smiled, and somehow—impossibly—Achamian saw Inrau in the iridescent cast of his look. "We are each other."

But I'm broken ... Something's wrong with me!

"Because you're a pious man born to a world unable to fathom your piety. But all that changes with me, Akka. The old revelations have outlived the age of their intention, and I have come to reveal the new. I am the Shortest Path, and I say that you are *not damned*."

Through the tumult of passion that rocked him, something old and arcane whispered the Mandate Catechism. *Though you lose your soul, you shall gain the—*

But Kellhus was talking again, speaking in intonations that seemed to resonate across the warm evening air, to ring out from the very heart of things.

"A sorcerer's words work miracles because they recall the God ... Think, Akka! What does it mean to see the world as sorcerers see it? What does it mean to apprehend the onta? The many see the world through one pair of eyes; they grasp Creation from but a single vantage—one *angle* among many. But the *Few*—those who recollect, no matter how imperfectly, the God's voice—possess an intimation of many angles, a memory of the thousand eyes that look out from this clearing we call 'here.' As a result everything they see is transformed, shadowed by insinuations of more.

"And think of the Mark ... For the many, sorcery is indistinguishable from the world—and how could it be otherwise, given they apprehend the world from but a single angle? For a man who cannot move, the façade simply *is* the temple. But for the Few, who glimpse many angles, sorcery must reek of incompleteness, for where the God's true voice speaks to the totality of angles, the Few are constrained by the murk and imperfection of their recollections. They can conjure façades only ..."

It seemed so obvious. All the analogies of sorcerers as blasphemers, as abusers of the divinity within, as those who ape the God's sacred song, were but crude approximations, tenuous glimpses of a truth that Kellhus held in his lap!

"And the Cishaurim," Achamian found himself saying, "what of them?"

The Warrior-Prophet shrugged. "Think of the way a fire will shroud the world in the course of illuminating a camp. Often the light of what we see blinds us, and we come to think there is one angle and one angle only. Though they know it not, this is why the Cishaurim blind themselves. They douse the fire of their eyes, pluck the one angle they see, to better grasp the many they *recollect*. They sacrifice the subtle articulations of knowledge for the inchoate profundities of intuition. They recall the tone and timbre, the *passion*, of the God's voice—to near perfection— even as the meanings that make up true sorcery escape them."

And there it was: the mysteries of the Psûkhe, which had baffled sorcerous thinkers for centuries, dispelled in a handful of words.

The Warrior-Prophet turned to him, clutched his shoulder with a shining hand. "The Truth of Here is that it is Everywhere. And this, Akka, is what it means to be in love: to recognize the Here *within the other*, to see the world through another's eyes. To be *here together*."

His eyes, luminous with wisdom, seemed unbearable.

The world had sloughed off the last of the sun, and the shadows pooled like ink. Night stalked the ruined ways of Charaöth.

"And *this* is why you suffer so … When what was here turns away from you, as *she* has turned away from you, it seems there's nowhere you might stand."

A mosquito dared whine through the air about their ears.

"Why are you telling me this?" Achamian cried.

"Because you are not alone."

Slavery agreed with her.

Even more than Yel or Burulan, Fanashila adored her new station in life. Fussing over her mistress in the mornings, snoozing in the afternoons, then fussing over her mistress again in the evenings. The gold. The perfume. The silk. The cosmetics Lady Esmenet let them use. The intimations of power—*great* power. The delicacies Lady Esmenet let them taste. Fanashila was *fami*, one of the original slaves from the Fama Palace in Caraskand. How could the freedom to chase goats compare with this?

Of course, Opsara cursed them whenever she could, the vicious old hag. "They're idolaters! Slavers! We must cut their throats, not kiss their toes!" Over and over, and on and on. But then, Opsara had *Kianene* blood in her—she was an *uftaka*—and everyone knew that uftaki were nothing more than menials who strutted like nobles. Their *own kind* even despised them. What did that say?

Besides, for all Opsara's talk, her ward, the infant Moënghus, seemed healthy enough. Fanashila even said as much one night in the slave mess.

They had been sitting in their accustomed corner—the one that marked their importance—mildly fingering rice from their bowls while Opsara ranted about killing their Inrithi masters. "Well," Fanashila blurted, "you go first!" How Yel and the others had howled with laughter. Without realizing, Fanashila had found the-way-to-shut-Opsara-up. Now she fairly shook with pride and giggles whenever Opsara started, because she knew her moment would shine again.

If anything troubled Fanashila, it was the Kneeling, when the overseers gathered her and the others and brought them to the Umbilica's shrine. First a Shrial Priest delivered a sermon—only bits and pieces of which Fanashila could understand—then they were forced to pray aloud to the half-circle of idols. Some were grotesque, like the severed head of Onkis upon a golden tree, others were obscene, like Ajokli with his chin propped upon his phallus, and several were even beautiful, like stern Gilgaöl or voluptuous Gierra—though the wide-thrown ankles of the latter made Fanashila blush.

The Shrial Priest called them Aspects of the God. But Fanashila knew better. They were demons.

But she prayed to them nonetheless, just as she was told. Sometimes, when the overseers were distracted, she would look away from the leering devil before her and search the brocaded panels that regaled the tarp walls for the Two Scimitars of Fane. They were all over, little signs of her people's faith. Then she would silently repeat the words she had heard so many times in Tabernacle.

One for the Unbeliever ... One for the Unseeing Eye ...

This, she decided, had to be enough. What harm could there be in praying to demons, when the Solitary God commanded all? Besides, the demons *listened* ... They actually answered *their* prayers. Why else would the idolaters be the slavers and the faithful the slaves?

After evening mess, the overseers herded the women to the Room of Mats, the large tent where they slept across fantastic carpets, which had been looted, the overseers said, from the strongholds of their dead Kianene masters. Some wept at night. Others, particularly those who were beautiful or those who caused trouble, were taken away in the dead of night. Sometimes they returned, sometimes not. But as far as Fanashila was concerned, they brought it on themselves. One need only *do* ... It was as simple as that. *Do* and you would be rewarded, or at the very least left alone.

This was what she reminded herself of the night she was taken away. Everything they told her, she did. That was the rule! They wouldn't make her disappear—not *her*! She had *washed the feet* of their Warrior-Prophet ...

Lady Esmenet would never allow it. Never!

The overseer, Koropos, a former Cironji slave of the Kianene, refused to answer any of her whispered questions. With a firm hand he guided her between the forms sprawled sleeping across the floor, then into the antechamber where the overseers slept and gamed. At first she assumed that they wanted to bed her. She had seen their evil grins when they watched her—especially that of Tirius, the freed Nansur. They had raped many of the others. But would they dare despoil her? All she had to do was cry to Lady Esmenet and their throats would be cut.

She said as much to Koropos.

"Tell *him*," the wiry old man snorted. With that, he shoved her through the curtain of hanging whips—the traditional entrance for Inrithi slave quarters—into the cool night air.

A man stood tall and indomitable in the night gloom. Beyond him, the encampment spread dark and labyrinthine across the distances. Because of the anonymous simplicity of his dress—a desert tunic beneath a Cironji chalmys—several heartbeats passed before she recognized him ... Lord Werjau of the Nascenti!

She fell to her knees, chin to her breastbone, as she had been trained.

"Look at me," he said, his tone firm yet gentle. "Tell me, my sweet, what's this rumour I hear?"

Relief swept through her. Fanashila looked away demurely. She loved gossip. Almost as much as attention. "Wha-what rumour would that be, my Lord?"

Werjau smiled down at her, stood so perilously near she could smell the sour of his crotch. He brought a callused thumb to her chin. She shuddered as he traced the outline of her lips.

"That they are lovers still," he said. Though his gaze remained remote, something seemed to ... smirk in his tone.

Fanashila swallowed, afraid once again. "They?" she asked, blinking tears. "Who?"

"The Prophet-Consort and the Holy Tutor."

CHAPTER ELEVEN

HOLY AMOTEU

Of all the Cants, none better illustrates the nature of the soul than the Cants of Compulsion. According to Zarathinius, the fact that those compelled unerringly think themselves free shows that Volition is one more thing moved in the soul, and not the mover we take it to be. While few dispute this, the absurdities that follow escape comprehension altogether.

—MEREMNIS, *THE ARCANA IMPLICATA*

As a miller once told me, when the gears do not meet, they become as teeth. So it is with men and their machinations.

—ONTILLAS, *ON THE FOLLY OF MEN*

Early Spring, 4112 Year-of-the-Tusk, Amoteu

They had come from the straw-floored manors of Galeoth, where dogs supped with their masters; from the frontier forests of Thunyerus, deep and great, where the Sranc waged their aimless and eternal war; from the mead-halls of Ce Tydonn, where long-haired thanes denounced mongrel races; from the great estates of Conriya, where dark-eyed Palatines made prizes of their pasts; and from the sultry plains of High Ainon, where painted caste-nobles beat paths through teeming streets. Eight seasons

220

previously, the Shriah of the Thousand Temples had called, and they had come ... the Men of the Tusk.

From Gerotha, they continued their march across a subdued land. Word of the Warrior-Prophet's Toll of Days had outrun them, and wherever they passed, they found Xerashi prostrate across the red-and-black earth. Hidden granaries were thrown open. Goat-milk, honey, dried peppers, and sugar cane, even entire herds of cattle, were willingly surrendered. Village elders acclaimed them, kissed their sandalled feet, and presented the most fair of their dark-skinned daughters. Anything that might appease the Lords of the Holy War.

The main column, consisting of Hulwarga, Chinjosa, Proyas, and Anfirig, followed the Herotic Way. One by one the coastal strongholds surrendered to them: Sabsal, Moridon, and even Horeppo, which had been a primary port-of-destination for Inrithi pilgrims in the years preceding the Holy War. More newcomers joined them, seafaring Galeoth—Oswentamen for the most part—driven ashore by Kianene marauders. Sweating in their hair shirts, they hauled their barks onto the rocky strands and burned them. They joined their kinsmen about their evening fires, only to be troubled by their strange garb and implacable stares.

Gothyelk, meanwhile, struck directly south to invest the great fortress of Chargiddo, using the intelligence provided by Athjeäri to secure his approach. Even here, word of the massacre at Gerotha had reached the heathen in advance, and after a largely ceremonial show of defiance, the famed citadel gave herself over to the uncertain mercy of the Tydonni.

Most Holy Prophet, the Earl of Agansanor would write, *Chargiddo has fallen, and with nary a death, save that of my cousin's nephew, who was taken by a stray shaft. Verily, you have boned this land like a fish! Praise be the God of Gods. Praise be Inri Sejenus, our prophet your brother.*

With each passing day, the sorrows of the long road seemed to fall away, and the Men of the Tusk recalled their old humour. Evenings became celebrations, pious bacchanals where toast after toast would be raised to their hallowed Warrior-Prophet. Hundreds of impromptu pilgrimages set out across the lush countryside, and the Xerashi wondered at these idolaters, who continually roamed ground stumped by ruins, arguing over passages in their scriptures.

Save for a handful of incidents, there were no atrocities like those that marred their earlier marches. In the Councils of Great and Lesser Names, the Warrior-Prophet made it clear that the Inrithi either kept or betrayed *his* word with their actions. "The Xerashi," he said, "need not love me to trust me. Just as we need not murder them to demonstrate our hate. Spare them, and their gates will be opened. Kill them, and you kill your brothers."

Though Xerash had been emptied of Kianene, Athjeäri found himself sorely pressed in Holy Amoteu. All across the Jarta Highlands, distant streamers of smoke plied the skies as the Fanim hastened to burn any and all structures possessing timber that could be used for siege engines. Taking Mer-Porasas as his base, the brash young Earl ranged to the very edges of the Shairizor Plains, visiting ruin upon the Fanim where he could. But after each encounter he returned with more empty saddles, until very soon his five hundred thanes and knights had dwindled to fewer than two hundred. Though he possessed daring in excess, he lacked the manpower required to secure his position, let alone fence with Fanayal and the heathen army that concentrated about Shimeh.

His missives to the Warrior-Prophet, which had begun as dispassionate appraisals of the situation in the field, soon became pleas for assistance. The Warrior-Prophet begged patience and fortitude, even as he exhorted the Great Names to hasten their march.

The main column climbed into the Jarta Highlands some ten days following the fall of Gerotha—a remarkable pace, given the size of the train, which included the perennially slothful Scarlet Spires, and the fact that they foraged as they marched. Then something peculiar happened.

Accounts of the incident would vary greatly, though all agreed that it involved an encounter between an old man—an old *blind* man—and the Warrior-Prophet. This in itself was extraordinary, since the Hundred Pillars were at great pains to either drive away or, failing that, kill every blind man found in the path of the Sacral Retinue. The nearer the Holy War drew to Shimeh, the more the Warrior-Prophet's Consort and Intricati feared the possibility of a Cishaurim attack.

Apparently, a blind Xerashi beggar had been overlooked, and as the Sacral Retinue passed through the Jartic town of Gim, he cried out to the Warrior-Prophet. In a letter to his father, Prince Nersei Proyas would write the following description:

*No one understood what he said, though Arishal and the other body-
guards understood the danger well enough. They immediately charged
toward the man, only to be brought up short by the resounding crack of
the Warrior-Prophet's voice. Everyone stood milling, confused, while the
Blessed One regarded the shambling old beggar. The man's skin was
almost black, so that his wild hair and beard seemed as white as a
Zeümi's teeth. As we watched, quite astonished, the Blessed One
dismounted and walked toward the old man—as though he were the
penitent! When he towered over the bent figure, he asked, "Who are
you to make demands?" to which the remarkable fool replied, "One who
has something to whisper into your ear." Cries of alarm erupted among
us. I know I, Father, was concerned to the point of terror. "And why,"
the Blessed One asked, "must you whisper?" to which the man
responded, "Because my words are the words of my doom. Truthfully,
you will kill me after you hear them." I know I shouted that this was a
trick of some kind, some foul Cishaurim deceit, and I know there were
many such shouts of apprehension, but the Blessed One did not listen.
He even kneeled, Father, to one knee, so that the blind man could
better reach his ear. We sat motionless, gutted by horror, while he
whispered his doom. And it was his doom, Father! For no sooner had
he finished than the Warrior-Prophet drew Enshoiya, his holy sword,
and struck the miscreant down, cutting him from his collar to his heart.
We had scarcely recovered our breaths when he commanded that the
Holy War halt and make camp across the fields of Gim. And to those
who dared ask for an explanation, he would say nothing.*

What did the old fool whisper?

There had been a time when he'd walked in glory and horror. Spear-Bearer
to mighty Sil, the great King After-the-Fall. He had dared the wrath of
Cu'jara Cinmoi on the plains of Pir Pahal. He had ridden the back of
Wutteät, Father of Dragons. He had wrestled Ciögli the Mountain—
thrown him from his feet! Sarpanur, the Nonmen of Ishriol had called
him at first, after the keystone that fixed their crude subterranean
arches. And then, following the Womb-Plague, Sin-Pharion, "the
Angel of Deceit."

Ah, the raucous glory of that age! He had been young then, before the accretions of graft after graft had sapped his monumental frame. And such a contest! But for Sil's impatience, he and his brothers would have won, and all this—this *world*—would be moot.

Driven from Min-Uroikas. Scattered. Hunted. So far they had dwindled!

And then, from nowhere, a second age of glory. Who would have guessed that the cunning of *Men* could resurrect their aborted designs, that the vermin could restore his destiny? Horde-General to dread Mog-Pharau, Breaker of Worlds. He had burned the Great Library of Sauglish. He had stormed the heights of Holy Trysë. He had made fires of their cities, beacons that shone through the very void. He had extinguished nations—bled whole peoples white! Aurang, the Norsirai of Kûniüri had called him "the Warlord." Perhaps the most far-seeing of his many names.

So how had it come to this? Bound to a *Synthese*, like a king to a leper's robes. Frail and fugitive. Skulking about the fires of a roused enemy. There had been a time when the screams of thousands had heralded his coming.

He circled the hilltop compound the way a vulture might, slow and high, and with a patience that could run out all life. To the west, the Hills of Jarta lay blanched and broken in the moonlight. To the east, the Plains of Shairizor fanned to the black horizon, scored by grove and field, pocked by barn and byre. Beyond, the Horde-General knew, lay Shimeh ...

The very heart of the mannish world. The Three Seas.

Everywhere, he could see the furtive mark of their generations, the residue of once-dominant themes and long-lost reprises. The shadows of the Shigeki fortress that had once commanded these heights. The Ceneian road that struck straight as a rule across the plain. The defensive sensibilities of the Nansur in the compound's concentric design. The frosting of Kianene ornament. Petalled battlements. Iron-fretted windows.

He was deeper than all this. Older than their blasted stone.

He spiralled downward, toward the outer courtyard, where he could see his children's horses. He alighted on one of the eaves, where the sun's warmth still radiated from the clay tiles. He called to them in the sacred pitch only they and rats could hear. They came leaping through dark and abandoned halls, faithful, faithless things. They grovelled before him, their groins slick from their victims. His eyes flared and they clutched themselves in anguish and ecstasy. His children. His flowers.

For decades, the Consult had assumed that the alien metaphysics of the Cishaurim had been responsible for uncovering their children in Shimeh. This had made the prospect of the Empire's fall to the Fanim intolerable. Half the Three Seas immune to their poison? The Holy War had seemed a rare opportunity.

But the plate had changed all too quickly. To realize that the Cishaurim were but a mask for a far more ancient foe. To come so very close, only to discover their sublime deceptions subverted by something *deeper*. Something new.

The Dûnyain.

There was more to this than a son hunting for his father—far more. Their devious methods and disconcerting abilities aside, these Dûnyain were *Anasûrimbor*. Even without the Mandate prophecies, enmity was a fact of their accursed blood. Who was this Moënghus? And if his son could seize the armed might of the Three Seas in a single year, what had he accomplished in *thirty*? What awaited the Holy War in Shimeh?

Despite the rank disorder of his soul, the Scylvendi had been right about one thing: these Dûnyain had seized too much already. They could not be allowed the Gnosis as well.

Aurang, his hoary soul wrenching at the seams of the Synthese that housed him, smiled an odd, bird-twitching smile. How long since his last *true* contest?

His children continued straining and clutching, their cracked faces bent to the stars.

"Prepare this place," he commanded.

"But, Old Father," the daring one, Ûssirta, said, "how could you be certain?"

He knew. He was the Warlord.

"The Anasûrimbor marches the Herotic Way. He will pause before crossing the plain, reorganize, revise his plans. The Scylvendi is right— he isn't like the others." A normal man—even an Anasûrimbor—would succumb to the eagerness that so quickened the legs of those who set eyes upon a hard-won destination. But not a Dûnyain.

Men. They had been little more than packs of wild dogs during the First Wars. How had they grown so?

"Is it *near*, Old Father?" the other, Maörta, exclaimed. "Does it come?"

He regarded the piteous thing, his wretched instrument. And so few of them remained.

"The sacrifice has been made," he said, ignoring its question. "The Anasûrimbor will be lulled into thinking he has already anticipated us. Then, when he comes to this place …"

Before the coming of these Dûnyain, the Consult could trust to their tools. Now Aurang had no choice but to intervene, to tyrannize what their tools could only mock, to possess what they could only mimic …

"Trust me, my children, he will be caught unawares when we strike. There is treachery in his wife's heart."

They would test the limits of this Prophet's penetration. They would deny him the Gnosis.

The thing gurgled and clacked its teeth.

"We probe their faces with pins," Eleäzaras said, affecting the droll tone that had once come so naturally to him.

"And that was how you found him?" Her tone was sharp and obviously sarcastic. Eleäzaras glanced derisively at Iyokus, even though all such looks were wasted upon him now. How little these menials knew of jnan!

"Need I explain it again?"

The painted lips smiled. "That depends whether *he* wishes to hear your story, now, doesn't it?"

Eleäzaras snorted, availed himself of his wine bowl once again, drinking deep. She was clever—he would cede her that. Damnably clever. *No-no … no need to bring* him *into this.*

The fact that she had learned of their discovery so quickly spoke not only to her ability but to the efficacy of the organization she had assembled following the Warrior-Prophet's ascendancy. He would not make the mistake of underestimating either her or her resources again. This whore-cum-Consort.

This … Esmenet.

She was attractive, though. Well worth rutting … To do to her what they had done to that thing's face. Yes, very attractive.

The slaves had finished pitching the pavilion no more than a watch previously. Eleäzaras had arrived with Iyokus to study the beast—the first live one they'd apprehended—when the Intricati had appeared in the wake of exclaiming and bewildered Javreh. She had just *walked in* ...

One of the Nascenti accompanied her, Werjau or something—Eleäzaras was too drunk to remember—as well as four of those Hundred-fucking-Pillars. All with Chorae bound to their palms, of course. They stood, a small and confrontational crowd, framed by the evening light that filtered through the entrance. Eleäzaras wondered if she even grasped the outrageousness of her presumption. Sweet Sejenus! They were the *Scarlet Spires*! No one simply intruded upon their affairs, no matter what their writ or who their lord and master. *Especially* a woman.

The chamber was both hot and foul, a result of all the felt the slaves had draped across the walls to muffle sound. Suspended face down, the thing lay shackled to the crude iron scaffold that propped the ceiling. A leather thong had been tied about the tip of each facial digit, drawing them out like the ribs of a parasol. In the corner of Eleäzaras's eye, it looked a grotesque parody of the Circumfix. Its crotch-face glistened in the lantern light, wet and vaginal.

Blood tapped the reed mats in a steady rhythm.

"We fully intended," Iyokus was saying, "to share any information we exacted."

Whether this was true or false, of course, depended entirely on the information exacted.

"Oh," the Intricati said, "I see ..." Despite her small stature, she cut an imposing figure in her Kianene gown and wrap. "And when might that have been?" she continued. "Sometime *after* Shimeh?"

Penetrating bitch. That was the thing, of course, the reason they had no hope of merely talking their way out of this small and likely inconsequential treachery: Shimeh lay mere days away.

The impossible had become imminent.

It was strange the way events had shown him the *divisions* in what had once been the singular morass of his soul. Even as he laughed at the thought of Shimeh—and the Cishaurim—something gibbered within him, panicked and sputtered, like that day his uncles had hauled him into the breakers to teach him how to swim. *Some other day, please … Some other day!*

Where was the justice? His contract with Maithanet and the Thousand Temples had been struck in a different world. There had been no mention of the Consult or the Second Apocalypse. No mention of the Mandate *being right* … And certainly nothing had been said about a *living prophet!*

How could they have been so deceived? And now to be bent upon murder, to have their knife drawn, only to discover that they had no motive … except self-preservation.

What have I done?

For weeks now, the members of the Scarlet Spires' privy council, the Two-Palms, had quarrelled over question after question. Is the Atrithau Prince truly a prophet? And if he is, why should the *Scarlet Spires* accede to his demands? And what of the Second Apocalypse? The Consult and their skin-spies … they had replaced *Chepheramunni!* They had ruled High Ainon in their name! What did that portend? And how should they respond? Should they retreat, abandon the Holy War? What would be the consequences of that?

Or should they continue prosecuting their war against the Cishaurim?

Burning questions, and all of them with no answer apart from decisive leadership—something that their present Grandmaster clearly lacked. The insinuations had already started, the niggling comments that accused all the more for their ambiguity. "Curse the implications!" he felt like screaming at Inrûmmi, Sarosthenes, and the others. "Just say what you mean!"

That said it all, he supposed. What was it the Conriyans said about an *Ainoni* demanding clarity?

It meant throats would be soon cut.

And Iyokus, especially, had become quarrelsome, despite the fact that Eleäzaras had renamed him to his old position. Who'd ever heard of a *blind* Master of Spies? Even before the bitch Intricati's arrival, the chanv addict had started, demanding that Eleäzaras parse the undecidable, that he recall his station, treat with the "new fanatics," as he called them, from a position of strength …

"Don't say it!" Eleäzaras had cried. "Don't even think it."

"So what? Are we to simply *endure* these indignities? You would yield our—"

"He *sees*, Iyokus! He reads our souls in our faces! What you say to me, you say to *him*, no matter what! All he need ask is, 'What does your Master of Spies make of all this?' and no matter what answer I give him, he will hear *these very words you speak!*"

"Pfah!"

There was strength in ignorance, Eleäzaras realized. All his life he had thought knowledge a weapon. "The world repeats," the Shiradic philosopher Umartu had written. "Know these repetitions, and you may intervene." Eleäzaras had taken this as his mantra, had used it as the hammer with which to pound cunning into his wit. *You may intervene*, he would tell himself, no matter what the circumstance.

But there was knowledge beyond hope of intervention, knowledge that mocked, degraded … gelded and paralyzed. Knowledge that only ignorance could contradict. Iyokus and Inrûmmi simply did not *know* what he knew, which was why they thought him castrate. They didn't even believe.

Perhaps it was inevitable that the Intricati appear here and now. That the *Warrior-Prophet* intervene.

"And why wasn't I summoned?" the Intricati was asking. "Why was the Warrior-Prophet not informed?"

"We thought it a School matter," Iyokus said.

"A School matter …"

Eleäzaras smirked. "It is *we* who face the Snakeheads, not you."

She actually had the temerity to take a step closer. "These things have nothing to do with the Cishaurim," she snapped. "I would ponder that word 'we,' Eleäzaras. I assure you, its meaning is more treacherous than even you might think."

Impertinent! Outrageous, impertinent whore! "Pfah!" he cried. "Why am I even speaking to the likes of you?"

Her eyes flashed. "The *likes?*"

Something, her tone or perhaps his own better judgement, caused him to reconsider. He felt his contempt drain away, his eyes dull with anxiety. He blinked, looked to the skin-spy, which writhed in the constrained way of couples making love with only blankets to conceal them. Suddenly everything seemed so … dreary.

So hopeless.

"I apologize," he said. Out of habit he had tried to sound scathing, but the words had sounded *scared* instead. What was happening to him? When would this nightmare end?

A smile of triumph crept across her face. She—a caste-menial whore!

Eleäzaras could feel Iyokus stiffen in outrage; apparently one did not need eyes to witness what had just happened. Consequences! Why must there always be consequences? He would pay for this ... this ... humiliation. To remain the Grandmaster, one had to *act* the Grandmaster ...

What did I do wrong? something churlish cried within.

"The creature will be transferred," she was saying. "These things have no soul for your Cants to compel ... Other means are required."

She spoke the language of edict, and Eleäzaras found himself understanding—though Iyokus, he knew, could not hope to follow. She *was* a handsome woman—beautiful, even. He would enjoy fucking her ... And the fact that she belonged to the Warrior-Prophet? Sugar on the peach, as the Nansur would say.

"The Warrior-Prophet," she continued, speaking his name like a well-worn threat, "wishes to know the details of your prep—"

"Is what they say true?" he blurted. "Is it true you once belonged to Achamian? *Drusas* Achamian?" Of course, he knew it was, but for some reason he needed to hear *her* say it.

She stared at him, dumbfounded. Suddenly Eleäzaras could actually hear the silence provided by the black felt walls—every stitch of it.

Tap-tap-tap-tap ... The thing bleeding faceless blood.

"Don't you see the *irony*?" he drawled on. "Surely you do ... I was the one who ordered that Achamian be abducted. I was the one who stranded you with ... with *him*." He snorted. "I'm the reason you're here at all, am I not?"

She didn't sneer—her face was far too beautiful—but her expression burned with contempt nonetheless. "More men," she said evenly, "should take credit for their mistakes."

Eleäzaras tried to laugh, but she continued, speaking as though he were nothing more than a creaking pole or barking dog. Noise. She continued telling *him*—the Grandmaster of the Scarlet Spires!—what he had to do. And why not, when he so obviously had abandoned decisions?

Shimeh was coming, she said. *Shimeh.*

As though names could have teeth.

———— ❧ ————

Rain. It was one of those showers that came sudden upon dusk, fore-shortening the sunlight and within moments casting the pall of woollen night. Water fell in sheets, vanishing into grasses, hissing across bare ground, bouncing across the dark welter of canvas slopes. Gusts made mist of the torrent, and sodden banners thrashed like fish on hooks. Hoarse shouts and curses echoed through the encampment. The delinquent battled to pitch their tents. Some few stripped and stood naked, letting the water cleanse the long, long road from their skin. Esmenet, like so many others, found herself running.

She was thoroughly drenched by the time she found the small pavil-ion. Standing stoic in the downpour, the guardsmen of the Hundred Pillars could only regard her with bemused sympathy. The canvas flap was slicked in cold. Kellhus already awaited her in the warmly illuminated interior—as did Achamian.

They both turned to her, though Achamian looked quickly back to the abomination—the skin-spy she had seized from Eleäzaras. It seemed to be muttering to him.

Rain drummed across the tarpaulin, an ambient and humid roar. Water dripped from dents in the ceiling.

The thing had been chained upright to the centremost post, its wrists hung high, its feet off the rush-covered ground to deny it leverage. Nude, it gleamed polished brown in the lantern light, the colour of the Sansori slave it had replaced. The wages of its captivity marred its skin: burns, welts, and inexplicable curlicues of broken skin, as though a child had scribbled upon it with an awl or knife. Its face disjointed and half clenched, it rolled its head as though dragging a weight. An expression of human astonishment seemed painted across its knuckled digits.

Iyokus had taken his toll, she realized, even in such a short time. She tried not to think of Achamian suffering the man's ministrations ...

"*Chigraaaa ... Ku'urnarcha murkmuk sreeee ...*"

"Some inborn impulse ..." Achamian was saying, as though he resumed an interrupted thought. "Like those caterpillars that curl into a ball whenever touched. The same must happen when they're captured."

Shuddering, Esmenet bent over to squeeze water from her hair, then gently dabbed her face with the inner lining of her surcoat, knowing from the stains that the lampblack about her eyes had scored her cheeks to the hollow. She blinked at the obscene image of the skin-spy, tried to steady her breath. She had to harden herself to such things!

Who are you fooling?

Was this how it was for others of high station? Perpetual fear? From everything, every word, every act, the consequences hung so heavy, swung so far and deep. *The Consult is real.*

"No," Kellhus said. "You're understanding them by reference to men." He shot Achamian a chiding smile that Esmenet found herself returning. "You're assuming they must possess some *self* to hide. But whatever subtlety of character they possess, they steal. Apart from that, they have only the bestial rudiments of self. They're shells only. The mockery of souls."

"More than enough," Achamian replied, grimacing.

The implications were clear: *More than enough to replace us ...*

"More than enough," Kellhus repeated, though his intonations—regret, sorrow, foreboding—made them seem entirely different words.

Still quite sodden, Esmenet took her place by Kellhus's side, making sure that he stood between her and Achamian. Suddenly she found herself at the dizzying centre of his attention.

"The man it replaced," he asked, "what was he?"

She tried to purge the adulation from her look. "One of their slave-soldiers," she replied. "Javreh ... He belonged to the Rhumkar."

"A Weeper," Achamian said, using the sorcerer's pejorative for Chorae archers—those who "shed" the Tears of God. The Rhumkari, Esmenet had been told, were widely considered the most deadly marksmen in all the Three Seas.

She nodded. "That was how he came to Eleäzaras's attention, in fact. The Scarlet Spires encourage liaisons between members of their most elite formations. His lover reported him to his superiors. Apparently they probed his face with pins." She looked to Kellhus with what she had assumed would be pride but felt like longing instead.

"Effective," he said, nodding, "but impractical on any useful scale."

Even though he didn't look at her, he gently squeezed her shoulder as he circled the monstrosity. The space between her and Achamian suddenly seemed ... nude.

"So what do you think?" Achamian asked. "Could we have caught them preparing for an assassination attempt?" Despite her discomfort, Esmenet turned to him, drawn by the quaver in his voice. He met her gaze for one round-eyed moment, then glanced away.

The anxiousness never lifted, she realized, the horror of making mistakes never went away.

Not for people like us.

"They know you bear the Mark now," she said to Kellhus. "They think you vulnerable."

"But the risks ..." Achamian said. "I can't think of anyone the Scarlet Spires scrutinize more than their Rhumkari. This thing's handler had to know as much."

"Indeed," Kellhus said. "It implies desperation."

Unaccountably, she thought of that day in Sumna arguing the significance of Maithanet's offer to the Scarlet Spires with Achamian and Inrau. The first day *men* had listened. "But think," she said, rallying what confidence she could. "Yours is the greatest soul, Kellhus, the most subtle intellect. You've come to thwart the Second Apocalypse. Wouldn't they do anything to deny you the Gnosis? Anything?"

"*Chigraaaaaaaa,*" the thing wheezed. "*Put hara ki zurot ...*"

Achamian glanced at Kellhus before turning to her with uncommon boldness. "I think she's right," he said, gazing with open admiration. "Maybe we can breathe easy, maybe not. Either way, we should probably keep you cloistered as much as possible." Though the patronage of his look should have offended her, there was apology in it as well, a heartbreaking admission.

She could not bear it.

<hr />

Darkness and drumming rain.

The thing lay motionless, though the scent of the guardsmen who doused the lanterns had pulled its phallus long and hard across its belly. The musk of terror.

The shackles chafed, but it felt no pain. The air chilled, but it was not cold.

It knew it had been sacrificed, knew the torments to come, yet it believed without contradiction that its Old Father would not abandon it. It had spoken long with its captive brothers. It knew the numbers that would guard it, the elaborate codes that would be required to see it. It was doomed, without hope of reprieve, and yet it would be saved—two certainties it could mull in what passed for its soul without any offence to consistency.

There was but one measure, one Truth, and it was warm and wet and bloody. The mere thought of it sent spasms through its member. How it yearned! How it *ached*!

It hung in the twilight it called thought, dreamed of mounting enemies ...

When the apportioned time had passed, it jerked its head upright and, still groggy, fumbled to assemble its face. As though out of reflex, it tested its bonds and shackles. Metal whined. Wood creaked.

Then it screamed, though not in any register mannish ears might detect.

"*Yut mirzur!*"

Shrill and piercing, ringing out across the army of Men, who slept huddled against the damp and chill, to where its brothers crouched like jackals in the rain.

"*Yut-yaga mirzur!*"

Two words in Aghurzoi, their holy tongue. "They believe."

From Gim, the Holy War struck across the Jarta Highlands. None could read the stele that marked their passage into Amoteu—though they somehow knew. Their scattered columns snaked across the dark and hazy hillsides, their arms and armour shining bright in the sunlight, their voices raised in booming song. They walked the ways of Holy Amoteu, and though the stacked landscape, with its pastures as flat as lakes across the valley floors, its slopes hunched about shale escarpments, was as novel as any they had crossed over the hard seasons, it seemed they had come *home*. Far more than Xerash, they knew this place. Its names. Its peoples. Its history.

They had been schooled in this earth since childhood.

By mid-afternoon of the following day, the Conriyans had reached the Anothrite Shrine, which lay some three miles off the Herotic Way. Seven men, Ankiriothi under Palatine Ganyatti, were drowned in the rush to bathe in the holy waters. With each day they trudged or rode across some greater threshold, some other marker of their great labour's end. Soon they would be in Besral, where they might glimpse the blood of the Latter Prophet's line in the eyes of the inhabitants. Then the River Hor. Then ...

Shimeh, it seemed, lay impossibly near. Shimeh!

Like a shout on the horizon. A whisper become voice in their hearts.

Meanwhile, a few days' march to the east, the Padirajah himself, Fanayal ab Kascamandri, took to the field with his several hundred Coyauri and hand-picked Grandees, bent on hunting down the man his people called Hurall'arkreet—a name they were forbidden to speak in his presence. Knowing that Athjeäri's numbers had dwindled, he ordered Cinganjehoi to ride in force across the south of the highlands with his Eumarnans. He guessed that the nimble Earl would skirt the Tiger's flank rather than withdraw, following the River Hor beneath the hoof-shaped hills the Kianene called the Madas, or the "Nails." Here he prepared an ambush, using, much to the disgust of the High Heresiarch, Seökti, a full cadre of Cishaurim to assure victory.

The young Earl of Gaenri, however, stood his ground and, though outnumbered ten to one, met Cinganjehoi and his Grandees in pitched battle. Despite the ferocity of the Inrithi, the situation was hopeless. The Red Horse of Gaenri vanished in the tumult. Crying out to his men, Athjeäri spurred toward it, battled his way into the heathen's midst, cowing them with shouts and hammering blows. Without warning, his Mongilean charger faltered, and an adolescent lancer, the son of a Seleukaran Grandee, stabbed him in the face.

Death came swirling down.

The Fanim keened in ululating triumph. Howling in outrage and horror, the Earl's householders charged into the heathen horsemen, who desperately tried to abscond with his body. At a horrible cost the Galeoth retrieved him, hacked and mauled—desecrated.

Bearing his body, the surviving Thanes and Knights of Gaenri fled westward, broken as few men could be. Within hours they encountered a strong band of Kishyati under Lord Soter, who scattered their pursuers. The Gaenri wept to know that deliverance had been so near, yet so very late. They would be called the Twenty, for out of hundreds no more than that number survived.

At the Council of Great and Lesser Names, the death of Athjeäri occasioned solemn remembrance and no little dread. For so long the young Earl had been the eyes of the Holy War, the longest and surest of their many lances. It was a disastrous omen. Since Cumor, the High Cultist of Gilgaöl, was dead, the Warrior-Prophet himself conducted the ceremony declaring him Battle-Celebrant, speaking the Gilgallic Rites without rehearsal.

"Inri Sejenus came after the Apocalypse," he told the grieving caste-nobles, "when the world's wounds had need of healing. I come before, when Men have need of warlike strength. Of all the Hundred Gods, far-striking Gilgaöl burns brightest within me, but not so bright as He burned within Coithus Athjeäri, son of Asilda, daughter of Eryeat, King of the Galeoth."

Afterward, the surviving priests of War washed his body and dressed him in clothing belonging to his recently arrived countrymen, so he wouldn't suffer the indignity of burning in the khalats of his enemy. He was laid upon a great pyre of cedar and set alight—a lone beacon beneath the arch of heaven.

The dirges of the Galeoth echoed long into the night.

The Holy War crossed the last of the Jarta Highlands, their mood sombre, their thoughts now filled with apprehension. Gothyelk joined them mere miles short of Besral, and though the Tydonni were dismayed to learn of Athjeäri's fall, the rest of the Holy War were heartened. Here, on the very land that had birthed the Latter Prophet, the Men of the Tusk had been reunited. Only one last task lay before them.

Then, the morning they wound down the last of the Jartic heights, they came to an abandoned Nansur villa at the end of the Shairizor Plains. Here the Warrior-Prophet called a halt, though hours of daylight remained. The Lords of the Holy War beseeched him to continue, so eager were they to at last lay eyes on the Holy City.

Denying them, he took up residence behind the fortified walls.

Esmenet begged him not to move.

She braced her hands against his hard chest, then, staring into his eyes, she slowly pressed down, taking him to his pelvis. He shuddered, and for a grinding instant she felt herself welded to him in singular bliss. He came, and she followed, bucking about iron and ringing heat, crying out …

"Thank you," she gasped in his ear afterward. "Thank you." It seemed she so rarely touched him anymore.

He sat on the edge of the bed, and though his breath was heavy, she knew he was not winded. He was never winded. He stood, and she watched him walk naked across the polished floor to the elaborate laver carved into the sill of the opposing wall. In the gloom, the tripods painted him in orange and crimson hues. As he washed, his shadow fell bloated across the frescoed walls. She lay watching, admiring his ivory form, savouring the memory of him slick between her thighs.

She hugged tight the sheets, suddenly greedy for what little warmth they offered. She stared across the suite, recognizing in its lines memories of her former home. The Empire. Centuries previous, she knew, some Patridomos had coupled in this very room, his thoughts miraculously innocent of words like "Fanim" or "Consult." He would have recognized "Kianene" perhaps, but only as the name of an obscure desert people. Not just individuals but entire ages, she realized, could be innocent of dreadful things.

She thought of Serwë. The perpetual anxiousness returned.

How had the joy of her new circumstances become so elusive? In her old life, she had often quizzed the priests who came to her, and in her darker moods she had even presumed to school them in what she saw as their hypocrisy. With some, those unlikely to return, she had asked what could be missing from their faith for them to find solace in whores. "Strength," they sometimes answered; several had even wept. But more often than not they denied missing anything at all.

After all, how could they be miserable, when Inri Sejenus had claimed their hearts?

"Many make that mistake," Kellhus said, standing at the side of the bed.

Without thinking, she reached out and grasped his phallus, began stroking its head with her thumb. He knelt on the edge of the bed and his great shadow encompassed her. A nimbus of gold outlined his mane.

Blinking tears, she looked to him. *Please … take me again.*

"They think misery inconsistent with faith," he continued, "and so they start to pretend. They act as others act, thinking they alone have doubts, they alone are weak … In the company of the joyous they become desolate, and hold themselves accountable for their own desolation."

He became hard and long beneath her touch, curved like a strung bow.

"But I have you," she murmured. "I lie with you. I bear your child."

Kellhus smiled, gently disengaged her hand. He leaned forward to kiss her palm. "I'm the *answer*, Esmi. Not the cure."

Why was she crying? What was wrong with her?

"Please," she said, clutching his member once again, as though it were her only purchase, her only possible hold on this godlike man. "Please take me."

This one thing I can give …

"There's more," he said, drawing back the sheets and placing a shadowy hand upon her belly. "So much more."

His look was long and sad. Then he left her for Achamian and the secrets of the Gnosis.

———— ✦ ————

She lay awake for some time, listening to the fragments of arcane voice that surfaced from the stonework about her. Then, the gloom thickening as the braziers failed, she stretched naked across the sheets and drowsed, her soul circling about sorrow after sorrow. The death of Achamian. The death of Mimara.

Nothing stayed dead in her life. Her past least of all.

"Walking between Wards is easy," a voice hummed, "when their author practises other arcana."

She awoke suddenly, if not completely, and through blinking eyes watched yet another man walk to the side of her bed … He was tall, dressed in a black cloak over a silvered brigandine. With relief she realized he was quite handsome. There was compensation of a different sort in—

His shadow had hooked wings.

She tumbled from the far side of the bed, shrank toward the far wall.

"And to think," he said, "that I thought twelve talents an outrage."

She tried to scream, but somehow he was there, pressed like a lover against her, his smooth hand clamped about her mouth. She felt the thick arch of him pressed against her buttocks. When he licked her ear, her body shuddered in treacherous delight.

"How," he gasped, "could the same peach command such different prices, hmm? Can the bruises be washed away? The juices sweetened?" His free hand roamed the planes of her body, and she could feel herself tense, not against him, but for ... as though her desires were as easily moulded as clay.

"Or is it simply the *vendor?*"

It seemed that fire had stolen her breath. "Please!" she gasped.

Take me ...

Stubble chafed the spit-softened skin below her ears. She knew that it was an illusion, but ...

"My children," he said, "only imitate what they see ..."

She whimpered into his suffocating hand—tried to cry out even as her legs slackened to the touch of his probing fingers.

"But *me*," he murmured in a voice that ran tickling over her skin, "I take."

HAPTER TWELVE

HOLY AMOTEU

Death, in the strict sense, cannot be defined, for whatever predicate we, the living, attribute to it necessarily belongs to Life. This means that Death, as a category, behaves in a manner indistinguishable from the Infinite, and from God.
　　　　　　　　　　—AJENCIS, *THE THIRD ANALYTIC OF MEN*

One cannot assume the truth of what one declares without presuming the falsity of all incongruous declarations. Since all men assume the truth of their declarations, this presumption becomes at best ironic and at worst outrageous. Given the infinity of possible claims, who could be so vain as to think their dismal claims true? The tragedy, of course, is that we cannot but make declarations. So it seems we must speak as Gods to converse as Men.
　　　　　　　　　　—HATATIAN, *EXHORTATIONS*

Early Spring, 4112 Year-of-the-Tusk, Amoteu

Incû-Holoinas, the Nonmen had called it. The Ark-of-the-Skies.

After his ancient victory over the Inchoroi, Nil'giccas had ordered a census of the vessel, the results of which were recorded in the *Isûphiryas*, the great annal of the Nonmen. Three thousand cubits in length, over two thousand of which were buried with the prow in the mangled depths. Five hundred in width. Three hundred in depth ...

It was a many-chambered mountain, wrought in a gold-gleaming metal that could not be scored, let alone broken. A city rolled into the warped planes of some misbegotten fish. A ruin that the world could not stomach, that the ages could not digest.

And, as Seswatha and Nau-Cayûti discovered, a great, gilded crypt.

They wandered its abandoned bowels, their steps creaking across the planks of rotted gopher wood that had been used to level the canted walls. Passage after winding passage, chamber after yawning chamber, some as wide as canyons. And everywhere they turned, they found bones—innumerable bones. Most were little more than chalk. They crumbled underfoot, hazing the air about their ankles with dust. The bones of Men or Nonmen, the remains of ancient warriors perhaps, or captives left to starve in the absolute dark. The fused bones of Bashrag, thick as a prophet's staff and grafted together in threes. The bones of Sranc, scattered like those of fish about an abandoned camp. And others they found impossible to identify, bones with singular shapes, some as small as earrings, others as long as a skiff's mast. They gleamed like oiled bronze, and could not be broken, despite the legendary strength of Nau-Cayûti's arms.

Never had Seswatha suffered such a horror, diffuse enough to ignore moment by moment, but possessing a tidal profundity, as though all that he cherished lay exposed, not just to harm, but to some horrifically contrary *truth*. Intellectually he understood the why and the wherefore, even as his viscera quailed. They walked the pits of Min-Uroikas, a place where the Inchoroi, in their wickedness, had gnawed at boundaries between the world and the Outside for thousands of years. And now the howl of their damnation lay near ... very near.

This was a topos, a place where hard lines of reality had become shading. They could hear it in the cavernous echoes. Gibbering screams in the scrape of their steps. Groaning multitudes in the rattle of their coughs. Inhuman roaring in the ring of their voices. And they could see it, as though images had been stitched to their periphery. Many-jawed faces, snapping out of the black. Weeping children ... Achamian lost count of the times he saw Nau-Cayûti abruptly whirl, trying to catch apparitions in the certainty of direct sight.

Where the going was not treacherous, Achamian staggered in Nau-Cayûti's wake, staring thoughtlessly at what little the light of his hooded lantern revealed. The husk of detritus, hanging in place like discarded skin. The walls of gold, their uterine curves skewed to the pitch of the Ark's final descent. The miniature panels of script stamped, it seemed, across every interior surface. Even their reflections, stretched grotesque across the surrounding walls and haloed with an unnatural nimbus of black.

Exhausted to the point of shambling steps and shaking hands, they finally paused, hoping to steal some furtive sleep. Achamian sat huddled in the crotch between bulkheads, at once drowsing and wringing his tight-clutched limbs in horror. He found himself revisiting every footstep, every gaping blackness, every mouldering passage, wondering where his hope had at last guttered out. How could they ever escape such a place? Even if they found what he searched for …

He could feel them, piling labyrinthine into the distances above and below him, the consuming hollows. It seemed hell itself roared inaudible about them.

This place.

"Bones," Nau-Cayûti spat between chattering teeth. "They had to be bones!"

Achamian cringed at the sound of his voice, looked to his forlorn shadow. The Prince hugged himself the same as he, as though shielding nakedness from blowing ice.

"There are some," Achamian whispered, "who argue that the entire Ark is a thing of bone, that vein and skin once pulsed across these walls."

"You mean the Ark once lived?"

Achamian nodded, even as he swallowed for dread. "The Inchoroi called themselves Children of the Ark. The most ancient Nonmen lays refer to them as the Orphans."

"So this thing … this *place* … mothered them?"

Seswatha smiled. "Or fathered … The fact is, we haven't the words for such things. Even if we could pierce the shroud of millennia, I fear this place would remain beyond our understanding."

"But I understand full well," the young Prince said. "You're saying that Golgotterath *is a dead womb.*"

Achamian stared at him, warred with the shame that threatened to break his gaze like lead upon glass.

"I suppose I am."

Nau-Cayûti peered through the surrounding gloom. "Obscenity," he muttered. "Obscenity. Why, Seswatha? Why would they bring war against us?"

"To close the world," seemed all he could muster.

To seal it shut.

The young man leapt forward, seized him about the shoulders. "She lives!" he hissed, his eyes bright with despair and suspicion. "You told me ... You promised!"

"She lives," Achamian lied. He even held the young man's cheek and smiled.

I've doomed us.

"Come," the High King's son said, standing tall in the dark. "I fear the dreams sleep might bring." Expressionless, he resumed picking his way through the black.

After a breath that seemed more ice than air, Seswatha stumbled after him, Nau-Cayûti, heir to Trysë, the greatest light of the dynasty that called itself Anasûrimbor.

The greatest light of Men.

<hr />

Kellhus reached ...

Out from the warmth of skin pressed in fabric, from the memory of arcane song ...

I have walked, Father, crossed the very world.

Ignoring the lacquered furniture, he sat cross-legged on the verandah floor, feeling the exhalation of stuffy rooms war with the cold air descending from the void of night. With sightless eyes he stared across the garden, which was both shadowy and haphazard, terraced and overgrown. The flower beds thronged with devil's claw and nettle. The cherry trees stood in thickets, the last of their delinquent blossoms hanging brown in the cool dew. There was the scent of caustic in the gutters where the slaves had poured wine that had gone to vinegar. There was the sharp musk of feral cats.

He reached …

Through masonry and burnt brick, over haggard slopes, across the Shairizor Plains …

I have followed the Shortest Path.

He saw not ceilings but distributions of hanging weights. He saw not walls but fears, a pageant of real and imagined enemies. He saw not a villa but a long-dead Imperial favour, the relic of a moribund race. Everywhere he turned, he apprehended the pillars among the pilasters, the ground beneath the scuffed floors …

Everywhere he looked, he saw what came before.

Soon, Father. Soon I will darken your door.

Without warning, the drafts became humid with the scent of jasmine and feminine lust. He heard bare feet—*her* bare feet—pad over marble. The bruise of sorcery was plain, almost rank, but he didn't turn to acknowledge her. He remained perfectly still, even when her shadow fell across his back.

"Tell me," she said in ancient Kûniüric, both fluid and precise, "what are the Dûnyain?"

Kellhus bent his thought backward, yoked the legion that was his soul. Likelihood chased likelihood, some to fruition, others to extinction. Esmenet, entwined in boiling light. Esmenet bleeding, broken at his feet. Words, winding and forking, calling out apocalypse and salvation. Of all his encounters since leaving Ishuäl, none demanded more … exactitude.

The Consult had come.

"We are Men," he replied. "Like other Men."

After looming over him for an instant, she turned and sashayed—quite naked—along the portico.

"I," she said as she reclined upon a black bamboo settee, "do not believe you."

In his periphery he saw her palm her breasts, press fingers down the slope of her belly. Her hands clawed her inner thighs. She drew up a knee, then with hooked fingers plumbed the depths of her sex. She cooed in pleasure, as though tasting a rumoured delicacy for the first time. Then, smiling, she withdrew two glistening fingers, raised them to the hollow of her mouth.

She swallowed them.

"Your seed," she murmured, "is *bitter* ..."

It means to provoke me.

He turned to her, drew her into the cauldron of his attention. Fluttering pulse. Shallow breath. Beads of sweat breaking into threads. He could smell her skin tingle in the night air, the residue of salt. He could even see the swelling of her breasts, the heat of her womb. But her thoughts ... It was as though the strings between her face and soul had been severed and refastened to something both sleek and alien.

Something not human.

Kellhus smiled as a father might when trying to teach a gentle lesson to an imperious child. "You cannot kill me," he said. "I'm beyond you."

She smirked. "How could you say this? You know nothing of me or my kind."

Though the roots of her tone and expression escaped him, the incipient sneer was unmistakable. It despised condescension.

It was proud.

She laughed. "Did you think Achamian's stories could prepare you? What the Mandate dream is but a *sliver* of what I've lived—of what I've *seen*. I've walked in the No-God's shadow. I've looked across the void and blotted your world by holding a fingertip before it ... No, you know nothing of me or my kind."

Pupils dilated. Nipples erect. An imperceptible flush about her neck and chest. Fingers curling the downy hair of her sex. Kellhus thought of the Sranc and their rutting frenzy for blood, of Sarcellus hardening to the promise of violence that night about the Galeoth fire ...

So similar.

They were the template of their creations, he realized. They had implanted their own carnal longings, made their own appetite the instrument of their domination.

"So what are you, then?" Kellhus asked. "What are the Inchoroi?"

"We," she cooed, "are a race of lovers."

The expected answer. Recollections cycled through his soul, not explicit and singular, but implicit and innumerable. Everything Achamian had said regarding these abominations ... He slackened his face in the simulacrum of profound sorrow. "And for this you are damned."

Flaring nostrils. A faint quickening of the pulse.

"We were born for damnation's sake," she said with deceptive calm. "Our very nature is our transgression. Look at this exquisite body. The heights of her bosom. The temple of her sex. I climb and I enter because I must." She fingered her pubis as she spoke, clutched tight her left breast. "And for this?" she gasped. "For this I am to heave and scream in lakes of fire? Because of boundaries of skin?"

Kellhus knew not the length or beam of its inhuman intelligence, but he knew it counted grievances. All souls, almost out of necessity, armed themselves with arguments and accusations of misunderstanding. A circle, after all, could have only one centre.

"Denial is the way," Kellhus said. "Boundaries are written into the order of things."

She matched his gaze in a way Esmenet never could, stared as though he were something pathetic and execrable. *It sees what I'm trying to do.*

"But you," she said with breathless sarcasm, "you could rewrite the scripture of my doom, hmm, *Prophet?*" She barked with laughter.

"There is no absolution for your kind."

She had raised her hips to the liquid flutter of her fingers. "Oh, but there isssss ..."

"So you would destroy the world?"

She shuddered, her body afire with arousal. She lowered her buttocks, crossed her legs about her fingers. "To save my soul, hmmm? So long as there are Men, there are crimes. So long as there are crimes, I am damned. Tell me, Dûnyain, what track would you follow? What would you do to *save your soul?*"

Track, it had said ... The Scylvendi.

I should have killed him.

She grinned at his silence. "You already know, don't you? I can feel the memory of you, the sweet ache of having hung from your bronze hook. Rutting is merely the way of things. Hunger. Appetite. Men gild. Men clothe. Men dance their blind pantomimes ... But it all comes to *love* in the end."

She abruptly stood and strolled toward him. Her hands wandered over the patterns the settee had pressed into her skin.

"Love is the Way ... And yet these little demons you call Gods decree otherwise? Dole out their rewards in proportion to our *suffering*? No." She paused before him, her slight form magnificent in the play of gloom and light. "I would save my soul."

She reached out to trace his lips with a shining fingertip. Esmenet, burning for congress. For all his breeding, all his conditioning, Kellhus could feel the ancient instinct rise ... *What kind of game?*

He caught her wrist.

"She doesn't love you," she said, tugging her wrist free. "Not truly."

The words jarred—but why? What was this darkness?

Pain?

"She worships," Kellhus found himself replying, "and has yet to understand the difference."

How many secrets could it see? How much did it know?

"Such a marvel," she said, "what you've accomplished ... So much *stolen.*"

It spoke as though knowing much warranted knowing all. *It tries to lure me, draw me into open discourse.*

"My father has been here thirty years."

"Long enough to require a Holy War to overcome him?"

"Long enough."

She smiled, drew two fingers across her sweaty breastbone. Though her body remained young, her eyes possessed an age not her own. "Again," she simpered, "I don't believe you ... You are your father's *heir*, not his assassin."

And the air reeked of sorcery.

Her hands found him through his robe, began fondling ... Kellhus stood bewildered. He wanted to seize her, thrust deep into her burning centre. He would show her! Show her!

His robe had been hiked—and by his own hand! The cool of her palms whisked across and against his flame.

"Tell meeee," she moaned again and again, and though Kellhus knew these to be her words, he found himself hearing, *Take me ...*

He lifted her with ease, spread her across the settee. He would pin her to the deep! He would plunge and hammer until she howled for release!

Who is your father? a voice whispered.

Still her hands milked him. Never had he suffered anything so sweet. Clutching her legs by the crotch of her knees, he pressed them out and back, bared her moist beauty. The world roared.

Tell me ...

With deft fingers she drew him across her slick fire.

What was happening? How could lightning be sparked in the brush of greased skin? How could moans, exhaled through the lips of a woman, sound so beautiful?

Who is Moënghus? the voice persisted. *What is his intent?*

Kellhus pressed through the fiery veil, into her arching cry ...

"To make manifest," he heard himself gasp, *"the Thousandfold Thought ..."*

For a heartbeat the world stopped. He saw *it*, old and hoary and rotted, staring out from his wife's eyes. The Inchoroi ...

Sorcery!

The Ward was simple—one of the first Achamian had taught him—an ancient Kûniüric Dara, proof against what were called incipient sorceries. His words racked the sultry air. For a moment the light of his eyes shone across her skin.

The darkness faltered and the shadow fell from his soul. He staggered back two steps, his phallus wet and chill and hard. She laughed as he covered himself, her voice guttural with inhuman intonations.

Bait it.

"Across the world in Golgotterath," Kellhus gasped, still stamping out the coals of his manic lust, "the Mangaecca squat about your true flesh, rocking to the mutter of endless Cants. The Synthese is but a node. You are no more than the reflection of a shadow, an image cast upon the water of Esmenet. You possess subtlety, yes, but you haven't the depth to confront me."

Achamian had told him of this creature, that its capacities would be largely restricted to glamours, compulsions, and possessions. The great shout that was its true form, the Schoolman had said, could be heard only as whispers and insinuations at such a distance. *I must own this encounter!*

"Come," she said, springing to her feet, stalking him as he retreated across the verandah, "kill me, then. Strike me down!"

A mask of counterfeit horror. Once again Kellhus unlaced the bindings of selfhood, rolled open the inner surfaces of his soul. Once again he reached ...

The past possessed weight. Where the young were like flotsam, forever drawn spinning into the current of passing events, the old were like stone. The proverbs and parables spoke of sobriety, restraint, but more than anything it was *boredom* that rendered the aged immune to the press of events. Repetition, not enlightenment, was the secret of their detachment. How did one move a soul that had witnessed all the world's permutations?

"But you *can't*," she cackled, "can you? Look upon this pretty shell ... these lips, these eyes, this cunny. I am *what you love* ..."

What was more, the Scylvendi had schooled it. The non sequiturs. The sudden questions. The thing had made *whim* the principle of its action—just as Cnaiür had ...

Kellhus reached.

"After all," she said, "what man would strike down his wife?"

He drew his sword, Enshoiya, pressed its point against the white tile floor between them. "A Dûnyain," he replied.

She stopped above the blade, close enough to pinch the tip between the toes of her right foot. She glared with ancient fury. "I am Aurang. Tyranny! A son of the void you call Heaven ... I am Inchoroi, a raper of *thousands*! I am he who would tear this world down. Strike, Anasûrimbor!"

Kellhus reached ...

... and saw himself through the obscenity's eyes, the enigma who would draw out his father, Moënghus. Kellhus reached, though with fingers lacking tips, palms without heat. He reached and he grasped ...

A soul that had snaked across all the world's ages, taking lover after lover, exulting in degradation, spilling seed across innumerable dead. The Nonmen of Ishoriol. The Norsirai of Trysë and Sauglish. Warring, endlessly warring, to forestall damnation ...

A race with a hundred names for the vagaries of ejaculation, who had silenced all compassion, all pity, to better savour the reckless chorus of their lusts. Stalking, endlessly stalking, the world they would make their shrieking harem ...

A life so old that only *he*, Anasûrimbor Kellhus, was unprecedented. Only the Dûnyain were new.

Who were these Men—these *Anasûrimbor!*—who hailed from Golgotterath's very shadow? who could see through masks of skin? who could subvert ancient faiths? who could enslave Holy Wars with nothing more than words and glances?

Who bore the name of their ancient foe ...

And Kellhus realized there was only one question here: Who were the Dûnyain?

They fear us, Father.

"Strike!" Esmenet cried, her arms back, her shining breasts pressed forward.

And he *did* strike, though with the flat of his palm. Esmenet sailed backward, rolled nude across the tiles.

"The No-God," he said, advancing, "he speaks to me in my dreams."

"I," Esmenet replied, spitting blood as she pressed herself from the floor, "don't believe you."

Kellhus seized the black maul of her hair, heaved her to her feet. He hissed into her ear. "He says that *you* failed him on the Plains of Mengedda!"

"Lies! Lies!"

"He comes, Warlord. For this world ... for *you!*"

"Strike me again," she whispered. *"Please ..."*

He threw her back to the floor. She writhed at his feet, thrusting her sex like an accusatory finger. *"Fuck me,"* she whispered. *"Fuck me."*

But the lustful glamour fell from him, deflected by the Dara Ward. He stood unmoved.

"Your secrets have been uncovered," he said in high oratorical tones. "Your agents are scattered, your designs overthrown ... You've *been defeated*, Warlord."

And for the first time she replied according to his anticipations.

"Ahhhh ... but there are as many battlefields as there are moments, Dûnyain."

Pause. The cycling of possibilities.

"You're a distraction ..." Kellhus said.

Esmenet herself had said it: they would do anything to deny him the Gnosis.

Her eyes flared white, and for an instant she looked like a leering Nilnameshi demon. A strange and preternatural laughter filtered through the overgrown garden, twined like snakes across the open spaces.

"Achamian," Kellhus whispered.

"Is already dead," the thing sneered. It rolled her head like a doll, then slumped across the cold stone.

———∞∞∞———

The sound of clinking stone, scarcely audible over the urgent counterpoint of voices in the garden beyond the iron-fretted windows.

A single plate of marble ran across the threshold of what once, back when the Nansur had ruled Amoteu, had been an ancestor shrine. As though of its own volition, it tipped upright then slipped aside, revealing a black slot scarcely large enough to fit a Tydonni shield. A foot swung out, its toes popping as they stretched. Rising like a stalk, the knee and thigh followed. Another foot appeared, then a hand, until all three limbs were bent and braced about the aperture like some deformed spider.

Then slowly, deliberately, the figure of a woman emerged, as though drawn from the pages of a book.

Fanashila.

She danced across the pallid floors, encountered a bleary-eyed Opsara shuffling back to the nursery from the latrine. She broke her neck, then paused, breathing, willing her erection to subside. At some point crossing shadows, she became Esmenet. It pressed her cheek against the bronze-strapped mahogany of his chamber door, heard nothing save the deep breathing of its quarry. The air fairly sang with residual odours: garlic from the kitchens, rotted teeth, armpits and anuses …

Soot, myrrh, and sandalwood.

It retrieved the Chorae from a pocket in her linen shift, then with deft movements tied it against her throat with leather string. It pressed open the door, leaning hard on the handle to silence the unoiled hinges. It had hoped to find him asleep, but of course his Wards had awakened him.

It stood at the dark entrance, her false face swollen with tears. Moonlight cast an oblong of pale squares across the floor at her feet. He was sitting in his bed, alarmed and ashen-faced. Though he peered, it could see him quite clearly: the astonished eyes, the thoughtful brow, the five white streaks of his beard.

He reeked of terror.

"Esmi?" he hissed. "Esmi? Is that you?"

Hunching its shoulders, it pulled her arms from the linen shift so that it fell to the cord tied about her waist. She heard his breath catch at the sight of her breasts.

"Esmi! What are you doing?"

"I need you, Akka ..."

"The Chorae about your throat ... I thought they were forbidden."

"Kellhus asked that I wear it."

"Please ... remove it."

Raising her arms to the back of her neck, she untied it, let it clatter to the floor. She stepped into the pale, fretted light, so that it mapped the contours of her stolen body. It knew she was a thing of beauty. "Akka," it whispered. "Love me, Akka ..."

"No ... this is wrong! He'll know, Esmi. He'll know!"

"He already knows," it said, crawling onto the foot of his bed.

She could smell his hammering heart, the promise of hot blood. There was such fear in him!

"*Please*," she gasped, drawing her breasts over the outline of his knees and thighs. His face so near, hanging in darkness.

The blow struck true, through the silken sheets, through her sternum, her heart and spine. Even still, it managed to heave forward across the blade, to strike his windpipe. And as the blackness swirled down, it saw him through the deceiving glamour, Captain Heörsa, thrashing in his very own death throes ...

The Dûnyain had outwitted them.

Traps within traps, the thing called Esmenet carelessly thought. *So beautiful ...*

In what passed for its dying soul.

Achamian ...

The lantern fell to the rotted floor, light rolled across heaped bones, and Seswatha felt himself lifted and thrown back into the blackness. Something hard cracked against the base of his skull. The world darkened, until all he could see was his student's raving face.

"Where is she?" Nau-Cayûti cried. "Where?"

And all he could think of was his voice pealing through the inhuman spaces, reaching, filtering—sealing their doom. They walked the halls of Golgotterath. Golgotterath!

Achamian! It's Zin …

"You lied!"

"No!" Achamian cried, shielding his eyes against the light hanging above him. "Listen! Listen!"

But it was Proyas before him, his face drawn, grave with the utter absence of expression.

"I'm sorry, old tutor," the Prince said, "but it's Zin … He's calling for you."

Without any real comprehension, he cast his blankets aside and bolted from his cot. For an instant he teetered: unlike the Incû-Holoinas, the canvas walls of the Prince's pavilion were square with the ground. Proyas steadied him, and they shared a long and sombre look. For so long the Marshal of Attrempus had stood at their borderlands, guarding the frontier across which the doubt of the one had warred with the certainty of the other. It seemed terrifying to stand face to face without him. But it also seemed true, a kind of human proof.

They had always stood this near, Achamian realized; they had merely stared off in different directions. Without warning, he found himself clasping the younger man's hand. It was not warm, but it seemed so very alive.

"I did not mean to disappoint you," Proyas murmured.

Achamian swallowed.

Only when things were broken did their meaning become clear.

Kellhus held her shaking in their bed.

"I do love you!" Esmenet cried. "I do!"

Shouts still echoed through the corridors. The Hundred Pillars, Kellhus knew, fanned across the grounds, searching for the Inchoroi's Synthese. But they would find nothing. Save for Captain Heörsa's death, everything had transpired as he'd expected. Aurang had sought only to deny him the Gnosis, not his life. So long as they knew nothing of the Dûnyain, the Consult were trapped in the pincers of a paradox: the more they needed to kill him, the more they needed to *learn* him—and to find his father.

Which was why Achamian had been their target—not Kellhus.

Kellhus hadn't known whether Esmenet would recall her possession, but the instant her eyes fluttered open, he'd realized that she not only remembered, she remembered as though *she herself* had spoken what was spoken, said what was said. There had been many hard words.

"I *do* love you," she wept.

"Yes," he replied, his voice far deeper, far wider, than she could possibly hear.

Quivering lips. Eyes parsed between horror and remorse. Panting breath. "But you said! *You said!*"

"Only," he lied, "what needed to be heard, Esmi. Nothing more."

"You have to believe me!"

"I do, Esmi … I do believe."

She clutched her cheeks, scratched welts across them. "Always the whore! Why must I always be the whore?"

He looked through her, past her bewildered hurt, down to the beatings and the abuse, to the betrayals, and beyond, out to a world of rank lust, shaped by the hammers of custom, girded with scripture, scaled by ancient legacies of sentiment and belief. Her womb had cursed her, even as it made her what she was. Immortality and bliss—this was the living promise all women bore between their thighs. Strong sons and gasping climax. If what men called truth were ever the hostage of their desires, how could they fail to make slaves of their women? To hide them like hoarded gold. To feast on them like melons. To discard them like rinds.

Was this not why he used her? The promise of sons in her hips?

Dûnyain sons.

Her eyes were like silver spoons in the gloom, shimmering with scarcely held waters. He looked through them and saw so much he could never undo …

"Hold me," she whispered. "Hold me, please."

Like so many others, she bore his toll. And it was only beginning …

Achamian had always thought it strange that so little was felt at the appropriate moment—only afterward, and even then it never seemed … proper.

When the Pederisk, the title given to Mandate Schoolmen devoted to finding the Few among Nron's children, had come to their hovel bent on taking Achamian—a boy with "great promise"—to Atyersus, Achamian's father had denied him—not for love of his son, Achamian would later decide, but for reasons both more pragmatic and more principled. Achamian had proven himself a quick study at sea, one who need not be hit as often as the others. And more importantly, Achamian was *his* son, and none other might have him.

The Pederisk, a willowy man with a face as hard and weathered as any mariner's, was neither surprised nor impressed by his father's drunken defiance. Achamian would never forget the way his smell— rosewater and jasmine—had owned the sour room. His father became violent, and with a dreadful air of routine the Schoolman's men-at-arms began beating him. Achamian's mother had shrieked. His brothers and sisters had squalled. But a strange coldness had settled upon Achamian, the monolithic selfishness of which only children and madmen are sometimes capable.

He had gloated.

Before that day, Achamian would never have believed his father could be so easily broken. For children, hard-hearted fathers were elemental, more deity than human. As judges, they seemed to stand beyond all possible judgement. Witnessing the humiliation of his father produced the first truly sorrowful day of his life—as well as a day of triumph. To see the great breaker broken ... How couldn't this transform the proportions of a young boy's world?

"Damnation!" his father had screeched. "Hell has come for you, boy! *Hell!*"

Only afterward, as they trundled up the coast in the Schoolman's cart, would he cry, overwhelmed by loss and delinquent regret.

Far, far too late.

"I see it, Akka ..." A voice barely more than a rasp. Xinemus. "Where I'm going. I see it now."

"And what do you see?" Humour them. This was what one did with the grievously ill ...

"Nothing."

"Shush. I'll describe it all to you. The Many-Eyed Walls. The First

Temple. The Sacred Heights. I'll be your eyes, Zin. You'll see Shimeh through me."

Through the eyes of a sorcerer.

Proyas's slaves had used screens to mark off an ad hoc sickroom for the Marshal of Attrempus. Embroidered pheasants cavorted across them, their tail feathers twining into the very trees they perched upon. Only two lanterns provided illumination, both of them hooded in blue cloth at the insistence of the physician-priests. Apparently Akkeägni was more discriminating with his colours than with his victims ... The result was peculiar, even eerie—something between firelight and moonlight. Everything in the spare chamber—the sagging canvas ceilings, the rush-matted ground, the blankets hanging from the Marshal's cot—possessed the nauseous pall of sickness.

Achamian knelt at the side of the cot, gently wiping his friend's brow with a wetted cloth. He dabbed the water pooled in his sockets, more because of the unnerving way it glinted in the gloom—like liquid eyes—than for the comfort of his friend.

Yet again he found himself at war with the urge to flee. Of all the unclean spirits, few were as terrifying or bloodthirsty as those belonging to dread Disease. Pulma had possessed him, the physician-priests had said, one of the most fearsome of Akkeägni's innumerable demons.

The lung-plague.

The Marshal jerked and convulsed. He arched across his cot as though his body were a bow taken up and drawn by something unseen. He made noises that could only be described as ... unmanly. Achamian clutched his bearded cheek, whispered words he could not recall afterward. Then, just as abruptly, Xinemus went slack. Once again his limbs were lost between the folds of his blankets.

Achamian wiped the sweat from the quivering planes of his face. "Shush," he whispered between the man's clawing breaths. "Shush ..."

"How the rules," the Marshal coughed, "have changed ..."

"What do you mean?"

"The game between us ... benjuka."

Achamian still had no clue as to his meaning, but he could think of nothing to say. It seemed a ... sin somehow, to question him twice.

"Remember how it was?" Xinemus asked. "The way you would wait in the dark while I took council with the Great?"

"Yes ... I remember."

"Now it's I who wait."

Again Achamian couldn't think of anything to say. It was as though words had come to their end, to the point where only impotence and travesty could follow. Even his thoughts prickled.

"Did you?" the Marshal abruptly asked.

"Did I what?"

"Did you ever win?"

"Benjuka?" Achamian blinked, stretched his face into an aching smile. "Not against you, Zin ... But someday ..."

"I think not."

"And why's that?" He hesitated, fearful of what answer this question might elicit.

"Because you try too hard," Xinemus said. "And when the plate doesn't yield—" He coughed, convulsed about pustulate lungs.

Achamian repeated, "When the plate doesn't yield ..." He humoured him no longer. *Selfish fool!*

"I see nothing," the Marshal gasped. "Sweet Sejenus! I see noth—" He cried out as though drowning in clotted blood, gagged, and thrashed. The sick-sweet flush of bowel filled the room.

Then he went slack. For several heartbeats all Achamian could do was stare. Without his eyes Xinemus seemed so ... *sealed in.*

"Zin!"

His friend's mouth worked soundlessly. Madly, Achamian thought of the fish heads heaped beneath his father's gutting table ... Mouths without stomachs, opening and closing, as slow as milkweed waving in the breeze.

"Leave ... me ..." his friend gasped. "Leave me ... be ..."

"This is no time for pride, you fool!"

"*Nooooo,*" the Marshal of Attrempus whispered. "This ... is ... the ... only ..."

And then it happened. One moment his complexion was mottled by the pallid exertions only the dying can know, and then, as quickly as cloth soaking water, it went purple-grey. A cooler air settled through the canvas spaces, the quiet of utterly inert things. Lice thronged from Xinemus's scalp onto his brow, across his waxy face. Achamian brushed at them, twitched them away with the numb fastidiousness of those who deny death by acting otherwise.

He clutched his friend's hand, began kissing his fingers. "In the morning Proyas and I will take you to the river," he said breathlessly. "Bathe you …"

Whining silence.

It seemed that his heart slowed, hesitated, like a boy unsure of the sincerity of his father's permission. His lips tightened, and a great void slowly opened in his chest, at first tugging and then lunging—demanding that he *breathe*.

With a shameful reluctance, he watched him in the darkness, Krijates Xinemus, this man who would be his older brother, this corpse with the face of an only friend. The first of the lice found him—Achamian could feel them. Like the tickle of insight.

He breathed, drew the rank air deep. And though his cry reached out across the plains, it fell far short of Shimeh.

———— ❧ ————

He pondered the plate, rubbing his hands together for warmth. Xinemus taunted him with a nasty chuckle.

"Always so dour when you play benjuka."

"It's a wretched game."

"You say that only because you try too hard."

"No. I say that because I lose."

With an air of chagrin, he moved the only stone among his silver pieces—a replacement for a piece stolen, or so Xinemus claimed, by one of his slaves. Another aggravation. Though pieces were nothing more than how they were used, the stone impoverished his play somehow, broke the miserly spell of a complete set.

Why do I get the stone?

———— ❧ ————

Achamian did not sleep that night.

One of the Hundred Pillars had come, summoning both him and Proyas to the villa in the encampment's heart. Apparently there had been some kind of attempt on Kellhus's life. Achamian refused outright. When Proyas made ready to leave, Achamian reproached him with words so harsh, so blasphemous, that the waiting Guardsman drew his sword, aghast. Achamian fled before the Prince could retort.

For a time he wandered the dark ways of the Holy War, thinking of the way the dew made his sandalled feet ache, of how the Nail of Heaven never moved, of the way the Men of the Tusk all slumbered beneath tents of Kianene manufacture, their differences, their heritages, shed like rubbish on the long path to redemption. He thought of everything, anything, save that which might drive the wedges of madness deeper.

Then, as dawn brightened over the promise of Shimeh in the east, he made his way back to the fortified villa. He climbed the slopes and passed unchallenged through the gates, and finally found himself walking the overgrown garden, heedless of the burrs and claws that snarled his robes, of the nettles that inflamed his skin. He waited below the verandah that fronted the main apartments—where his wife moaned about the cock of the man he worshipped.

He waited for the Warrior-Prophet.

A lark called out from the dried stump of a cedar. Fiddle-necks, their orange blooms bent along hairy stems, trembled in the breeze.

He drowsed, dreamed of Golgotterath.

"Akka?" a blessed voice said as though from nowhere. "You look horrible."

Achamian found himself instantly awake, thinking, *Where is she? I need her!*

"She sleeps," Kellhus said. "She suffered grievously last night ... much as you did."

The Warrior-Prophet stood above him, his flaxen hair and white gown glaring in the morning sunlight. Achamian blinked at his figure. Despite the beard, the resemblance to Nau-Cayûti, his ancient cousin, was unmistakable.

For some reason Achamian felt his fury and resolve crumble, as a child's might before a mother or a father. A grimace stole across his face.

"Why?" he croaked. At first he feared the man would misunderstand him, think that he asked after Esmenet, and his monstrous decision to use her as a tool to sound the Consult.

"Our end does not give meaning to our life, Akka. The manner of Zin's de—"

"No!" he cried, leaping to his feet. "Why didn't you *heal him?*"

For the briefest instant Kellhus seemed taken aback—but then all was as it should be. Comfort glittered in his eyes. Understanding shouted from the line of his smile, sad and faint.

Achamian's ears roared with such violence that he heard nothing of Kellhus's reply, save that it was false. He literally stumbled, such was the force of the revelation. Strong hands drew him upright. Kellhus—grasping him by the shoulders, staring intently into his face. But the intimacy, that eroticism of awe that had braced all their exchanges, had vanished. A vacancy, cold and heartless, shouted from the beloved face.

How?

And somehow, unaccountably, Achamian knew that he was truly *awake*—perhaps for the very first time. No longer was he that hapless child in this man's gaze.

Achamian pulled away—not horrified, just ... blank.

"What are you?"

Kellhus's gaze did not falter. "You flinch from me, Akka ... Why?"

"You are *not* a prophet! *What are you?*"

The transformation of his expression was subtle enough that someone standing three or more paces away would have missed it, but for Achamian it was enough to send him stumbling back in horror. As one, Kellhus's every facial nuance went *dead*—utterly dead.

Then, in a voice as cold as winter slate:

"I am the Truth."

"Truth?" Achamian struggled to regain his composure, but the horror spilled through him, unlooping like entrails. He fought for his breath, to see past the glaring sky, to hear through the buzzing world. "Tru—"

An iron grip around his throat. His head yanked back, his face thrust to the sun, like a doll hoisted to the sky. He hadn't even seen Kellhus move!

"Look," the dead voice said. No strain. Nothing of this physical cruelty in his voice. Nothing.

The sun speared Achamian's eyes, seemed blinding even with them clenched shut.

"Look," without added emphasis, except for the finger which caressed his trachea in such a way that bile began to burn the back of his throat.

"*Can't ... see ...*"

Abruptly he dropped face forward against the ground. Before he'd regained his knees, he'd begun his arcane muttering. He knew his capabilities. He knew he could destroy him still.

But the voice would not relent.

"Does this mean the sun is empty?"

Achamian paused, turned his face from the grass and scree, squinted at the figure looming above.

"*Do you think,*" a voice crackled across every possibility of hearing, "*the God would be anything other than remote?*"

Achamian lowered his forehead to the biting weeds. Everything spinning, slumping ...

"*Or do I lie, in that, since I am all souls, I choose the one that will turn the most hearts?*"

And tears answered. *Don't hit me ... Please, Papa, please. Don't—*

"*Or should it speak of treachery that my purposes move beyond yours? Encompass yours?*"

He raised shaking hands to his ears. *I'll be good! I swear!* He fell to his side, sobbed against hard, bristling earth. The road so long. So painful. The hunger ... Inrau ... Xinemus dead.

Dead.

Because of me! Oh, dear God ...

The Warrior-Prophet sat next to him as he wept, gently holding one of his hands, his face impassive, eyes closed and turned to the sun.

"Tomorrow," he said, "we march on Shimeh."

CHAPTER THIRTEEN

SHIMEH

What frightens me when I travel is not that so many men possess customs and creeds so different from my own. Nay, what frightens me is that they think them as natural and as obvious as I think my own.

—SERATANTAS III, *SUMNI MEDITATIONS*

A return to a place never seen. Always is it thus, when we understand what we cannot speak.

—PROTATHIS, *ONE HUNDRED HEAVENS*

Spring, 4112 Year-of-the-Tusk, Atyersus

Shouts of consternation drew Nautzera to the unshuttered colonnade that adjoined the Rudiments Library, high above the western ramparts of Atyersus, where students often gathered on mild and sunny days. Several young initiates stared and pointed across the dark straits, along with Marmian, an Auditor on furlough from their Mission in Oswenta. Nautzera waved them away, leaned out over the stone balustrade. As tired as his eyes were, he could see the cause of the commotion quite clearly: fifteen yellow-painted galleys anchoring in the straits, poised across the cerulean blue less than a mile from the mouth of Atyersus's scarped

262

harbour. Distant seamen climbed the rigging, lowering beams on sails adorned with Tusks, long and vertical and golden.

Atyersus was thrown into an uproar. Initiates and officers bawled commands. The fortress's soldiery stamped down the narrow corridors, rushing to man far-flung walls and turrets. Nautzera joined the other members of the Quorum on the heights of the Comoranth Tower, where they could view the fleet of interlopers without obstruction. They made a ludicrous sight: seven old men—two in nightshirts, one still wearing an ink-stained scriptor's apron, and the rest, like Nautzera, in full ceremonial garb—waving liver-spotted hands as they bickered back and forth. Most of them assumed the obvious: that the ships were part of a blockade meant to prevent their imminent departure for Shimeh. But just who were they? The colours and tusks suggested the Thousand Temples ... Did the Shrial ingrates think themselves a match for the *Gnosis*?

Simas counselled immediate attack. "As far as we know," he cried, "the Second Apocalypse has already begun! No matter who owns the deed to these galleys, we can only assume that the Consult commands them. We've always known they would attempt to destroy us in the opening days. And now, with the Harbinger, this so-called Warrior-Prophet ... *Think*, my brothers. What would the Consult do? Wouldn't they risk anything to prevent us from joining the Holy War? We must strike!"

But Nautzera wasn't so rash. "To act in ignorance," he fairly screeched, "is always folly, whether at war or not!"

Ultimately, however, word that a launch rowed toward shore settled the matter. Despite his protestations, Simas was overruled. The Quorum agreed they should at least treat with the strangers. Slaves hastened to make ready their litters, and soon Nautzera was staring at the mysterious vessels through the veils of his palanquin. The slaves fairly ran down the switchback road running from Atyersus's main gate to the stone quays that jutted into the fortress's small natural harbour.

Surrounded by confused throngs of guards and adepts, the Quorum assembled on the ancient stone of the one jetty not crowded with berthed ships. The launch had drawn near enough for them to cluck in astonishment. They traded rapid conjectures, but it was clear that no one knew what was happening. Their voices trailed as the dock men caught the ropes thrown from the approaching launch. The rowers pulled their oars skyward; the boat was pulled in and secured. Nautzera and the others stood rigid with shock. Complete silence fell across the surrounding copse of masts and rigging. The Nroni seamen crowding the railings of the neighbouring ships stared down in wonder, not only at their sorcerous masters, but at the retinue that climbed from the launch.

The Quorum stood, seven old scowling men, watching as their visitors assembled on the tip of the finger of stone. Expressionless, their silvered helms and chain bright in the sun, five Shrial Knights formed a wordless line, screening the figures behind. Their Chorae murmured dark beneath their white silk surcoats. Of those behind, Nautzera could only glimpse faces—most of them clean-shaven. Then an imposing black-bearded figure pressed past the Knights into the Quorum's astonished view. With the exception of Nautzera, he loomed over all of them, dressed in a stately gown of white that had been hemmed about the collar and sleeves with golden tusks the size of finger bones. Though his face seemed middle-aged, his blue eyes were surprisingly young. He too wore a Chorae against his breast.

"Holy Shriah," Nautzera said evenly.

Maithanet *here?*

Smiling with radiant warmth, the man studied their faces, raised his eyes to the dark bastions of Atyersus behind them ... He lunged forward. Then somehow—his movement had been too quick for surprised eyes to comprehend—he was holding Simas by the base of the skull.

The air was riven with sorcerous muttering. Eyes flared with Gnostic light. Wards whisked into shimmering existence. Almost as one, the members of the Quorum fell into defensive posture. Dust and grit trailed down the sloped sides of the jetty.

Simas had gone limp as a kitten, his white-haired head lolling against the fist bunched at the back of his neck. The Shriah seemed to hold him with impossible strength.

"Release him!" Yatiskeres cried, scrambling back with the others.

Maithanet spoke as though showing them how to slaughter rabbits. "If you pinch them here," he said, jerking the old man as if in emphasis, "they are thoroughly incapacitated."

"Releas—"

"Release him!"

"What's this madness?" Nautzera exclaimed. He alone hadn't cast any

Wards. Neither had he retreated down the jetty with the others. In fact he stepped *between* the Shriah and his fellow Schoolman, as though interposing himself to protect the man.

"And if you *wait*," Maithanet continued, now staring directly at Nautzera, "if you wait, their true aspect will be revealed."

The old sorcerer struggled for his breath. There was something about the way Simas shook. Something not *old*. Something not ...

"He's killing hi—"

"Silence!" Nautzera shouted.

"We learned of this one through our interrogations of the others," Maithanet said, his voice possessing a resonance that brushed aside the alarmed prattle. "It's an accident, an anomaly that, thankfully, its architects have been unable to recreate."

It?

"What are you saying?" Nautzera cried.

Thrashing slack limbs, the thing called Simas began howling in a hundred lunatic voices. Maithanet braced his feet, rocked like a fisherman holding a twisting shark. Nautzera stumbled back, his hands raised in Warding. With abject horror, he watched the man's oh-so-familiar face crack open, clutch at the skies with hooked digits.

"A skin-spy with the ability to work sorcery," the Shriah of the Thousand Temples said, grimacing with exertion. "A skin-spy with a soul."

And the grand old sorcerer realized he had known all along.

Spring, 4112 Year-of-the-Tusk, Shimeh

Ecstatic shouts rang out over the whisk and thud of galloping horsemen. Someone let go a long, low whistle. Proyas reined his horse to a halt at the fore of his household knights. His face blank in the manner of knotted stomachs, he stared dumbstruck at the eastern horizon.

At first he struggled with a dismaying sense of banality. For days now he'd known this vista lay just beyond the horizon. Unseen, it had seemed something at once dark and golden, a monument so terrible with holiness that he could do naught but fall on his belly when confronted by its aspect. But now ...

He felt no urge to fall. In fact he felt no urge to do anything whatsoever, save to breathe and to watch. When he glanced at his fellow Men of the Tusk, they seemed little more than brigands appraising a victim, or wolves watching the herd that would fatten them for winters to come. He found himself wondering if this was always the way when dreams confronted the actuality that conceived them. He felt the customary wonder of sighting a great city from a great distance, he supposed, the sense of standing far from the carnival of brick and humanity that would soon encompass him. Nothing more.

The tears struck before the passion. He tasted them first. When he reached up to wipe his lips, the length and thickness of his beard surprised his hand. Where was Xinemus? He'd promised to describe …

His shoulders hitched in silent sobs. Sky and city reeled through broken sunlight. He clutched tight his saddle's iron pommel. He thumbed the frayed knots that secured his canteen.

Finally he cleared his throat, blinked, and looked about. He heard and saw other men weeping. He sighted a sunburned man farther down the line of accumulating Inrithi, kneeling shirtless in the grasses with his arms thrown wide, screaming at the city as though confessing hatred to a tyrannical father.

"Sweet God of Gods," someone behind Proyas began intoning, "Who walk among us … Innumerable are your hallowed names."

The words swelled with deep-throated resonance, became ever more implacable and embalming as horseman after horseman took them up. Soon the slopes thrummed with cracked voices. They were the faithful, come with arms to undo long centuries of wickedness. They were the Men of the Tusk, bereaved and heartbroken, laying eyes on the ground of countless fatal oaths … How many brothers? How many fathers and sons?

"*May your bread silence our daily hunger …*"

Proyas joined them in their prayer, even as he grasped the reason for his turmoil. They were the swords of the Warrior-Prophet, he realized, and this was the city of Inri Sejenus. Moves had been made, and rules had been changed. Kellhus and the Circumfixion had hamstrung all the old points and purposes. So here they stood, signatories to an obsolete indenture, celebrating a destination that had become a waystation …

And no one knew what it meant.

"Judge us not according to our trespasses ..."

Shimeh.

"But according to our temptations ..."

Shimeh at long last.

If she was not holy before, Proyas decided, Xinemus and all the uncounted dead had made her such. There was no working back from what was final.

The Ainoni of Moserothu stood scattered across the shallow heights, watching their Palatine, the hard-hearted Uranyanka, lead the Warrior-Prophet to the best vantage. The two men paused beside a wall so ancient that grasses thronged along its broken crest—one of several ruined mausoleums set across the hillside.

Before them stretched the Plains of Shairizor, still blackened from the recent burning of fields and plantations. The River Jeshimal bisected the distances, winding like a rope into the violet and mauve foothills of the Betmulla Mountains. A great city occupied the heart of the plain, gathered about a pair of promontories overlooking the Meneanor. Her curtain walls, which had been tiled in white, gleamed in the sunlight. Great eyes, each as tall as a tree, marred their circuit and seemed to stare back at them.

Shimeh. The Sacred City of the Latter Prophet. At long last.

Some fell to their knees, bawling like children. But most simply stared, their faces blank.

Names were like baskets. Usually they came to men already filled, with refuse, banalities, and valuables mixed in various measures. But sometimes the passage of events overthrew them. Sometimes they came to bear different burdens. Heavier things. Darker things.

Shimeh was such a name.

From the four corners of Eärwa they had come. They had hungered about the walls of Momemn. They had survived the great bloodlettings of Mengedda and Anwurat. They had cleansed Shigek with their fury, walked the furnace plains of the Great Carathay. They had endured pestilence, starvation, and insurrection. They had nearly murdered the

God's own Prophet. Now, at last, they apprehended the *purpose* of their heartbreaking labour.

For the pious and the sentimental, this was a moment of consummation. But for those scarred by their innumerable trials, this could only be a time of *measure*. What could be worth what they had suffered? What could repay what they had exacted? This place? This chalk-white city?

Shimeh?

Somewhere, somehow, the name had been overturned.

But as always, the words of the Warrior-Prophet circulated among them. "This," he was said to have said, "is not your destination. It's your*destiny.*"

Parties of knights struck across the plain, while more and more Men of the Tusk crowded the hillside. Soon the entire Holy War stood arrayed along the summits, staring and pointing.

There, to the south, was the Shrine of Azoroa, where Inri Sejenus had given the first of his sermons. And there was the High Round, the great fortress raised by Triamarius II, its black concentric walls overlooking the Meneanor. And to its right, with its ochre stone and cyclopean pillars, was the Mokhal Palace, the ancient seat of the Amoti Kings. And that line, running from the hills to the city across the Shairizor Plain, marked the remnants of the Skiluran Aqueduct, named after the most gluttonous of Amoteu's Nansur rulers.

And there, on the Juterum, the Holy Heights, stood the First Temple, the great circular gallery of columns that marked the site of the Latter Prophet's Ascension. And to its right, with a gold-flaring dome above a façade of stacked colonnades, was the dread Ctesarat, the cancer they had come to excise ...

The great tabernacle of the Cishaurim.

Only as the sun drew their shadows to the footings of the many-eyed walls did they abandon the hillsides to strike camp on the plain below. Few slept that night, such was their confusion. Such was their wonder.

Spring, 4112 Year-of-the-Tusk, Amoteu

Every Biaxi breathing, the Exalt-General—the *Emperor*—had said. *I shall burn you all alive.*

General Biaxi Sompas found himself obsessing over these words. Would he do such a thing? The answer to that question was obvious. Ikurei Conphas was capable of anything—one need only spend a day in his company to know that. And there was always Martemus to remember. But *could* he? That was the question. Old Xerius would never dare. He understood, even respected, the power of House Biaxi. There would be uproar in the Houses of the Congregate, even insurrection. If one House could be scratched from the Lines, then any House could be.

Besides, the Ikureis had enough enemies as it was ... Conphas wouldn't dare!

But he would. Sompas could feel it in his bones. Conphas would dare. And what was more, the other Houses would simply stand by and watch. Who would raise arms against the *Lion of Kiyuth*? Sweet Sejenus, the Army had chosen him over a *prophet*.

No. No. He did the right thing, the only thing he could do ... under the circumstances.

"We've come too far east," Captain Agnaras said in his dour, matter-of-fact way.

Of course, you idiot! That's the idea ...

They had been fleeing for several days now: himself, his Captain, his sorcerer, and some eleven other Kidruhil. They still called it "hunting," but, with the possible exception of the Saik Schoolman, they knew: they were being hunted. He could no longer remember the last contact they'd had with any of the other parties, though he knew others had to be out there, somewhere. They still rode across the wrinkled feet of the Betmulla, though the forests had become temple deep, almost reminiscent of those beneath the Hethanta Mountains. The sun had drawn low on the western horizon, its warmth and light baffled by the soaring canopy. Their horses trod across soft and uneven humus. The deepening shadows seemed to whine with horror.

He had panicked, he realized that now. He'd felt the Scylvendi slipping away, so he'd divided his search parties into even smaller units, telling himself he needed a finer net. That was when things began falling apart, when the trail they followed became strewn with Kidruhil, dead and desecrated. Riders were dispatched to muster the scattered parties, never to return. The sense of dread had grown, like a rash made gangrenous from scratching. Then one morning—Sompas could no longer remember which—they had woken up fugitives.

But how could he have known?

No. No. Demons hadn't been part of the bargain, Saik or no Saik.

"We've come too far," the weather-beaten Captain repeated, peering through the darkness that bloated through the towering cedars. "The Holy War must be near ... either them or the Fanim."

According to Agnaras, they had passed out of Xerash some time ago.

Holy Amoteu, he found himself thinking. *The Sacred Land* ...

His men pretended not to notice his strange laugh. Ouras, however, snorted in disgust. The Schoolman—one of those sallow, impudent types—had stopped disguising his contempt several days ago.

He pressed on, though he could sense their growing impatience. Swaying to the pitch of their saddles, they passed between the great low-forking trunks, riding in loose formation. Cones crunched beneath hooves. Resin bittered the air. The sun fell, and with every passing moment the depths of the forest became less distinct, as though black gauze had been strung between the trees. This, Sompas decided, had to be the Forest of Hebanah, as it was called in the days of *The Tractate.* But since Temple, for him, had been little more than an excuse to carouse and politick, he remembered little of what the scripture had to say of the place.

Without warning, and quite without permission, Captain Agnaras called a halt. They had come to a clearing of sorts, a broad expanse beneath the bowers of an ancient cedar more massive than any the General had ever seen. Weary and wordless, his cavalrymen dismounted and set about their assigned tasks. Not one dared look at him.

The horses were attended to, the fires kindled, and the tents pitched. Soon the darkness was near absolute, and smoke pillared the clearing, winding high into the heart of the sheltering cedar. Sitting upon one of the humped roots, the General could only watch, idly pinching the hem of his blue mantle.

Very little was said.

When the sorcerer slipped away to relieve himself, Sompas found himself joining him. He was not quite willing things to happen anymore—they just ... happened.

I have no choice!

They stood side by side amid some scrub just outside the circle of firelight.

"This has been a disaster," the Schoolman snapped, watching him in the indirect way of urinating men. "An absolute disaster. You can be assured, General, that all this will find its way to official parch—"

It had quite possessed a soul of its own. Rising and falling with nary a glimmer.

Such a naughty knife.

Sompas cleaned it on the twitching man's leggings, then joined his men, his glorious Kidruhil, about the fire. Them he could trust to understand—enough of them, anyway. But a sorcerer?

Please.

He had no choice. It simply *had* to happen.

It wasn't just his own skin at stake, it was his entire *line*. He couldn't allow his ill fortune—for it was nothing more—to blot out all of House Biaxi. Conphas *would do it*—without scruple or compunction. His only hope, Sompas had realized, was to see him dead. His only hope was to find the Holy War, to throw himself on the mercy of the Warrior-Prophet ... to let him know.

And who knew? With the accursed Ikurei wiped out, perhaps a Biaxi might find his way to the Mantle. An Emperor conspiring against his faith with the *Fanim*? The more Sompas had considered it, the more it seemed that honour and righteousness bound him to this course. He had no choice ...

Surprised at his own calm, Sompas joined Agnaras, who sat alone at the officers' fire. The man seemed to work hard not to look at him.

"Where's Ouras?" Sompas asked, as though annoyed at a generally acknowledged fool.

"Who knows?" the Captain replied. "In the woods, shitting ..." *Who cares?* his tone said. There was relief in that.

Sitting on his camp stool, the General clutched his hands together before the flames lest the hard-boiled soldier see them shake. Agnaras was a Threesie in the classic mould. He understood weakness, which was far more dangerous than simply holding it in contempt—for Sompas, anyway. The General glanced at the other, larger fire, where the others congregated, and a number of looks clicked instantly away. They were too silent, and their faces, etched in the kindling firelight, were far too blank. Suddenly he could *feel* it. They were *waiting* ...

For an opportunity to cut his throat.

Sompas returned his gaze to the fire, thought of Ouras lying crumpled in the undergrowth mere lengths away. He would have to pick his moment carefully ... and his words.

Or perhaps he should just slip away ...

"Who guards the perimeter?" he asked Agnaras, making his decision even as he spoke.

Yes-yes-slip-away-run-run—

Shouts brought him and Agnaras to their feet.

"There's something in the tre—"

"I hear it! I hear—"

"Shut up!" the Captain roared. "All of you!" He held his hands out to either side, as though literally holding their voices down. The fires seemed to cackle. A coal popped. Sompas jumped.

Weapons drawn, they stood listening for a dreadful moment, peering into the canopy but seeing only the limbs that raftered air immediately above them—those painted by firelight. The smoke seemed to roll up into oblivion.

Then they heard it: a rasp from the blackness above. There was a small rain of grit, then bark twirled across the clearing.

"Sweet Sejenus!" one of the cavalrymen gasped, only to be silenced by barks of anger.

There was a sound, like that of a little boy pissing across leather. A sizzling hiss drew their attention to the main fire. It seemed all their eyes focused upon it at once: a thread of blood unwinding across the flames ...

Followed by a plummeting shadow. Fiery wood and coals exploded outward. Smoke billowed. Men cried out in the sudden twilight, stumbled back. Some frantically beat at sparks on cloaks and clothing. Sompas could only stare at Ouras, bent backward over the heaped fire, broken and bleeding.

The horses screamed and reared beneath the trees, little more than dancing shadows in the greater black. Agnaras bawled out orders—

But she had already dropped into their midst, falling like rope.

All Sompas could do was stagger backward. He had no choice …

The Captain fell first, tripping to his knees, coughing, gagging, as if trying to dislodge a chicken bone. Two more followed, clutching wounds that glittered black. Sompas could scarce see her longsword, it moved so fast.

Blonde hair whisked like silk in the gloom, chasing a pale face of impossible beauty. And the General realized he *recognized* her … the Prince of Atrithau's woman. The one whose corpse had been hung with the man in Caraskand.

She had come down from her tree.

The Kidruhil retreated before her whirling figure, flailing with their blades. She leapt after them, catching a man's throat like an orange on the tip of her sword. Howling out of the darkness, the Scylvendi barrelled into their flank, hewing them with great sweeping strokes. Men fell in gouts.

Then it was over, save for a gagging that might have been a shriek.

Shirtless, slicked in sweat, the Scylvendi turned to him and spat, a thing of scars and cuts that would be scars. Despite his prodigious size, he seemed scarecrow thin, like something starved of far more than food. His eyes glinted from beneath his battered brow.

His stance wide, the barbarian stood before Sompas while the beautiful woman circled behind. From nowhere, it seemed, a third figure leapt from the blackness beyond the fires, landing in a crouch to the Scylvendi's left. A man Sompas did not recognize.

A shudder seized the Nansur General, and he found himself, absurdly, thankful he had relieved his bladder just moments earlier. He hadn't even drawn his sword.

"She saw you murder the other," the Scylvendi said, wiping spattered blood into a smear across his cheek. "Now she wants to fuck."

A warm hand snaked along the back of his neck, pressed against his cheek.

That night Biaxi Sompas learned that there were rules for everything, including what could and could not happen to one's own body. These, he discovered, were the most sacred rules of all.

Once, in the screaming, snarling misery of it all, he thought of his wives and children burning.

But only once.

Spring, 4112 Year-of-the-Tusk, Shimeh

In the dawning light, the Judges led great trains of the faithful to bathe in the River Jeshimal. Many beat their own backs with branches, an impromptu rite of penance. Parties of mounted knights watched over the worshippers, wary of marauders from the city, whose white turrets loomed in the near distance. But the black gates remained shut, and no heathen dared molest them.

Their hair wet and their eyes bright, most returned to the encampment singing, certain they had been cleansed. But some were unnerved, for the many-eyed walls seemed to mock them. The Tatokar Walls, they called them, though few knew the significance of the name.

Along with Kyudea, her ruined sister to the northwest, Shimeh had been the ancestral seat of the Amoti Kings. In the time of Inri Sejenus, the city was far smaller, encompassing only the heights to the east of the Jeshimal. By the time Triamis I declared Inrithism the official faith of the Ceneian Empire, the city had doubled in size, swollen by the influx of pilgrims and markets. But unlike Caraskand, which was at once a strategic caravan entrepot and exposed to the unruly tribes of the Carathay, the Aspect-Emperors saw no need to raise walls about the greater city; after all, the entire Three Seas lay under Cenei's heavy but prosperous hand. Even in the turbulent days following the Empire's collapse, during Amoteu's brief and contentious independence, no defences—save the Heterine Wall about the Sacred Heights—were constructed.

It was Surmante Xatantius I, the warlike Nansur Emperor famous for his endless wars against Nilnamesh, who first walled the outer city, taking ancient representations of Mehtsonc's many-towered fortifications as his model. The white-glazed tile was added centuries later by the Cishaurim under Tatokar I: apparently the High Heresiarch disapproved of Xatantius's quarries. The towering eyes were the responsibility of Tatokar's successor, the famed poet Hahkti ab Sibban. When a visiting Ainoni dignitary asked him for an explanation, he reportedly said they were to remind the idolaters that "the Solitary God does not blink"—to shame them, in effect. Even then, the silting of Shimeh's harbour had forced Inrithi pilgrims to enter the city via her gates.

Origins aside, the eyes became the subject of ceaseless debate among the Men of the Tusk. Sometimes they seemed to gaze with bland curiosity, and at others to glare in a kind of entranced fury. The longer the Inrithi pondered them, the more Shimeh took on the aura of a living thing, until she seemed some great and unfathomable beast, like a vast, ramshackle crab sunning onshore after crawling up from the deep. It made the prospect of assaulting the city ... uncertain.

Who knew what living things might do?

Where there had been many voices, many wills, now there was but one. With the Logos he had sown, and now with the Logos he would reap.

Soon, Father. I will see you soon.

Turning from Esmenet, Kellhus held out his radiant hands, and a hush passed through the vast congregation. Earlier, he had sent messengers announcing a final Council of Great and Lesser Names on the slopes above the teeming encampment. As he had expected, far more than the caste-nobility had answered his call. Fairly half the Holy War had massed on the incline before him, clotting the summit, perched like crows along the rims of those ruined sepulchres near enough to afford a view.

He stood partway down the slope so that, for those above, Shimeh would rise like a halo about his head and shoulders. The Lords of the Holy War occupied an oblong clearing immediately before him, sitting in the grass. Their look was at once eager and chaste, brimming with enthusiasm yet wary of the cauldron to come. To their right, forming a south shore for the sea of faces rising behind them, the Nascenti stood stiff with uncertain pride, doing their best to convey the impression that they alone knew what was about to happen. Eleäzaras, Iyokus, and several other Scarlet Schoolmen stood on the opposite shore, their faces blank with anxiousness. Kellhus saw Eleäzaras lean to listen to the bandaged Iyokus. The Grandmaster's gaze momentarily clicked to Achamian, who stood—as usual—on Kellhus's left.

"I turn," Kellhus cried, "and I see you in your thousands, the Holy War, the great Tribe of Truth. But I also see thousands upon thousands more, assembled in gleaming ranks, filling the plains, the distant slopes ... I see the ghosts of the fallen, standing among us, watching with pride those who will make good their heartbreaking sacrifice."

There could be no forgetting. They had paid for this moment in terror and blood.

"Those who will reclaim my brother's house."

He could remember, perfectly, what it had been like those three years past, stepping from the shadow of Ishuäl's Fallow Gate. Countless tracks had fanned out from his feet, leading to countless possible outcomes. But unlike a tree, he could war only in one direction. With every step he murdered alternatives, collapsed future after future, walking a line too thin to be marked on any map. For so long he had believed that line, that track, belonged to him, as though his every footfall had been a monstrous decision for which he alone could be called to account. Step after step, annihilating world after possible world, warring until only this moment survived …

But those futures, he now knew, had been murdered long before. The ground he travelled had been Conditioned through and through. At every turn, the probabilities had been summed, the possibilities averaged, the forks impossibly predetermined … Even here, standing before Shimeh, he executed but one operation in the skein of another's godlike calculation. Even here, his every decision, his every act, confirmed the dread intent of the Thousandfold Thought.

Thirty years …

A soft-eyed grin. "I'm reminded of our first Council," he said, "so very long ago on the Andiamine Heights." They smiled at his rueful scowl. "I recall that we were fat."

Laughter, at once thunderous and intimate, as though they were dozens instead of thousands, listening to a beloved uncle tell well-worn jokes. He was their axle, and they were his wheel.

"Proyas," he called, grinning like a father at a son's beloved foibles. "I remember you were bent upon winning your contest with Ikurei Xerius. You mourned the straits that forced you, time and again, to sacrifice principle for convenience, scripture for politics. For your entire life you sought a purity you thought you could glimpse but could never grasp. For your entire life you yearned for a *bold* God, not one who skulked in scriptoriums, whispering the inaudible to the insane."

Now you rail at the old habits, and mourn the toll of the new ...

He looked to the Earl of Agansanor, who sat like a youth, his knees held in the burly circle of his arms. "Gothyelk, you wished only to die absolved. The water of your life was running dry, and it seemed all you could taste was the salt of your sins. What old caste-warrior doesn't turn to counting his crimes? And you, looking back on your life, decided that the hoard was too great, that only your blood could tip the scales of redemption."

Now, thinking my finger on the balance, you dare dream of a quiet death ...

"And Gotian, sweet Gotian, you desired only to be told, not out of some base desire to grovel at the feet of another, but to shape your life into the very mould of God's will. Despite your power and prestige, you were forever haunted by your ignorance. You could not, like so many others, take comfort in the pretence of knowledge."

I have become your rule and revelation, the very incarnation of the certainty you seek.

This exercise had become a custom of his. By calling out the truth of a few faces, he made them all feel known—watched.

"Each of you," he continued, sweeping his gaze across the assembly, "had your reasons for joining the Holy War. Some of you came to conquer, some to atone, some to boast, to avenge, to flee ... But I wonder, can any one of you say that you came for Shimeh *alone?*"

For several moments he heard nothing but the discordant hammering of their hearts. It was as though their breasts had become ten thousand drums.

"Is there no one?"

What he wrought here had to be perfect. There had been no mistaking the words of the old man who had accosted him in Gim. The sails of the Mandate fleet could appear any day now, and the Gnostic Schoolmen would not yield their war lightly. Everything had to be complete before their arrival. Everything had to be inevitable. If they had no hand in the work that they witnessed, they would be that much more reluctant in advancing their claims. *"Your father bids me tell you,"* the blind hermit had said, *"'There is but one tree in Kyudea ...'"*

The question was whether the Men of the Tusk could prevail without him.

"None of you!" he cried in a voice like a crossbow bolt. "None of you came simply for Shimeh, because you're Men, and the hearts of Men are not simple." He looked from face to face, inviting them to see the obvious. "Our passions are a morass, and because we lack the words to name them, we pretend our words are the only true passions. We make our impoverished schemes the measure. We condemn the complicated and cheer the caricature. What man does not yearn for a *simple* soul, to love without recrimination, to act without hesitation, to lead without reservation?"

He saw the recognition sparking in a thousand eyes.

"But there is *no such soul.*"

To speak was to pluck the lute strings of another's soul. To *intone* was to strum full chords. He had long ago learned how to speak past meanings, to mine passion with mere voice.

"*Conflict* is what we are in truth. Conflict. We think it an affliction, an obstruction, an adversary to be overcome, when in fact it is the very quintessence of our souls. Think back on your life. Have *any* of your motives been pure? Ever? Or is this one more lie you use to appease your gluttonous vanity? Think! Is there anything you've done for the love of God alone?"

Again silence, both shamefaced and willing.

"No. There's nothing simple in your hearts. Even the adoration you bear me is marbled with fear, avarice, doubt … Werjau worries he's lost my favour because I've laid eyes upon Gayamakri thrice. Gotian despairs, for he's aspired to purity his entire life." A smattering of laughter. "The shadows of conflict darken *all* of your faces! *Conflict.* Does this mean that you're impure, wicked, or unworthy?"

The final word rang like an accusation.

"Or does it mean that you are *Men*?"

A wind had dropped into the silence, and the scent of the onlookers filled his nostrils: the bitter of rotting teeth, the ink of armpits, the honey of unwashed anuses, all shot through with strands of balsam, orange, and jasmine. And for a moment it seemed he stood within a great circle of apes, hunched and unwashed, watching him with dark and dumbfounded eyes. Then he glimpsed another circle, this one far different, where the Men of the Tusk stood as they stood now, only with their backs turned to him so that they looked outward, while he occupied the shadowy heart of them all—unseen, unguessed ...

He knew their incantations. The words that could burn them, that could bring down their cyclopean walls. But more importantly, he knew the words that could *wield* them, that spoke from the darkness that came before. He need only speak to make men blubber, to make them cut their own throats. What did it mean to make instruments of men? And what did it matter, so long as they were wielded in the name of the God?

There was only mission.

"There's nothing deeper," he said with a sudden, apologetic melancholy. "There's no undiscovered purity lying obscured in our souls. We are legion, both within and without. Even our God is a God of warring Gods. We are conflict—to our very pith!

"We. Are. *War*."

Towering above the heads of his wild countrymen, the giant Yalgrota, his hair crazed in the humidity, raised his bloodstained axe and howled. Within moments the air shivered with cries, and brandished weapons dazzled the hillside with reflected sunlight. Everywhere Kellhus looked, he saw honed edges and clenched teeth, beating fists and rolling eyes. Even Esmenet daubed tears from the kohl about her eyes. Only Achamian stood apart from the spectacle ...

"The Book of Songs," Kellhus continued, "tells us that 'war is heart without harness.' Or think of Protathis, who says that 'war is where the gag of the small is cut away.' Why do you think the only true simplicity we ever find—the only *peace*—is on the field of battle? The blow fended. The blow struck. The howling chorus. The bestial dance. The pendulum of horror and exultation. Can't you see? War is *our soul made manifest*. In it we are called out and condensed, and we burn so very bright."

He held the Holy War in the palm of his intent. The Orthodox had all but dissolved in the face of his manifest divinity. As his Intricati, Esmenet had effectively silenced the remaining dissenters. Both Conphas and the Scylvendi had been removed from the plate ...

Only Achamian yet dared look at him in alarm.

"Tomorrow you shall descend upon the last of a wicked people. Tomorrow you shall wrest my brother's house from their depraved fury."

He looked directly to Nersei Proyas. "Tomorrow you shall raise arms to Shimeh! And I, the Prophet of War, shall be your prize!"

For months now he had trained them, teaching them cues that they recognized without realizing. When to speak, and when to hush. When to cry out, and when to cease breathing.

"But Most-Blessed!" Proyas exclaimed, using one of the many honorifics that he and others had devised. "You speak as though ..." A guileless frown. "Are you not leading the morning assault?"

Kellhus smiled as though caught withholding a glorious secret.

"Every brother is a son ... and every son must first visit my father's house."

Again the look from Achamian. Again the need to subdue the man's endless misgivings.

———⁂———

Gathered on the slopes above the encampment, the Lords of the Holy War unanimously agreed they must assault the city. Starving the Sacred City to force her defenders—both arcane and mundane—to battle outside the walls wasn't an option. The Inrithi no longer possessed the numbers to effectively surround Shimeh. Any determined heathen sortie, they knew, could win their way through. And even though Shimeh's harbour was silted in due to the neglect of her Kianene masters, supplies still could arrive by sea.

The only points of contention turned on the Warrior-Prophet's demand that they attack the city on the morrow, and the dismaying revelation that they must do so *without him*. Of the latter he refused to speak, but of the former he said: "We attack a foe still reeling from disaster, a foe who are many. But now that we've arrived ... Think on your experience: in the face of enemies, time welds the hearts of men. Certainty, righteousness—these things strike *first*!"

The previous day, outriders had scoured the surrounding hills, searching for any sign of Fanayal and the reassembled Fanim host. The Amoti, as a rule, knew nothing, and those Kianene they captured told tales of varying outlandishness: Cinganjehoi, the Tiger of Eumarna, waited in the Betmulla, ready to descend upon them at any moment. Or the Kianene fleet, which supposedly had been destroyed, had stormed the Xerashi coast, disgorging an army that even now approached from their rear. Or Fanayal had commanded a mass exodus, and even now retreated with the Cishaurim to the great city of Seleukara. Or all the strength of Kian lay coiled in Shimeh like a snake in a basket, poised to strike the instant the Inrithi raised the lid …

No matter what the tale, the idolaters were either assured victory or doomed.

The consensus among the Great Names was that none of these tales were true. The Warrior-Prophet disagreed, pointing out that the captives repeated the *same* half-dozen stories. "Fanayal has planted these rumours," he said. "He makes noise to obscure truth's call." He admonished them to remember the man who strove against them. "Don't forget his daring on the fields of Mengedda and Anwurat. Fanayal may be the son of Kascamandri," he said, "but he's a student of Skauras."

The decision was made to confine their assault to Shimeh's westward walls, not only because the encampment lay to the west of the city but because the Juterum lay on the west bank of the Jeshimal, and everyone agreed that the Sacred Heights must be their first objective. So long as the Cishaurim remained undefeated, they knew, all was jeopardy.

Proyas and Gotian then petitioned the Blessed One, begging to lead the assault in advance of the Scarlet Spires. Though the Tusk's condemnation of sorcery had been rescinded, they still loathed the thought of sorcerers being the first to set foot in the Sacred City. But Chinjosa and Gothyelk vehemently disagreed. "I've lost one son to Scarlet sloth," the old Tydonni Earl exclaimed, referring to the death of his youngest in Caraskand. "I shall not lose another!"

But as always, the Warrior-Prophet decided the issue. "We—*all of us*—will attack together," he said. "Who attacks first, who stands where in the order of battle: these things mean nothing. Surely, after so much suffering, *success* can be our only point of honour … Success."

Meanwhile, the Men of the Tusk occupied themselves with preparations, threw themselves at their tasks with sweat and song. Parties were sent into the hills for timber—though not much was required. Raiders were dispatched down the Amoti coast, ordered to secure what supplies they could. Knights wove mantlets from olive branches; for miles, surrounding groves were stripped to their gnarled trunks. Haphazard ladders were constructed of poplars and palm. Great stones were gathered from the shoreline to be used as ammunition. The siege engines built at Gerotha, which the Warrior-Prophet had ordered disassembled and borne by Xerashi captives in the host's train, were brought forward and rebuilt, some even in darkness.

Late that night, as they stretched their limbs before their fires, they talked long of the strangeness of it all, their words and manner somewhere between exhaustion and exultation. They traded accounts of the Warrior-Prophet's words at the Council of Great and Lesser Names. And though they took heart, many Men of the Tusk found their haste troubling, as though they, like the inconstant and the irresolute, had lost heart at the moment of consummation, and sought only to bring the ordeal to a swift conclusion.

And as the fires went out, leaving only the most stubborn and thoughtful awake, the sceptics dared argue their misgivings.

"But think," the faithful retorted. "When we die surrounded by the spoils of a long and daring life, we will look up to those who adore us and we will say, 'I knew him. I knew the Warrior-Prophet.'"

CHAPTER FOURTEEN

SHIMEH

Some say I learned dread knowledge that night. But of this, as with so many other matters, I cannot write for fear of summary execution.
—DRUSAS ACHAMIAN, THE COMPENDIUM OF THE FIRST HOLY WAR

Truth and hope are like travellers in contrary directions. They meet but once in any man's life.
—AINONI PROVERB

Spring, 4112 Year-of-the-Tusk, Shimeh

Esmenet dreamed that she was a prince, an angel fallen from the dark, that her heart had beaten, her loins had ached, for tens of thousands of years. She dreamed that Kellhus stood before her, an outrage to be blotted, an enigma to be dissected, and above all a burning question ...

Who are the Dûnyain?

When she awoke, several moments passed before she recognized herself. Reaching out through the gloom, she clutched only cool sheets where Kellhus should have been. For some reason she was unsurprised, as well as uncommonly concerned. There was an oppressive sense of finality in the air, like the smell of drying ink.

Kellhus?

Ever since reading *The Sagas*, a foreboding had grown within her, an accumulation that had filled her heart and limbs with a sense of rolling heaviness. The night in the Nansur villa—the night of her possession— had stained this listless dread with a bewildering urgency. Every time she blinked, she saw things penetrated and penetrating. She could still feel the creature's hands upon her flesh, and the memory of her obedient lust seemed ever-present. The hunger she had suffered that night! A thirst that only terror could touch, and that no horror could slake. At once bestial and remote, it had been a wantonness that eclipsed obscenity ... and became something pure.

The Inchoroi had taken her, but the *want*, the insatiable desire ... those had been hers.

Of course, Kellhus had tried to console her, even as he plied her with endless questions. He said much the same thing Achamian had said when explaining Xinemus's torment: that the self never stood apart when one was compelled, because it was the very thing possessed. "You can't distinguish yourself from him," Kellhus explained, "because for a time, he *was* you. That's why he tried to provoke me into killing you, because he feared the memories you might have of his memories."

"But the things!" she could only reply. "The things I ached for!" Grimacing faces. Grinning orifices and gaping wounds. The rush of hot fluids.

"Those desires weren't yours, Esmi. They only seemed to be yours because you couldn't see where they came from ... You simply suffered them."

"But then, how does any desire belong to me?"

When she learned of Xinemus's death, she told herself that *he* had been the cause of her distress, that her sense of encroaching doom was nothing more than concern for his well-being. But the lie was too obvious for even her to believe, and she spent hours cursing herself for her inability to mourn the man who had been such an uncompromising friend. And when, shortly after, Achamian moved with his things out of the Umbilica, she once again tried to wrap explanations around the chill morass of her heart. And even though this lie, through force of partial truth, had lasted a day and a night, it collapsed the instant she had laid wondering eyes on the actual origin of her misapprehension.

Shimeh.

This, she had thought as the great eyes of the city walls stared her down, *is where we all die.*

Her head buzzing, she threw aside her sheets, called to the crane-embroidered screen behind which Burulan sometimes slept. Moments later she was dressed and interrogating Gayamakri. He knew only that Kellhus had left the Umbilica to wander on foot through the camp. Apparently, the dark-eyed man said with a frown, he had refused any escort.

There had been a time, not so long ago, when Esmenet would have feared walking alone through the encamped Holy War, but now she could imagine no place safer. The moon was bright, and save for the odd guy rope strung across her path, she found the going easy. Most firepits either were dark or tinkled with orange coals, but an inevitable few remained awake, carousing to no purpose or drinking in sullen circles. Those who recognized her fell immediately to their knees. None had seen the Warrior-Prophet.

Then she fairly collided with a man, an Ainoni knight by the look of him, and with horror she realized he had bedded her several times before her ... renewal. Before then she had continually told herself that *she* ruled her coupling, not her custom. But the smirk on his face told her otherwise. The smirk on *all* their faces told her otherwise. Instantly she understood that he took great pride in using her, the Prophet-Consort, as his sheath.

He caught her elbows and pressed her back. "Yes," he said, as though to confirm her mortification. He was very drunk. His leash, they would have said back in Sumna, had been soaked in liquor. Decorum. Honour. He could easily slip these things.

"Do you know who I am?" she said sharply.

"Yes," he repeated, his manner lurid. "I *know* you ..."

"Then you know how close you stand to death."

A look of dank puzzlement. She advanced and struck him with an open palm.

"Insolent *dog*! Kneel!"

He stared, stunned, unmoving.

"Kneel! Or I'll have you *flayed alive* ... Do you understand?"

It took several heartbeats for his astonishment to lurch into terror. And several more for his knees to buckle. Drink always added to the momentum of such things. He fairly blubbered his apologies. And more importantly, he told her he'd seen Kellhus leave the camp to climb the westward slopes.

Esmenet left him, hugging her shoulders to keep from shaking. She could understand her clenched teeth, but her smile baffled her. She thought about having her agents hunt the man down on the morrow. Though she had always detested the brutality that her new station had forced upon her, the thought of his screams thrilled her for some reason. Scenarios roiled through her thoughts, and though she knew they were both petty and absurd, she exulted in them nonetheless.

What was it? Her shame? His smirk? Or was it the mere fact that she *could do* these things?

I am, she breathlessly thought, *his vessel*.

Lost in her worries, she climbed the shallow hillside, bemoaned the hem of her gown as she waded through thistles and moist grasses. High over the Meneanor Sea, the Nail of Heaven flashed against the greater black. Twice she turned to stare at Shimeh in the moonlight.

It scarcely seemed real.

She discovered Kellhus sitting perched upon the ruins of one of the mausoleums that dotted the hillside, staring intently across the Shairizor at the dark city. She thought of climbing the collapsed portion then using the wall like a catwalk, but she recalled the life she bore within her. She strode to the mossy foundations beneath him instead. He sat cross-legged, his hands upturned and clasped in his lap. He had tied his hair into a Galeoth war-knot. His face looked marmoreal in the moonlight, which gleamed across the curls of his beard. As always, there was something indefinable about his pose or his manner that seemed to dwarf his immediate surroundings. Where others would seem lonely, even desolate, he seemed an unfaltering sentinel, white in the moonlight, black in its shadow.

Without looking away from Shimeh, he said, "You think of Caraskand. You remember the way I withdrew from you before the events leading to the Circumfix. You fear that I do the same for similarly perilous reasons."

Hands on her hips, she stared upward, scowled in mock disapproval. "I'm trying not to."

He smiled. His eyes glittered when he looked down.

"Why this?" she asked. "Why here?"

"Because soon I must leave." He crouched and held down his hand.

She reached up to his wrist, then suddenly found herself standing beside him, steadied by his powerful arms. For a moment it seemed they stood perched on the point of a needle. She glanced nervously about, at the slopes dropping toward the plain, at the blackness between the thin poplars that thronged from the interior of the ruined mausoleum. She breathed deep his smell: oranges, cinnamon, the musk of masculine sweat. Despite the fear his words had engendered, she savoured him as she always did. His beard seemed white in the moonlight.

She gingerly stepped back, the better to look up into his eyes. "Where are you going?"

He studied her for a moment. In the distance beyond him, Shimeh looked both intricate and stone-ancient, a great fossil uncovered by the wash of tides.

"To Kyudea."

Esmenet scowled. Kyudea was Shimeh's dead sister, destroyed long ago by some Ceneian Aspect-Emperor whose name she couldn't remember. "Your father's house," she said sourly.

"Truth has its seasons, Esmi. Everything will be made clear in due course."

"But, Kellhus ..." What did it mean that they had to assail Shimeh without him?

"Proyas knows what must be done," he said decisively. "The Scarlet Spires will act as they see fit."

Desperation welled through her. *You can't leave us.*

"I must, Esmi. I answer to a different voice."

Not *her* voice, something fragile within her realized. But then neither did he answer to her customs, her concerns, or even her hopes ... The things that moved her simply didn't touch him. Though they stood together, Kellhus had planted his feet across a far more unfathomable ground. What moved him moved on the scale of the planets and their cycles across the night sky.

Suddenly he seemed a wild stranger, like the Scylvendi ... The son of something terrible.

"And Akka?" she asked quickly, hoping to cover this moment of weakness. "Shouldn't he accompany you?"

You must stay safe!

"Where I walk, no one can follow," he said. "Besides, I'm beyond his protection. He knows that now." Despite the onerous implications of what he said, he spoke with matter-of-fact ease.

"He'll want to know where you've gone."

Kellhus smiled and nodded as though to say, *That Akka* ... "He knows. Do you think you're the only one who stalks me with well-meaning questions?"

For some reason his gentle humour made her want to cry. Suddenly she was bending her knees to the broken stone, lowering her face to the moss at his sandalled feet. How absurd she must look, she thought, kneeling atop a wall's broken lip, playing out in pantomime what others did on solid ground. A wife before her husband.

But she didn't care. He was the only measure. The only judgement ...

Use me.

No matter where they turned, men found themselves encircled by greater things. Usually they ignored them. And sometimes, moved by pride and base hunger, they warred against them. But either way, those things remained just as great, and men, no matter how lunatic their conceit, remained just as small. Only by kneeling, by offering themselves as one might offer the haft of a weapon, could men recognize their place in this world. Only by submitting could they recognize themselves.

There was rapture in submission. The vulnerability of another towering overhead—precarious, like letting a stranger touch one's face. The sense of profound communing, as though only those who acknowledged their insignificance could themselves be acknowledged. The relief of surrender, the disburdening that accompanied the yielding of responsibility.

The paradoxical sense of *licence*.

The nattering voices fell silent. The exhaustion of endless posturing melted away. She found it narcotic, even arousing ... the domination of another.

With a forbearing laugh, Kellhus helped her to her feet. He even bent to brush the grit from her gown. "Do you know," he said, looking up, "that I love you?"

She smiled, and though part of her gushed like an adolescent, something older and wiser watched him with a whore's callused eyes. "I know," she said. "But I ... I ..."

"You *should* fear what's about to happen," he said. "All Men should fear."

She hesitated. "I couldn't survive without you."

Hadn't she told Akka the same thing?

He placed a warm and radiant hand upon the swell of her belly, and it seemed that he blessed her womb. "Nor I without you."

He enclosed her in his arms, stole her worries with a deep kiss. Though he held her with a strange fierceness afterward, she could feel his gaze drift back to Shimeh. She clutched his hard frame, thinking of the strength coiled within his heart, within his limbs. She thought of the gift of prophecy, and how it seemed to kill all those who dared wield it.

Never let go, she told herself. *Never.*

And somehow he heard. He always heard.

"Fear for the future, Esmi, not me." Fingers combed through her hair, drew tingling lines across her scalp. "This flesh is but my shadow."

How far had he walked?

Kellhus thought of snow-hooded mountains, the flash of sunlight across glacial heights. He thought of deep forests and lost cities, of moss-limned statuary leaning from the humus. He thought of unmanned walls ...

It seemed he could hear someone shrieking his name through frozen forest arcades.

"Kellhus? *Kelllhuuss!*"

How far had he come?

After sending Esmenet back to the encampment, he'd travelled westward across the broken pasture, climbing the ramped hillsides. At the very summit he paused amid several dead oaks, turned his back to the Nail of Heaven, which now lay over Shimeh and the Meneanor, so that he could follow its axis across the dark landscape before him ...

Toward Kyudea.

"I know you can hear me," he said to the world, dark and sacred. "I know that you listen."

A sourceless wind pulled the grasses into streamers, drawing them to the southwest. Against the constellations, dead branches clacked and creaked without rhythm.

"What was I to do?" he replied. "They attend only to what lies before their eyes. They listen only to what pleases their ears. Things unseen, things unheard ... they trust to you."

The wind subsided, leaving an unearthly silence in its wake. He heard the pasty hiss of maggots squirming through the gut of a dead crow some five paces to his right. He heard the chatter of termites seething beneath the bark of the surrounding oaks.

He tasted the sea on the air.

"What was I to do? Tell them the *truth*?"

He stooped, pulled a twig from the straps of his right sandal. He studied it by moonlight, followed the thin, muscular branchings that seized so much emptiness from the sky. Tusk sprouting from tusk. Though the trees about him had died seasons previously, the twig possessed two leaves, one waxy green, the other brown ...

"No," he said. "I cannot."

The Dûnyain had sent him into the world as an assassin. His father had imperilled their isolation, had threatened Ishuäl, the great sanctuary of their hallowed meditations. They had no choice but to send Kellhus, even knowing that they served Moënghus's ends ... What else could they do?

So Kellhus had walked the length of Eärwa, from the ruined wastes of the North to the raucous cities of the South. Every advantage had been exploited, be it a single smile or a thousand fists. Every liability had been minimized. He had learned as much as the world would yield: languages, histories, factions, the peculiarities of innumerable hearts. He had mastered her mightiest weapons ... Faith. War. Sorcery.

He was Dûnyain, one of the Conditioned. At every turn he followed the Logos, the Shortest Path.

And yet he had come *so far*.

Bound to the Circumfix, slowly turning beneath Umiaki's dark bowers. Serwë gaping past him, as cold as stone against his nakedness. Her face swollen and black.

I wept.

Casting aside the twig, Kellhus leaned into the night and began sprinting across the grasses, toward the Betmulla Mountains piling black across the horizon before him. He leapt thickets, pedalled into black ravines, then lunged up broken slopes.

He ran. Not once did he stumble, nor did he slow to determine his bearings. The ground was *his* ... Conditioned.

Everywhere, all about him, one world. The crossings were infinite, but they were not equal.

They were not equal.

To those few Kianene and Amoti who heard the noise, it sounded like tapestries being beaten by slaves in the distance. But it moved above, against the stars.

Along the walkways of the First Temple, it became a shadow, crept along vault and ceiling fresco. For a moment it obscured what lay beneath, then it was gone. It drank with its eyes, while its soul dreamed a million years. Wise and cunning. Animal in its fury. How this place cut with its endless edges and cramped skies.

Thorns. Its every glimpse speared like thorns.

The stone is weak. We could wash it away ...

Do nothing, the Voice replied. *Just watch.*

They know we are here. If we do not move, they will find us.

Then test them.

The Ciphrang fell to the floor and huddled, cringed from all things exterior, all things *surface*. It waited, longed for the pitching deeps. Soon one of them came. The manling had no eyes, and yet saw ... saw as it did, though without the pain. But the salt of his fear tasted no different.

It rose and revealed its Form. Zioz, his face as bright as the sun.

The manling made noise in terror, then unleashed his own light: a thread of raw energy. With one hand, Zioz grasped the thread, curious. When he pulled, the soul was yanked from the manling. The light vanished. The meat slapped the floor.

Weak ...

There are others, the Voice said. *Far, far stronger.*

Perhaps I will die.

You are too mighty.
Perhaps you will die with me ... Iyokus.

Something—a pendulous absence—circled above Achamian ... He should be awake.

But the smell had pummelled Seswatha to his knees, forced him to retch again and again. Burning spittle was the most he could manage, but still his innards heaved and heaved. Standing in the gloom above, Nau-Cayûti watched him, too weary for expression.

Through endless dark they had climbed, higher and higher, knowing that sooner or later the emptiness had to yield to horrors. It began with raining waste: urine, excrement, trailing from seams, spilling in skirts they had to leap through. They passed wells that had once been corridors, where streams of slurry toppled down into endless dark. They circled great pits of rotting flesh, where corpses—some fetal and malformed, others full-grown—had been thrown from unknown heights. And once, they had even crossed a lake filled with brackish water—what must have been the accumulation of thousands of years of rain.

They had wept for relief while bathing. It was no mean thing to be cleansed in such a place.

Of course, Seswatha had heard rumours. Once he'd even had occasion to speak at length with Nil-Giccas, who had battled through the halls of this place thousands of years before. But nothing could prepare Seswatha for the horrid immensity of the Incû-Holoinas. According to the Nonman King, not one in a hundred Inchoroi survived the Ark's fall from the heavens, and yet a thousand thousand of them had warred against the Nonmen over the course of their innumerable wars. The Ark, Nil-Giccas insisted, was an ingrown world, a labyrinth of labyrinths. "Be wary," the white lips had intoned. "No matter how deep, the cup of evil always overflows."

Nau-Cayûti had seen the light first, a pale glimmer hanging at the terminus of a side passage. Dousing their own light, they crept along the incline. Silence came easily. The planks that righted the skewed floors had long since given way to a kind of earth, the accretion, Seswatha decided, of detritus shed and packed over the ages. With every step the reek became more pungent. The roaring clamour swelled only as they crossed the last few paces.

The passage simply ended. What had been a single light was broken into thousands and pitched across yawning space. Nau-Cayûti had gasped and cursed, while Seswatha, after gaping for several breathless moments, had fallen to his knees and vomited. What he smelled was *human*, and it seemed the most unbearable stench of all.

A city. They found themselves staring across a city. The steaming heart of Golgotterath.

He should be awake!

A cavernous void opened before them. It reminded Seswatha of a ship's ribbed hold, though pitched on its end, and far too vast to truly resemble any work of Men. Sheer golden faces reared into obscurity, hazed by the smoke of countless fires. Structures of mortise and hacked stone climbed their foundations, crusting their sides like stacked hornets' nests, not dwellings but open cells, squalid and innumerable. It all would have looked like something revealed by low tide were it not for the fires and the figures teeming like mites across it. Lumbering files of Bashrag. Gibbering masses of Sranc. And among them, human captives, untold numbers of them, some shackled to sledges in great groaning trains, others scattered across the open-air harems of their captors, gagging beneath convulsing shadows, their mouths working, their eyes rolled up to the dark, pink and naked and bloodied, countless men, women, and children. The bodies of the broken choked the alleys below.

He should be awake ...

The pealing roar, screams upon screams, wailing across heights of alien gold, reverberating through bones and heart, reverberating, reverberating ...

Nau-Cayûti slumped to his knees. "What is this?" More of a breath than a whisper.

He turned to his teacher, his pupils ringed by crazed white. *"Th-this?"*

Spoken like a bereaved child.

Awake!

Seswatha felt himself hoisted and thrown back into shadow. Something cracked his skull, and murk encompassed everything until he could see only his beloved student's anguish—his lunatic hurt!

"Where is she? Whe—"

Awake, you fool!

With a gasp Achamian clawed his way to consciousness. *Shimeh!* he thought. *Shimeh!* There was a shadow above him, framed by the whining ring of his unanswered Wards. And there was a great and crushing absence, swinging in small circles from the end of a leather string. A Trinket, hanging the breadth of a finger above his breast ...

"Some time ago," the Scylvendi grated, "during all the empty hours thinking, I understood that you die as I do ..." A tremor passed through the hand holding the string.

"Without Gods."

Even from this distance, Eleäzaras could see the faint glow of lights spilling from the Ctesarat Tabernacle upon the Sacred Heights. He sat with Iyokus beneath the open canopy that flared from the south face of his pavilion. Circles of blood had been painted across the flattened grasses. Tomorrow they would at last engage their mortal enemy, and though the meaning of that engagement now escaped him, he would see it through.

Which meant he would use every weapon at his disposal—no matter how wicked.

"The Cishaurim flee," Iyokus said, his mouth aglow with the Diamotic Communion. "As we suspected, they have no Chorae upon the Juterum. But they call ... they call."

The Snakeheads had no choice. They would disperse their Trinkets to guard against further incursions by Ciphrang, which meant that tomorrow his brother Schoolmen would face fewer in their initial assault.

Eleäzaras leaned forward. "We shouldn't have used a Potent when a Debile would have suited our purposes just the same. And especially *not* Zioz! You told me yourself he was becoming dangerous."

"All is well, Eli."

"You grow reckless ..."

Have I become such a coward?

Iyokus turned to him. Blood soiled his bandages where they pressed against his translucent cheeks.

"They must fear us," the man said. "Now they do."

The bizarre terror of awakening to a mortal threat: a pang wrapped round with a sluggish incredulity, as though something deep believed he still slept. Like a knife probing wool.

"Scylvendi!" Achamian gasped. It seemed he mouthed ice more than sound. The stink of the man filled the cramped confines of his tent, a smell somewhere between horse and dog.

"*Where*," the voice growled from the darkness, "*is he?*"

Achamian knew he referred to Kellhus, either because of the intensity with which he said "he" or perhaps because he could scarcely think of anyone else himself. But then, all men searched for Kellhus, even those who knew him not.

"I don't—"

"*Lies!* You are always with him. You are his protector—I know this!"

"*Please* ..." he gasped, tried to cough without raising his chest. The Chorae had become unbearable. It seemed his heart might crack his sternum, leap into its absence. He could feel the stinging of his skin about his right nipple, the beginnings of the Salt. He thought of Carythusal, of Geshrunni, now long dead, holding a Trinket above his hand in the Holy Leper. Strange how this one seemed to have a different ... *taste*.

I was never meant to escape.

The shadow hunched over him in fury, seemed to growl. Though he could see no more than the man's outline limned in the faintest moonlight, Achamian saw him clearly in his soul's eye: the strapped arms, the neck-breaking hands, the face rutted by murderous wrath.

"I will not ask again."

What was happening here? *Don't panic, old fool.*

"You think," Achamian managed, "I would betray *his* trust, Scylvendi? You think I value my life *over his?*" Desperation, not conviction, had animated these words, for he did not believe them. Even still, they seemed to give the Scylvendi pause.

A moment of brooding dark, then the barbarian said, "I will trade, then ... barter."

Why the sudden reversal? And the man's voice ... had it actually quavered? The barbarian yanked the Chorae into his palm, like a child with a well-practised toy. Achamian fairly cried out in relief. For a moment he lay panting, still terrified and utterly dumbfounded. The shadow watched, motionless.

"Trade?" Achamian exclaimed. For the first time he noticed the two figures sitting behind the barbarian, though the gloom was such that he could tell only that one was a woman and the other a man. "Trade *what*?"

"Truth."

This word, intoned as it was with exhaustion and a profound, barbaric candour, struck him like a blow. Achamian pressed himself onto his elbows, glared at the man, his eyes wild with outrage and confusion.

"And what if I've had my fill of Truth?"

"The truth of *him*," the Scylvendi said.

Achamian peered at the man, squinted as if into the distance, even though he loomed so very near. "I already know that truth," he said numbly. "He's come to—"

"You know *nothing*!" the barbarian snarled. "Nothing! Only what he has let you know." He spat in the corner next to Achamian's uncovered feet, wiped his lips with the hand holding his Chorae. "The same as all his slaves."

"I'm no sla—"

"But you are! In his presence *all men are slaves*, sorcerer." With the Chorae clutched tight in his fist, the Scylvendi leaned back to sit cross-legged. "He is *Dûnyain*."

Never had Achamian heard such shaking hate in a word, and the world was filled with such epithets: Scylvendi, Consult, Fanim, Cishaurim, Mog-Pharau ... It sometimes seemed there were as many hatreds as there were names.

"That word," Achamian said carefully, "'Dûnyain' ... it simply means 'truth' in a dead tongue."

"The tongue is not dead," Cnaiür snapped, "and the word no longer means 'truth.'"

Achamian recalled that first meeting outside Momemn, the Scylvendi standing proud and savage before Proyas, while Kellhus had held Serwë amid Xinemus's knights. He hadn't believed Cnaiür then, but the revelation of Kellhus and his name, *Anasûrimbor*, had overturned all his suspicions. What was it Kellhus had said? That the

Scylvendi had accepted his wager? Yes, and that he had dreamed of the Holy War from afar ...

"What you told us," Achamian said, glimpsing the sheen of teeth, "that first day with Proyas ... you lied."

"I lied."

"And Kellhus?" For some reason, asking this made his throat ache.

A pause. "Tell me where he went."

"No," Achamian said. "You promised me Truth ... I will not barter untested wares."

The barbarian snorted, but it didn't strike Achamian as an expression of derision or contempt. There was a pensiveness to the man, a vulnerability of movement and manner that contradicted the violence of his aspect. Somehow Achamian knew that Cnaiür *wanted* to speak of these things, as though they burdened him in the way of crimes or powerful grievances. And this realization terrified him more thoroughly than any Trinket ever could.

"You think Kellhus was sent," the Scylvendi said in a hollow voice, "when he was *summoned.* You think he is unique, when he is but one of a number. You think he is a saviour, when he is nothing more than a slaver."

These statements clawed all blood and sensation from Achamian's face.

"I don't understand—"

"Then *listen!* For thousands of years they have hidden in the mountains, isolated from the world. For thousands of years they have bred, allowing only the quickest of their children to live. They say you know the passing of ages better than any, sorcerer, so think on it! *Thousands of years* ... Until we, the natural sons of true fathers, have become little more than children to them."

What followed was too ... naked not to be true. The two shadows sitting behind him did not move while he talked, not by the slightest measure. The Scylvendi's voice was harsh, marred by the guttural cadences of his mother tongue, but he spoke with an eloquence that gave the lie to the severity of his race. He told the story of a boy just outgrowing his native fragility, who found himself captured by the words of a mysterious slave, and led across trackless expanses between sane acts and upright men.

A story of patricide.

"I was his accomplice," the Scylvendi said. Toward the end of his story he had slouched in thought, speaking more and more to his palms, as though each word were a pebble added to a back-breaking load. Suddenly he raised his fists to his temples. "I was his accomplice, *but I was not willing!*"

He lowered his forearms to his knees, held his fists out, as though snapping a bone.

"They see our thoughts through our faces—our hurts, our hopes, our rage, and our passion! Where we guess, they *know*, the way herdsmen can read the afternoon's weather in the morning sky ... And what men know, men dominate."

Somehow it seemed a shaft of light had found his face, so bright was the anguish in his voice. Achamian could hear his tears, his sneering grimace.

"He chose me. He raised me up, and he shaped me, the way women shape flints to scrape their hides. He used me to kill my father. He used me to secure his escape. He used me ..."

The shadow crossed his fists over his bull chest.

"Shame! *Wutrim kut mi'puru kamuir!* I could not stop thinking! I could not stop thinking! I laid eyes upon my degradation, I *understood*, and I stamped my heart with that understanding!"

Without realizing, Achamian wrung finger against finger, joint against joint. There was the Scylvendi's shadow and the pit that was his Chorae. Nothing else existed.

"He was intellect ... He *was war!* *That* is what they are! Do you not see? With every heartbeat they war against circumstance, with every breath they conquer! They walk among us as we walk among dogs, and we yowl when they throw out scraps, we whine and whimper when they raise their hands ...

"They make us love! They make us love!"

Vast was the night. Great was the ground.

And yet they yielded. They yielded.

Step-step-leap. Incantations of space. World crossing world.

The hares darted from his path. The thrushes burst from his feet, hurtling into the stars. The jackals raced at his side, their tongues lolling, their loping limbs tiring.

"Who are you?" they panted as their hearts failed them.

"Your master!" cried the godlike man as he outdistanced them. And though humour was unknown to him, he laughed. He laughed until the sky shook.

Your master.

How could a heart hold such outrage?

The sorcerer rocked back and forth in the candlelight, to and fro, muttering, muttering ...

"Back-back ... m-must start at beginning ..."

But he could not—no, not yet. Never had he been party to such an exchange. Never had such words been thrown upon the balance of his heart.

He knew the Scylvendi meant to kill *him,* his final, greatest student. He knew what the two shadows behind the barbarian had been. As they exited his tent, he had seen *her* face in a shaft of moonlight, as perfect as that night it had swayed and moaned above *him.* Serwë ...

You gave him up. The Warrior-Prophet ... You told the barbarian where he goes!

Because he lies! He steals what is ours! What is mine!

But the world! The world!

Fie on the world! Let it burn!

"The beginning!" he cried. *Please.*

Before him, spread across his silk bedding, were sheaves of parchment. He dipped his quill in his inkhorn, murmuring, murmuring ... Quickly he wrote all the names of all the factions that had so bedevilled him, redrawing the map that had burned in the Sareotic Library.

He paused over,

INRAU

searching for the memory of his sorrow, struck by remembrances that no longer mattered—or so it seemed. And he shuddered so violently at writing,

THE CONSULT

he was forced to set his quill down and hold his arms tight to his chest.

You gave him up!

No! No!

When he was finished, it seemed he held the very same parchment he had lost, and he pondered the identity of things, the way words did not discriminate between repetitions. They were immortal, and yet they cared.

With a bold stroke, he crossed out,

THE EMPEROR

and inked,

CONPHAS

underneath, thinking of all the Scylvendi had said regarding the new Emperor, of how even now he marched on the Holy War from the west— or from the sea. *"Warn them,"* the leering shadow had said. *"I would not see Proyas dead."*

He quickly scratched a welter of new lines, all the connections he had ignored since his abduction by the Scarlet Spires. Then, in a hand too steady to be his own—for he *was* mad, he knew that now—he wrote,

THE DÛNYAIN

in the open space to the left of,

ANASÛRIMBOR KELLHUS

He held his quill above the ancient word for some time. Two drops of ink—tap-tap—marred the script. He watched them bleed outward, chasing a million infinitesimal veins, obliterating the word.

And for some reason, that spurred him to write,

ANASÛRIMBOR MOËNGHUS

above. The name, not of Kellhus's son by Serwë, but of his *father*—the man who had summoned him to the Three Seas ...

Summoned!

He dipped his quill into his inkhorn, his hand as light as an apparition. Then, as though crowded forward by dawning apprehension, he slowly wrote,

ESMENET

against the top left margin.

How had her name become his prayer? Where did she fall in these monstrous events?

Where was his own name?

He stared at the completed map, insensible to the passage of time. The Holy War roused about him. Shouts and the chunk-chunk of hooves passed through his tent—passed through him. He had become a ghost that stared and stared, not really pondering but *watching*, as though the secret lay hidden in the ink's immobility ...

Men. Schools. Cities. Nations.

Prophets. Lovers.

There was no pattern to these breathing things. There was no encompassing thought to give them meaning. Just men and their warring delusions ... The world was a corpse.

Xinemus's lesson.

Without knowing why, he began connecting each of the names to,

SHIMEH

where it lay centre bottom. Lines. One after another, drawn to the city that was about to devour so many, guilty and innocent alike. The bloodthirsty city.

Her name he connected last of all, for he knew she needed Shimeh more than any other—save perhaps himself. Once the black thread was drawn tight, he returned the tip of his quill and drew it out once more.

And again. And again. And again. Quicker and quicker. Until he slashed the vellum sheet in a frenzy. Cut after cut after cut—

For he was sure that his quill had become a knife …

And that flesh lay beneath the tattooed skin.

CHAPTER FIFTEEN

SHIMEH

If war does not kill the woman in us, it kills the man.

—TRIAMIS I, *JOURNALS AND DIALOGUES*

Like so many who undertake arduous journeys, I left a country of wise men and came back to a nation of fools. Ignorance, like time, brooks no return.

—SOKWË, *TEN SEASONS IN ZEÜM*

Spring, 4112 Year-of-the-Tusk, Shimeh

Soundless light broken through beads of dew. Dark canvas faces steaming. Shadows stretching from engines of war, slowly shrinking. Hues of grey bleeding into a panoply of colours. The far tracts of the sea flashing gold.

Morning. The beginning of the world's slow bow before the sun.

Slaves stirred smoke from the firepits, used dried grass to conjure flames from buried coals. The sleepless roused themselves, sat in the chill, watching the twining smoke, disbelieving ...

The first of the horns pealed raw across the distances.

The day had come. Shimeh awaited, black against a fan of rising light.

———⟨∞⟩———

"Your father," the old man in Gim had rasped, *"bids me tell you ..."*

Kyudea rose from the pastures like a scattered cairn. Foundations snaked through the grasses. Weathered stone crowned the peaks of rambling mounds. Here and there, toppled columns breached the turf, as though the wrecked city had been swamped by the swells of an earthen sea.

The Warrior-Prophet wandered the debris, a future mapped with each exhalation. His soul forked into the blackness of possibility, following the calculus of inference and association. Thoughts branching, shoot after shoot, until he filled the immediate world and struck beyond, down into the exhausted soil of the past, out across the ever-receding horizon of the future.

Cities burned. Entire nations took flight. A whirlwind walked ...

"'There is but one tree in Kyudea ...'"

Though only dead stone lay scattered about him, Kellhus could see what had come before: the grand processionals, the thronging thorough-fares, the ponderous temples. Kyudea had been as great as Shimeh, if not greater, in the days when the provinces south of the River Sempis had been nations. Now she was mute and fallow, a place for shepherds to shelter their flocks in time of storm.

Glories had dwelt here once. Now there was nothing. Only overturned stone, the whisk of grasses beneath the wind ...

And answers.

"'There is but one tree,'" the old man had said, his voice not his own, *"'and I dwell beneath it.'"*

And Kellhus had struck, cleaving him to the heart.

He had been used, deceived—all along, from the very beginning ... That had been the Scylvendi's claim.

"But I'm not like the others!" Achamian had protested. *"I don't believe for my heart's sake!"*

A shrug of powerful, many-scarred shoulders. *"Which is why he would concede you your concerns ... make them the ground of an even deeper devotion. Truths are his knives, and we are all of us cut!"*

"What are you saying?"

Ink-bloodied parchment in hand, Achamian wandered through the camp, pressed through masses of armed and arming Inrithi, neither seeing nor hearing those who bowed and addressed him as "Holy Tutor." He passed from the radial avenues of the Conriyan encampment to more haphazard ones of the Tydonni. He saw an armoured man, an aging Meigeirish knight, his beard long and grey, on his knees before the smoking pit of his fire.

"Take my hand," Achamian heard the man sing, *"and kneel before ..."*

Without warning, the knight opened his eyes, glared at him even as he wiped away his tears. The ensuing verse, *He who raises light ...,* seemed to hang unsung in the air between them. Then he turned, angrily collected his weapons and gear. Horns brayed in the morning distance.

"Take My Hand" ... One of a hundred hymns to the Warrior-Prophet, most of which Achamian knew by heart.

He gazed down the length of the congested avenue, saw others kneeling, some alone, others in groups of two or three. Where the avenue curved out of sight, he could see a Judge exhort dozens of penitents. Everywhere he looked he saw Circumfixes, painted across kite-shields, wired into necklaces, embroidered across chests and high banners. The entire world seemed to rumble with devotion.

How had this happened?

What Kellhus had said in the Apple Garden was true: to kneel low before the God was to stand high among the fallen. The servants of an absent king invariably ruled in his stead. "What I do," the pious said, "I do for *Him*," calling on writs so ancient, so metaphoric, that any hatred or conceit could be interpreted into them. It was as though what *transcended,* what stood outside the dim and slovenly circle of this life, was nothing more than a sheath hidden beyond the horizon. One needed only reach out to draw weapons ...

Kneeling! What was it but another outrageous gluttony? Who begrudged sweets when flesh so soon would be served? Even the *world* found itself on the table, its clamour become music, its caprice become courses served for the sake of the pious alone. Everything was for *them.*

And the others? They need only beg.

"What are you saying?" he had cried to the Scylvendi.

"That even you, the proud naysayer, are his slave. That he hunches at the springs of your every thought, draws you as water to his cup."

"But my soul is my own!"

Laughter, dark and guttural and vicious, as though all sufferers, in the end, were no more than fools.

"He prizes no thought higher."

Achamian had found certainty in Kellhus, despite losing Esmenet to him. He'd even made his torment into a kind of *proof*. So long as his charge pained him, he told himself, *it must be real*. He did not, as so many did, believe for flattery's sake. Seswatha's Dreams assured that his importance would be more a thing of terror than pride. And his redemption had been a thing too ... abstract.

To love one who had wronged him—that was his test! And he had been *rooted*—so rooted ...

Now everything toppled, hurtled across steepening moments in an avalanche of hungers and hatreds, rushing toward ... toward ...

Shimeh.

He knew not what.

"Truths are his knives, and we are all of us cut ..."

What was happening?

To know anything was to know, in some measure, *where one stood*. Small wonder he clutched his chest for fear of falling, even here on the wide ground of Shairizor—in the long shadow of Shimeh.

"Ask yourself, sorcerer ... What do you have that he hasn't taken?"

He had much preferred his damnation.

The fires along the walls of Shimeh dulled in dawn's early light. Soon they were little more than orange smears between the battlements.

The Fanim upon the walls stared out in wonder across the fields. The impossible sight of the four siege-towers, two to either side of the Massus Gate, had dismayed them, for everyone had agreed it would take the idolaters weeks to prepare any assault. Now they watched at the strange formations gathering before the gate proper. Most of them were conscripts, armed with tools or relics of forgotten wars, but some two thousand survivors of the long backward battle from Mengedda stood among them, and even they were perplexed by the idolaters. Their lord, Hamjirani, was called to the turrets so that he might see for himself. For some time he argued with lesser Grandees, only to finally withdraw in disgust.

Arrayed across the slopes of the Juterum, the Hill of Ascension, the heathen drummers began beating their skins. As though in reply, Inrithi horns brayed loud, hanging for the length of a man's lungs.

Opposite the gate the Fanim called Pujkar and the Inrithi called Massus, small clots of men began advancing over the fields. Across the walls, men cried out for their officers, assuming the idolaters sought to parley. But the nobles among their number shouted them down. Archers were called to the ready.

Spread out across a hundred or more yards, the formations approached, some forty of them, each some ten paces from the others, and consisting, the defenders could now see, of six men—five abreast and one back, garbed in crimson beneath silver corselets. Small pennants fluttered from a horn set into their battlecaps, a different colour and sign adorning each cadre. All their faces were painted white, as was the manner of the Ainoni in war. The outermost men bore heavy crossbows, as did a lone man who trailed in the rear. Two like-armoured men marched on the inside of the flanking crossbowmen, bearing immense basketwork shields that almost entirely obscured them from anything but the most extreme angles. Save shadows, not much could be seen of the figures who marched between and behind the shields.

The more ignorant among the watching Fanim began jeering, but a whisper circulated among them, passing from ear to ear until all was rigid silence. A single Kianene word that even the most ignorant of the Amoti knew and feared: *qurraj* ...

Sorcerer.

As though answering a pause in conversation, an otherworldly chorus droned out from the approaching formations, not so much through the air as under the scorched crops and razed structures, and up through the bones of Shimeh's mighty curtain wall. The engines cast the first of the firepots. Eruptions of liquid flame revealed the Wards curving about each cadre. A cloud swallowed the sunlight, and as one the defenders saw the foundations of spectral towers.

True horror struck them then. Where were Indara's Water-bearers?

Those Fanim who tried to run were cut down by their own officers. The unholy chorus grew louder. The forward cadres halted some fifty lengths from the ramparts. The odd panicked arrow winked into smoke against their Wards. Columns of foot soldiers streamed forward between the cadres. To the rear of the formations, out of bowshot, several solitary figures stepped into air, their crimson gowns flapping, their eyes and mouths shining bright.

There was a collective intake of breath along the battlements ...

Then glittering light.

——— ⊷⊶ ———

The great siege-tower Proyas's men called Tippytoes groaned and creaked as the oxen and slaves pressed it forward across the fields. As the construction neared completion the previous dusk, Ingiaban had wondered aloud whether the siege-tower—which had been constructed to breach Gerotha's walls—would be tall enough "to give Shimeh's towers a kiss." With typical wit Gaidekki had replied that "she need only stand on her tippytoes." Somehow the name had stuck.

The great structure dipped and righted itself. Standing upon its packed crown, Proyas tightened an already white-knuckled grip on the railing. Men shouted, both about him and throughout the floors below. The crack of whips rose from behind. Before him, he could see the siege-tower's path marked in the raw dirt the sappers had used to level the irrigation ditches runnelling the fields. At the track's end, the white-and-ochre walls of Shimeh waited, their heights bristling with heathen men and heathen spears.

To his left, Tippytoes' counterpart, which the men had come to call Sister, lumbered forward as well, matching their progress. Taller than most any tree, she had been sheathed in mats of sodden seaweed, so that she seemed something otherworldly, a limbless beast. Hatches had been propped open along each of her six floors, behind which, Proyas knew, dozens of ballistae stood cocked and waiting, prepared to rake the parapets of the Tatokar Walls as soon as they entered range. The carpenter-overseers who had directed the assembly of both towers swore they were miracles of engineering—as they should be, given that the Warrior-Prophet had designed them.

Tippytoes teetered and advanced, her axles and joints screaming. The white-tiled walls and their giant eyes loomed closer …

Please God, Proyas found himself praying, *let this one thing be!*

The first of the stones arced toward them, flung by great engines hidden in the city. They fell wide, thumping into the earth short of their positions, but there was something surreal about watching them, as though the soul refused to believe weights so great could be cast so high. Men hollered in warning. A missile whooshed over them—close enough to touch! It missed, but crashed with deadly effect into the long train that drove them forward. Tippytoes lurched still for a moment, long enough for Sister to pull ahead. Proyas could see her runged back-side, which was naught but a giant ladder. Then Tippytoes heaved forward again.

Count-Palatine Gaidekki suddenly appeared among the men crowding the rear of Sister's top platform, his dark face beaming.

"Glory goes to the fleet of foot!" he cried. "We'll wash up the blood so you don't slip when you arrive!"

Though teeth remained clenched, all laughed, and a number began shouting for more speed. The laughter redoubled when a near hit forced Gaidekki and his men to fairly dive.

Then the first of the lights flashed about Massus Gate, and all heads turned. It seemed they could hear screams …

Even if sorcery was no longer anathema, few men among the pious—especially among the Conriyans—wished to follow the Scarlet Spires anywhere, let alone to Holy Shimeh. Proyas watched numb as great gouts of flame washed across the barbicans …

There was a chorus of plank-muffled shouts from directly beneath him, followed by a staccato snap, as though someone had broken a dozen twigs over his knee. Iron-tipped bolts whirred out from the ballistae arrayed behind the hatches below him, fanned across the teeming parapets. Moments later, Sister responded in kind. Save for those that exploded in small ceramic showers against the wall, the missiles seemed to vanish into the defenders crowding the battlements.

"Shields!" Proyas cried, not because they would help against the heathen artillery, but because they had come within extreme bow range.

Something dimmed the morning sun … Clouds?

The first hail of arrows fell upon them and those heaving them forward.

"Fire!" Proyas cried to the archers about him. "Clear the walls!"

The Massus Gate had become a mad play of lights in his periphery. But there was no time to watch. With every heartbeat, the unblinking eyes of Shimeh's walls drew closer and the air grew thicker with missiles. When he dared lower his shield, he could discern individual heathen in the bristling mass of defenders. He glimpsed one old man, a kettle bound to his head, taken in the throat by a bolt and carried backward into the city. Flaming pots crashed about the towers. Two smashed into the side of Sister, flinging burning tar across the seaweed. Suddenly smoke wreathed every sight, and the roar of fire bloated every sound. There was a crack and a concussion that brought all of them to their knees. One of the mighty stones had found its target. But miraculously, Tippytoes groaned onward. The floor beneath Proyas heaved like the deck of a ship. He hunched under his shield. The archers about him nocked, stood, fired, then crouched to nock once again. Every second man, it seemed, fell backward, swatting at a jutting shaft. The knights dragged them, dropped them over the side to make room for the others surging up from the lower floors. There was a roar, then a titanic clacking of stones that could only come from the Massus Gate. But a chorus of shrieks drew his attention to his left, to Sister, where a pot had exploded across the upper deck. Burning knights dove, heedless of the height, crashed onto their comrades below.

"Gaidekki!" Proyas screamed across the interval. "*Gaidekki!*"

The Count-Palatine's scowling face appeared between the timber hoardings, and Proyas actually smiled, despite the arrows buzzing between them. Then Gaidekki was gone. Proyas slipped to his knees, blinking against the image of the man's neck and shoulders snapping about an unstoppable stone.

The sky blackened. Closer and closer the siege-towers lumbered, though Sister had become a shining inferno. Then there were the white-tiled walls, close enough to hit with thrown clothing, crammed with arms and howling faces. Proyas could see a great eye opening across the white-tiled planes below, glimpse the wide expanse of street and structure reaching out to the Sacred Heights. There! There! There was the First Temple!

Shimeh! he thought. *Shimeh!*

Proyas lowered his silver war-mask, glimpsed his stooped kinsmen doing the same. The flying bridge dropped, its iron hooks biting the battlements. Tippytoes was tall enough to kiss after all.

Crying out to Prophet and God, the Crown Prince leapt into the swords of his enemy ...

The tree could not be missed.

It stood at the edge of a greater hill near the heart of the debris fields, the twin of black Umiaki in girth and height. Its great tendons were stripped of their bark, and its limbs reached into the air like winding tusks.

Climbing the remnants of a monumental stair set into the hillside, Kellhus soon found himself beneath its massive sinews. Beyond the tree, upturned blocks and rows of headless pillars stretched across the levelled summit. Save in the direction of Shimeh, where the ground had given way altogether, paving stones encircled the tree's base, rising and cracking about the immense roots.

He placed a hand against the immovable trunk, ran his fingertips across the lines that scored its surface. The spoor of old worms. He paused where the ground sheered away, staring at the black clouds that had accumulated on the horizon—above Shimeh. It seemed he could hear the thrum of distant thunder. Then he lowered himself over the fall, using exposed roots to anchor his descent.

Sheets of gravel clattered across the slopes below.

He found his footing. Above him, the tree soared, its trunk smooth and phallic, its boughs curved like canines, reaching far into the airy heights. Before him, roots twined like cuttlefish limbs. At some point—many years ago, from the look of the hatchet work—an opening had been hacked through them. Peering into the excavated gloom, Kellhus saw the lines of stonework, stairs dropping into blackness ...

He pressed his way forward, descended into the belly of the hillside.

Holding out his hand to alert Serwë and her brother, Cnaiür reined his stolen horse to a hard stop. Four vultures took soundlessly to the sky. On the slopes of a neighbouring rise, five saddled but riderless horses momentarily raised their heads, then continued grazing.

The three of them had paused on a low rise overlooking the carnage. The Betmulla Mountains rose grey and hunched in the distances before them—and there was still no sign of Kyudea, though Serwë insisted they followed the Dûnyain's path exactly. She could smell him, she said.

Cnaiür dismounted, strode into the midst of the sprawled bodies. He hadn't slept for days, but the exhaustion that buzzed through his limbs seemed an abstract thing, as easily ignored as a philosopher's argument. Ever since his discussion with the Mandate sorcerer, a strange intensity had seized him—a vigour he could only identify with hate.

"*He goes to Kyudea,*" the fat fool had finally said.

"*Kyudea?*"

"*Yes, Shimeh's ruined sister. It lies to the southwest, near the headwaters of the Jeshimal.*"

"*Did he tell you why?*"

"*No one knows ... Most think he goes to speak with the God.*"

"*Why do they think that?*"

"*Because he said he goes to his father's house.*"

"Kidruhil," Cnaiür called back, identifying the dead. "Likely hunting us."

He stared at the tracks across the ground, then stooped to examine several of the corpses. He pressed knuckles against the cheek of one, gauging its warmth. The skin-spies watched impassively, stared with unnerving directness as he walked back and remounted his horse.

"The Dûnyain surprised them," he said.

How many seasons had he pined for this moment? How many thoughts scattered and broken?

I shall kill them both.

"Are you sure it was him?" her brother asked. "We smell others ... Fanim."

Cnaiür nodded and spat. "It's him," he said with weary disgust. "Only one had time to draw his weapon."

War, she realized—war had given the world to men.

They had fallen to their knees before her, the Men of the Tusk. They had beseeched her for her blessing. "Shimeh," one man had cried. "I go to die for Shimeh!" And Esmenet did, though she felt foolish and so very far from the idol they seemed to make of her; she blessed them, saying words that would give them the certainty they so desperately needed—to die or to kill. In a voice she knew so well—at once soothing and provoking— she repeated something she had heard Kellhus say: "Those who do not fear death live forever." She held their cheeks and smiled, though her heart was filled with rot.

How they had thronged about her! Their arms and armour clattering. All of them reaching, aching for her touch, much as they had in her previous life.

And then they left her with the slaves and the ill.

The Whore of Sumna, some had called her, but in tones of exaltation, not condemnation, as though only by falling so far could one be raised so high. She found herself thinking of her namesake from *The Chronicle of the Tusk*, Esmenet, wife of Angeshraël, daughter of Shamanet. Was that her fate, to be a reference buried among holy articles? Would they call her Esmenet-allikal, or "Esmenet-the-other," the way *The Tractate* distinguished those with namesakes from the Tusk? Or would she simply be the Prophet-Consort ...

The Whore of Sumna.

The sky darkened, and the murderous roar swelled on the morning breeze. At long last it was *happening* ... and she could not bear it. She could not bear it.

Ignoring several entreaties to go watch the assault from the edge of the encampment, she returned to the Umbilica. It was deserted save for a handful of slaves gathered about their breakfast fires. Only one of the Hundred Pillars—a Galeoth with a bandaged thigh—stood guard. He bowed low and stiff as she barged past him into the closeted murk of the interior. She called out twice as she walked the tapestried halls, received no reply. All was quiet, still. The clamour of the Holy War seemed impossibly distant, as though she listened to another world through the joints of this one. Eventually she found herself in the dead Padirajah's bedchamber, staring at the great gilded bed where she and Kellhus slept and coupled. She piled her books and scrolls on it, then, crawling across the covers, surrounded herself with them. Rather than read, she touched, savoured their smooth and dry surfaces. Some she held until they became as warm as her skin. Then, for no reason she could fathom, she counted them, like a child jealous of her toys.

"Twenty-seven," she said to no one. Distant sorceries cracked faraway air, made the gold and glass settings hum with their rumble.

Twenty-seven doors opened, and not one way out.

"Esmi," a hoarse voice said.

For a moment she refused to look up. She knew who it was. Even more, she knew what he looked like: the desolate eyes, the haggard posture, even the way his thumb combed the hair across his knuckles ... It seemed a wonder that so much could be hidden in a voice, and an even greater wonder that she alone could see.

Her husband. Drusas Achamian.

"Come," he said, casting a nervous glance about the room. He did not trust this place. "Please ... come with me."

Through the canvas warren, she could hear Moënghus's infant wail. She blinked tears and nodded.

Always following.

<hr/>

Screams. Men combusting, burning like autumnal leaves, trailing oily ribbons of black. Thunder upon thunder, a chorus roaring at depths only the shivering stone could hear. Those cringing along the inner base of the fortifications saw the shadows of battlements flicker across the nearby tenements.

The heads of ghost dragons reared from the forward Scarlet Cadres, then like dogs straining for their master's hand, they bent forward and vomited incendiary streams. Fire gushed up across masonry, orange and gold in the gloom, blazing between crenellations, swirling down stair and ramp, rolling over men and transforming them into flailing shadows.

Within heartbeats, the Fanim packed across the barbican and adjacent walls ceased to exist. Stone cracked, exploded. The bastions of the gate buckled, and men winced, as though watching knees fold backward. The towers leaned out through the smoke, then dropped into obscurity. A great hemisphere of dust and debris rolled out and over the sorcerers and their unearthly song.

At long last, the Scarlet Spires marched.

Kellhus climbed through deeper ruins.

At the base of the stair he found a lantern made of horn and translucent paper—something neither Kianene nor Nilnameshi in manufacture. When ignited, it cast a diffuse orange glow ...

The halls were not human.

The drafts came to him, murmuring their secrets. His soul reached out, calculating probabilities, transforming inferences into space. About him, the galleries scrawled on and on into the immured blackness.

So like the Thousand Thousand Halls ... So like Ishuäl.

Kellhus forged ahead, the scattered detritus cracking beneath his feet. He watched the walls resolve from cold blackness, studied the mad detail that thronged across them. *Statuary*, not reliefs, had been carved into them: figures no taller than his knee, posed in narratives that outran the light of his lantern, and stacked one atop another, even across the vaulted ceiling, so that it seemed he walked through stone grille work. He paused, held his lantern before a string of naked figures raising spears against a lion, then realized that another frieze had been carved *behind* this first. Peering through miniature limbs, he saw deeper, more licentious representations, depicting all manner of poses and penetrations.

The work of Nonmen.

A trail had been scuffed across the hide of ancient dust—and by someone, Kellhus realized, who possessed a stride and gait identical to his own. Following it, he pressed deeper into the derelict mansion, knowing that he walked in his father's very footsteps. After descending several hundred paces, he entered a domed vestibule where the renderings across the walls were chiselled large as life but continued telling the same twofold tale of martial exploit and priapic excess. Copper bands, their bright green bleeding into the limestone, had been set into the walls, bearing a strange wedge script. But whether they were benedictions, explanations, or recitations of some hallowed text, Kellhus could not say.

He knew only that the inhabitants of this place had celebrated deeds in all their ambivalent complexity, rather than—as was the wont of Men—reproducing only flattering surfaces.

Ignoring the alternate passages, Kellhus continued following the track through the dust. It wound deep into the abandoned labyrinth, always descending. Save for the pitted remains of bronze arms, he found no artifacts, only chamber after florid chamber, each as ornate as the last. He passed through a vast library where scroll-racks towered higher than his lantern light could reach, and where queues and twining stairs—all exquisitely carved from living rock—loomed from the darkness as though from the ocean deeps. He did not pause, though he held out his lantern to each room he passed by or through: infirmaries, granaries, barracks, and personal apartments—warrens of them. Everything he saw, he pondered, knowing he understood nothing of the souls for whom these things were natural and immediate.

He pondered four thousand years of absolute dark.

He crossed a vast processional gallery where sculptured *events* spilled from the walls, epic scenes of strife and passion: nude penitents prostrate before the court of a Nonman King, warriors striving against mobs of Sranc or Men. Though Moënghus's trail often passed through these grand dioramas, Kellhus found himself walking around—heeding some voice from nowhere. Towering columns soared into the darkness, worked with arms gripping arms, twining upward and around, squared with bent-back wrists and open hands that cast the shadow of fingers. The ceilings remained cloaked in black obscurity. The silence was that of mighty hollows, at once oppressive and fragile, as though the clatter of a single stone might thunder.

Upraised palms braced his every step. Blank eyes studied his every angle. The Nonmen who had authored this place had possessed more than a fascination with the living form; it had been their obsession. Everywhere, they had cut their image into the dead stone about them, transforming the suffocating weights that hemmed them in into extensions of themselves. And Kellhus realized: the *mansion itself* had been their devotional work—their Temple. Unlike Men, these Nonmen had not rationed their worship. They did not distinguish between prayer and speech, idol and statue ...

Which spoke to their terror.

Collapsing possibilities with every step, Anasûrimbor Kellhus followed his father's trail into the blackness, his lantern raised to the issue of artisans, ancient and inhuman.

———⚉———

Where are you taking me?

Nowhere … Nowhere good.

He said nothing as he led her through the encampment, away from Shimeh, toward the greening heights to the west. She too said nothing, and spent much of the journey watching the grass stain the toes of her white silk slippers. She even made a game of it, kicking through the tangle of blades and stalks purposefully. Once she even wandered to her right so that she might walk across untrod ground, and for a moment it almost seemed they were Achamian and Esmenet once again, condemned and derided rather than exalted or revered. The sorcerer and his melancholy whore. She even dared clutch his chill hand.

What harm could come of it?

Please … keep walking. Let us flee this place!

Only when they passed through the final battery of tents did she actually *notice* him, the forward-fixed eyes misted by inscrutable thoughts, the strong jaw working beneath the plaits of his beard. They began climbing—toward the very gutted mausoleum where she had found Kellhus the night previous.

It seemed different in daylight, somehow. The walls …

"You never came to Zin's funeral," he finally said.

She squeezed his hand. "I couldn't bear to." Her voice faltered, speaking the words. They seemed cruel, horribly so, despite what she herself had suffered the night the Marshal of Attrempus died.

His only friend.

"Was the fire bright?" she asked. The customary question.

He climbed several more steps, his sandalled feet swishing through yellow-blooming bitterweed. Several bees spun in angry circles, buzzing through the thunder that rumbled across the distances—the clamour of battle. Through some trick of sound, the faint raving of one man floated to the fore, at once hoarse and metallic.

"The fire was bright."

The bricked ruin rose before them, its foundations ringed with thronging sumac and weeds. Poplars shot young and straight from the interior, brushing the highest of the truncated walls with their branches. She wondered at details that had escaped her in the gloom with Kellhus. At the webbed nest of caterpillars bobbing in the breeze. At the ovals which might once have been faces, set into the eastward walls.

What am I doing?

For an absurd instant she found herself fearing for her life. Many men would have murdered her for crimes she had committed ... What about Achamian? Could loss have unearthed such a man within him? But then, unaccountably, she was angry at the way he had yielded her. *You should have fought for me!*

"Why are we here, Akka?"

Oblivious to her mad thoughts, he turned with one arm held wide, as though boasting of hard-won lands.

"I wanted you to see this," he said.

Following his hand, she looked out across the encampment, whose tent-enclosed avenues wheeled out in broken seashell patterns, over the razed groves, fields, and buildings of the intervening ground. And there it was, scored by pluming smoke, motionless and gloomy beneath the preternatural dark of the sky ... Shimeh.

From their seaward faces the Tatokar Walls wound white as teeth about the warren of street and structure that engulfed the heights of the Juterum. Both the ground and the parapets winked with flashing arms. The two siege-towers given to Proyas were pressed against the ramparts, surrounded by lines and squares of men. The northern one burned like a miniature paper votive. A great pillar of smoke rose from what had been the Massus Gate, leaning low over the city, its nethers burnished by the wicked glare of sorceries. To either side, several of the great eyes had been broken, and the towers appeared abandoned. Farther to the south, on the far side of the ruined aqueduct, the two siege-towers given to Chinjosa had also reached the walls, and dark masses of Ainoni teemed about their bases, queuing to climb their runged backs.

And in the near distance, clear through passing sheets of smoke, stood the First Temple.

She raised a balled fist to her brow. Perhaps it was some trick of scale or perspective, but it all seemed so *slow,* as though it happened through water—or something more viscous than human understanding.

Nevertheless, it *happened* ...

"We've gained the heights," she said—a murmur that somehow became a cry. "The city is ours!" She turned to Achamian, who seemed to watch with the same horror and wonder—*awe*—that numbed her expression.

"Akka ... Can't you see? Shimeh falls! *Shimeh falls!*"

There had been so much in these words—far more than fervour, far more than the tears that clotted her eyes. Love. Rape and revelation. Disease, starvation, and massacre. Everything they had survived. Everything she had endured.

But he shook his head, his eyes still fixed on the vista before them. "It's all a lie."

Horns pealed to the lowing clouds.

"What?"

He turned to her, his look possessed by a terrifying blankness. She recognized it, for the same blankness had owned her eyes the night he had returned to Caraskand.

"The Scylvendi came to me last night."

Fanim drums throbbed. The clouds continued to darken, answering to the Cishaurim and their malevolent will.

Urged on by the cries of their Captains, phalanxes of Javreh charged the slopes, clambered across the heaped ruin of the Massus Gate, then sprinted into the towering veils of smoke that slowly drifted across the city. The first of the Scarlet Cadres followed, picking their way forward carefully, keeping their sorcerers shielded at all times.

The outlines of the surviving walls resolved from the haze, and as the formations passed beneath them, geysers of glittering fire reached up to lave their heights. More stonework came tumbling to ground. The world itself seemed to mutter curses.

Sarothenes was the first of the Scarlet Schoolmen to set foot in Shimeh, followed by Ptarramas the Older and Ti, who, despite his great age, continually scolded his Javreh for their sloth. Before them loomed a warren of alleyways and buildings that stretched to the foot of the Juterum. Their Javreh pickets fanned out in their hundreds, cutting down hapless Amoti, sifting through the buildings. Screams pealed out from hidden places.

Ptarramas the Older was the first to die, struck in the shoulder by a Chorae as he pressed his cadre forward. He fell to the street, cracked like statuary. Bellowing arcana, Ti sent flocks of burning sparrows into the black windows of the adjacent tenement. Explosions spit blood and debris across the street. Then, from the ruins of the outer wall, Inrûmmi struck the building's westward face with brilliant lightning. The air cracked. Burnt brick walls sloughed to the ground. In an exposed room, a burning figure stumbled over the lip of the floor and plummeted to the ruin below.

Sheltered by his Javreh and their wide shields, Eleäzaras gained the summit of the ruined Massus, surveyed his cadres deploying before him. He leaned against the iron prongs jutting from the debris at his feet—the remains of the portcullis. Though he couldn't see Ptarramas, he knew that something had already happened.

They had hoped to draw the Snakeheads out in a decisive engagement, but Seokti was too canny. The Shigeki fiend, it appeared, hoped to bleed them. Pick them off one by one.

Eleäzaras looked across the maze of structures before him, the welter of walls and rooftops extending to the slopes of the Juterum and marble bastions of the First Temple upon its summit. He could sense the Chorae out there, buried in cellars, crouched in lethal vantages, waiting …

Everywhere. Hidden enemies.

Too much … too many.

"Fire cleanses!" he cried. "Raze it! Burn it all to ash!"

※

The long-awaited horns sounded, a coarse peal over the throb of heathen drums. Towering amid his shield-brothers, Yalgrota Sranchammer raised his axe to the darkling sky, howled bloodthirsty oaths to Gilgaöl—mighty War. His kinsmen answered with raucous shouts. Then the Thunyeri surged into the Scarlet Schoolmen's wake, racing over the smoking ruins of the Massus Gate. Shattered tile cracked beneath their booted feet.

To their north, Proyas and his Conriyans battled across the parapets. Of their two siege-towers, one had been lost to inferno, but hundreds clambered up the back of the other, dashing through arrows to reinforce their Prince. To their south, Chinjosa and his Ainoni watched with amazement as the Fanim defenders fled the ponderous approach of their two siege-towers. Bellicose Uranyanka and his Moserothi would be the first of their number to set foot upon the Tatokar Walls.

The black-armoured Thunyeri spilled unopposed into the city. Prince Hulwarga and Earl Goken struck south, leading the Skagwi and the wild-haired Auglishmen into the unruined streets behind the Ainoni section of the wall. Earl Ganbrota, meanwhile, drove north with his Ingraulish, their shields adorned with shrunken heads. The east they left to the Scarlet Gurwikka and their dark-skinned slaves.

Soon the Kianene and Amoti were dissolving in panic. Everywhere they looked, they saw chain-armoured myriads, loosed like blond wolves into the streets.

The lantern faltered, and for a moment Kellhus cradled it as though trying to coax it to life with the fire of his own body. With a final hiss, it faded into nothing.

But that was not the end of light. He saw the faintest of glimmers off to his right, toward the sound of booming water. Rather than use any Cant that might announce his presence, he continued in blackness.

The sound grew more and more thunderous as he followed the pitch hallway. A fine mist sheened his skin, matted his hair and robe. The light grew more and more distinct: orange shining across the black of wet stone. Twice he stooped, drew his fingers across the floor to ensure that he still followed his father's trail.

The hallway opened onto a balcony that overlooked a vast cavern. At first all he could discern were the mighty curtains of water tumbling from abyssal blackness, and on such a scale that the flooring beneath him seemed to float upward. Then he noticed the points of light below, several of them, arrayed across a platform beyond the waterfalls' reach, and reflected in the oily surface of some kind of pool. Braziers, he realized, dim-burning because of the sodden air.

Father?

Kellhus descended a broad stair hewn from the walls. As elsewhere in the mansion, every surface had been rendered with heroic carvings across more pornographic reliefs, though on a far greater scale. Kellhus could make out immense vaults, their tangled figures encrusted with the mineral residue of water and millennia. The falls themselves towered into darkness, raucous, white foam wheeling, dropping with the weight of glaciers, so tall they threatened to press him to his knees.

A series of chutes, like halved versions of the long curved horns the Thunyeri used to communicate in battle, had been raised to the tumbling skirts of the waterfalls. There were dozens of them, hooking outward and downward, arranged to convey water to the sprawling floor below, though only three still reached into the crashing white, the others having broken. Green about the edges, they gleamed copper where the water still runnelled them.

The stair wound away from the falls, curled across the back of the vast chamber, where it met its mirror image and broadened in a monumental fan. Bronze weaponry and armour lay scattered across the steps, remnants of the ancient battle that had been lost here. As he neared the stair's base, the sounds of smaller waters were braided into the background roar: the gurgling of eaves, and the slap and whish of small streams across stone. A cavernous must permeated the air.

"They gathered here in the hundreds," a voice called across the gloom, clear despite the ambient rumble. "Even thousands, in the days before the Womb-Plague ..."

A Kûniüric voice.

Kellhus paused on the steps, searched the gloom.

At last.

As broad as the Siricus Arena in Momemn, the floor opened before him, matted with detritus and the small mounds which were all that remained of the fallen. Ripples dilated in endless procession across the broad pool set in the floor's centre. Like a black mirror, it reflected the braziers burning along its far rim, the fat bronze faces looming over them, and the great cascading column of the waterfall. At the terminus of the chutes, a series of immense bronze statues had been erected: kneelers, obese and naked, with channels cut into their backs and with heads hollowed into great-jowled masks. They squatted in a broad semi-circle facing the pool, their expressions lurid in the orange light. Water streamed from the eyes and mouths of three of them, slapping across the stone. The hollowed head of one had broken off altogether. It now rested near the far end of the pool, its single unsubmerged eye staring across the black waters.

"Bathing was holy for them," the voice continued.

Kellhus descended the last of the monumental stair, slowly walked across the floor. He had grown accustomed to listening through voices, but this one was smooth as porcelain—seamless and inscrutable. Even still, he knew it very well. How could he not, when it was his own?

Advancing around the pool, he saw a pale figure, sitting cross-legged behind the sheets of water that poured from one of the monstrous faces. A man, white-skinned, obscured by rushing translucence.

"The fires are for you," the figure said. "I have lived in darkness for a long, long time."

Her calm terrified Achamian almost as much as the clamour on the horizon. The very wind stank of sorcery.

"So he uses everyone," she finally said. "His every word is bent upon manipulation ..." She stared as though her eyes had forgotten how to blink. "Don't you mean he uses *me*?"

"I—I haven't thought it all through yet, but I think he wants ... *children* ... Children with his strength, his intellect, and you—"

"So he *breeds*. Is that it? I'm his prized mare?"

"I know how hateful these words must—"

"Why would you think that? I've been used my whole life." She paused, glared at him with as much remorse as outrage. "My whole life, Akka. And now that I've become the instrument of something *higher*, higher than men and their rutting hunger—"

"But why? Why be an instrument at all?"

"You speak as if we had a choice—you, a *Mandate Schoolman*! There's no escape. You know that. With every breath, we are used!"

"Then why the bitterness, Esmi? Shouldn't a prophet's vessel sound ex—"

"Because of you, Akka!" she cried with alarming ferocity. "*You!* Why can't you just let me go? You know that I love you, so you cling to that, you dig in with grubby nails and you yank and yank and yank, you bruise and batter my heart, and you refuse to let me go!"

"Esmi ... I asked and you came."

Long silence.

"All this," she said, her voice almost inaudible for the crack of faraway sorceries, "everything Cnaiür said ... what makes you think that Kellhus hasn't already told me?"

Achamian swallowed, ignored the lights that flashed across his periphery.

"Because you say you love him."

Cymbals crashed in a relentless tempo, measuring the hellish advance of the Scarlet Spires. They laid waste to all before them. Whatever resistance the heathen mustered, they puffed out like candle flames. Companies of horsemen, bowmen arrayed across the rooftops—all mummified in Anagogic fire.

Save for the adept Watchers who walked the sky in their wake, most of the seventy-four surviving sorcerers of rank marched on foot through the conflagration, sheltering themselves and their Javreh shield-men with Wards. Bathed in the light of successive Cants, each cadre trailed a flickering array of shadows. They climbed ramps of blackened stone, mounds of smashed brick, found their footing, and worked more thunderous devastation. Stones arced skyward, trailing streamers of smoke. Cornices and pillars collapsed upon their footings, swallowed by the black-billowing issue of their destruction. The whole world seemed rendered in luminous bloods and abyssal blacks. They stepped over sizzling limbs.

Above towering flames and through curtains of smoke, the First Temple and the Ctesarat loomed ever closer, until they encompassed the horizon. Again and again the Scarlet Schoolmen called out with destruction, but none would answer.

The Fanim ran before them, like flame-maddened beasts.

Only the sky ...

Of all this world, only the sky offered them surcease, a momentary reprieve from spikes of terrestrial congestion. Through furnace eyes they gazed across the world's dark curvature. The sun flared white and preternaturally bright. Thunderheads roiled beneath, trailing into nothingness in the distance, like snow kicked across ice. They saw pale coastlines, vast tracts of bleached ochre and blue. They flexed their frames in languorous vanity, beat their air-scooping wings.

Zioz. Setmahaga. Sohorat ...

Only here, at the limits of this cursed world.

Then the Voice called them, crackling with torment and rebuke. As one, they bent their elephantine heads back, howled into the indigo depths, then plunged backward, diving into the skein of angry clouds. Wind burned eyes that could not tear.

Like stones, they dropped from the belly of the clouds.

Shimeh encircled the nearing ground, dark save where fires scored her. They sensed the mortals, loping like monkeys down murky streets, raping, murdering, warring ...

Would that they could devour it all.

But the Voice! The Voice! Like a thing of needles. More agonizing than the million teeth of this surrounding world.

They soared toward the city's heart, following the yaw and pitch of the eastern wind, then alighted, one after another, on the eaves of the First Temple.

The Voice approved.

They flattened like beetles against the slate. They could sense the eyeless ones within, waiting.

Fall upon them! the Voice screeched. *Rend them! Only in their midst will you be safe from the Chorae!*

They smashed through the shingles, tore aside the braces, cracked the great stone lintels asunder, then dropped in a hail of debris. A dozen saffron-robed men scrambled about them, blue lights flashing from their foreheads. Great arcs of energy sizzled across their incandescent hides.

Sohorat roared, and plaster rained throughout the forest of columns. Flies burst from his maw. Raving wolves bubbled from his palms, smashed the sheets of light, gorged on those cringing behind them. Zioz swept burning threads into his fist, wrenched souls from their housing meat. Setmahaga clawed aside flimsy defences, struck heads from bodies, gloried in the blood that smoked across his limbs. He squealed like a thousand pigs, such was his exultation.

"*Demon!*" A voice like a thunderclap.

They turned from the blood-soaked marble, saw an old, eyeless man approach from the deeper temple. Something flashed from his forehead, like a stolen star. Others spilled between the flanking columns. More blind men.

Flee, the Voice whispered in his soul.

Setmahaga fell first, struck in the eye by an *absence* affixed to the end of a stick. An explosion of burning salt ...

Flee!

Then Sohorat, his slavering form caught in torrents of light, screamed. Zioz leapt into the clouds.

Return me, manling! Throw off these chains!

But the Scarlet Schoolman was obstinate.

One last task ... One more offending eye ...

Water everywhere, falling in thundering cataracts, singular drops, and draping sheets. Kellhus paused next to one of the shining braziers, peered beneath the bronze visage that loomed orange and scowling over his father, watched him lean back into absolute shadow.

"You came to the world," unseen lips said, "and you saw that Men were like children."

Lines of radiance danced across the intervening waters.

"It is their nature to believe as their fathers believed," the darkness continued. "To desire as they desired ... Men are like wax poured into moulds: their souls are cast by their circumstances. Why are no Fanim children born to Inrithi parents? Why are no Inrithi children born to Fanim parents? Because these truths are *made*, cast by the particularities of circumstance. Rear an infant among Fanim and he will become Fanim. Rear him among Inrithi and he will become Inrithi ...

"Split him in two, and he would murder himself."

Without warning, the face re-emerged, water-garbled, white save the black sockets beneath his brow. The action seemed random, as though his father merely changed posture to relieve some vagrant ache, but it was not. *Everything*, Kellhus knew, had been premeditated. For all the changes wrought by thirty years in the Wilderness, his father remained Dûnyain ...

Which meant that Kellhus stood on conditioned ground.

"But as obvious as this is," the blurred face continued, "it escapes them. Because they cannot see what comes before them, they assume *nothing* comes before them. Nothing. They are numb to the hammers of circumstance, blind to their conditioning. What is branded into them, they think freely chosen.

So they thoughtlessly cleave to their intuitions, and curse those who dare question. They make ignorance their foundation. They confuse their narrow conditioning for absolute truth."

He raised a cloth, pressed it into the pits of his eyes. When he withdrew it, two rose-coloured stains marked the pale fabric. The face slipped back into the impenetrable black.

"And yet part of them fears. For even unbelievers share the depth of their conviction. Everywhere, all about them, they see examples of their own self-deception ... 'Me!' everyone cries. 'I am chosen!' How could they *not* fear when they so resemble children stamping their feet in the dust? So they encircle themselves with yea-sayers, and look to the horizon for confirmation, for some *higher sign* that they are as central to the world as they are to themselves."

He waved his hand out, brought his palm to his bare breast. "And they pay with the coin of their devotion."

"And what of you, Akka?" Esmenet said, her voice become scathing. "Haven't you yielded your precious Gnosis as readily as I've yielded my womb?" Why couldn't she just hate him, this drab and broken sorcerer? It would all be so much easier then.

Achamian cleared his throat. "Yes ... yes, I have ..."

"Then tell me *why*, Holy Tutor. Why would a Mandate Schoolman do such an unthinkable thing?"

"Because the Second Apocalypse ... It comes ..."

"The very world is at stake and you *complain* that he makes weapons of all things? Akka, you should rejoi—"

"I'm not saying he's not the Harbinger! He may even be a prophet for all I know …"

"Then what *are* you saying, Akka? Do you even *know*?"

Two tears threaded his cheeks.

"That he *stole* you from me! Stole!"

"Picked your purse, did he? That's funny, because I feel more shit than gold."

"It's not like that."

"Isn't it? You love me, yes, Akka, but I've never been anything more than a—"

"But you're *not thinking*! You see only your love for him. You're not thinking of what he sees *when he gazes upon you*."

A moment of silent horror.

"But he lies! The Scylvendi lies! I'm *Nansur*. I know—"

"Tell me, Esmi! Tell me *what he sees*!"

She shook. Why was she shaking? The earth seemed like stone beneath her knees.

"The truth," she murmured. "He sees the truth!"

Somehow his arms had scooped her to her feet. And she clutched him, sobbed and wailed into his shoulders.

He whispered into her ear. "He doesn't *see*, Esmi … He watches."

And the words were there, at once deafening and unspoken.

… *without love.*

She looked up to him, and he stared at her with an intensity, a desperation, she knew she would never find in Kellhus's endless blue eyes. He smelled warm … bitter.

His lips were wet.

Eleäzaras gazed across the infernal landscape. He could hear himself cackle, but he knew not the voice. What was this he felt? Glee, dark and gloating, like watching a hated sibling struck at last. Remorse, and fear—terror, even! It was as though he dropped and dropped and never struck ground.

And, yes … *omnipotence*. Like liquor burning through his veins, or opium sweltering his soul.

Like the spectres of decapitated snakes, dragonheads reared above various cadres and masticated about streaming fire. To his immediate right, someone—Nem-Panipal?—sang boiling clouds of black. Lightning flashed out in a blinding skein. Stone exploded outward. Sheering along a diagonal, a tower fell onto the ruins of its own foundation, where it lay like an overturned hull.

The Grandmaster cackled as the wave of dust rolled over him. Shimeh burned! Shimeh burned!

Somehow Sarothenes, his shield-bearers nowhere to be seen, had found his way to his side. Why would the fool risk—

"You press too hard!" the rail-thin sorcerer cried. Lines of black scored his rutted face, where he had wiped at flecks of soot, no doubt. "You exhaust us on women, children, and dumb stone!"

"Kill them!" Eleäzaras spat. "I care not!"

"But the *Cishaurim,* Eli! We must conserve ourselves!"

For some reason, he thought of all the slaves who had swallowed his member, of clutching tight silken sheets, of the luxurious agony of release. This was what it was like, he realized. He had seen them, the Men of the Tusk, filing back from battle, matted in blood, smiling with those terrifying eyes ...

As though to show those eyes to Sarothenes, he turned to the man, held out a hand to the sulphurous calamity before them.

"Behold!" he spat contemptuously. "Behold what we—*we!*—have wrought."

The soot-stained sorcerer stared at him in horror. Lights flashed across his sweaty cheek.

Eleäzaras turned back to exult in the wages of his impossible labour. Shimeh burned ... *Shimeh.*

"Our power," he grated. "Our *glory!*"

From the parapets of the Mirraz Gate, Proyas gazed in disbelief.

A vast plate of clouds—dark, churning in unnatural, ingrown ways—moved in ponderous revolutions about the city, taking the Sacred Heights as its axis. Simply staring at it dizzied his footing. From where he stood, the First Temple seemed impossibly near. He could even see armoured men—Fanim—emerge from the darkness beyond the outermost ring of pillars, bounding down stairs and across landings before disappearing behind the battlements of the Heterine Wall. But what dismayed him was the great curtain of smoke and fire that approached the Heights from the ruins of the Massus Gate. Chalk-white streamers. Mists of ochre dust. Rolling veils of grey. Plumes like liquid basalt, solid and black. And through them, glowering fires, threads of lightning, and flying cataracts of gold. Whole tracts of the city had been blasted and consumed, reduced to a great thumb of smouldering ruin.

Ingiaban laughed maniacally. "Have you ever seen such a thing!"

Proyas turned to rebuke him, only to glimpse a figure draped in shimmering crimson picking his way over the matted dead immediately behind them. The man teetered for a moment, skidding in blood. His iron-grey braid swung across his left shoulder.

"What are you doing?" Proyas cried.

The Scarlet Schoolman ignored him, took up a position facing west, and stretched his arms wide beneath the sky.

"You're destroying the city!"

The old man whirled, so quickly that his ornate gowns were a heart-beat in following. Despite his phlegmatic eyes and stooped frame, his voice was as forceful as it was furious. "Conriyan ingrate! The Cishaurim own the skies. They use the darkness to hide their Chorae! If we lose this contest, then *all is lost*, do you understand? *Holy Shimeh* ... Fie on your fucking city!"

Shocked as much by the man's bearing as by his vehemence, Proyas retreated a step, speechless. Cursing, the Schoolman returned to his task, and Proyas found himself peering down the wall to the nearest tower. Tiny figures teemed atop the parapet, and among them, another white-bearded Schoolman stood leaning against the battlements, his arms held out to the west, his eyes flaring bright as he sang. Black clouds ribbed the sky above, though the Meneanor beyond still winked blue and white, bathed in distant sunshine.

The sorcerer before Proyas began singing as well. A sudden wind bellied his gaping sleeves.

And a voice whispered, *No ... not like this.*

Screens of tumbling water, breaking the world beyond them into glittering lines and smeared shadows. Kellhus had ceased trying to penetrate them.

"Power," Anasûrimbor Moënghus said, "is always power *over*. When an infant may be either, what is the difference between a Fanim and an Inrithi? Or between a Nansur and a Scylvendi? What could be so malleable in Men that anyone, split between circumstances, could be his own murderer?

"You learned this lesson quickly. You looked across Wilderness and you saw thousands upon thousands of them, their backs bent to the field, their legs spread to the ceiling, their mouths reciting scripture, their arms hammering steel ... Thousands upon thousands of them, each one a small circle of repeating actions, each one a wheel in the great machine of nations ...

"You understood that when men stop bowing, the emperor ceases to rule, that when the whips are thrown into the river, the slave ceases to serve. For an infant to be an emperor or a slave or a merchant or a whore or a general or whatever, those about him *must act accordingly*. And Men act as they *believe*.

"You saw them, in their thousands, spread across the world in great hierarchies, the actions of each exquisitely attuned to the expectations of others. The identity of Men, you discovered, was determined by the beliefs, the assumptions, of others. *This* is what makes them emperors or slaves ... Not their gods. Not their blood.

"Nations live as Men act," Moënghus said, his voice refracted through the ambient rush of waters. "Men act as they *believe*. And Men believe as they are conditioned. Since they are blind to their conditioning, they do not doubt their intuitions ..."

Kellhus nodded in wary assent. "They believe absolutely," he said.

He found himself clutching her hand, pulling her away, toward the derelict mausoleum. He saw her smile despite her tears, her face so heartbreakingly beautiful, while beyond her, just to the left of her cheek, the First Temple, freckle-small in the distance, presided over smoke and burning streets.

The walls had collapsed to their footings at the mausoleum's south-eastern corner. He stepped over them, sweeping weeds flat with a sandalled foot. He drew her into the interior, into the dappled gloom where the young trees had rooted. Insects whirred up into the last of the sunlight. They kissed again, embraced in a more profound manner. Then they were upon the ground, cold, hard, and matted with living things.

No, something whispered within him. *Not like this ... not like this!*

And he knew—they both knew!—what it was they were doing: blotting one crime with another ... But he couldn't stop. Even though he knew she would hate him afterward. Even though he knew *that was what she wanted ...*

Something unforgivable.

She was weeping, whispering things—inaudible things. It seemed the roaring of ache and need and accusation was all Achamian could hear. *What am I doing?*

"I can't hear you," he murmured, fumbling with the tails of her gown that had bunched between her legs. Why so frantic? What was this terror he felt?

Sweet Sejenus! How could a heart pound so hard?

Please. Please.

Beneath him, she rocked her face back and forth, bit the knuckle of her thumb.

"We're dead," she gasped. "*He does love me ... He will kill ...*"

Then Achamian was inside her.

⌘

They fled the walls, the Amoti and their Kianene overseers, and ran into the darkening streets. The iron men had come with blistering sorceries and shrieking horns. The accursed idolaters. And it seemed that none could resist them. Where was the Padirajah? Where were his Wellkeepers? His Grandees and their shining horses? And the Water-bearers! Where were they?

Smoke drifted faint and sheer over Shimeh's western quarters. Ash fell like snow. Here and there, panicked groups were run down by the Conriyans and their silver-masks-without-expression. The encounters were as disastrous as they were brief. Some careered into their countrymen running in the opposite direction. Words of breathless horror were exchanged, descriptions of the crimson qurraji who blasted everything in their path, of the black-mailed northmen swinging severed heads and hooting in animal voices. The idolaters seemed to be everywhere.

But many stumbled onto the expanse of the Esharsa Market, where the triangular pennant of a *real* Grandee, Prince Hûkal of Mongilea, awaited them, along with four hundred riders, true desert men from the unforgiving plains of the Great Salt. The Amoti conscripts found themselves arrayed in new ranks across the open cobble, while the black-garbed Prince cried out reminders of Fane and his indomitable courage. Soon, some two thousand faithful occupied the open cobble, their shoulders squared, their hearts renewed.

And not a moment too soon. Melee had already engulfed the surrounding streets, where the Fanim defended hasty barricades against unmounted Conriyan knights. The idolaters' numbers swelled as more and more of the bands ranging the streets joined the fracas. Those who came upon the market paused, and only ventured to attack when several hundred of them had gathered. The Anpleian barons and knights led the assault, eager to avenge the death of Shressa Gaidekki, their beloved Count-Palatine, but they were undone, driven back by the charges of Hûkal and his Mongileans. Only when the Prince Nersei Proyas arrived with the Palatines Ingiaban and Ganyatti were they able to organize a determined assault. The Amoti broke easily enough, fled into the eastern streets, many of which the Conriyans had already overrun on the flanks. But the Mongilean horsemen proved far more stubborn, and their charges exacted a horrible toll. Even as their horses failed them, they fought with ferocious zeal. Lord Ganyatti, the Palatine of Ankirioth, traded blows with mighty Prince Hûkal himself. The heathen lord beat aside his shield and cracked his collarbone with a blow that snapped his scimitar. Lord Ganyatti toppled back, was crushed by pummelling hooves.

Death came swirling down.

Led by the fury of Lord Proyas, the Conriyans broke the heathen horsemen and recovered the Palatine's ravaged corpse. The Mongileans melted into the surrounding streets. Howling mighty oaths, the bereaved Ankiriothi raced after them.

But the Prince pulled Ingiaban aside.

"What is it?" the burly Palatine said, his voice ringing through his war-mask.

"Where are they?" Proyas asked. "The Fanim."

"What do you mean?"

"They only pretend to defend their city."

———— ∞ ————

All Kellhus could see of his father were two fingers and a thumb lying slack upon a bare thigh. The thumbnail gleamed.

"As Dûnyain," the disembodied voice continued, "you had no choice. To command yourself, you had to master circumstance. And to master circumstance, you had to bind the actions of the worldborn to your will. You had to make limbs of nations. So you made their *beliefs* the object of your relentless scrutiny. It was axiomatic.

"You realized those truths that cut against the interests of the powerful were called lies, and that those lies that served those interests were called truths. And you understood that it had to be this way, since it is the *function* of belief, not the veracity, that preserved nations. Why call an emperor's blood divine? Why tell slaves that suffering is grace? It is what beliefs *do*, the actions they license and prohibit, that is important. If men believed all blood was equal, the caste-nobility would be overthrown. If men believed all coin was oppression, the caste-merchants would be turned out.

"Nations tolerate only those beliefs *that conserve* the great system of interlocking actions that makes them possible. For the worldborn, you realized, truth is largely irrelevant. Why else would they all dwell in delusion?

"Your first decision was elementary. You claimed to be a member of the caste-nobility, a prince, knowing that, once you convinced some, you could demand that all act accordingly. And through this simple deception, you secured your independence. No other would command you, because they believed they had no *right* to command you.

"But how might you convince them of *your* right? One lie had made you their equal; what further lie might make you their master?"

———— ∞ ————

Whatever their old ardour, their bodies remembered. When he closed his eyes, she was *there*, beneath him, *about* him, enclosing his every languorous thrust, gasping and crying out, gasping and crying out. He could feel himself balled like a fist within her, alive to her heat, her liquid clutch.

She reached out for his face, pulled him down to her hot mouth. She sobbed as she kissed him.

"You were dead!"

"I came back for you ..."

Anything. Even the world.

"Akka ..."

"For you."

Esmi. Esmenet. Gasping and crying out ...

Such a strange name for a harlot.

Sheets of mist wheeled out from the mighty subterranean cataract, soaking his hair to his scalp, his robes to his skin. False tears slipped down his cheeks as he listened.

"You understood that beliefs, like Men, possessed hierarchies, that some commanded more than others, and that *religious belief* commanded most of all. What better demonstration could there be than the Holy War itself? That the actions of so many could be pitched with single purpose against so many native weaknesses: fear, sloth, compassion ...

"So you read their scriptures, scrutinized the authority of words over men. You saw the primary function of Inrithism: to anchor belief in what cannot be seen, and so assure the repetition of the manifold actions that give nations their form. To doubt the order, to question *the way things are*, is to question the God-who-was-their-creator. The God becomes the warrant of Men and their station, and the arbitrary relations of power that are the truth of the Emperor and the Slave are covered over, nary to be seen. Not only do questions become hazards, heresies, they also become *futile*, for their answers lie nowhere in this world. The servant shakes his fist at the heavens, not his master."

His father's voice—so much like his own—swelled to seize all the dead Nonmen spaces.

"And here you saw the Shortest Path ... For you understood that this trick, which turns the eyes of the oppressed skyward and away from the hand that holds the whip, could be usurped to your ends. To command circumstance, you must command action. To command action, you must command belief. To command belief, you need only speak *with the voice of heaven.*

"You were Dûnyain, one of the Conditioned, and they, with their stunted intellects, were no more than children."

From the heights of the ruined Shrine of Azoreah, Inrithi hornsmen, Tydonni belonging to Gothyelk's own household, saw it first: a twinkle followed by a thunderous roar.

The Lords of the Holy War had scoured the surrounding plains, had even sent scouting parties into the cloven roots of the Betmulla, but they had found no sign of Fanayal or his heathen army. Aside from yielding Shimeh, which the Inrithi commanders found difficult to believe, this could mean only one thing.

The scouts, stationed across what heights the Shairizor Plains offered, were ready, as was Earl Gothyelk, who held his several thousand surviving Tydonni in reserve, though for years assailing Shimeh's walls had been his heart's most ardent dream. They had expected the Kianene to take the field, where their speed and mobility could be exercised to their full advantage.

The *manner*, however, confounded them.

Reports were sent to the Earl, who waited with his men just to the east of the encampment, describing heathen activity in the southeastern quarters of the Holy City—the vicinity of the Tantanah Gate. He dispatched messengers to Chinjosa's Ainoni, whose flanks lay nearest to the movement, then ordered a general advance. Should the Fanim host begin issuing from one of the eastern gates, he was, as per the Warrior-Prophet's hallowed instructions, to assemble along the River Jeshimal, securing its two bridges and one—quite treacherous—whitewater ford. Following standards bearing the Circumfix, black on gold, the mail-draped Tydonni knights took the lead, trotting forward on their stolen horses. To their left, Holy Shimeh boomed and smoked. Men laughed and pointed to

Ainoni pennants on the many-towered Tatokar Walls. The pace was practised, leisurely even. The inveterate old Earl did not consider time an issue, since it would take hours for the heathen to trickle through the gates, let alone form up for battle.

But the gates were not thrown open.

For weeks the sappers had laboured, undermining the foundations of their own defences. Walls meant nothing, their bright-eyed Padirajah assured them, when Schools went to war. Mathematicians from Nenciphon were consulted, as was the great architect Gotauran ab Suraki. Then the Cishaurim were employed.

For a time the hornsmen at Azoreah could only stare in astonishment. Light flashed, white haloed by blue and indigo, then the faraway Tantanah Gate and tracts of adjoining wall simply *dropped*, dissolving into gigantic blooms of dust. The breeze was slow in drawing the obscuring clouds sheer. Several heartbeats passed where they could see only lumbering shadows. Then they saw them—mastodons, dozens of them, ramping the debris with broad timber rafts. By the time the hornsmen sounded their pealing alarm, the first of the Kianene horsemen were already racing across the Shairizor Plains.

The sound of the heathen drums suddenly redoubled.

"You need only convince them that the distance between their intellect and yours was the distance between the World and the Outside. Do this, and they would yield to you absolute authority, cede to you their utter devotion.

"The path was narrow, to be certain, but it was very clear. You cultivated their awe and their inklings, telling them things *no man* could know. You appealed to the spark of Logos within them. You mapped the logic of their commitments, showed them the implications of the tenets they already held. You showed them beliefs fixed by *truth* rather than function. You made their fears and weaknesses plain—you showed them *who they were*—even as you exploited those weaknesses to your advantage.

"You gave them certainty, though all the world is mystery. You gave them flattery, though all the world is indifference. You gave them purpose, though all the world is anarchy.

"You taught them *ignorance*.

"And throughout, you insisted that you were only a man like any other. You even feigned anger when others dared voice their suspicions. You did not impose, and you never presumed. You *conditioned*. You gave one man a wheel, another an axle, another a harness or a box, knowing that sooner or later they themselves would put the pieces together—that *the revelation would be theirs*. You bound them with inferences, knowing that someday they would make *you* their conclusion."

The clean-shaven face leaned into the uncertain light. It seemed a grinning skull through the veiling water.

"That they would make you their Prophet.

"But even this wasn't enough," the lips continued. "Those without authority lost nothing by inserting you between them and their Gods, for they already yielded their actions to others. Servitude is the most instinctive of habits. But those with authority ... To rule in the name of an absent king is to rule outright. Sooner or later the caste-nobility had to move against you. Crisis was inevitable ..."

Moënghus stood, pale, indistinct, like a vapour exhaled by the earth. He stepped beneath the spouting eyes. For a moment water sluiced about his figure, then he was clear, dripping, standing eye to socket with his son, naked save for his sodden loincloth.

Pubic curls darkened the linen. Steam coiled about his beaded skin.

"This," the eyeless face said, "was where the Probability Trance failed me ..."

"So you did not anticipate the visions?" Kellhus asked.

His father's face remained absolute and impassive.

"What visions?"

—————————⊗⊗⊗—————————

It seemed that he had screeched his throat raw. Several moments passed, but eventually the red-robed sorcerers ceased their fell singing. The glitter of sorceries dampened, then dulled into nothingness. Drums throbbed beneath the cackling rush of fires.

Red fires.

Eleäzaras no longer laughed. Behind the forward cadres, he stood in the heart of the great swath of hell his School had hacked from the city.

Fumes steamed about the shell of foundations, fires twined into roaring towers, walls rose like fins from mounds of smashed brick; on and on, through slow-rolling veils of smoke, back to the battered ridge that had been the mighty Tatokar Walls. The slopes of the Juterum reared above the curtains of flame, its heights fenced by the ramparts of the Heterine Walls. So close! He had to crane his neck to see the dome and cornices of the Ctesarat above the battlements.

There they would find them ... the assassins.

The Cishaurim had sent their invitation, and they had come. After innumerable miles and deprivations—after all the humiliation!—they had come. They had kept *their* end of the bargain. Now it was time to balance the ledgers. Now! Now!

What kind of game do they play?

No matter. No matter. He would raze all Shimeh if he had to. Upend the very earth!

Eleäzaras pressed a crimson sleeve against his face. It came away dark with soot and sweat. Despite the protestations of Shalmessa, his Javreh Captain, he pushed aside the tall woven shields and strode to the tip of a monolithic finger of stone that jutted from the debris. Waves of heat buffeted him.

"Fight!" he howled at the wavering images in the distance above. The black sky wheeled. "*Fight!*"

Someone's hands pulled at him. He slapped them away.

Sarothenes.

"There are Chorae near, Eli! Great numbers of them ... Can't you feel them?"

It would be good to bathe, Eleäzaras thought inanely. To scrub this madness from him.

"Of course," he snapped. "Beneath the ruin. Held fast by the dead."

The world about him seemed black and hollow and glittering white. Kellhus raised his palm. "My hands ... when I look upon them, I see haloes of gold."

Scrutiny. Calculation.

"I have not my eyes with me," Moënghus said, and Kellhus understood instantly that he referred to the asps used by his Cishaurim brethren. "I walk these halls by memory."

For all the signs he betrayed, this man who was his father could be a statue of stone. He seemed a face without a soul.

"The God," Kellhus said. "He doesn't speak to you?"

Scrutiny. Calculation.

"No."

"Curious ..."

"And from where does his voice hail?" Moënghus asked. "From what darkness?"

"I know not ... Thoughts come. I know only that they're not mine."

Another infinitesimal pause. *He dips in the Probability Trance, the same as I ...*

"The mad say much the same," Moënghus said. "Perhaps your trials have deranged you."

"Perhaps ..."

Scrutiny. Calculation.

"It's not in your interest to deceive me." A stone-faced pause. "Unless ..."

"Unless," Kellhus said, "I've come to assassinate you, as our Dûnyain brothers have decreed ... Is this your apprehension?"

Scrutiny. Calculation.

"You have not the power to overcome me."

"But I do, Father."

Another pause, imperceptibly longer.

"How," his father finally said, "could you know this?"

"Because I know *why* you were compelled to summon me."

Scrutiny. Calculation.

"So you have grasped it."

"Yes ... the Thousandfold Thought."

Chapter Sixteen

Shimeh

*Doubt begets understanding, and understanding begets compassion.
Verily, it is conviction that kills.*

—PARCIS, *THE NEW ANALYTICS*

Spring, 4112 Year-of-the-Tusk, Shimeh

Oily torchlight. Orange faces, slack with anxiety. Orange brickwork
stained and smeared with offal. Hunched ceilings, so low that even the
shortest of the bowmen had to stoop. Men coughed, some continuously,
but not because of the sewage soaking their boots. The fires above were
eating the air …

Or so the Waterbearer had said.

The Cishaurim stood beneath the exit. The asps wound about his neck
peered upward, their thumb-sized heads a silvery black. The idolaters had
fallen silent. The vaulted ceiling no longer thrummed with impact and
explosion. Grit no longer tinkled across their helms.

He cocked his shaved pate, as though listening …

"Douse the light," he commanded. "Cover your eyes."

They dropped their torches into the slop. For a moment, sputtering
blue light illuminated their shins. Everything went black …

Then impossibly bright. A thunderous crack.

"Move!" the Waterbearer cried. "Climb! Climb!"

Suddenly all was blue, illuminated by a coin of incandescence that flared on the Waterbearer's brow. They jostled forward, spitting at the dust. One by one they shouldered their way past the blind man, struggled up a slope of broken and blistering stone, then found themselves dashing through fiery ruins.

"This voice you hear," the old Dûnyain said, "is not part of the Thousandfold Thought."

Kellhus ignored these words. "Take me to them."

"To whom?"

"To those you hold captive."

"And if I refuse?"

"Why would you refuse?"

"Because I need to revise my assumptions, to explore these unforeseen permutations. I had discounted this possibility."

"What possibility?"

"That the Wilderness would break rather than enlighten. That you would come to me a madman."

Water, endlessly dropping, pounded air and stone. The thunder of inevitability.

"Refuse me anything, and I *will* kill you, Father."

Hunched low on their saddles, the Kianene raced from the ruins of the Tantanah Gate to the River Jeshimal, their many-coloured khalats slapping against the rings of their mail, at first just a few dozen, then hundreds, in a long arrow-shaped stream. Still others filed out the Jeshimal Gate, which lay so close to the Ainoni flank.

The Tydonni hornsmen, who could see the Fanim quite clearly from the Shrine, sounded their alarums again and again. But the old Earl of Agansanor plodded onward at a trot. He could see the great cloud rising from the far quarters of the city, but the half-ruined arches of the Skilura Aqueduct, which was very near, obscured his view. When the horns continued to sound, he cursed and sent scouts forward.

By then it was too late.

The first of the Kianene, their horses lathered by the sprint, had reached the Jeshimal. They began to secure the crossings. For the horns-men watching from the Shrine of Azoreah, it seemed that Shimeh had been tipped so that war itself might spill from it. Soon numbers that dwarfed the Tydonni reserves were racing across the Shairizor. Several of the mastodons, which had been the first to cross the toppled wall, were now tramping in their wake, dragging the same timber rafts that had been used to bridge the low ridge of debris. And the hornsmen saw it with far more clarity than any could—the cunning of the Padirajah's plan.

By now, Earl Gothyelk had urged his knights into a ranging gallop, leaving his more numerous footmen behind. As he picked his way past the aqueduct, he saw his dilemma immediately, for hundreds of heathen had already crossed the river and were forming up over the razed fields and groves. Raising his mace high, he called his kinsmen to formation. When he saw that his peers, the Earls Iyengar, Damergal, and Werijen Greatheart, had also cleared the ruined aqueduct, he cried out and charged headlong toward the seething banks of the River Jeshimal.

Raising a mighty shout, the thanes and knights of Ce Tydonn followed.

In absolute darkness they walked, through halls more ancient than the Tusk. A father leading his son.

The roar of the waterfall receded, became a wash as featureless as the black. The scuff of their steps echoed across walls as pitted with representation as those that had come before. And Kellhus talked, explained all that inference had taught him of his father. He spoke in generalities, mostly. The details he hazarded, particularly with regard to Moënghus's manipulation of Cnaiür, he secured through the assignation of probabilities.

"After fleeing the Utemot, you turned south rather than east. You knew the same swazond that would see you survive the Steppe would also see you dead in the Nansurium. This was how you found yourself in Fanim lands.

"They imprisoned you at first, for though their hatred fell short of the Nansur's homicidal fury—the Battle of Zirkirta had not yet happened—they had no love of the Scylvendi. After learning their language, you professed your devotion to Fane. Because of your literacy, it was easy to convince your captors to sell you as a slave. You fetched a respectable price.

"Not long after, you were freed, for the love you instilled in your masters quickly became awe. Not even the Fanic Priests could match your command of the *pillai-a-fan*, or any of the other subsidiary scriptures you were able to obtain. Those who would whip you now implored you to travel to Shimeh ... to the Cishaurim, and the possibility of power beyond anything the Dûnyain had conceived."

Five steps. Kellhus could smell the water drying across his father's bare skin.

"My inference was warranted," Moënghus said from the black before him.

"Indeed. We dwarf the worldborn. They are *less* than children to us. No matter what we encounter, be it their philosophy, their medicine, their poetry, or even their faith, we see so much deeper, and our strength is that much greater.

"So you assumed taking up the Water would be no different, that becoming one of the Indara-Kishauri would make you godlike in comparison. And since the Cishaurim themselves scarcely understand the metaphysics of their practice, there was nothing you could learn that would contradict this assumption. You couldn't know that the Psûkhe was a metaphysic of the *heart*, not the intellect. Of *passion* ...

"So you let them blind you, only to find your powers proportionate to your vestigial passions. What you thought to be the Shortest Path was in fact a dead end."

The air shivered to the rhythm of hammering drums.

High above the wreckage of street and structure, those Scarlet Schoolmen designated Watchers waited, standing upon the ground's echo in the sky. Plumes towered between them. Firestorms raged beneath their slippered feet. The black clouds wheeled above. Only with difficulty could they see the cadres of their brothers, spread across forward limits of the tossed and broken landscape. They sensed the Chorae before they saw the first of the Thesji Bowmen: absences like wraiths, weaving across the shattered ground below. Shouts of warning were traded, but no one knew what to do. Not since the Scholastic Wars had the Scarlet Spires waged such a battle.

There was a flash, white ringed with a nacre of black. One of their number, Rimon, plummeted to ground, where he shattered salt.

The others ran across sky.

Dismayed shouts drew Eleäzaras's attention to the cloudscape behind him. He saw gouts of flame falling from the hanging heights, roaring across already scourged ground. He glanced about, saw the fright and bewilderment of his people. But for some reason his own terror was nowhere to be found. Instead, hot tears burned down his cheeks. Great and intangible weights fell away, so quickly he thought he might pop into the sky, like a bladder of air released from drowning waters.

It happened ... It happened!

He looked up to the heights looming before them, to the gilded dome of the Ctesarat, the Cishaurim Tabernacle, wavering in the heat of the intervening fires. Then he swept his gaze to either flank, to the burning buildings that ringed the arena they had created. They were all around him—as they had always been. Cishaurim filth. Surrounding. Surrounding.

"*They come!*" he boomed in a laughing, sorcerous voice. "*At long last, they come!*"

Arrayed across the pitched ruin, so small beneath the fires they had kindled, the Schoolmen of the Scarlet Spires cried out in exultant acclaim. Their Grandmaster had come back to them.

Then threads of incandescence, blinding blue and white, lashed through the encircling walls of flame.

"Seökti and the others respect you," Kellhus continued. "Indeed, as Mallahet you have a reputation that reaches across Kian and beyond. And you shine in the Third Sight. But secretly, they all think you cursed by the Solitary God. Why else would the Water elude you?

"And without your eyes, your ability to discern what comes before is much reduced. The snakes are but pinholes. For years you waged futile war against your circumstance, and though your intellect could astound those about you and earn you access to their most privileged counsels, the instant they found themselves beyond the force of your presence, the undermining whispers were rekindled. 'He is weak.'

"Then, about twelve years ago, you discovered the first of the Consult skin-spies—probably through discrepancies in their voices. The Cishaurim were thrown into an uproar, that much is certain. And even though no one knew the slightest thing about the creatures, the blame was placed on the Scarlet Spires. For only the greatest of the Schools, they thought, could dare, let alone execute, such an outrage. Infiltrate the *Cishaurim*?

"But you were Dûnyain, and though our brothers know nothing of the arcane, our understanding of the *mundane* is without peer. You realized that these things weren't sorcerous artifacts, that they were engines of the flesh. But you couldn't convince the others, who sought to instruct the Scarlet Spires on the perilous course they had taken. There must be consequences. So the Cishaurim assassinated the Grandmaster of the Scarlet Spires, prompting a war that will find its conclusion this very day ..."

Just then, Kellhus inadvertently kicked something lying upon the graven floor. Something hollow and fibrous. A skull?

"But you," he continued without hesitation, "kept the creatures, and over years of torment you eventually broke them down. You learned of Golgotterath, her ramparts heaped about the horns of an ancient derelict, a vessel fallen from the void in the days when Nonmen yet ruled Eärwa; of the Inchoroi and the great war they waged against long-dead Nonmen Kings. You learned how the last survivors of that fell race, Aurang and Aurax, perverted the heart of their Nonman captor, Mekeritrig, and how he corrupted Shauriatis, the Grandmaster of the Mangaecca, in his turn. You learned how this wicked cabal broke the glamour about Golgotterath, and made its horrors their own ...

"You learned of the Consult."

"These words you speak," Moënghus said from the black, "'wicked,' 'corrupted,' 'perverted' ... why would you use them when you know they are nothing more than mechanisms of control?"

"Of course, you had heard of the Consult," Kellhus continued, ignoring his question. "And like most in the Three Seas, you thought them long dead—the stuff of Mandate delusions. But the stories you extracted from your captives ... there was too much consistency, too much detail, for them to be fabrications.

"The deeper you probed, the more troubling the story became. You had read *The Sagas*, and you had doubted them, thinking them too fanciful. Destroying the world? No malice could be so great. No soul could be so deranged. After all, what could be gained? Who follows paths over precipices?

"But the skin-spies explained it all. Speaking in shrieks and howls, they taught you the why and wherefore of the Apocalypse. You learned that the boundaries between the World and the Outside were not fixed, that if the World could be cleansed of enough souls, it could be *sealed shut*. Against the Gods. Against the heavens and the hells of the Afterlife. Against redemption. And, most importantly, against the possibility of damnation.

"The Consult, you realized, were labouring to *save their souls*. And what was more, if your captives could be believed, they were drawing near the end of their millennial task."

In the absence of light, Kellhus studied his father through the lens of different senses: the scent of naked skin, the displacement of drafts, the sound of bare feet scuffing through the dark.

"The Second Apocalypse," Moënghus said simply.

"Only you knew their secret. Only you could detect their spies."

"They have to be stopped," Moënghus replied. "Destroyed."

"So you brooded over what the skin-spies told you, spent years immersed in the depths of the Probability Trance."

From the very first, ever since descending the glaciers into the wastes of Kûniüri, Kellhus had pondered the man now leading him through these galleries of darkness. Scheme after probabilistic scheme. The branching of innumerable alternatives, waxing and waning with each mile walked, with every insight and apprehension.

I'm here, Father. In the house you have prepared for me.

"You began," Kellhus said, "contemplating what would become the Thousandfold Thought."

"Yes," Moënghus replied, a simple affirmation. Even as he said this, Kellhus sensed the changes—in acoustics, odours, even ambient temperature. The pitch-black corridor had opened onto a chamber of some kind. One where things still lived, and where things had died—many things.

"We have arrived," his father said.

———— ⬥ ————

Beneath the eaves of the clouds, the Inrithi knights of Ce Tydonn thundered across dead fields and stumped orchards. Pennants slapped against the smoking expanse of Shimeh: the Three Black Shields of Nangaelsa, the White Stag of Numaineiri, the Red Swords of Plaideol, and other ancient marks of northern peoples. Beneath the black and gold Circumfix, Lord Gothyelk, Earl of Agansanor, galloped before them, and all the world rumbled.

The distance closed. More and more Fanim climbed the ramped banks of the Jeshimal and hastened to join the milling ranks. Arrows began falling among the Inrithi, disorganized volleys that either clattered harmlessly from their great kite-shields or were stilled by thick pads of felt. Several horses fell screaming, throwing their riders to earth, but the masses simply parted about them and pounded on. Spurs urged chargers faster. Lances were lowered. Long-bearded warriors began roaring out to Gilgaöl—mighty War.

The heathen began charging toward them, haphazardly at first, like clutches of seed falling from laden trees, then en masse. The whole horizon moved, at once dark and many-coloured. Among the Tydonni some glimpsed the triangular standard of Cinganjehoi, the famed Tiger of Eumarna.

The Men of the Tusk leaned into their lances, both grinning and grimacing. It seemed they rattled the world to its foundations. "Shimeh!" a voice pealed out—the grizzled old Earl, riding hard in their lead. Soon they were all shouting, "Shimeh! Shimeh! Shimeh!"

Then all was snapping wood and screaming horses, hacking swords and pummelling maces. Men shouting, dying. Gauslas, son of Earl Cerjulla, was the first of the caste-nobility to fall, beheaded by silver-helmed Cinganjehoi himself. But his Warnutishmen, howling in grief, could not be broken, nor could any of the Tydonni. The iron men hammered down shields and smashed faces. They shattered scimitars with their long notched swords. They brained shrieking horses.

Then, like a miracle, they were reining to stop before blue and black waters. They had taken the riverbank.

The Grandees of Eumarna were broken, killed or beaten away, but there was no respite. Like angry bees the Fanim reassembled beyond their flanks, even behind them, riding in hard arcs, loosing arrow after arrow. Across the ground, the wounded howled through forests of stamping legs. The bridgeheads were retaken, and the Inrithi Earls thundered at their men, exhorting them to hold them. Vicious melees raged across the bridges and the rapids. But the Fanim were already uncoupling the timber rafts that their mastodons had dragged from the levelling of the Tantanah Gate. On the Jeshimal's far bank all the world seemed to throng with the enemy. Fanim riders crowded onto the first of the rafts. More and more arrows fell among the Inrithi.

Earl Gothyelk looked to the white-tiled walls of the city, saw that King-Regent Chinjosa and his Ainoni were yet in disarray. Many still crowded the parapets.

Cursing, he commanded his hornsman to sound the retreat. They had lost the Jeshimal.

Kellhus spoke a sorcerous word and a point of light appeared, sheeting low-vaulted walls in illumination. Though ornate by Inrithi standards, the chamber was more austere than any he'd encountered since plumbing the darkness beneath Kyudea. The friezes that panelled the walls did not screen deeper carvings. They seemed more reserved in theme and content as well, as if the product of an older, more stolid age—though Kellhus decided it had more to do with the room's function. It had been some kind of access chamber for the mansion's ancient sewers.

Workbenches and strange iron and wood mechanisms littered the walls with shadow. At the far end of the chamber, where the ceiling sloped so low a man would have to stoop, a cistern opened beneath converging chutes, as dust-dry as everything else in the room. Nearer, two wells or pits had been dropped into the floor, each possessing graven lips that, perversely, had been carved into the semblance of hands reaching out of the darkness to tear at four spread-eagled figures, one for each point of the compass. With heads bent back in soundless howls, each clutched at the ground with stationary desperation.

The two skin-spies hung suspended above these pits, their arms and legs shackled in chains of pitted iron.

Kellhus approached the nearer one, stepping past a hanging funnel— part of a rust-grooved force-feeding mechanism. How many years had the thing hung here, dangling in absolute black, flinching from instruments, listening to the insistent cooing of his father's voice?

With a gesture he drew the point of light closer. Shadows swung like steepled fingers.

Their facial limbs were drawn perpetually open with rust-brown wire affixed to an iron ring. A contraption of cords and pulleys allowed the things' inner faces to be pulled back or down.

"When did you realize you didn't possess the strength," Kellhus asked, "that more was needed to avert the No-God's second coming?"

"From the very first I recognized that it was probable," Moënghus said. "But I spent years assessing the possibilities, gathering knowledge. When the first of the Thought came to me, I was quite unprepared."

Their braincases had been sawed open, revealing lobes and milky convolutions hazed by hundreds of silver needles. Neuropuncture. Kellhus reached out a finger, brushed the tip of one near the brain's base. The creature jerked and stiffened. Excrement slopped down into the pit. The reek of it swelled through the room.

"I assume," Kellhus continued, "that you're not entirely without Water ... that this was how you were able to reach out to Ishuäl, to send dreams to those Dûnyain you knew before your exile."

Through intersecting chains he saw his father nod, as hairless as the ancient Nonmen who had hewn the stone surrounding them. What secrets had he learned from these captives? What dread whispers?

"I have some facility for those elements of the Psûkhe that require more subtlety than power. Scrying, Calling, Translating ... Even still, my summons to you nearly broke me. Ishuäl lies across the world."

"I was the Shortest Path."

"No. You were the only path."

Kellhus examined the two squares of oak that had been laid across the floor on the far side of the wells. They looked like doors, only stripped of their hinges and handles and set with hooks in each corner so that they could be hung directly beneath the skin-spies. The child and woman nailed across them—tools his father had used either to fan or to sate the creatures' lusts—hadn't been dead long. Their blood gleamed like wax.

An interrogation technique, or another feeding mechanism?

"And my half-brother?" Kellhus asked. In his soul's eye it seemed he could almost see him—the pomp, the authoritarian grandeur—so many times had he heard him described. Kellhus stepped around the far side of the skin-spies to gain a clear view of his father. The man seemed wizened, all but naked in the glaring light. Strangely bent ... or broken.

He uses every heartbeat to reassess. His son has returned to him insane.

Moënghus nodded and said, "You mean Maithanet."

Her head in the crook of his shoulder, Esmenet stared up through the trees. She breathed deep and slow, tasting the salt of her tears, smelling the dank of mossy stone, the bitter of pinched green. Like little flags, the leaves swung and fluttered, their waxy clatter so clear against the background roar. It seemed marvellous and impossible. Twigs upon branches, branches upon limbs, all upward fanning, at once random and perfectly radial, all reaching for a thousand different heavens.

She sighed and said, "I feel so young."

His chest bounced in silent laughter beneath her cheek.

"You are ... Only the world is old."

"Oh, Akka, what are we going to do?"

"What we must."

"No ... that's not what I mean." She cast an urgent look to his profile. "He'll *see*, Akka. The instant he glimpses our faces, he'll see us here ... He'll *know*."

He turned to her. The scowling hurt of old fears unearthed.

"Esmi—"

The snort of a horse, loud and near, interrupted him. They looked to each other in confusion and alarm.

Achamian crept back along the bruised V that marked their path through the weeds, crouched behind the scabbed masonry. She followed. Over his shoulder she glimpsed a row of cavalry—obviously Imperial

Kidruhil—arrayed in a long line across the heights. Dour, expressionless, the mailed horsemen stared out to the roaring city. Their horses stamped and snorted in nervousness. From the gathering clamour she knew that more, very many more, approached from behind.

Conphas? Here? But he was supposed to be dead!

"You're not surprised," she whispered in sudden understanding. She leaned close to him. "Did the Scylvendi tell you about this? Does his treachery run this deep?"

"He told me," Achamian said, his voice so hollow, so dismayed, that her skin prickled in terror. "And he told me to warn the Great Names ... H-he didn't want any harm to befall the Holy War—for Proyas's sake as much as anything else, I think ... B-but ... after he left, all I could think about was ... was ..." He trailed, then turned to her, his eyes round. "Stay here. Stay hidden!"

She shrank backward, such was the intensity of his tone. She pressed her back against the forking of slender trunks. "What are you talking about? Akka ..."

"I can't let this happen, Esmi. Conphas has an entire army ... Think of what will happen!"

"That's *exactly* what I'm thinking about, you fool!"

"Please, Esmi. You're *his wife* ... Think of what happened to Serwë!"

In her soul's eye she glimpsed the girl trying to palm blood back into the gash about her throat. "Akka!" she sobbed.

"I love you, Esmenet. The love of a fool ..." He paused, blinked two tears. "That's all I've ever had to offer."

Then suddenly he stood tall. Before she could speak, he had stepped over the broken foundation. There was something nightmarish to his movements, an urgency that couldn't be contained by his limbs. She would have laughed had she not known him so well.

He walked out and among the cavalrymen, calling ...

His eyes shining. His voice a thunderclap.

Emperor Ikurei Conphas I was in an uncommonly jubilant mood.

"A holy city afire," he said to the grave faces to either side of him. "Masses locked in battle." He turned to the old Grandmaster, who seemed to slump in his saddle. "Tell me, Cememketri—you Schoolmen pretend to be wise—what does it say of men that we find such things beautiful?"

The black-robed sorcerer blinked as though trying to clear the rheum from his eyes. "That we are bred to war, God-of-Men."

"No," Conphas replied, his tone at once playful and cross. "War is intellect, and men are stupid. It's *violence* we're bred to, not war."

Astride his horse, the Emperor gazed down across the Inrithi encampment, out to where Shimeh smoked and flickered with warring lights. In addition to the ailing Saik Grandmaster, General Areamanteras, several sundry officers, and members of the messenger corps accompanied him, arrayed along the summit of the mounded ridge. His Kidruhil fanned out before him, forming ranks lower on the slopes, near a series of ruined structures he couldn't be troubled to identify. His Columns approached from behind, already drawn out into red and gold battle lines. Their timing had been impeccable. They had debarked from the fleet the night before, in a miraculous little harbour mere miles up the coast. Even the winds had been blessed. And now ...

He fairly cackled at what he saw. The Scarlet Spires engaged in the shadow of the Juterum. Half the Holy War running heedless and amok through the smoking streets. Fanayal striking to the south of the city, trying to outflank the stubborn Tydonni. Everything was exactly as his scouts had informed him.

The Men of the Tusk had no inkling of his arrival. Which meant that Sompas, wherever he was, had succeeded in stopping the Scylvendi. Four full Columns! A veritable spear in the small of the Holy War's back.

Whom do the Gods favour now, hmm, Prophet?

A defect carried from the womb ... Please.

He laughed aloud, utterly unperturbed by the ashen looks of his officers. Suddenly it seemed he could see the future to its very limit. It wouldn't end here, oh my, no! It would *continue*, first to the south, to Seleukara, then onward to Nenciphon, west to Invishi—all the way to Auvangshei and the legendary gates of Zeüm! He, Ikurei Conphas I, would be the new Triamis, the next Aspect-Emperor of the Three Seas!

He turned scowling to his retinue. How could they not see it? It was all so *clear*. But then, they peered through the smoke of mortality. All they could see now was their precious Holy City. But time would show. In the meantime, they need only foll—

"Who's that?" General Areamanteras abruptly muttered.

Conphas found and recognized the man immediately. *Drusas Achamian*, walking through the grass, turning toward them, his eyes and mouth ablaze—

Groping for his Chorae, he screamed, "Cememket—"

But heat sucked all air from his lungs. He heard screams dissolve like salt into boiling broth. He was falling.

"To me, Emperor!" an aged voice cried. "To me!"

He was on the ground, rolling through grasses that had become black ash. Somehow the Grandmaster of the Imperial Saik was standing above him, his white hair whipping in convections, his sorcerous voice strong despite his unsteady stance. Ethereal ramparts distorted the air between them and the Mandate sorcerer, who'd turned to the breaking ranks of Kidruhil. Lines of light swept out, more perfect than any rule, flashing across the nearest of the Imperial Heavy Cavalry, who ... collapsed, not bodily but in sopping *pieces* that rolled between the hummocks and weeds.

A blinding light rewrote all the shadows, and through upraised fingers Conphas saw a sun falling from black-bellied clouds, plummeting onto the figure of the Mandate Schoolman. Bursting fire, ribbons of it, arcing off in all directions. Conphas heard himself cry out in relief, elation ...

But as his eyes adjusted, he saw the flames twining away into nothingness about an invisible sphere, and he glimpsed *him*, as clear as that night beneath the Andiamine Heights, or in the Sapatishah's Palace in Caraskand: Drusas Achamian, unharmed, *untouched*, laughing about incandescence as he sang.

From nowhere, a massive concussion. The air just *cracked*.

Cememketri fell to one knee, made a curious gasping sound. Parabolas of light parsed the air about his half-shattered Wards. The sound of iron teeth, grinding at the world's very bones ... Cememketri's voice wavered in old-man panic—words wrapped around gasps.

Another concussion, and Conphas found himself face-first in the ash. His ears shrieked, but he could still make out the hoarse old voice howling ...

"Run!"

And the Emperor ran, screaming.

The Saik Grandmaster's blood was blown like sleet across his back.

Cursing, the lone guardsman before the Umbilica's silk and canvas entrance shot to his feet. He blinked at the approaching figure, which did not ... move right. At moments it seemed a man, but at others it seemed something else, like a moth's pupa or a bundle of collapsing cloth—something flattened from all directions, though it did not grow smaller.

And the air seemed to ... crackle, as though somewhere, just out of sight, sheaves of papyrus burned.

He stood rigid, breathless. Everything in his body—deeper, even—clamoured for him to run.

But he was one of the Hundred Pillars. It was shame enough to be left behind, but to fail in this? He drew his longsword, cried out "Halt!" more from bewilderment than anything else.

And miraculously, the thing ceased moving.

Forward, anyway, because it somehow clawed *outward*, as though soft inner surfaces were being peeled back, exposed to the needling sky.

A face like summer sunlight. Limbs barked in fire.

Reaching out, the thing grasped his head, skinned it like a grape.

Where, bolted a voice through his smoking skull, *is Drusas Achamian?*

Fire and light, burnishing the underside of black-wheeling clouds, carving the outer pillars of the First Temple bright against a heart of inscrutable black.

Heeding the thunder of their Grandmaster's voice, the flanking cadres of the Scarlet Spires drew back before the flailing lights, falling into a great circle across the devastation they had brought to the foot of the Sacred Heights. The more numerous Cishaurim assailed them, the snakes about their throats craning forward. In trios, the weaker crouched and dashed through the ruins, white-blue energies spilling from their foreheads like water toppling toward unseen grounds. The stronger floated proud, dispensing great scourging torrents. All across the levelled streets, there were blinding points of contact where pure light broke against the ghosts of cracking stone.

Between singing Cants and renewing Wards, the sorcerers of rank cried instructions and encouragement to their Javreh shield-bearers. Now and again, when one of the slave-soldiers stumbled across the treacherous footing, a Chorae would whir out of the fire and darkness. Hem-Arkidu was struck, so perfectly balanced he remained standing as incandescent lashes snapped through his fading defences, a pillar of salt amid sizzling, screaming ruin.

The circle closed. The Schoolmen abandoned their Encircling Wards and began fencing the spaces before them with far more robust Directional Wards: the quick-spoken Portcullis, the difficult yet mighty Ramparts of Ur.

Then they responded in kind.

To its bones, Shimeh shivered with unholy reverberations. The terrible majesty of the Dragonhead. The scalding horror of the Memkotic Furies. The air-sucking whoosh of the Meppa Cataract. Dozens of lesser Cishaurim vanished in gold-boiling torrents. Others were dragged smoking from the sky. Abandoning their positions to the rear of their cadres, many Rhumkari, the Scarlet Spires' famed Chorae crossbowmen, crept forward through the rubble, began shooting bolts at those mighty few who seemed immune to sorcerous fires. They blinked at glimpses of snakes and faces, black against sheeted white.

But the crossbowmen within the circle turned, their eyes drawn skyward by shouts, and saw Cishaurim dropping through smoke, landing in their midst. Within moments, before the flying walls of debris crashed over them, they had killed more than a dozen. But the Cishaurim neither relented nor faltered. For they were Indara's Water-bearers, the Firstborn of the Solitary God, and unlike their wicked foemen, they cared not for their lives.

In the midst of their enemy, they spilled their Water.

The slaughter was great.

The Fanim jeered and pelted them with arrows as they fled the banks of the River Jeshimal. The retreat quickly became a rout. Soon scattered bands of Tydonni were careering across the fields, racing toward the line of arched ruin that was the Ceneian aqueduct. Some riders halted to save their unhorsed thanes, only to be overrun by the pursuing tides of heathen horsemen. Save for the thunder of sorcery, Kianene drums and ululations owned the skies.

But the sturdy footmen of Ce Tydonn, under the command of Gothyelk's eldest son, Gotheras, were already assembling beneath the aqueduct. With every passing moment, more spears and many-coloured shields spanned the gaps between the crumbling pylons. To the north, where the aqueduct trailed into a linear mound before the Tatokar Walls, the Ainoni were also drawing into defensive positions. Palatine Uranyanka howled at his Moserothi to close the gap with the Tydonni— Nangaels under Earl Iyengar. Lord Soter led his bloodthirsty Kishyati in a desperate charge from the north.

Trailing skirts of dust, the knights of Ce Tydonn thundered haphazardly into the ranks of their countrymen. Most pressed their way to the rear, seeking respite. But some, like Werijen Greatheart, wheeled with their households and, roaring out encouragement, braced for the heathen onslaught.

Missiles rained among them, like hail across tin.

"Here!" Earl Gothyelk of Agansanor roared. *"Here we stand!"*

But the Fanim parted before them, content to release storms of whirring arrows. The knights of Kishyat, their faces painted dread white above their square-plaited beards, had exacted a terrible toll on their flank. But even more, Cinganjehoi recalled well the obstinacy of the idolaters once their heels touched ground. As yet only a fraction of the Fanim army had crossed the Jeshimal.

Fanayal ab Kascamandri was coming. Lord of the Cleansed Lands. Padirajah of Holy Kian.

⸻

Past the Esharsa Market, through slums and tangled alleyways, the Conriyans battled and chased the Fanim, losing more and more of their number to rapine and plunder, drawing up only when they reached the broad reed marshes that had once been Shimeh's great harbour. Proyas had long since abandoned any attempt to impose order or restraint on his men. The madness of battle was on them, and though his heart grieved it, he understood what it meant to wager one's life, and the bestial licence that men took as their prize.

Shimeh, it seemed, was no exception.

It wasn't ...

Separated in the pursuit, he found himself wandering the murky streets. He came upon a small market square where the escarpment of façades and cornices fell away, allowing him to see the heights of the Juterum: the Heterine Walls painted in flickering lights, the tall columns of the First Temple a motionless blue. Smoke rose from the heights' footings to the west, great tattered curtains of it, climbing the way sand might fall through clear water. Boiling upward, it passed into and merged with the unnatural clouds, so that the whole of heaven seemed a thing of smoke spilling outward across the plane of an immense ceiling.

It wasn't ...

He looked across the abandoned kiosks sunk into the buildings before him, only to glimpse what seemed to be a *tusk* in the shadowy confines of one. Scowling against the press of his war-mask, he wandered past the threshold, past ropes hung with workaday pottery, shelves cluttered with wooden bowls and plates.

There it was ... the size of his forearm perhaps, painted in pitch across a humble door. The crude simplicity of it struck a pang in the back of his throat. A giddiness, something like fear or expectation, made haze of his heart and limbs, the same as when his mother had brought him to temple as a child.

He raised a hand, felt the wood through the iron links about his fingertips. He caught his breath when the door swung open.

Aside from sleeping mats, the room was unfurnished—the abode of debt-slaves, perhaps. A man, a common Amoti by the look of him, sat slumped against the wall to his right, where he appeared to have bled to death. The haft of a knife lay just beyond the reach of his purple fingers. Another man, one of the Kianene they had fought across the Esharsa, lay sprawled across the floor, face downward. The floor listed toward the far wall, so that the blood spilled away, sheeting the planks, gumming about wood shavings, stretching thin claws along the grouted seams. Almost invisible in the murk, a woman and a juvenile girl cringed in the far corner, watching him with horror-round eyes.

He remembered his silver war-mask, raised it. He savoured the sudden cool across his face. The fear of the women did not diminish, though he had thought that it would. He looked down, and as though for the first time saw the blood daubed and smeared across his white and blue khalat. He raised his gauntleted hands. They too had been slicked in crimson.

Memories of savagery, of hacking death, of screams and horrified curses. Memories of Sumna, his forehead pressed against Maithanet's knee, weeping as one reborn. How had he come so far?

Despite the rumbling drums and the distant horns, his footsteps seemed to burst across the silence. Thud. Thud. The mother wailed and rocked as he approached, began babbling something … something …

"… *merutta k'al alkareeta! Merutta! Merutta!*"

She desperately pawed at the blood across her lower lip and chin, then smeared

across the floor at his booted feet. A tusk?

"*Merutta!*" she bawled, though whether she meant "tusk" or "mercy" he could not tell.

They screamed and shrank as he reached for them. He pulled the girl to her feet, found her lightness at once terrifying and arousing. She flailed at him ineffectually, then went very still, as though his hands might be jaws. The mother bawled and beseeched, smeared tusk after tusk across the gritty floor.

No, Prosha …

It wasn't supposed to be … Not like this.

But then, it never was.

It seemed he could smell the girl over the reek of smoke and entrails—no perfumes, at once sour and musky and clean, the smell of young promise. He turned her to the sourceless light. Cropped black hair. Brimming eyes. Swollen cheeks. By the Gods, she was lovely, this daughter of his enemy. Narrow hips. Long legs …

If he were to strike her, would he feel death at the end of his arm? If he were to grow hot upon her ...

An enormous crack shivered the air, thrummed through the building's bones.

"Run," he murmured, though he knew she wouldn't understand. He pulled her back, held a soiled hand out to raise the mother. "You must find a better place to hide."

This was Shimeh.

"In this world," Moënghus said, "there's nothing more precious than our blood—as you have no doubt surmised. But the children we bear by worldborn women lack the breadth of our abilities. Maithanet is not Dûnyain. He could do no more than prepare the way."

Her name arose like a pang from the darkness: *Esmenet.*

"Only a true son of Ishuäl could succeed," his father continued. "For all the Thousandfold Thought's innumerable deductions, for all its elegance, there remained countless variables that could not be foreseen. Each of its folds possesses a haze of catastrophic possibilities, most of them remote, others nearly certain. I would have abandoned it long ago, were not the consequences of inaction so absolute.

"Only one of the Conditioned could follow its path. Only *you*, my son."

Could it be? A tincture of sorrow in his father's voice? Kellhus turned from the hanging skin-spies, once again enclosed his father within the circle of his scrutiny.

"You speak as though the Thought were a living thing."

He could see nothing in the eyeless face.

"Because it is." Moënghus stepped between the two hanging skin-spies. Though blind, he unerringly reached out to run a finger down one of the many hanging chains. "Have you heard of a game played in southern Nilnamesh, a game called *viramsata*, or 'many-breaths'?"

"No."

"Across the plains surrounding the city of Invishi, the ruling caste-nobles are very remote, very effete. The narcotics they cultivate assure them of the obedience of their populations. Over the centuries they have elaborated jnan to the point where it has eclipsed their old faiths. Entire lives are spent in what we would call gossip. But viramsata is far different from the rumours of the court or the clucking of harem-eunuchs—far more. The players of viramsata have made games of truth. They tell lies about who said what to whom, about who makes love to whomever, and so on. They do this *continually*, and what is more, they are at pains to *act out* the lies told by others, especially when they are elegant, so they might make them true. And so it goes from tongue to lip to tongue, until no distinction remains between what is a lie and what is true.

"In the end, at a great ceremony, it is the most *compelling* tale that is declared *Pirvirsut*, a word that means 'this breath is ground' in ancient Vaparsi. The weak, the inelegant, have died, while others grow strong, yielding only to the Pirvirsut, the Breath-that-is-Ground.

"Do you see? The viramsata, they become living things, and *we are their battle plain*."

Kellhus nodded. "Like Inrithism and Fanimry."

"Precisely. Lies that have conquered and reproduced over the centuries. Delusional world views that have divided the world between them. They are twin viramsata that even now war through shouts and limbs of men. Two great thoughtless beasts that take the souls of Men as their ground."

"And the Thousandfold Thought?"

Moënghus turned to him, as precisely as if he could see. "An instigator that goads them, that bleeds them even as we speak. A formula of events that will rewrite the very course of history. A great transition rule that will see Inrithism and Fanimry transformed. The Thousandfold Thought is all these things.

"Beliefs *beget action*, Kellhus. If Men are to survive the dark years to come, they must all act *of one accord*. So long as there are Inrithi and Fanim, this will not be possible. They must yield before a new delusion, a new Breath-that-is-Ground. All souls must be rewritten ... There is no other way."

"And the Truth?" Kellhus asked. "What of that?"

"There is no Truth for the worldborn. They feed and they couple, cozening their hearts with false flatteries, easing their intellects with pathetic simplifications. The Logos, for them, is a tool of their lust, nothing more ... They excuse themselves and heap blame upon others.

They glorify their people over other peoples, their nation over other nations. They focus their fears on the innocent. And when they hear words such as these, they recognize them—but as defects belonging to others. They are children who have learned to disguise their tantrums from their wives and their fellows, and from themselves most of all …

"No man says, 'They are chosen and we are damned.' No worldborn man. They have not the heart for Truth."

Stepping from between his faceless captives, Moënghus approached, his expression a mask of blind stone. He reached out as though to clasp Kellhus's wrist or hand, but halted the instant Kellhus shrank back.

"But why, my son? Why ask me what you already know?"

She clutched the crumbling walls, ducked to see past the fronds of sumac.

Something, a high wind perhaps, worried the darkling clouds that shadowed the Holy City. A corona of gold had formed along their outer rim, and sunlight showered across the slopes above the Holy War's encampment, upon the ruined mausoleums of the ancient Amoti Kings. Even still, the sorcerer flared with impossible brilliance. His eyes bright-burning orbs. His mouth working about glaring white.

From where Esmenet watched, Achamian was no longer Achamian, but something altogether different, something godlike and all-conquering. Multiple spheres of light englobed him, each bisected with further, shielding discs. Brilliant lines webbed the slopes surrounding him, glittering geometries that sundered all but the thickest bodies and the hardest steel. The Abstractions of the Gnosis. The War-Cants of the Ancient North.

His voice—and no matter how unearthly, it remained his voice—had become a singsong mutter that descended from all directions, that tingled against her fingertips when she pressed the stone. Despite her terror and confusion, she knew that at long last she saw him, the one whose long shadow had always chilled their hopes, darkened their love.

The Mandate Schoolman.

From what she could see, the Nansur were in utter confusion. The Kidruhil had broken, dispersed into the distances, where still the far-flung lines of the Gnosis found them. The air rang with frantic alarms.

She was no fool. She knew there would be Chorae, that it was only a matter of time before the units of crossbowmen or some such fought their way through the confusion. But how long would it take? How long could he survive?

She was about to watch him die, she realized. The only man who truly loved her.

From nowhere, it seemed, golden fires rolled over him, burning the earth about his Wards to glass. Then lightning struck, brilliant spasms of it, scrawling across the glowing planes. She stumbled along the interior of the ruined wall, struggled to find a footing, then pulled herself up to look westward.

Her heart caught at the sight of the Imperial Columns, their ranks piling across the distances. Then she saw *them*: along the crest, standing the height of a tree above the ground, four black-robed sorcerers, wrapped in spectral bastions of stone. They sang dragons. They sang lightning, lava, and sun. Twice the concussions knocked her from her perch.

One by one the Mandate Schoolman pulled them down, each with blistering precision.

The Holy Water of the Indara-Kishauri fell sideways across the heaped earth, spiralling from souls that had become fissures. Dozens of Scarlet Schoolmen, too engrossed or startled to sing new Encircling Wards, screamed in the scalding light. Entire cadres were swept away in deluge after glittering deluge. Narstheba. Inrûmmi ...

Death came swirling down.

Cishaurim were struck down with Chorae—quick, soundless flashes, like tissue cast into flame—but then so too were Schoolmen, by the Thesji Bowmen who dashed through the smoke-hazed ruin. Within heartbeats the circle was broken, and organized battle became sorcerous melee. Each Schoolman found himself warring alone with his stunned cadre, both to live and to kill. Their shouts were lost in the thunder of their destruction. The Cishaurim were everywhere among them, standing in clutches, behind broken walls, upon mounded debris—blue-burning beacons. Geysers erupted along the sheer brick surfaces, leaving deep pocks that trailed dust and gravel. Bricks fell like powdered plaster.

Many of the Cishaurim, the Secondaries and Tertiaries, they killed with single Dragonheads. The Primaries they hammered and hammered, either singly or in concert, only to find themselves falling to their knees, screaming out Ward after desperate Ward.

The Scarlet Spires knew of the Nine Incandati, those Primaries whose backs could bear the most Water, but they had no inkling as to their true strength. Now the greatest of the Psûkari assailed them: Seökti, Inkorot, Hab'hara, Fanfarokar, Sartmandri ... And they could not cope.

Within moments of closing with Inkorot, Sarosthenes was singing Wards only. Dazzling light crashed all about him, striking with such force that it seemed the very joists of the world must crack. His Javreh shield-bearers wailed about him, struggling to find their feet. The ghost stone cracked, was torn away in sheets. His song ran out, and all was brilliant agony.

Eleäzaras had been very near the Cishaurim's surprise descent. Beset by Fanfarokar and Seökti, the High Heresiarch himself, he too could do no more than sing Ward after Ward. The Heresiarch hung over half-windows directly before him, his asps curved to watch the surrounding ruin, his figure bleached white by his impossible dispensations. Fanfarokar assailed him from the right, shielded in the crotches of a ruined tabernacle. The words. The words! The Grandmaster bent all his craft and cunning to the words, both silent and spoken. The world beyond his defences was rocked and blasted by deafening light. He sang and he sang to keep his narrow circle safe.

He had not the luxury of despair.

Then a moment of miraculous respite. The world went dark save for the wicked glow of the fires. Through the whoosh and crackling, Eleäzaras heard a horn, lonely and crude, crying out over the fields of ruin. All, sorcerer and Cishaurim alike, peered about in blinking confusion. Then Eleäzaras saw them, demon-red in the gloom, assembled in a long line across the broken ground: the Thunyeri, their black armour sheened in blood, their cornsilk beards tousled by the wind of great fires burning. He saw the Circumfix, black on red, pinned to the standard of Prince Hulwarga.

Men of the Tusk, come to save them.

Masses of Kianene horsemen encompassed the fields before them, line after rumbling line of them, trotting directly toward the ruined aqueduct. Waiting with butted spear and hoisted shield, the Men of the Tusk watched them, marking the standards of foes now well known. The Khirgwi tribes, bent on completing the work of the desert. The Grandees of Nenciphon and Chianadyni, who had suffered so terribly beneath the walls of Caraskand. The Girgashi of King Pilaskanda, leading some two dozen of their dread mastodons. The survivors of Gedea and Shigek under Ansacer. The long-suffering horsemen of Eumarna and Jurisada under Cinganjehoi, who time and again had driven the Inrithi before him. And beneath the Padirajah's own banner, the fearless Coyauri, the ringlets of their mail gleaming gold where open sky found them.

All that remained of a proud and fierce nation, come for a final reckoning.

To the left of the Inrithi, over the heart of the city, smoke trailed like gauze in water, obscuring the First Temple and the Sacred Heights. Lights glowered and flickered from within, glimpses of brilliance through rags of black. Booms and thunder broke across the distances, more fell than the pulse of heathen drums.

The braided Nangaels began singing first, then the Numaineiri, one of the Warrior-Prophet's unearthly hymns. Soon the entire Inrithi line was awash with deep warrior voices, singing

> We, the sons of past sorrow,
> We, the heirs of ancient trow,
> Shall raise glory to the morrow,
> And shall deliver fury to the now ...

The Kianene quickened to the pace of crashing cymbals, rank after rank of them, roping field and pasture with dark colour. Then suddenly the cohorts were racing as though one against another. Riding at the fore, the Sapatishahs thrust their scimitars high and cried out. Their Grandees and the fiercest of their kinsmen answered, and soon all howled in outrage and injury.

So many wrongs suffered. So many deaths unavenged.

The ground swept beneath them. Not fast enough. Not fast enough.

Men wept for awe and hatred. And it seemed the Solitary God heard them ...

The Skilura Aqueduct stretched before them, a perfect line that ran from city to horizon, long tracts of it intact, arches piled across arches, and sections completely collapsed. Crowded between the ruined pilings and about the scree, ranks of the Inrithi barricaded its foundations, a wall of shields and wicked men. The distance closed. The moments thinned to impossibility. For a heartbeat, song warred with inarticulate clamour ...

We shall raise glory to the morrow?

Then all the world erupted.

Lances snapped. Shields cracked. Some horses shied and reared, while others bulled through. Men stabbed and hooked. Song and cry both faltered, and shrieks claimed the sky. From the heights of the aqueduct, Inrithi archers rained incessant ruin. Others heaved blocks and stones onto the heaving masses below. Here and there, heathen burst through to the far side, where the waiting Tydonni and Ainoni knights instantly charged into them. Bloodshed and melee seethed along the length of the Inrithi line.

"Even the Dûnyain," Moënghus said, "possess vestigial versions of these weaknesses. Even me. Even *you*, my son."

The implication was clear. *Your trial has broken you.*

Was this what had happened beneath the black boughs of Umiaki? Kellhus could remember rising from Serwë's corpse, the hands wrapping him in white linen. He could remember blinking at the flash of sunlight through the leafy gloom. He could remember *walking* when he should be dead, and seeing them in their thousands, the Men of the Tusk, crying out in astonishment and relief and exultation—in *awe* ...

"There's *more*, Father. You're Cishaurim. You must know this."

He could remember the voice.

WHAT DO YOU SEE?

Even without eyes, his father's face still seemed to *scrutinize*. "You refer to your visions, the voice from nowhere. But tell me, where is your proof? What assures your claim over those who are simply mad?"

TELL ME.

Assurance? What assurance did he have? When the real punished, the soul denied. He had seen it so many times in so many eyes ... So how could he be so certain?

"But on the Plains of Mengedda," he said. "The Shrial Knights ... What I prophesied came to pass." To the worldborn these words would have sounded blank, devoid of concern or occasion. But to a Dûnyain ...

Let him think I waver.

"A fortuitous Correspondence of Cause," Moënghus replied, "nothing more. That which comes before yet determines that which comes after. How else could you have achieved all that you have achieved? How else could you be possible?"

He was right. Prophecy *could not be.* If the ends of things governed their beginnings, if *what came after* determined what came before, then how could he have mastered the souls of so many? And how could the Thousandfold Thought come to rule the Three Seas? The Principle of Before and After simply *had to be true,* if its presumption could so empower ...

His father had to be right.

So what was this certainty, this immovable conviction, *that he was wrong?*

Am I mad?

"The Dûnyain," Moënghus continued, "think the world closed, that the mundane is all there is, and in this they are most certainly wrong. This world is *open,* and our souls stand astride its bounds. But what lies Outside, Kellhus, is no more than a fractured and distorted reflection of what lies within. I have searched, for nearly the length of your entire life, and I have found nothing that contradicts the Principle.

"Men cannot see this because of their native incapacities. They attend only to what confirms their fears and their desires, and what contradicts they either dismiss or overlook. They are bent upon affirmation. The priests crow over this or that incident, while they pass over all others in silence. I have *watched,* my son, for years I have *counted,* and the world shows no favour. It is perfectly indifferent to the tantrums of men.

"The God *sleeps* ... It has ever been thus. Only by striving for the Absolute may we awaken Him. Meaning. Purpose. These words name not something given ... no, they name our task."

Kellhus stood motionless.

"Set aside your conviction," Moënghus said, "for the *feeling* of certainty is no more a marker of truth than the feeling of will is a marker of freedom. Deceived men *always think themselves certain*, just as they always think themselves free. This is simply what it means to be deceived."

Kellhus looked to the haloes about his hands, wondered that they could be light and yet cast no light, throw no shadow ... The light of delusion.

"But *we*, my son, do not have the luxury of error. Void ... void has come to this world. It fell from the skies thousands of years past. Twice it has reared from the ashes of its falling: the first time in what the Mandate call the Cûno-Inchoroi Wars, the second time in what they call the First Apocalypse. It is about to arise a third time."

"Yes," Kellhus murmured. "He speaks to me as well."

WHAT AM I?

"The No-God?" Moënghus asked. He paused momentarily. Had his father possessed eyes, Kellhus was certain he would have seen them fall in and out of focus as the consciousness within rose and submerged. "Then you truly *are* mad."

The shouts were everywhere, descending from blinding, blinking sunlight.

"*Emperor! God-of-Men!*"

His men ... his glorious Columnaries, come to save him.

"*He's dead! No-no-no!*"

"*Sweet Sejenus, our prayers have been answered!*"

"*Sedition! I should run you—*"

"*What? You think I value my skin over my so—!*"

"*He's right! We all know it. We've all been thinking—*"

"*Then you're all guilty of treason!*"

"*Are we? And what of this madman? What kind of fool would trade souls for ink and glo—*"

"*Exactly! I'll be hanged before I fight for Fanim pigs! What? Risk my life to fight for my own damnation?*"

"*He's right! He's ri—*"

"Look!" a voice cried immediately above him. "He moves!"

For a moment Conphas could hear nothing for the ringing in his ears. Then there were arms and hands, many of them, dragging him by his harness. His heels bounced over turf. All he could think was to hold fast his Chorae. What had happened? What had happened?

He glimpsed his hands, which he had raised to his face, saw his Trinket, greasy with blood. He cried out, sick with sudden certainty of his doom. His heart felt like a sparrow battling in his breast.

I'm dead! I've been slain!

Then he remembered, and he was fighting, striking away hovering hands.

Drusas Achamian.

"Kill him!" he barked, pressing himself to his feet. Columnaries and officers surrounded him, gawking in wonder and terror. Men of the Selial Column. Conphas snatched the cloak of one, used it to mop the blood from his face and neck. Cememketri's blood—the imbecile! Useless! Feeble!

"Kill him!"

But only a few matched his gaze; the others looked past him, toward the rounded summit. He noticed the strange shadows that played about all of their feet. The ringing in his ears fell away and Conphas heard it, the thrum of their otherworldly song. Whirling, he saw Saik Schoolmen astride the sky, pitching sorcerous ruin over the far side of the humped pasture. As he watched, one of the black-robed sorcerers foundered, his Wards crumbling beneath a calligraphy of linear lights. He fell flaming to the ground.

As would the others. Four Anagogic sorcerers would not be enough, not against the Gnosis. Conphas cursed himself for dividing the Imperial Saik between the Columns. With the Cishaurim and the Scarlet Spires locked in mortal struggle, he had assumed that ... that ...

This isn't happening ... not to me!

"My Chorae," he said numbly. "Where are my crossbowmen?"

No one could answer—of course. All was in disarray. The Mandate filth had obliterated his entire command. The Emperor's *own standard* had vanished in an eruption of fire. The sacred standard destroyed! He turned from the spectacle, scanned the surrounding fields and pastures.

Kidruhil fled to the south—fled! Three of his Columns had halted, while the phalanxes of the farthest, the Nasueret, actually seemed to be withdrawing.

They thought he was dead.

Laughing, he pressed his way through the clutch of soldiers, opened his bloodied arms to the far-flung ranks of the Imperial Army. He hesitated at the sight of white-garbed horsemen cresting the far rise, but only for a heartbeat.

"Your Emperor has survived!" he roared. *"The Lion of Kiyuth lives!"*

Flames, tongues wrapped about golden tongues, spitting plumes of smoke into the sky.

Without any apparent signal, the Thunyeri began advancing, hundreds of them, spilling into the trenches, climbing debris slopes, leaping through windows stranded in solitary walls. They raised no battle cry. Like wolves, they floated soundlessly forward.

The Cishaurim recollected themselves. Gouts of light plummeted across the smashed landscape, fell among the rushing Norsirai warriors. Keening screams. Shadows thrashing in boiling light. For heartbeats, all the Grandmaster could do was stare dumbfounded. He saw one barbarian, his beard and hair aflame, stumble across the pitch of fallen walls, still holding a Circumfix banner high.

Without warning, the deluge found Eleäzaras once again, arcs of inchoate energy that cracked and shattered his Wards. He cried out his song, propping and renewing, all the while knowing it would not be enough. How had their foemen become so strong?

But then the dread lights were halved, then halved yet again. Gasping, Eleäzaras glimpsed the giant Yalgrota, soot-blackened and blood-smeared, heaving Fanfarokar into the air by the throat. The asps flailed. Fist closed about a Chorae, the Thunyeri giant hammered the shaven skull into sopping ruin. Eleäzaras whirled, searching the heaped darkness for threats, saw Seökti floating backward before a rush of black shadows ... toward the fires that fenced the sloped foundations of the Sacred Heights. He saw the remaining cadres of his brothers— so few!—light up in renewed fury.

"Fight!" he thundered in a sorcerous voice. "Fight, Schoolmen, *fight!*"

Out of his entire cadre, only one of his shield-bearers remained, cringing at his feet. He had no idea what had happened to the others.

Cursing the fool, the Grandmaster of the Scarlet Spires stepped into the smoke-rent sky.

The white roar of battle.

Felled by heathen arrows, men toppled from the heights of the aqueduct onto the straining masses below. Swords and scimitars rising and falling, throwing blood into black skies. Shields braced against the necks of maddened horses. Astonished men, gauntlets pressed against mortal wounds. Raging men, hacking and hammering at the crush before them. Weeping men, dragging the lolling corpses of their lords.

Then the Fanim fell back, leaving the fallen curled and stretched across the ground behind them. They retreated as waters might from the breakers. All along the Skilura Aqueduct, the Inrithi roared in exultation. One of the Numaineiri stepped forward and, waving his sword back and forth, cried, "Wait! You forgot your blood!"

Hundreds laughed.

The dead were culled from the ranks. Messengers were dispatched along the rear of the line. For seven seasons the Men of the Tusk had lived and breathed war. The routines seemed as near to them as their bones and blood. More Inrithi climbed to the rutted heights of what had become their wall, where the sight of the Fanim massing and reforming across the fields stole their breath.

Horns signalled. Someone, somewhere, resumed their song.

We shall raise glory to the morrow,
we shall bring fury to the now.

Out of bowshot, the Fanim congregated anew about their bright banners. For a short time, only the south saw battle as Ansacer led his cohorts, men as hard-bitten as the idolaters, up the pastures that ramped the Shrine of Azoreah. Though dreadfully outnumbered, Lord Gotian and his Shrial Knights sailed down the slopes toward him. "*God,*" the warrior monks cried, *"wills it!"* And they met, hammer to hammer. Along the length of the aqueduct, the Men of the Tusk cheered at the sight of heathen fleeing back down the slopes.

Then the rhythm of the drums slowed, and with a clash of cymbals the great masses of heathen before them began trotting forward. The first of the Inrithi arrows climbed into the sky, fired by the Agmundrmen with their powerful yew bows. The archers of other nations soon joined them, though it seemed their volleys fell for naught into the slow-advancing tide.

Suddenly, in the disjointed manner of great assemblies, the Fanim host reined to a halt a mere hundred paces before the ranks drawn across the aqueduct's foundations. Everywhere, stitched across flapping banners, painted across round shields, the horsemen bore the Two Scimitars of Fanimry. Their horses, caparisoned in skirts of fine iron rings, stamped and snorted, but beneath their helms the expressions of the Fanim possessed a murderous calm. Struck by wonder, the Men of the Tusk let their song trail. Even the archers lowered their bows.

With no more than the dead and slender tracts of ground between them, the sons of Fane and Sejenus regarded one another.

Sunlight showered across the fields, gleamed from clammy metal. Blinking, men looked to the heavens, saw vultures circling the glare.

Mastodons screamed among the Girgashi. An anxious rustling passed through the lines, both heathen and idolater. Spotters along the aqueduct's crown shouted out warnings: heathen horsemen seemed to be repositioning themselves behind their motionless brethren. But all eyes were drawn to the Coyauri, where the banner of the Padirajah himself pressed forward through the ranks—the Maned Desert Tiger, embroidered in silver on a triangular bolt of black silk. The rows parted and, draped in golden mail, Fanayal himself spurred his black onto the intervening ground.

"Who?" he cried to the astonished onlookers—and in Sheyic no less. *"Who is the true voice of God?"*

His voice was youthful and strident, but it was also a signal to his kinsmen. Thousands erupted forward, lances lowered, mouths howling.

Limbs numb in shock, the Inrithi braced themselves. The sun's heat now seemed to sicken.

Fanayal led a hurtling wedge of Coyauri into the Gesindalmen and their Galeoth brothers—all those who had elected to abandon King Saubon in Caraskand. Earl Anfirig cried out to his blue-tattooed countrymen, but the surprise was too much. All seemed confusion. The forward ranks had been bowled under, and the heathen cavalrymen hacked and slashed in their very midst. The Padirajah fought his way into the shadow of the arches, while his bowmen raked the summit of the aqueduct above.

A sudden cheer boomed out among the heathen, for Cinganjehoi had broken through the Ainoni farther to the north and now fenced with Lord Soter and his merciless Kishyati knights. Heeding the calls of their Padirajah, the Coyauri redoubled their fury, battled their way forward, through to the sunlight on the far side. Then suddenly they were galloping across open turf, cutting down the scrambling survivors. The glorious Grandees of Nenciphon and Chianadyni streamed into their wake.

But the thanes and knights of Ce Tydonn awaited them. In wave after wave, the iron men crashed into the expanding mass of heathen. Lances shattered arms, threw men from saddles. Horses jostled neck to neck, hoof to hoof. Swords and scimitars rang. Kissing the golden Tusk that hung about his neck, Earl Gothyelk charged directly toward the Padirajah's standard. His householders scattered several dozen Coyauri, fought their way forward. The Earl, whom his men called "the Old Hammer," laid low all who dared oppose him. Then he found himself knee to greave with golden Fanayal.

According to witnesses, the confrontation was short-lived. The Earl's famed mace was no match for the Padirajah's swift blade. Hoga Gothyelk, the red-faced Earl of Agansanor, leader of the Tydonni-over-the-Sea, slumped from his saddle.

Death came swirling down.

———— ❧ ————

There was a sterility to the sorcerous light, a pallor that refused to discriminate the stone of the Nonman carvings from the flesh of his father's face and limbs.

"Tell me, Father ... what is the No-God?"

Moënghus stood motionless before him. "The trial broke you."

His time, Kellhus knew, was running short. He could no longer afford his father's distractions. "If it was destroyed, if it no longer exists, how could it send me dreams?"

"You confuse the madness within you for the darkness without—the same as the worldborn."

"The skin-spies—what have they told you? What is the No-God?"

Though walled in by the flesh of his face, Moënghus seemed to scrutinize him. "They do not know. But then, none in this world know what they worship."

"What are the possibilities you've considered?"

But his father would not relent. "The darkness comes before you, Kellhus—*it owns you*. You are one of the Conditioned. Surely you—" He paused abruptly, turned his blind face to open air. "You have brought others ... Who?"

Then Kellhus heard them as well, creeping through black toward their light and their voices. There were three of them. The Scylvendi he recognized by his heartbeat ... But who accompanied him?

"I have been *chosen*, Father. I *am* the Harbinger."

The quiet of alternating breaths. The sound of grit beneath palm and heel.

"These voices," Moënghus said with slow deliberation, "what do they say of *me*?"

His father, Kellhus realized, had finally grasped the principles of this encounter. Moënghus had assumed that his son would be the one requiring instruction. He had not foreseen it as possible, let alone inevitable, that the Thousandfold Thought would outgrow the soul of its incubation—and discard it.

"They warn me," Kellhus said, "that you are Dûnyain still."

One of the captive skin-spies convulsed against its chains, vomited threads of spittle into the pit below.

"I see. And this is why I am to die?"

Kellhus looked to the haloes about his hands. "The crimes you've committed, Father ... the *sins* ... When you learn of the damnation that awaits you, when you come to *believe*, you will be no different from the Inchoroi. As Dûnyain, you will be compelled to master the consequences of your wickedness. Like the Consult, you will come to see tyranny in what is holy ... And you will war as they war."

Kellhus fell back into himself, opened his deeper soul to the details of his father's nearly naked form, assessing, appraising. The strength of limbs. The speed of reflexes.

Must move quickly.

"To shut the World against the Outside," the pale lips said. "To seal it through the extermination of mankind ..."

"As Ishuäl is shut against the Wilderness," Kellhus replied.

For the Dûnyain, it was axiomatic: what was compliant had to be isolated from what was unruly and intractable. Kellhus had seen it many times, wandering the labyrinth of possibilities that was the Thousandfold Thought: The Warrior-Prophet's assassination. The rise of Anasûrimbor Moënghus to take his place. The apocalyptic conspiracies. The counterfeit war against Golgotterath. The accumulation of premeditated disasters. The sacrifice of whole nations to the gluttony of the Sranc. The Three Seas crashing into char and ruin.

The Gods baying like wolves at a silent gate.

Perhaps his father had yet to apprehend this. Perhaps he simply couldn't see past the arrival of his son. Or perhaps all this—the accusations of madness, the concern over his unanticipated turn—was simply a ruse. Either way, it was irrelevant.

"You are Dûnyain still, Father."

"As are—"

The eyeless face, once perfectly obdurate and inscrutable, suddenly twitched in the ghost of a grimace. Kellhus pulled his knife from his father's chest, retreated several steps. He watched his father probe the wound with his fingers, a weeping perforation just beneath his rib cage.

"I am more," the Warrior-Prophet said.

A broad swath of ground cooked and smoked about him.

Achamian whirled, turned in a half-circle, saw the last of the fleeing Kidruhil, the Inrithi encampment congesting the nearer reaches of the plain, and Shimeh, still dark beneath the clouds, bleeding smoke. He looked back to the crest, to where two of the four Saik Schoolmen lay burning. The whole of the Imperial Army, he realized, climbed the far side. Any second now their banners would float above the grasses and wildflowers. He recalled his Mandate training ...

Just below high ground.

He needed to run. To where the approach of Chorae bowmen could be seen, and where the earth provided the most cover. But part of him already mourned the futility of it. The only reason he had survived this long was that he'd caught them so entirely unawares. That wouldn't last, not with Conphas still breathing.

I'm dead.

Then he remembered Esmenet. How could he forget? He looked to the ruined mausoleum, took fright that it lay so near. Then he saw her, her face small and boylike, peering through the shadowy recesses of the sumac that thronged about the foundation. She had seen it all, he realized ...

It shamed him for some reason.

"Esmi, no!" he cried, but it was too late. She had already leapt the foundations, had already started sprinting toward him across the browned and blackened turf.

He saw it *twinkle* first—a flash in his periphery. Then the Mark, gouged nauseatingly deep.

He looked up ...

"*Nooo!*" he howled. Glass cracked beneath his feet.

Long-winged, black scales about molten limbs, scimitar talons, an eye-encircled maw ...

A Ciphrang, called from the hellish bowels of the Outside. A sulphurous godling.

A gust swept up her skirts, knocked her to her knees. Esmenet turned her face skyward ...

A demon descending.

Iyokus ...

Proyas found himself on the roof of an ancient fullery—the only structure overlooking the Juterum's westward approaches that wasn't aflame. Though sunlight ringed the distances, all was smoke and twilight. If he looked at the sky overlong, he could feel himself spin, so he concentrated on the clay tiles beneath his feet. He scrambled across the shallow pitch, stumbled once, kicking free sheaves of rotted tile. He lowered himself onto his stomach, crawled out onto a south-facing pediment.

Gazed across Shimeh.

Streamers and veils of smoke lent the sky the perspective of city streets, making it easy to judge the relative distance of the hanging sorcerers and their warring lights. Below, all was black ruin and smouldering fire. Free-standing walls, as ragged as ripped parchment. Guttered foundations. The wounded crying out, waving pale hands. The charcoal dead.

Untouched on the heights, the First Temple observed with monumental repose.

There was a stupendous crack, and Proyas fairly toppled from his perch. He hugged the roof to the point of breathlessness, blinked the dazzle from his eyes.

Almost immediately below him he saw two crimson-robed Schoolmen, one old and decrepit, surrounded by headless pillars in the gallery of a destroyed temple, the other middle-aged and corpulent, balanced upon a crest of tossed debris. Their Wards shone, like silver in moonlight, or steel in dark alleys. Mouths flaring, they sang, and fires whooshed and thundered. Some fifty paces out, the ground exploded as if hammered by a rod the size of a great netia pine. Showers of smoking gravel rained across the wreckage.

Somehow, impossibly, a figure cloaked in saffron floated through it. Blue incandescence surged from his forehead, plummeted *over* the ground, sweeping away pillars like sticks, breaking across the Wards of the old Scarlet Schoolman. Proyas threw a forearm across his eyes, so bright was the contact.

The Cishaurim climbed skyward until he hung level with Proyas, flew out and around, all the while assailing the old sorcerer with gouts of blue-flashing energy. Black clouds had boiled into being in the air behind him, discharging lines of lightning like cracks in glass, but the Cishaurim ignored them, intent on overcoming the Scarlet Schoolman below. The air hummed with crashing reverberations, the clacking of mountain-sized stones. Against this tumult the screams of men could be no more than the chirps of infant mice. Or nothing at all.

Trailing thunder. Fading light. The hanging figure had relented, turning both face and serpents to the other madly singing Schoolman. His robes boiled a shimmering ochre in the wind. His asps fanned like iron hooks from about his neck.

Proyas didn't have to look to know the old sorcerer was dead, or that the other soon would be. He found himself standing windswept on the pediment, perched on the very ledge, ruined streets and blasphemous fire careering across the distances before him.

"Sweet God of Gods!" he cried to the acrid wind. With bare hands he tore the Chorae from the chain about his neck.

"Who walk among us ..." He drew back his sword-weary arm, secured his footing.

"Innumerable are your holy names ..." And he cast his Tear of God, a gift from his mother on his seventh birthday.

It seemed to vanish against the iron horizon ...

Then a flash, a black-ringed circle of light, from which the saffron figure plummeted like a sodden flag.

Proyas fell to his knees on the brink, leaned out over the fall. His holy city gaped before him. And he wept, though he knew not why.

Again and again the thanes and knights of Ce Tydonn charged, but they could not staunch the breach. Soon they were engulfed in howling desert horsemen, beset on all sides. In an endless stream, silk-garbed Kianene galloped beneath the arches and into view of the Inrithi encampment. Hundreds of them climbed the teetering pilings, gained the summit of the aqueduct, where pitched battles were waged beneath the withering fire of the heathen horse-archers. Others charged the length of the stonework, into Earl Damergal and his hard-pressed Cuärwethi trying to roll back the flanks of the breach. Still others beat their horses toward the stunned crowds of onlookers about the rim of the encampment.

A shout was raised among the Nangaels, where a spear took down King Pilaskanda, and set his Girgashi reeling back in disorder. The mastodons panicked in the withdrawal, began stomping through their own lines. The Ainoni cheered Palatine Uranyanka, who rode along their lines holding high the severed head of Cinganjehoi, who had been trapped behind the

Moserothi after being driven back by Lord Soter and his Kishyati.

But the doom of the Inrithi rode with Fanayal ab Kascamandri, who led his shimmering Grandees far behind the lines of the idolaters. To the north and the south, cohorts of Kianene spread across the Shairizor Plain, shrugging past clots of battling knights and hooking back to the east, to charge into the far side of the ancient aqueduct. Earl Damergal was killed by a block thrown from the arches above. Earl Iyengar found himself stranded with his household to the rear of his Nangaels. Howling oaths, he watched his kinsmen broken into warring clots. A Mongilean Grandee silenced him with an arrow through the throat. Death came swirling down.

The Fanim wept with fury, with outrage, as they cut down the Inrithi invaders. They cried out glory to Fane and the Solitary God, even as they wondered that the Men of the Tusk did not flee.

Think-think-must-think!

An Odaini Concussion Cant, knocking her clear of the thing's monstrous descent, back toward the mausoleum.

It landed hard and leaden, as though it had been wrought of twisted anchors, yet it moved as if its limbs floated in some unseen ether. The thing turned to him, hunched and slavering.

"The Voice," it wheezed, taking one dread step forward. All life crumbled to tan dust about it.

"It says, an eye for an eye."

Waves of heat rolled outward, as dry as bone become ash.

"Then the hurting ends ..."

And Achamian knew this was no common demon. Its Mark was like light, concentrated to the point where the parchment of the world blackened, curled, and burned. The Daimos ...

What had Iyokus loosed?

"Esmi!" he cried. "Flee! Please! I beg you! *Flee!*"

The thing leapt toward him.

Achamian began singing—the deepest of the Cirroi Looms. Glorious Abstractions knitted the air about and before him, a thresher of light. The demon laughed and screamed.

---⊗⊗⊗---

His father staggered against the panels that pitted the walls. Snakes curled out of the recesses, shining and black. They curled about his throat, like eyes that strangled.

Kellhus stepped back, focused his eyes on a point the size of a thumbnail held at arm's length. What was one became many. What was soul became *place*.

Here.

Calling out from bones of things.

With *three voices* he sang, one utteral pitched to the world and two inutterals directed to the *ground*. What had been an ancient Cant of Calling became something far, far more ... A Cant of *Transposing*.

Blue fractal lights mapped the air about him, cocooned him in brilliance. Through scribbling filaments he saw his father press himself upright, turn with his asps to the girded corridor. Anasûrimbor Moënghus ... that he could look so pale in the light of his son!

Existence cringed before the whip of his voice. Space cracked. Here was pried into there. Beyond his father he saw *Serwë*, her blonde hair tied into a war-knot. He saw her leap out of the black ...

Even as he toppled into one far greater.

---⊗⊗⊗---

Drusas Achamian shouted out destruction. Light scored the creature, parabolas of knifing white. Molten blood flecked the grasses. Chits of fiery flesh sailed like kicked coals.

Waves of heat burned Esmenet's cheeks. She stared as one transfixed, though she could not bear to watch. Surrounded by withered, burning grasses, he stood behind his sheets of light, at once glorious with power and dreadful with frailty. But the thing was upon him, a raving nightmare, hammering and clawing, blows that cracked the stone about her, that brought blood to her nose. Wards buckled and fractured. Achamian called out great concussions and the demon's head was battered. Horns snapped. Spider-eyes ruptured light.

Its assault became a frenzy, a jerking blur of violence, until it seemed hell itself tore and gnashed at his gates.

Achamian staggered, blinked white-burning eyes, cried out—

An instant of wasted voice.

Rats screamed through its exultant roar. Achamian falling, his mouth working. The closing of dragon claws …

Achamian falling.

She could not scream.

The monstrosity leapt into the sky, punishing the air with rent wings. She could not scream.

⊶⊷⊷⊷

"I live!" Ikurei Conphas cried one more time, only to hear nothing above the crack and thunder of sorcerous battle, both near and far. No resounding cheer, no individual shouts of relief or acclaim. They couldn't see him—that was it! They mistook him for one of their own. For a man …

He whirled back to his stunned rescuers.

"You!" he shouted to a dumbstruck Selial Captain. "Find General Baxatas. Tell him to join me here at once!"

The man hesitated—for scarcely an eye-blink, but it sparked a cold fire in Conphas's belly. Then the fool was off, sprinting through grass and clover toward distant formations.

"And you!" Conphas snapped at a run-of-the-mill Columnary. "Find some hornsmen. Quick-quick! Tell them to signal the general advance!"

"And y—" He broke off. There *was* shouting on the wind. Of course! It had just taken them time to recover their hearts. To gather their wits. The hapless fools …

They thought me dead!

Grinning, he turned back to the vista of his army …

Only to see the horsemen he had glimpsed earlier, several hundred of them, riding unchallenged along the stationary flanks of the Selial Column. *"There are no more nations!"* a voice cried from their galloping midst. *"There are no more nations!"*

For several moments Conphas could scarce credit his eyes—or even his ears, for that matter. They were obviously Inrithi, despite their white-and-blue khalats. The banner of the Circumfix hung above the forward riders, trailing a skirt of golden tassels. And behind it … the Red Lion.

"Kill them!" Conphas howled. "Attack! Attack! Attack!"

For an instant it seemed nothing would happen, that nobody had heard. His army continued to mill in imbecile crowds; the interlopers continued to ride unmolested among them.

"There are no more nations!"

Then the white-clad knights abruptly changed direction, began riding toward *him*.

Conphas turned to the remaining Columnaries, at once laughed and snarled. And he remembered his grandmother, back when her beauty had yet burned as bright as legend. He remembered her drawing him up onto her lap and laughing at the way he squirmed and kicked his legs.

"It's good you prefer to keep your feet on the ground! For an Emperor that is the first thing ..."

"And what is the second?"

A laugh like a clear fountain. *"Ahhh ... The second is that you must ceaselessly measure."*

"Measure what, gramama?"

He could remember tapping his fingers on her cheek. How small his fingernails had been ...

"The purses of those who serve you, my little godling. For if you ever find them empty ..."

Of the dozen Nansur Columnaries who faced him, two fell to their knees, weeping, and three offered their swords. Five ran like madmen, and two simply walked away. He could hear the rumbling climb into the sky behind him.

"I defeated the Scylvendi," he said to the remainder. "You were there ..."

Hooves pounding the turf. The ground shivered through his sandals.

"No *man* could do such a thing," he said.

"No man!" one of the kneelers cried. The soldier clutched his hand, kissed his Imperial Ring.

Such a *deep* sound, the charge of the Inrithi. Thunder about horses snorting, gear clanking. So this was what the heathen heard.

The Emperor of Nansur turned, not really believing ...

He saw King Saubon leaning from his saddle, his face ruddy with murderous intent. More than sun glinted in the man's blue eyes.

He saw the broadsword that took his head.

Striding through smoke and over towering bonfires, Eleäzaras advanced on the Heresiarch of the Cishaurim. Seökti ravaged the ground before him, raising up skirts of smoking debris, tossing and breaking the black-armoured Thunyeri that surged toward him.

His voice bleeding, Eleäzaras shouted out the most powerful of the Great Analogies. He was the Grandmaster of the Scarlet Spires, the greatest School of Near Antiquity. He was Heir to Sampileth Fire-Singer, to Amrezzer the Black. He would avenge his beloved teacher! His School!

"Sasheoka!" he screamed between Cants.

Dragon fire buffeted the Heresiarch earthward, and for a moment the man rolled in golden fire, sheathed in foaming blue, fouled in his shimmering yellow gowns. Again and again Eleäzaras smote him. Magma burst from the earth beneath him. Suns crashed from the heavens. Great burning palms slapped about his alien defences, a fiery crush, into which Eleäzaras sang more and more power, until he saw the blind face cry out. His feet braced across smoke and sky, Eleäzaras laughed as he sang, for vengeance had made hatred a thing of rapture and glory.

But from a different direction, flurries of blue plasma, the Holy Water of the Indara-Kishauri, rained across his Wards, rocking them, then glancing off into the clouds above, where they vanished in smudges of glowing blue. The ghosts of cracks appeared. Sheets of ethereal stone fell away ...

Another Incandati soaring up from the ruin, disgorging world-cracking power ... Eleäzaras turned back to his Wards, singing deeper Ramparts, sturdier Shields. He glimpsed Seökti, climbing back into the sky. Glaring cataracts flaring from an impossible point between his missing eyes ...

Where were his brother Schoolmen? Ptarramas? Ti?

All about him the world had become a tidal surge of brilliant white and blue, tearing, pounding. Markless, as virginal as the Godspun world.

Tearing. Pounding.

The Grandmaster of the Scarlet Spires grunted, cursed. Jets of incandescence exploded through his Wards, immolating his left arm even as he screamed deeper defences. A fissure opened before him. Light blew across his scalp and brow. Like a doll, he was thrown backward.

His corpse toppled into the burning tracts below.

All along the length of the Skilura Aqueduct, the Fanim enveloped the despairing Men of the Tusk. Horsemen swept in flurries about the pilings, loosing shafts from point-blank range. Others charged into haphazard shield-walls, hacking their way past pikes and spears. Lord Galgota, the Palatine of Eshganax, fell to the merciless fervour of the Kirgwi.

Lord Gotian charged into the fray with all that remained of his Shrial Knights. At first their conviction and fury won them long expanses of ground, but they were too few. The heathen swarmed about their flanks, shot their horses out from under them. The Knights of the Tusk fought on, singing hymns that no calamity could break. Gotian fell, struck by an arrow in his armpit as he held his sword high, and still the warrior-monks sang.

Until death came swirling down.

Then horns sounded from the west. For a moment all those across the Shairizor, heathen and idolater alike, turned to the heights where the ancient Amoti had buried their Kings. And there, above the encampment, they saw the Imperial Army assembled in long lines along the crest.

The Men of the Tusk boomed in jubilation. At first the heathen raised ragged cheers of their own, and jeered at the arm-waving Inrithi, for their Grandees had told them not to fear should the Nansur arrive. But a presentiment of doom was traded among them, passing from band to slowing band. More than a few had seen the Circumfix and the Red Lion among the sacred standards of the Nansur Columns.

This wasn't the treachery of an Emperor—an Ikurei—come to seal a pact with their Padirajah. The hated standard of the Exalt-General, with its distinctive Kyranean disc, was nowhere to be seen.

No. This wasn't Ikurei Conphas. It was the Blond Beast …

King Saubon.

The Kianene horsemen withdrew from the surviving clots of Inrithi, milled in confusion across the plain. Even the Golden Padirajah seemed uncertain.

From the shadow of the aqueduct, Lord Werijen Greatheart cried out to the Tydonni of Plaideol. Raising a great shout, the blond-bearded warriors charged across the corpse-strewn turf, ran hacking into their wicked enemy's midst. Others followed, heedless of wounds or numbers.

Black-robed Schoolmen stood astride the sky: the Imperial Saik, the Sorcerers of the Sun, advancing on the massed formations of their hated, ancestral foe.

Horse and man thrashed black in descending fire.

⁂

The Scylvendi fairly gagged for breath. There *he* was, slumped against the mad walls of this place, in a white-illuminated chamber that opened at the end of the corridor. Pale. Naked save a loincloth. *There he was ...*

For hours Cnaiür had climbed through these obscene halls, following Serwë and her brother as they tracked Kellhus's scent. Apart from the braziers beneath the cavernous waterfall, all had been black. Deep into deep. Dark into dark. Through an underworld of vile images. They passed through ruins, Serwë said, the mines of the Cûnuroi, long murdered by the ancestors of Men. And Cnaiür had known that no track could lead him farther from the Steppe. His heart had hammered in his ears. He had glimpsed his father, Skiötha, beckoning through the black. And now ...

There he was—*Moënghus!*

Serwë assailed him first, her limbs and blade a whirring blur. But he stopped her with blue-flashing hands, swatted aside her slender figure ...

Just as her brother descended, slashing at impossible palms, spinning and kicking, lunging and probing—only to be seized about the throat, to gape and thrash as the blind man lifted him off his feet, to blister and burn as blue light consumed his head, made a candle of his body. The thing's face cramped open and the blind man threw him slack to the ground.

Throughout this, Cnaiür had advanced down the corridor, walking steadily, though the numbness of his gait made it seem that he shambled. He remembered approaching Kellhus the same way, that day he'd found him half dead upon his father's barrow, surrounded by circles of lifeless Sranc. He remembered the limb-hollowing air of nightmares. The breath like needles. But this was different! That had been the point of departure, from his homeland, from his people, from everything he had thought hallowed and strong. This was his destination. This was him ...

Him!

Three black snakes coiled about his throat, one hooked above either shoulder, another curled above his gleaming scalp. Cnaiür glimpsed the wound in his abdomen, the blood soaking pink across his loincloth, but he couldn't recall seeing him cut.

"Nayu," the blind face said in recognition. Kellhus's voice! Kellhus's features! When had the son become the father's mould?

"Nayu ... You have returned to me ..."

The snakes watched him, their tongues lapping the air. Even without eyes, the face beseeched him, tugged with a look of long remorse and astonished joy.

"Just as I knew you would."

Cnaiür stopped at the threshold, mere paces from the man who had butchered his heart. He glanced uneasily about the room, saw Serwë splayed motionless to his right, her long blonde hair swept across a bloodied floor, and the captive skin-spies hanging abject within a curtain of pulleys and chains. The walls warred with inhuman images. He squinted at the light that hung impossibly beneath the graven vaults.

"Nayu ... put down your sword. Please."

Blinking, he saw the notched blade in the air before him, though he had no recollection of drawing it. The light rolled like liquid across it.

"I am Cnaiür urs Skiötha," he said. "The most violent of all men."

"No," Moënghus said softly. "That is but a lie that you use to conceal your weakness from other men, just as weak."

"It is you who lie."

"But I see it within you. I see ... the truth of you. I see your love."

"*I hate!*" he screamed, so loud that the halls returned the words to them as a thousand whispers.

Though blind, Moënghus somehow managed to look to the ground in pensive pity. "So many years," he said. "So many seasons ... Everything I showed you has scarred your heart, set you apart from the People. Now you hold me accountable for what I taught."

"Desecration! Deceit!" Spittle burned his unshaven chin.

"Then why does it torment you so? Surely lies, when uncovered, fade like smoke. It is *truth* that burns, Nayu—as you know ... for you have burned in it for uncounted seasons."

Suddenly Cnaiür could feel it: the miles of earth heaped above them, the clawing inversion of *ground*. He had come too far. He had crawled too deep.

The sword dropped from the stranger's senseless fingers, rang like something pathetic across the floor. His face broke, like a thing wrapped about twitching vermin. The sobs whispered across the pitted stone.

And Moënghus was holding him, enclosing him, healing his innumerable scars.

"*Nayu* ..."

He loved him ... this man who had *shown* him, who had led onto the trackless steppe.

"*I am dying, Nayu.*" Hot whispers in his ear. "*I need your strength ...*"

Abandoned him. Forsook.

He had loved only him. In all the world ...

Weeping faggot!

The kiss was deep; the smell strong. His heart hammered. Shame bled from his every pore, skittered across his trembling limbs, and somehow ignited an even deeper ardour.

He breathed shuddering air into Moënghus's hot mouth. The snakes twisted through his hair, pressed hard and phallic against his temples. Cnaiür groaned.

So unlike Serwë or Anissi. A wrestler's clasp, firm and unyielding. The promise of surrender, of shelter in stronger arms.

He reached beneath his girdle, into his breeches ...

His eyes leaden with ardour, he murmured, "I wander trackless ground."

Moënghus gasped, jerked, and spasmed as Cnaiür rolled the Chorae across his cheek. White light flared from his gouged sockets. For an instant, Cnaiür thought, it seemed the God watched him through a man's skull.

What do you see?

But then his lover fell away, burning as he must, such was the force of what had possessed them.

"Not again!" Cnaiür howled at the sagging form. He stumbled to his knees, weeping, raving. "How could you leave me?"

His screech pealed through the derelict halls, filled the very earth.

And he laughed, thinking of the final swazond he would cut into his throat. One last thought too many ... *See! See!*

He cackled with grief.

He knelt over his lover's corpse—for how many heartbeats, he would never know. Then, just as the sorcerous light began to fade, a cool hand fell upon his cheek. He turned and saw Serwë ... For an instant her face cracked, as though gasping for air. But then it was seamless once again. Seamless and perfect.

Yes. Serwë ... The first wife of his heart.

His proof and prize.

Absolute darkness engulfed them.

The walls of flame that fenced the great swath of destruction wrought by the Scarlet Spires crawled outward, leaving smoking husks in their wake. But somehow, miraculously, the ancient fullery, with its open galleries and queued basins, had escaped unscathed. Kneeling on the lip of its southern pediment, Proyas had seen it all, as though from the edge of a mighty cliff.

The destruction of the Scarlet Spires.

The drums of the heathen had replaced the unearthly thrum of incantations. Even now the last of the Cishaurim—he could see only five—floated over the charred and derelict landscape, the asps about their necks hooked downward, searching for survivors. Every several heartbeats, brilliance fell from them and crackling booms rifled through the darkling sky.

He knew not what it meant. He knew nothing ...

Save that this was Shimeh.

He turned his face skyward. Through the haze he glimpsed the first vestiges of blue, a rim of gold about fleecy black.

There was a flash, a sparkle in the corner of his eye. He looked to the Sacred Heights, saw a point of light hanging above the eaves of the First Temple. The point lingered, painting the slate shingles of the dome white, then it burst, so bright that it struck circles across the firmament. Like sails cut from the mast, great sheets of smoke bloomed outward, swept over the hanging Cishaurim and out across the devastation.

And Proyas saw a *figure* standing where the light had been, so distant he could scarce make out his features, save that his hair was gold and his gown billowed white.

Kellhus!

The Warrior-Prophet.

Proyas blinked. Shivers splashed across his skin.

The figure leapt from the Temple's edge, soared over the astonished Fanim manning the Heterine Wall, then down the slopes, through the rim of burning buildings. Even from so far, Proyas could hear his world-reaming song.

As one, the scattered Cishaurim turned. With eyes like twin Nails of Heaven, the Warrior-Prophet walked across the heights toward them. With every step, it seemed, debris flew from the ground toward him, where it was drawn into circling loops, one after another, smaller circles bisecting the orbits of those larger, until rings of spinning ruin fairly obscured him.

The sun burst forth, as after the deluge. Mountainous shafts of white pillared the streetscape, made pearl of the fallen, burnished the plumes that still piled black and grey into the sky. And Proyas saw the reason for the rings: heathen bowmen scrounging the ruin for Chorae. The Warrior-Prophet cried out, and sequential explosions fanned across the ground beneath him, making missiles of snapping stone and brick. Even still, Proyas glimpsed bolts rising toward him. Some sailed wide; others glanced from the rings, cracking the sorceries that bound them, flinging debris across the city.

More and more ground-raking explosions. Bodies were tossed. Foundations shattered. The thunder of it silenced the relentless throbbing of the drums.

Soaring over the haze, their saffron robes flashing in the sunlight, the five Cishaurim closed with Kellhus. Like cataracts of water, blinding energies crashed across his spherical Wards, burning with a brilliance that forced Proyas to throw up a hand against the glare. Somehow, perfect lines flickered from the maelstrom, coiled into knifing geometries about the nearest of the Cishaurim. The blind man seemed to claw the air with his hands, then rained across the ground in blood and pieces.

But Kellhus's Wards were failing, cracked and shattered by tempests of unholy light. No more Gnostic lines glittered out to assail the hanging Cishaurim. And Proyas realized that Kellhus could not win, that he could only cry out Wards lest he be swept away. That it was only a matter of time.

Then—impossibly—it was over. The Cishaurim relented, and the roar of their assault trailed away like distant thunder. Proyas could see nothing ... only smoke, ruin, and sunlight.

He found himself gaping for breath—or was it a soundless howl?

Sweet God ... Sweet God of Gods!

There was a flash behind one of the assailants, and suddenly Kellhus *was there*, a hand clamped about the Cishaurim's jaw, Enshoiya's blade jutting bright through the saffron across his breast. Proyas stumbled to his feet, nearly teetered in a fatal fall. He caught himself, laughed through his tears. Cried out.

Then Kellhus was gone and the body dropped. The three remaining Cishaurim hung motionless, dumbstruck. Had they eyes, Proyas was certain they would have blinked.

And the Warrior-Prophet was behind another, beheading him, halving his snakes, in the space of a heartbeat. Proyas saw Kellhus jerk as the body tumbled down, realized he had caught a crossbow bolt fired from below. In a single snapping motion, he threw it like a knife at the nearest sorcerer-priest. There was a burst of incandescence rimmed by a nacre of black. The figure dropped.

Proyas whooped. Never had he felt so renewed, so young!

And Anasûrimbor Kellhus was singing the Abstractions once again. White robes boiled in the clearing sun. Planes and parabolas crackled about him. The very ground, to the pith of its ruin, hummed. The surviving Cishaurim floated in a broad and wary circle. He knew he had to keep moving, Proyas realized, to avoid the fate of his brothers. But it was already far too late ...

There was no escaping the Warrior-Prophet's holy light.

The sun slipped red into the iron west. The clouds crumbled in the southern winds and were dragged into purple streamers over the Meneanor. The gloom reared from the gullies and ravines of the devastation. Blood cooled across pitted stone.

In the dying light, something clink-clinked over the wheezing of subterranean fires. Amid stone heaped and tossed about unmoving foundations, a small boy hunched over a shattered figure of white, using a stone to chip salt into the palm of his little hand. Though the battle was over, he cast terrified looks over his shoulder. When he had filled his purse, he turned to the dead sorcerer's face, regarded it with an eerie blankness that a grown man might have confused with sorrow but his mother, had she still breathed, would have known as hope.

He stood, bent to study a small cut on his knee. He smeared the blood away with his thumb, watched a new bead well in its place. Then, spooked by some sound, he whirled and saw the strange human-headed bird that regarded him.

"Would you like to know a secret?" a thin voice cooed. The miniature face grinned, as though finding unexpected pleasure in playing a half-hearted game.

Too numb to be terrified, the young boy nodded, clutched tight the salt that would be his fortune.

"Come closer."

Chapter Seventeen

Shimeh

*Faith, they say, is simply hope confused for knowledge. Why believe
when hope alone is enough?*

—CRATIANAS, NILNAMESHI LORE

Ajencis, in the end, argued that ignorance was the only absolute.
According to Parcis, he would tell his students that he knew only
that he knew more than when he was an infant. This comparative
assertion was the only nail, he would say, to which one could tie
the carpenter-string of knowledge. This has come down to us as the
famed "Ajencian Nail," and it is the only thing that prevented the
Great Kyranean from falling into the tail-chasing scepticism of
Nirsolfa, or the embarrassing dogmatism of well-nigh every philosopher
and theologian who ever dared scratch ink across parchment.

But even this metaphor, "nail," is faulty, a result of what happens
when we confuse our notation with what is noted. Like the numeral
"zero" used by the Nilnameshi mathematicians to work such
wonders, ignorance is the occluded frame of all discourse, the unseen
circumference of our every contention. Men are forever looking for
the one point, the singular fulcrum they can use to dislodge all
competing claims. Ignorance does not give us this. What it provides,
rather, is the possibility of comparison, the assurance that not all
claims are equal. And this, Ajencis would argue, is all that we need.

392

For so long as we admit our ignorance, we can hope to improve our claims, and so long as we can improve our claims, we can aspire to the Truth, even if only in rank approximation.

And this is why I mourn my love of the Great Kyranean. For despite the pull of his wisdom, there are many things of which I am absolutely certain, things that feed the hate which drives this very quill.

—DRUSAS ACHAMIAN, THE COMPENDIUM OF THE FIRST HOLY WAR

Spring, 4112 Year-of-the-Tusk, Shimeh

The Ciphrang had sailed drunken across the skies, shrieking at the pinch of the needle world. Hanging from its claws, Achamian glimpsed lines and blots that were warring men, and the smudge of a burning city. The thing's blood trailed earthward, burning like naphtha.

The ground spiralled closer and closer ...

He awoke scarcely alive, breathing dust he could not lick from his teeth. With the one eye he could open, he saw sand cupped about the base of waving reeds. He heard the sea—the Meneanor Sea—pounding nearby shores.

Where were his brothers? Soon, he thought, the nets would be dry and his father would shout across the wind, summoning his nimble fingers. But he couldn't move. He wanted to weep at the thought of the beating his father would administer, but it seemed one more thing that did not matter.

Then something was dragging him, drawing him across the sand; he could see the clots where his blood blackened it. Dragging him, a shadow leaning against the sun, drawing him down into the darkness of ancient wars, into Golgotterath ...

Into a golden labyrinth of horrors more vast than any Nonmen Mansion, where a student, who was more a son, gazed at him with horror and incredulity. A Kûniüric Prince, just beginning to fathom his surrogate father's betrayal.

"She's dead!" Seswatha shouted as much at the unbearable expression as at the man. "She's gone to you now! And if she lives, then what you find *you will not keep*, no matter how deep you think your passion!"

"But you said," Nau-Cayûti cried, his brave face broken in grief. "You said!"

"I lied."

"How? How could you do this? You were the only one, Sessa! *The only one!*"

"Because *I couldn't succeed*," Achamian said. "Not alone. Because what we do here is more important than truth or love."

Nau-Cayûti's eyes gleamed like bared teeth in the gloom. This, Seswatha knew, was the look that had sealed the final heartbeat of so very many—Man and Sranc alike.

"And what do we do here, old teacher? Pray tell."

"We search," Achamian murmured. "We search for the Heron Spear."

Then there was rinsing water—fresh water, though the air smelled of salt. And the mutter of voices, concerned and compassionate, but calculating as well. Something soft daubed his cheeks. He glimpsed a wisp of cloud, and beneath it a little girl's face, both brown and freckled, like Esmenet's. He watched her pick at the long strands of hair the wind had drawn across her lips.

"*Memest ka hoterapi,*" a voice cooed from some other place. It was too matronly to belong to the girl. "Shhhh … shhhh …"

The sea rolled white into unseen breakers. He thought of the lice that would abandon him when finally, irresistibly, he breathed his last.

Wakefulness, true wakefulness in the sense of being still and watchful, was slow in coming. For the first few days it seemed he rolled, as though he had been bound to a great spinning wheel, only a small portion of which breached the surface of hot, amniotic waters. There was the pallet upon which he tossed and writhed, the murky room where the woman and her daughter came with water and basin, and sometimes fish ground into a stomach-warming gruel. And there were the nightmares, drawn into a grinding slurry of torment and loss. An ancient world ending without ending, just wound stacked upon immortal wound, and endless screaming.

He suffered the Fevers, as he had once so very long ago. He recalled them well enough.

When they broke, he found himself alone, blinking at the palm-thatched ceiling. Sheaves of spring herbs hung from the rafters, which were little more than poles. Old nets hung from the walls. There was a table heaped with dried fish like the soles of sandals. He could see the stains and smell the odours of countless guttings. Above the crash of breakers, he could hear the walls creak and rattle in the wind. Twine fluttered in the drafts. In the corner, a momentary dust devil spun flecks of chaff ...

Home, he thought. *I've come home*. And he slept his first true sleep.

In the chariot of the Kyranean High King, he stood dumbfounded.

For years now, an inexplicable sense of doom had hung upon the horizon, a horror that had no form, only direction ... All Men could feel it. And all Men knew that it bore responsibility for their stillborn sons, that it had broken the great cycle of souls.

Now at last they could see it—the bone that would gag Creation.

Bashrag beat the ground with their great hammers, while Sranc heaved in imbecile masses. They swallowed the surrounding plains, loping in armour of tanned human skin, gibbering like apes, throwing themselves at the ramparts the Men of Kyraneas had made of Mengedda's ruins. And behind them, *the whirlwind* ... a great winding rope sucking the dun earth into black heavens, elemental and indifferent, roaring ever nearer, come to snuff out the last light of Men.

Come to seal the World shut.

The storm clouds firmed their grip on the sun, and all became twilight and thunder. Clutching their groins, the Sranc fell to their knees, heedless of the mannish swords that fell upon them. Then, through the snarling mouths of its children, Seswatha heard it, the million-throated voice of Tsuramah, the No-God ...

WHAT DO YOU SEE?

"What," Anaxophus said, "do you see?"

Seswatha gaped at the High King. Though the man's tone and expression were entirely his own, he had spoken the selfsame words as the No-God.

"My Lord High King ..." Achamian knew not what else to say.

The surrounding plains writhed and warred. As tall as the horizon, the dread whirlwind approached, *the No-God walked*, so vast that it made gravel of Mengedda's ruin, motes of men.

I MUST KNOW WHAT YOU SEE

"I must know what you see ..."

The painted eyes fixed him, honest and intent, as though demanding a boon whose significance had yet to be determined.

"Anaxophus!" Seswatha cried through the clamour. "The Spear! You must take up the Spear!"

This isn't what happens ...

A chorus of roars. The men about them were leaning into the wind, crying out to their Gods. Sand pelted bronze plates. The No-God walked, rising with yawning dimension, transcending the span of a single look, upending the hierarchy of the moving and the immovable, so that it seemed the whirlwind stood still while all Creation flew about it.

TELL ME

"Tell me ..."

"By all that's holy, Anaxophus! Anaxophus! Take up the Spear!"

No ... this can't be ...

The No-God advanced across the Mengedda Plain, sweeping up legions of Sranc, tossing them about its thunderhead base like dolls knitted of cheap flesh. And in its winding heart Seswatha glimpsed it, the glint of the Carapace, hanging like a black jewel ... He turned back to the Kyranean High King.

WHAT AM I?

"What am I?" the dark and regal face said, frowning. His oiled braids thrashed like snakes about his shoulders. The last of the light glimmered across the lions wrought into his bronze armour.

"The World, Anaxophus! *The very World!*"

This isn't how it happens!

The whirlwind towered over them, a mountainous pillar of fury so high one had to kneel to see the cloud-shrouded summits. Cycling winds roared over them. The horses screamed and kicked from side to side. The chariot rocked beneath their feet. All had become ochre shadow. More scouring gusts, buffeting them with the power of riptides, bottomless and all-encompassing. The grit peeled the skin from his knuckles, from his cheeks.

The No-God walked.

Too late ...

Strange ... the way passion flickered out before life.

Horses shrieking. Chariot tipping.

TELL ME, ACHAMIA—

He bolted awake, crying out.

The woman, who happened to be standing at the door, dropped her basin and ran to him. Instinctively, he grabbed her arms, the way a dismayed husband might. When she tried to pull away, he clutched her tighter, used her to find his unsteady feet. She cried out, but he did not let go. He felt his fingers cramp into her arms, so hard they had to hurt— but he couldn't let go!

The door crashed open. A man rushed in, fists high and swinging.

There was a blow that Achamian couldn't recollect afterward. He only saw the man draw his wife away as he struggled to regain his feet. His cheek throbbed. The man hollered in some language, gesticulated wildly, while the woman seemed to plead with him, clutching at his left arm even though he shrugged her hands away each time.

Achamian stood, quite naked. There was something wrong, he realized, with his right leg. He grabbed a rough blanket from his pallet, wrapped himself with it. Then, bewildered, he circled the man and his wife, made his way to the door, stumbled backward out into the sunlight, felt his heels kick hot sand. He raised a hand against the brightness of sun, beach, and heaving sea. He saw the little girl with the freckles, cringing behind the back wall. Then he saw others, far out, past where the black rocks broke the white sand, drawing their boats through the diamond foam.

He turned and, as fast as he could manage, fled across the shore.

Please don't kill me! he wanted to cry out, though he knew he could burn them all.

He began walking east, to Shimeh. It seemed the only direction he knew.

It was morning, and the sun seemed to flee the very earth he yearned to reach, as though fearing he might somehow catch it. So long as the sand lay hard and flat, he followed the seashore, savouring the warm rush of the Meneanor about his ankles. Red-throated gulls hung motionless in the gaping sky. Everything moved both faster and slower, as they always did on the earthly edges of a great sea. The vast planes of water heaved ponderously before a motionless horizon, and yet lights sparkled across the slow-rolling surfaces, and the frayed edges of things trembled in a never-ending wind.

He paused four times. Once to make a staff of some sea-worn wood. Once to tie a section of rotted rope about his black blanket, which he had folded into what the Nansur called a "hermit's robe." A third time to inspect his leg, which had been gashed about his shin and ankle. He had no recollection of receiving the wound, though he clearly remembered gasping a Skin Ward the instant before the demon had overcome his defences. Perhaps he hadn't gasped quickly enough.

He paused a fourth time just before the piling breakers forced him from the beaches. He came upon a tidal pool so sheltered from the wind that its surface seemed glass. He knelt at its edge to study the reflection of his face. He saw that the Two Scimitars had been drawn in soot or lampblack across his forehead—the work of his caregivers, he supposed. A charm or blessing or prayer of some sort.

For some reason he was loath to wash it away, so he only rinsed his matted beard.

When the water settled, he studied his reflection again—the dark, smallish eyes, the beard climbing high on his cheeks, the five white streaks. He pressed his finger into the image, watched it bend and waver about the intrusion, a thing of pure surface. How could men feel so deep?

He struck inland, carefully picking his way through the pasture to avoid thistles. Though the wind continued to blow—he could see its gusts in the shadows it chased across the rolling distance—it seemed to miss him more and more, the way it always was when one left the shore. The heat of thronging green embalmed him, and insects wended to and fro with aimless precision. Once, he startled a thrush, and nearly cried out as it exploded from his feet, battling its dry way to some other crotch in the grasses.

The ground swelled before him, and he came across a broad swath of trampled earth, the residue of passing horsemen—hundreds of them. He was not so very far after all.

He crossed the summit, where the mausoleums of the ancient Amoti Kings wasted in the sunlight. The glass of burnt earth cut his bare feet.

He crossed the worn and packed expanses where the Holy War had pitched its encampment.

He walked through the fields of battle, near the ruined aqueduct, where stench and yellowed grass marked the points where man and horse had fallen.

He walked through the ruins of the Massus Gate, and across an overturned fragment of wall he saw an iris wrought in black tile on white.

He picked his way through the blasted streets, and paused to stare at a Scarlet Schoolman who jutted from the debris, poised in his final moment, salted to the pith.

He climbed the great stair cut into the side of the Juterum, though he did not pause at any of the pilgrim's stations.

He saw no one until he reached the western gates of the Heterine Wall, where two Conriyans he vaguely recognized stood guard. Crying out "Truth shines!" they fell to their knees before him, implored him for his blessing.

He spat on them instead.

As he climbed toward the First Temple, he gazed across the still-smoking foundations of the Ctesarat, the High Tabernacle of the Cishaurim. It meant nothing to him.

The First Temple loomed so very near, its circular façade soaring white over the thousands of Inrithi congregated about it. The sun rained down. The shadows were sharp. The sky was cloudless, a turquoise bowl marked only by the Nail of Heaven, which glittered like something lost and precious glimpsed in the deeps.

Leaning heavily on his staff, Achamian climbed the last stretch. Without exception, the Men of the Tusk made way for him. He was more important than they were—more important by far. He stood at the centre of the world—teacher to their Warrior-Prophet. He brushed past them, indifferent to their entreaties. Finally he paused on the topmost stair and glared at them. Glared and laughed.

Turning his back, he limped into the airy gloom, passed beneath the blessing tablets strung from the lintels. So different, he thought, from the templed gloom of Sumna, where all was garish and painted. The marble soothed his bleeding feet.

All were kneeling as he passed through the outer ring of pillars. Pressing through their murmuring midst, he found himself thinking of the strange ... *hollow* that had opened within him. He stood, he breathed, which meant his heart still beat within his breast, but its pulse was lost to him. He thought of the lice that would soon spill from his scalp.

Then he heard stern proclamations, the kind that made so many shiver with awe. And he recognized the voice of *Maithanet*, the Holy Shriah of the Thousand Temples. He could almost glimpse him through the concentric forest of pillars.

"Arise, Anasûrimbor Kellhus, for all authority now resides in thee ..."

A moment of silence, sullied by the gentle sound of weeping.

"Behold, the Warrior-Prophet!" the obscured Shriah bellowed. "Behold, the High King of Kûniüri!"

"Behold, the *Aspect-Emperor of the Three Seas*!"

The words winded Achamian as surely as a father's blow. While the Men of the Tusk leapt to their feet, crying out in rapture and adulation, he staggered against one of the white pillars, feeling the cool of engraved figures pressed against his cheek.

What was this hollow that had so consumed him? What was this yearning that felt so like mourning?

They make us love! They make us love!

Some time passed before he realized that Kellhus himself was speaking. Achamian found himself drawn forward—irresistibly, inevitably. Dressed in the silk khalats of their enemy, thanes and knights pressed clear of his path, staring as though he were a leper.

"With me," Kellhus declared, "everything is rewritten. Your books, your parables, and your prayers, all that was your custom, are now nothing more than childhood curiosities. For too long has Truth languished in the vulgar hearts of Men. What you call tradition is naught but artifice, the fruit of your vanity, of your lust, of your fear and your hate.

"With me, all souls shall find a more honest footing. With me, all the world is born anew!"

Year One.

Achamian continued to limp forward. With every tap, his staff hummed and tingled in his palm. Cracked ... like everything else in this miserable world. "The old world is dead!" he cried out. "Is this what you say, Prophet?"

The silence of gasps and rustling silk.

The last of the obscuring figures parted, more astonished than scandalized. And at last Achamian could see ... He blinked, struggling to separate what was familiar from the pomp and the glory.

The Holy Court of the Aspect-Emperor.

He saw Maithanet, draped in the golden vestments of his station. He saw Proyas, Saubon, and other surviving Lords of the Holy War, a new caste-nobility, less numerous but more radiant than the old. He saw the Nascenti and other high-ranking apparati of the Ministrate, decked in the glory of their fraudulent station. He saw Nautzera and the Quorum, flashing crimson-gold in the Mandate's finest ceremonial robes. He even saw Iyokus, standing as pale as glass in Eleäzaras's magisterial gowns.

He saw Esmenet, her mouth open, her painted eyes shining with tears that spilled ... a Nilnameshi Empress once again.

He could not see Serwë. He could not see Cnaiür or Conphas.

Neither was Xinemus anywhere to be found.

But he saw *Kellhus*, sitting leonine before a great hanging Circumfix of white and gold, his hair flashing about his shoulders, his flaxen beard plaited. He saw him drawing the nets of the future, just as the Scylvendi had said, measuring, theorizing, categorizing, penetrating ...

He saw the *Dûnyain*.

Kellhus nodded to him, his frown amiable and perplexed. "This is what I *decree*, Akka. The old world is dead."

Leaning against his staff, Achamian glanced across the astonished assembly. "So you speak," he said without urgency or rancour, "of an apocalypse."

"It's not so simple. You know that ..." His voice, his expression—everything about him—beamed indulgent good humour. He raised a welcoming hand, gestured to the space to his right. "Come ... take your place at my side."

Just then Esmenet cried out, flew from the dais toward Achamian, only to stumble and fall weeping ... Her palms to the floor, she raised her face to him, hopeless and beseeching.

"No," Achamian said to Kellhus. "I've returned for my wife. Nothing more."

A moment of crushing, monolithic silence.

"Preposterous!" Nautzera cried out. "You will do as he commands!"

Even though Achamian heard the grand old sorcerer, he did not heed him. Years had passed since he last understood his scholastic brothers. He held out his hand. "Esmi?"

He watched her find her feet, saw the crescent of her belly. She was showing ... How could he not have seen that before?

Kellhus simply ... watched.

"You're a Mandate Schoolman," Nautzera grated with admirable menace. "A *Mandate Schoolman!*"

"Esmi," Achamian said, his eyes and outstretched hand directed only at her. "Please ..."

This was the only thing that could *mean* anymore.

"Akka," she sobbed. She glanced about, seemed to wilt beneath the rapt gazes that encircled them. "I'm the mother of ... of ..."

So the hollow could not be shut. Achamian nodded, wiped the last tear he knew he would ever shed. He would be heartless now. A perfect man.

She approached him—with longing, yes, but with wariness and horror as well. She clutched the hand he had held out, the one that did not lean against his staff. "The *world*, Akka. Don't you see? The very world hangs in the balance!"

What will it be the next time I die?

With a savagery that both thrilled and frightened him, he snatched her left wrist, twisted and bent it back, so that she could see the blurred tattoo that blackened the back of her hand. He thrust her away from him.

The crowd erupted in outrage. But strangely, no one moved to seize him.

"No!" Esmenet shrieked from the floor. "Leave him alone! Leave him! You don't know him! You don't kn—"

"*I renounce!*" Achamian roared, sweeping his scathing gaze across all assembled. "I renounce my station as Holy Tutor, as Vizier to the court of the Anasûrimbor Kellhus!" He glanced at Nautzera, not caring whether the old man sneered or no.

"*I renounce my School!*" he continued. "As an assembly of hypocrites and murderers."

"Then you sentence yourself to death!" Nautzera cried. "There's no sorcery outside the Schools! There are no—"

"*I renounce my Prophet!*"

Gasps and sputters filled the galleries of the First Temple. He waited for the uproar to subside, staring for what seemed an unblinking eternity at the otherworldly aspect of Anasûrimbor Kellhus. His last student.

Nothing passed between them.

Somehow his gaze found Proyas, who looked so ... *aged* with his beard squared. There was prayer in his handsome brown eyes, the promise of return. But it was far too late.

"And I renounce ..." He trailed, warred with errant passions. "I renounce my *wife*."

His eyes fell upon Esmenet, stricken upon the floor. *My wife!*

"*Noooo*," she wept and whispered. "*Pleeaaase, Akka ...*"

"As an adulteress," he continued, his voice cracking, "and a ... a ..."

His face a mask of nimil, he turned without leave, began walking back the way he came. The Men of the Tusk stared at him dumbstruck, their outrage as bright as sparks in their eyes. But they fell away before his approach. They fell away.

Then, through the sound of Esmenet weeping ...

"*Achamian!*"

Kellhus. Achamian did not condescend to turn, but he did pause. It seemed the future itself leaned inscrutable against him, a yoke about his neck, a spear point against his spine ...

"The next time you come before me," the Aspect-Emperor said, his voice cavernous, ringing with inhuman resonance, "you will kneel, Drusas Achamian."

Retracing his bloody footprints, the Wizard limped on.

Encyclopedic Glossary

AUTHOR'S NOTE

Steeped in the classics, Inrithi scholars commonly rendered names in their Sheyic form, opting for native forms only in the absence of antique Sheyic analogues. So, for instance, the surname Coithus (which is mentioned twice by Casidas in *The Annals of Cenei*) is in fact a Sheyic version of the Gallish "Koütha," and so is rendered as such here. The surname Hoga, on the other hand, has no extant Sheyic form, and so is rendered in the original Tydonni. Kyranean place names (such as Asgilioch, Girgilioth, or Kyudea) are a notable exception.

The vast majority of the following proper names, then, are simply transliterated from their Sheyic (and in some instances Kûniüric) form. They have been translated only where their Sheyic (or Kûniüric) version does likewise. So, for instance, the Ainoni "Ratharutar," which has the Sheyic form "Retorum Ratas," is given as "the Scarlet Spires," the literal meaning of *ratas* ("red") and *retorum* ("towers"). The etymological provenance and translated meaning of place names can be found bracketed at the beginning of certain entries.

These would be the names as Drusas Achamian knew them.

A

Abenjukala—The classic treatise on benjuka, written anonymously in Near Antiquity. Because of its emphasis on the relation between benjuka and wisdom, many consider it a classic philosophical text as well.

Absolute, the—Among the Dûnyain, the state of becoming "unconditioned," a perfect self-moving soul independent of "what comes before." See *Dûnyain* and *Conditioning, the*.

Abstractions—An epithet for Gnostic sorceries.

Adûnyani—"Little Dûnyain" (Kûniüric from Ûmeritic *aŕtûnya*, or "little truth"). The name taken by the followers assembled by Kellhus in Atrithau.

Aëngelas (4087–4112)—A Werigdan warrior.

Aethelarius VI (4062–)—(Sheyic form of Athullara) The King of Atrithau, last of the line of Morghund.

Agansanor—A province of south central Ce Tydonn, noted for the martial zeal of its sons.

Age of Bronze—Another name for Far Antiquity, during which bronze was the dominant technology of Men.

Age of Cenei—The era of Ceneian dominance of the Three Seas, from the conquest of Nilnamesh in 2478 until the Sack of Cenei in 3351.

Age of Kyraneas—The era of Kyranean dominance of the northwestern Three Seas.

Age of Warring Cities—The era following the dissolution of Kyraneas (*c.* 2158) until the rise of Cenei, characterized by perpetual warfare between the cities of the Kyranae Plain.

Aghurzoi—"Cut Tongue" (Ihrimsû) The language of the Sranc.

Agmundr—A province of northeastern Galeoth, located beneath the Osthwai Mountains.

Agnotum Market—The main bazaar of Iothiah, dating back to the days of Cenei.

agoglian bulls—Ancient Kyranean symbols of virility and fortune. The most famous examples are found in the Hagerna opposite the Vault-of-the-Tusk.

Agongorea—"Fields of Woe" (Kûniüric) The blasted lands to the west of the River Sursa and north of the Neleost Sea.

Agonic Collar—A sorcerous artifact of the Ancient North, reputedly crafted by the Mihtrulic Gnostic School. According to Mandate scholars, the purpose of the Agonic Collar was analogous to that of the Uroborian Circle utilized by the Anagogic Schools of the Three Seas, namely, to inflict excruciating pain on the wearer should he attempt to utter any sorcerous incantation.

Agonies—The name for the Gnostic Cants of Torment, a reputed specialty of the Mangaecca.

Ainoni—The language of High Ainon, derived from Ham-Kheremic.

Ajencis (*c.* 1896–2000)—The father of syllogistic logic and algebra, held by many to be the greatest of all philosophers. Born in the Kyranean capital of Mehtsonc, he is reputed to have never once left his city, even during the horrific plagues of 1991, when his advanced age made his death a near certainty. (According to various sources, Ajencis bathed on a daily basis and refused to drink water drawn from city wells, claiming that these practices, combined with a distaste for drunkenness and a moderate diet, were the keys to his health.) Many commentators, both antique and contemporary, complain that there are as many Ajencises as there are readers of Ajencis. Though this is certainly true of his more speculative works (such as *Theophysics* or *The First Analytic of Men*), his work does possess a discernible and consistent sceptical core, primarily exemplified in *The Third Analytic of Men*, which also happens to be his most cynical work. For Ajencis, Men by and large "make their weaknesses, not reason or the world, the primary measure of what they hold true." In fact, he observed that most individuals possess no criteria whatsoever for their beliefs. As a so-called critical philosopher, one might have supposed he would eventually share the fate of other critical philosophers, such as Porsa (the famed "Philosopher-Whore" of Trysë) or Kumhurat. Only his reputation and the structure of Kyranean society saved him from the vicissitudes of the mob. As a child, he was allegedly such a prodigy that the High King himself took notice of him, granting him what was called Protection at the unprecedented age of eight. Protection was an ancient and hallowed Kyranean institution; the "Protected" were those who could say anything without fear of reprisal, even to the High King. Ajencis continued speaking until he suffered a stroke and died at the venerable age of 103.

Ajokli—The God of thievery and deception. Though listed among the primary Gods in *The Chronicle of the Tusk*, there is no true Cult of Ajokli, but rather an informal network of devotees scattered across the great cities of the Three Seas. Ajokli is oft mentioned in the secondary scriptures of the different Cults, sometimes as a mischievous companion of the Gods, other times as a cruel or malicious competitor. In the *Mar'eddat*, he is the faithless husband of Gierra.

Ajowai—A mountain fastness in the north Hinayati Mountains that serves as the administrative capital of Girgash.

akal—The base monetary unit of Kian.

Akkeägni—The God of disease. Also known as the God of a Thousand Hands. Scholars have oft noted the irony that the Priesthood of Disease provides the primary repository of physicians for the Three Seas. How can one at once worship disease and war against it? According to the scriptures of the Cult, the *Piranavas*, Akkeägni is a so-called Bellicose God, one who favours those who strive against him over sycophants and worshippers.

Akksersia—A lost nation of the Ancient North. Though the White Norsirai of the north shore of the Cerish Sea lacked any sustained contact with the Nonmen, they gradually became the second great seat of Norsirai civilization. Akksersia was founded in 811 by Salaweärn I, following the dissolution of the Cond Yoke. Though confined to the city of Myclai, her commercial and administrative capital, the nation gradually extended its hegemony, first along the length of the River Tywanrae, then across the plains of Gâl and the entire north shore of the Cerish Sea. By the time of the First Great Sranc War in 1251, it was the largest of the ancient Norsirai nations, incorporating almost all the White Norsirai tribes save those of the Istyuli Plains. It fell to the No-God after three disastrous defeats in 2149. Akksersian colonists on the Cerish Sea's heavily forested south shore would form the nucleus of what would become the Meörn Empire.

Akksersian—The lost language of ancient Akksersia, and "purest" of the Nirsodic tongues.

Akkunihor—A Scylvendi tribe of the central Steppe. As the tribe closest to the Imperial frontier, the Akkunihor are the traditional brokers of Three Seas rumour and knowledge among the Scylvendi.

Algari (4041–4111)—A body-slave to Prince Nersei Proyas.

Alkussi—A Scylvendi tribe of the central Steppe.

"All heaven cannot shine through a single crack ..."—The famous line attributed to the poet Protathis suggesting that no man can be trusted with divine revelation.

Allosian Forum—The great judicial galleries located at the foot of the Andiamine Heights.

Am-Amidai—A large Kianene fortress located in the heart of the Atsushan Highlands, raised in 4054.

amicut—A ration used by Scylvendi warriors on the trail, consisting of wild herbs and berries beaten into dried sections of beef.

Ammegnotis—A city on the south bank of the River Sempis, raised during the Kyranean New Dynasty.

Amortanea—The merchant carrack that bore Achamian and Xinemus to Joktha.

Amoteu—A governorate of Kian, located on the southern edge of the Meneanor Sea. Like all the nations in the shadow of the Betmulla Mountains, Amoteu, or Holy Amoteu as it is sometimes called, grew in the influential shadow of Old Dynasty Shigek. According to extant inscriptions, the Shigeki referred to both Xerash and Amoteu as Hut-Jartha, the "Land of the Jarti," or as Huti-Parota, the "Middle-Lands." The Jarti were the dominant Ketyai tribe of the region, to which the Amoti and several others were tributaries before the Shigeki conquest. But with the extensive cultivation of the Shairizor Plains, and the slow rise of Shimeh and Kyudea along the River Jeshimal, the balance of power slowly shifted. For centuries the Middle-Lands found themselves the battle-ground between Shigek and her southern competitors, Eumarna across the Betmulla Mountains and ancient or Vapartic Nilnamesh. In 1322, Anzumarapata II, the Nilnameshi King of Invishi, crushed the Shigeki and, in an effort to secure his conquests, transplanted hundreds of thousands of indigent Nilnameshi on the Plains of Heshor, an act that would long outlive his brief empire (the Shigeki reconquered the Middle-Lands in 1349). With the collapse of Shigeki regional dominance in 1591, the Jarti attempted to reassert their ancestral control—with disastrous consequences. The resulting war gave rise to a brief Amoti Empire, which reached the length of the Betmulla to the frontier of the Carathay Desert. All the Middle-Lands would fall under the power of Kyraneas in 1703.

With the dissolution of Kyraneas, *c.* 2158, Amoteu enjoyed its second—and last—period of independence, though now the Xerashi, the descendants of Anzumarapata's settlers, had become its primary competitors. This second "golden age" would witness Inri Sejenus, and the slow growth of the faith that would eventually come to dominate the Three Seas. After a brief period of Xerashi occupation, Amoteu would suffer a long succession of foreign overlords, each leaving its own stamp: first the Ceneians, who conquered the Middle-Lands in 2414, then the Nansur in 3574, and finally the Kianene in 3845. Despite the peace and prosperity enjoyed by other conquered provinces, the early years of Ceneian rule would prove particularly bloody for Amoteu. In 2458, while Triamis the Great was still in his infancy, Inrithi fanatics led the province in a vicious rebellion against Cenei. As punishment, Emperor Siaxas II butchered the inhabitants of Kyudea and razed the city to the ground.

Amoti—The language of Amoteu, a derivative of Mamati.

Anagkë—The Goddess of fortune. Also known as "the Whore of Fate." Anagkë is one of the primary "Compensatory Gods," which is to say, one who rewards devotion in life with paradise in the afterlife. Her Cult is extremely popular in the Three Seas, especially among the higher, political castes.

Anagogis—A branch of sorcery that turns on the resonance between meanings and concrete things.

Analogies—An alternate name for Anagogic sorceries.

Anasûrimbor Dynasty—The ruling dynasty of Kûniüri from 1408 to 2147. See *Apocalypse*.

Anaxophus V (2109–56)—The Kyranean High King who wielded the Heron Spear against the No-God at Mengedda in 2155.

ancestor scroll—A scroll kept by most pious Inrithi, bearing the names of all the dead ancestors who might intercede on their behalf. Since the Inrithi believe that honour and glory in life brings power in the afterlife, they are particularly proud of renowned ancestors and ashamed of known sinners.

Ancient North—The name given to the Norsirai civilization destroyed in the Apocalypse.

Ancilline Gate—One of the so-called Lesser Gates of Momemn, located to the immediate south of the Girgallic Gate.

Andiamine Heights—The primary residence and principal administrative seat of Nansur Emperors, located on the seaward walls of Momemn.

Anfirig, Thagawain (4057–)—The Galeoth Earl of Gesindal.

Angeshraël (?–?)—The most famed Old Prophet of the Tusk, responsible for leading the Five Tribes of Men into Eärwa. Also known as the Burnt Prophet for bowing his face into his fire after confronting Husyelt at the foot of Mount Eshki. His wife was Esmenet.

Angka—The ancient Norsirai name for Zeüm.

animas—The "moving force" of all existence, typically analogized as the "breath of God." Much ink has been spilt over the question of the relation between animas, which is primarily a theological concept, and the sorcerous concept of "onta." Most scholars are of the opinion that the latter is simply a secular version of the former.

Anissi (c. 4089–)—The favourite wife of Cnaiür urs Skiötha.

Ankaryotis—A demon of the Outside, one of the more manageable Potents controlled by the Scarlet Spires.

Ankharlus—A famed Kûniüric commentator and high priest of Gilgaöl.

Ankirioth—A province of south central Conriya.

Ankmuri—The lost language of ancient Angka.

Ankulakai—The mountain on the southern limit of the Demua that cradles the city of Atrithau.

Anmergal, Skinede (4078–4112)—A Tydonni thane, slain at the Battle of Tertae Fields.

Annals of Cenei, The—The classic treatise of Casidas, covering the history of Cenei and the Ceneian Empire from the Imperial City's legendary foundation in 809 to the time of Casidas's death in 3142.

Annand—A province of north central Conriya, known primarily for its silver and iron mines. "All the silver in Annand" is a common Three Seas expression, meaning "pricelessness."

Anochirwa—"Horns Reaching" (Kûniüric) An early mannish name for Golgotterath.

Anphairas, Ikurei—See *Ikurei Anphairas I.*

Anplei—The second-largest city in Conriya after Aöknyssus.

anpoi—A traditional drink throughout the Three Seas, made of fermented peach nectar.

Ansacer ab Salajka (4072–)—The Sapatishah-Governor of Gedea. The Black Gazelle is his totem.

Ansansius, Teres (c. 2300–2351)—The most famed theologian of the early Thousand Temples, whose *The City of Men*, *The Limping Pilgrim*, and *Five Letters to All* are revered by Shrial scholars.

Anserca—The southernmost province of the Nansur Empire.

Antanamera—A province of High Ainon, located on the highland frontier of Jekk.

Anwurat—A large Kianene fortress to the south of the Sempis Delta, constructed in 3905.

Anyasiri—"Tongueless Howlers" (Ihrimsû) An early Cûnuroi name for the Sranc.

Aöknyssus—The administrative and commercial capital of Conriya. Once the capital of the long-lost Shiradi Empire, Aöknyssus is perhaps the most ancient of the Three Seas' great cities, with the possible exception of Sumna or Iothiah.

Aörsi—A lost nation of the Ancient North. Aörsi was founded in the 1556 partitioning of Greater Kûniüri between the sons of Anasûrimbor Nanor-Ukkerja I at his death. Even contemporaries recognized Aörsi as the most warlike of the ancient Norsirai nations, though her ambitions remained uniquely defensive rather than expansionist. Sparsely populated save for the regions surrounding her capital, Shiarau, Aörsi faced considerable and unrelenting pressure from the Sranc and Bashrag tribes of the Yimaleti Mountains to the north, not to mention the Consult legions of Golgotterath across the River Sursa to the west—a challenge that would spur the construction of Dagliash, the greatest fortress of the age. It is no accident that the word *sursa* came to mean "front line" across the Ancient North.

Aörsi's history is one of ingenuity and determination in the face of never-ending crises. Perhaps it is fitting that her destruction in 2136 (see *Apocalypse*) was due more to the betrayal of her southern Kûniüric cousins than to any real failure on the part of Anasûrimbor Nimeric, her final King.

Apocalypse—The protracted wars and atrocities that obliterated the Ancient North. The roots of the Apocalypse are many and deep. Mandate scholars (who, popular opinion to the contrary, are not the recognized authorities on the subject) argue that they are older than recorded history. More sober accounts reach back no further than the so-called Nonman Tutelage, which eventually led the Gnostic School of Mangaecca to the site of the Incû-Holoinas, the Ark-of-the-Skies, where it lay protected, hidden by Nonmen glamours in the shadow of the western Yimaleti Mountains. Accounts are incomplete, but it seems clear that what were called the Great Sranc Wars were a consequence of the Mangaecca occupation of what would come to be called Golgotterath.

Traditionally, scholars date the beginning of the Apocalypse with Anasûrimbor Celmomas's call for a holy war against Golgotterath, his Great Ordeal, which is to say, with the beginning of the accounts found in *The Sagas*, the primary historical source text for this cataclysmic event. Legend has it that Nonmen Siqu informed the Grandmaster of the Sohonc (the pre-eminent Sauglish School) that the Mangaecca, or Consult as they had come to be called, had uncovered lost Inchoroi secrets that would lead to the world's destruction. Seswatha in turn convinced Celmomas to declare war on Golgotterath in 2123.

There has been much debate regarding the next twenty years, and much severe criticism of the pride and bickering that would eventually destroy the Ordeal. What most fail to realize is that the threat facing the High Norsirai of Kûniüri and Aörsi at this time was entirely hypothetical. In fact, it is surprising that Celmomas was able to hold his coalition, which included Nonmen as well as token contingents of Kyraneans, together for as long as he did.

The first great battle, fought in 2124 on the Plains of Agongorea, was indecisive. Celmomas and his allies wintered in Dagliash and forded the River Sursa the following spring, catching their foe unawares. The Consult withdrew to Golgotterath, and so began what would be called the Great Investiture. For six years the Ordeal attempted to starve the Consult into submission, to no avail. Every assault proved disastrous. Then, in 2131, after a dispute with King Nimeric of Aörsi, Celmomas himself abandoned his own Holy War. The following year disaster struck. Consult legions, apparently utilizing a vast subterranean network of tunnels, appeared in the Ring Mountains to the rear of the Ordeal. The coalition host was all but destroyed. Embittered by the loss of his sons, Nil'giccas, the Nonman King of Ishterebinth, withdrew altogether, leaving the Aörsi to war alone.

The following years witnessed a string of further disasters. In 2133 the Aörsi were defeated at the Passes of Amnerlot, and Dagliash was lost soon after. King Nimeric withdrew to his capital of Shiarau. A year passed before Celmomas acknowledged his folly and mobilized to relieve him. By then it was too late. In 2135, Nimeric was mortally wounded in the Battle of Hamuir, and Shiarau fell to the Consult legions the following spring. The Aörsic House of Anasûrimbor had perished forever.

Now it was Kûniüri that stood alone. His credibility destroyed, Celmomas was unable to rally any allies, and for a time the situation seemed bleak. But in 2137 his youngest son, Nau-Cayûti, managed to rout the Consult at the Battle of Ossirish, where he earned the name Murswagga, or "Dragonslayer," for killing Tanhafut the Red. His next victory, within sight of Shiarau's ruins, was more complete still. The Consult's remaining Sranc and Bashrag fled across the River Sursa. In 2139 the young Prince besieged and recaptured Dagliash, then launched several spectacular raids across the Plains of Agongorea.

Then, in 2140, Nau-Cayûti's beloved concubine, Aulisi, was abducted by Sranc marauders and taken to Golgotterath. According to *The Sagas*, Seswatha was able to convince the Prince (who was once his student) that she could be rescued from the Incû-Holoinas, and the two of them embarked on an expedition that is almost certainly apocryphal. Mandate commentators dispute the account found in *The Sagas*, where they successfully return with both Aulisi and the Heron Spear, claiming that Aulisi was never found. Whatever happened, at least two things are certain: the Heron Spear was in fact recovered, and Nau-Cayûti died shortly after (apparently poisoned by his first wife, Iëva).

In 2141, the Consult returned to the offensive, wrongly thinking the Kûniüri crippled by the loss of their greatest and most beloved son. But Nau-Cayûti's mead-brothers proved themselves able, even brilliant, commanders. At the Battle of Skothera, the Sranc hordes were crushed by General En-Kaujalau, though he died of mysterious causes within weeks of this victory (according to *The Sagas*, he was another victim of Iëva and her poisons, but again this is disputed by Mandate scholars). In 2142, General Sag-Marmau inflicted yet another crushing defeat on Aurang and his Consult legions, and by the fall of that year he had hounded the remnant of their horde to the Gates of Golgotterath itself.

But the Second Great Investiture proved far shorter than the first. As Seswatha had feared, the Consult had been merely playing for time, nothing more. In the spring of 2143 the No-God, summoned by means unknown, first drew breath. Across the world, Sranc, Bashrag, and Wracu—all the obscene progeny of the Inchoroi—hearkened to his call. Sag-Marmau and the greater glory of Kûniüri were annihilated.

The effect of his coming cannot be overestimated. As numerous independent accounts attest, all Men could sense his dread presence on the horizon, and all infants were born dead. Anasûrimbor Celmomas II had little difficulty gathering support for his Second Ordeal. Nil'giccas and Celmomas were reconciled. Across Eärwa, hosts of Men began marching toward Kûniüri.

But it was too late.

Celmomas and his Second Ordeal were destroyed on the Fields of Eleneöt in 2146. The Heron Spear, which could not be used because the No-God refused to give battle, was lost. Kûniüri and all the great and ancient cities of the River Aumris were destroyed the following year. The Nonmen of Injor-Niyas retreated to Ishterebinth. Eämnor was laid waste the year after, though its capital, Atrithau, raised on anarcane ground, managed to survive. The list continues. Akksersia and Harmant in 2149. The Meöri Empire in 2150. Inweära in 2151, though the city of Sakarpus was spared. The Shiradi Empire in 2153.

The Battle of Kathol Pass, fought primarily by the remnants of the Meöri and the Nonmen of Cil-Aujas in the autumn of 2151, would be mankind's only victory during these dark years, one which was entirely undone when the Meöri turned on their benefactors and sacked the ancient Nonman Mansion the following spring (which gave birth to the myth that the Galeoth, the descendants of those Meöri refugees, were forever cursed with treachery and fractiousness).

Though defeated at the Battle of Mehsarunath in 2154, Anaxophus V, the High King of Kyraneas, managed to save the core of his host and fled southward, abandoning Mehtsonc and Sumna to the Scylvendi. The Tusk was evacuated and brought to ancient Invishi in Nilnamesh. Though the historical record is scant, Mandate scholars insist that it was at this time that the High King admitted to Seswatha that his knights had rescued the Heron Spear from the Fields of Eleneöt eight years previously.

Perhaps no single event from these dark times has inspired more acrimony and debate among Three Seas scholars of the Apocalypse. Some historians, the great Casidas among them, have called this the most monstrous deception in history. How could Anaxophus conceal the only weapon that could defeat the No-God while the greater part of the world died? But others, including many belonging to the Mandate, argue precisely the opposite. They admit that Anaxophus's motive—to save Kyraneas and Kyraneas alone—was more than a little suspect. But they point to the fact that had he not hidden the Heron Spear, it would surely have been lost in the catastrophes following the Fields of Eleneöt and the destruction of the Second Ordeal. According to extant accounts, not once did the No-God expose himself to battle during this time. It was the years of attrition that forced him to intercede in the Battle of Mengedda.

Whatever the case, the No-God, or Tsuramah as the Kyraneans called him, was destroyed by Anaxophus V in 2155. Freed of his terrible will, his Sranc, Bashrag, and Wracu slaves dispersed. The Apocalypse had ended, and Men set out to recover what they could of a ruined world.

apples—Galeoth slang for severed heads gathered as trophies.

Araxes Mountains—A range forming the eastern frontiers of both Ce Tydonn and Conriya.

Architect—An epithet used by skin-spies to describe their Consult makers.

Arithmeas—The Prime Augur to Ikurei Xerius III.

Ark-of-the-Skies—See *Incû-Holoinas.*

Arweal (4077–4111)—One of the Nascenti, formerly a client thane of Earl Werijen, claimed by disease at Caraskand.

Ascension—The direct passage of Inri Sejenus to the Outside as described in "The Book of Days" in *The Tractate.* According to Inrithi tradition,

Sejenus ascended from the Juterum, or the Sacred Heights, in Shimeh, though *The Tractate* seems to suggest that Kyudea and not Shimeh was the location. The First Temple was purportedly raised on the very location.

Asgilioch—"The Gate of Asga" (Kyranean from Kemkaric *geloch*) The great Nansur fortress, dating back to Far Antiquity, guarding the so-called Southron Gates in the Unaras Spur. Perhaps no Three Seas fortress can claim such a storied past (which includes, most recently, stopping no fewer than three Fanim invasions). Over the years the Nansur have coined many epithets for the famed stronghold, among them Hubara, or "the Breakers."

Aspect-Emperor—The title taken by Triamis the Great in the twenty-third year of his rule (when the Shriah, Ekyannus III, formally institutionalized the so-called Emperor Cult) and adopted by all his successors.

Athjeäri, Coithus (4089–)—The Earl of the Galeoth region of Gaenri, and nephew to Coithus Saubon.

Atkondo-Atyoki—The language group of the Satyothi pastoralists of the Atkondras Mountains and surrounding regions.

Atkondras Mountains—Perhaps the greatest range west of the Kayarsus, running from the Sea of Jorua to the Great Ocean, and effectively sealing Zeüm from the rest of Eärwa.

Atrithau—The ancient administrative and commercial capital of what was once Eämnor, and one of two Norsirai cities to have survived the Apocalypse. Atrithau is peculiar in that it is built upon what is called "anarcane ground," which is to say, ground that renders sorcery impotent, found at the foot of Mount Ankulakai. It was originally founded *c.* 570 as the fortress Ara-Etrith ("New Etrith") by the famed Umeri God-King Carû-Ongonean.

Atrithi—The language of Atrithau, derived from Eämnoric.

Atsushan Highlands—The arid hill country of the Gedean interior.

Attong Plateau—"Missing Tower" (from Kyranean *att anoch*) Also known as the Attong Gap. The famous opening in the Hethanta Mountains, and the traditional invasion route of the Scylvendi.

Attrempus—"Tower of Respite" (Kyranean) The sister fortress of Atyersus, founded in 2158 by Seswatha and the nascent School of Mandate, and held in trust by House Nersei of Conriya since 3921.

Atyersus—"Tower of Warning" (Kyranean) The sister fortress of Attrempus, founded in 2157 by Seswatha and other Gnostic survivors of the Apocalypse. Atyersus is the primary stronghold of the Mandate.

Auja-Gilcûnni—The lost "ground tongue" of the Nonmen. See *Languages of Nonmen*.

Aujic—The lost tongue of the Nonmen Aujan Mansions.

Aumri-Saugla—The language group of the ancient Norsirai peoples of the Aumris Valley.

Aumris River—The primary river system of northwest Eärwa, draining the greater Istyuli basin and emptying into the Neleöst Sea. The River Aumris is also the cradle of Norsirai civilization. Over a relatively brief period of time, the High Norsirai tribes that settled the rich alluvial plains along the lower Aumris founded the first cities of Men, including Trysë, Sauglish, Etrith, and Ûmerau. As the result of trade with the Nonmen of Injor-Niyas, the power and sophistication of the Aumris River civilization grew quickly, culminating in the Trysean Empire under the God-King Cûnwerishau in the fourth century.

Aurang (?–)—A surviving Prince of the Inchoroi and Horde-General to the No-God during the Apocalypse. Very little is known of Aurang, save that he is a ranking member of the Consult and the twin brother of Aurax.

Aurax—(?–)—A surviving Prince of the Inchoroi. Very little is known of Aurax, save that he is a ranking member of the Consult and the twin brother of Aurang. Mandate scholars speculate that it was he who first taught the Tekne to the Mangaecca.

Auvangshei—Famed Ceneian fortress on the extreme western frontier of Nilnamesh, often symbolically invoked as the limit of the known world, which is to say, the Three Seas.

Avowels—The classic text by Olekaros, which poses as a "spiritual exploration" but is in actual fact little more than a collection of wise sayings from various thinkers in various nations. Its Sheyic translation enjoys widespread popularity among caste-noble lay readers in the Three Seas.

B

bagaratta—The "sweeping way" of Scylvendi sword fighting.

Bajeda, Straits of—The straits separating the southwestern tip of Nron from the southeastern extremities of Cironj.

Balait urs Kututha (4072–4110)—A Scylvendi warrior of the Utemot tribe, and Cnaiür urs Skiötha's brother-in-law.

Bannut urs Hannut (4059–4110)—A Scylvendi warrior of the Utemot tribe, and Cnaiür urs Skiötha's uncle.

Bardic Priest—In the traditional folk religions of the Ancient North, a type of wandering priest who earned his living reciting scriptural lays and performing priestly functions for various gods.

Barisullas, Nrezza (4053–) The King of Cironj, at once admired and maligned throughout the Three Seas for his mercantile ingenuity. He is notorious for surviving and managing to reverse Shrial Censure not once but three times.

Batathent—A ruined fortress-temple dating back to pre-classical Kyraneas, and destroyed by the Scylvendi shortly after the fall of Cenei in 3351.

Battle-Celebrant—An honour bestowed by the Gilgallic Priesthood on those most responsible for victory in battle.

Battlemaster—Among the Inrithi, the traditional rank assigned to those commanding coalitions.

Battle of Anwurat—A pivotal battle of the First Holy War, fought in the summer of 4111 about the fortress of Anwurat south of the Sempis Delta. Despite early setbacks, the Inrithi under Cnaiür urs Skiötha managed to rout the Kianene host of Skauras ab Nalajan, allowing the subsequent conquest of southern Shigek and opening the road to Caraskand.

Battle of Caraskand—Sometimes called the Battle of Tertae Fields. The desperate and pivotal battle in 4112 between the host of Kascamandri ab Tepherokar, the Padirajah of Kian, and the First Holy War under Anasûrimbor Kellhus, where the Fanim, despite outnumbering the diseased and starved Inrithi, found themselves incapable of slowing or stopping the First Holy War's general advance. Many attribute the Inrithi victory to the intercession of the God, though a more likely explanation is to be found in the revelatory events immediately preceding the battle. Nersei Proyas is particularly effective in his descriptions of the maniacal morale enjoyed by the Inrithi as a result of the Warrior-Prophet's Circumfixion and subsequent vindication. That the Kianene were over-confident is amply demonstrated by the Padirajah's decision to allow the First Holy War to assemble its ranks unmolested.

Battle of Eleneöt Fields—The great battle between the Horde of the No-God and the Second Ordeal on Kûniüri's northeastern frontier in 2146.

Despite having assembled the greatest host of their age, Anasûrimbor Celmomas and his allies were unprepared for the vast numbers of Sranc, Bashrag, and Wracu gathered by the No-God and his Consult slaves. The battle was an unmitigated catastrophe, and signalled the eventual destruction of Norsirai civilization.

Battle of Kiyuth—An important battle between the Imperial Army of Nansur and the Scylvendi, fought in 4110 on the banks of the River Kiyuth, a tributary of the Sempis river system. The overconfident Scylvendi King-of-Tribes led his people into a trap laid by Ikurei Conphas, the Nansur Exalt-General. The resulting defeat was unprecedented, given that it occurred on the Jiünati Steppe.

Battle of Maän—A minor battle fought between Conriya and Ce Tydonn in 4092.

Battle of Mehsarunath—The first great battle fought between the gathered might of Kyraneas and the host of the No-God on the Attong Plateau in 2154. Though Aurang, the No-God's Horde-General, won the battle, the Kyranean High King, Anaxophus V, was able to escape with much of his host intact, setting the stage for the far more decisive Battle of Mengedda the following year.

Battle of Mengedda, the Second—The desperate battle where Anaxophus V and his southern tributaries and allies made their victorious stand against the Horde of the No-God in 2155. Thought by many to be the most important battle in history.

Battle of Mengedda, the Fourth—The battle where the so-called Vulgar Holy War under Nersei Calmemunis suffered utter destruction at the hands of the Kianene under Skauras ab Nalajan in 4110.

Battle of Mengedda, the Fifth—The first decisive battle fought between the First Holy War and the Kianene, in 4111. Plagued with organizational problems and dissension among its commanders, the First Holy War, under the nominal command of Prince Coithus Saubon, was caught by Skauras ab Nalajan and his Kianene host on the Plains of Mengedda with only half of its available strength. From morning to late afternoon, the Inrithi managed to beat back innumerable Kianene charges. When the remainder of the First Holy War arrived on the Fanim flank, the will of the Kianene broke and they were routed.

Battle of Paremti—A minor battle fought between Conriya and Ce Tydonn in 4109, and the first military victory of Prince Nersei Proyas. Historically significant because Proyas had his cousin, Calmemunis, whipped for impiety, an act that many historians claim precipitated Calmemunis's decision to prematurely march with the so-called Vulgar Holy War.

Battle of the Slopes—Name given to the prolonged contest between the Kianene and the Ainoni at the Battle of Anwurat.

Battle of Trantis Bay—The decisive sea battle where the Kianene fleet, using Cishaurim, was able to annihilate the Imperial Nansur fleet under General Sassotian in 4111, thereby denying the First Holy War its primary source of water for its march across Khemema.

Battle of Tywanrae Fords—One of three disastrous defeats suffered by Akksersia and its allies at the hands of the Horde of the No-God. Tywanrae is often evoked by Mandate scholars as an example of the limitations of using Chorae alone to cope with enemy sorcerers in battle.

Battle of Zirkirta—A major battle fought between the Kianene host of Hasjinnet ab Skauras and the Scylvendi under Yursut urs Muknai on the Jiünati Steppe in 4103. Though their cavalry proved no match for the Scylvendi, and Hasjinnet himself was slain, the Kianene were quick in recovering, and most of the ill-fated expedition survived.

Battleplain—See *Mengedda Plains*.

Battles of Agongorea—See *Apocalypse*.

Bengulla (4103–12)—Son of Aëngelas and Valrissa.

benjuka—A subtle and ancient game of strategy played by caste-nobility throughout the Three Seas. A derivative of the more esoteric *mirqu* played by Nonmen, the first extant references to benjuka date back to the so-called Nonmen Tutelage (555–825).

Betmulla Mountains—A minor mountain range forming the southwestern frontier of both Xerash and Amoteu.

Biaxi, House—One of the Houses of the Congregate, and traditional rival to House Ikurei.

blood-of-the-onta—A common term for what Zarathinius called the "ink" of the Mark.

Bogras, Praxum (4059–4111)—The general of the Selial Column, slain at Anwurat.

Bokae—An old Ceneian fort on the western frontier of Enathpaneah.

Boksarias, Pirras (2395–2437)—The Ceneian Emperor who standardized trading protocols within the empire and established a thriving system of markets in its major cities.

Book of Circles and Spirals, The—The magnum opus of Sorainas, providing an entertaining blend of philosophical commentary and religious aphorism.

Book of Devices, The—An oft-revised Nansur military manual depicting the banner devices of their ancestral foes.

Book of Divine Acts, The—The magnum opus of Memgowa, the famed Zeümi sage and philosopher. Though not as commonly read or copied as his *Celestial Aphorisms*, most scholars consider it a vastly superior work.

Bowl, the—The name given to Caraskand's central quarter, which is surrounded by five of the city's nine heights.

Breaking of the Gates—The name given to the assault on the Gates of Eärwa, a series of fortified passes through the Great Kayarsus, by the Men of Eänna. Since *The Chronicle of the Tusk* ends with the determination to invade Eärwa, or the Land of the "Uplifted Sun," and since the Nonmen Mansions most involved in resisting the Tribes of Men were all destroyed, very little is known either of the Breaking of the Gates or of the subsequent migratory invasions.

Bukris—The God of famine. As one of the so-called Punitive Gods, who command sacrifices through threat and the imposition of suffering, Bukris has no real Cult or priesthood. According to Kiünnat tradition, Bukris is the older brother of Anagkë, which is why Anagkean Cultic Priests typically administer the rites of propitiation during times of hunger.

Burning of the White Ships—One of the more famous acts of treachery during the Apocalypse. Falling back before the Consult legions, Anasûrimbor Nimeric dispatched the Aörsic fleet in 2134 to shelter in the Kûniüri port of Aesorea, where it was burned by agents unknown mere days after its arrival, deepening the feud between the two peoples, with tragic consequences. See *Apocalypse*.

Burulan (4084–)—One of Esmenet's Kianene body-slaves.

Byantas—A near antique writer of the Ceneian Empire.

C

Calasthenes (4055–4111)—A sorcerer of rank in the Scarlet Spires, slain by a Chorae at Anwurat.

Calmemunis, Nersei (4069–4110)—The Palatine of the Conriyan province of Kanampurea, and nominal leader of the Vulgar Holy War.

Cants—The name given to offensive sorcerous incantations. See *sorcery*.

Cants of Calling—The family of incantations that enable communications over distance. Though the metaphysics of these Cants is only loosely understood, all long-distance Cants of Calling seem to turn on the so-called Here Hypothesis. One can call only to slumbering souls (because they remain open to the Outside) and only to those residing someplace where the Caller has physically been. The idea is that the "Here" of the Caller can only reach a "There," or other location, that has been a "Here" sometime in the past. The degree of similarity between Anagogic and Gnostic Cants of Calling has led many to suspect that they hold the key to unravelling the Gnosis.

Cants of Compulsion—The family of incantations that control the movements of an individual's soul. Typically these include the so-called Cants of Torment, though not always. An insidious aspect of these Cants is that their subject often has no way of distinguishing sorcerously compelled thoughts from his own thoughts. This has spawned a whole literature on the very notion of "will." If the compelled soul feels every bit as uncompelled as the free soul, then how can anyone truly know himself to be free?

Canute—A Province of Ce Tydonn, one of the so-called Deep Marches of the Upper Swa.

Caphrianus I (3722–85)—Commonly called "the Younger" to distinguish him from his Ceneian namesake. The Nansur Surmante emperor famed for his wily diplomacy and far-reaching reforms of the Nansur legal code.

Cara-Sincurimoi—"Angel of Endless Hunger" (Ihrimsû) An ancient Nonman name for the No-God. See *No-God*.

Caraskand—A major city and great caravan entrepot of the southwestern Three Seas. The administrative and commercial capital of Enathpaneah.

Carathay Desert—Vast arid region of dunes and gravel flats occupying southwestern Eärwa. Large oases are primarily found along the eastern regions of the desert, but there are skeletal river systems throughout.

Caro-Shemic—The language of the scriptural pastoralists of the Carathay Desert.

Carythusal—Also known as "the City of Flies." The most populous city in the Three Seas, and the administrative and commercial capital of High Ainon.

Casidas (3081–3142)—A famed philosopher and historian of Near Antiquity, best known for his magisterial *The Annals of Cenei*.

caste-apparati—A term for hereditary officials in Three Seas bureaucracies.

caste-menial—A term for the suthenti, or the hereditary labourer caste.

caste-noble—A term for the kjineta, or the hereditary warrior caste.

caste-priest—A term for the nahat, or the hereditary priest caste.

castes—Inherited social statuses. Though weaker in the so-called Middle-North, the Inrithi caste system is one of the central institutions of Three Seas society. In a technical sense, there are almost as many castes as there are occupations, but in practice they fall into roughly four different groups: the suthenti or labouring castes, the momurai or transactional castes, the nahat or priestly castes, and the kjineta or warrior castes. Elaborate protocols supposedly govern all interactions within and between castes to ensure the observances of various privileges and obligations, as well as to minimize ritual pollution, but in practical terms they are rarely adhered to unless in the pursuit of advantage.

caünnu—The Scylvendi name for the hot southwestern winds that cross the Jiünati Steppe during the height of summer.

Celestial Aphorisms—One of Memgowa's most celebrated texts.

Celmomas II, Anasûrimbor (2089–2146)—The implacable foe of Golgotterath in the early days of the Apocalypse, and last of the Kûniüric High Kings. See *Apocalypse*.

Celmomian Prophecy—The dying words of Anasûrimbor Celmomas II to Seswatha on the Fields of Eleneöt in 2146 to the effect that an Anasûrimbor would return at "the end of the world." Given that the prevention of the so-called Second Apocalypse is the Mandate's entire reason for existence, it is perhaps no surprise that most Mandate scholars think the Celmomian Prophecy authentic. Few others in the Three Seas credit their claims, however.

Cememketri (4046–)—The Grandmaster of the Imperial Saik.

Cenei—A city of the Kyranae Plain that arose from the Age of Warring Cities to conquer the entire Three Seas. Cenei was destroyed by the Scylvendi under Horiötha in 3351.

Ceneian Empire—The greatest Ketyai empire in history, embracing the entirety of the Three Seas at its greatest extent, from the Atkondras

Mountains in the southwest, to Lake Huösi in the north, to the Kayarsus Mountains in the southeast. The primary agent in the creation and maintenance of this empire was the Ceneian Imperial Army, which was perhaps the best trained and organized in history.

No more than a minor river trading town in the days of Kyraneas, Cenei emerged from the Age of Warring Cities as the pre-eminent city of the Kyranae Plain. The conquest of Gielgath in 2349 sealed the city's regional dominance, and in the ensuing decades the Ceneians under Xercallas II would secure the remnants of what had once been Kyraneas. Xercallas's successors continued his aggressive, expansionist policies, first pacifying the Norsirai tribes of Cepalor, then waging three consecutive wars against Shigek, which fell in 2397. Then, in 2414, after conquering Enathpaneah, Xerash, and Amoteu, General Naxentas staged a successful coup and declared himself Emperor of Cenei. Though he would be assassinated the following year, all his successors would avail themselves of the Imperial institutions he created.

Triamis I became Emperor in 2478, beginning what most scholars consider the Ceneian Golden Age. In 2483 he conquered Nilnamesh, and then Cingulat the following year. In 2485 he defeated a great Zeümi host at Amarah, and would have invaded the Satyothi nation had not mutinies among his homesick troops prevented him. He spent the next decade consolidating his gains, and striving against the internecine religious violence between followers of the traditional Kiünnat sects and the growing numbers of "Inrithi." It was in the course of negotiating settlements that he became friends with the then Shriah of the Thousand Temples, Ekyannus III, and in 2505 he himself converted to Inrithism, declaring it the official state religion of the Ceneian Empire. He spent the next ten years putting down religious rebellions, while at the same time invading and occupying both Cironj (2508) and Nron (2511). He then spent ten years campaigning across the eastern Three Seas against the successor nations of the old Shiradi Empire, first conquering Ainon (2518), then Cengemis (2519), and finally Annand (2525).

Ensuing Aspect-Emperors would marginally add to the extent of the empire, but its boundaries remained fairly stable for nearly eight hundred years, during which time the language and institutions of Imperial Cenei and the Thousand Temples would be stitched into the very fabric of Three Seas society. Aside from periodic wars with Zeüm, and the interminable wars against the Scylvendi and Norsirai tribes across the empire's northern frontier, this would be an age of unprecedented peace, prosperity, and commerce. Only the periodic civil wars, usually fought over succession, posed any real threat to the empire.

Though Cenei itself was destroyed by the Scylvendi under Horiötha in 3351, historians traditionally date the collapse of the Ceniean Empire in 3372, when General Maurelta surrendered to Sarothesser I in Ainon.

Cengemic—The language of Cengemis, a derivative of Sheyo-Kheremic.

Cengemis—The province that once marked the northern limit of the Eastern Ceneian Empire. After the collapse of the Eastern Empire in 3372, it enjoyed independence until overrun by Tydonni tribes in 3742.

Cepalor—A region of temperate, semi-forested plains extending east of the Hethantas from the Nansur frontier to the southwestern marches of Galeoth. Since the fall of Kyraneas, Cepalor has been inhabited by Norsirai pastoralists known as the Cepalorae, who have long been tributaries of the Nansurium.

Cepaloran—The language group of Norsirai pastoralists of the Cepaloran Plains.

Cerish Sea—The largest of Eärwa's inland seas.

Cerjulla, Sheorog (4069–4111)—The Tydonni Earl of Warnute, claimed by disease at Caraskand.

Cern Auglai—A fortress and pirate entrepot located on the coast of Thunyerus.

Cet'ingira (?–)—See *Mekeritrig*.

Ce Tydonn—A Norsirai nation of the Three Seas, located north of Conriya on the eastern shoreline of the Meneanor, founded in 3742 in the wake of Cengemis's collapse. The first mention of the Tydonni is found in Casidas's *Annals of Cenei*, where he mentions their raids across the River Swa. Descendants of White Norsirai refugees from the Apocalypse, the Tydonni are thought to have occupied the southern regions of the Dameori Wilderness for centuries, prevented by their native fractiousness from causing much difficulty for their southern Ketyai neighbours. At some point in the thirty-eighth century, however, they united, and with little difficulty overwhelmed the Men of Cengemis at the Battle of Marswa in 3722. It wasn't until King Haul-Namyelk finally succeeded in unifying the various tribes under his absolute authority in 3741 that Ce Tydonn proper came into existence.

Perhaps the most peculiar and distinctive predilection of the Tydonni is found in their racial beliefs. *Ti dunn* literally means "struck iron" in their tongue, reflecting their belief that their people have been purified by the crucible of their long wandering through the Dameori wildernesses. They hold that this gives them "privileged blood," rendering them morally, intellectually, and physically superior to other races. This has made the Tydonni cruel overlords of the Cengemi, who have often rebelled against them.

chanv—An addictive narcotic popular among the Ainoni aristocracy, although many eschew it because of its uncertain origins. Chanv reputedly sharpens the intellect, extends one's lifespan, and drains the body of all its pigment.

Charamemas (4036–4108)—The famed Shrial commentator and author of *The Ten Holies*. Achamian's replacement as Proyas's tutor in exoterics in 4093.

Charcharius, Trimus (4052–)—The Patridomos of the House Trimus.

Chargiddo—A large fortress located on the frontier of Xerash and Amoteu beneath the Betmulla Mountains.

Chemerat—An ancient Kyranean name for Shigek, meaning "Red Land."

Chepheramunni (4068–4111)—The King-Regent of High Ainon, nominal leader of the Ainoni during much of the First Holy War, claimed by disease at Caraskand.

Chiama—Walled town on the River Sempis, destroyed by the First Holy War in 4111.

Chianadyni—A governorate of Kian and one-time tributary of the Nansur Empire. Located to the west of Eumarna and east of Nilnamesh, Chianadyni is the traditional homeland of the Kianene and, after Eumarna, the wealthiest and most populous governorate in Kian.

Chigra—"Slaying Light" (Aghurzoi) An ancient Sranc name for Seswatha.

Children of Eänna—An epithet for Men in *The Chronicle of the Tusk*.

Chinjosa, Musammu (4078–)—The Count-Palatine of the Ainoni province of Antanamera, appointed King-Regent of High Ainon shortly after Chepheramunni's death in the winter of 4111.

Chorae—Artifacts of the Ancient North, also known as "Trinkets" (to the Schools) and "The Tears of God" (to the Inrithi). In appearance, Chorae are small iron spheres, one inch in diameter, that are banded by runes written in Gilcûnya, the holy tongue of the Nonmen Quya. Chorae are extraordinary in that they render their bearer immune to all sorcerous Cants and instantly kill any sorcerer who comes into contact with them. Although the principles behind their creation (they belong to a lost branch of sorcery called the Aporos) are no longer understood, thousands are believed to circulate in the Three Seas alone. The Chorae play a pivotal role in the political balance of power in the Three Seas, insofar as they allow the non-scholastic Great Factions to check the power of the Schools.

Chorae bowmen—Specialized units that use Chorae affixed to the end of arrow shafts or crossbow bolts to kill enemy sorcerers. Chorae archers are a staple of almost every military organization in Eärwa.

Chronicle of the Tusk, The—The most ancient extant human text in Eärwa, and the scriptural foundation for all mannish faiths save Fanimry. As the oldest literate work, its provenance is almost entirely unknown. Many Inrithi commentators have pointed out that it must have been a collective work, cobbled together from many (likely oral) sources over a period of many years. Like most scriptures, its popular interpretation is highly selective and idealized. It consists of the following six books:

Book of Canticles—The old "Tusk Laws" regarding every aspect of personal and public life, which were superseded in the Inrithi tradition by the revised strictures of *The Tractate*.

Book of Gods—The primary scripture of the Cults, enumerating the various gods, and explaining the rites of purification and propitiation basic to each.

Book of Hintarates—The story of Hintarates, an upright man plagued with apparently undeserved adversity.

Book of Songs—A collection of verse prayers and parables extolling the virtues of piety, manliness, courage, and tribal loyalty.

Book of Tribes—The extended narrative of the first Prophets and Chieftain-Kings of the Five Tribes of Men before the invasion of Eärwa.

Book of Warrants—The account of the observances governing the interactions between castes.

Cil-Aujas—A lost Nonman Mansion, located in the shadow of the Osthwai Mountains.

Cincûlic—The undeciphered tongue of the Inchoroi, which the Nonmen call *Cincûl'hisa*, or "the Gasp of Many Reeds." According to the *Isûphiryas*, communication between the Cûnuroi and the Inchoroi was impossible until the latter "birthed mouths" and began speaking Cûnuroi tongues.

Cinganjehoi ab Sakjal (4076–)—Famed Kianene Saptishah-Governor of Eumarna, known among his people as "the Tiger of Eumarna."

Cingulat—A Ketyai nation of the Three Seas, located on the northwestern coast of Kutnarmu, just south of Nilnamesh.

Cinguli—The language of Cingulat, a derivative of Sapmatari.

Cironj—A Ketyai island nation located at the juncture of all three of the Three Seas, and possessing a strong mercantile and maritime tradition.

Cironjic—The language of Cironj, a derivative of Sheyo-Kheremic.

Cishaurim—The notorious priest-sorcerers of the Fanim based in Shimeh. According to Fanim religious tradition, the Prophet Fane became the first of the Cishaurim after he went blind in the desert. Given Fane's claim that the true power of the Solitary God cannot be exercised so long as one sees the profane world, Cishaurim initiates voluntarily blind themselves at a certain point in their study, enabling them to dispense the "divine water" of the "Psûkhe," as the Cishaurim refer to it. Little is known about the metaphysics of the Psûkhe beyond the fact that it cannot be perceived by the Few and that it is in many ways almost as formidable as the Anagogic practice of the Schools.

   The Scarlet Spires categorize individual Cishaurim according to their power: Tertiaries, or those with only the most rudimentary strength, Secondaries, or those with strength comparable to sorcerous initiates, and Primaries, those with strength exceeding that of initiates (but still, according to the Scarlet Magi, short of the strength possessed by true Anagogic sorcerers of rank).

Citadel of the Dog—The great redoubt of Caraskand as named by the Men of the Tusk. Raised by Xatantius in 3684, it was originally called Insarum, until it fell to the Fanim in 3839, who called it Il'huda, "the Bulwark."

Cleansed Lands—A Kianene epithet for nations where Fanimry is predominant.

Cmiral—The great temple complex of Momemn, located near the heart of the city, adjacent to the Kamposea Agora.

Coithus, House—The ruling dynasty of Galeoth.

Cojirani ab Houk (4078–4112)—The Grandee of Mizrai, famed for his enormous strength and size, slain by Prince Nersei Proyas at the Battle of Caraskand.

College of Luthymae—The College of the Thousand Temples responsible for spying and intelligence.

College of Marucee—A College of the Thousand Temples destroyed in the Sack of Shimeh in 3845.

College of Sareöt—A College of the Thousand Temples dedicated to the preservation of knowledge, destroyed in the Fall of Shigek in 3933.

Colleges—Organizations of priests directly subordinate to the Thousand Temples, with mandates ranging from caring for the poor and sick to the collection of intelligence.

come after, to—For the Dûnyain, "to come after" means to be victimized by events over which one has no control. See *Dûnyain*.

come before, to—For the Dûnyain, "to come before" means to master the passage of events. See *Dûnyain*.

Commerce of Souls, The—Ajencis's classic treatise on politics.

Condic—The language group of ancient pastoralists of the Near Istyuli Plains.

Conditioned, the—A term used to refer to the Dûnyain.

Conditioning, the—Specifically, the arduous physical, emotional, and intellectual training undergone by Dûnyain monks, though the term has more general and far-reaching connotations as well. The Dûnyain believe that everything is conditioned in some way, but they draw a principled distinction between the arbitrary conditioning of the world and the rational conditioning of Men. Conditioning in the light of the Logos, they believe, allows *more* such conditioning, which in turn leverages more such conditioning, and so on. This virtuous circle, they believe, finds its apotheosis in the Absolute: the Dûnyain believe that, using reason, they can condition themselves to the point of becoming *unconditioned*, a perfect, self-moving soul. See *Dûnyain.*

Conphas, Ikurei (4084–)—The nephew of Emperor Ikurei Xerius III and heir apparent to the Imperial Mantle.

Conriya—A pre-eminent Ketyai nation of the eastern Three Seas, located south of Ce Tydonn and north of High Ainon, founded in 3374 (after the collapse of the Eastern Ceneian Empire) around Aöknyssus, the ancient capital of Shir. Of the four successor nations to the Shiradi Empire (Cengemis, Conriya, Ainon, and Sansor), none has worked so hard to reclaim and preserve its ancient traditions. Nowhere are the caste divisions more rigidly observed, and nowhere are the codes governing caste-noble behaviour more strict. Though many, particularly the Ainoni, scoff at what they consider the affectation of antique ways, there can be little doubt that the resulting social discipline has served the Conriyans well. Since gaining independence, Conriya has successfully weathered innumerable incursions, invasions, blockades, and embargoes, almost all of them due to the machinations of High Ainon.

Conriyan—The language of Conriya, a derivative of Sheyo-Kheremic.

Consult—The cabal of Magi and Generals that survived the death of Mog in 2155 and has laboured ever since to bring about the return of the No-God.

Coyauri—The famed elite heavy cavalry of the Kianene Padirajah, first organized by Habal ab Sarouk in 3892 as a response to the Nansur Kidruhil. The White Horse on Yellow is their standard.

Csokis—A derelict Inrithi temple complex located in Caraskand.

Cuärweth—A province of interior Ce Tydonn, located to the north of Meigeiri.

Cuäxaji (4069–)—The Sapatishah-Governor of Khemema.

Cu'jara Cinmoi (?–?)—The greatest of the Nonman Kings and first great foe of the Inchoroi. See *Cûno-Inchoroi Wars*.

Cultic Deities—See *Hundred Gods*.

Cultic Priests—Those priests, usually hereditary, devoted to the service and worship of one of the Hundred Gods.

Cults—The collective name of all the various sects devoted to the individual Gods of the so-called Kiünnat. In the Three Seas, the Cults have been administratively and spiritually subordinate to the Thousand Temples since Triamis I, the first Aspect-Emperor of Cenei, declared Inrithism the official state religion of the Ceneian Empire in 2505.

Cumor, Haarnan (4043–4111)—The High Cultist of Gilgaöl in the Holy War, claimed by disease at Caraskand.

Cûno-Halaroi Wars—The wars between Nonmen and Men following the Breaking of the Gates, of which very few accounts exist. See *Breaking of the Gates*.

Cûno-Inchoroi Wars—The protracted series of wars between the Nonmen and the Inchoroi following the ancient arrival of the latter.

　　According to the *Isûphiryas*, the Incû-Holoinas, the "Ark-of-the-Skies," plunged to earth to the west of the Sea of Neleost in land ruled by Nin'janjin, the Nonman King of Viri. The letter sent by Nin'janjin to Cû'jara-Cinmoi, the King of Siöl, is recorded as follows:

The Sky has cracked into potter's shards,
Fire sweeps the compass of Heaven,
The beasts flee, their hearts maddened,
The trees fall, their backs broken.

Ash has shrouded all sun, choked all seed,
The Halaroi howl piteously at the Gates,
Dread Famine stalks my Mansion.
Brother Siöl, Viri begs your pardon.

Rather than send aid to Nin'janjin, Cû'jara-Cinmoi assembled an army and invaded the lands of Viri. Nin'janjin and his Ishroi capitulated without battle; Viri became a bloodless tributary of Siöl. The western lands of Viri, however, remained shrouded in cloud and ash. Survivors from the region spoke of a fiery vessel streaking across the skies. So Cû'jara-Cinmoi commanded Ingalira, a hero of Siöl, to lead an expedition to find this Ark. What happened to Ingalira on this expedition is not recorded, but he returned to Siöl some three months later and presented two inhuman captives to Cû'jara-Cinmoi. Ingalira called these captives *Inchoroi*, or "People of Emptiness," both because the sounds they made were empty of meaning and because they fell from the emptiness of the sky. He spoke of flattened forests and gouged plains, of mountains thrown into a ring, and of two golden horns rearing from a molten sea, so mighty they brushed the clouds.

Repelled by the obscene aspect of the Inchoroi, Cû'jara-Cinmoi had them put to death, and set a Watch upon the Incû-Holoinas, the Ark-of-the-Skies. Years passed, and the power of Cû'jara-Cinmoi and the High Mansion of Siöl waxed. The Mansion of Nihrimsul was subdued, and her King, Sin'niroiha, "First Among Peoples," was forced to wash the sword of Cû'jara-Cinmoi. With the subsequent conquest of Cil-Aujas to the south, Siöl and her High King commanded an empire that ranged from the Yimaleti Mountains to the Sea of Meneanor.

During this time, the Watch was kept on the Ark. The land cooled. The skies cleared.

Either because of original inconsistencies or because of subsequent corruptions, extant versions of the *Isûphiryas* are unclear as to the subsequent order of events. At some point a secret embassy of Inchoroi reached Nin'janjin at Viri. Unlike the Inchoroi brought to Cû'jara-Cinmoi by Ingalira, these possessed the ability to speak Ihrimsû. They reminded Nin'janjin of Cû'jara-Cinmoi's treachery in his time of need, and offered an alliance to break the yoke of Siöl over Viri. They would undo, the Inchoroi said, the misfortune their coming had wrought upon the Cûnuroi of Viri.

Despite the warnings of his Ishroi, Nin'janjin accepted the Inchoroi terms. Viri revolted. The Siölan Ishroi within its halls were slain; the rest were enslaved. At the same time, the Inchoroi swarmed from the Ark, overwhelming the Watch. Only Oirinas and his twin, Oirûnas, survived, riding hard to warn Cû'jara-Cinmoi.

Sil, the Inchoroi King, and Nin'janjin assembled their hosts to meet Cû'jara-Cinmoi on the fields of Pir-Pahal, which Men would call Eleneöt in a later age. According to the Isûphiryas, the Nonmen of Viri were dismayed by the sight of their allies, who wore fierce and festering bodies as garments of war. Gin'gûrima, the greatest hero among them, pointed to Nin'janjin and declared, "Hate has blinded him." This treason within a treason was repeated by others, until it became a thundering chorus. Nin'janjin fled, seeking protection from Sil. The Inchoroi then turned upon their allies, hoping to destroy the host of Viri before Cû'jara-Cinmoi and the great host of Siöl could close with them.

Overmatched by the Inchoroi and their weapons of light, the Nonmen of Viri were driven back with horrendous losses. Only Cû'jara-Cinmoi and his Ishroi Chariots saved them from utter destruction. The chroniclers of the *Isûphiryas* claim the battle raged through the night and into the following morning. Eventually, all but the most powerful of the Inchoroi were overwhelmed by the valour, sorceries, and numbers of the host of Siöl. Cû'jara-Cinmoi himself struck down Sil, and wrested from him his great weapon, Suörgil, "Shining Death," which Men in a latter age would call the Heron Spear.

Much reduced, the Inchoroi fled back to their Ark, taking Nin'janjin with them. Cû'jara-Cinmoi hunted them within sight of the Ring Mountains, but was forced to abandon his pursuit when word of further disasters reached him. Emboldened by Siöl's distraction, Nihrimsul and Cil-Aujas had revolted.

Weakened by the Battle of Pir-Pahal, Cû'jara-Cinmoi was hard pressed to recover his empire. A Second Watch was put upon the Holoinas, but no attempt was made to breach the gold-grooved faces of the Ark. After years of hard campaigning, Cû'jara-Cinmoi finally brought the Ishroi of Cil-Aujas to heel, but King Sin'niroiha and the Ishroi of Nihrimsul continued to resist him. The *Isûphiryas* chronicles dozens of bloody yet indecisive confrontations between the two Kings: the Battle of Ciphara, the Battle of Hilcyri, the Siege of Asargoi. Proud beyond reason, Cû'jara-Cinmoi refused to relent, and put to death every embassy Sin'niroiha sent to him. Only when Sin'niroiha became King of Ishoriöl through marriage did the High King of Siöl concede. "A King of Three Mansions," he is said to have declared, "may be Brother to a King of Two."

The *Isûphiryas* mentions the Inchoroi only once during this time. Unwilling to assign desperately needed Ishroi to the Second Watch, Cû'jara-Cinmoi had charged Oirinas and Oirûnas, the sole survivors of the First Watch, with recruiting Men for the duty. Among these Halaroi was a "criminal" named Sirwitta. Apparently Sirwitta had seduced the wife of a high-ranking Ishroi and conceived by her a daughter named Cimoira. The Judges of the Ishroi were perplexed: such a thing had never happened before. The truth of Cimoira was suppressed, and despite her mannish blood she was accepted as Cûnuroi. Sirwitta himself was banished to the Second Watch.

Somehow (the *Isûphiryas* does not go into detail) Sirwitta managed to enter the Incû-Holoinas. A month passed, and all thought him lost. Then he reappeared, deranged, screeching claims so alarming that Oirinas and Oirûnas brought him directly to Cû'jara-Cinmoi. What was said between Sirwitta and the High King of Siöl is not recorded. The chroniclers say only that Cû'jara-Cinmoi, after hearing Sirwitta speak, ordered him put to death. A later entry, however, describes Sirwitta as "tongueless and imprisoned." It appears the High King, for some unknown reason, had rescinded his warrant.

Many years of peace followed. From their fortresses in the Ring Mountains, the Ishroi of Siöl guarded the Ark. Whether the Inchoroi lived still or had perished, no one knew. Cû'jara-Cinmoi grew old, for the Nonmen of those days were still mortal. His eyesight dimmed, and his once-mighty limbs began to fail him. Death whispered to him.

Then Nin'janjin returned. Invoking the ancient codes, he appeared before Cû'jara-Cinmoi begging Mercy and Penance. When the High King of Siöl bid Nin'janjin come near so he might see him, he was astonished to discover his old adversary had not aged. Then Nin'janjin revealed his true reason for coming to Siöl. The Inchoroi, he said, were too terrified of Cû'jara-Cinmoi's might to leave their Ark, so they dwelt in confinement and misery. They had sent him, he claimed, to sue for peace. They wished to know what tribute might temper the High King's fury.

To which Cû'jara-Cinmoi replied: "I would be young of heart, face, and limb. I would banish Death from the halls of my people."

The Second Watch was disbanded and the Inchoroi moved freely among the Cûnuroi of Siöl, becoming their physicians. They ministered to all, dispensing the remedies that would at once make the Nonmen immortal and doom them. Soon all the Cûnuroi of Eärwa, even those who had initially questioned Cû'jara-Cinmoi's wisdom, had succumbed to the Inchoroi and their nostrums.

According to the *Isûphiryas*, the first victim of the Womb-Plague was Hanalinqû, Cû'jara-Cinmoi's legendary wife. The chronicler actually praises the diligence and skill of the High King's Inchoroi physicians. But as the Womb-Plague killed more and more Cûnuroi women, this praise becomes condemnation. Soon all the women of the Cûnuroi, wives and maidens both, were dying. The Inchoroi fled the Mansions, returning to their ruined vessel.

Ishroi from across Eärwa answered Cû'jara-Cinmoi's call to war, even though many held the High King responsible for the deaths of their beloved. Grieved almost to madness, the High King led them through the Ring Mountains and arrayed them across the Inniür-Shigogli, the "Black Furnace Plain." Then he laid Hanalinqû's corpse before the unholy Ark and demanded the Inchoroi answer his fury.

But the Inchoroi had not been idle over the long years since the Battle of Pir Pahal. They had delved deep into the earth, beneath the Inniür-Shigogli and out into the Ring Mountains. Within these galleries they had massed hordes of twisted creatures unlike any the Cûnuroi had ever seen: Sranc, Bashrags, and mighty Dragons. The Ishroi of the Nine High Mansions of Eärwa, who had come to destroy the diminished survivors of Pir Pahal, found themselves beset on all sides.

The Sranc withered before the sinew and sorcery of the Ishroi, but their numbers seemed inexhaustible. The Bashrags and the Dragons exacted a horrifying toll. More terrible still were those few Inchoroi who ventured out into battle, hanging above the tumult, sweeping the earth with their weapons of light, apparently unaffected by the sorceries of the Ishroi. After the disaster of Pir Pahal, the Inchoroi had seduced the practitioners of the Aporos, who had been forbidden from pursuing their art. Poisoned by knowledge, they devised the first of the Chorae to render their masters immune to Cûnuroi magic.

But all the heroes of Eärwa stood upon the Black Furnace Plain. With his bare hands, Ciögli the Mountain, the strongest of the Ishroi, broke the neck of Wutteät the Black, the Father of Dragons. Oirinas and Oirûnas fought side by side, working great carnage among the Sranc and Bashrags. Ingalira, the hero of Siöl, strangled Vshikcrû, mighty among the Inchoroi, and cast his burning body into the Sranc.

The mighty closed with the mighty, and innumerable battles were fought. But no matter how hard the Inchoroi pressed, the Cûnuroi would yield no ground. Their fury was that of those who have lost wives and daughters.

Then Nin'janjin struck down Cû'jara-Cinmoi.

The Copper Tree of Siöl fell into pitching masses of Sranc, and the Cûnuroi were dismayed. Sin'niroiha, the High King of Nihrimsul and Ishoriöl, fought his way to Cû'jara-Cinmoi's position, but found only his headless body. Then the hero Gin'gûrima fell, gored by a Dragon. And after him Ingalira, who had been the first to lay eyes upon the Inchoroi. Then Oirinas, his body sundered by an Inchoroi spear of light.

Realizing their plight, Sin'niroiha rallied his people and began fighting his way into the Ring Mountains. A greater part of the surviving Cûnuroi followed him. Once clear of their foe, the glorious Ishroi of Eärwa fled, gripped by a mad fear. Either too weakened or suspecting a trap, the Inchoroi did not pursue.

For five hundred years the Cûnuroi and the Inchoroi waged a war of extermination, the Cûnuroi to avenge their murdered wives and the eventual death of their race, and the Inchoroi for reasons they alone could fathom. No longer did the Cûnuroi speak of the Incû-Holoinas, the Ark-of-the-Skies. Instead they spoke of Min-Uroikas, "the Pit of Obscenities"—what would later be called Golgotterath by Men. For centuries it seemed the abominations had the upper hand, and the poets of the *Isûphiryas* record defeat after defeat. But slowly, as the Inchoroi exhausted their fell weapons and relied more and more on their vile slaves, the Cûnuroi and their Halaroi servants gained the advantage. Then at long last the surviving Ishroi of Eärwa trapped the last of their diminished foe within the Incû-Holoinas. For twenty years they warred through the Ark's labyrinthine halls, finally hunting the last of the Inchoroi into the deep places of the earth. Unable to destroy the vessel, Nil'giccas instructed the remaining Quya to raise a powerful glamour about the hated place. He and the surviving kings of the Nine Mansions forbade their peoples from mentioning the Inchoroi or their nightmarish legacy. The last Cûnuroi of Eärwa withdrew to their Mansions to await their inevitable doom.

Cûnuroi—See *Nonmen.*

"Cut from them their tongues ..."—The famous phrase from *The Chronicle of the Tusk* condemning sorcery and sorcerers.

Cynnea, Braelwan (4059–4111)—The Galeoth Earl of Agmundr, claimed by disease at Caraskand.

D

Dagliash—The ancient Aörsic fortress overlooking the River Sursa and the Plains of Agongorea. It changed hands several times in the wars preceding the Apocalypse. See *Apocalypse.*

Daimos—Also known as noömancy. The sorcery of summoning and enslaving agencies from the Outside. For both political and pragmatic reasons, many Schools forbid its practice. Some esoteric scholars claim that

Daimotic sorcerers condemn themselves to eternal torment at the hands of their erstwhile slaves when they die.

Dakyas—A semi-mountainous district of Nilnamesh.

Dameöri Wilderness—A vast tract of forested, Sranc-infested wilderness extending from the Tydonni frontier in the south and running northeast of the Osthwai Mountains to the Sea of Cerish.

Dark Hunter, the—A common epithet for Husyelt, the God of the Hunt.

"[the] darkness which comes before"—A phrase used by the Dûnyain to refer to the congenital blindness of individuals to the worldly causes that drive them, both historical and appetitive. See *Dûnyain*.

Daskas, House—One of the Houses of the Congregate.

Daybreak—Achamian's mule.

Dayrut—A small fortress in the Gedean interior, built by the Nansur after the fall of Shigek to the Fanim in 3933.

Dead-God, the—See *Lokung*.

Defence of the Arcane Arts, A—The famed sorcerous apologia of Zarathinius, which is as widely cited by philosophers as by sorcerers because of its pithy critiques not only of the Inrithi prohibition of sorcery but of Inrithism itself. The work has long been banned by the Thousand Temples.

Demua Mountains—An extensive range located in northwestern Eärwa, forming the frontier between Injor-Niyas and what was once Kûniüri.

denotaries—In Gnostic sorcery, the "primer" Cants given to students to practise "dividing their voice," which is to say, saying and thinking two separate things.

Detnammi, Hirul (4081–4111)—The Palatine of the Ainoni province of Eshkalas, slain at Subis under dishonourable circumstances.

Dialogues of Inceruti, The—One of the most famous "missing works" of Far Antiquity, frequently referenced by Ajencis.

Dinchases (4074–4111)—A Captain of Attrempus and lifelong comrade-in-arms to Krijates Xinemus, slain at Iothiah. Also known as "Bloody Dinch."

"Doff your sandals and shod the earth ..."—A common saying meant to remind listeners not to project their failings onto others.

Domyot—(Sheyic version of "Torumyan") Also known as the Black Iron City. The administrative capital of Zeüm, famed for the cruelty of its rulers and for its iron-skirted walls. For most in the Three Seas, Domyot is as much a place of legend as Golgotterath.

Dragons—See *Wracu*.

Dreams, the—The nightmares experienced by Mandate Schoolmen of the Apocalypse as witnessed through Seswatha's eyes.

Dunjoksha (4055–)—The Sapatishah-Governor of Holy Amoteu.

Dûnyain—A severe monastic sect that has repudiated history and animal appetite in the name of finding enlightenment through the control of all desire and all circumstance. Though the origins of the Dûnyain are obscure (many think them the descendants of the ecstatic sects that arose across the Ancient North in the days preceding the Apocalypse), their belief system is utterly unique, leading some to conclude their original inspiration had to be philosophical rather than religious in any traditional sense.

Much of Dûnyain belief follows from their interpretation of what they consider their founding principles. The Empirical Priority Principle (sometimes referred to as the Principle of Before and After) asserts that within the circle of the world, what comes before determines what comes after without exception. The Rational Priority Principle asserts that Logos, or Reason, lies outside the circle of the world (though only in a formal and not an ontological sense). The Epistemological Principle asserts that knowing what comes before (via the Logos) yields "control" of what comes after.

Given the Priority Principle, it follows that thought, which falls within the circuit of the before and after, is also determined by what comes before. The Dûnyain therefore believe the will to be illusory, an artifact of the soul's inability to perceive what comes before it. The soul, in the Dûnyain world view, *is part of the world*, and therefore as much driven by prior events as anything else. (This stands in stark contrast to the dominant stream of Three Seas and Ancient North thought, where the soul is taken to be, in Ajencis's words, "that which precedes everything.")

In other words, Men do not possess "self-moving souls." Far from a given, such a soul is an *accomplishment* for the Dûnyain. All souls, they claim, possess *conatus*, the natural striving to be self-moving, to escape the circle of before and after. They naturally seek to *know* the world about them and so climb out of the circle. But a host of factors make outright escape impossible. The soul men are born with is too obtuse and clouded by animal passions to be anything other than a slave of what comes before. The whole point of the Dûnyain ethos is to overcome these limitations and so become a self-moving soul—to attain what they call the Absolute, or the Unconditioned Soul.

But unlike those exotic Nilnameshi sects devoted to various other forms of "enlightenment," the Dûnyain are not so naive as to think this can be attained within the course of a single lifetime. They think of this, rather, as a multi-generational process. Quite early on they recognized that the instrument itself, the soul, was flawed, so they instituted a program of selective breeding for intellect and dispassion. In a sense the entire sect became a kind of experiment, isolated from the world to maintain control, with each prior generation training the next to the limit of their capabilities, the idea being that over the millennia they would produce souls that could climb further and further from the circle of before and after. The hope was that eventually they would produce a soul utterly transparent to Logos, a soul capable of apprehending all the darknesses that come before.

Dûnyanic—The language of the Dûnyain, which remains very close to the original Kûniüri from which it is derived.

E

Eämnor—A lost White Norsirai nation of the Ancient North. The roots of Eämnor reach back to the days of Aulyanau the Conqueror and the Cond Yoke. In 927, Aulyanau conquered the fortress of Ara-Etrith ("New Etrith") and, struck by the anarcane characteristics of Mount Ankulakai, settled several Cond tribes in the vicinity. These tribes flourished, and under the influence of the nearby cities of the Aumris they quickly abandoned their pastoral ways. In fact the Cond were so effectively assimilated into Aumris culture that their White Norsirai cousins, the Scintya, took them for High Norsirai during the time of the Scintya Yoke (1228–1381).

Eämnor proper emerged from the Scintya Yoke as one of the preeminent nations of the Ancient North. Though laid waste in 2148, Eämnor could be considered the sole surviving nation of the Apocalypse, insofar as Atrithau survived. Due to the concentrations of Sranc, however, Atrithau has never been able to recover more than a fraction of the lands constituting historical Eämnor.

Eämnoric—The lost language of ancient Eämnor, a derivative of Condic.

Eänna—"[Land of the] Uplifted Sun" (Thoti-Eännorean) The traditional name of all the lands to the east of the Great Kayarsus.

Eärwa—"[Land of the] Felled Sun" (Thoti-Eännorean) The traditional name of all the lands to the west of the Great Kayarsus.

Ebara—A small fortress in the Gedean interior, built by the Nansur after the fall of Shigek to the Fanim in 3933.

Ecosium Market—The main "wares market" of Sumna, located just south of the Hagerna.

Ej'ulkiyah—A Khirgwi name for the Carathay Desert meaning "Great Thirst."

Ekyannus I (2304–72)—The first "institutional" Shriah of the Thousand Temples, and the author of the widely admired 44 *Epistles*.

Ekyannus III, "the Golden" (2432–2516)—The Shriah of the Thousand Temples who converted Triamis the Great in 2505 and thus assured the predominance of Inrithism in the Three Seas.

Eleäzaras, Hanamanu (4060–)—The Grandmaster of the Scarlet Spires.

Eleneöt, Fields of—See *Battle of Eleneöt Fields*.

elju—The Ihrimsû word for "book," referring to someone, either Man or Sranc, who accompanies a Nonman to aid with his failing memory.

Empire-behind-the-Mountains—A Scylvendi name for the Nansurium.

Emwama—The indigenous Men of Eärwa, who, as slaves of the Nonmen, were massacred by the Five Tribes following the Breaking of the Gates. Very little is known of them.

Enathpaneah—A governorate of Kian and former province of the Nansur Empire. Located at the hinge of Khemema and Xerash, Enathpaneah is a semi-mountainous, semi-arid land whose wealth is predominantly derived from the caravans that pass through Caraskand, its administrative and commercial capital.

Ennutil—A Scylvendi tribe of the northwestern Steppe.

Enshoiya—Sheyic for "certainty." The Zaudunyani name for the Warrior-Prophet's sword.

ensolarii—The base monetary unit of High Ainon.

Eöthic Garrison—The primary fortress and barracks of the Emperor's personal guard, dominating Momemn's northern quarter.

Eöthic Guard—The personal heavy infantry guard of the Nansur Emperors, consisting primarily of Norsirai mercenaries from Cepalor.

Epistemologies, The—A work oft attributed to Ajencis but more likely a redacted compilation drawn from his other works. Many consider it his definitive philosophical statement on the nature of knowledge, but some argue that it distorts his position since it presents a unitary vision of views that actually evolved quite dramatically over the course of his life.

Eritga (4092–4111)—A Galeoth slave-girl belonging to Cutias Sarcellus, slain in the deserts of Khemema.

Eryeat, Coithus (4038–)—The King of Galeoth, and father of Coithus Saubon.

Eshganax—A Palatinate of High Ainon, located across the north Secharib Plains.

Eshkalas—A Palatinate of High Ainon, famed for the quality of its cotton, located on the western edge of the Secharib Plains.

Eumarna—The most populous governorate of Kian and former province of the Nansur Empire. Located to the south of the Betmulla Mountains, Eumarna is a large, fertile land that is primarily known for its exports of wine and horses.

Eumarni—The language of Eumarna, a derivative of ancient Mamati.

eunuchs—Men castrated either before or after the onset of puberty, but usually before. Eunuchs have become something of an informal caste in the Three Seas, both in the management of harems and also in high administrative posts, where their lack of progeny, the belief is, renders them more immune to influence and less likely to harbour dynastic ambitions.

Exalt-General—The traditional title of the Imperial Army's supreme commander.

Exhortations—The sole surviving work of Hatatian. See *Hatatian*.

"Expect not, and you shall find glory everlasting ..."—*The Tractate*, Book of Priests, 8:31. The famed "Expect Not Admonition" of Inri Sejenus, where he urges his followers to give without hope of exchange. The paradox, of course, is that by doing this, they hope for eternal paradise in exchange.

F

Fallow Gate—The northernmost gate of Ishuäl.

Fama Palace—The residence and administrative seat of the Warrior-Prophet while the First Holy War remained in Caraskand, located on the Heights of the Bull.

Fanashila (4092–)—One of Esmenet's Kianene body-slaves.

Fanayal ab Kascamandri (4075–)—The first-born son of the Padirajah, and leader of the Coyauri, his famed elite heavy cavalry.

Fane (3669–3742)—The Prophet of the Solitary God and founder of Fanimry. Initially a Shrial Priest in the Nansur province of Eumarna, Fane was declared a heretic by the ecclesiastical courts of the Thousand Temples in 3703 and banished to certain death in the Carathay Desert. According to Fanim tradition, rather than dying in the desert, Fane went blind, experienced the series of revelations narrated in the *kipfa'aifan*, the "Witness of Fane," and was granted miraculous powers (the same powers attributed to the Cishaurim) he called the Water of Indara. He spent the remainder of his life preaching to and consolidating the desert tribes of the Kianene, who after his death would launch the White Jihad under the leadership of Fane's son, Fan'oukarji I.

Fanim—The name used by the Inrithi to refer to the followers of Fanimry.

Fanimry—A monotheistic faith founded upon the revelations of the Prophet Fane. The central tenets of Fanimry deal with the solitary nature and transcendence of the God, the falseness of the Gods (who are considered demons by the Fanim), the repudiation of the Tusk as unholy, and the prohibition of all representations of the God.

Fan'oukarji I (3716–71)—"Peerless son of Fane" (Kianni) The son of the Prophet Fane and the first Padirajah of Kian. Fan'oukarji is credited with the fantastic success of the White Jihad against the Nansur Empire.

Far Antiquity—The historical period beginning with the Breaking of the Gates and ending with the Apocalypse in 2155. See *Near Antiquity*.

Feast of Kussapokari—A traditional Inrithi holiday marking the summer solstice.

fevers—A generic name for various forms of malaria.

Few, the—Those born with the innate ability to sense the onta and work sorcery. See *sorcery*.

Finaöl, Weofota (4066–4111)—The Earl of the Tydonni province of Canute, slain at Anwurat.

First and Final Word—A common epithet for the words of Inri Sejenus.

Five Tribes of Men—The five rough cultural and racial groups that migrated into the Eärwic subcontinent at the beginning of the Second

Age; respectively, the Norsirai, the Ketyai, the Satyothi, the Scylvendi, and the Xiuhianni.

Flail, the—A constellation in the northern sky.

flat-place, the—According to Scylvendi custom, the ideal spiritual state wherein the Scylvendi warrior, freed of all passion and desire, becomes the very expression of the land.

Forbidden Road—A secret military road connecting the Scylvendi and Kianene frontiers of the Nansur Empire.

44 Epistles—The magnum opus of Ekyannus I, consisting of forty-four "letters" written to the God, including commentary and confession as well as philosophical inquiry and critique.

Fourth Analytic of Men, The—Also known as *The Book of Maxims*. One of the more famous works of Ajencis, containing several hundred not so very flattering "Observations of Men" and the corresponding maxim outlining the practical way to deal with each of the Men so observed.

Fourth Dialogue of the Movements of the Planets as They Pertain to Astrology, The —One of the famed "lost works" of Ajencis.

Fustaras (4061–4111)—An Orthodox agitator and proadjunct from the Selial Column.

G

Gaenkelti (4068–4111)—The Exalt-Captain of the Palatial Eöthic Guard.

Gaenri—A fiefdom of Galeoth, located to the northwest near the Hethantas.

Gaeterius (2981–3045)—The Ceneian slave-scholar celebrated for his commentaries on *The Chronicle of the Tusk* collected under the title *Contemplations on the Indentured Soul*.

Gaethuni—A fiefdom of Ce Tydonn, located on the southwestern coasts.

Gaidekki, Shressa (4062–)—The Palatine of the Conriyan district of Anplei.

Gâl, Plains of—A great expanse of grasslands to the north of the Cerish Sea.

Galeoth—A Norsirai nation of the Three Seas. Following the Apocalypse, countless thousands of Meöri refugees settled the environs north of Lake Huösi. Though nominally tributary to the Ceneian Empire, surviving records indicate that the "Galoti," as the Ceneians called them, were a fractious and warlike people. At some point in the thirty-fifth century, sedentary kingdoms began to displace the pastoral tribes along the Vindauga and Sculpa rivers. Galeoth proper did not arise until *c.* 3683, when King Norwain I reputedly concluded twenty years of campaigning and conquest by having his captive foes butchered en masse in the reception hall of Moraör, the great palace complex of the Galeoth Kings.

Galeoth Wars—The wars fought between Galeoth and the Nansur Empire, first in 4103–4, then again in 4106. In each case the Galeoth, under the generalship of Coithus Saubon, enjoyed early successes, only to be subsequently defeated in more decisive engagements, the last of which was the Battle of Procorus, where Ikurei Conphas commanded the Imperial Army.

Galgota, Nisht (4062–)—The Palatine of the Ainoni palatinate of Eshganax.

Gallish—The language of Galeoth, derived from Old Meoric.

Ganbrota, Murworg (4064–)—The Earl of the Thunyeri fiefdom of Ingraul.

gandoki—"shadows" (Gallish) A traditional Galeoth sport where two men, their wrists bound to either end of two poles, attempt to knock each other off their footing.

Ganrelka II, Anasûrimbor (2104–47)—The successor of Celmomas II and the last reigning High King of Kûniüri.

Ganrikka, Warthût (4070–)—A client thane of Gothyelk.

Ganyatti, Amurrei (4064–)—The Conriyan Palatine of the district of Ankirioth.

Gaörtha—The true name of the second skin-spy to pose as Cutias Sarcellus.

Garsahadutha, Ram-Sassor (4076–4111)—A Tributary Prince of Sansor, leader of the Sansori in the Ainoni contingent of the Holy War, slain at the Battle of Anwurat.

Gate of Horns—One of Caraskand's main gates.

Gate of Pelts—One of Sumna's famed Nine Great Gates, opening onto the Karian Way.

Gaumum, House—A Nansur House of the Congregate, with holdings scattered across the western Kyranae Plain.

Gayamakri, Sattushal (4070–)—One of the Nascenti, formerly an Ainoni baron.

Gedea—A governorate of Kian and former province of the Nansur Empire. Located between Shigek and the Anaras Spur, Gedea is a semi-arid land with interior plateaus and semi-mountainous coasts. Historically, Gedea is primarily known as the battleground between ancient Shigek and Kyraneas.

Gekas—A palatinate of High Ainon, located on the upper River Sayut.

Gerotha—The administrative and commercial capital of Xerash.

Geshrunni (4069–4110)—A Shield-Captain of the Javreh, slain in Carythusal.

Gesindal—A fiefdom of Galeoth located to the immediate northwest of Oswenta. A disproportionate number of Gesindalmen belong to the so-called Tattoo Cult of Gilgaöl—a subsect common among the Galeoth and Cepalorans—believing that skin tattooed with the sacred signs of War is immune to injury.

Ghoset—An ancient Wracu spawned during the Cûno-Inchoroi Wars.

Gielgath—An important Nansur city located on the Meneanor coast.

Gierra—The God of carnal passion. One of the so-called Compensatory Gods, who reward devotion in life with paradise in the afterlife, Gierra is very popular throughout the Three Seas, particularly among aging men drawn to the "aphrodisica," Cultic nostrums reputed to enhance virility. In the *Higarata*, the collection of subsidiary writings that form the scriptural core of the Cults, Gierra is rarely depicted with any consistency, and is often cast as a malign temptress, luring men to the luxury of her couch, often with fatal consequences.

Gilcûnya—The tongue of the Nonmen Quya and the Gnostic Schools, thought to be a debased version of Auja-Gilcûnni, the so-called "ground" (or first) tongue of the Cûnuroi.

Gilgallic Gate—An immense gate located at the westernmost point of Momemn's walls.

Gilgaöl—The God of war and conflict. One of the so-called Compensatory Gods, who reward devotion in life with paradise in the afterlife, Gilgaöl is perhaps the most popular of the Hundred Gods. In the *Higarata*, the collection of subsidiary writings that form the scriptural core of the Cults, Gilgaöl is depicted as harsh and sceptical of Men, continually demanding proof of worth from those who would follow him. Though subordinate to the Thousand Temples, the Gilgallic Cult boasts nearly as many priests, and perhaps receives more in the way of sacrificial donations.

Ginsil (2115–c. 2147)—The wife of General En-Kaujalau in *The Sagas*, who pretended to be her husband to fool the assassins coming to kill him.

Girgalla (1798–1841)—An ancient Kûniüric poet famed for his *Epic of Sauglish*.

Girgash—A nation of the Three Seas, located on the mountainous northern frontier of Nilnamesh, and the only Fanim nation aside from Kian.

Girgashi—The language of Fanic-Girgash, a derivative of Sapmatari.

Girgilioth—A ruined city on the south bank of the River Sempis, which was once the capital of Kyranean-occupied Shigek but was destroyed following Kyraneas's demise in the Apocalypse.

gishrut—A traditional Scylvendi drink made from fermented mare's milk.

Gnosis—The branch of sorcery once practised by the Gnostic Schools of the Ancient North but now known only to the Schools of Mandate and Mangaecca. Unlike Anagogic sorcery, Gnostic sorcery is leveraged through the use of the Abstractions, which is why Gnostic sorcerers are often referred to as Philosopher Magi. The Gnosis was first developed by the Nonmen Quya, who imparted it to the early Norsirai Anagogic sorcerers during the Nonman Tutelage, 555–825.

    Several Gnostic Cants are: the Bar of Heaven, the Bisecting Planes of Mirseor, the Cirroi Loom, the Ellipses of Thosolankis, the Odaini Concussion Cant, the Seventh Quyan Theorem, and the Weära Comb.

    See *sorcery*.

Gnostic Schools—Those Schools that practise the Gnosis. Only two such Schools, the Mangaecca and the Mandate, survive, though prior to the Apocalypse some dozen or so Gnostic Schools were in existence, the Sohonc foremost among them.

Goat's Heart, The—The famed book of fables by Protathis.

God, the—In Inrithi tradition, the unitary, omniscient, omnipotent, and immanent being responsible for existence, of which Gods (and in some strains Men) are but "aspects." In the Kiünnat tradition, the God is more an abstract placeholder than anything else. In the Fanim tradition, the God is the unitary, omniscient, omnipotent, and *transcendent* being responsible for existence (thus the "Solitary God"), against which the Gods war for the hearts of men.

Gods, the—Supernatural inhabitants of the Outside possessing human characteristics and figuring as objects of ritual and worship. See *Hundred Gods*.

Goken the Red (4058–)—The notorious pirate and Thunyeri Earl of Cern Auglai.

Golgotterath—The nigh impregnable stronghold of the Consult, located to the north of Neleöst Sea in the shadow of the Yimaleti Mountains. Called Min-Uroikas by the Nonmen during the Cûno-Inchoroi Wars, Golgotterath did not become significant to human history until its occupation by the Mangaecca School in 777, who excavated the Incû-Holoinas and raised vast fortifications about it. See *Apocalypse*.

Gonrain, Hoga (4088–)—The second-eldest son of Earl Gothyelk.

gopa—A red-throated gull common to the southern Three Seas, and notoriously ill-mannered.

Gotagga (*c.* 687–735)—Great Umeri sorcerer credited with the birth of philosophy apart from what had been purely theological speculation. According to Ajencis, Men explained the world with characters and stories before Gotagga and with principles and observations after.

Gotheras, Hoga (4081–)—The eldest son of Earl Gothyelk.

Gothyelk, Hoga (4052–)—The Earl of Agansanor, and leader of the Tydonni contingent of the Holy War.

Gotian, Incheiri (4065–)—The Grandmaster of the Shrial Knights and Maithanet's representative in the Holy War.

Grandmaster—The title bestowed upon the administrative rulers of the Schools.

Great Desert—See *Carathay Desert*.

Great Factions—The general term used to refer to the most powerful military and political institutions of the Three Seas.

Great Kayarsus—The vast system of mountain ranges that forms the eastern frontier of Eärwa.

Great Library of Sauglish—The archive founded by Carû-Ongonean, the third Umeri God-King, *c.* 560, and transformed by Nincaerû-Telesser II (574–668) into the cultural heart of the Ancient North. At the time of its destruction in 2147, it was rumoured to be as large as some small cities.

Great Names—The epithet for the ranking caste-nobles leading the various contingents of the First Holy War.

Great Ocean—The ocean to the west of Eärwa, largely uncharted beyond the coastline, though some claim the Zeümi have mapped its extent.

Great Pestilence—Also known as the Indigo Plague. The devastating pandemic that swept Eärwa following the death of the No-God in 2157.

Great Ruiner—A folkloric name of the No-God among the surviving tribes of Men in the Ancient North.

Great Salt—A particularly harsh region of the Carathay Desert bordering traditional Chianadyni.

Great Ziggurat of Xijoser—The largest of the Shigeki Ziggurats, raised by the Old Dynasty God-King Xijoser *c.* 670.

Griasa (4049–4111)—A slave belonging to House Gaunum, and a friend of Serwë's.

Gunsae—A long-abandoned Ceneian fortress located on the Gedean coast.

Gurnyau, Hoga (4091–4111)—The youngest son of Earl Gothyelk, slain in Caraskand.

H

haeturi—The Nansur name for the bodyguards assigned to high-ranking officers in the Imperial Army.

Hagarond, Raeharth (4059–4111)—The Galeoth Earl of Usgald, slain at Mengedda.

Hagerna—The vast temple complex located in Sumna, housing the Junriüma, the many Colleges, and the administrative machinery of the Thousand Temples.

Hamishaza (3711–83)—A renowned Ainoni dramatist, remembered for his *Tempiras the King* and his jnanic wit, which was rumoured to be unparalleled.

Ham-Kheremic—The lost language of ancient Shir.

Hamoric—The language group of the ancient Ketyai pastoralists of the eastern Three Seas.

"[the] hand of Triamis, the heart of Sejenus, and the intellect of Ajencis"—The famous saying attributed to the poet Protathis, referring to the qualities all men should strive for.

Hansa—A slave-girl belonging to Cutias Sarcellus.

Hapetine Gardens—One of many architectural idylls on the Andiamine Heights.

Hasjinnet ab Skauras (4067–4103)—The eldest son of Skauras ab Nalajan, slain by Cnaiür urs Skiötha at the Battle of Zirkirta in 4103.

Hatatian (3174–3211)—The infamous author of the *Exhortations*, a work that eschews traditional Inrithi values and espouses an ethos of unprincipled self-promotion. Though long censured by the Thousand Temples, Hatatian remains popular among the caste-nobility of the Three Seas.

Haurut urs Mab (4000–4082)—An Utemot memorialist when Cnaiür was a child.

Heights of the Bull—One of the nine heights of Caraskand.

hemoplexy—A common disease of war characterized by intense fevers, vomiting, skin irritation, severe diarrhea, and, in the most extreme cases, coma and death. Also known as "the hollows" or "the hemoplectic hand."

Heörsa, Dun (4078–)—A Shield-Captain of the Hundred Pillars, formerly a Galeoth thane.

Heresiarch—The title of the leader of the Cishaurim.

Heron Spear—A powerful artifact of the Inchoroi Tekne, so named because of its unique shape. The Heron Spear first appears in the *Isûphiryas* as Suörgil (Ihrimsû, "Shining Death"), the great "spear of light" taken by Cu'jara Cinmoi from the corpse of Sil, the Inchoroi King, at the battle of Pir Pahal. For millennia the Heron Spear lay in the possession of the Nonmen of Ishoriol, until it was stolen by Cet'ingira (see *Mekeritrig*) and delivered to Golgotterath *c.* 750. Then in 2140 it was stolen again by Seswatha (see *Apocalypse*), who believed it to be the only weapon capable of destroying the No-God. For a brief time it was thought destroyed at the catastrophic Battle of Eleneöt Fields, but it reappeared in 2154 in the possession of Anaxophus V, High King of Kyraneas, who used it to slay the No-God at the Battle of Mengedda. For centuries it resided in Cenei, a treasured possession of the Aspect-Emperors, only to be lost once again when the Scylvendi sacked Cenei in 3351. Its whereabouts are presently unknown.

Hethanta Mountains—A large mountain range located in central Eärwa.

Hifanat ab Tunukri (4084–4111)—A Cishaurim sorcerer-priest and servant of Anasûrimbor Moënghus, slain at Caraskand.

High Ainon—A Ketyai nation of the eastern Three Seas, and the only nation to be ruled by one of the Schools, the Scarlet Spires. Founded in 3372 after Sarothesser I defeated General Maurelta at the Battle of Charajat, High Ainon has long been one of the most populous and power-ful nations of the Three Seas. The agricultural production of the Secharib Plains combined with that of the Sayut Delta and River Valley supports both an extensive caste-nobility (noted for their wealth and their obses-sion with jnan) and an aggressive mercantilism. Ainoni ships can be found berthed in every port in the Three Seas. During the Scholastic Wars (3796–3818), the School of the Scarlet Spires, which is based in the capital, Carythusal, managed to destroy the army of King Horziah III and assumed indirect control of the nation's primary institutions. The nominal head of state, the King-Regent, answers directly to the Grandmaster.

High Kunna—The debased version of Gilcûnya used by the Anagogic Schools of the Three Seas.

High Sakarpean—The language of ancient Sakarpus, a derivative of ancient Skettic.

High Sheyic—The language of the Ceneian Empire, a derivative of ancient Kyranean.

High Vurumandic—The language of the Nilnameshi ruling castes, a deriva-tive of Vaparsi.

Hilderath, Solm (4072–)—One of the Nascenti, formerly a Tydonni thane.

Hinayati Mountains—A large system of mountain ranges located in south-western Eärwa, sometimes called "the spine of Nilnamesh."

Hinnant—A palatinate of High Ainon, located in the heart of the Secharib Plains.

Hinnereth—The administrative and commercial capital of Gedea, located on the Meneanor coast.

History (Dûnyain)—The movement of human events through time. The significance of History for the Dûnyain is found in the fact that past circum-stances dominate and determine present actions, such that individuals continually find themselves "coming after," which is to say, at the mercy of events over which they have no control. The Dûnyain believe that utter detachment from history is a necessary precondition for absolute awareness.

History (Inrithism)—The movement of human events through time. The significance of History for the Inrithi is that the God is manifested within it. The Inrithi believe that certain configurations of events express the truth of the God while certain other configurations are inimical to such expression.

Hoga, House—The ruling dynasty of Agansanor. The Black Stag on Green is their traditional device.

Hoga Brood—The name given in the Conriyan court to Hoga Gothyelk's sons.

hollows—See *hemoplexy*.

Holy Precincts—See *Hagerna*.

Holy War—The Inrithi host summoned by Maithanet that invaded Kian in 4111 bent upon the reconquest of Shimeh.

Home City—A common Nansur epithet for Momemn.

Hortha, Sonhail (4064–)—A Galeoth knight, client to Prince Coithus Saubon.

Houses of the Congregate—A quasi-legislative assembly consisting of the primary landholding families of the Nansur Empire.

Hulwarga, Hringa (4086–)—The second son of King Hringa Rauschang of Thunyerus, and leader of the Thunyeri contingent of the First Holy War after the death of his older brother, Prince Hringa Skaiyelt, in Caraskand. Called the Limper because of his uneven gait.

Hundred Gods—The collective name of the Gods enumerated in *The Chronicle of the Tusk* and worshipped either under the auspices of the Cults (which is to say, subordinate to the Thousand Temples), or in the traditional versions of the Kiünnat. In the Inrithi tradition, the Hundred Gods are thought to be aspects of the God (whom Inri Sejenus famously called "the Million Souled"), much the way various personality traits could be said to inhabit an individual. In the far more variegated Kiünnat tradition, the Hundred Gods are thought to be independent spiritual agencies, prone to indirectly intervene in the lives of their worshippers. Both traditions recognize the differences between the Compensatory Gods, who promise direct reward for worship and devotion, the Punitive Gods, who secure sacrifices through the threat of suffering, and the more rare Bellicose Gods, who despise worship as sycophancy and favour those who strive against them. Both the Inrithi and Kiünnat traditions see the Gods as indispensable to eternal life in the Outside.

The esoteric apologist Zarathinius is infamous for arguing (in *A Defence of the Arcane Arts*) the absurdity of worshipping deities as imperfect and capricious as mere Men. The Fanim, of course, believe the Hundred Gods are renegade slaves of the Solitary God—demons.

Hundred Pillars—The Warrior-Prophet's personal bodyguard, named after the one hundred men rumoured to have surrendered their water—and their lives—to him on the Trail of Skulls.

Huösi, Lake—A large freshwater lake draining the Vindauga and Sculpa river systems, and emptying into the Wutmouth.

hustwarra—The Galeoth name for camp wives.

Husyelt—The God of the hunt. One of the so-called Compensatory Gods, who reward devotion in life with paradise in the afterlife, Husyelt comes after only Yatwer and Gilgaöl in Cultic popularity, particularly in the Middle-North. In the *Higarata,* the collection of subsidiary writings that form the scriptural core of the Cults, Husyelt is depicted as the most anthropocentric of the Hundred Gods, as intent upon enabling his worshippers as he is upon securing their obedience and devotion. The Cult of Husyelt is rumoured to be extraordinarily wealthy, and high-ranking members of the Husyeltic priesthood often possess as much political clout as Shrial apparati.

Huterat—A town on the Sempis Delta, destroyed by the First Holy War in 4111.

I

idolaters—A term commonly used by Fanim to refer to Inrithi.

Ihrimsû—The tongue of Injor-Niyas.

Ikurei, House—A Nansur House of the Congregate, with holdings concentrated in and about Momemn. The Imperial House since 3941.

Ikurei Anphairas I (4022–81)—The Emperor of Nansur from 4066 to 4081, and grandfather of Ikurei Xerius III, assassinated by persons unknown.

Ikurei Dynasty—Always one of the more powerful Houses of the Congregate, the Ikurei seized the Imperial Mantle in 3941, capitalizing on the turmoil following the loss of Shigek and then Gedea to Kian in the Dagger Jihad. Ikurei Sorius I became the first of a line of shrewd yet defensive Ikurei Emperors. See *Nansur Empire.*

Ikurei Xerius III (4059–)—The Emperor of the Nansur Empire.

Imbeyan ab Imbaran (4067–4111)—Sapatishah-Governor of Enathpaneah and son-in-law of the Padirajah, slain at Caraskand.

Imperial Army—A common name for the standing Nansur army.

Imperial Precincts—The name given to the grounds of the Andiamine Heights.

Imperial Saik—The School indentured to the Nansur Emperor.

Imperial Sun—The primary symbol of the Nansur Empire.

Impromta, The—The anonymously written collection of the Warrior-Prophet's earliest sermons and aphorisms.

Imrothas, Sarshressa (4054–4111)—The Palatine of the Conriyan province of Aderot, claimed by disease at Caraskand.

Inchoroi—"People of Emptiness" (Ihrimsû) A mysterious and obscene race that, according to legend, descended from the void in the Incû-Holoinas. Very little is known about them, aside from their apparently limitless capacity for cruelty and their malignant obsession with the carnal. See *Cûno-Inchoroi Wars*.

Incû-Holoinas—"Ark-of-the-Skies" (Ihrimsû) The great vessel that brought the Inchoroi from the heavens and became the golden heart of Golgotterath.

Indara-Kishauri—The "tribe" of the Cishaurim. The "Indara" refer, in the Kianene tradition, to the "tribe of water-bearers," a legendary band that supposedly wandered the dunes dispensing water and mercy to the faithful. The designation is critical (according to the *kipfa'aifan*, it saved Fane's life), given the importance of tribal affiliation in desert Kianene society.

Indenture, the—The infamous document used by Ikurei Xerius III in his attempt to secure the lands conquered by the First Holy War.

Indigo Plague—According to legend, the pestilence swept up from the No-God's ashes after his destruction at the hands of Anaxophus V in 2155. Mandate scholars dispute this, claiming that the No-God's body was recovered by the Consult and interred in Golgotterath. Whatever the cause, the Indigo Plague ranks as among the worst in recorded history.

Indurum Barracks—A lodging for soldiers located in Caraskand and dating back to the Nansur occupation of the city.

Ingiaban, Sristai (4059–)—The Palatine of the Conriyan province of Kethantei.

Ingoswitu (1966–2050)—A far antique Kûniüric philosopher, famed in his own day for his *Dialogia* but primarily known in the Three Seas through

Ajencis and his famed critique of Ingoswitu's *Theosis* in *The Third Analytic of Men*.

Ingraul—A fiefdom of the Thunyeri Sranc Marches.

Ingusharotep II (*c.* 1000–*c.* 1080)—The Old Dynasty Shigeki King who conquered the Kyranae Plains.

Injor-Niyas—The last remaining Nonmen nation, located beyond the Demua Mountains. See *Ishterebinth*.

Inrau, Paro (4088–4110)—A former student of Drusas Achamian, slain in Sumna.

Inri Sejenus (*c.* 2159–2202)—The Latter Prophet and spiritual (although not historical) founder of the Thousand Temples, who claimed to be the pure incarnation of Absolute Spirit ("the very proportion of the God"), sent to emend the teachings of the Tusk. After his death and supposed ascension to the Nail of Heaven, his disciples recounted his life and teachings in *The Tractate*, the text that is now considered by the Inrithi to be as holy as *The Chronicle of the Tusk*.

Inrithi—The followers of Inri Sejenus, the Latter Prophet, and his amendments to the Tusk.

Inrithism—The faith founded upon the revelations of Inri Sejenus, the Latter Prophet, which synthesizes elements of both monotheism and polytheism. The central tenets of Inrithism deal with the immanence of the God in historical events, the unity of the individual deities of the Cults as Aspects of the God, and the role of the Thousand Temples as the very expression of the God in the world.

Following the alleged ascension of Inri Sejenus, Inrithism slowly established itself throughout the Ceneian Empire as an organized hierarchy independent of the state—what came to be called the Thousand Temples. Initially, the existing traditionalist Kiünnat sects simply dismissed the new religion, but as it continued to grow, a number of attempts were made to circumscribe its powers and prevent its further spread, none of them particularly effective. Escalating tensions eventually culminated in the Zealot Wars (*c.* 2390–2478), which, although technically a civil war, saw battles fought far outside the boundaries of what then constituted the Ceneian Empire.

In 2469, Sumna capitulated to Shrial forces, but hostilities continued until Triamis was anointed Emperor in 2478. Though himself Inrithi (converted by Ekyannus III), and despite enacting the constitution governing the division of powers between the Imperium and the Thousand Temples, he refrained from declaring Inrithism the official state religion until 2505. From that point the ascendancy of the Thousand Temples was assured, and over the ensuing centuries the remaining Kiünnat "heresies" of the Three Seas would either wither away or be forcibly stamped out.

Inshull (?–?)—One of the Chieftain-Kings named in the Tusk.

Inskarra, Saweor (4061–4111)—The Earl of the Thunyeri province of Skagwa, slain at Anwurat.

Inûnara Highlands—A region of foothills to the northeast of the Unaras Spur of the Hethanta Mountains.

Invishi—The commercial and spiritual capital of Nilnamesh, and one of the most ancient cities of the Three Seas.

Iothiah—A great Old Dynasty city located on the Sempis Delta.

Irreüma—A so-called "all-Gods temple" located in the administrative quarter of the Hagerna. Though its architecture belongs to the classical Kyranean period, its provenance is unknown.

Iryssas, Krijates (4089–)—The young and impetuous majordomo of House Krijates, and cousin to Krijates Xinemus.

Ishoiya—Sheyic for "uncertainty." The so-called Day of Doubt, an Inrithi holy day celebrated in late summer, commemorating the spiritual turmoil and renewal undergone by Inri Sejenus during his imprisonment in Xerash. Among the less pious, Ishoiya is renowned as a day of copious drinking.

Ishroi—"Exalted Ones" (Ihrimsû) The name given to the Nonmen warrior castes.

Ishterebinth—"Exalted Stronghold" (Ihrimsû) The last of the Nonmen Mansions, located to the west of the Demua Mountains. Known as Ishoriöl ("Exalted Hall") in the Isûphiryas, Ishterebinth was considered one of the premier cities of the Cûnuroi after Siöl and Cil-Aujas. See *Cûno-Inchoroi Wars*.

Ishuäl—"Exalted Grotto" (Ihrimsû) The secret fastness of the Kûniüric High Kings, located in the Demua Mountains, and subsequently inhabited by the Dûnyain.

Istriya, Ikurei (4045–)—The mother of Emperor Xerius III, once famed for her legendary beauty.

Istyuli Plains—A vast and largely semi-arid tableland running from the Yimelati Mountains in the north to the Hethanta Mountains in the south.

Isûphiryas—"Great Pit of Years" (Ihrimsû) The great work chronicling the history of the Nonmen prior to the Breaking of the Gates. In all likelihood it is the most ancient text in existence. Sometime in the fourth century, a copy of the *Isûphiryas* was given to Cûnwerishau by Nil'giccas, the Nonman King of Ishoriöl (Ishterebinth), as part of the ancient treaty between their two peoples—the first between Nonmen and Men. During the reign of the God-King Carû-Ongonean, five Ûmeri translations of the *Isûphiryas* were bequeathed to the Library of Sauglish. Four of these were destroyed in the Apocalypse. The fifth was saved by Seswatha, who delivered it to the scribes of the Three Seas.

Ivory Gate—The northernmost gate of Caraskand, so named because of the pale limestone used to construct it (as well as the Gate of Horns).

Iyokus, Heramari (4014–)—A Daimotic sorcerer of rank within the Scarlet Spires, and, despite his chanv addiction, Master of Spies to Hanamanu Eleäzaras.

J

Jahan Plains—The large, arid tableland that makes up the western frontier of Eumarna.

Jarutha—A small agricultural town some twenty miles southwest of Momemn.

Javreh—The slave-soldiers of the Scarlet Spires, famed for their ferocity in battle. The first unit was created in 3801 by Grandmaster Shinurta at the height of the Scholastic Wars.

Jekhia—A tributary nation of High Ainon, famed as the mysterious source of chanv, located at the headwaters of the River Sayut in the Great Kayarsus. The Men of Jekhia are unique in that they exhibit Xiuhianni racial characteristics.

Jeshimal River—The primary river system of Amoteu, draining the Betmulla Mountains and emptying into the Meneanor Sea at Shimeh.

Jihads—Fanim holy wars. Since the inception of Fanimry, the Kianene have waged no fewer than seven jihads, all of them against the Nansur Empire.

Jirux—A great Kianene fortress on the north bank of the River Sempis.

Jiünati Steppe—A vast region of semi-arid plains extending northward from the Carathay Desert to the Istyuli Plains, and inhabited by Scylvendi pastoralists since the early years of the Second Age.

jnan—An informal code of manner and speech understood by many to be a "war of word and sentiment." Adeptness at jnan is understood, particularly by the more refined subcultures of the Three Seas, to be the key determinant of status among individuals who are otherwise of equal caste or station. Given that the God is believed to be manifested in the movement of history, and history is determined primarily by the disparate statuses of men, for many jnan is understood as a sacred and not simply an instrumental enterprise. Many others, however, especially the Norsirai of the Three Seas, regard jnan with contempt, as a "mere game." Jnanic exchanges are typically characterized by concealed antagonism, the appreciation of irony and intellect, and the semblance of detached interest.

Joktha—A port city on the Enathpanean coast.

Jorua Sea—A great inland sea located in mid-western Eärwa.

Journals and Dialogues—The collected writings of Triamis I, greatest of the Ceneian Aspect-Emperors.

Judges—The name given to Zaudunyani missionaries.

Jukan—The God of sky and season. One of the so-called Compensatory Gods, who reward devotion in life with paradise in the afterlife, Jukan rivals Yatwer in popularity among subsistence farmers yet is scarcely represented in major urban centres. The priests of Jukan are readily recognizable by their blue-dyed skin. The Marjukari, an extreme ascetic branch of the Jukanic Cult, are notorious for living as hermits in the mountains.

Junriüma—Also known as the Vault-of-the-Tusk, the ancient fortress-temple that houses the Tusk, located in the heart of the Hagerna in Sumna.

Jurisada—A governorate of Kian and former province of the Nansur Empire. Located on the southeastern end of the Eumarnan Peninsula, Jurisada is an intensively agricultural region, densely populated, and thought to be a land of "spiritual sloth" by many Kianene.

Juru—God of virility and fertility. One of the so-called Compensatory Gods, who reward devotion in life with paradise in the afterlife, Juru is popular among aging caste-noble men, and possesses only a handful of temples, most of them found in major cities. It is often mocked as the Mistress Cult.

Juterum, the—The so-called Sacred Heights in Shimeh, where, according to scripture, Inri Sejenus ascended to the Nail of Heaven.

K

Kahiht—The name given to so-called World-Souls in the Inrithi tradition. Since the God manifests himself in the movement of historical events in Inrithism, to be Kahiht, or a world historical individual, is considered sacred.

Kalaul—The great campus of the Csokis temple complex in Caraskand.

Kamposea Agora—A great bazaar adjacent to the temple complex of Cmiral in Momemn.

Kanampurea—A palatinate in the Conriyan interior, famed for its agricultural productivity, traditionally held by the brother of the Conriyan King.

Kanshaïva—A district of Nilnamesh.

Karian Way—An old Ceneian road running through the province of Massentia that once linked Sumna to Cenei during the reign of the Aspect-Emperors.

Karyot—A palatinate of High Ainon, located on the upper Sayut and forming the Jekhian frontier.

Kasalla, Porsentius (4062–)—One of the Nascenti, formerly a Captain in the Imperial Army.

Kasaumki, Memshressa (4072–)—One of the Nascenti, formerly a Conriyan knight.

Kascamandri ab Tepherokar (4062–4112)—The Padirajah of Kian, slain by the Warrior-Prophet at the Battle of Tertae Fields.

Kayarsus Mountains—See *Great Kayarsus*.

Kelmeöl—The ancient capital of the Meöri Empire, destroyed in the Apocalypse in 2150.

Kemkaric—The language group of the ancient Ketyai pastoralists of the northwestern Three Seas.

Kengetic—The language group of the Ketyai peoples.

Kepfet ab Tanaj (4061–4112)—The Kianene officer who betrayed Caraskand to Coithus Saubon and the First Holy War in 4111.

Kerathotics—The native Inrithi minority of Shigek.

Kerioth—A major port city on the south coast of Eumarna.

Kethantei—A palatinate located in south central Conriya, noted for its wine and fruit production.

Ketyai—The typically black-haired, brown-eyed, dark-skinned race predominantly concentrated about the Three Seas. One of the Five Tribes of Men.

Khemema—A region of Kian and former province of the Nansur Empire. Located to the south of Shigek, Khemema marks the point where the great Carathay Desert reaches the Meneanor Sea. Sparsely inhabited by desert tribesmen (see *Khirgwi*), Khemema's only source of wealth derives from the regular trade caravans that travel between Shigek and Caraskand.

Khirgwi—The tribesmen of the eastern Carathay Desert, tributary to the Kianene but ethnically distinct.

Kian—The most powerful nation of the Three Seas, extending from the southern frontier of the Nansur Empire to Nilnamesh. The Kianene were originally a desert people from the fringes of the Great Salt. Various Ceneian and Nilnameshi sources refer to them as cunning and audacious raiders, the target of several different campaigns and punitive expeditions. In his monumental *The Annals of Cenei*, Casidas describes them as "courtly savages, at once disarmingly gracious and murderous in the extreme." Despite their reputation and apparent numbers (Nansur records indicate several attempts to gauge their numbers by concerned provincial governors), the Kianene spent most of their time battling amongst themselves over scarce desert resources. Their conversion to Fanimry (c. 3704–24) would change this, and with drastic consequences.

Following the unification of the Kianene tribes under Fane, Fan'oukarji I, Fane's eldest son and the first of Kian's Padirajahs, led his countrymen in the so-called White Jihad, winning a series of spectacular victories over the Nansur Imperial Army. By the time of his death in 3771, Fan'oukarji I had conquered all of Mongilea and had made serious inroads into Eumarna. He had also founded his capital, Nenciphon, on the banks of the River Sweki.

Successive Jihads would see Eumarna (3801), Enathpaneah (3842), Xerash and Amoteu (3845), then finally Shigek and Gedea (3933) all fall to Kian. Though the Nilnameshi would successfully thwart several different Kianene invasions, Fanic missionaries would succeed in converting the Girgashi to Fanimry in the thirty-eighth century. By the end of the fourth millennium Kian was easily the pre-eminent military and commercial power of the Three Seas, and a source of endless consternation not only for the much-diminished Nansur Empire but for Inrithi Princes in every nation.

Kianni—The language of Kian, a derivative of Caro-Shemic.

Kidruhil—The most celebrated cohort of heavy cavalry in the Three Seas, primarily constituted by Nansur caste-nobles from the Houses of the Congregate.

Kig'krinaki—A Sranc tribe from the Plains of Gâl.

Kimish (4058–)—The Prime Interrogator to Ikurei Xerius III.

King-Fires—The ritual bonfires signifying kingship among the Galeoth.

King-of-Tribes—The title given to the individual elected by the Scylvendi chieftains to lead the gathered tribes in war.

kipfa'aifan—"Witness of Fane" (Kianni) The holiest scripture of Fanimry, chronicling the life and revelations of the Prophet Fane from his blinding and exile into the Great Salt in 3703 to his death in 3742. See *Fane*.

Kishyat—A palatinate of High Ainon, located on the south bank of the River Sayut on the Sansori frontier.

Kiskei, House—A Nansur House of the Congregate.

Kisma—The adoptive "father" of Mallahet.

Kiyuth River—A tributary of the River Sempis, running deep into the Jiünati Steppe.

kjineta—See *castes*.

Kneeling Heights—One of the nine heights of Caraskand and the location of the Sapatishah's Palace.

knight-commander—The rank directly subordinate to the Grandmaster in the Shrial Knights.

Knights of the Tusk—See *Shrial Knights*.

Knights of Trysë—Also known as the Knights of the Ur-Throne. An ancient order of knights sworn to defend the Anasûrimbor Dynasty, thought destroyed in 2147 with the Sack of Trysë.

Koraphea—The most populous city of High Ainon after Carythusal, located on the coast north of the Sayut Delta.

Korasha—Also known as the White-Sun Palace. An extensive palace complex in Nenciphon, and traditional residence and administrative seat of the Kianene Padirajahs.

Kothwa, Hargraum (4070–4111)—The Tydonni Earl of Gaethuni, slain at Mengedda.

Kumeleus, Sirassas (4045–)—A staunch supporter of House Ikurei, and Exalt-General prior to Ikurei Conphas.

Kumrezzar, Akori (4071–4110)—The Palatine of the Ainoni district of Kutapileth, and one of the leaders of the Vulgar Holy War.

Kûniüri—A lost nation of the Ancient North and the last of the ancient Aumris empires. High Norsirai city-states developed along the River Aumris and from c. 300 were united under Cûnwerishau, the God-King of Trysë. From c. 500 the city of Umerau gained ascendancy, leading to the Umerau Empire and the cultural efflorescence of the Nonman Tutelage under Carû-Ongonean. Ancient Umeria thrived until defeated by the Cond tribesmen of Aulyanau the Conqueror in 917. The rapid collapse of the so-called Cond Yoke led to a second period of Trysean dominance of the Aumris, this one lasting until 1228, when another series of White Norsirai migratory invasions resulted in the so-called Scintya Yoke.

The Kûniüric period proper did not begin until 1408, when Anasûrimbor Nanor-Ukkerja I, exploiting the confusion surrounding the collapse of the Scintya Empire, seized the Ur-Throne in Trysë, declaring himself the first High King of Kûniüri. Over the course of his long life (he lived to the age of 178, the reputed result of the Nonman blood in his veins), Nanor-Ukkerja I extended Kûniüri to the Yimelati Mountains in the north, to the western-most coasts of the Cerish Sea in the east, to Sakarpus in the south, and to the Demua Mountains in the west. At his death, he divided this empire between his sons, creating Aörsi and Sheneor in addition to Kûniüri proper.

Kûniüri became, largely by virtue of its cultural inheritance, the centre of learning and craft for all Eärwa. The Trysean court hosted what were called the Thousand Sons, the scions of Kings from lands as far away as ancient Shigek and Shir. The holy city of Sauglish hosted pilgrim scholars from as far away as Angka and Nilnamesh. High Norsirai fashions were emulated throughout Eärwa.

This golden age came to an end with the Apocalypse and the defeat of Anasûrimbor Celmomas II on the Fields of Eleneöt in 2146. All the ancient cities of the Aumris would be destroyed the following year. The surviving Kûniüri were either enslaved or scattered.

See *Apocalypse*.

Kûniüric—The lost language of ancient Kûniüri, derived from Umeritic.

Kuöti—A Scylvendi tribe of the northwestern Steppe.

Kurigald—A fiefdom of Galeoth, located on the eastern shores of Lake Huösi.

Kurrut—A small fortress in the Gedean interior, built by the Nansur after the fall of Shigek to the Fanim in 3933.

Kushigas (4070–4111)—The Palatine of the Conriyan province of Annand, slain at Anwurat.

Kusjeter (4077–4111)—The Count-Palatine of the Ainoni province of Gekas, slain at Anwurat.

Kussalt (4054–4111)—The groom to Prince Coithus Saubon, slain at Mengedda.

Kutapileth—An administrative district of eastern High Ainon, noted for its iron and silver mines.

Kutigha (4063–4111)—A Thousand Temples informant for the Scarlet Spires.

kut'ma—In benjuka, the "hidden move" that seems insignificant but actually determines the outcome of the game.

Kutnarmu—The generic name for the unexplored continent south of Eärwa.

Kyranae Plains—A fertile region drained by the River Phayus and extending from the southern Hethanta Mountains to the Meneanor Sea. Its peoples have given birth to three great empires: ancient Kyraneas, the Ceneian Empire, and most recently the Nansur Empire.

Kyranean—The lost language of ancient Kyraneas, derived from ancient Kemkaric.

Kyraneas—A lost nation of the ancient Three Seas, located on the River Phayus, with a capital first at Parninas then at Mehtsonc. Culturally linked and long tributary to Shigek, Kyraneas expanded to include much of her erstwhile ruler's empire, and was at the height of her power at the time of the Apocalypse. With the loss at Mehsarunath in 2154 and the destruction of Mehtsonc shortly after, the fate of the ancient kingdom was sealed, even though the Kyranean High King, Anaxophus V, managed to defeat the No-God the following year. See *Apocalypse*.

L

Labyrinth—See *Thousand Thousand Halls*.

Lance, the—A Scylvendi constellation in the northern sky.

Languages of Men—Until the Breaking of the Gates and the migration of the Four Nations from Eänna, the Men of Eärwa—called the Emwama in *The Chronicle of the Tusk*—were enslaved by the Nonmen and spoke debased versions of their masters' tongues. No trace of these languages remains, nor does any trace of their original, pre-bondage language. The great Nonman history, the *Isûphiryas*, or the "Great Pit of Years," suggests the Emwama originally spoke the same tongue as their kin across the Great Kayarsus. This has led many to believe that Thoti-Eännorean is indeed the primeval language of all men.

Languages of Nonmen—Without doubt, the Nonmen, or Cûnuroi, tongues are among the oldest in Eärwa. Some Aujic inscriptions predate the first extant example of Thoti-Eännorean, *The Chronicle of the Tusk,* by more than five thousand years. Auja-Gilcûnni, which has yet to be deciphered, is far older still.

Latter Prophet—See *Inri Sejenus*.

"[to] laugh with Sarothesser"—An Ainoni phrase expressing their belief that laughter at the moment of death signifies triumph. This tradition stems from the legend that Sarothesser I, the founder of High Ainon, laughed at death the moment before it claimed him.

Law of the Tusk—The traditional law as laid out in the Book of Canticles in *The Chronicle of the Tusk*. Though largely superseded by *The Tractate*, it is still referred to in cases on which Inri Sejenus was silent.

Legion—A Dûnyain term referring to the preconscious sources of the conscious thought.

Leweth (4061–4109)—A trapper in the abandoned Atrithan province of Sobel.

Library of Sauglish—The famed temple complex and text repository found in ancient Sauglish. According to legend, the Library had grown to the size of a city within the city by the time of Sauglish's destruction in 2147.

Library of the Sareots—See *Sareotic Library*.

Ligesseras, House—One of the Houses of the Congregate.

Logos—The name used by Dûnyain to refer to instrumental reason. The Logos describes the course of action that allows for the most efficient exploitation of one's circumstances in order "to come before," that is, to precede and master the passage of events.

"[The] Logos is without beginning or end."—A Dûnyain phrase referring to the so-called Rational Priority Principle. See *Dûnyain*.

Lokung—The "Dead-God" of the Scylvendi. See *No-God*.

Low Sheyic—The language of the Nansur Empire and lingua franca of the Three Seas.

M

Maëngi—The true name of the first skin-spy to pose as Cutias Sarcellus.

Magga, Hringa (4080–4111)—A cousin of Prince Hringa Skaiyelt of Thunyerus.

Maithanet—The Shriah of the Thousand Temples, and primary instigator of the First Holy War.

Mallahet—A notorious member of the Cishaurim.

Mamaradda (4071–4111)—The Javreh Shield-Captain assigned to execute Drusas Achamian.

Mamati—The language of scriptural Amoteu, a derivative of Caro-Shemic.

Mamayma (?–?)—One of the Chieftain-Kings named in *The Chronicle of the Tusk*.

Mamot—A ruined Ceneian city located near the mouth of the River Sweki.

Mandate, School of—The Gnostic School founded by Seswatha in 2156 to continue the war against the Consult and to protect the Three Seas from the return of the No-God. Based in Atyersus, the Mandate maintains missions in several different cities about the Three Seas and embassies in the courts of all the Great Factions. Aside from its apocalyptic calling, the Mandate is distinct from the other sorcerous Schools in several respects, not the least of which is its possession of the Gnosis, a monopoly it has been able to protect for almost two thousand years. The Mandate also differs in the fanaticism of its members: apparently, all sorcerers of rank continuously dream Seswatha's experiences of the Apocalypse every night, the effect of a sorcerous rite called the Grasping, where initiates reputedly submit to incantations while holding Seswatha's mummified heart. Also, the members of the Mandate elect an executive council (called the Quorum) rather than an individual Grandmaster to further guard against deviations from their core mission.

Typically, the Mandate can boast between fifty and sixty sorcerers of rank, and perhaps twice that number of initiates. These numbers, which are typical of minor Anagogic Schools, are deceptive, however, since the power of the Gnosis makes the Mandate more than a match for Schools as large as, say, the Scarlet Spires. Because of this power, the School has long been courted by the Kings of Conriya.

Mandate Catechism—The ritual set of questions and answers on Mandate doctrine, recited by teacher and student at the beginning of each day of study. The first thing learned by all Mandate Schoolmen.

Mangaecca—The ancient rival to the School of Sohonc, and last of the four original Gnostic Schools. From its founding in 684 by Sos-Praniura (the greatest student of Gin'yursis), the School of Mangaecca had pursued a predatory ethos, regarding knowledge as the embodiment of power. Though this earned the School an ambiguous reputation, the Mangaecca managed to avoid running afoul of the High Gnostic Writ, the edict of Nincama-Telesser circumscribing sorcerous conduct. Then, in 777, at the behest of a Nonman Erratic named Cet'ingira, they discovered the Incû-Holoinas, the dread Ark of the Inchoroi. Over the following centuries they continued their excavations of the Ark and their investigations of the Tekne. In 1123 rumours began spreading that Shaeönanra, then Grandmaster of the Mangaecca, had discovered a catastrophic means to undo the scriptural damnation of sorcerers. The School was promptly outlawed, and the remainder of the School fled to Golgotterath, abandoning Sauglish forever. By the time of the Apocalypse, they had transformed into what would be called the Consult. See *Apocalypse*.

Manghaput—A major port city in Nilnamesh.

Mansions—The mannish name for the great subterranean cities of the Nonmen.

Mantraitor—See *Mekeritrig*.

Mark, the—The name for what is otherwise known as the "bruising of the onta." Aside from the Psûkhe, which may or may not be a true sorcery, all sorcerous manifestations and practitioners exhibit what is called the Mark. Various descriptions of the Mark have come down through history, but there seems to be little consistency in the accounts, apart from the experience's ephemeral nature. According to religious accounts, the Mark is akin to the disfiguring of criminals, the way the God reveals the blasphemers in the presence of the righteous. But apologists such as Zarathinius point out that if this is indeed the case, then it is more than a little ironic that only the *blasphemers* can see the Mark. In secular accounts, textual analogies are typically resorted to: seeing the Mark is akin to seeing where text has been scratched away and overwritten in ancient documents. In the case of sorcery, since the amendments to reality are as flawed as the Men who do the amending, it stands to reason that some essential difference would be visible.

Marsadda—The former capital of Cengemis, located on the coast of Ce Tydonn.

Martemus (4061–4111)—A Nansur General, and aide to Ikurei Conphas.

Massentia—A province of the central Nansurium, called "the Golden" because of the bounty of her wheat fields.

Meärji (4074–)—A Galeoth thane, client to Prince Coithus Saubon.

Mehtsonc—The ancient administrative and commercial capital of Kyraneas, destroyed in the Apocalypse in 2154.

Meigeiri—The administrative and spiritual capital of Ce Tydonn, founded in 3739 about the Ceneian fortress of Meigara.

Meigon (4002–)—A member of the Dûnyain Pragma.

Mekeritrig (?–)—"Traitor of Men" (Kûniüric) The mannish name for Cet'ingira, the Nonman Siqu who revealed the location of Min-Uroikas to the School of Mangaecca in 777, and who would become a ranking member of the Consult during the Apocalypse. See *Mangaecca* and *Apocalypse*.

Memgowa (2466–2506)—The famed near antique Zeümi sage and philosopher, primarily known in the Three Seas for his *Celestial Aphorisms* and *The Book of Divine Acts*.

memorialists—Those members of a Scylvendi tribe, typically the old and infirm, entrusted with the memorization and recitation of the Scylvendi oral tradition.

memponti—A Sheyic term meaning "fortuitous turn." In jnan, the most auspicious moment to make one's purposes clear.

Men—With the possible exception of the Sranc, the dominant race of Eärwa.

Meneanor, Sea of—The northernmost of the Three Seas.

Mengedda—A ruined city in the heart of the Mengedda Plains, famed as the battleground where Anaxophus V struck down the No-God with the Heron Spear in 2155.

Mengedda Plains—The natural geographical frontier between Shigek and Nansur, just south of the Unaras Spur and north of the Gedea Highlands. As the site of innumerable battles, the fields are widely reputed to be haunted.

Men of the Tusk—The warriors of the First Holy War.

Meöri Empire—A lost nation of the Ancient North. Founded as a trading stronghold by Akksersian colonists *c.* 850, the city of Kelmeöl grew rapidly, and its people, the Meöri, progressively asserted more and more authority over the neighbouring White Norsirai tribes. By the time Borswelka I was declared King in 1021, it had become an aggressive, militaristic city-state. By the time his grandson Borswelka II died in 1104, it had conquered most of the Vosa River Basin and had established trading contacts with Shir to the south through a series of forts along the River Wernma. Strategically situated, and without any regional competitors, the Meöri Empire, as it came to be called, flourished as a mercantile nation. It collapsed with the destruction of Kelmeöl in 2150 during the Apocalypse.

metaphysics—Generally, the study of the ultimate nature of existence. More specifically, the study of the operative principles behind the various branches of sorcery. See *sorcery*.

Meümaras (4058–)—The Captain of the *Amortanea*.

Middle North—A term sometimes used to refer to the Norsirai nations of the Three Seas.

Mimara (4095–)—Esmenet's first-born daughter.

Mimaripal (4067–)—A client baron of Chinjosa.

Ministrate—The Zaudunyani organization dedicated to the conversion of the Orthodox.

Min-Uroikas—"Pit of Obscenities" (Ihrimsû) The Nonman name for Golgotterath. See *Cûno-Inchoroi Wars*.

Miracle of the Circumfixion—The second of the Warrior-Prophet's three so-called "Miracles," referring to his survival of the Circumfix in Caraskand.

Miracle of Water—The first of the Warrior-Prophet's three so-called "Miracles," referring to his discovery of water in the wastes of Khemema.

Misarat—An immense Kianene fortress located on the northwestern frontier of Eumarna.

Mog-Pharau—The ancient Kûniüric name for "No-God." See *No-God*.

Mohaïva—A district of Nilnamesh.

Momas—The God of storms, seas, and chance. One of the so-called Compensatory Gods, who reward devotion in life with paradise in the afterlife, Momas is the primary deity worshipped by seamen and merchants, and is the patron divinity of Cironj (and to a lesser extent Nron). In the *Higarata*, he is depicted as cruel, even malicious, and obsessed with minute matters of propriety—leading some commentators to suggest he is in fact a Bellicose, as opposed to a Compensatory, God. His primary device is the White Triangle on Black (representing the Shark's Tooth worn by all devotees of Momas).

Momemn—"Praise Momas" (Kyranean) The administrative and commercial capital of the Nansurium. Heavily fortified, Momemn houses the residence of the Nansur Emperor, as well as one of the busiest harbours on the Three Seas. Historians have oft noted how each of the three capitals (Mehtsonc, Cenei, and Momemn) of the three great empires to arise from the Kyranae Plain have stood along the River Phayus, each closer than the last to the Meneanor. Some claim that Momemn, which stands at the river's mouth, will be the last, thus leading to the common phrase "running out of river" to indicate changing fortunes.

Mongilea—A governorate of Kian and former province of the Nansur Empire, located along the coasts adjacent to the River Sweki. Long a tributary land, Mongilea has exchanged masters many times. As the original conquest of Fan'oukarji I (3759), it has become the "Green Homeland" of the Kianene, and a famed producer of horses.

Moraör—"Hall of Kings" (Old Meoric) The famed palace complex of Galeoth's rulers, located in Oswenta.

Morghund, House—The ruling dynasty of Atrithau since 3817.

Moserothu—An Ainoni city located in the heart of the populous Secharib Plains.

Mother-of-Cities—See *Trysë*.

Mount Eshki—The legendary "Mountain of Revelation" where, according to *The Chronicle of the Tusk*, the Prophet Angeshraël received the call to lead the Tribes of Men into Eärwa.

Mount Kinsureah—The legendary "Mountain of Summoning" where, according to *The Chronicle of the Tusk*, the Prophet Angeshraël sacrificed Oresh, the youngest of his sons by Esmenet, to demonstrate his conviction to the Tribes of Men.

Mouth-of-the-Worm—A Yatwerian temple in Carythusal, so named because of its proximity to the slums commonly called the Worm.

Munuäti—A powerful Scylvendi tribe from the interior of the Jiünati Steppe.

Muretetis (2789–2864)—An ancient Ceneian scholar-slave famed for his *Axioms and Theorems*, the founding text of Three Seas geometry.

Mursiris—"Wicked North" (Ham-Kheremic) The ancient Shiradi name for the No-God, so named because his presence was for so long sensed only as an intimation of doom on the northern horizon.

Myclai—The ancient administrative and commercial capital of Akksersia, destroyed in 2149 during the Apocalypse.

Mygella, Anasûrimbor (2065–2111)—The famed Hero-King of Aörsi, whose deeds are recounted in *The Sagas*.

Mysunsai—"The Bond of Three" (Vaparsi) The self-proclaimed "mercenary School," which sells its sorcerous services across the Three Seas. Perhaps the largest of the Anagogic Schools, though far from the most powerful, the Mysunsai are a commercial result of the 3804 defensive amalgamation of three minor Schools during the Scholastic Wars: the Mikka Council from Cironji, the Oaranat from Nilnamesh, and the (Cengemic) Nilitar Compact from Ce Tydonn. Under the terms of the infamous Psailian Concession during the Scholastic Wars, the Mysunsai assisted the Inrithi in their Ainoni campaigns, an act for which the School was never forgiven, though it did much to confirm the School's exclusive commercial interests to its customers.

N

Nabathra—A mid-sized town in the province of Anserca, whose markets control the regional distribution of wool, the province's primary commodity.

Nagogris—A large New Dynasty city on the upper River Sempis, famed for her red sandstone fortifications.

nahat—See *castes*.

Nail of Heaven—The northern star that, aside from being the brightest in the night sky (it is sometimes visible in daylight), provides the axis from which all other stars revolve.

Naïn (4071–4111)—A sorcerer of rank in the Scarlet Spires, slain by Chorae at Anwurat.

Nangael—A fiefdom of Ce Tydonn, located along the Swa Marches. Nangael warriors can be readily identified by their tattooed cheeks.

Nanor-Ukkerja I (1378–1556)—"Hammer of Heaven" (Kûniüric from Umeritic *nanar hukisha*) The first Anasûrimbor High King, whose defeat of the Scintya in 1408 would lead to the founding of Kûniüri and begin what most scholars regard as the longest-reigning dynasty in recorded history.

Nansur—See *Nansur Empire*.

Nansur Empire—A nation of the Three Seas and self-proclaimed inheritor to the Ceneian Empire. At the height of its power the Nansur Empire extended from Galeoth to Nilnamesh, but it has been much reduced by centuries of warfare against the Fanim Kianene.

Though the Nansur Empire has witnessed its fair share of usurpers, palace revolts, and short-lived military dictatorships, it has enjoyed a remarkable degree of dynastic stability. It was under the Trimus Emperors (3411–3508) that the "Nansur" (the traditional name for the district surrounding Momemn) emerged from the chaos following Cenei's destruction to unify the Kyranae plains. But true Imperial expansion did not occur until the Zerxei Dynasty (3511–3619), which, under the rule of successive and short-lived Emperors, managed to conquer Shigek (3539), Enathpaneah (3569), and the Sacred Lands (3574).

Under the Surmante Emperors (3619–3941), the Nansurium enjoyed its greatest period of growth and military ascendancy, culminating in the rule of Surmante Xatantius I (3644–93), who subdued the Cepaloran tribes as far north as the Vindauga River, and who even managed to capture the ancient Nilnameshi capital of Invishi, thus very nearly restoring all the so-called Western Empire that had once belonged to Cenei. But his practice of debasing the talent in order to finance his endless wars fairly wrecked the empire's economy. By the time Fan'oukarji I embarked on his White Jihad in 3743, the empire still had not recovered from Xatantius's excesses. His Surmante descendants found themselves embroiled in never-ending wars they could ill afford, let alone win. Scarce resources and an intransigent commitment to the Ceneian model of warfare, which seemed incapable of coping with Kianene tactics, conspired to render the empire's decline an inevitability.

The dynasty of the most recent claimants to the Imperial Mantle, the Ikurei, arose as the result of a coup brought about by the turmoil following the loss of Shigek to the Kianene in 3933 (in the so-called Dagger Jihad of Fan'oukarji III). A former Exalt-General, Ikurei Sorius I reorganized both the Imperial Army and the empire, changes that allowed him and his descendants to defeat no fewer than three full-scale Fanim invasions. The Nansur Empire has enjoyed a precarious stability ever since, though it remains continually fearful of the prospect that the Scylvendi tribes might unite once again.

Nansurium—See *Nansur Empire.*

Narradha, Hringa (4093–4111)—The youngest brother of Prince Hringa Skaiyelt, slain at Mengedda.

Nascenti—The nine primary disciples of Anasûrimbor Kellhus, the so-called "Thanes of the Warrior-Prophet."

Nasueret Column—Also known as the "Ninth Column." A Column of the Nansur Imperial Army, traditionally stationed on the Kianene frontier. Their device is the Black Imperial Sun halved by an eagle's wing.

Nau-Cayûti (2119–40)—"Blessed Son" (Umeritic) The youngest son of Celmomas II and the famed "scourge of Golgotterath." Nau-Cayûti is famed for his heroism and martial brilliance during the dark days after the fall of Aörsi (2136), when Kûniüri stood alone against Golgotterath. Many of his exploits, such as the Slaying of Tanhafut the Red and the Theft of the Heron Spear, are recounted in *The Sagas.*

Naures River—An important river system in eastern Nilnamesh.

Nautzera, Seidru (4038–)—A senior member of the Mandate Quorum. See *Mandate, School of.*

Near Antiquity—Sometimes called the Ceneian Age. The historical period beginning in 2155 (the end of the Apocalypse) and ending with the Sack of Cenei in 3351. See *Far Antiquity.*

Neleöst Sea—A large inland sea located in northwestern Eärwa that formed the traditional northern frontier for those nations arising from the Aumris River Valley.

Nenciphon—The administrative capital of Kian, and one of the great cities of the Three Seas, founded by Fan'oukarji I in 3752.

Nergaöta—A semi-mountainous fiefdom in northwestern Galeoth, renowned for the quality of its wool.

Nersei, House—The ruling House of Conriya since the Aöknyssian Uprisings of 3942, which saw the entire line of King Nejata Medekki murdered. The Black Eagle on White is their device.

Nerum—A minor port city and the administrative capital of Jurisada, located on the coast just south of Amoteu.

Neuropuncture—The Dûnyain art of producing various behaviours by probing the exposed brain with fine needles.

Ngarau (4062–)—The Grand Seneschal to Ikurei Xerius III.

Nil'giccas (?–)—The Nonman King of Ishterebinth.

Nilnamesh—A populous Ketyai nation on the extreme southwest edge of the Three Seas, famed for its ceramics, spices, and stubborn refusal to relinquish its exotic versions of Kiünnat either to Inrithism or to Fanimry. Primarily for geographical reasons, the fertile plains to the south of the Hinayati Mountains have long enjoyed cultural and political independence from the Three Seas. Casidas was the first to remark that the Nilnameshi were an "inward people," both in the sense of their obsession with the plight of their souls and in their utter disdain for outland Princes. Only two periods in their history cut against this tendency. The first is the Old Invishi period (1023–1572), when Nilnamesh was united under a series of aggressively expansionist Kings based in Invishi, which is now the traditional spiritual capital of Nilnamesh. In 1322 and then again in 1326, Anzumarapata II inflicted crushing defeats on the Shigeki, and for some thirty years compelled tribute from the proud river kingdom. Then, in 2483, Sarnagiri V, leading a coalition of Princes, was routed by Triamis the Great, and Nilnamesh found itself a province (albeit an unruly one) for more than a thousand years.

    The era following the collapse of the Ceneian Empire is commonly called the New Invishi period, though none of the ancient city's Kings has been able to hold more than a fraction of Nilnamesh for more than a generation.

Nimeric, Anasûrimbor (2092–2135)—The High King of ancient Aörsi before its destruction in the Apocalypse. See *Apocalypse*.

nimil—The Nonmen steel forged in the sorcerous furnaces of Ishterebinth.

Nincaerû-Telesser (c. 549–642)—The fourth God-King of the Umeri Empire, and famed patron of the ancient Gnostic Schools.

Nin-Ciljiras (?–)—The last surviving Nonman King.

Nine Great Gates—The epithet given to the main gates of Sumna.

Nirsodic—The language group of ancient Norsirai pastoralists ranging from the Sea of Cerish to the Sea of Jorua.

No-God—Also known as Mog-Pharau, Tsurumah, and Mursiris. The entity summoned by the Consult to bring about the Apocalypse. Very little is known about the No-God, save that he utterly lacks remorse or compassion and possesses terrible power, including the ability to control Sranc, Bashrag, and Wracu as extensions of his own will. Because of his armour (the so-called Carapace), which eyewitnesses describe as an iron sarcophagus suspended in the heart of a mountainous whirlwind, it is not even known whether he is a creature of flesh or of spirit. According to Mandate scholars, the Inchoroi worship him as their saviour, as do—according to some—the Scylvendi.

Somehow, his mere existence is antithetical to human life: during the entirety of the Apocalypse, not one infant drew breath—all were stillborn. He is apparently immune to sorcery (according to legend, eleven Chorae are embedded in the Carapace). The Heron Spear is the only known weapon that can harm him.

See *Apocalypse.*

Nomur (?–?)—One of the Chieftain-Kings named in the Tusk.

Nonman King—The poetic name of Cu'jara Cinmoi in the High Norsirai bardic tradition.

Nonmen—At one time the pre-eminent race of Eärwa, but now much reduced. The Nonmen call themselves *ji'cûnû roi,* "the People of Dawn," for reasons they can no longer remember. (They call Men *j'ala roi,* "the People of Summer," because they burn so hot and pass so quickly.) *The Chronicle of the Tusk,* which records the coming of Men to Eärwa, generally refers to Nonmen as Oserukki, the "Not Us." In the Book of Tribes, the Prophet Angeshraël alternately refers to them as "the Accursed Ones" and "the sodomite Kings of Eärwa," and he incites the Four Nations of Men to embark on a holy war of extermination. Even after four millennia, this xenocidal mission remains part of the Inrithi canon. According to the Tusk, the Nonmen are anathema:

Hearken, for this the God has said,
"These False Men offend Me;
blot out all mark of their Passing."

But Cûnuroi civilization was ancient even before these words were carved into the Tusk. While the Halaroi, Men, wandered the world dressed in skins and wielding weapons of stone, the Cûnuroi had invented writing and mathematics, astrology and geometry, sorcery and philosophy. They dredged mountains hollow for the galleries of their High Mansions. They traded and warred with one another. They subdued all Eärwa, enslaving the Emwama, the soft-hearted Men who dwelt in Eärwa in those early days.

Their decline is the result of three different catastrophic events. The first, and most significant, was the so-called Womb-Plague. In the hope of achieving immortality, the Nonmen (specifically, the great Cu'jara Cinmoi) allowed the Inchoroi to live among them as their physicians. The Nonmen did in fact attain immortality, and the Inchoroi, claiming their work done, retired back to the Incû-Holoinas. The plague struck shortly after, almost killing males and uniformly killing all females. The Nonmen call this tragic event the Nasamorgas, the "Death of Birth."

The following Cûno-Inchoroi Wars further sapped their strength, so that by the time the first Tribes of Men invaded, the Nonmen had not the numbers or, some say, the will to resist their advance. Within the course of a few generations they were nearly exterminated. Only the Mansions of Ishoriol and Cil-Aujas survived.

See *Cûno-Inchoroi Wars*.

Nonmen Tutelage—The great period of Norsirai–Cûnuroi trade, education, and strategic alliances, beginning in 555 and ending with the Expulsion in 825 (following the famed Rape of Omindalea).

Norsirai—The typically blond-haired, blue-eyed, fair-skinned race predominantly concentrated along the northern fringe of the Three Seas, although they once ruled all the lands north to the Yimaleti Mountains. One of the Five Tribes of Men.

noschi—A Kûniüric term meaning "source of light," but used in the sense of "genius" as well.

Noshainrau the White (c. 1005–72)—The founding Grandmaster of the Sohonc and author of the *Interrogations*, the first elaboration of the Gnosis by Men.

Nron—A minor island nation of the Three Seas, nominally independent but in fact dominated by the School of Mandate in Atyersus.

Nroni—The language of Nron, a derivative of Sheyo-Kheremic.

Numaineiri—A populous and fertile fiefdom of interior Ce Tydonn, located to the west of Meigeiri. Numaineiri warriors are known to paint their faces red whenever they believe themselves doomed in battle.

number-sticks—A means of generating random numerical results for the purposes of gambling. The first references to number-sticks reach as far back as ancient Shigek. The most common variations consist of two sticks typically referred to as the Fat and the Skinny. A groove is carved all the way through the Fat so that the Skinny can drop up and down its interior length. The Skinny is then capped on either end to prevent it from falling out. Numerical values are marked along the length of the Fat, so that when the sticks are thrown, the Skinny can indicate a result.

Numemarius, Thallei (4069–4111)—The Patridomos of House Thallei, and General of the Kidruhil until his death in Nagogris.

Nymbricani—A tribe of Norsirai pastoralists who range southern Cepalor.

Nyranisas Sea—The easternmost of the Three Seas.

O

Oknai One-Eye (4053–4110)—The inveterate chieftain of the Munuäti, a powerful federation of Scylvendi tribes.

Okyati urs Okkiür (4038–82)—The cousin of Cnaiür urs Skiötha, who first brought Anasûrimbor Moënghus as a captive to the Utemot camp in 4080.

Old Ainoni—The language of Ceneian Ainon, a derivative of Ham-Kheremic.

Old Father—An epithet used by skin-spies to describe their Consult makers.

Old Meöric—The lost language of the early Meöri Empire, a derivative of Nirsodic.

Old Name—A term referring to the original members of the Consult.

Old Science—See *Tekne*.

Old Scylvendi—The language of ancient Scylvendi pastoralists, a derivative of Skaaric.

Old Zeümi—The language of Angka (ancient Zeüm), a derivative of Ankmuri.

Olekaros (2881–2956)—A Ceneian slave-scholar of Cironji descent, famed for his *Avowals*.

omen-texts—The traditional indexes, usually specific to each of the Cults, detailing the various omens and their meaning.

Omiri urs Xunnurit (4089–4111)—The lame daughter of Xunnurit and wife of Yursalka.

Oncis Sea—The westernmost of the Three Seas.

111 Aphorisms—A minor work of Ekyannus VIII, consisting of 111 aphorisms that primarily deal with matters of faith and integrity.

"one lamb for ten bulls"—A saying that refers to the relative difference in value between a witting and an unwitting sacrificial victim.

Onkis—The Goddess of hope and aspiration. One of the so-called Compensatory Gods, who reward devotion in life with paradise in the afterlife, Onkis draws followers from all walks of life, though rarely in great numbers. She is only mentioned twice in the *Higarata*, and in the (likely apocryphal) *Parnishtas* she is portrayed as a prophetess, not of the future, but of the motivations of Men. The so-called "shakers" belong to an extreme branch of the Cult, where the devotees ritually strive to be "possessed" by the Goddess. Her symbol is the Copper Tree (which also happens to be the device of the legendary Nonman Mansion of Siol, though no link has been established).

"Only the Few can see the Few"—The traditional expression used to refer to the unique ability of sorcerers to "see" both the practitioners and the products of sorcery.

Onoyas II, Nersei (3823–78)—The King of Conriya who first forged the alliance between the School of Mandate and House Nersei.

onta—The name given by the Schools to the very fabric of what is.

On the Carnal—The most famous of Opparitha's exhortatory works, popular among lay readers though widely derided by Three Seas intellectuals.

On the Folly of Men—The magnum opus of the famed satirist Ontillas.

On the Temples and Their Iniquities—A quasi-heretical Sareot text.

Ontillas (2875–2933)—The near antique Ceneian satirist most famous for his *On the Folly of Men*.

Opparitha (3211–99)—The near antique Cengemian moralist most famous for his *On the Carnal*.

Opsara (4074–)—A Kianene slave who serves as the infant Moënghus's wet nurse.

Ordeal, the—Sometimes referred to as the Great Ordeal. The tragic holy war Anasûrimbor Celmomas called against Golgotterath in 2123. See *Apocalypse*.

Orthodox—The name taken by the Inrithi opponents of the Zaudunyani during the siege of Caraskand.

Osbeus—A basalt quarry used in Near and Far Antiquity, located near the ruins of Mehtsonc.

Osthwai Mountains—A major mountain range located in central Eärwa.

Oswenta—The administrative and commercial capital of Galeoth, located on the north coast of Lake Huösi.

Other Voice—The name given to the "voice" used to communicate in all Cants of Calling.

Othrain, Eorcu (4060–4111)—The Tydonni Earl of Numaineiri, slain at Mengedda.

Ottma, Cwithar (4073–)—One of the Nascenti, formerly a Tydonni thane.

Outside—That which lies beyond the World. Most commentators follow Ajencis's so-called Dyadic Theory when characterizing the World and its relation to the Outside. In *Meta-Analytics*, Ajencis argues that it is the relation between subject and object, desire and reality, that underwrites the structure of existence. The World, he argues, is simply the point of maximal objectivity, the plane where the desires of individual souls are helpless before circumstance (because it is fixed by the desire of the God of Gods). The many regions of the Outside then represent diminishing levels of objectivity, where circumstances yield more and more to desire. This, he claims, is what defines the "spheres of dominance" of Gods and demons. As he writes, "the greater will commands." The more powerful entities of the Outside dwell in "sub-realities" that conform to their desires. This is what makes piety and devotion so important: the more favour an individual can secure in the Outside (primarily through the worship of Gods and the honouring of ancestors), the greater the chance of finding bliss rather than torment in the afterlife.

Over-Standard—The sacred military standard of the Nansur Exalt-General, decorated with the disc-shaped breastplate of Kuxophus II, the last of the ancient Kyranean High Kings. Imperial Columnaries often refer to it as "the Concubine."

P

Paäta (4062–4111) A body-slave belonging to Krijates Xinemus, slain in Khemema.

Padirajah—The traditional title of the ruler of Kian.

Palpothis—One of the famed Ziggurats of Shigek, named after Palpothis III (622–78), the Old Dynasty God-King who raised her.

Panteruth urs Mutkius (4075–4111)—A Scylvendi of the Munuäti tribe.

Parrhae Plains—A region of fertile tablelands located in northwestern Galeoth.

Pasna—A town on the River Phayus, known for the quality of its olive oil.

pembeditari—A common pejorative used for camp prostitutes, meaning "scratchers."

pemembis—A wild bush prized for its fragrant blue blooms.

peneditari—A common name given to camp prostitutes, meaning "long-walkers."

perrapta—A traditional Conriyan liquor, often used to inaugurate meals.

Persommas, Hagum (4078–)—One of the Nascenti, formerly a Nansur blacksmith.

Pharixas—A disputed island stronghold in the Meneanor Sea.

Phayus River—The primary river system of the Kyranae Plains, draining the south central Hethanta Mountains and emptying into the Meneanor Sea.

Pherokar I (3666–3821)—One of Kian's earliest and fiercest Padirajahs.

pick—A derogatory term often used by Norsirai when referring to Ketyai. The word comes from the Tydonni *pikka*, or "slave," but has come to have broader, racial connotations.

Pilaskanda (4060–)—The King of Girgash and a tributary ally of the Kianene Padirajah.

Pirasha—An old Sumni whore befriended by Esmenet.

Pisathulas—The personal eunuch attendant of Ikurei Istriya.

Plaideöl—A fiefdom of Ce Tydonn, one of the "Deep Marches" above the eastern headwaters of the River Swa. Plaideölmen are famed for their ferocity in battle, and are easily distinguished by their great beards, which they never trim.

Pon Way—An old Ceneian road that runs northwest from Momemn parallel to the River Phayus and serves as one of the Nansurium's primary commercial arteries.

Poripharus—An ancient Ceneian philosopher and adviser to Triamis the Great, famed for drafting the Triamic Code, the body of laws that forms the basis of legal practice in most Three Seas nations (with the notable exception of Kian).

Possessors of the Third Sight—An alternate name for the Cishaurim, so called because of their reputed ability to see without their eyes.

Pragma—The title given to the most senior of the Dûnyain.

Prima Arcanata, The—The magnum opus of Gotagga, representing the first sustained examination of sorcerous metaphysics by Men.

Prince of God—One of several names given to the Warrior-Prophet by the Men of the Tusk.

Principle of Before and After—Also known as the Empirical Priority Principle. See *Dûnyain*.

Proadjunct—The highest non-commissioned rank in the Imperial Nansur Army.

Probability Trance—A meditation technique used by the Dûnyain to assess consequences of hypothetical acts in order to determine the course of action that will most effectively allow them to master their circumstances.

Prophet of the Tusk—The name given to the prophets depicted in *The Chronicle of the Tusk*.

Prophilas, Harus (4064–)—The commander of Asgilioch.

Protathis (2870–2922)—A famed near antique poet of Ceneian descent, celebrated for many works, including *The Goat's Heart*, *One Hundred Heavens*, and the magisterial *Aspirations*. Protathis is regarded by many as the greatest Ketyai poet.

Proto-Caro-Shemic—The language group of the ancient pastoralists of the Eastern Carathay Desert, a derivative of Shemic.

Psailas II (4009–86)—The Shriah of the Thousand Temples from 4072 to 4086.

Psammatus, Nentepi (4059–)—A Sumni Shrial priest of Shigeki descent, and regular customer of Esmenet's.

Psûkalogues, The—The magnum opus of Imparrhas, sorcerer of the Imperial Saik and esoteric metaphysician primarily interested in the Psûkhe of the Cishaurim.

psûkari—Practitioners of the Psûkhe.

Psûkhe—The arcane practice of the Cishaurim, much like sorcery, though cruder in its exercise, and distinguished by its invisibility to the Few. See *sorcery*.

Pulit—A tribe of Scylvendi from the southern desert fringes of the Jiünati Steppe.

Q

Quandary of Man—The classic Dûnyain problem referring to the fact that Men, though beasts like other beasts, can apprehend the Logos.

Quorum—The ruling council of the Mandate.

Quya—The generic name for Nonmen Magi.

R

Rash (4073–4112)—The nickname of Houlta, a caste-menial Zaudunyani agitator, slain in the Battle of Caraskand.

Rauschang, Hringa (4054–)—The King of Thunyerus and father of Skaiyelt and Hulwarga.

Restored Empire—For some in Nansur, the cherished goal of restoring all the "lost provinces" (the territories seized by the Kianene) to the Nansur Empire.

Ring Mountains—The range that encircles Golgotterath.

Rite-of-the-Spring-Wolves—A rite of passage marking the transition of Scylvendi adolescent boys to manhood.

Rohil River—The easternmost of the three major river systems draining into Lake Huösi.

Ruminations—The magnum opus of Stajanus II, the so-called Philosopher-Emperor who ruled Cenei from 2412 to 2431.

Ruöm—The innermost citadel of Asgilioch, often called the High Bull of Asgilioch, destroyed by an earthquake in 4111.

S

Sacred Lands—A name for Xerash and Amoteu, the two lands that figure directly in *The Tractate*.

Sagas, The—A collection of epic lays that recount the Apocalypse. It primarily consists of "The Kelmariad," the story of Anasûrimbor Celmomas and his tragic Ordeal; "The Kayûtiad," the account of Celmomas's son, Nau-Cayûti, and his heroic exploits; "The Book of Generals," the story of the deceptive events following Nau-Cayûti's murder; "The Trisiad," which recounts the great city's destruction; "The Eämnoriad," the story of ancient Atrithau's expulsion of Seswatha and subsequent survival; "The Annal Akksersa," which recounts the Fall of Akksersia; and lastly, "The Annal Sakarpa," or "The Refugee's Song" as it is sometimes called, the strange account of the city of Sakarpus during the Apocalypse.

Despite the scorn of Mandate scholars (or perhaps because of it), *The Sagas* possess an almost scriptural reputation in the Three Seas.

Saik—The Anagogic School based in Momemn and indentured to the Nansur Emperor. The Saik, or the Imperial Saik as they are often called, are the institutional descendants of the Saka, the notorious state-sanctioned School of Imperial Cenei, who for a thousand years dominated the Three Seas under the aegis of the Aspect-Emperors. Though still considered a Major School, the Saik have dwindled in strength, their resources limited by Nansur's losses and their numbers diminished by continual skirmishing with the Cishaurim. Also known as "Sorcerers of the Sun."

saka'ilrait—"Trail of Skulls" (Khirgwi) The Khirgwi name for the route taken by the Holy War across Khemema.

Sakarpic—The language of Sakarpus, a derivative of Skettic.

Sakarpus—A city of the Ancient North located in the heart of the Istyuli Plains, and, aside from Atrithau, the only city to survive the Old Wars.

Sakthuta—A mountain in the Hethantas overlooking the River Kiyuth.

Sanathi (4100–)—The daughter of Cnaiür and Anissi.

Sancla (4064–83)—Achamian's cellmate and lover during his adolescence in Atyersus.

Sansor—A nation of the Three Seas tributary to High Ainon.

Sansori—The language of Sansor, a derivative of Sheyo-Kheremic.

Sapatishah-Governor—The title of the regional, semi-autonomous rulers of the various provinces of Kian.

Sapatishah's Palace—The name given by the Men of the Tusk to Imbeyan's palace in Caraskand, located on the Kneeling Heights.

Sapmatari—The lost language of Nilnameshi labouring castes, a derivative of Vaparsi.

Sappathurai—A powerful mercantile city in Nilnamesh.

Sarcellus, Cutias (4072–99)—A Knight-Commander of the Shrial Knights, murdered and replaced by Consult skin-spies.

Sareotic Library—In the time of the Ceneian Empire, one of the greatest libraries in the known world. The so-called "script law" of Iothiah forced, on punishment of death, all visitors bearing books to surrender them for copying and inclusion in the Library. Though the Sareots were massacred when Shigek fell to the Fanim in 3933, Padirajah Fan'oukarji III spared the Library, thinking it the will of the Solitary God.

Sarothesser I (3317–3402)—The founder of High Ainon, who overthrew the yoke of the Ceneian Empire in 3372 and ascended the Assurkamp Throne as the first Ainoni King.

Sasheoka (4049–4100)—The Grandmaster of the Scarlet Spires, assassinated in 4100 by the Cishaurim for reasons unknown, and predecessor to Eleäzaras.

Saskri River—A major river system in Eumarna, with headwaters in Eshgarnea and draining the Jahan Plains.

Sassotian, Pomarius (4058–4111)—The General of the Imperial Fleet during the First Holy War, slain at the Battle of Trantis Bay.

Sathgai—The Norsirai name for Uthgai, Chieftain of the Utemot and legendary Scylvendi King-of-Tribes, who led the People under the No-God during the Apocalypse.

Satiothi—The language group of the Satyothi peoples.

Satyothi—The black-haired, green-eyed, black-skinned race predominantly concentrated in the nation of Zeüm and the southern extremities of the Three Seas. One of the Five Tribes of Men.

Saubon, Coithus (4069–)—The seventh son of King Coithus Eryeat of Galeoth and titular leader of the Galeoth contingent of the Holy War.

Sauglish—One of the four great ancient cities of the Aumris Valley, destroyed in the Apocalypse in 2147. From the early days of the Nonmen Tutelage, Sauglish was established as the intellectual capital of the Ancient North, home to the first Gnostic Schools and to the Great Library of Sauglish. See *Library of Sauglish* and *Apocalypse*.

Sayut River—One of the great rivers of Eärwa, originating in the Southern Great Kayarsus and draining into the Nyranisas.

Scaralla, Hepma (4056–4111)—The ranking high priest of Akkeägni during the First Holy War, taken by disease at Caraskand.

Scarlet Magi—A name for Schoolmen belonging to the Scarlet Spires.

Scarlet Spires—The most powerful School of the Three Seas and de facto ruler of High Ainon. The roots of the Scarlet Spires reach as far back as ancient Shir (to this day traditionalists within the School refer to themselves as the "shiradi"). In many ways the development of the Scarlet Spires exemplifies the development of every Three Seas School, that of loose networks of sorcerous practitioners becoming progressively more organized and insular in the face of chronic, religiously motivated persecution. Originally called the Surartu—"Hooded Singers" (Ham-Kheremic)—the Scarlet Spires secured the river fortress of Kiz in Carythusal *c.* 1800, and emerged from the chaos surrounding the Apocalypse, the collapse of Shir, and the Great Pestilence as one of the most powerful factions in ancient Ainon. Sometime around 2350, Kiz was severely damaged in an earthquake and subsequently covered with red enamel tiles in the reconstruction, thus leading to the School's now-famous moniker.

Scholastic Wars—A series of holy wars waged against the Schools from 3796 to 3818. Called by Ekyannus XIV, the Scholastic Wars saw the near-destruction of several Schools and the beginning of the Scarlet Spires' hegemony over High Ainon.

Schoolmen—Sorcerers belonging to the Schools.

Schools—Given the Tusk's condemnation of sorcery, the first Schools, in both the Ancient North and the Three Seas, arose out of the need for protection. The so-called "Major Schools" of the Three Seas are the Circle of Nibel, the Imperial Saik, the School of Mandate, the Mysunsai, and the Scarlet Spires. The Schools are among the oldest institutions in the Three

Seas, surviving, by and large, both because of the terror they inspire and by their detachment from the secular and religious powers of the Three Seas. With the exception of the Mysunsai, all the Major Schools predate the fall of the Ceniean Empire.

Scindia—The Scylvendi-dominated land to the immediate west of the Hethanta Mountains.

Scorpion Braid—A mummer's trick, consisting of a rope soaked in a poison that makes the jaws and claws of scorpions seize when they grasp it.

Scoulas, Biaxi (4075–4111)—The second Knight-Commander of the Shrial Knights, slain at Mengedda.

Scuäri Campus—The main parade ground of the Imperial Precincts in Momemn.

Sculpa River—The northernmost of the three major river systems draining into Lake Huösi.

Scylvendi—The dark-haired, pale-blue-eyed, and fair-skinned race predominantly concentrated in and around the Jiünati Steppe. One of the Five Tribes of Men.

Seat, the—A symbolic name for the station of Shriah.

Secharib Plains—The vast alluvial tablelands that sweep north from the River Sayut in High Ainon, noted for their fertility (sixty- to seventy-fold crop yields) and dense population.

Second Apocalypse—The hypothetical catastrophe that will inevitably befall Eärwa should the No-God ever walk again. According to the Mandate tradition, Anasûrimbor Celmomas, the High King of Kûniüri during the Apocalypse, prophesied that the No-God will in fact return. The prevention of the Second Apocalypse is the Mandate's ultimate goal.

Seleukara—The commercial capital of Kian, and one of the great cities of the Three Seas.

Selial Column—A division of the Imperial Nansur Army traditionally stationed on the Kianene frontier.

"selling peaches …"—A common Three Seas euphemism for selling sex.

Sempis River—One of the great river systems of Eärwa, draining vast tracts of the Jiünati Steppe and emptying into the Meneanor Sea.

Seökti (4051–)—The Heresiarch of the Cishaurim.

Sepherathindor (4065–4111)—The Count-Palatine of the Ainoni palatinate of Hinnant, claimed by disease at Caraskand.

Seswatha (2089–2168)—The founder of the School of Mandate and implacable enemy of the Consult throughout the Apocalypse. Born the caste-menial son of a Trysean bronzesmith, Seswatha was identified as one of the Few at a very young age and brought to Sauglish to study with the Gnostic School of Sohonc. A prodigy, he became the youngest sorcerer of rank in the history of the Sohonc at the age of fifteen. During this time he became fast friends with Anasûrimbor Celmomas, a so-called "Hostage of the Sohonc," as the School referred to its resident exoteric students. As this strategic friendship might suggest, Seswatha proved an adroit political operator, both before becoming Grandmaster and after, forging relationships with important personages across the Three Seas, including Nil'giccas, the Nonman King of Ishterebinth, and Anaxophus, who would become the High King of Kyraneas. These skills, in addition to his peerless command of the Gnosis, would make him the natural, if not the titular, leader of the various wars waged against the Consult before the Apocalypse. He and Celmomas would become estranged during this time, apparently because Celmomas resented Seswatha's influence over his youngest son, Nau-Cayûti, but legends have long circulated that Nau-Cayûti was in fact Seswatha's son, the product of an illicit union between him and Sharal, the most prized of Celmomas's wives. They would not be reconciled until the eve of the Apocalypse—after it was far too late. See *Apocalypse*.

Seswatha's Dreams—See *Dreams, the.*

Seswatha's Heart—The mummified heart of Seswatha, which is the key artifact in the so-called Grasping, the sorcerous rites that transfer Seswatha's memories of the Apocalypse to Mandate Schoolmen. See *Mandate, School of.*

Setpanares (4059–4111)—The General in command of the Ainoni contingent of the First Holy War, slain by Cinganjehoi at Anwurat.

Shaeönanra (*c.* 1086–)—"Gift of Light" (Umeritic) The Grandvizier of the Mangaecca who, according to legend, went mad studying the Incû-Holoinas, and whose subsequent acts would eventually see him convicted of impiety and his School outlawed in 1123. The greatest prodigy of his age, Shaeönanra claimed to have rediscovered a means of saving the souls of those damned by sorcery. He reputedly spent his life investigating various soul-trapping sorceries in the hope of avoiding passage to the Outside—and to great effect, given that he allegedly continues to live some three thousand years afterward, though in an obscene and unnatural manner. By the fourteenth century the Trysean annals began referring to him as Shauriatas, the "Cheater of Gods."

Shakers—The name given to extreme devotees of Onkis who claim that their fits of shaking are the result of divine possession.

Shanipal, Kemrates (4066–)—The Baron of Hirhamet, a district in south central Conriya.

Shaul River—The second most important river system in the Nansur Empire, after the Phayus.

Shauriatas (*c*. 1086–)—"Cheater of Gods" (Umeritic) See *Shaeönanra*.

Shelgal (?–?)—One of the Chieftain-Kings named in the Tusk.

Shemic—The language group of the ancient non-Nilnameshi pastoralists of the southwestern Three Seas.

Shem-Varsi—The language group of the proto-Nilnameshi pastoralists of the southwestern Three Seas.

Sheyic—The language of the Ceneian Empire, which still serves, in debased form, as the liturgical language of the Thousand Temples and as the "common tongue" of the Three Seas.

Sheyo-Buskrit—The language of Nilnameshi labouring castes, a derivative of High Sheyic and Sapmatari.

Sheyo-Kheremic—The lost language of the lower castes of the Eastern Ceneian Empire.

Sheyo-Xerashi—The language of Xerash, a derivative of Xerashi and High Sheyic.

Shield-Breaker, the—A common name for Gilgaöl, God of War.

Shigek—A governorate of Kian and former province of the Nansur Empire. Located on the fertile delta and alluvial plains of the River Sempis, Shigek was the ancient competitor of Kyraneas and the first civilized nation of the Three Seas.

Shigek reached the height of her power during the so-called Old Dynasty period, when a succession of Shigeki God-Kings extended their dominion to the limits of the Kyranae Plains in the north and to ancient Eumarna to the south. Great cities (of which only Iothiah survives) and monumental works, including the famed Ziggurats, were raised along the River Sempis. At some point in the twelfth century various Ketyai tribes began asserting their independence on the Kyranae

Plains, and the God-Kings found themselves waging incessant war. Then, in 1591, the God-King Mithoser II was decisively defeated by the Kyraneans at Narakit, and Shigek began its long tenure as a tributary to greater powers. It was most recently conquered in 3933 by the Fanim hosts of Fan'oukarji III. Much to the dismay of the Thousand Temples, the Kianene method of simply taxing non-believers—as opposed to out-and-out persecuting them—led to the wholesale conversion of the populace to Fanimry within a few short generations.

Shikol (2118–2202)—The King of ancient Xerash, famed for sentencing Inri Sejenus to death in 2198, as recounted in *The Tractate*. For obvious reasons, his name has become synonymous with moral corruption among the Inrithi.

Shimeh—The second-holiest city of Inrithism, located in Amoteu, and the site of Inri Sejenus's ascension to the Nail of Heaven.

Shinoth—The legendary main gate of ancient Trysë.

Shir—An ancient city-state on the River Maurat that eventually became the Shiradi Empire. See *Shiradi Empire*.

Shiradi Empire—The first great nation to arise in the eastern Three Seas, where it ruled much of what is now Cengemis, Conriya, and High Ainon for much of Far Antiquity. By *c.* 500 a number of Hamori Ketyai tribes had settled the length of the River Sayut and the Secharib Plains, becoming more sedentary and socially stratified as they exploited the rich cereal yields afforded by the fertile soils of the region. But unlike Shigek, where the first God-Kings were able to unify the Sempis River Valley quite early, Seto-Annaria, as it came to be called (after the two most dominant tribes), remained a collection of warring city-states. Eventually the balance of power shifted to the north, to the city-state of Shir on the River Maurat, and sometime in the thirteenth century it managed to subdue all the cities of Seto-Annaria, though its rulers would spend generations putting down rebellions (the Seto-Annarians apparently thought themselves superior to their uncouth cousins from the north). Then, sometime in the fifteenth century, Xiuhianni invaders from Jekk ravaged the empire and Shir was razed to the ground. The survivors moved the capital to ancient Aöknyssus (the present administrative capital of Conriya), and after some twenty years managed to oust the Eännean invaders. Centuries of stability followed, until 2153, when the forces of the No-God inflicted a disastrous defeat on the Shiradi at the Battle of Nurubal. The following two hundred years of chaos and internecine warfare effectively destroyed what remained of the empire and its central institutions.

The influence of ancient Shir is evident in many respects in the eastern Ketyai nations of the Three Seas, from the revering of beards (first cultivated by caste-nobles to distinguish themselves from the Xiuhianni, who were reputed to be unable to grow beards) to the continued use of a Shiradi-derived pictographic script in High Ainon.

Shortest Way—See *Logos*.

Shriah—The title of the Apostle of the Latter Prophet, the administrative ruler of the Thousand Temples, and the spiritual leader of the Inrithi.

Shrial Apparati—The generic term for career and hereditary functionaries in the Thousand Temples.

Shrial Censure—The excommunication of Inrithi from the Thousand Temples. Since it rescinds all rights to property and vassalage as well as to worship, the worldly consequences of Shrial Censure are often as extreme as the spiritual. When King Sareat II of Galeoth was censured by Psailas II in 4072, for instance, fairly half of his client nobles rebelled, and Sareat was forced to walk barefoot from Oswenta to Sumna in contrition.

Shrial Knights—Also known as Knights of the Tusk. The monastic military order founded by Shriah Ekyannus the Golden in 2511, charged with prosecuting the will of the Shriah.

Shrial Law—The ecclesiastical law of the Thousand Temples, which in a labyrinthine variety of forms serves as the common law for much of the Three Seas, particularly for those areas lacking any strong secular authority.

Shrial Priests—Inrithi clerics who, as opposed to Cultic Priests, are part of the hierarchies of the Thousand Temples, and perform the liturgies of the Latter Prophet and the God rather than those of the Gods.

Shrial Remission—A writ issued by the Thousand Temples absolving an individual of sin. Remissions are commonly awarded to those who accomplish some act of penance, such as joining a pilgrimage or a sanctioned war against unbelievers. Historically, however, they are primarily sold.

Shrial Warrant—A writ issued by the Thousand Temples authorizing the arrest of an individual for the purpose of trial in the ecclesiastical courts.

Sign of Gierra—The twin serpents that Sumni harlots must have tattooed on the back of their left hand, apparently in imitation of the Priestesses of Gierra.

Simas, Polchias (4052–)—Achamian's old teacher and a member of the Quorum, the ruling council of the School of Mandate.

Sinerses (4076–)—A Shield-Captain of the Javreh and favourite of Hanamanu Eleäzaras.

Singer-in-the-Dark—See *Onkis*.

Siqu—Generally, the term referring to Nonmen who find themselves in the service of Men, usually as mercenaries or in some advisory capacity. Specifically, those Nonmen who participated in the so-called Nonmen Tutelage from 555 to 825. See *Nonmen Tutelage*.

Sirol ab Kascamandri (4004–)—The youngest daughter of Kascamandri ab Tepherokar.

Skafadi—A Kianene name for the Scylvendi.

Skafra—One of the principal Wracu, or Dragons, of the Apocalypse, finally slain by Seswatha at Mengedda in 2155.

Skagwa—A fiefdom on the Thunyeri Sranc Marches.

Skaiyelt, Hringa (4073–4111)—The eldest son of King Rauschang of Thunyerus and leader of the Thunyeri contingent of the Holy War. Claimed by disease at Caraskand.

Skalateas (4069–4111)—A member of the Mysunsai School, murdered in the Ansercan countryside by the Scarlet Spires.

Skauras ab Nalajan (4052–4111)—The Sapatishah-Governor of Shigek and the first principal antagonist of the First Holy War, slain at Anwurat. A veteran of many wars, he was deeply respected by both his allies and his enemies. The Nansur called him Sutis Sutadra, the "Southern Jackal," because of his Black Jackal standard.

Skavric—The language group of the Scylvendi peoples.

Skettic—The language group of ancient pastoralists of the Far Istyuli Plains, a derivative of Nirsodic.

Skilura II (3619–68)—Also called "the Mad." The most cruel of the Surmante Emperors of Nansur, whose deranged antics led to the Granary Revolts of 3668 and the accession of Surmante Xatantius I to the Mantle.

Skiötha urs Hannut (4038–79)—The father of Cnaiür urs Skiötha, and former Chieftain of the Utemot.

Skogma—An ancient Wracu thought destroyed during the Cûno-Inchoroi Wars.

Skuthula the Black—An ancient Wracu spawned during the Cûno-Inchoroi Wars, one of the few Dragons known to have survived the Apocalypse, though his present whereabouts are unknown.

Snakeheads—An Inrithi epithet for the Cishaurim.

Sobel—An abandoned province north of Atrithau.

Sodhoras, Nersei (4072–4111)—A Conriyan Baron and cousin of Prince Nersei Proyas.

Sogian Way—A Nansur coastal road first constructed in the age of Kyraneas.

Solitary God—"Allonara Yulah" (Kianni) The name used by Fanim to denote the transcendent singularity of their supreme deity. According to Fanim tradition, the God is not, as the Inrithi claim, immanent in existence, nor is He manifold in the way described by the Latter Prophet.

Sompas, Biaxi (4068–)—The General of the Kidruhil following the death of General Numemarius in Nagogris. Sompas is the eldest son of Biaxi Coronsas, Patridomos of House Biaxi.

Sorainas (3808–95)—A celebrated Nansur scriptural commentator, and author of *The Book of Circles and Spirals*.

sorcerer of rank—Though practices differ extensively between Schools, generally the title given to a sorcerer who is qualified to teach sorcery to another.

Sorcerers of the Sun—A common epithet for the Imperial Saik. See *Saik*.

sorcery—The practice of making the world conform to language, as opposed to philosophy, the practice of making language conform to the world. Despite the tremendous amount of apparently unresolvable controversy surrounding sorcery, there are several salient features that seem universal to its practice. First, practitioners must be able to apprehend the "onta," which is to say, they must possess the innate ability to see, as Protathis puts it, "Creation *as created*." Second, sorcery also seems to involve a universal commitment to what Gotagga calls "semantic hygiene." Sorcery requires precise meanings. This is why incantations are always spoken in a non-native tongue: to prevent the semantic transformation of crucial terms due to the vagaries of daily usage. This also explains the extraordinary "double-think" structure of sorcery, the fact that all incantations require the sorcerer to say and think two separate things *simultaneously*. The spoken segment of an incantation (what is often called the "utteral string") must have its meaning "fixed" or focused with a silent segment (what is often

called the "inutteral string") that is simultaneously thought. Apparently
the thought incantation sharpens the meaning of the spoken incantation
the way the words of one man may be used to clarify the words of another.
(This gives rise to the famous "semantic regress problem": how can the
inutteral string, which admits different interpretations, serve to fix the
proper interpretation of the utteral string?) Though there are as many
metaphysical interpretations of this structure as there are sorcerous
Schools, the result in each case is the same: the world, which is otherwise
utterly indifferent to the words of Men, *listens*, and sorcerous transformations of reality result.

Soroptic—The lost language of ancient Shigek, a derivative of Kemkaric.

Soter, Nurbanu (4069–)—The Palatine of the Ainoni district of Kishyat.

"[The] soul that encounters Him passes no further."—A line from *The
Sagas* referring to the Battleplain and the belief that all those who perish
there remain trapped.

Southern Columns—Those divisions of the Imperial Nansur Army stationed
on the Kianene frontier.

Southron Gates—The series of passes through the Unaras Spur guarded by
Asgilioch.

Sranc—The violent, inhuman creatures first created by the Inchoroi as
instruments of war against the Nonmen. According to the *Isûphiryas*, the
Sranc are one of the "Weapon Races" created by the Inchoroi to prosecute
their war of extermination against the Nonmen and their Emwama slaves.

    The motivations of the Sranc seem to be as base as imaginable, in that
they seem to find sexual gratification in acts of violence. There are innumerable accounts of the indiscriminate rape of men, women, children, and
even corpses. They seem to know nothing of mercy or honour, and though
they do take prisoners, very few are known to have survived captivity,
which is said to be savage beyond imagining.

    They reproduce rapidly. Though no outward physical differences are
readily visible, female Sranc seem to have roles identical to those of male
Sranc. Apparently, a great number of Sranc in various stages of pregnancy
were observed in battle over the course of the Apocalypse. Though generally
inferior to Men in individual combat, they are ideal logistically, as they are
able to live for sustained periods on little more than grubs and insects.
Survivors recount tales of vast tracts of ground overturned and rooted by
passing Sranc hordes. Under the command of the No-God they are utterly
fearless, and seem to strike with unerring control and coordination.

Typically, Sranc stand no higher than the average caste-menial's shoulder. Their skin is devoid of pigment, and despite the refined—to the point of repulsiveness—beauty of their faces, their physiognomy is bestial (though hairless), with pinched shoulders and deep, almond-shaped breasts. They are exceedingly fast across both open and broken terrain, and their sheer viciousness is said to compensate for their slight stature.

Mandate scholars are prone to make dire warnings about the present numbers of Sranc in Eärwa. Apparently the ancient Norsirai had reduced the Sranc, pressing them to the margins of Eärwa, and the No-God was still able to summon hosts that reportedly blackened the horizon. Now Sranc dominate half the continent.

Sranc Pits—The famed gladiatorial arena of Carythusal, where human slaves are typically pitted against Sranc.

Stajanas II (2338–95)—The famed "Philosopher-Emperor" of Cenei, whose *Ruminations* has remained an important work in the Three Seas literary canon.

Stalker, the—A common epithet for Husyelt.

Steppe, the—See *Jiünati Steppe*.

Subis—A once-fortified oasis in Khemema, frequented by caravans passing between Shigek and Eumarna.

Sudica—A province of the Nansur Empire, largely depopulated by 4111 but among the wealthiest districts of the Kyranae Plain during the ages of Kyraneas and the Ceneian Empire.

"suffer not a whore to live ..."—The passage from Canticles 19:9, *The Chronicle of the Tusk*, condemning prostitution.

summoning horns—The great horns of bronze used to signal the "prayer watches" to the Inrithi faithful.

Sumna—The site of the Tusk and the holiest city of Inrithism, located in Nansur.

Surmante, House—A former Nansur House of the Congregate, and the Empire's ruling dynasty from 3619 to 3941.

Surmantic Gates—The great northern gate of Carythusal, whose construction was financed in 3639 by Surmante Xatantius I to commemorate the ill-fated Treaty of Kutapileth, a short-lived military pact between Nansur and High Ainon.

Sursa River—The river system that once formed the crucial frontier between Agongorea and Aörsi before the Apocalypse.

Suskara—A vast region of broken plains and highlands between Atrithau and the Jiünati Steppe, inhabited by numerous tribes of Sranc, some of which are tributary to the so-called Sranc King of Urskugog.

suthenti—The menial castes. See *castes*.

Sutis Sutadra—See *Skauras ab Nalajan*.

Swa River—The river that forms the northern frontier of Ce Tydonn.

Swarjuka (4061–)—The Sapatishah-Governor of Jurisada.

swazond—The ceremonial scars used by Scylvendi warriors to denote foes slain in battle, believed by some to be markers of stolen strength.

Swazond Standard—The name given to Cnaiür's banner at the Battle of Anwurat.

Sweki River—"The Sacred" (Kianni) The so-called "miracle river," revered as holy by the Kianene, who claim that its waters arise from nothing by the will of the Solitary God. Before the first Jihads, Nansur cartographers made several attempts to locate its headwaters in the Great Salt, none of them successful.

Synthese—Artifacts of the Inchoroi Tekne, thought to be living "shells" specifically designed to house the souls of senior Consult figures.

syurtpiütha—A Scylvendi euphemism for life, meaning "the smoke-that-moves."

T

talent—The base monetary unit of the Nansur Empire.

Tamiznai—A fortified oasis two days south of the River Sempis, frequented by caravans.

Tears of God—See *Chorae*.

Tekne—Also known as the Old Science. The non-sorcerous craft of the Inchoroi, used to mould abominations out of living flesh. According to various Nonman sources, the Tekne proceeds on the presumption that everything in nature, including life, is fundamentally mechanical. Despite the absurdity of this claim, few dispute the efficacy of the Tekne, as the Inchoroi and the Consult after them have time and again demonstrated the ability to "manufacture flesh." Mandate scholars claim that the fundamental principles of the Tekne have been long lost, and that the Consult can only proceed in a trial-and-error fashion, on the basis of an incomplete understanding, and using ancient and ill-understood instruments. This ignorance, they claim, is all that preserves the world from the No-God's return.

Tempiras the King—A work widely thought the greatest of Hamishaza's satiric tragedies.

Temple of Exorietta—A notorious temple in Carythusal.

Temple Prayer—Also referred to as the High Temple Prayer. The prayer, beginning "Sweet God of Gods" and attributed to Inri Sejenus in *The Tractate*, that has become the standard among the Inrithi.

Tendant'heras—An extensive fortress located on Nilnamesh's frontier with Girgash and Kianene.

Tertae Plains—The heavily cultivated alluvial plain bordering northeast Caraskand.

tesperari—A Nansur term for naval captains who retire to command merchant ships.

Thampis, Kemetti (4076–)—A Conriyan Baron from the Anpleian frontier.

Tharschilka, Heänar (4068–4110)—The Galeoth Earl of Nergaöta, and one of the three leaders of the Vulgar Holy War.

Therishut, Gishtari (4067–4111)—A Conriyan Baron from the Ainoni frontier, murdered by persons unknown.

Thesji Bowmen—An elite Kianene unit of Chorae archers.

Third Analytic of Men, The—Regarded by many as Ajencis's magnum opus, the *Third Analytic* interrogates the aspects of human nature that make knowledge possible, as well as the human weaknesses that make knowledge so difficult to attain. As Ajencis notes, "if all Men disagree on all matters, then most Men confuse deception for truth." He investigates the reasons, not only for deception in general, but for the erroneous sense of conviction that sustains it, giving what has come to be called the "selfish knower" thesis, the idea that convenience, conditioning, and appeal (as opposed to evidence and rational argumentation) are the primary motivation for the beliefs of the vast majority.

Thoti-Eännorean—The alleged mother tongue of all Men, and the language of *The Chronicle of the Tusk*.

"Though you lose your soul, you shall gain the world."—The penultimate answer in the Mandate catechism, referring to the fact that Mandate Schoolmen, unlike other Schoolmen, damn themselves for a purpose.

Thousand Temples—The ecclesiastical and administrative framework of Inrithism, based in Sumna but omnipresent throughout most of the Three Seas. The Thousand Temples first became a dominant social and political institution during the reign of the first Aspect-Emperor, Triamis the Great, who declared Inrithism the official faith of the Ceneian Empire in 2505. Authority is nominally centralized in the person of the Shriah, who is regarded as the Latter Prophet's living representative, but the sheer size and complexity of the Thousand Temples often renders that authority ceremonial. Aside from the management of the temples proper, there are the ecclesiastical courts, the political missions, the various Colleges, and the labyrinthine interconnections with the Cults to administer. As a result, the Thousand Temples often suffers from weak leadership, and is regarded with cynicism by many in the Three Seas.

Thousand Thousand Halls—The labyrinth constructed by the Dûnyain beneath Ishuäl and used by them to test their initiates. Those who become lost in the Thousand Thousand Halls invariably die, ensuring that only the most intelligent survive.

Three-Headed Serpent—The symbol of the Scarlet Spires.

Three Hearts of God—A term referring to Sumna, the Thousand Temples, and the Tusk.

Three Seas—Specifically, the seas of Meneanor, Oncis, and Nyranisas, located in south central Eärwa. More generally, the (primarily Ketyai) civilization that has thrived in this region since the end of the Apocalypse.

Threesie—The name given to Nansur who sign on for a third fourteen-year term of service in the Imperial Army.

Throseanis (3256–3317)—A late Ceneian dramatist, famed for his *Triamis Imperator*, a dramatic account of the life of Triamis I, the greatest of the Ceneian Aspect-Emperors.

Thunyeric—The language of Thunyerus, a derivative of Meoric.

Thunyerus—A Norsirai nation of the Three Seas located on the northeastern coasts of the Meneanor Sea. According to Thunyeri legend, their peoples migrated down the length of the Wernma River, continually pressured by the Sranc tribes that largely rule the great forests of the Dameori Wilderness. For two hundred years the Thunyeri plied the Three Seas as pirates and raiders. Then, in 3987, after three generations of Inrithi missionaries had largely converted them from their traditional Kiünnat beliefs, the tribes elected their first King, Hringa Hurrausch, and began adopting the institutions of their Three Seas neighbours.

Tirummas, Nersei (4075–4100)—The eldest brother of Nersei Proyas, and Crown Prince of Conriya until his death at sea in 4100.

Tokush (4068–4111)—The Master of Spies to Ikurei Xerius III.

topoi—Locations where the accumulation of trauma and suffering has frayed the boundaries between the World and the Outside.

Tractate, The—The writings of Inri Sejenus and his disciples, forming the second part of the Inrithi scriptural canon. The Inrithi believe *The Tractate* to be the prophesied culmination of *The Chronicle of the Tusk*, an amendment of the Covenant of Gods and Men for the realities of a new age. Among its seventeen books are various accounts of the life of the Latter Prophet, many parables for the purposes of moral instruction, and Inri Sejenus's own explanation of the "Intervention" he himself represents: that mankind, as it matures, will become more and more able to worship the God in His "singular multiplicity." Given that *The Tractate* was written more as a testament to the divinity of Inri Sejenus's vision than out of any real commitment to historical rigour, it is impossible to assess the veracity of the text. Zarathinius and, more recently, Fanim commentators have pointed out several glaring inconsistencies in the text, but nothing that Inrithi apologists have not been able to explain away.

Trail of Skulls—See *saka'ilrait*.

Triamarius I (3470–3517)—The first of the Zerxei Emperors, acclaimed by the Imperial Army following the assassination of Trimus Meniphas I in 3508. See *Nansur Empire*.

Triamarius III (3588–3619)—The last of the Zerxei Emperors of Nansur, murdered by palace eunuchs. See *Nansur Empire*.

Triamic Walls—Caraskand's outermost fortifications, raised by Triamis the Great in 2568.

Triamis Imperator—The famed drama by Throseanis, based on events in the life of Triamis the Great.

Triamis the Great (2456–2577)—The first Aspect-Emperor of the Ceniean Empire, famed for his conquests and for declaring Inrithism the official state religion in 2505. See *Ceneian Empire*.

Triaxeras, Hampei (4072–)—The Captain of Ikurei Conphas's bodyguard.

Trimus, House—A Nansur House of the Congregate.

Trinkets—See *Chorae.*

Trondha, Safirig (4076–)—A Galeoth thane, client to Earl Anfirig of Gesindal.

Trucian Dramas, The—The magnum opus of Xius, a near antique poet and playwright.

Truth Room—An interrogation chamber located deep in the catacombs beneath the Andiamine Heights.

Trysë—The ancient administrative capital of Kûniüri, destroyed in the Apocalypse in 2147. Arguably the greatest city of the Ancient North and, with the exception of Sauglish, Umerau, and Etrith, also the oldest.

Tshuma (4073–)—One of the Nascenti, formerly a Kutnarmu mercenary.

Tsuramah—"Hated One" (Kyranean) The ancient Kyranean name for the No-God. See *No-God.*

Tusam—A village in the Inûnara Highlands destroyed by Fanim raiders in 4111.

Tusk, the—The premier holy artifact of both the Inrithi and Kiünnat traditions, and the most unholy in the Fanim tradition (where it is referred to as Rouk Spara, or "Cursed Thorn"). Since the Tusk bears the oldest extant version of *The Chronicle of the Tusk*, which in turn is the oldest human text, its provenance remains an utter mystery, though most scholars agree that it predates the coming of the Tribes to Eärwa. It has been installed in the holy city of Sumna throughout most of recorded history.

Twin Scimitars—The primary holy device of Fanimry, symbolizing the "Cutting Eyes" of the Solitary God.

Tydonni—The language of Ce Tydonn, a derivative of Meoric.

Tywanrae River—A major river system in north central Eärwa, draining the Gâl basin and emptying into the Cerish Sea.

U

Uän, Samarmau (4001–)—One of the Dûnyain Pragma.

Ukrummu, Madarezer (4045–4111)—A sorcerer of rank in the Scarlet Spires, slain by Chorae at Anwurat.

Ulnarta, Shaugar (4071–)—One of the Nascenti, formerly a Tydonni thane.

Umeri Empire—The first great nation of Men, encompassing the length of the River Aumris, founded after the overthrow of the Trysean God-Kings, *c.* 430. See *Kûniüri.*

Umeritic—The lost language of ancient Umerau, a derivative of Aumri-Saugla.

Umiaki—The name of the ancient eucalyptus tree located in the heart of the Kalaul in Caraskand, famed as the tree from which the Warrior-Prophet was hung on the Circumfix.

"umresthei om aumreton"—Kyranean for "possessing in dispossession." Ajencis's term for those moments where the soul comprehends itself in the act of comprehending other things, and so experiences the "wonder of existence."

Unaras Spur—The low mountain range that extends from the southern terminus of the Hethantas to the Meneanor coast, marking the geographical frontier between the Kyranae Plain and Gedea.

Unclean, the—A name, derived from *The Chronicle of the Tusk*, commonly used by Inrithi as a pejorative for sorcerers.

Unmasking Room—A chamber located in the labyrinth below Ishuäl where Dûnyain children are taught the connections between facial musculature and passions.

Unswolka, Goeransor (4079–)—The Tydonni thane of Hagmeir in Numaineiri.

Uranyanka, Sirpal (4062–)—The Palatine-Governor of the Ainoni city of Moserothu.

Uroborian Circle—A so-called "artifactual Cant" used to prevent the utterance of sorcery and thought to turn on the same aporetic principles that make Chorae possible.

Uroris—A constellation in the northern sky.

Usgald—A fiefdom in the Galeoth interior.

Uskelt Wolfheart (?–?)—One of the Chieftain-Kings named in the Tusk.

Utemot—A tribe of Scylvendi located in the northwest extremes of the Jiünati Steppe. Among the Scylvendi, the Utemot are noted as the tribe of both Uthgai and Horiötha, the two greatest conquerors in their history.

Utgarangi ab Hoularji (4059–)—The Sapatishah-Governor of Xerash.

Uthgai (*c*. 2100–*c*. 2170)—The folklore hero and Scylvendi King-of-Tribes during the Apocalypse, whose deeds are oft recited in the Scylvendi oral tradition.

V

Valrissa (4086–4112)—A daughter of the Werigda and wife of Aëngelas.

Vaparsi—The lost language of ancient Nilnamesh, a derivative of Shem-Varsi.

Vasnosri—The language group of the Norsirai peoples.

Vault-of-the-Tusk—See *Junriüma*.

Venicata—An Inrithi holy day celebrated in late spring, commemorating the so-called First Revelation of Inri Sejenus.

Vindauga River—The westernmost of the three major river systems draining into Lake Huösi, and the primary geographical boundary between Galeoth and Cepalor.

Vulgar Holy War—The name given to the first contingent of the Holy War to march against the Fanim.

W

Wainhail, Swahon (4055–4111)—The Galeoth Earl of Kurigald, slain at Mengedda.

war, Scylvendi mode of—Despite their illiteracy, the Scylvendi possess an extensive war nomenclature that provides them with a thorough understanding of battle and its psychological dynamics. They call battle *otgai wutmaga*, a "great quarrel," wherein the point is to convince the foe of their defeat. The concepts central to the Scylvendi understanding of war are as follows:

unswaza—envelopment
malk unswaza—defensive envelopment
yetrut—penetration
gaiwut—shock
utmurzu—cohesion
fira—speed
angotma—heart

utgirkoy—attrition

cnamturu—vigilance

gobozkoy—moment of decision

mayutafiüri—ligaments of conflict

trutu garothut—flexible unit cohesion (literally, "men of the long chain")

trutu hirthut—inflexible unit cohesion (literally, "men of the short chain")

War-Cants—The Gnostic sorceries developed in Sauglish (primarily by Noshainrau the White) for the express purpose of waging war and overcoming opposing sorcerers.

Wards—The name given to defensive sorceries in contradistinction to offensive sorceries, or Cants. See *sorcery*. The most common types of Wards (found in both Anagogic and Gnostic sorceries) are: Wards of Exposure, which provide advance warning of intruders or imminent attacks; Shield-Wards, which provide direct protection against offensive sorceries; and Skin-Wards, which provide "protection of last resort" against all types of threat.

Warnute—A fiefdom of Ce Tydonn, one of the so-called Deep Marches of the Upper Swa.

"war of word and sentiment"—The explanation of jnan found in Byantas's *Translations*.

Wathi Doll—A sorcerous artifact common to Sansori witches, also known as a "murder doll," either because a human sacrifice is required for its manufacture (a soul is imprisoned as the artifact's animus) or because the Dolls are often used as remote assassins.

Werigda—A Norsirai tribe from the Plains of Gâl.

Werijen Greatheart, Rilding (4063–)—The Tydonni Earl of Plaideöl.

Werjau, Sainhail (4070–)—One of the Nascenti, formerly a Galeoth thane.

Wernma River—An extensive river system in east central Eärwa, draining vast tracts of the Dameori Wilderness and emptying into the Meneanor Sea.

Whelming—A hypnotic trance instrumental to Dûnyain Conditioning, and a purificatory rite of induction for the Zaudunyani.

"When sorcerers sing, men die."—The traditional expression used to refer to the fact that sorcery is destructive rather than constructive.

White Jihad—The holy war waged against the Nansur Empire by Fan'oukarji I and the Kianene from 3743 to 3771. See *Kian*.

White Lord of Trysë—An honorific of the Kûniüric High King.

White-Sun Palace—See *Korasha*.

White Yaksh—The traditional tent of Scylvendi tribal chieftains.

Whore, the—A popular name for the Goddess Anagkë. See *Anagkë*.

witches—The name given to women who practise sorcery, despite their persecution by both the Thousand Temples and the Schools.

wizards—The name given to men who practise sorcery independent of any School, despite their persecution by both the Thousand Temples and the Schools.

World Between—The world as it exists "between" our perceptions of it, or "in itself."

World-Breaker—A name for the No-God. See *No-God*.

Worldhorn—A ceremonial sorcerous artifact belonging to the Aörsic House of the Anasûrimbor and lost in the destruction of Shiarau in 2136.

Worm, the—A vernacular name for the great slums of Carythusal.

Wracu—Also known as Dragons. Immense, fire-spitting, winged reptilian monstrosities created by the Inchoroi during the ancient Cûno-Inchoroi Wars to destroy the Nonmen Quya, then subsequently wielded by the No-God during the Apocalypse. Very few are thought to have survived.

Wrigga (4073–)—A caste-menial Zaudunyani agitator.

Writ of Psata-Antyu—The proclamation issued by the high clergy of the Thousand Temples at the Council of Antyu (3386) that limits the power of the Shriah. The Writ was motivated by the cruel excesses of Shriah Diagol, who held the Seat from 3371 until his assassination in 3383.

Wutmouth River—The immense river joining Lake Huösi to the Meneanor Sea.

wutrim—A Scylvendi word meaning "shame."

X

Xatantian Arch—The triumphal arch marking the ceremonial entrance to the Scuäri Campus, which depicts the military exploits of Emperor Surmante Xatantius. See *Xatantius I*.

Xatantius I (3644–93)—The most warlike of the Surmante Emperors of Nansur, Xatantius enlarged the Nansur Empire to its greatest extent, pacifying the Norsirai tribes of the Cepalor and for a time even managing to hold the far southern city of Invishi (though he failed to entirely subdue the Nilnameshi countryside). Despite his military successes, his continual wars exhausted both the Nansur people and the Imperial Treasury, inadvertently laying the groundwork for the disastrous wars against the Kianene following his death. See *Nansur Empire*.

Xerash—A governorate of Kian and former province of the Nansur Empire. Located north of Eumarna on the Meneanor coast, Xerash is primarily known, through *The Tractate*, as the violent and debauched neighbour of Amoteu during the time of Inri Sejenus. See *Amoteu*.

Xerashi—The lost language of scriptural Xerash, a derivative of Vaparsi.

Xerius—See *Ikurei Xerius III*.

Xiangic—The language group of the Xiuhianni peoples.

Xijoser (*c.* 670–*c.* 720)—An Old Dynasty God-King of Shigek, known primarily for the Ziggurat bearing his name.

Xinemus, Krijates (4066–)—The Conriyan Marshal of Attrempus.

Xiuhianni—The black-haired, brown-eyed, olive-skinned race that still dwells beyond the Great Kayarsus. One of the Five Tribes of Men, who, according to *The Chronicle of the Tusk*, refused to follow the other four tribes into Eärwa.

Xius (2847–2914)—The great Ceneian poet and playwright, famed for *The Trucian Dramas*.

Xoägi'i—A Sranc tribe from the Plains of Gâl.

Xothei, Temple of—The primary edifice of the Cmiral temple complex, famed for its three great domes.

Xunnurit (4068–)—The Scylvendi chieftain of the Akkunihor tribe, infamous for leading the Scylvendi to defeat at the battle of Kiyoth.

Y

yaksh—The conical tents of the Scylvendi, made of greased leather and poplar branches.

Yalgrota Sranchammer (4071–)—The Thunyeri groom of Prince Hringa Skaiyelt, famed for his giant stature and ferocity in war.

Yasellas—A prostitute acquaintance of Esmenet.

Yatwer—The Goddess of fertility. One of the so-called Compensatory Gods, who reward devotion in life with paradise in the afterlife, Yatwer is far and away the most popular Cultic deity among caste-menials (as Gilgaöl is among caste-nobles). In the *Higarata,* the collection of subsidiary writings that form the scriptural core of the Cults, Yatwer is depicted as a benefi- cent, all-forgiving matron, capable of seeding and furrowing the fields of nations with a single hand. Some commentators have noted that Yatwer is anything but revered in either the *Higarata* or *The Chronicle of the Tusk* (wherein "tillers of soil" are often referred to with contempt). Perhaps this is why Yatwerians tend to rely on their own scripture, the *Sinyatwa,* for their liturgical rites and ceremonies. Despite the vast numbers of adher- ents enjoyed by the Cult, it remains one of the more impoverished, and seems to generate a large number of zealous devotees as a result.

Year-of-the-Tusk—The primary dating system for most mannish nations, which takes the legendary Breaking of the Gates to be year zero.

Years of the Crib—A common term for the eleven years of the No-God's manifestation during the First Apocalypse, wherein all infants were still- born. See *Apocalypse.*

Yel (4079–)—One of Esmenet's Kianene body-slaves.

Yellow Sempis River—A tributary of the River Sempis.

Yimaleti Mountains—An extensive mountain range located in the extreme northwest of Eärwa.

Ysilka—The wife of General Sag-Marmau in *The Sagas,* whose name is often used as a euphemism for "adulteress" in the Three Seas.

yursa—A Galeoth liquor made from fermented potatoes.

Yursalka (c. 4065–4110)—A Scylvendi warrior of the Utemot tribe.

Yutirames—A sorcerer of rank in the Scarlet Spires, slain by Achamian in the Sareötic Library.

Z

Zarathinius (3688–3745)—The famed author of *A Defence of the Arcane Arts.*

Zaudunyani—"Tribe of Truth" (Kûniüric) The name taken by Kellhus's followers during the First Holy War.

Zealot Wars—The prolonged religious conflict (c. 2390–2478) between the early Inrithi and the Kiünnat, which eventually led to the ascendancy of the Thousand Temples in the Three Seas.

Zenkappa (4068–4111)—A Captain of Attrempus, formerly a Nilnameshi slave belonging to the household of Krijates Xinemus, slain at Iothiah.

Zerxei, House—A former Nansur House of the Congregate, and the empire's ruling dynasty from 3511 to 3619, when Zerxei Triamarius III was assassinated by his palace eunuchs.

Zeüm—A mysterious and powerful Satyothi nation beyond Nilnamesh, and the source of the finest silks and steel in the Three Seas.

Zeümi—The language of the Empire of Zeüm, a derivative of Old Zeümi.

Zeümi Sword-Dancers—The members of an exotic Zeümi Cult that worships the sword and has developed sword fighting to an almost supernatural level.

Ziek, Tower of—The prison, located in Momemn, used by the Nansur Emperors to incarcerate their political foes.

Ziggurats of Shigek—The immense stepped pyramids found to the north of the Sempis Delta and raised by the ancient God-Kings of Shigek to serve as their mortuary tombs.

Zirkirta—See *Battle of Zirkirta*.

Zohurric—See *Aghurzoi*.

Zursodda, Sammu (4064–4111)—The Palatine-Governor of the Ainoni city of Koraphea, claimed by disease at Caraskand.

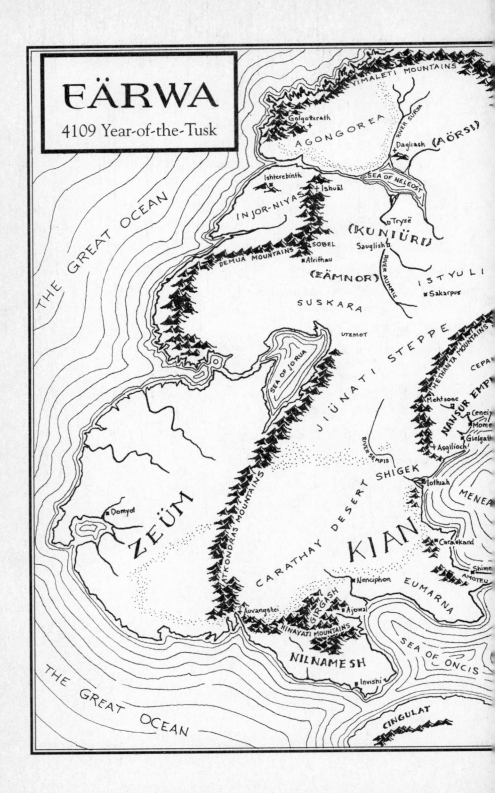

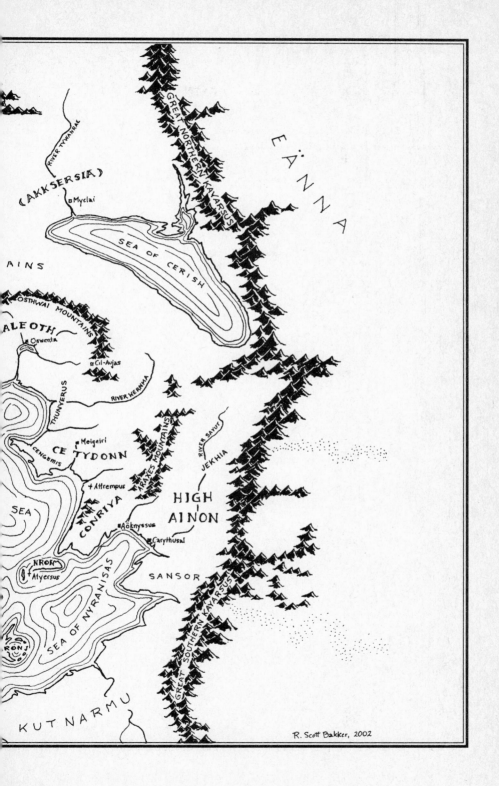

EÄNNA

GREAT NORTHERN KAYARSUS

RIVER TYWANRAE

(AKKSERSIA)

□ Myclai

SEA OF CERISH

AINS

OSTHWAI MOUNTAINS

ALEOTH

∟ Oswenta

□ Cil-Aujas

RIVER WERNMA

THUNYERUS

RIVER SAYUT

JEKHIA

CENGEMIS

CE TYDONN

■ Meigeiri

ANDES MOUNTAINS

HIGH
AINON

✝ Attrempus

CONRIYA

■ Aöknyssus

SEA

■ Carythusal

NROK

SANSOR

⸰ Atyersus

SEA OF NYRANISAS

GREAT SOUTHERN KAYARSUS

RONJ

KUT NARMU

R. Scott Bakker, 2002

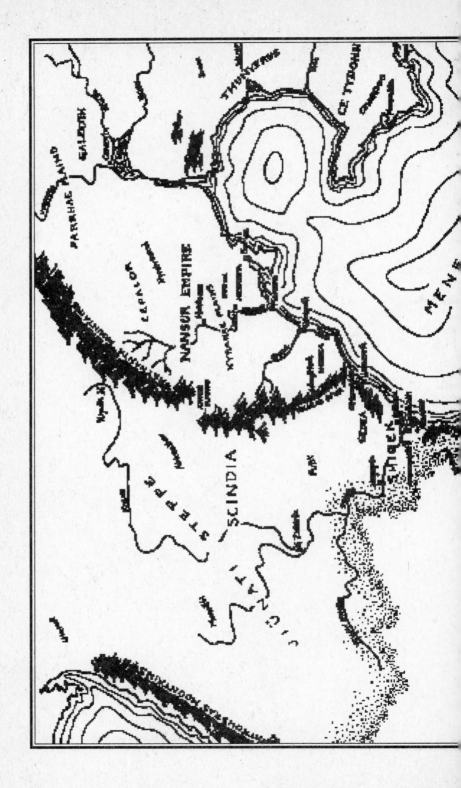

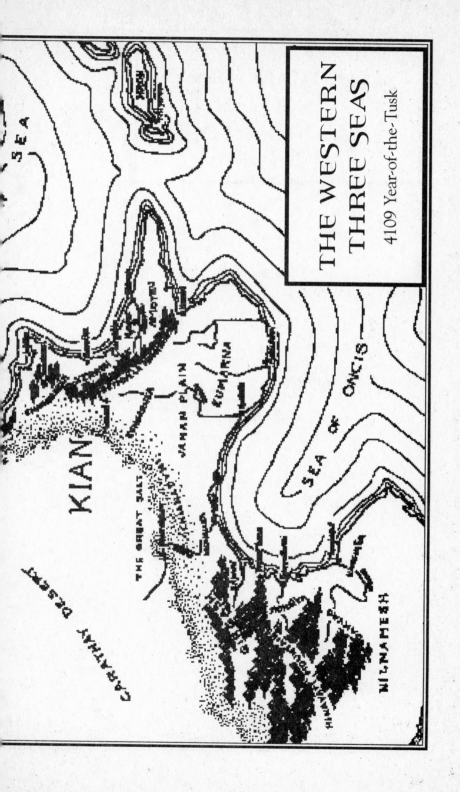

THE WESTERN
THREE SEAS

4109 Year-of-the-Tusk

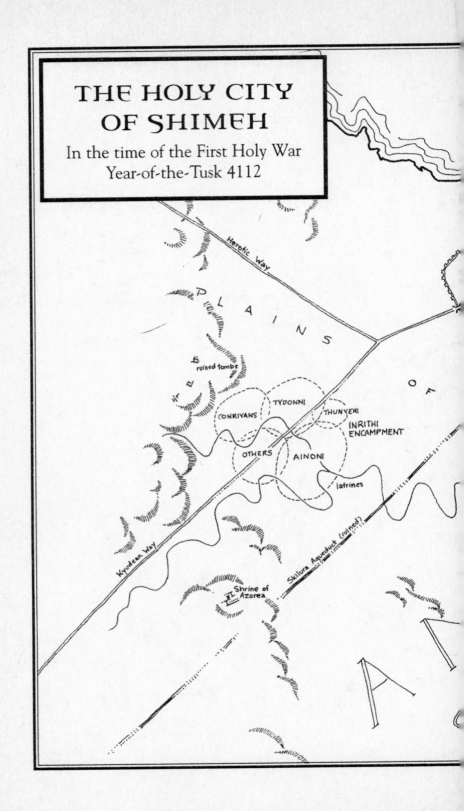

THE HOLY CITY
OF SHIMEH

In the time of the First Holy War
Year-of-the-Tusk 4112

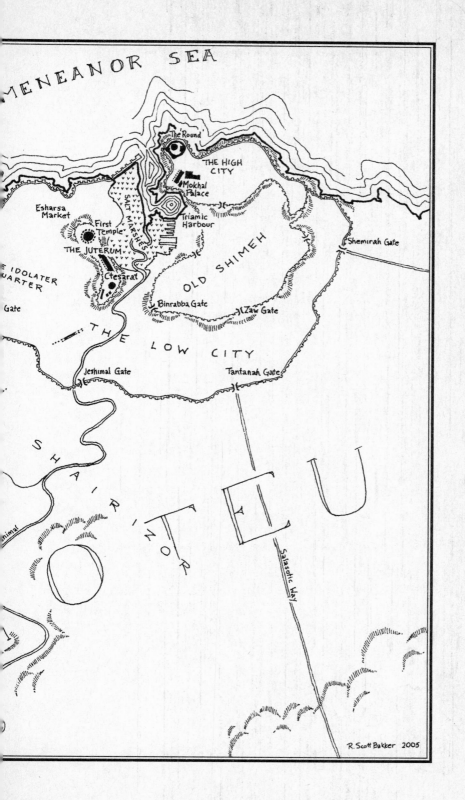

MENEANOR SEA

The Round

THE HIGH CITY

Mokhal Palace

Esharsa Market

First Temple

Triamic Harbour

THE JUTERUM

SALT MARSHES

E IDOLATER QUARTER

Ctesarat

Shemirah Gate

OLD SHIMEH

Gate

Binrabba Gate

Zaw Gate

THE LOW CITY

Jeshimal Gate

Tantanah Gate

SHAIRIZOR

SHIMEH

himal

Sassastic Way

R. Scott Bakker 2005

ACKNOWLEDGMENTS

To think I started this journey almost twenty years ago …

If anyone had told me years back that the summer of 2005 would find me completing *The Prince of Nothing*, I likely would have coughed beer out of my nose. But here I am, and I have a long list of debts to prove it.

First, to my wife, Sharron, who has literally supported me unto the brink of insolvency. I stand tallest when she's at my side.

Then, the usual suspects: my brother, Bryan Bakker, for the gift of second sight; my friend Roger Eichorn, for the gift of his second sight; and my agent, Chris Lotts, for his honesty and his acumen—not to mention the odd eleventh-hour bombshell!

I would also like to thank:

Steve Erikson.

My family and friends, for indulging my obsession in conversation after conversation. Joe Edmiston, for his squash-court criticisms. And my neighbour Mike Brown, for helping me sort out the difference between mystery and obscurity.

But the people I most need to thank are the *fans* of the series. This includes everyone at www.three-seas.com and the "other author" forum at sffworld.com. The names that come immediately to mind are: Jack Brown, Wil Horsley, Gary Wassner, White Lord, Dylanfanatic, Ainulindale, Mithfanion, Leiali, Texmex, and, of course, Saintjon. Through innumerable discussions across several different venues, you have all made your mark.